"R. F. Delderfield has dared to revive the saga. . . . This is a novel in which we can take our ease, a refreshing change from the bewildering complexities of brilliant avant-garde fiction."
—*The New York Times*

"A HORSEMAN RIDING BY has a robust and honest quality . . . the story is a rollicking good one. . . . Delderfield handles time factors, suspense threads, characterizations, and plotting with the flair and solidity of an accomplished and professional storyteller." —*Denver Post*

"Magnificent." —*Columbus Dispatch*

". . . every satiny page is a delight. . . . [Craddock's] marriage to Claire is one of fiction's most endearing love stories . . . a beautiful novel."
—*Minneapolis Tribune*

"An extraordinary achievement. . . . It is both breathtaking in scope and at the same time moving on a personal level."
—*Fort Worth Star-Telegram*

[continued on next page]

R. F. Delderfield's

A HORSEMAN RIDING BY

is a saga on the grand scale, detailing the human drama of English country life during the most turbulent years of this restless century.

LONG SUMMER DAY, the first volume, spans the period from 1902 to 1911, the charmed interval between Queen Victoria's death and the approach of World War I, a time that seemed indeed like a "long summer day" to the generation that lived through it. Among these was Paul Craddock, Squire of Shallowford and veteran of the Boer War. The peace that prevailed in England and abroad contrasted sharply with the tumbling succession of dramatic events in Paul's own life—his marriage to Grace Lovell, the headstrong champion of the new women's rights movement; the daily personal drama of birth and death that seemed to mirror the country seasons, and his deeply fulfilling second marriage to the lovely Claire Derwent. But their idyllic way of life could not last forever. Soon it, too, would be swept away in the mightiest storm of hardship and destruction the world had ever known. . . .

LONG SUMMER DAY
is Volume I of *A Horseman Riding By,*
originally published in the U.S.A.
by Simon and Schuster.

Long Summer Day

R. F. Delderfield's A HORSEMAN RIDING BY—of which
Long Summer Day is the first volume—is a vast,
panoramic novel of English country life from the Boer
War to the Battle of Britain, from the death of Queen
Victoria to the battlefields of World War II. Filled
with narrative energy, robust action, and fully drawn
characters, this novel summons up the traditions of a
vanished world of cottagers and landed gentry clinging
to a feudal way of life, Members of Parliament, and
restless "new women" freed from the sexual and
intellectual restraints of the Victorian Era. Above all,
the reader is plunged into the world of the families
whose lives are rooted in the green acres of Shallowford—the Craddocks, the leading family of the
beautiful valley, and their neighbors and tenants—
the Codsalls, the Derwents, and the Willoughbys.
Against the passion of their lives—their births, deaths,
marriages, triumphs and failures—is mirrored the whole
stirring range of the strength and grace of a period
that will vanish under the onslaught of a violent century.
But now, through the story-telling magic of R. F.
Delderfield, the clock is stilled, and we are once again
in that Golden Era when people believed in patriotism
and men lived with goodness, dignity and honor. . . .

Long Summer Day, 1902–1911

The Queen is dead, Long live the King! An era is gone and now begins the tumultuous years of the new century—the Long Summer Day that begins with Victoria's death and ends just before the blast of war and the death of a generation. The theme of this saga is embodied in Paul Craddock, invalided out of the Boer War, who becomes the Squire of Shallowford. To this neglected Westcountry estate, he brings an immense enthusiasm and vision of prosperity for the entire countryside. For Paul, his family, and his tenants and neighbors in the valley, the years are filled with a tumbling succession of events—his marriage to headstrong Grace Lovell, who abandons him and their young son to take an active part in the suffragette campaigns convulsing England; and his happy, love-filled second marriage to the beautiful Claire Derwent. But the idyllic way of life of Paul, Claire, and the tenants and neighbors of Shallowford is soon to end. For on the horizon are the inexorable drumbeats of the Great War—a war that will bring tragedy and hardship to a generation, and cataclysmic challenge to all the values that Paul Craddock holds dear. . . .

Books by R. F. Delderfield

The Adventures of Ben Gunn
All Over the Town
The Avenue Goes to War
Bird's Eye View
Cheap Day Return
Diana*
The Dreaming Suburb
Farewell the Tranquil Mind*
God Is an Englishman*
The Green Gauntlet
Long Summer Day (Volume I of A Horseman Riding By)*
The March of the Twenty-six
Mr. Sermon*
Napoleon in Love
Nobody Shouted Author
On the Fiddle
Post of Honor (Volume II of A Horseman Riding By)*
The Retreat from Moscow
Seven Men of Gascony
Theirs Was the Kingdom*
There Was a Fair Maid Dwelling
Too Few for Drums*
To Serve Them All My Days*
The Unjust Skies

*Published by POCKET BOOKS

R. F. DELDERFIELD

Long Summer Day

Volume I

of

A Horseman Riding By

PUBLISHED BY POCKET BOOKS NEW YORK

LONG SUMMER DAY

Simon and Schuster edition published 1967

POCKET BOOK edition published August, 1974

L

This POCKET BOOK edition includes every word contained
in the original, higher-priced edition. It is printed from
brand-new plates made from completely reset, clear, easy-to-
read type. POCKET BOOK editions are published by POCKET
BOOKS, a division of Simon & Schuster, Inc., 630 Fifth
Avenue, New York, N.Y. 10020. Trademarks registered
in the United States and other countries.

Standard Book Number: 671-78672-5.
Library of Congress Catalog Card Number: 67-20800.
Front cover illustration by Lou Marchetti.

Printed in the U.S.A.

For Deirdre Gibbens
and
Sir Geoffrey Harmsworth,
both old friends, with a genuine
love for the Westcountry.

In all corners of the West there are Craddocks and Potters, Codsalls and Pitts, Tozers and Stokes, Timberlakes and Willoughbys; no person in this book is intended to represent a living character but rather a race of people in a corner of the country as old as time. Similarly there are hundreds of Shallowfords, scores of Sorrell Valleys. If any reader is looking for identification let him seek it in the national spirit that, even in this day and age, still quickens the people of provincial England.

At Shallowford House   Paul Craddock = (1) Grace Lovell (m. 1903)
                         Simon (1904)

                         (2) Claire Derwent (m. 1907)

| Stephen and Andrew (The Pair, 1908) | Mary (1910) | Karen ("Whiz") (1913) | Claire (1918) | John (1934) |

Ikey Palfrey (adopted 1902)

At Four Winds   Martin Codsall = Arabella (until 1904)
                 Will   Sydney

                 Norman Eveleigh = Marian (until 1932)

| Gilbert | Deborah | Rachel | Harold | Robbie | Esther | Mavis | Susan |

                 Harold Eveleigh = Connie (after 1932)

At Hermitage Farm   Arthur Pitts = Martha
                      Henry = Gloria
                      David   Prudence

At Perewinkle Farm   Will Codsall = Elinor Willoughby (until 1931)
                       Mark   Queenie   Floss   Richard

                       Rumble Patrick Palfrey = Mary Craddock (1934 onwards)
                       Jerry

At High Coombe   Edward Derwent = Liz (second wife)
                   Hugh   Rose   Claire   (all by first wife)

IN THE SORREL VALLEY, 1902-40

At Deepdene Farm   Edwin Willoughby

Francis   Elinor

At Low Coombe   Tamar = Meg

Sam = Joanie   Smut = Marie   Hazel = Ikey

Cissie = Brissot   Violet = Jumbo
Bellchamber

Pansy = (1) Walt Pascoe
         (2) Dandy Timberlake.
         (3) Reg Willis

At Home Farm   Old Honeyman

Nelson = Prudence Pitts

Estate Workers (1902–40)   John Rudd, agent = Maureen O'Keefe, lady-doctor
Horace Handcock, gardener == Ada Handcock
                             (housekeeper)
Thirza Tremlett, parlourmaid and nurse
Chivers, groom
Matt and Luke, shepherds
The Timberlake family, sawyers
Gappy Saunders, gardener's boy

At Coombe Bay   Parson Bull
Parson Horsey
Keith Horsey = Rachel Eveleigh
Abe Tozer, smith
Ephraim Morgan, builder
Tom Williams, fisherman
James Grenfell, M.P.
Walt Pascoe, labourer
Professor Scholtzer
Bruce and Cecia Lovell
Aaron Stokes, reed-cutter
Willis, wheelwright

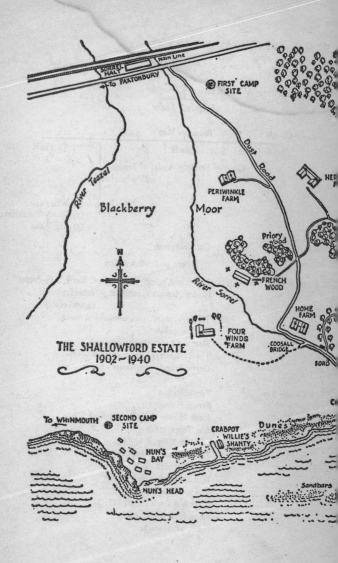

THE SHALLOWFORD ESTATE
1902~1940

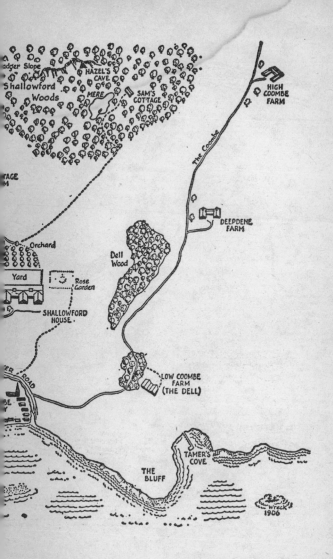

Long Summer Day

CHAPTER ONE

I

HE left the carriage, ascended the short flight of steps and walked briskly past the dozing porter sitting in the deep shade of the portico; a small, neat man, in dark, well-cut clothes and glossy topper. He did not look incongruous out here in the open country under a blistering sun, but like a confident rook, or perhaps a raven, with years of combative experience well behind him; a sleek, utterly self-possessed and in a subdued sense, deadly raven, with a bill best avoided.

The porter did not see him until he was inside the cool hall and in the act of turning the polished handle of the door, marked "MATRON: PRIVATE". The man rubbed sleep from his eyes and shouted "Hi there! You can't . . ." but the dapper man with the jutting Van Dyke beard was already inside with the door closed behind him, and the porter, baffled and dismayed, hesitated, bemused by the visitor's arrogance.

The matron, fourteen stone of starched linen, was almost equally disconcerted, at least for the moment. She was accustomed to deference, advertised by timid knocks, downcast eyes, abject mumbles and not merely because, as matron, she was Queen Empress of the Hospital for Convalescent Officers, but because, as a Countess who had given her country seat to the nation in its hour of need, she had been basking in a golden glow of patriotism ever since Black Week, in December 1899, when every capital in Europe was whooping at the spectacle of a few thousand Boer farmers trouncing the British Empire. Here she had sat ever since, flirting decorously with the Harley Street men, patronising the nameless doctors, cosseting heroes, and resolutely bullying her volunteer nurses. She had never realised a war could be so richly rewarding.

1

She looked up from her tea-pouring and saw the little man with the beard standing in front of her desk and his leisured removal of his hat was no more than a token courtesy. She was so astonished that she forgot to be outraged and could only suppose the insolent intruder had lost his way and blundered in here by mistake. But while she was waiting for the porter to arrive and remove him he actually sat down. Actually seated himself, in the leather swivel chair, used by Sir Brian Wilmott, and all the other famous physicians who paid calls on her, and before she could exclaim he said, in a hoarse voice she could only describe as singularly common, "Lieutenant Craddock: Lieutenant P. Craddock, of the Yeomanry. He arrived here a day or so ago. I should like the latest report on him!", and he pushed a visiting card across the table.

She made a slight gobbling sound, handling the card as though it was a live cockroach. It read, "Franz Zorndorff, Zorndorff & Craddock, Ltd." and underneath, in neat script, "Canal Place, E.4 and Belsize Mansions, N.W.3." She found her voice at last, just as the porter, after a perfunctory knock, sidled into the room and looked at her for inspiration.

"How dare you? You had no appointment . . . ?"

"No," Zorndorff said, blandly, "none!", and then smiled in the most insolent and embarrassing way possible.

The porter arrived, passing a hand over his jowls. "He walked past!" he began, "he walked right past . . ." and then the little man looked at him and suddenly the Countess did not seem nearly as formidable and he retreated, muttering, so that the matron was abandoned to make what head she could against the visitor's armoury of invincible insolence.

She said, weakly, "Craddock, you said?", and made a miserable pretence of shuffling among the papers on her desk, whereupon the little man smiled, this time a charming although by no means ingratiating smile, and said, "Perhaps I should be more explicit, Countess; I am at present serving on the Board of Voluntary Hospitals in the London area. I have been a generous subscriber but in view of Lieutenant Craddock's presence here, I have decided to particularise. I have here a banker's draft for five

2

hundred guineas, earmarked for this institution, together with a guarantee of another five hundred to be paid over the day my late partner's son is removed from the dangerously ill list!", and he took from his pocket a stiff, foolscap envelope, laying it beside the visiting card.

All the tension went out of the atmosphere and although the matron began to gobble again it was not with suppressed indignation but the effusiveness she hitherto reserved for Harley Street visitors, men like Sir Brian, known to have been consulted on royal births at Windsor Lodge and York House. Her blunt fingers shook as she withdrew the cheque from the envelope and all the time Franz Zorndorff watched her; with relish.

She began to bustle then, so that suddenly the room was full of the whisper of starched linen. Bells rang in far off corners of the mansion and a sister appeared, and then a hollow-eyed young man in a white coat, and finally the Chief Medical Officer, inclined to be irritable and impatient until the matron waved the cheque under his nose, after which he became almost cordial and produced a gold cigarette case from under his white coat, offering the visitor an Egyptian cigarette which was declined. He thought, "A Jew, almost certainly! And a Continental Jew at that! But who the devil am I to quibble? If we can nail that other five hundred we can expand and beat Marylebone's intake by fifty patients, what might that mean? Publicity if nothing else; and with the war virtually over and private practice in the offing, that will be one up on quacks like Sir Brian!" His mind began to juggle with the new cases in "H" Ward, whence all the recent arrivals had been sent but he found it difficult to isolate a Lieutenant Craddock, and held the visitor at bay with vague rumbles of "Craddock! Ah yes, Craddock. Leg wound, I believe. Smashed knee-cap. One of the stretcher cases that came in from the *Mondego Castle* on Monday . . . Monday was it, or Tuesday? . . . We've been inundated, Mr. Zorndorff, inundated . . ." and then, mercifully, the matron (who at last seemed to have grasped the urgency of the occasion) placed the file in front of him, and he could stop floundering and seriously address himself to manoeuvring this big fish to the bank. "Craddock!" he exclaimed, "Lieutenant

Craddock, P. Why, of course, Mr. Zorndorff! Give Mr. Zorndorff some tea, Countess!", and he relaxed in his chair, like an ageing athlete who, against all probability, has breasted the tape an inch ahead of odds-on competitors.

Zorndorff watched the interplay with quiet enjoyment, looking more than ever like a raven, with deep-set, hooded eyes and supercilious beak. These people, he thought, were such tyros at the game. They gave themselves away so easily and they had no reserves of subtlety, no real knowledge of the blasting power of money. As if he would be here, scattering them all like a fox in a hen-run, if he had not made it his business to reconnoitre in advance, and satisfy himself that the rivalry between the various members of the minor aristocracy and their medical cliques had not already reached a point where, one and all, they were ready to bankrupt themselves, and submerge their entire professional lives in outbidding one another in patriotic endeavour, just so long as whispers of their efforts appeared in *The Bystander* and *Illustrated London News*. Patriotism, he reflected, was a kind of illness itself, and one that would respond to no other drug but public acclaim, public adulation. Before the war it had been who gave the largest house parties, and whose equipage attracted most notice at Ascot, but now only the slow-witted, clinging to Victorian traditions, raised these faded banners. Ever since Black Week, ever since national prestige had been spat upon by Kruger and his Bible-thumping peasants, these people had been at work on a new banner that was no more than a Union Jack; a man like himself, who knew that even Union Jacks had to be paid for, would be a fool not to take every possible advantage of their gavottes. He said, very civilly, "What are his chances? That's what I must know before I leave," and waited.

The Medical Officer was now in command of the situation. Lieutenant Craddock was on the touch-and-go list; Lieutenant Craddock's wound originated from a Mauser bullet entering on an upward course, half-an-inch below the right knee-cap and received whilst patrolling the blockhouses along the Pretoria-Bloemfontein railway. Two operations had already been performed, one in South Africa,

4

one during the voyage home. Both were badly botched. The patient's condition had deteriorated during the voyage but he was now reported to be "holding his own". If gangrene was confirmed then the leg would certainly have to be amputated. So far his youth and health had served him well but he would appear to have rather less than a fifty-fifty chance. Everything that could be done for the boy was being done. The M.O. closed the file and searched the visitor's face for reactions. Seeing none he said, without malice, "His next of kin is given as 'father', Mr. Zorndorff."

"I buried his father yesterday," Zorndorff said without looking at doctor or matron for he appeared to be thinking so deeply that the process was almost visible.

The Countess said, in a voice entirely free from disappointment, "Poor laddie! You are a relative, Mr. Zorndorff?"

Zorndorff must have arrived at his decision for he looked up, brightly, and said, "No relative at all. I am his executor. His father was my oldest friend and business partner. He left his son the sum of twenty-eight thousand pounds, plus a third share in our joint undertaking."

He did not seem in the least interested in the effect of this statement and the ensuing silence in the room was embarrassing for the subdued. They waited, each conscious of the loudly ticking clock; there was nothing else they could do. When Zorndorff rose, asking, or rather demanding, to be led to the patient, they stood up as one and the Countess would have demurred if her half-hearted protest had not been cut short by the M.O.'s gesture. The gesture did not escape Zorndorff, who smiled grimly, standing aside for the surgeon to lead the way through a maze of corridors to a small ward, on the south side of the house.

There were ten or twelve patients lying there and it was insufferably hot, the strong May sunshine beating in at tall, half-curtained windows. One or two voluntary nurses stood about listlessly but straightened themselves as the surgeon strode in, with Zorndorff mincing behind. They went along the beds until they came to one containing a man with his right leg suspended in a cradle that looked like a miniature gallows. The patient was asleep, but fitfully so, for as

Zorndorff looked down at him he moved his head left and right half-a-dozen times and his breathing was irregular. Zorndorff studied the face without emotion and the surgeon, watching him, thought, "He's a damned coldblooded customer! I wonder if the money reverts to him if the boy dies?" and then he flushed slightly, being half-persuaded that the Jew could read his thoughts.

Zorndorff stood by the bed looking down for more than a minute. He saw a narrow face, with a long jaw-line and slightly hollowed cheekbones sprouting a half-inch of blue-black stubble. It was a strong, obstinate face, still boyish under the flush of fever and a man's beard. The dark hair was thick and plentiful, the forehead high, the mouth rather thin and somehow fastidious, like the shapely fingers drumming feebly on the turned-back sheet. It had, he thought, very little in common with the squarish, stolid features of old Josh Craddock, whom he had first met when he was about this boy's age, but there was, Zorndorff suddenly realised, a strong resemblance to the dark, silent woman, who had married Josh the Plumber and had watched him moulded, clinging desperately to his artisan background, into Josh the Merchant. It was the first time he had thought of Josh Craddock's wife in years and he did so now with reluctance and the merest flicker of guilt. He had forgotten even her name, for she had never been linked in his mind to the man who came forward out of nowhere to stand resolutely and illogically between him and deportation to Austria, at the time of his bankruptcy. Yet he recalled her face now and one other thing about her; she had been a countrywoman who had wandered into the city and never found her way out again. He remembered this clearly, and also that she had loathed the city and the claims it made upon her and that her loathing had broken her heart at the age of twenty-eight.

He said, without looking up, "You have private wards here?"

The M.O. said they had indeed, a few, but they were occupied.

"Be so good as to move someone out," Zorndorff said, "someone with a better chance of recovery." Then, before the surgeon could either agree or disagree, "Can you

6

recommend a specialist, a good one, who will make himself available for a second opinion?"

The surgeon hesitated, clutching the rags of his pride, but the prospect of the honours list jogged his elbow just in time and he said, sourly, "I was at Barts under Sir Jocelyn Ferrars but he would be extremely expensive!"

"His fee would not, I think, amount to more than twenty-eight thousand pounds," Zorndorff said, and the surgeon's resentment was swamped by a grudging tide of admiration for such preposterous insolence.

They were out in the cool hall again, where the smell of disinfectant followed them but the temperature was twenty degrees lower and suddenly Zorndorff was being very civil again, thanking him gravely for his courtesy, and begging him to convey his respects to the Countess. Then, in a twinkling, he was gone, and the porter lumbered forward to open the door and run down the steps to the visitor's carriage. The M.O. waited just long enough to see the fellow get a tip for his pains, and from the man's expression it was at least a florin, possibly as much as a crown.

He thought, as he plunged his hands into his cluttered overall pockets, "Damn him! I ought to have torn out a handful of beard and thrown it in his face!" but the mood of bitterness did not last as far as the matron's door for by then his attention was fully occupied with other matters. Who could be ejected from a private ward with the least fuss? And how much should he offer Sir Jocelyn on that arrogant little bastard's behalf?

II

For a man lying flat on his back, with one leg suspended from a pulley, the ceiling looked incredibly far off, yet not so far as to prevent Craddock conjuring fantasies from stains etched into the plaster by leaks that were stopped a century ago; during the long, hot afternoons, when pain and drugs were doing battle with one another inside him, the ragged edges of the damp areas resolved themselves into charging lines of infantry and squadrons of cavalry, with here the burst of a bombshell, there an angled standard.

The battle overhead distressed him far more than the pain or weakness resulting from his wound, for in the months between the present, and the day he had pitched headlong into the dry watercourse beside the railway line, he had come to terms with pain. There never seemed to have been a time when small, darting flames were not searing the nerves between shin and groin. The battle overhead was something different. It would never resolve itself. The opposing armies were always on the point of advancing but when he looked again they were still ranged in lines, with bayonets advanced, officers' swords upraised, drums beating, bugles braying, and the smoke from the batteries billowing between the two hosts. It was a setpiece, but there was about it an immediacy that compelled him to cock an ear for the sob of breathless men and the screams of wounded. It exhausted him but unless he closed his eyes he found it difficult to look elsewhere, for the pulley, and the narrowness of the cot, exacted a penalty in terms of pain. Yet often enough he paid the fee, pressing his left cheek to the pillow to bring his right eye in line with the French windows opposite and staring out at the prospect beyond the terrace, where convalescents played their interminable games of pontoon.

Beyond them he could see the park sloping down a field or two, then up to a line of woods on the horizon. Nothing much happened out there. Sometimes a cow browsed into view, and occasionally a farm waggon crawled along the hillside track, moving so slowly that it seemed to take a very long time to cross his restricted line of vision. He could see clouds drifting above the elms, and patches of blue through the rents and somehow, as though to counter the poised strife overhead, the view brought peace and sanity, for he was aware that the stillness outside was real, whereas the battle on the ceiling was not.

Gradually he began to relate the two vistas, the one fraught with anxiety and stress, the other bringing him joy and tranquillity, so that, as the days passed, and the hillside view slowly began to assume mastery over the armies above, he knew that he would live, drawing more

8

reassurance from the contrast than from anything the surgeon said or the soothing remarks made by the plump nurse who brought him drinks. And with this growing belief in his survival the battle on the ceiling lost its horrid significance, and the vision of serenity framed in woods resolved itself into a kind of Promised Land where he, Lieutenant Paul Craddock, whom they had given up for dead, roamed in the splendour of his youth.

That was after they had moved him to a private ward upstairs, a small room where his view was greatly enlarged and he could lie hour upon hour looking across at the great bow of the woods, and the brown, green, drowsing patchwork, between woods and park. By then the tide of pain had receded a very long way, but had been displaced by boredom and acute discomfort, arising from the angle of his leg, slung to the damned gallows at the foot of the bed. Dressings brought pain but also relief from the tedium of lying there alone. If it had not been for the magnificent view he would, he thought, have died of boredom. Yet there were adequate compensations. The leg, they told him, had been saved after all, and although the surgeon warned him that he would almost certainly suffer a permanent disability resulting from partial atrophy of the joint, it would not be much more than stiffness and he would walk with a slight limp, and could certainly ride; in fact, the more exercise he took the better. He had, they said, been extraordinarily lucky, not solely to have escaped amputation above the knee but to be alive at all. His cure, they explained, was due to a third operation performed by one of the most brilliant surgeons in the country, brought here at enormous cost at the instance of a Mr. Franz Zorndorff, some five days after his arrival from South Africa. He noticed that they all spoke of Mr. Zorndorff with awe and this puzzled him, for all he recalled was a secretive and rather flashy little Austrian Jew who, during his boyhood and youth, had been in close partnership with his father.

They let him ponder this for a day or so and then, with every manifestation of sympathy, they broke the news that his father had died the day he had landed in England. He was shocked by the news but not overwhelmed. He had

9

not seen his father in almost three years and, on the last occasion they had met before he embarked for South Africa, their mutual antipathy, so long banked down by mutual distrust had flared into a shouting match, with Joshua Craddock calling his son every kind of a fool to stick his nose into the Imperial quarrel, and Paul talking a good deal of vainglorious nonsense about his patriotic duty to assist in the chastening of Kruger and Kruger's Bible-thumping farmers. Since then there had been a letter or two, and an occasional draft of money after his commissioning, but no exchange of affection, no show of warmth on the part of either one of them.

After they had left him with what they imagined to be his grief Paul found that, for the first time in his life, he could think of his father impersonally, a big, broad-shouldered, taciturn man, with a squarish face, deliberate hands, a large, walrus moustache, a deep voice that disguised his Bermondsey accent, and above all, a baffling inaccessibility due, as Paul now realised, to his obsession with business affairs that never seemed to bring him any real satisfaction for all the time he lavished on them. He had never, for instance, told Paul anything of his mother, who had died when the child was five, or how it came that he, Joshua, had fought his way from the top strata of the artisan class, a plumber with two or three men in his employ, to that of city merchant, or a kind of city merchant, for Paul had no knowledge of how his father earned a living, apart from some connection with scrap metals near the centre of his original endeavours as a plumber. It seemed to him, lying trussed up under this infernal gallows, a very strange thing that he should know so little about his family, particularly as Joshua had been insistent that he should come into the business on leaving the undistinguished little private school, where he had been sent as a boarder when he was eight years old. He had resisted this pressure solely because he had a strong disinclination to work in an office under artificial light, and had dismayed his father by announcing his intention of entering the artillery. He had already made application for entry to Woolwich when the War offered all young men a chance of immediate service overseas. One of the few accomplishments he had learned at the pretentious little school he attended (Joshua, in his ignorance, had always referred to it as "a public school") was how to sit a horse, so that it had been easy, under the impetus of Black Week and its humiliating defeats, to join the Yeomanry. Later, because of the gaps torn in the ranks by the enteric fever epidemic, it had been almost as easy to get a temporary commission, but for all that he had not seen much active service. By the time his training period had expired the war had degenerated into ding-dong encounters between patrols and Boer Commandos and it was in one of these scuffles that he had received his wound. Before that, however, he had changed his mind about a military career. He was unable, he discovered, to take pleasure in harassing the wretched Veldt farmers and their families, and it was not long before doubts obscured his vision of Imperial infallibility. He wondered sometimes, what he would do with his life now that a gammy leg barred him from most outdoor occupations, yet his prospects did not dominate his thoughts during the earliest stage of his convalescence, when he was learning to walk again on sticks and a network of lines rigged along the terrace. What occupied his mind more often was the curious deference shown him, not only by the volunteer nurses but the Countess, the Chief Medical Officer, and the junior physicians. It puzzled him, for instance, that he alone, apart from one or two high-ranking casualties, had a room to himself, and also that any request he made—for a book, a magazine, or a variation of hospital diet—was granted, when in the crowded general wards below other junior officers, especially the non-professionals like himself, were treated like tiresome children and reacted accordingly, cursing the impulse that had involved them in a war for which many serving soldiers now felt a slight disgust, causing them to ask themselves if, after all, the pro-Boer Lloyd George and his following had not been justified in condemning the adventure from the outset.

He found the key to all this within a few minutes of receiving his first visit from Franz Zorndorff.

The little man strode on to the terrace unannounced

about a week after Paul had been allowed downstairs. He was not wearing his city clothes today but had got himself up in what he imagined to be correct country-house attire, a pepper-and-salt Norfolk suit, a wide grey cravat with a diamond pin, and a billycock hat sporting a pheasant's feather. The staff made way for him as though he had been the Emperor of Japan or, at the very least, a racegoing friend of the new king, Edward. He seated himself in a creaking basket chair and opened his pigskin attaché case, producing a sheaf of papers tied with pink tape.

"Delighted to see you're making such excellent progress my boy!" he began, gaily. "We've a little signing to do first of all. I trust you read all the letters the solicitors sent on?"

"No," Paul admitted, a little irritated by Zorndorff's brashness and the fact that he made no mention at all of his partner's death. "I began to read them but I found it difficult to concentrate. You wrote promising you would come over soon, so I decided I'd ask you to summarise them. They looked damned dull to a man who has read nothing heavier than the *Strand Magazine* for three years."

He saw to his amusement that he had succeeded in disconcerting the Jew, who now looked somewhat startled and then, recovering himself, uttered a short, neighing laugh.

"Then you won't know? Unless, of course, the whisper has gone round, as I rather thought it might!"

Paul asked him to explain, adding that visitors were only allowed a bare half-hour before the bell rang and the terrace had to be cleared.

"Oh, don't concern yourself over that!" Zorndorff said, contemptuously, "I've tamed everybody in this charnel-house, including that fraud of a matron! They won't shoo me out, I can assure you!" And then, placing his shapely hands on his knees and looking directly at Paul, he added, "You'll probably be surprised at the extent of your patrimony. I was myself, somewhat, although I realised of course that Josh spent very little over the years. That was his trouble, I think; he could never cease to think in sixpences, or free himself from the notion that

12

he was still waiting on a plumber's harvest—a hard frost that is!"

"You haven't told me how my father died," Paul said, not altogether liking the half-veiled patronage of the man yet understanding now why he had been treated as a favoured patient.

The Jew lost a little of his ebullience. He said, seriously, "I suppose I owe it to you to admit that Josh Craddock died fulfilling what he imagined an obligation to me. As to the facts, he killed himself heaving a two hundred-weight water-cistern from a cart!" He hissed through his teeth, one of the few Continental habits he had retained after forty years in England. "Imagine that! Josh Craddock, with cash and assets totalling something like forty-five thousand pounds, killing himself to help a lazy oaf of a carter empty a cart!"

The figure stunned him and Zorndorff, enjoying the confusion his casual announcement caused, smiled as he waited for Craddock to recover a little. The Jew had a well-stocked wardrobe of smiles; this was an occasion for his thin one. He said, finally, "Well, and how much did you think he was worth?"

Never having given any thought to the matter Paul guessed, reckoning the ugly house in Croydon, at £750 and his father's share of the business at about £3,000. "Certainly not more than five," he said, "and hardly any of it in cash! You wouldn't be having a little quiet fun at my expense, Mr. Zorndorff?"

"I don't joke about money!" the Austrian said, sharply. "As to the estate, I based Joshua's share of the business on half our last offer to sell, a little over fifteen thousand; the rest is in hard cash, or readily saleable assets, and you are the sole beneficiary. That was something I insisted on when I witnessed the will."

He began to forage in his case but Craddock checked him, saying, "Never mind the documents, Mr. Zorndorff! I should much prefer you to explain, and as simply as you can! Am I to understand that the whole of this sum, including a half-share in the business, comes to me and that I can do as I wish with it?"

"By no means," Zorndorff said. "Your father remained

13

an artisan all his life but he was no fool. We talked it over and agreed that you should inherit a third share of the business and the whole of the capital sum, but you won't receive more than five thousand until you are twenty-eight. That last provision was no suggestion of mine!"

Because Paul still appeared bemused the Jew became a little impatient. "Come now," he said, "even you must realise that the coarse metal trade prospers in wartime. We were doing well enough on sub-contracts before the war, but three years ago, when army contracts were put about, we forged ahead in relation to the blunders the generals made over there! I was optimistic from the start but I must confess that even I hardly expected a three-year war. The point is, we seem to be set fair indefinitely for the Kaiser has obliged the trade by entering the naval race. If you applied yourself I daresay you could soon convert your thirty thousand working capital into two hundred thousand."

Paul, who had heard nothing but the last few words, said slowly, "What the devil do I know of the scrap metal business? Or any business?"

"I would be prepared to teach you," the Jew said, earnestly now, and without a trace of patronage. "Joshua was the only friend I ever had and I have every intention of paying my debt to him, whether you like it or not, my friend!"

"Then you must find some other way of paying it," Paul said. "I may be half a cripple but I'm damned if I intend to devote my life to scrap metal, Mr. Zorndorff!"

The Jew did not seem surprised or disappointed. He looked thoughtful for a moment, drawing his brows together and contemplating his beautifully manicured hands. "With that capital you could do almost anything you liked," he said, at length. "Have you any preferences? Or is it something you would prefer to think about during the time you remain here?"

Paul said, briefly, "First I intend to learn to walk, Mr. Zorndorff; properly, without sticks; like any other person, you understand? I think they have exaggerated my disability. In the meantime, would you care to buy me out at any figure you considered fair?"

The naïveté of the offer stirred Zorndorff. His head shot up and his eyes sparkled as he said, crisply, "Be satisfied with your loose change, and oblige me by allowing me to fulfill my obligations any way I choose!" and he stood up so suddenly that Paul made sure he was deeply offended but he was not, for his smile betrayed him and somehow, because of it, Paul was convinced of the man's fundamental honesty, and of the genuineness of the obligation he felt for the son of the man who had once stood between him and ruin. He said, half apologetically, "I know you have my interests at heart, Mr. Zorndorff, you have proved that already. I daresay I should have croaked in the general ward without first-class attention but the truth is I never expected this kind of opportunity and it alters everything. I had some idea of farming, in a small way, in one of the Dominions perhaps, but it's something I need to think about very deeply. I don't imagine I shall be out of here for a month or more. May I come to you then? Or write, if I form any decision?"

"By all means, by all means," Zorndorff said, expansive and avuncular again, and without any gesture of farewell except a vague pat on the shoulder he picked up his case, strolled along the terrace and went down the steps to the carriage park behind the forecourt.

Paul watched him go, thinking, "Whatever he does is part of a charade. What could he and a dull dog like my father have had in common? Were they the complement of one another? And was my mother somehow involved in the improbable association?" His involvement with the dapper, enigmatic Austrian was to endure for another forty years but this was something he never discovered.

III

As the weeks passed and the sun continued to beat on the baking facade of the great house, there were many things he discovered about himself and not the least important of them was the durability of the bright crystals of thought left in the recesses of his brain by the long, ex-

15

hausting fever duel between the static army on the ceiling and the serenity of the view of the park and downland, seen through the windows of the two wards he had occupied. Somehow the latter came to represent his future, and all that was pleasant and rewarding in life, and he saw it not simply as a pleasing vista of fields, woods and browsing cattle, but as a vision of the England he had remembered and yearned for out there on the scorching veldt. And this, in itself, was strange, for he was city born and bred, and although he had never shared the Cockney's pride in the capital neither had he been conscious, as a boy, of a closer affinity with the woods and hedgerows of the farmland on the Kent-Surrey border, where he had spent his childhood and boyhood. Yet the pull existed now, and it was a very strong pull, as though he owed his life to nectar sucked from the flowers growing wild out there across the dreaming fields near the rim of the woods, and with this half-certainty came another—that it was in a setting like this that he must let the years rescued for him unwind, yielding some kind of fulfillment or purpose. He had never had thoughts like this before and it occurred to him that pain, and a prolonged flirtation with death, had matured him in a way that had been leap-frogged by the other convalescents, many of whom had had more shattering experiences in the field. Some the war had left cynical and a few, among them the permanently maimed, bitter but all the regular officers seemed to have emerged from the war with their prejudices intact and talked of little else but sport, women, and the military lessons learned from the campaigns. They continued, Paul thought, to regard England as a jumping-off ground for an eternal summer holiday in the sun among lesser breeds, looking to them and the Empire for protection and economic stability, but had little or no sense of kinship with the sun-drenched fields beyond the terrace, or the chawbacons seen toiling there, taking advantage of the Coronation weather to cut and stack the long grass. He began to keep very much to himself, reading and browsing through the long afternoons on the terrace, and it was here, about a fortnight after Zorndorff's visit, that he came across the two-page advertisement in the *Illustrated*

16

London News that gave him at least a glimmering of an idea concerning his future.

It was a detailed announcement of the forthcoming sale by auction of a thirteen hundred acre Westcountry estate, owned by a family called Lovell, that seemed to have been very hard-hit by Boer marksmanship, for the heir, Hubert Lovell, had been killed at Modder River after winning a Victoria Cross, and his brother, Ralph, in a skirmish outside Pretoria. Their father, Sir George Lovell, had been a considerable landowner, with other and larger estates in Cumberland and Scotland, and the Devon manor-house, the home farm and five tenant farms, together with areas of surrounding woodland and common, were destined to come under the hammer at the end of the month unless disposed of, either as a whole or in parcels, by private treaties.

It was an impressive and, he would judge, an expensive advertisement, for there were pictures of the house and the three dead Lovells, and a potted history of the family. The house looked impressive but neglected, a sprawling, porticoed building, built on the shallow ledge of a long slope crowned by woods, and seemed to Paul to be mainly Tudor, with Carolean or Georgian extensions east and west. It was approached by a sharply curving tree-lined drive and had clusters of spiralling chimneys that he associated with Elizabethan buildings. It looked squat, comfortable, weatherbeaten and commodious but it was not, in the first instance, the house that attracted his attention, so much as descriptions of the outlying farms, each of between four hundred and two hundred acres. The agents handling the sale announced that they would be open to separate sales of these properties, each of which had its own farmhouse and farm-buildings, and their names read like an Arcadian rent-roll—Four Winds, The Hermitage, Deepdene, High Coombe and Low Coombe.

The oval portraits of the three Lovells interested him. The old man, Sir George, was a bearded, heavy-featured man, with bulging eyes and, Paul would judge, a sensual, bullying mouth. He looked more like an evangelist than a country squire. His elder son, Hubert, was handsome in an unremarkable and slightly effeminate

17

way, with a smooth face and rather vacuous expression, whereas Ralph, the younger boy, was an almost comic caricature of a Regency rake, with his sulky mouth, mop of dark, unruly hair, and an expression that suggested willfulness and a certain amount of dash.

He mulled over the advertisement all the afternoon, wondering how much one of the larger farms would cost, and whether, in fact, a serious bid could be made in advance. Four hundred acres, he felt, was a large enough bite to begin with, and at length, almost on impulse, he tore the two pages from the magazine and enclosed them in a brief, tentative letter to Zorndorff. He would be discharged, they said, in time to accept Zorndorff's invitation to watch the Coronation procession from a private stand rented by the Austrian, and in his note he suggested that they might discuss the matter on that occasion if, in the meantime, his father's solicitors could extract some relevant information from the agents of the sale. He was still only half-serious and wondered, as he sealed the letter, if Zorndorff would pour scorn on the notion, and employ arguments to launch him as a more genteel farmer in Malay or Africa, but after the letter had gone he felt curiously elated, as though at last he had done something positive to convert his fever dreams into reality. He watched the post eagerly during the week but all that arrived from Zorndorff was a telegram bearing the cryptic message, "Letter received; will discuss later; expecting you midday, Club, 24th instant", proving that Zorndorff, for all his apparent neglect, knew rather more regarding his immediate future than he knew himself. The Austrian's club was an establishment in St. James' and the address was on one of the cards he had left with the sheaf of documents that Paul had read with wandering attention. He thought, laying the telegram aside, "Damn the man, why does he have to go out of his way to dominate everybody?" and then he thought he knew the answer in his case. He had, after all, been baulked by the flat rejection of the offer to launch his old friend's son on a money-making career in the metal trade and was still, in his insufferable arrogance, determined to have his way in the matter. "And I daresay the little devil will in the end!" Paul thought, glumly, "for he seems to have acquired the knack of making everyone bow the knee to him!" He had, at that stage, a great deal to learn about Franz Zorndorff's way of doing business.

IV

The newsvendor's cry reached the cab as a continuous high-pitched whine, at the junction of the Strand and Waterloo Bridge Road, and Paul leaned out to wave so that the man dived into the traffic and seemed almost to come at the cab from under the bellies of two enormous horses dragging a brewer's dray. The headline, in the heaviest black type, confirmed the rumour he had heard in the train; the new King was seriously ill, and the Coronation had been postponed indefinitely.

Craddock read the news unemotionally. The King was well over sixty and at that age any exalted man who took his pleasures as strenuously as Teddy might well be taken ill, might even die and be buried in Westminster Abbey. The cab swung into Trafalgar Square, merging into the solid stream of traffic debouching from the Mall, Whitehall and Northumberland Avenue, and here, over the Admiralty Arch, hung two huge portraits, framed in gilt ovals, of Edward and Alexandra, gazing out over chestfuls of decorations and diamonds at the traffic below. Craddock glanced up at them, remembering the barrack-room jokes he had heard about the King's philanderings. He was, they said, the most persistent royal woman chaser since Charles II, but she was a woman whose regality made jokes about them seem in bad taste. He had waited, Paul reflected, forty years to mount the throne and now, at the very last minute, he was lying in bed awaiting a chancy operation. All the stands and scaffolding, the tinsel and bunting, were ready but now there would be no procession, no cheering crowds and no military bands but in their stead an orgy of impersonal grief for a bearded, corpulent man, fighting for his life and a chance

19

to justify himself as man and monarch. Paul studied the faces of the people on the pavements but found there little indication of a national catastrophe, only the stress of scurrying through a whipped-up sea of horse traffic, pounding along to the accompaniment of a low-pitched roar. The sun continued to blaze overhead and the stink of fresh manure, blending with clouds of thick white dust, made Craddock's nostrils twitch. They shook free of the mêlée about halfway down Pall Mall and turned into St. James' Street, where Zorndorff awaited him at his Club.

"I suppose you've heard the news," Paul said, as he paid off the cabby, and the man grinned. "Couldn't 'elp it, could I, Sir? Been screaming their 'eads orf since first light! D'you reckon he'll make it, Sir?"

"Why not?" Craddock heard himself say, "he's Vicky's son; that ought to help!"

The cabby nodded eagerly and Paul noticed that he was no longer grinning. As he pocketed Craddock's tip he said, "Funny thing, can't seem to get used to the idea of a king. Kind o' permanent she was, like the Palace over there, or Nelson back in the square! You keep forgettin', gov'nor—you know, when they play 'God Save the Queen—King'!" and he saluted, flicked his whip and bowled away towards Piccadilly.

Craddock stood on the Club steps pondering for a moment. The man was right of course. Post-Victorian London was not the city he remembered of less than three years ago but he would have found it difficult to put the changes into words. The streets had always been jam-packed with slow-moving traffic, and reeking with odours of horse-sweat and dust, but the changes seemed to lie in the mood of passers-by, more brash and brittle than he remembered, with a little of the class rigidity gone, more audacity among the vendors, porters and draymen, less assurance in the stride of those two cigar-smoking, top-hatted gentlemen, as they walked down the hill towards St. James' Palace. He went on into the plush-lined lobby and when he mentioned Mr. Franz Zorndorff the doorman at once became obsequious, and directed him to the dining-room, a vast, crowded rectangle, where the clatter of cutlery and the roar of conversation was as oppressive as the uproar outside. Zorndorff appeared through a cloud of waiters, calling, "Ah, my boy! Not in here, not in this babel! I've booked lunch in the members' dining-room upstairs," and he seized Craddock by the arm and steered him up a broad staircase and along a corridor to a smaller room, with the words "Members Only" painted in gilt letters on the swing-doors.

"You'll have heard the news, Paul? It must be a big disappointment for you," Franz said as the waiter, without waiting for the order, brought them two very dry sherries.

"It might have been this morning," Craddock told him, "but after crossing London from King's Cross I don't mind admitting it's a relief. Maybe I should have done it by stages, like a diver coming up from a great depth, but the noise and stink terrified me! I'm sorry for the Cockneys, though, they deserve a bit of glitter after putting up with this day and night."

"Come, you're a Cockney yourself, Paul. You were born in Stepney and that's within earshot of Bow, isn't it?"

"I'm not proud of it," Craddock said. "How the devil can you make decisions in such a hellish uproar?"

"Far more expertly than I could make them beside the old rustic mill," Franz told him jovially, "for in London wits are whetted every time one crosses the street and as for this," he waved his hand in the general direction of Piccadilly, "this is nothing, my friend, to the midday congestion beyond Temple Bar, or south of the river on a weekday. We shall wait until evening before going there and drive back to my house in Sloane Street at sunset. You can stay there as arranged. I shall be busy except for today, but I imagine you have things to attend to."

He went on to talk of general matters, the food, the King's chances of a recovery, the effect of his illness on the political scene, Paul's wound and the post-hospital treatment prescribed for it, anything, Paul soon realised, to steer away from the subject of purchasing a West-country farm, but by now Paul had, to some extent, the

21

measure of the man and felt reasonably secure in his affections, so that when the coffee and brandy had been served, and the waiter had ceased to make his swift, discreet dashes upon the table, he said, grinning, "Look here, Mr. Zorndorff, if you think I'm an ass to have written that letter you can say so! You don't have to avoid the subject, like a cat walking through puddles!" Zorndorff twinkled, put on his avuncular look and replied, amiably, "There is a side to you that indicates a latent business acumen, my boy! You possess a quiet obstinacy wedded to a somewhat shattering directness of manner, a formidable combination under certain circumstances!" He sipped and savoured his brandy, as Paul waited and then, carefully setting down the glass, he said seriously, "I hadn't forgotten the letter and enclosures but before I even discuss it you must do something for me. A very small thing, but also an obligation of a kind, I think."

"Well?"

"You must come down to the scrapyard. This evening, after my siesta. If you have really made up your mind to stick your nose in the dirt then you should give yourself the chance of deciding on the spot whether it is the three-percent-barring-acts-of-God dirt of a provincial farm, or the gilt-edged dirt of a bone yard! Afterwards? Afterwards we might get around to discussing your absurd proposition. Is that agreed?"

"Certainly I'll come to the yard with you. As a matter of fact I should like to, out of curiosity. I've never once been there, at least, not to my recollection."

"That," Zorndorff said, affably, "I already know, for your father fell into the error common to all artisans who have risen in the world. He was determined to ensure that his son wore a clean collar to work. This is very excellent brandy, but the flavour is a little elusive I think."

"Certainly no more so than you, Mr. Zorndorff," Paul said, smiling, to which Zorndorff replied, "From now on, my boy, it would flatter me if you would address me as 'Uncle Franz'. I have cohorts of indigent nephews but none, alas, with a float of five thousand and expectations."

The curious thing about this pronouncement, Paul

noticed, was that, although larded with Zorndorff's brand of laboured irony it was uttered in all sincerity.

They paid off the cabby at Tower Bridge, walking southeast into the maze of streets running between the Old Kent Road and the canal, and as they went along Paul was aware of a stronger and more tangible security than he had ever known. He did not understand why this should be so, only that, in some way, it emanated from the dapper little man tripping along beside him, an utterly incongruous figure here in his tweeds and billycock hat, twirling his cane to emphasise points in his flow of conversation. Zorndorff was obviously very much at home in this part of London, turning left or right without hesitation when, to Craddock, every seedy little street seemed the same and even their names ran in sets, the battles of the Crimea, the battles of the Indian Mutiny, the seacoast towns of the Cornish peninsula and a variety of flowering shrubs that had not been seen hereabouts for generations. The complexity of the brick labyrinth astonished him, for it went on and on until it melted into the bronze sky, under which the stale summer air was battened down by a pall of indigo smoke, rising from ten thousand kitchen-ranges behind the yellow brick terraces. The houses all looked exactly alike, narrow, two-storeyed little dwellings, bunched in squat, yellowish blocks, like rows of defeated coolies awaiting their evening rice issue. Here and there the occupiers (none were owners Franz told him) stood at the doors, obese, shirtsleeved men with broad, pallid faces, wrinkled old crones with furtive eyes and nutcracker jaws, shapeless, blowsy women in aprons, their moon faces curtained by great hanks of hair, and sometimes a very old man, like a Chelsea pensioner stripped of his uniform. The evening heat hung level with the chimney pots and although the litter cars were at work in the streets most of the rubbish escaped their revolving brooms and was whirled into the gutter. The curious thing was that Craddock did not shrink from the scene, as he had from the comparatively clean streets of the West End, for although, on this side of the river, there was airlessness, and evidence of an appalling poverty, there was also a

23

sparkle and vitality that intrigued and interested him, as though he was exploring the seamier section of a foreign city. Watching the West End crowds that morning he had seen individuals hurrying past in isolation but down here, where the yards spilled into one another, and the house numbers ran up to two hundred in stretches of less than a hundred yards, the Londoners were obviously a community and, as far as he could judge, a more or less contented community. It was the urchins in the street that interested him the most, bedraggled little ragamuffins, with the zest and impudence of city gamins all over the world. He watched them spill out of their narrow houses, calling to one another in their strong nasal accents, to torment the carter in charge of the water-sprinkler who was doing a very little towards laying the dust. Every time the carjets sprayed the urchins dashed within range of the nipples, accepting the flick of the carter's whip as part of the sport. Franz said, "It astonishes you? The richest city in the richest country in the world? Perhaps you find it difficult to believe but it is far more salubrious than it was. When I came here in the 'sixties no man dressed like us would have dared to walk these streets, not even in daylight. You have read your Dickens, I imagine?" and when Craddock told him that he had, he added, "There is still squalor to spare but not nearly so much vice, I think. That is largely because there is plenty of work within easy walking distance of these hovels. It is only down nearer the Docks that a man can get knocked on the head nowadays, and then only at night."

As they went along, moving further south of the river, Franz pointed out various local landmarks. There was Peek Frean's biscuit factory, employing over a thousand, and nearby the "Grenadier" match factory, where there had been a national scandal over a number of operatives who had contracted the dreaded "phossy-jaw", from contact with phosphorus. He did not need to point out the Tannery for the stench assailed them as they rounded the corner of the high boundary wall and then, within a quarter-mile of this enormous building, they passed through the double-gates of the scrapyard and Craddock looked with amazement at his inheritance.

It was about two to three acres of wasteland, enclosed on three sides by the backs of terraced houses, and on the fourth by an eight-foot wall, surmounted with broken glass. Debris lay on all sides, strewn in what at first seemed utter confusion but when he looked more closely was seen to be stacked according to some kind of plan. The junk rose in a series of twenty-foot pyramids, built row upon row, like a terrible parody of a cornfield full of stooks, and round the base of each pyramid was a patch of cinders rutted by cart wheels. Every imaginable article of hardware was represented. Craddock saw brass bedsteads, buckled bicycles, tin baths, skeins of twisted, rusting pipes, holed and handleless pails, cracked lavatory pans, stoves, both whole and in fragments, stripped perambulator frames and at one point, between two mounds of rubbish, the better part of a tanker engine, looking like a dying dinosaur in a swamp.

"Great God!" he exclaimed, "you say my father actually *liked* working here?"

"Most of the men and boys on piecework like it, at all events, they much prefer it to a steady job in a factory. We had a Salvation Army Unit here last summer, and about a dozen of them were talked into attending a free camp on the Downs. Most of them were back here before the week was out, and even those who stayed spent their time looking for scrap."

"How much do you pay casual labour for this kind of rubbish?"

"That depends on what they bring in. Certain metals, like copper, carry a bonus, but an average barrowload earns them about a shilling. If it comes by the cartload we weigh it on the weighbridge there by the office."

Craddock glanced in the direction indicated and saw that one half of the yard was dotted by a dozen, slow-burning fires. In the still evening air the smoke ascended vertically and all the time smuts floated across his vision, drifting by like cockroaches in a trance. The wooden hut that did service as an office was built on a steep concrete ramp and under the ramp were several carts, awaiting their turn to move on to the weighbridge. Franz led the way over, mincing along the narrow tracks between the rubble stacks, lifting his cane to acknowledge the checker's respectful greeting. Craddock followed him up the ramp and stood on the platform looking out over the vast desolation. It was like, he thought, an illustration of Dante's *Inferno,* that he had seen among sale catalogues that his father had kept in the glass-fronted bookcase at home, and the orange glow of the setting sun, lighting up acres of slate roofs to the west, shed an unlikely radiance on the squalor. Franz had gone into consultation with a beefy man in the office and Craddock stood quite still, looking across the yards to the vast huddle that surrounded St. Paul's, in the far distance. He thought, "Twenty-eight thousand pounds out of this! It's an ugly joke but the laugh is on poor devils who comb through refuse heaps at a shilling a barrowload!" and as he thought this his ear caught the pleasant warble of a mouth-organ, playing "Lily of Laguna" and he looked down beyond the weighbridge to see a boy aged about ten or eleven sitting on the nearside shaft of one of the carts, his bare legs swinging free, his hands cupped to his mouth so that Craddock could only see the upper part of a face, crowned by a mop of black hair. The child's face and air of rapt concentration arrested him, so that for a moment he forgot his disgust for the place and concentrated on the musician, noting the boy's breadth of forehead, large, thoughtful eyes, and above all, the statuesque set of head cocked sideways, as though listening intently to the wail of his own music.

Then something happened that made him shout a warning, for a carter ducked between the tailboard of the foremost cart and the head of the horse harnessed to the cart in charge of the boy, so that the animal, startled, threw up its head and the overloaded cart tilted, sending its load of scrap metal cascading over the tailboard and producing a clatter that set the terrified horse rearing, its hooves flailing within inches of the carter now boxed between the wall of the ramp and the rear of his own cart.

The boy must have moved at fantastic speed, for when Craddock turned his head he was missing from his seat on the shaft and Craddock could only suppose him to have been thrown down between the footboard and the hindquarters of the frantic horse. He turned to run down the

26

steps but at that moment he saw the boy bob up on the far side and spring on the animal's back, where he hung on with his knees as he tore off his jacket, leaned far over the neck and flung it over the animal's head, holding it there as his body was flung backwards and forwards by the violent heaves. Gradually the animal quietened, straining outward away from the ramp and then, after what seemed to Craddock a long interval, the checker came running round to the far side of the queue and grabbed the bridle, throwing his weight on the horse's head and then wheeling the cart out of line away from the ramp, so that the carter could rise shakily to his knees and stagger past his own vehicle to the weighbridge. The boy with the mouth-organ then swung his legs and slid to the ground and Craddock, to his amazement, saw that he was not only grinning, but still had his harmonica clutched in his right hand.

"Serve yer bloody well ri'!" he jeered at the man, "doncher know better'n to come on 'er from the blind side?" whereupon he perched himself on a bollard beside the scales and at once proceeded to suck at his mouth-organ, until such time as the foremost cart moved off the weighbridge and it was his turn to follow it across the grating.

Craddock, spellbound by the incident, now saw that Franz was standing beside him.

"That boy!" he said, "I've never seen anyone react as quickly and intelligently! Who is he? I . . . I'd like to give him something."

Franz glanced into the yard.

"I heard a lot of shouting," he said, "what happened?" and when Craddock described the incident he said, carelessly, "Oh, they're always getting and giving hard knocks down there. You don't have to come here distributing your largesse!" and plunging a hand into his pocket, he called over the guard rail—"Here boy! That's one of Sophie's horses isn't it?" and the boy grinned up at them and said, "Yerse, Mr. Zorndorff, it's ole Betty, an' she's blind in one eye! Foster come up on 'er blind side so she turned nasty! She's orlri' now tho', Mr. Zorndorff!" but when Zorndorff continued to frown he lost a little of his perkiness, pocketed his harmonica and ran over to help the men clearing away the litter that had spilled on the carriageway.

"Never mind that, come up here at once you rascal!" Zorndorff called and the boy, looking like a pupil answering a headmaster's summons, came slowly up the steps to the platform and stood before them, now looking furtive and dejected.

"You're one of Sophie Palfrey's boys yourself, aren't you?" asked Franz sharply and the boy nodded, throwing back his mop of hair and converting the gesture into a surreptitious wipe of his nose. "I'm the oldest. Me Dad's laid orf fer a bit, so Ma said to load up an' bring what was waiting out back from las' week!"

"All right," said Zorndorff, gruffly, "I'm not blaming you for what happened but that horse of your mother's is past working and we'll have trouble with the inspector if you don't send her to the knacker's and get another. You'd best tell your mother that, you understand? Here . . ." and he tossed the boy a coin, which the child caught expertly and thrust into his pocket.

"Cor, thanks Mr. Zorndorff," he said, carefree again, and skipped down the steps to help reload his cart.

"What did you give him?" asked Craddock, a little annoyed by Zorndorff's cavalier handling of the situation, and when Franz told him sixpence he said it wasn't enough whereupon Franz turned on him fiercely and said, "It's more than enough! You don't know these people! Show them kindness and they'd be on top of you, with their tricks and excuses in two minutes! I know that family well. As a matter of fact that boy is a relation of a sort."

"A relation?"

"He's one of Sophie Carrilovic's brood. She came over here and married a tanner called Palfrey, a thorough-going scoundrel who drinks all he earns and beats her regularly every Saturday night. She's a Croat, one of the many who got word of me and migrated for pickings! It happens with every expatriate, the moment he gets his head above water! I've had them clamouring for work and somewhere to live for years, and at first I did what I could, remembering my own troubles, but there comes a time when a man has to harden his heart or go under."

"But the boy's speed and courage saved that carter's life," Paul protested.

"I don't doubt it," Franz grunted, "but something of that kind happens here every day of the week. They have a saying, south of the river; there are only two kinds of folk—the quick and the dead! Damn it man, the mortality rate among children of his kind is forty per cent up to the age of five and it doesn't depreciate much in the next ten years."

Craddock was silent and they moved into the office, an airless little building, littered with spiked invoices, price-lists and grimy box files. Here, and among all that debris below, thought Craddock, his father had lived out his life, accumulating thousands of pounds but ultimately bursting his heart lifting a piece of rubbish from a cart. It seemed a pitiful waste of energy and initiative and his wife, the woman Craddock had never known, must have loathed it, and perhaps taken refuge in dreams of open country until the day she died. Down here, he reflected, the children of the poor fought for coppers, risking their lives handling half-blind horses and counting the acquisition of an extra sixpence a triumph. He thought again of all the men who had died in South Africa to maintain the momentum of the machine that opportunists like Franz Zorndorff thought of as a modern, highly-industrialised state. Well, at least the volunteers in South Africa had spent their final moments breathing fresh air, and under a sun that was not blotted out by sulphurous smoke and floating smuts but surely—surely to God there was a compromise between the England of yesterday, with its fat farms and thriving local industries, and the grinding, impersonal money-machine that England had become in the last few decades? Surely somewhere, somehow, the industrial skills of the Watts and Stephensons and Faradays could be applied to a land that could still grow good corn and breed the best cattle in Europe? He said, deliberately:

"Well, coming here has resolved any doubts I had, Uncle Franz. I'll sell all my interests in this graveyard at once! I'll accept whatever terms you propose, purchase

29

over a period, or money down for a bargain price outright! And I won't have second thoughts on this! You can get the lawyers to make out the papers tomorrow."

He expected immediate protests, arguments, scorn, for down here, safe on his home ground, there was an edge to the Croat that was blunted in the West End, but Zorndorff only sighed and, lifting his case, spilled its contents on to the littered trestle table, poking among the papers until he found a slim clip of letters, with a buff telegram form on top. He said, with a shrug, "I had no real hope you would recant but at least I've done my duty by your father; it was always his wish you would take over this place and perhaps mould it into something as profitable but somewhat more conventional. However, I suppose I have a duty to your mother as well. You never knew her, did you?"

"No," Paul said, "and very little about her, except that she was a countrywoman."

"She came, I believe, from somewhere in the Severn Valley but I am not familiar with the English provinces. That would be a hundred miles or so due east of this Shallowford place you wrote about? Well," he smiled his thin smile, "what is a hundred miles to a ploughboy, eh? You'll see that I have secured an option on the place. You can go and look over it tomorrow, now that the Coronation is cancelled!" and he handed Paul the papers which included the original advertisement from the *Illustrated London News*. Paul glanced at the telegram. All it said was, *"Will meet Lieutenant Craddock Sorrel Halt 3.30 p.m. 24th instant. Latest information is thirteen thousand acceptable. Will confirm later. John Rudd, Agent."*

"What the devil does it mean, Uncle Franz? It doesn't make sense! I asked for a price on one of the farms, not the entire damned acreage and house!"

"My boy," Franz said, "I told you your father found it impossible to stop thinking in sixpences. If you must farm then farm big! Don't nibble! Take the biggest bite offered you! And when you get there don't let this joker of an agent bluff you. They'll take thirteen thousand gladly, if only to save the extra delay in selling off by lots. It's clearly the best offer they've had. I should have stuck fast at twelve!"

"But hang it," Paul exclaimed, exasperation with the Croat's patronage overcoming his nervousness, "I haven't got more than five thousand, have I? And I don't know a damned thing about running an estate of this size! My idea was to learn farming, not set up as a squire over thirteen hundred acres!"

"Oh, you'll learn," Zorndorff said, with maddening unconcern. "This agent seems to know his business and doubtless he'll stay on for a year or two. As to the money, you can leave that side of it to me. I'll waive a point and release another eight thousand, plus a working capital of a thousand or two to tide you over until the rents come in. As to disposing of your share in this bone-yard, you'll find me far less co-operative! You'll keep your interest as long as I think fit, and remember you can't sell to anyone but me until your twenty-eighth birthday and I daresay you'll be very glad of the income during the intervening period! It looks to me as if the place is badly run down."

Paul sat on one of the office stools, trying to grapple with the magnitude of the new situation and finding it difficult not to succumb to panic.

"How far am I committed?" he demanded and the Jew, looking at him kindly, said, "You aren't committed at all. This is an option, not a contract, boy. Go down and look at it. Ride about, ask questions, listen at keyholes if necessary. With this amount of money involved any safety device is permissible! But I'll tell you one thing! Don't come back here and admit that your nerve isn't equal to it, and start hedging your bets by becoming a pennypiece freeholder among a crowd of tenant-farmers, all of whom, I daresay, would buy their land if they had the guts and capital! If you do that you'll soon be squeezed out and make a mess of it. In other words, stay there as boss or not at all! There's only one way to farm in this country —on a big scale, with lesser men doing all the donkey work. That talk of starting at the bottom is put about by people at the top; those at the bottom stay there!"

"You didn't!" Paul argued, chuckling in spite of himself, "my father told me the pair of you started with a working capital of less than a hundred!"

"Ah," Zorndorff said, "that was before this country sold

its soul to the devil! It's very different nowadays. The day of the small man is over, I'm afraid!" He pointed through the begrimed window to the weighbridge, where the line of carters was still awaiting their turn. "Do you imagine any of those ruffians will ever sip brandy in St. James', as we did today? Only if there is another war, on a far vaster scale than the South African affair, and then only the gamblers among them!"

"Why are you so eager to push me into this?" Paul asked, suddenly, "you know it can never make money, not as you understand money?"

Franz said, shrugging, "That's so, but apart from pro-pitiating one's involuntary sleeping partner and one's sole, solvent nephew, I like a young man to follow his destiny even if it leads to the Official Receiver!"

It was some kind of answer but it was very far from being a complete or even an honest answer. Franz Zorn-dorff's contempt for sentiment was genuine enough, but as he looked sidelong at Paul Craddock's strong, narrow face and obstinate mouth it was not of his old friend that he thought but of the stately, aloof woman, who had been Josh Craddock's country-bred wife. He fancied that, for the first time in all the years that had passed since he and Josh had thrown down their challenge to the world, she was regarding him with tolerance, or at least without disdain.

CHAPTER TWO

I

JOHN RUDD recognised him the moment the little train emerged from the cutting, a lean young man with a rather sallow face, head and shoulders thrust enquiringly through the window of a first-class compartment. Recognition did nothing to reassure the chunky, ruddy-faced man sitting the piebald cob and holding the grey gelding by a leading rein. Rudd thought, as the face disappeared, and the train ran alongside the platform, "That's him all right, an ex-Yeomanry show-off, still wearing uniform a month after peace has been signed! A kid too, by the look of him, with plenty of somebody else's money to burn, and all the answers in his narrow little head!", and he kicked the flanks of the cob and moved forward, deciding that he would be damned before he dismounted and went into the booking-office to help The Prospect with his luggage. He couldn't carry it anyway, since the idiot had told the Jewboy to wire asking for horses, and why should he have done that? Probably in order to cut a dash in his uniform so that now the luggage would have to come over on the carrier's cart, a service that would cost him a florin. Rudd waited, glumly, more than ever convinced that he would be paid off and turned loose within the next month or so. After all, an ex-Yeomanry poop would not be likely to need an agent to run a six-farm estate. He would be sure to imagine he could do the job better himself.

Craddock had seen Rudd and been intimidated by the man's moody stare, and the squareness of his seat on the piebald. He looked like a man who knew his business but also a person unlikely to give unprejudiced advice on matters involving his personal future. Craddock slipped on his rucksack, all the luggage he had brought with him, and left the train, noting that nobody else got out at the halt but that his arrival caused a ripple among stationmaster, porter and two or three idlers sunning themselves on platform seats. They looked at him incuriously but steadily, so that he had to walk the gauntlet of their stares, surrendering his ticket and stalking through the booking-hall and into the station-yard, which was more like a garden with its tall hollyhocks, sunflowers and neat beds of geranium growing under the stationmaster's windows. Rudd touched his low crowned hat.

"Lieutenant Craddock?"

"Only 'lieutenant' until the first week of July," Craddock said, making a determined effort to smile as he shook the agent's hand. "I'm in uniform because I was discharged from hospital yesterday and didn't stop to buy civilian togs."

Rudd surveyed him coolly, a little disconcerted by his youth and cordiality. "Maybe I'm wrong," he reflected, "maybe he's a poop that can be handled with a little care," and he nodded briefly, swinging his leg over the cob and dismounting to slip the gelding's stirrup-irons down the leathers.

"She's fat but you'll find her comfortable, Mr. Craddock. Been out to grass since early spring. Nobody to hunt her back end of the season," and he stood holding the crupper, while Craddock hoisted his stiff leg across the grey's back. He managed it but not without a grimace and Rudd said, casually, "You got it in the leg then?"

"Knee joint," Craddock told him, "it doesn't look much but it's given everybody a hell of a lot of trouble."

This seemed all there was to say so they set off down the curving white road side by side. It was not until they had crossed the main highway, and pushed on down a stony track leading across a wide stretch of gorse moor, that Rudd spoke again. To Craddock, who still found him intimidating, he seemed to do so with reluctance.

"Maybe it was a good idea riding back. At least I can show you some of the country before you look at maps. Our boundary begins down there in the hollow, a mile or so on. We shall go pretty well the entire length of our western border and pass two of the farms, Hermitage and Four Winds, both around three-fifty acres."

"How far is it?" Craddock asked for something to say, and Rudd told him that the distance from Shallowford to Sorrel Halt, their nearest rail point, was a little over six miles. "It would have been much shorter," he added, "if the family hadn't opposed the Great Western Railway crossing their land. As it is the branch line was kept to the far side of that main road that we crossed just now. That's one reason that has kept us in the Middle Ages."

He said this with a sneer and Craddock looked at him again, noting the firm flesh of his jaw which had the strength of a steel trap and the bleakness of hard, light blue eyes, now gazing straight ahead. He looked and rode, thought Craddock, as though he had seen service in a cavalry regiment and he might have been a year or so short of fifty. He said, without curiosity, "Have you been in the Army, Mr. Rudd?"

The agent's reaction was immediate. He swung round so sharply that the cob threw up its head and pranced a step or two as Craddock's grey, evidently accustomed to its tantrums, neatly sidestepped giving Craddock's leg a sharp twinge. They stopped, half-facing one another.

"So they haven't lost much time telling you!" snapped Rudd and Craddock saw that his cheeks were a network of tiny blue veins and that a pulse beat in his temples. He decided that he disliked the man on sight and replied, crisply, "Nobody's told me anything, Mr. Rudd. I explained that I was in hospital until forty-eight hours ago. All the arrangements were made by my father's executor, Mr. Franz Zorndorff, and neither he nor I have met or corresponded with anyone down here, save yourself."

The anger went out of the agent's face and he looked confused and shamefaced. He gave the reins a twitch and they moved on.

"Then I beg your pardon," he said after a pause, "I had no cause to say anything like that, no cause at all! Damned bad manners on my part! I apologise, Mr. Craddock."

"Very well," said Paul, his resentment ebbing, for the man now looked both depressed and uneasy, "we'll forget I asked, except to say that it was a perfectly innocent remark on my part. While we are at it, however, am I right in imagining you resent me coming here? If so, it might help us both if you explained why?"

Rudd reined in again and sat quite still, staring over the hillside to a great sprawl of woods on the far edge of the moor and it seemed to Craddock that he was almost willing the nearest clump of oaks to topple and crash. Suddenly he looked directly at Craddock and his full lips twitched in an unexpectedly frank smile.

"I don't blame you thinking me a rum 'un," he said, "but the fact is I'm pretty much on edge these days and there's reason enough for that right enough! I've been waiting here ever since Sir George died up north, and even before that I had no kind of instructions from him or his solicitors. They even let me read about Mr. Hubert's death in the newspapers. I suppose Shallowford means little enough to them but they might have had the decency to reassure me about my own future. After all I've served them well for close on twenty years, and if they had any complaints I've yet to hear of them!"

"You mean your position as agent has neither been confirmed nor terminated since the estate was put up for sale?"

"I've not had a word, one way or the other, nothing except a telegram about the furniture sale from the solicitors."

"It all seems a bit casual," Craddock said, "and I can understand you feeling touchy about it. Did you intend leaving when Shallowford is sold?"

"I've nothing else in the offing at the moment," Rudd said grimly, "but it would be unreasonable to discuss that with you at this stage. In any case," he paused a moment, looking down at the cob's bristles, "to be honest it wasn't my position here that made me fly off the handle just now. I jumped to the wrong conclusion, that's all."

"That the Lovell family had written to me about you?"

"Yes, and rather more than that."

"You can't expect me to follow you there, Mr. Rudd. Either tell me what's in your mind or let's ride on and we can discuss your position as agent when I've had a chance to make up my mind. It isn't made up in advance, you know."

Rudd said, breathing heavily, "No . . . wait, Mr. Craddock! You've served overseas, so it isn't like talking to a complete stranger. I'd rather tell you at once why that 'innocent question' of yours encouraged me to make an ass of myself! The fact is, I *have* served in the Army. Until I was twenty-eight I held a commission in the Light Cavalry and I too served in Africa but another part of Africa." He paused a moment and then said, flatly, "I was cashiered, more or less."

"How can an officer be cashiered 'more or less'?" Craddock asked.

"What I mean is it wasn't official but it was a drumming out just the same," Rudd said, "and it wasn't for debt either but something a damned sight worse! It was that

36

that gave the Lovells, father and sons, the edge on me all these years, and they still have it, even though all three of them are dead now, damn them! And on top of it all Hubert had to win a V.C.! Well, thank God I wasn't called upon to congratulate him on that!"

"Then the Lovells were bad people to work for?"

"They were but I don't hate them for that," Rudd said, "any more than do the rest of the people around here, folk dependent upon them for one reason or another." He seemed to rise slightly in his stirrups and survey the whole sweep of the moor as far as the sea. "This has been a bad place to be," he said quietly, "rotten bad for three generations if you had no means to escape from it! It need not have been but it was, for they made it so, one and all! It took me years to make up my mind about that, that it was them and not the place itself. However, that doesn't explain my touchiness does it?", and unexpectedly he smiled again and kicked his heels, so that the cob began to walk on down the slope and the well-mannered grey followed.

"I don't see that you are under the slightest obligation to explain things to me at this stage," Paul said.

"Oh come, Mr. Craddock," said Rudd, good-humouredly now, "suppose I left it there? You would only get to wondering and wondering and be driven to find out one way or another. Anyone would, especially a lad your age, who could never imagine it happening to him."

"A good deal has happened to me already," Paul said. "I only pulled through by a miracle. They gave me up time and again and I got in the habit of hearing my chances chewed over by doctors and nurses. That can teach you a thing or two if you'll let it."

Rudd looked frankly at him and for the first time there was tolerance in his eyes.

"Exactly what did it teach you that was new, Mr. Craddock?"

"Patience, I suppose, and gratitude for being alive. Also respect for people who seemed to go to a great deal of trouble to improve one's chances—those kind of things."

"I was a pupil at a different kind of school," Rudd said. "Did you ever hear of the Prince Eugène Napoleon? The 'Painted Emperor's' son, the one killed in the Zulu War?"

37

"Certainly. He was killed on June 1st, 1879, whilst on reconnaissance during the advance on the Zulu capital."

"Now, how the devil do you come to know that?" exclaimed Rudd and Craddock chuckled. "Because it happens to have been the day I was born, so naturally I made a mental note of it when I'd read an account in one of the *Strand Magazine*s we had at home."

"Now that's very odd," said Rudd, musing, "that's damned odd! If I was a superstitious man I'd say that was some kind of omen but good or bad I wouldn't know. Do you recall the circumstances?"

"No, I'm afraid I don't," said Craddock, "but I imagine you liked the Prince Imperial as much as you seem to have liked your late employers."

"About even I should say," retorted Rudd easily, "for both had a peculiar propensity for winning notoriety at other people's expense! That young man had nobody but himself to blame for what happened. He off-saddled in shoulder-high grass out of range of the camp, with one wretched lieutenant and six troopers as escort. The Zulus jumped the troop and they had to bolt for it. Everyone got away but the Prince. He was riding a nervous horse and couldn't get a leg over when the firing started. He had about a dozen assegai wounds when they found him. All in front. Very proper."

"How were you involved?"

"I was sent after the patrol by an officer who should never have sent it out in the first place, and when I met them coming back hell for leather I turned and rode in with them. Was that so odd? What is a man supposed to do when he sees a reconnaissance patrol riding for their lives? Stop them and ask for a written report?"

It was strange, Craddock thought, how time had done nothing to dull the man's memory of that single moment of panic, now twenty-three years behind him. It was as though, up to that moment, nothing of importance had occurred to him, and after it he had lived a kind of half-life in which the most sensational event came a poor second to a wild gallop across the veldt, with troopers gasping out news that the Prince Imperial was back there, speared through by assegais.

"Why are you telling me all this, Mr. Rudd?" he asked and Rudd said, "God knows! I haven't mentioned it to anyone else in twenty years! Not that everyone here doesn't know about it, Sir George and Hubert saw to that."

"But they continued to employ you as their agent."

"That's *why* they employed me and also why I stayed. What kind of future was open to a man who had turned tail and abandoned a Prince Imperial to a few savages?"

They rode silently for a moment and then Craddock said, "Very well, now you've told me, but as far as I'm concerned I don't give a damn what bad luck you ran into all that time ago. I've done my share of dodging tricky situations and so has every other soldier, unless he's a fool, or a bit slow off the mark! I was hoping to rely on you for straightforward advice on my chances of making some kind of success with this place; if I decided to buy that is, but you ought to know right away that it wasn't my idea at all but Zorndorff's. I can't even legally buy it for another five years."

Rudd looked surprised. "You mean your money is tied up until then?"

"That's so but it needn't necessarily stop a purchase. Mr. Zorndorff seems anxious that I should take the plunge, although administration of an estate this size was only a vague notion at the back of my mind, something I used to think about when I knew I would be invalided out. I've had no previous experience and wanted a single farm. The only qualifications I have are that I should be interested and I can ride. I'm not a crock either. When this stiffness eases I'll be as fit as the next man. I wanted an open-air life and Mr. Zorndorff seemed to think this was as good an opportunity as any."

Rudd was smiling again. The man had almost as wide a range of expression as Zorndorff. No trace remained of his previous sullenness and he looked, Craddock now felt, like a man one could trust.

"Well, I suppose you might do worse, things being what they are and I mean your circumstances, not those of the estate. It's badly run down and peopled with backward, lazy rascals but they ought to welcome you; if they have any sense that is! The Lovells took their rents every quarter day for a century or more and cursed them if they asked for a new tile on the roof. You'll need to put money into it for a spell but the land on this side is as good as any in Devon and there's good timber behind the house. The Home Farm is in shape, for I've seen to that, and Honeyman is a good farmer. It's in the Coombe area that you've got layabouts and they're mostly confined to one family, the Potters, of Low Coombe. However, there's no point at all in my influencing you one way or the other at this stage, you'll have to make up your own mind after you've gone the rounds." He chuckled and glanced sidelong at Craddock through half-closed eyes. "Well, this is a rum do I must say! I expected all kinds of developments when I got the enquiry but nothing quite like this, I can assure you." And then he seemed to brace himself in the saddle, assuming a paternal, businesslike air. "We're about halfway down," he said, "so I'll do what I should have done at first instead of crying on your shoulder, Mr. Craddock!" He pointed left towards the steep wood that bounded the moor. "That's Hermitage Wood, close-set oak and beech mostly but with a big fir plantation higher up. This moor is called Blackberry Down and it's common land, used by us and also by the Gilroy Estate, our nearest neighbour across the Teazel. That's the smaller of the two streams, this one on your right is the Sorrel that flows through our land as far as the sea at Coombe Bay, four miles from here. Coombe Bay isn't much more than a small village but we own some property there, held on long leases. The road runs beside the river here for a mile or more and the park wall is over there on your left, beyond Hermitage Farm. Martin Codsall's farm, Four Winds, is down there across the river, the biggest we've got, and fairly well run. Above you, hidden by that clump, is Hermitage, farmed by Pitts and his son, sound enough chaps but very unenterprising. Beyond the park wall . . ."

He broke off as Paul, lifting his head, trotted forward and reined in on the very brow of the hill where he could look across the long, rolling slope to the sea.

"One minute, Mr. Rudd," he called, "I've never seen anything quite like this before!" and he swept the prospect from west to east, from the thin sliver of the Teazel marking Gilroy's boundary on the right, to the high, wooded bluff above the outfall of the River Sorrel, that ran below in a wide curve to the left. He could sniff the sea breasting the scent of heather and gorse, a smell of summer released from the bracken by the grey's hooves, and hear the light breeze shaking Martin Codsall's corn on the slope where Four Winds' meadows met the great sweep of the woods and the Sorrel, ten yards wide, and spanned by a wooden bridge, began its final curve to the sea. He could even see the sun glinting on a roof in the distant village and as his eyes followed the course of the shallow stream a kingfisher flashed and then disappeared into the brake.

Rudd said, "Ah, it looks tame enough now, Mr. Craddock, but some of its moods are damned ugly! You should see it when the sou'westers come roaring in from over the Whin, and sleet drives at you from every point of the compass!", and he led the way down on to the track that followed the bend of the river, a broad path thick with spurting white dust that swept up in clouds and then settled to bow the stalks of cowparsley in the hedgerow on their side of the river.

It was this tall bank that held Paul's attention until they passed the angle of the grey stone wall, bordering the park, for its colour defied the dust every yard of the way. Tall ranks of foxgloves grew there, and at their roots a thick carpet of stitchwort, ragwort, dandelion, honeysuckle, dog rose and campion. The air throbbed with the hum of insects and huge bumble bees droned from petal to petal, like fat, lazy policemen checking the doors of silent premises. As they trotted past the wooden bridge Rudd told him that it was the only one spanning the Sorrel between the railway and the sea, and rightly belonged to Codsall of Four Winds but was used by everyone when the ford from which the estate derived its name was impassable. As the little grey lodge came in view beyond the Home Farm buildings, he added, "I took the liberty of getting Mrs. Handcock, the housekeeper, to make you up a bed in my lodge. There used to be a lodgekeeper of course, and I lived up at the house, but when he left I moved in and have been too lazy to shift. I'm a widower, and can look after myself although one of Tamer Potter's sluts looks in to clean up every once in a while. I live a solitary life down there and get sick of my own company, so you'll be welcome to stay with me as long as you are here. The guest rooms up at the big house are in poor shape. If we get a wet spell after this long drought the ceilings will leak."

"The lodge will suit me very well," Paul said but absently for he was still a prey to pleasurable excitement and nagging anxiety, sparring one with the other just below his belt. The whole place, he thought, was so immense, and not only vast and awesome but overpowering. By acquiring suzerainty of such a domain, he would be shouldering the cares of a small kingdom and that without a notion of how to rule unless he placed himself under the thumb of this square-faced, unpredictable agent, a man who rode with a chip on his shoulder, a chip the size of a French Prince. He must, he told himself, take plenty of time to think this out, and do his thinking in solitude.

The park gates looked as if they had remained open for years and hung by rusting hinges to a pair of fifteen-foot stone pillars, crowned by stone eagles. A stone's throw from the entrance was the ford, paved with flat stones and no more than six inches deep where the river ballooned into a pond. Geese honked among buttercups and anemones growing on the margin and the lodge, a snug little house with a pantiled roof and trim muslin curtains stood only a few yards inside the drive. All that Paul could see of the house itself was a cluster of chimney pots soaring above the last few chestnuts of the drive which curved sharply at the top of the steep ascent, where grew huge clumps of rhododendron, now in flower.

Mrs. Handcock, the housekeeper, came waddling to the lodge door as they clattered up and Rudd, dismounting, introduced Paul, giving the horses to a boy about twelve who somehow contrived to hoist himself on to the cob and rode away across the paddock to the Home Farm. The housekeeper was a large, pink-faced woman about fifty, with greying hair and a rich Westcountry brogue, the first purely Devon accent Paul had ever heard. She was respectful in her approach but by no means humble, as she shepherded him into the parlour where the table was laid for tea, a traditionally Devonshire tea of scones that Mrs. Handcock called "chudleys", and huge bowls of home-made strawberry jam, served with thick, yellow cream. Paul was too elated to do justice to her hospitality but he did his best and was afterwards shown to his room which was very small but scrupulously clean, with a copper can of hot water set ready for his use. He listened a moment to the rumble of Rudd's voice below, guessing that the agent was giving Mrs. Handcock his first impressions of The Prospect but then he thought that this was taking mean advantage of them and having washed, came down-stairs again, to find Rudd very much at ease in his big armchair, with jacket off, feet up and a Meerschaum pipe between his teeth. Paul lit his own pipe and tried to pretend that he too was at ease but Rudd was not fooled. He said, "I didn't tell you the conditions of the furniture sale, Mr. Craddock. The curtains and carpets, together with various fittings labelled 'R', go with the property; all the other stuff is up for sale the day after tomorrow. Coombes and Drayton are doing it from Whinmouth, that's our nearest town, some three miles west of Gilroy's place, across the Teazel. If you have made your decision before the auction you can bid for anything you want, or I'll get someone to bid for you. Would you like to go up there now, or will you wait until morning?"

"I should like to go now," Paul said, "and if it's all the same to you, Mr. Rudd, I'd prefer to poke around on my own. I can make notes of anything I might want to ask and I expect you've got plenty to do."

"I've got an inventory to make out," Rudd told him. "The lawyers have been pestering me for it ever since the sale notices went up. The place is locked so you'll need the front-door key," and he handed Craddock a key that looked as if it would have opened a country gaol. "I usual-ly have a toddy before bed," he added, "would you care to join me, after dusk?"

"Very much," Craddock said, "and convey my thanks to Mrs. Handcock for the tea." He left then, more than ever anxious to be alone, yet conscious of a growing liking for the agent and climbed the steep drive, discovering that the brazen heat had gone from the day and that long, evening shadows were now falling across the smaller paddock, beyond which he could just see what looked like a formal garden enclosed by ragged box hedges. It was so quiet that he could hear the rustle of birds in the rhododendron thickets and then, as he rounded the curve, there was the house twenty yards distant, looking like a great grey rock, with the last rays of red-gold sunlight lighting up its westerly windows but its eastern wing blank, as though such life as remained in the pile had gone to watch the sunset.

It was easier to assess its age and character than had been possible by studying the picture in the *Illustrated London News;* Craddock saw at once that it was really two houses, of widely separated periods. The centre block, notwithstanding its portico and Doric columns, was a stone Tudor farmhouse, with two squarish windows set low in the wall. The massive front door was the kind of entrance suggested by the key and although at first sight the two styles represented in the frontage seemed incongruous yet they seemed to have learned to tolerate one another over the years, the marriage having been accomplished by a mantle of creeper running wild along the whole front of the building. The main windows, opening on to the terrace, looked as if they gave upon spacious rooms and the terrace itself was unpretentious, divided in half by the semi-circular approach fronting the pillars, and bounded by a low stone wall spaced with stone cranes or herons.

Craddock stood looking up at it for several minutes, watching the west windows turn ruby in the sun and as he stared, eyes half closed against the sun, the silent building began to stir with life, so that he saw it as an ageing and once beautiful woman, awaiting the return of sons who had marched away centuries since and been swallowed up in a forgotten war. There was patience here, patience and a kind of desperate dignity, as though all hope of their return had never been abandoned, and that one day all the windows would glow with candles. Craddock tried to relate this dignity and repose with the little that Rudd had told him of the family who had lived here for a century or more but he found this very difficult, for somehow the house did not strike him as morose, merely forsaken and resigned. Yet about the middle section of it, the oldest, Elizabethan block, vitality lingered, the older tenants still seeming to exert more influence than the Lovells and this conviction was so real that Craddock would not have been surprised if, as he watched, lights had flickered in that part of the house leaving each wing dark and lifeless.

He climbed the stone steps and wrestled with the giant key, the lock turning more easily than he had anticipated, and the great door swung back with a sound like an old man's cough. He left the door open, for it was dim in the slate-slabbed hall and here he saw that the early-Victorian architect's work on the interior had been more bold than outside, for beyond the great empty fireplace a stair ran up in a well-contrived curve and each step was so broad and shallow that it promised an easy ascent to those short of wind. There was not much furniture in the hall and what there was was shrouded in green dust-sheets. Some of the portraits had lot numbers attached to them and Craddock, recalling the hard faces of Sir George and younger son, guessed they were portraits of Lovells from 1806 onwards; they had the same bleakness of eye and stiff formality of dress that he had noted in the photographs in the magazine.

He glanced in two reception-rooms, one on each side of the hall, finding them half-full of shrouded furniture, most of which was lotted, but here and there was a piece labelled with an "R". The reserved pieces, he noticed, were mostly heavy oak or draperies, like the big refectory table and the faded curtains looped with silk ropes as thick as cables. He went back into the hall and down the stone passage leading to the kitchens but the light was bad so he returned and ascended the stairs, hesitating at the top where there was a kind of minstrel gallery, trying to decide whether to take the left- or the right-hand corridor.

He was standing here when he heard the sound of a footfall on a wooden floor, and hearing it repeated identified the sound of someone walking in one of the rooms in the west wing. He was on the point of retracing his steps, and locking the door behind him, when he remembered that he was as authorised to be here as anyone else, so he walked quietly in the direction of the sounds until

45

he came to the door at the very end of the corridor. It was slightly ajar but when he stopped and listened again the sounds had ceased, so after a preliminary cough he walked into what had obviously been a nursery, for there were toys strewn about, including a large dappled rocking-horse and over in the corner a vast three-fold children's scrap screen of the kind that every upper-class nursery possessed. Then, over by the tall window, where the square panes had turned to stained glass in the setting sun, he saw the girl.

Astonishment made him the trespasser. He stood just inside the door gaping, and she stared back, an instinctive defiance stemming from anger rather than alarm. She was, Craddock decided on the spot, the most exciting woman he had ever seen. Not in illustrated books, nor in the course of his visits to picture galleries or in his dreams, did he recall having seen anyone who made such an immediate impact upon his senses. She was wearing a light blue riding habit, hitched at one side, a white silk blouse frilled at the throat to give the impression of a stock and was bareheaded, her dark hair gathered in a broad grey ribbon. Her eyes matched her costume exactly, her nose was short and straight and her small but very resolute chin had a large dimple an inch below a small, red mouth. But what impressed him more than her good features or bearing, was the texture of her skin, which was pale and waxlike, very firm and entirely without blemish. Her hair, removed from the strong rays of ruby light that flooded the window, would have seemed jet black, giving the taut skin of her cheeks and forehead an almost phosphorescent glow. She was not much above five feet in height but the cut of her habit, enclosing a small waist and emphasising the upward sweep of her breasts and downsweep of her sturdy thighs, added a fictitious inch or so to her figure.

He stood staring at her and she stared back, one hand gripping the curtain, the other holding a riding switch, and perhaps thirty seconds passed before she said, sharply: "Who are you? What are you doing here?" The voice betrayed no trace of fear, or even surprise, only a leashed and rather daunting anger.

He said, uncertainly, "My name is Craddock, Paul Craddock. I'm looking over the house. Mr. Rudd, the agent, gave me the key," and he held it up as though it had been his ticket of admission and she was the janitor. She considered him and the key for a moment but her expression did not relent. She still glowered at him, as though he had been a strange male who had blundered into her bedroom, so he tried again, this time a little hoarsely, for his throat was dry and his heart was pounding.

"I arrived this afternoon, Rudd and I rode over from the station."

"Why?"

She spat the word at him so sharply that it converted his uncertainty into indignation.

"Why not? My father's trustee has an option on the estate!"

Her expression softened and there was curiosity in the eyes.

"Does he intend buying the place? Buying the estate as a whole?"

"He might," Paul said, "and on my behalf but it's far from settled yet." Then, tentatively, "Do you live here? Rudd said the house had been empty some time."

Her eyes left him for the first time since he had entered the room. She glanced first at the bare floor, then out of the window.

"No," she said, less aggressively, "I don't live here. I used to come here a great deal; some time ago, before . . . before the war!"

Her reluctance to speak the word gave him a clue. He said, lightly, "Ah, you knew the Lovells then?"

"Of course!", and that seemed to be all the information she was prepared to give for suddenly she seemed to slump a little, as though bored with the conversation. After a pause, however, she went on, "I must go now, it'll be dusk before I'm home. I've got a horse in the yard and four miles to ride. I'm sorry I startled you, I should have asked Rudd for the key. I only came here to look at some furniture." Then, in a few long strides, she was past him and before he could think of an excuse to detain her she was half-way along the passage, her high-heeled riding boots clacking on the bare boards. A door banged somewhere behind the kitchens and after that there was silence, a slightly eerie silence he thought, as though she had been a ghost and he had imagined the encounter.

He crossed to the window asking himself impatiently why a chance meeting with a pretty girl in an empty house should disturb him, both emotionally and physically. She was obviously here without authority and had probably decided to bluff. He wondered briefly how she had managed to unlock the back door and why she should have seemed so resentful of him. She had, he decided, been musing and had made her way to this particular room for that purpose. Her pose over there by the window had betrayed as much and his sudden appearance, breaking into her reflections, had startled her so that, in a sense, her anger had been counterfeit. He remained standing where she had stood, wondering if she would circle the west wing and appear at the crest of the drive, but when he heard or saw nothing of her he fell to thinking about women in general and his relations with them in the past.

His experience with women had been limited but although technically still a virgin he was not altogether innocent. There had been a very forward fourteen-year-old called Cherry, who had lived in an adjoining house in Croydon, when he came home for school holidays and Cherry had succeeded in bewitching but ultimately terrifying him, for one day when they were larking about in the stable behind her house, she had hinted at the mysterious differences between the sexes and when, blushing, he had encouraged her to elaborate, she had promptly hoisted her skirt and pulled down her long cotton drawers, whereupon he had fled as though the Devil was after him and had never sought her company again, although he watched her closely in church on successive Sundays, expecting any moment to see forked lightning descend on her in the middle of "For all the Saints". Then there had been a little clumsy cuddling at Christmas parties, and after that a flaxen-haired girl called Daphne whom he had mooned over as an adolescent and had thought of a good deal in the Transvaal but now he had almost forgotten what Daphne looked like and had not recalled her name until now. Finally there had been an abortive foray across the frontier in the company of a self-assured, toothy officer, called Prescott-Smythe, the two having ventured into a brothel at Capetown, where Paul spent a few embarrassing moments with a Hottentot whore. The experience was something he would have preferred to forget and indeed, almost had forgotten save for the girl's mousey smell and repellent gestures. After that the Veldt and the exclusive company of men until he was wounded, and in the hospital any attempts to establish extra-professional relationships with volunteer nurses had been nipped in the bud by the Countess who regarded every officer as her personal prerogative. So he stood thinking, glancing round the musty nursery and wondering what compulsive memories had directed the girl here when she had every reason to suppose that the house would be empty. The rocking horse and the faded scrap screen offered no answer and apart from the few scraps of peeling wallpaper there was little else in the room. Then, unexpectedly, he saw her again, riding a neat bay round the south-western corner of the house below the window and as he watched she flicked the horse into a slow canter at the head of the drive and they passed out of sight under the avenue chestnuts. He saw a swift flash of blue as she passed the gate pillars and then nothing more, so that excitement ebbed from the day and he made his way down the shallow stairs, letting himself out and carefully re-locking the door.

Dusk was falling outside and a blue mist lay under the woods enclosing the house from the back. The front windows were blank and there was no life in the house, not even the original block beyond the pillars. He noticed also that paint and plaster were peeling from parts of the façade and that the old building now looked more like a near-ruin than a dignified woman awaiting the return of dead men. Yet the vivid memory of the girl's eyes and pale, waxlike skin remained as he made his way back to the lodge and as soon as he had settled over a toddy with Rudd he told the agent of his encounter, expecting surprise and possibly indignation at a trespass but Rudd only shrugged when he described the girl and her curiously aggressive reception.

"That'll be Grace Lovell," he said, carelessly, and when

Paul asked if she was a granddaughter of the old Squire, Rudd chuckled.

"By no means," he said, "simply a family hanger-on of a kind, although perhaps that's a bit unfair to the girl. Her father, Captain Bruce Lovell, is the family ne'er-do-well and even he is only a cousin. He took one of the Lovell houses at Coombe Bay after his retirement from the Gunners and was quite a charge on them all until he remarried. His wife was a Voysey, very wealthy family from Derbyshire I understand. But in marrying her Bruce bit off more than he could chew, or so I'm told. The girl's been very troublesome too. She was to have married Ralph, the younger son of the old man, but Kruger put paid to that of course."

As always when he discussed the Lovells Rudd's manner hardened but somewhere at the back of Paul's mind a shutter opened and the girl's display of anger at being discovered in the empty house began to make sense.

"Was it a family match or were they fond of one another?" he asked but at that the agent's casualness left him and he looked at Paul with a kind of exasperation.

"Look here, if you've been smitten by Grace Lovell my advice is forget her. She's tarred with the same old brush, an indiscipline that can show itself in obstinacy, bloody mindedness, or a sort of madness. There's congenital rottenness in that family somewhere along the line. Sometimes I used to dismiss it as arrogance coming from always having had too much money, but other times . . . well, I'm not going to bore you with more confessions. They're all dead now, at least, the three I had to do with are, and I'm done with them, thank God, so take another glass before you go to bed and tell me what you thought of the house up yonder."

They talked for a spell of the fabric of the building and Rudd told him something of its growth from a manor farmhouse, older by far than any other farm on the estate, to its present unmanageable size. The main changes were made in the early eighteen-twenties, on the proceeds of prize-money won by the first Lovell's brother, who had been lucky during the long war with France. Paul listened with assumed interest but his mind was not much

50

exercised by Rudd's estimates of how much it would cost to put Shallowford and surrounding property in order after two decades of neglect. It was engaged in following a flash of blue beyond the ford and across country to the sea. "Smitten" was the word the agent had used, and Paul was regretting now that he had betrayed interest in the girl. Rudd, however, interpreted his polite affirmatives as a desire for bed and presently arose, knocking out his pipe.

"We'll do the round tomorrow," he said. "I'll show you the worst part first, over in the Coombe, and then we'll look for something better at Hermitage and Four Winds in the west. Good night to you, Mr. Craddock. There's a candle on the hall tray."

He went up and Paul soon followed but it was a long time before he slept. His wound ached from the long ride and the owls in Hermitage Wood were hunting and making a great deal of noise about it. Soon the moon rose, flooding the tiny chamber with a silver light, and at last Craddock slept, most of his doubts unresolved.

II

Nobody could have said with certainty how the Potters of Low Coombe received warning of The Prospect's visit. They were usually the first to get news, even of insignificant events and Smut Potter, the poacher, who saw Craddock's arrival at the station probably passed the word around. The Potters lived with a communal ear to the ground and could hear and interpret every rustle of rumour between the sea and the far side of the moor beyond the railway line. The green basin they occupied under the wooded, sandstone bluff suggested a gypsy encampment but in place of caravans were ramshackle buildings centred on a ruinous cob farmhouse and life revolved around the pump which, at this time of year, was hidden by docks, chickweed and shoulder-high nettles. A long clothes-line stretched from pump to the nearest oak and along it, on any fine day, hung an astonishing array of threadbare garments, all the way down from Old

51

Tamer's long woollen pants to the pinafore of Hazel, the youngest of the Potters, a half-witted nine-year-old, as wild as any animal in the woods.

Nobody, not even Tamer himself or his brown-faced, handsome wife Meg, could give the full strength of the clan at any given time. Potter boys and Potter girls were always coming or going and as often as not some of Meg's Romany kinfolk were encamped in the Coombe, although, under Sir George, this had been forbidden upon penalty of eviction, for it gave every local poacher an alibi. Tamer and his wife had been living at Low Coombe for as long as most Valley folk could remember, sometimes farming the ninety-odd acres between the sea and Edwin Willoughby's farm, higher up the Coombe, but subsisting in the main upon the driblets of money the children brought in, Sam, the eldest boy, from the sale of firewood, Smut, the second boy, from poaching and the three older girls from what they earned as part-time domestics and the occasional sale of their lusty, unwashed bodies. But for all their improvidence the Potters were a happy-go-lucky brood, each with their father's eye for a quick profit and their mother's resilience, nurtured by the systematic persecution of Romanies. They were ragged, dirty, thieving and irrepressible but they seldom went short of food and not one of them had ever been laid aside by a day's illness. Peasant cunning on the part of Tamer, allied to possession of the Evil Eye on the part of his wife, may have contributed to their survival, for although they were despised and avoided by respectable families like the Codsalls, the Pitts and the Derwents, and treated with tolerance by their immediate neighbours, the Willoughbys, few in the Sorrel Valley cared to incur the hostility of the men, or the witchcraft of Meg, who was credited with the power to distribute blessings or blights, according to her inclination.

The scene in Low Coombe that morning was akin to the scurry in a Highland glen after word had arrived that redcoats were arriving to search for arms and Jacobites. At first there was a wave of panic, showing itself in wildly disordered attempts to clear away litter, strip the clothesline and shore up tottering walls but the Potters could never engage in sustained activity and after half-an-hour's running here and there Old Tamer called a conference round the pump, pointing out that perhaps, in the circumstances, it would be more profitable to advertise extreme poverty, rather than create an impression that the Potters were sober, industrious farmers. Rudd, the agent, would never be taken in by a last-minute spit-and-polish whereas the new young Squire (the Potters, one and all, already thought of Paul as such) should be given no excuse for thinking the family was self-sufficient and could survive without a reduction of rent and perhaps a loan of draught animals from the Home Farm.

"Us'll get nowt if us makes out us needs nowt!" Tamer reasoned, "zo us might as well let un zee us is down to our last varden!", and the family, standing in a semi-circle in the nettles, sanctioned this realistic approach with enthusiastic nods and grunts before dispersing to their various occupations, nine-year-old Hazel having been posted half-way up the cart-track to give immediate warning of the approach of the visitors.

She came flying down the path in less than ten minutes, shrieking the news that Rudd and New Squire were on their way and Cissie, the eldest girl, cuffed her for making such an outcry, whereupon Hazel kicked her sister in the buttocks as she bent to replenish the fire and then fled to the safety of the oak which she climbed with the speed of a chimpanzee until she could look down on the dell from a height of some fifty feet. Meanwhile, all older Potters adopted expressions of deep humility, and the postures of absorbed artisans, Mother Meg at the huge washtub, Sam at the woodpile, the three elder girls at the osier frames and Tamer presiding over the tribe from the porch steps, his patriarchal belly clasped in his hands. Only Smut, the rebel of the tribe, continued what he was doing, skinning a rabbit taken from the Gilroy warrens across the Teazel in the small hours. Smut, twenty now, and as muscled as a professional wrestler, made no compromises with the enemy. His was a war without truce.

Half-a-mile or so higher up the Bluff, where the ascent flattened out to form a tiny valley east of the Coombe,

Edwin Willoughby of Deepdene had also received warning of the inspection, for the Potters were on affectionate terms with Willoughby, a Christian who took the Sermon on the Mount literally. Willoughby was a Methodist lay-preacher, as well as a farmer, but his God tested him sorely. On the one hand he had, willy-nilly, to live with the Potters, and north of his border lived the dour Edward Derwent, who abominated the gypsy family. Thus Willoughby's land, a poor and stubborn two hundred acres, was a no-man's-land between two hostile clans and Edwin enjoyed little of the forbearance he preached each Sunday in one or other of the little tin chapels along the coast. He persisted, however, for he had experienced worse in the lifetime of his wife, Ada, now at rest in the Coombe Bay Methodist burial ground. There were many in and about the Sorrel Valley who declared that Edwin's devotion to the Almighty stemmed from His mercy in removing Ada in the fifteenth year of their marriage, for it was generally admitted that she had tormented her husband with tongue by day and loins by night and for good measure occasionally let fly at him with a saucepan or flat-iron. Since her death he had grown to look rather like a saint, with his long silky hair, white as hoar frost, high, pale forehead, and mild, deepset eyes that burned with love for all mankind, even such wayward sons as Tamer Potter and his crusty neighbour, Derwent. His sermons, although spiced with the traditional touch of brimstone, expressed his deep belief in an era when lions would lie down with lambs, and reformed Potters would hoe harmoniously alongside Derwents. He was fortified in his faith by the example of his sister Mary, who had made her home with him after his wife's death and now divided her time between keeping Deepdene farmhouse spotless and presiding over a small school for Valley children too young to travel to the nearest elementary school, at Whinmouth, or the Church School, in Coombe Bay. All the children of the surrounding country had been Mary's pupils and among the present generation were Codsalls, of Four Winds, Derwents, of High Coombe, and Honeymans, from the Home Farm. Mary Willoughby was a sweet-faced woman, several years older than Edwin and had been mother to Edwin's children, Francis and Elinor, both of whom helped to run the little farm.

News of The Prospect's tour was leaked across the hedge to Edwin by Smut Potter but the Willoughbys had no need to prepare against the arrival of a new squire. Their land was poor but their buildings and outbuildings were in good trim and their livestock a credit to the hardworking Edwin and his prudent eighteen-year-old daughter, Elinor, who was responsible for the poultry. Edwin thought it wise, however, to tramp back to the farm where his sister was reading *Alice in Wonderland* to the children and inform her of the visit of a new master of Shallowford but all Mary exclaimed was, "There now, I do hope he'll zettle an' be happy yer," and went on reading of the Cheshire Cat, while Edwin crossed the Deepdene fields to see how his modest barley crop was coming along and pass the news to one of Farmer Derwent's labourers, hard at work diverting a small stream that ran along the Deepdene-High Coombe boundary into a shallow trench inside the Derwent holding. The man was rather outfaced to see Edwin's saintly face loom over the hedge but he need not have been. Edwin saw what he was about and offered him the loan of a larger spade.

Edward Derwent, his big son Hugh, and his two daughters, Rose and Claire, discussed the news over their breakfast after they had finished an early morning stint in fields east of the farm and in the stables, where the girls had their riding school. Neither husband nor children addressed a word to the second Mrs. Derwent, a nonentity at High Coombe who was not included in family councils. Hugh, broad and swarthy like his father, dismissed the news as a Potter-inspired rumour.

"No one with money to burn would buy this white elephant," he declared, "he could do better up country if he was looking for land. Big house is leaking bad, I hear, and apart from us, the Codsalls and the Pitts, what of us got to offer but flint, dirt farmers and a tangle of woods? It's probably nowt but a swell from London after some o' they antiques upalong." Whereupon he wolfed his rashers

55

and three eggs with the despatch of a man who has been forking hay since first light, and at once returned to the fields.

The two girls, Rose and Claire, were far more intrigued.

"Gregory had it from Mr. Willoughby that Mr. Craddock is an army officer wounded in the war," Rose said. "I wonder if he's married, and if so what his wife can be thinking of to bury herself down here?"

Edward Derwent, always inclined to speak scornfully of the estate, was not prepared to extend the same privilege to his children. He was a powerful, dark-jowled man, with bushy black brows that met over a strong nose in a broad "V" and gave him an expression of permanent irritation.

"Why the devil does everyone here talk as if we lived in a desert?" he demanded aggressively, and his wife lowered her gaze penitently as though she too had erred in this respect. "We've done pretty well here, haven't we?" Claire, the pretty daughter, giggled. As her father's favourite this called for no reproof so he continued, rumblingly, "White elephant! Flint and woodlane! A backwater! What kind of talk is that? There's nothing wrong with my land and if the riding stable books are to be believed we're showing a good profit on liveries, so why all this belittling of the place?"

Rose and Claire were well accustomed to their father's rhetorical questions and paid them no attention at all but continued to speculate on the possibilities of the new man's patronage.

"If he's a cavalry officer he'll be sure to hunt," Rose said, "and if he's wealthy enough to buy Shallowford he'll probably keep a second hunter, carriage horses and at least one hack!"

"He might even have a motor," suggested Claire but not seriously, for the lunatic improbability of this made Rose laugh aloud and even their stepmother gave a nervous little smile. Nobody in the Sorrel Valley had ever seen a motor, except in the illustrated magazines. The new King was said to own one but the Derwents thought it a clownish substitute for the royal coach.

The girls went on gossiping about a possible successor

to the Lovells after they had returned to the yard to muck out and clean tack. Rose, big boned and freckled, confined herself to the more practical aspects of the situation—whether the new man was likely to prove as reckless a rider to hounds as the late Ralph Lovell, who had ridden horses to death and broken limbs in the process, but her sister, fair-haired and soft mouthed, with dimples in place of her sister's rash of freckles, continued to harp on the possibility of the new squire being a bachelor. She had read and enjoyed *Jane Eyre,* and the prospect of a Mr. Rochester at large in the Valley offered all kinds of possibilities. They were still speculating when the hired man, Gregory, stumped into the yard and confirmed the presence of Agent Rudd and his "Lunnon gent, in Yeomanry togs".

" 'Er's down wi' the Potters now, Misses," he said, "an' they ole varmints'll be in a proper ole flummox, if I knaws aught about it!"

The embarrassment of the Potter clan was wishful thinking on Gregory's part. As a Derwent employee he naturally embraced Derwent politics, nurturing a dutiful hate for his master's principal enemies. The truth was, however, very different, for Old Tamer and his family had played fish like Paul Craddock far too long to lose the advantage of an hour's warning of the approach. Rudd and Craddock rode into the Coombe about nine o'clock and Paul was impressed by the scene of virtuous industry in the Dell. All the Potters except Smut genuflected and Tamer went so far as to reach for a forelock that was not there.

"Well, you damned rascals," Rudd said jovially, "you'll have to stir your lazy stumps round here! Mr. Craddock is considering buying Shallowford. *Considering,* mind you! Don't broadcast it up and down the Valley. God help me," he went on aloud, glancing round the Dell, "did you ever see people make such a tip of a place? Look at that yard, and those outbuildings?"

Tamer simpered and rubbed his hands, as though overjoyed to hear the agent enjoy a harmless jest at his family's expense, but inwardly Paul was obliged to agree, for what with the washing, the forest of nettles, empty tins and broken boxes, a smouldering ashtip, and the presence of a saddleback pig rooting under the trees, the natural beauty of the green basin was grotesquely camouflaged. As far as Paul could see the Potters were not farmers at all but down-at-heel vagrants, living on their wits. The two things that did impress him, however, was the heroic industry of Meg at the washtub, and the shining health of the three girls, weaving baskets beside the fire. He did not see Hazel Potter, perched forty feet above his head but she saw him and tried, unsuccessfully, to hit him with an acorn. She was lying full length on a great limb of the oak, her mop of hair swinging free, her face pressed close to the bark, and as she looked down on the group she composed one of her secret prose poems about the newcomer, singing it softly under her breath and exulting in the fecundity of her imagination.

"He be tall and thin, like a birch in winter," she sang, "and the silvery bits on his soldier's clothes look like the birch bark I can peel in strips . . .", but then the new squire dismounted stiffly, and so did Mr. Rudd, and they all moved out of her range of vision so that she forgot them and turned her attention to the tiny brown stains oozed from the crown of the uncupped acorn in the palm of her hand. Hazel Potter was even less trammelled by the demands of duty and industry than her sisters. Some said she was short of wits, and this had kept her from attending school but others declared she had inherited her mother's powers of witchcraft and were careful to give her skimmed milk or a halfpenny when they heard her crooning to herself at their doors.

With Tamer as guide, and Sam bringing up the rear, Rudd and Paul were shown around the holding. Hens fled squawking at their approach, for a sudden turn of speed was a condition of survival to all birds and animals in the Potter farmyard. As they poked about among the sheds and litter Tamer maintained a running commentary of the difficulties of life at Low Coombe and Rudd, who cherished for him the amused tolerance law-abiding citizens show the picturesque burglar, let him whine to his heart's content.

"Us needs all manner o' things to maake a praper start yerabouts," Tamer explained, as they entered a stable half-full of rubbish and containing no beast of any kind. "You'll mind, Maister, that the military commandeered the ole mare us 'ad, and 'er 've never been replaaced, so as us must needs do our own haulin' from the shore."

"They use seaweed for manure on the Coombe farms," Rudd told Paul, "and most of our horses were bought up by the Army, in the first year of the war. I've made a note of this kind of thing so you needn't bother to memorise it all, I just want you to get a general impression."

"Be'ee reely going to taake Squire Lovell's place, Maister?" Sam Potter asked reverently, but Paul said, "I really don't know, it's too early to say but I'd prefer you didn't discuss it outside the estate."

He said this earnestly but he was already enjoying the sensation his presence had occasioned in the Valley. From the moment he had opened his eyes that morning, and looked over the ford to the long downslope to the sea, he had been uplifted by an elation that had eluded him since childhood and this was not caused by the novelty of the occasion or even by the beauty of Shallowford's southern vista but by a feeling akin to that of home-coming to a place and people who seemed, in some improbable way, to need and want him. He looked over the golden vista basking in slanting sunlight, noting the steep hedgerows and their riot of colour, and inhaling the scent of the baked, red earth, spiced with the whiff of the sea. He warmed to the soft burr of the Devon accent and the sharp hiss of indrawn breath that men like Tamer Potter used as an expression of assent, but buried deeper than this, glowing like a small, bright coal, was the memory of Grace Lovell and her pale, shining skin and he wondered if the tour would take them through the village of Coombe Bay, where he might see her again, although he was careful to say nothing of this to Rudd.

They left the Dell by the broken gate, taking the path across parched fields to the headland, east of the river. A few pigs rooted on the edge of Coombe Brake, and half a dozen lean cows browsed in the meadow. Rudd shook his head over the Potters' domain; "Lovell was always on the point of turning the rascals loose," he said, "but somehow he never did and I think I know why. People like the Potters have the power of survival and would endure under any system. They're a dirty, dishonest and thoroughly worthless bunch, but somehow one goes on tolerating them as a kind of counterpoise to stolid, law-abiding tenants, like the Pitts and the Willoughbys. Take those girls now—a trio of handsome, tawny animals; how do they manage to keep strong and healthy? It's probably on account of them that Old Tamer never got his marching orders, for young Ralph used to ride over this way rent-collecting and they probably took turns to pay him in a dry ditch every quarter day! We're crossing to the Willoughby boundary now—he's a harmless enough chap, notwithstanding a touch of religious mania, and his sister Mary is a credit to the Valley. If it wasn't for Mary Willoughby half the children round about wouldn't be able to read or write!"

"Aren't they compelled to attend school nowadays?" Paul asked but Rudd chuckled. "Common law doesn't operate in places like this as it does in cities, Mr. Craddock. We're four miles from the nearest main road, and six from the railway. Whinmouth, on the estuary yonder, is a two-hour ride, and there is not even a village bobby between us and Paxtonbury, twelve miles inland. No, the folk about here are pretty well as self-contained as they were in the eighteenth century, and have their own ways of doing things. Mary Willoughby started that little school of hers twenty years ago and dispensed all the schooling Valley children have ever had or wanted. Listen!", and he reined in on the northern slope of the cliff field, pointing to a white cluster of buildings about half a mile below them. "That's Deepdene, the farm that keeps the Potters at Low Coombe and the Derwents at High Coombe from tearing at one another's throats! You can hear the children singing. I always like to listen when I ride out this way in the forenoon. It cheers me up after calling on the Potters."

Paul listened but at first could hear nothing but the slow suck of the sea on the pebbles below. Then, very faintly, the sound of children's voices reached him across

Willoughby's barley field, and after a moment or so he could identify the strains of "John Peel". It had, as Rudd implied, a refreshing innocence and as they came to the road nearer the farm Willoughby's daughter Elinor came out of the henroost to greet them. She was a shy, slim girl and on being introduced to Craddock, lowered her glance and said she would warn Auntie Mary of the visitors' approach, using this as an excuse to escape. Paul saw her dart into the schoolroom, a long, half-timbered barn adjoining the house and was struck by the speed with which her bare feet covered the ground.

"How old is that girl?" he asked and Rudd said she was eighteen, and being courted by Will Codsall, the elder of the Codsall boys at Four Winds, just across the river.

"The Codsalls are against the match," he added, "for Arabella is a snob and thinks her Will could do better. I daresay she's right, but Elinor Willoughby will make a good farmer's wife for somebody. I've never seen her idling or flirting, and she's damned clever with her poultry strains. There's nothing much wrong with this farm, although it's too small to be profitable. Derwent, beyond the crest up there, has all the best acreage this side of the river."

The singing stopped in the middle of a bar and they dismounted, giving their horses to Francis Willoughby and going into the barn. Paul felt far less at ease here than he had in the Porters' Dell for the children, about a dozen of them, stared at him in curiosity, sitting on forms with their arms folded and expressions blank. When he was introduced to them as "a soldier gentleman friend of Mr. Rudd's" they rose like so many clockwork figures and piped "Good morning, sir!", after which they subsided, again in concert.

Rudd brought a flustered Mary Willoughby over to shake hands but instead of doing so she dropped a swift curtsy, so that Paul was struck by the tug of feudalism among the Lovell tenantry.

"I heard the children singing," he said, for something to say and Mary Willoughby replied, eagerly, "Will you have them sing for you here, Sir? I'm sure they'd like to, wouldn't you, my dears?" and the children chanted "Yes, Miss Willoughby," opening and closing their mouths like two rows of puppets, then fixing their eyes on their teacher who picked up a tuning fork, tapped it on the desk and said, "Softly then! Watch the baton! One chorus of 'The British Grenadiers', because Mr. Rudd tells me Mr. Craddock is just home from the wars!"

The children, one and all, received this news with respect, their eyes leaving the tuning fork and returning to Paul. They sang in shrill, clear voices, the boys grinning, the girls repressing giggles, and when they had finished Paul said, hoarsely, "Thank you, that was splendid! Er— how many are there here, Miss Willoughby?" and Mary said there were fourteen today because two of the older boys were out helping with the harvest and little Hazel Potter was playing truant again.

Paul, on impulse, pulled out a handful of loose change, saying that everyone present was to have a reward for singing so well but before the squeal of delight had died away a bullet-headed little boy in the rear row shot up his hand and demanded, "Sir, sir! Did you kill ole Kruger?", a question that made even the demure Mary Willoughby laugh.

"No," said Paul, "nobody killed Kruger, because he got away before anyone could catch him!", but his questioner was not satisfied with this and saw Paul's presence as a means of beguiling a tedious hour's instruction. He followed up with, "Did *all* the Boers run away, please sir?", and Paul glanced at Rudd, hoping for some inspiration but getting none said, deliberately, "The Boers didn't run away at all. They were very brave. After all, they were farmers fighting for their country, just as we would!", and Paul again glanced at Rudd who was now studying a knothole on the schoolroom floor. Feeling miserably embarrassed he got up and tried to smile. "I'm sure Miss Willoughby won't want me to stay and interrupt your lessons any longer," he said, "so Mr. Rudd and I will have to say good-bye, because we have to ride over and see all the other farms."

When they were clear of the farm, and riding along

the ridge parallel with the woods Paul said, "Did I do wrong to tell them the truth?"

"If you're only a visitor passing through it doesn't matter a damn what you say," Rudd told him, "whereas if you become 'New Squire', as the Potters rather hope, you can say anything you like! After all, they'll be tenants, and if a Tory doesn't mince his words with them why should a Radical?"

"I'm not sure that I am a Radical," Paul told him. "I never gave a thought to politics until I began to convalesce, and had nothing better to do than read the Parliamentary debates in the newspapers."

"Well," pursued Rudd, with one of his quizzical sidelong glances, "and what conclusions did you arrive at?"

"I don't know, one can't help admiring that chap Lloyd George's nerve defying the whole weight of public opinion about the war, and there were fellows out there who came around to agreeing with him, after they took part in chivvying the Boers from Hell to Hackney. It seemed to me, however, that once we were in it we had to choose going through with it or becoming the laughing stock of the world. Apart from that it now looks as if they'll get a better deal from us than they would have got from anyone else. What would have happened to them if the Germans or French had been in our situation?"

"Ah," said Rudd evasively, "that would be telling!" and Paul thought: "Damn him, he gave so much away yesterday that he'll be a clam from now on! However, I'd lay six to four that he's pro-Lloyd George, if only because the Lovell family were Tories!" and then he forgot politics, surrendering himself to the beauty of a long, easterly slope stretching from Willoughby's boundary, across the Derwent holding to the cloudless sky over the county border.

They met Willoughby on the ridge and introductions were exchanged. Rudd, glancing over the hedge, saw the evidence of Gregory's excavations alongside the stream and at once remarked on it.

"Derwent had no right to siphon off your water," he told the saint-like farmer. "You may need it badly later on, even if you don't now."

63

"Why, God bless you, Mr. Rudd," Willoughby said, "who am I to begrudge a neighbour water for his cattle in weather like this?"

Rudd said, "Well, it's your concern I suppose, but I doubt if he'd do the same for you!", and they rode on down the slope and through the fir copse that shaded the freshly whitewashed buildings of the Derwent farm, Rudd saying that Paul was not to expect forelock-pulling from Derwent, who was anxious to become a freeholder and probably had the means to purchase his land if a new owner was willing to sell it.

"He's a cagey fellow, with a poor wisp of a second wife," he told Craddock. "Frankly, I've never liked him much but both he and his son Hugh are first-class farmers, and the two daughters are the leading lights of the local hunt. One's a very fetching girl but the other looks like a horse. They'll all be civil to you when I tell him why you're here, but don't be fooled by the Derwents. They're like the Codsalls; money and land are the only things they care about and after that, Independence Day!"

Paul's reception at High Coombe was much as Rudd had predicted, both father and children making a show of hospitality and the faded Mrs. Derwent bringing out glasses of sherry and some appetising little pikelets on a large, silver tray.

The house was well furnished, the stock in good condition and the farm buildings in repair. Paul was particularly impressed by the spotlessly clean stables where Rose, the daughter with a face like a horse, showed him a magnificent four-year-old gelding she intended hunting next season. Rose cared for nothing but horses but her sister Claire showed great solicitude when Rudd told her that Paul had been wounded in action. She was extraordinarily pretty, Craddock decided, with golden hair piled high on a small head, dark blue eyes and an undeniably kissable mouth. She pretended to scold Rudd for encouraging a convalescent man with a leg wound to undertake such a long ride on a hot day, and when she took Paul's glass to refill it her long fingers caressed his but in the nicest possible way. Craddock, somewhat to his surprise, found he was able to relax at High Coombe, notwithstanding Derwent's dourness. The yard and enclosures were pleasant places in which to linger after the seediness of the Potter farm, and there were no children to embarrass him with leading questions about Kruger and the war. They resisted an invitation to stay for lunch, however, and pressed on under a blazing midday sun, breasting the northern spur of the ridge and entering the blessed coolness of Shallowford Woods.

Craddock at once decided that this was the most enchanting part of the estate, a great belt of old timber rising from a jungle of undergrowth that covered the entire south-eastern section of the estate, two miles across and about a mile deep, with a dip in the middle filled by a shallow mere. He had not noticed the lake on the map Rudd had shown him before they set out and thus came upon it by surprise, an oval of reed-fringed water enclosed by oaks and beeches, some of which must have been centuries old. Waterlilies floated here and a tiny islet, half-way across, was the haunt of wild duck and moorhen, who took to the reeds as soon as the horses emerged from the trees. Paul saw that there was a building of mock oriental design on the islet and Rudd told him it was known as "The Pagoda" and had been built, half a century ago, by Amyas Lovell, father of the late baronet. Amyas, Rudd said, had been wounded in the head campaigning in Lower Burma and had been very eccentric towards the end of his life. The pagoda was supposed to be a miniature replica of a temple in Mandalay, and the old soldier had been in the habit of punting himself across the lake and painting atrocious water-colours from the pagoda steps.

They rode on through the murmurous woods, Rudd making estimates of the value of the timber, Paul telling himself that if ever he owned Shallowford he would prefer to sell Derwent his farm rather than fell any of the trees. Some of the beeches rose to a height of over a hundred feet and on the western edge of the wood, where they towered above younger trees, they had been planted according to plan for they were evenly spaced along the rides.

They emerged into glaring sunshine again east of the steeper and fas less dense Hermitage Wood that rose behind the house. Paul could now see the back view of the manor lying in the little valley as they crossed rough ground heading for Hermitage Farm, which lay in open country between the curve of the Sorrel and the main road they had crossed the previous afternoon.

"You'll like Arthur and young Henry Pitts," Rudd told Paul, "they're a genial, hardworking pair and I don't ever recall having had a dispute with them all the twenty years I've been here. Although Arthur is no more than my age his father and grandfather farmed here before him and his father, Old Gaffer Pitts, is still living, although he's got Parkinson's disease, poor old chap, and now sits mumbling in the chimney corner. He can remember the harvest failures of the 'forties, and riots over the Corn Laws away in Whinmouth and Paxtonbury. He was in the militia at the time and broke heads on behalf of the Lovells, but his son and grandson are very easy-going and we'll stop off there for a bite of lunch, if you've room for it after all those pikelets Claire Derwent pressed on you. That girl is about desperate for a husband, Mr. Craddock! I daresay you noticed she made a dead set at you. What did you think of her? More fetching than the little dark ghost you disturbed in the nursery last night?"

Paul smiled but said nothing, determined to give the agent no opening in this particular field but as they urged their horses into a trot at the top of Hermitage he reflected that the Sorrel Valley seemed very well endowed with pretty girls, for he had encountered six in a single morning's ride and any one of them would have stood out in a crowd among the overdressed young women he had noticed in London. Musing on them as they jogged down the track he made comparisons, measuring the aloof appeal of Grace Lovell with the pink and white prettiness of Claire Derwent and the shy charms of the Willoughby girl, now courted by young Will Codsall. He recalled also the frankly sensual appeal of the three Potter girls and it came into his mind that they had the generous proportions of the Hottentot prostitute from whom he had fled in Capetown but looked infinitely more wholesome. Then he was required to face yet another series of introductions, this time to Arthur Pitts and his wife Martha, their son

Henry, and Pitts' old father, The Gaffer. He took to this family at once, for there was a lack of ceremony about Hermitage that had been absent elsewhere, or perhaps it only appeared so, because Rudd was on more friendly terms with the Pitts than with the other tenants and he and Arthur began talking of the drought, and the harvest while Paul was faced with vast helpings of ham and tongue and mountains of green salad, served with a stone jug of potent, home-brewed cider.

Henry, Arthur's son, a thick-set young man with a pallor at odds with a farmer who had been out in a heat-wave for a month was exceptionally welcoming and solemnly wished Paul well if he did in fact buy, reinforcing Rudd's hints that "the plaace would require a praper ole shower o' money" if it was to be put on a profitable basis. Martha, Arthur's busy little wife, had a brogue as broad or broader than Tamer Potter's and Paul had some difficulty in catching the drift of her conversation, spiced as it was with so many strange words, like "thicky" and "giddon" which he interpreted as "that" and "go along with you", whereas all animals, male and female, were referred to as " 'Er". She expressed her deep thankfulness that "they ole Boers were now parcelled up an' vinished with", and that no more young men would be required to "get theirselves shot to tatters", pointing out that if a man had a mind to die from gunshot wounds he might, with more profit, "stand the blind side of thicky hedge, when us iz rabbiting!" Her husband, Arthur, who happened to overhear this remark, said, "Dornee talk so daft, mother! You get a blamed sight more pay chasin' they Boers than us gets for the rabbits us knocks over hereabouts!" One way and another Paul delighted in their cheerful company and was sorry when Rudd said they must press on to Four Winds to meet the Codsalls; his failure to do so that same day would surely stir up jealousy in the Valley.

"Well youm right there," confirmed Martha, "but dornee let that Arabella Codsall give herself airs and you can depend on it she'll try, seeing as she can't never forget her father left her the best-dowered daughter in the Valley."

Rudd, laughing, said he would mind her advice and off they went again, Paul making light of the growing stiffness in his knee, which pained him somewhat when he swung his leg over the grey.

"I think they're delightful people," he told Rudd, when they were trotting down to the river road and Rudd said he had planned the tour this way because it had a natural rhythm, all the way from sleazy rascality in the Potters' Dell, to the farcial pretentiousness of Arabella Codsall, "the best-dowered woman in the Valley".

"Four Winds is the largest farm in the area," he told Paul as they went along, explaining that it had been stocked on Arabella's money, nearly two thousand left by her father, a Paxtonbury draper. "Mind you," he added, "Martin paid dearly for his stake, for Arabella never lets him forget that she married beneath her and considers herself a cut above any other farmer's wife in the Valley. Martin is a harmless sort of chap but of less account at Four Winds than Derwent's wife is at High Coombe. At least Mrs. Derwent can handle a knife and fork how she likes and that's more than Martin can when there's company. She's a tiresome, garrulous, over-weening bitch is Arabella, for she not only nags her husband from morning to night but discriminates between the boys. Will, the elder, is an amiable blockhead, who would make a good enough farmer if he was left to himself, but he isn't and his mother makes a pet of Sydney, her younger son, who she is determined to make into a gentleman. How the hell she'll do that with Codsall blood and bone I can't imagine, for the Codsalls have been farming there for a century and Codsall's father, old Jeremiah, died in the infirmary after falling in the Sorrel dead drunk on New Year's night. However, we'd best call and round off the day by taking a quick look at the village itself. You can see the Home Farm any time, tomorrow if you like, if you don't want to hang about the sale."

Paul, elated at the prospect of riding down to the sea before the heat went out of the day, now addressed himself to the impossible task of sorting out the various families he had met so far but his memory boggled at so many Potters and Willoughbys and Derwents and Pitts, with here a husband who bullied his wife, and there a wife who nagged her husband, of the rivalries and jealousies and a bevy of pretty, chirrupy girls and their lumping great brothers, so that he gave it up as they clattered over the wooden bridge into Codsall territory and saw the sprawling cluster of buildings round the long, low farmhouse close to the western boundary.

It was obvious that word of his presence had reached the fifth farm, for the four Codsalls awaited them in the yard, dressed in their Sunday broadcloth and Rudd, spotting Martin Codsall's silk waistcoat from afar, let out a guffaw and shouted, "Codsall! You never tog yourself up for me when I come for the rent!", a jest that Arabella Codsall, towering half-a-head above her husband, and holding little Sydney by the hand, ignored but bobbed an abbreviated curtsy in Paul's direction, exclaiming, "Look now, Sydney! The gentleman's in uniform, and an officer's uniform, I declare! Welcome to Four Winds, Mr. Craddock!" Then, in a higher key that carried as far as the river—"Will! Don't stand gawping! Take the gentleman's horse! Martin! What are you about? Show the visitors into the parlour this minute!", and the Codsalls moved into action like a sullen detail surprised by a visiting staff-officer and watched by a zealous sergeant-major.

III

Arabella Codsall, notwithstanding her comparative affluence, was almost certainly the most unhappy woman in the Valley and her discontent stemmed from her disgust of the poor material with which she was obliged to work. Under no circumstances could she have proved a success as a farmer's wife. She had been born over a linen-draper's shop and brought up within the tight circle of a cathedral city's tradesmen's community, so that she thought of farmers as hobbledehoys in a social bracket equivalent to that of roadsweepers, lamplighters and Irish navvies. For all that she had been glad to marry Martin Codsall some twenty years before when she was then twenty-eight and towered nearly six inches above most of the eligible tradesmen's sons, in her native Paxtonbury. She had the additional handicap of looking rather like an indignant goose, with a large, curving nose, small startled eyes, sharply receding chin and a mouth that was always half-open, as though honking with fury. She had arrived at Four Winds with a supply of linen and one hair trunk but any chance she had of making the most of her situation was shattered by her father's death and surprise legacy of nearly two thousand pounds. She had not expected anything like this amount for Alderman Blackett had been notoriously secretive concerning his savings. Moreover, there had originally been two other children and the Alderman, having made his will early, had not altered it when these two died in a scarlet-fever epidemic in the early 'nineties, so that the words "or surviving progeny thereof" trebled Arabella's patrimony. She at once set about the task of hoisting the cumbersome Codsalls into a niche above that occupied by their neighbours, and only a peg or two below that of the Lovells, but it had been a wearisome, thankless task, for neither Martin nor her elder son Will seemed able or willing to exploit their opportunities. Arabella mistook the symbols and rituals of her linen-draper's background for reliable handholds along the haul towards gentility, instituting at Four Winds such incongruous items as four o'clock tea sipped from thin china, linen napkins, a maid with a cap, and even a tablecloth at breakfast, novelties that bewildered Martin Codsall and ultimately converted both him and his son Will into farmyard fugitives, who stayed out of doors whenever possible. Yet she persisted; year after year she prodded and planned, and words of advice and admonition gushed from her goosey little mouth like a cataract, so that in order to survive her menfolk were driven to raise all kinds of defences against her nagging. Martin took refuge in a weak man's obstinacy and a warren of bolt holes. Will adopted the characteristics of a deaf mute, so that at last Arabella was driven to direct most of her energy upon Sydney, the younger boy. Sydney was more pliant—or so it seemed—and his pliancy soon won for him the adoration of his mother. The moment Arabella had word of Craddock's visit, and the possibility of his succeeding as Squire, Four Winds erupted. She dressed Sydney in his best, set the hired hands to scour the yard, instituted a spring-clean inside the house (where most of the work was done by a befrilled half-witted child, called Minnie), flushed Martin and Will from their hiding-places and ordered them to don their Sunday serge. Martin, mumbling that he had work to do, took his revenge by somewhat overdoing the transformation and appeared downstairs in a starched dickey when it was too late to go back and change his shirt. Son Will, his mind still searching for a permanent escape route from this hell upon earth, said nothing at all but eyed Craddock with interest when he rode into the yard, perhaps seeing in him some glimmer of hope for the future; for Will Codsall, madly in love with Elinor Willoughby and reduced to the status of an automaton, any change at Shallowford would be for the better.

Within two minutes of being seated in the Codsall's airless parlour, listening to Arabella's uninterrupted flow of domestic clichés, Paul realised that Rudd had not exaggerated in his description of Arabella as an insufferable woman. Her approach to him was at once over-weening and apologetic, overbearing yet grotesquely cringing, vain to the point of idiocy, yet voluble in her demands as a long-suffering tenant, so that Rudd, after listening to her gobbling for ten minutes, cut in with a terse, "It's not the slightest use burdening Mr. Craddock with all this, Mrs. Codsall! He hasn't even made up his mind to buy Shallowford and if you make everything sound run down I don't suppose he will!"

This remark had some effect upon her, inasmuch as she converted her flood of complaints into a detailed description of Sydney's astonishing progress under a private tutor, at Whinmouth, whereupon Craddock, taking his cue from the agent, said, "I really came over to look at the farm, Mrs. Codsall," and on that Martin bobbed up like a hare and led the way out into the sunshine with Will breathing down his neck and Mrs. Codsall, still gobbling, bringing up the rear. Sydney did not follow his parents into the yard. He was a well-schooled little boy and his Sunday suit anchored him to the parlour.

They inspected Codsall's excellent Friesian herd, then his pigs and finally his sheep down by the river. Here Martin disappeared, seemingly into a haystack, but Arabella and Will followed every step of the way, so that Paul had the impression he was being dogged by a goose and a soft-footed St. Bernard dog. Soon both he and Rudd ceased to comment, for the most innocuous remark increased the clack of Arabella's tongue and finally they made their escape, the honking of Arabella following them as far as the swing gate that led to the bridge. It seemed then that they had spent a long afternoon at Four Winds but on glancing at his watch Paul saw that their visit had occupied no more than forty-five minutes.

Neither of them spoke for a while and the silence in the river meadows was like a balm but at length Rudd said, "One understands under what terrible provocation some murders are committed! I've often thought how willingly I would give evidence on Martin's behalf, if he appeared at Paxtonbury Assizes one fine day charged with drowning that wife of his in a duckpond. Justifiable homicide! That's what the verdict would be." Paul asked if he knew the cause of Arabella Codsall's terrible volubility and he replied with a wry smile, "Well, I suppose I might quote our friend Donne about a woman's mouth only being full of words when she is empty elsewhere, but it doesn't apply in Arabella's case. I think it has something to do with the dismal nineteenth-century cult of 'self-improvement', foisted upon us by all those crackpot writers and philosophers, like Ruskin, Bentham, and all the rest of them! Buried down there for the past two decades I've seen less changes than most men but what I have seen could have taught those city sociologists something! It's a great mistake to teach everybody to read and write, Craddock, maybe the greatest mistake western civilisation has ever made, for it'll do for us all in the end, mark my words!"

"Now how can you possibly justify that?" Paul demanded, recalling the squalor of the area beyond Tower Bridge, "surely some of a nation's wealth ought to be ploughed back into its population. From what I've seen since I came home precious little of our industrial profits

72

are being invested in the welfare or the fabric of the country. Isn't a compulsory education the key to a nation's progress?"

"It's a key all right," Rudd said sadly, "but does it unlock? When I was a boy the social scale here and in the cities was not adjustable. In the main you stayed what you were born, artisan, tradesman, professional man, gentleman. Hardly anyone in a district like this *could* read or write, or wanted to, but they were contented enough, they didn't resent the patronage of people like the Lovells. They got all they needed by hard work and peasant cunning, by making themselves indispensable to their so-called betters, and they didn't quarrel with the pattern either. People like Arabella Codsall wouldn't have been tolerated for a moment, but that isn't so any more. Arabella is laughed at by old-timers like Martha Pitts, but only behind her back! I've seen Arabella at village socials, queening it over all the other wives but impressing them, in spite of themselves. Nobody challenges her, not even me or you. And if her husband took an ashplant to her backside as he ought he'd be up before the magistrates. If Arabella hadn't been taught to read and write would she have had the impudence to complain to us about her damned rights-of-way or her roof tiles?"

"What do you think will happen in backwaters like this eventually then?"

"I can tell you that, now that we have universal male suffrage. The whole ediffice will come crumbling down in a single life's span and the land, as we know it today, will go to pot, with nobody left to tend it. All the children you saw with their noses in books at Mary Willoughby's school will drift away to the cities and become an army of frustrated little clerks and busybodies. They'll all be Arabella Codsalls, wringing their hands over their neighbours' possessions, living in little brick boxes with a few square feet of garden. You might regard the talkative Mrs. Codsall as a local pioneer."

"Altogether too pessimistic," Paul argued. "Damn it all, we're all subject to evolution. Things never stay the same for long, either nationally or locally."

"That's so," pursued Rudd, "but my point is things are

changing far too quickly. People can't absorb the social and economic changes of the last century. When technology leaves the mass of population far enough behind there's going to be a God-Almighty explosion."

"What kind of explosion?"

"How do I know? Go back to your history books. A revolution of some kind, or a war."

"We've just finished a war," Paul argued, "and it hasn't turned civilisation inside out."

"I'm not talking about colonial wars," Rudd said, "I'm talking about Armageddon."

They rode on in silence for a spell, the flashing stream on their left and the church spire of Coombe Bay rising clear of Codsall's cornstalks. It occurred to Paul that there was an affinity of a kind between Rudd and Zorndorff, both of an age, both addicted to sensational generalisations. He wondered what each man expected of him, and whether Rudd would be interested in Zorndorff's advocacy of the purchase of the estate but before he could continue the discussion they entered the steep village street of Coombe Bay and he found himself looking about him for any signs of Grace Lovell riding her neat bay mare.

There were none. Coombe Bay was deep in its afternoon siesta and the broad, single street was quite deserted. It was not much of a village, a double row of thatched cottages curving away from the river and, lower down, a straggle of tiny shops, and a few Georgian terrace houses, with window boxes and polished knockers.

Rudd told him that the estate owned some of these houses let at fifty pounds a year, and that a larger house on the headland was occupied by Grace Lovell's father, the family parasite. They ambled down to the beach where the Sorrel, no more than thirty feet across, gushed into the sea under a rounded, sandstone bluff. There was a boat shelter, one or two blue jerseyed fishermen pottering about their nets, and further west, where the sand swept in a wide curve as far as a landslip, some children paddling and shrimping under the breakwater. It was all very quiet and still under the hot afternoon sun, so quiet that Paul could hear the splash of tiny wavelets falling on the white sand. They sat there resting the horses and Paul would have liked to have dismounted and bathed his stiff leg in the sea but was too lazy to dismount and pull off his boots. Presently a yellow gig, driven at a spanking pace swept out of the High Street and turned west along the waterfront, disappearing up a side-street beyond the inn, which had a double-headed bird on its signboard and the name "The Raven" in Gothic lettering.

"That's Doctor O'Keefe," Rudd said, "he never drives that poor beast at anything under a canter. He does it to spread the impression that he's conscientious when, in fact, he's usually half-pickled. He's a likeable old rascal though, and I daresay you'll meet him if you stay long enough. Came here years ago, after some kind of scandal in his native Dublin but he's a good doctor, drunk or sober. I've seen him do some remarkable patchwork in my time here," and then, as though he had suddenly made up his mind to be done with small talk and come to the point, "How do you feel about the place as a whole, Mr. Craddock? Is it anything like you imagined? Are you still serious about taking up your option?"

"Which question do you want answered first?" Paul asked, smiling, but Rudd said, rather peevishly, "It makes small enough odds to me one way or the other. You won't need an overseer like me if you intend living here and not leaving us to our own devices for years on end like the Lovells."

"Well," said Paul, "as to making up my mind I'd rather leave it until tomorrow if you've no objections. I'd like to think over what I've seen so far and I owe it to Mr. Zorndorff to discuss it with him. Is there a telephone on the estate?"

"Good God, no!" said Rudd, "what would anybody here want with a telephone? The nearest one is in Whinmouth Post Office, nine miles to the west."

"Very well," said Paul, "I'll decide before the sale opens tomorrow. As to what I feel about the place, I admit it intrigues me. It's so utterly unlike anything I imagined after reading that article in the *Illustrated London News*."

"Can't you be a bit more specific?" asked Rudd, and

because he seemed genuinely concerned Paul added, "I think it's a private world, populated by a few hundred castaways from a wreck about a century ago! On your own admission its commercial prospects are very thin but frankly I'm not much concerned about that. I should expect to put money into any property I took and it boils down to this in the end; what kind of person are these farmers and their families looking for as a landlord, or 'squire' if you like? What would be his responsibilities to them? Or theirs to him? Wouldn't they prefer to buy their farms cash down or over a period? Do they really want a city stranger breathing down their necks?"

Rudd's spurt of irritation had spent itself, as it usually did in a matter of seconds.

"How can I answer that?" he said smiling. "They haven't confided in me all the time I've been here. I was little more than a rent-collector for the Lovells."

"That isn't quite true," Paul told him, "because it's obvious that you've formed an opinion about every one of them. Is Derwent the only one keen to become a free-holder? Wouldn't Mrs. Codsall jump at the chance of being her own squireen?"

"I doubt it," said Rudd, "she likes the link with Quality, you being Quality if you follow me. Derwent is an exception, and I daresay he'd quibble at the price you asked him. Neither Potter nor Willoughby would care to stand on their own feet, and Arthur Pitts is happy with things as they are. No, they'd jog along if they got a man prepared to put the estate in order. They'd all rather leech on somebody like you, so I'm afraid you would have the monopoly of obligations, Mr. Craddock."

"Well, that's honest enough," Paul said, "and I'll bear it in mind when I give you my answer tomorrow. Have you got a hip bath up at the lodge? I've overdone it a bit I think, and I'd like to soak this leg and take it easy for the rest of the day."

Rudd was instantly solicitous and swung his cob around.

"I'm an idiot!" he exclaimed, "I ought to have thought of that but the truth is I've enjoyed myself today in an odd sort of way. It's long enough since I saw Shallowford tenants hang out flags. We'll go home and Mrs. Handcock will fix you up with some soda."

An hour later Paul was enjoying a soda soak in the wash-house behind the lodge and after a high tea, and a smoke in the parlour, the ache of his wound left him and he surrendered to a pleasant drowsiness as the shadows moved across the paddocks. Rudd, sharing the silence with him, avoided reopening discussion on the sale but when Paul, on the point of going to bed, asked if the grey would be available early in the morning he promised to have Honeyman's lad see to it and tether the horse in the yard behind the wash-house by six-thirty. Paul thanked him and after a moment's hesitation, said, "I should like to own that horse in any case, Mr. Rudd. He isn't included in the sale, is he?" and Rudd said no, although the stable tack was, adding that Ralph Lovell had bought the gelding for fifty pounds shortly before he left for South Africa.

"I'd gladly give that for him," Paul said, "he's quiet and very well-mannered for a young horse, and I don't intend to take any chances until my leg is right."

"Then consider it sold," Rudd said, "you might go further and fare a great deal worse!", and with that Paul left him sitting in his big armchair, looking out of the open window across the paddock. "It's odd," he thought, as he mounted the little stair to his room, "but the prospect of leaving here is making him miserable notwithstanding all his grousing about the Lovells."

CHAPTER THREE

I

THE cock at the Home Farm awakened him soon after first light and on going to the window he saw that it promised to be another scorcher. A curtain of pale, blue mist veiled the downslope to the sea and wisps of cloud, coral pink over the sandstone cliff of the Coombe, were translucent and very still. Over in the rhododendron thickets the bird chorus was beginning and as Paul dressed the steady rhythm of its twitter built into a continuous murmur, like the patter of rain on glass. He stood at the window sniffing the morning and thinking that this might be a day he would remember all his life, yet he was free of qualms and felt as fit as he ever remembered, with little stiffness resulting from his twenty-mile ride the previous day.

The grey was tethered to the rail of the big paddock, stirrups high on the leathers, reins tucked under the crupper, and as he climbed into the saddle he thought that Honeyman's boy must be a very early riser, for it was still only six-forty and the boy was already a figure on the skyline, plodding the mile or so back to the farm.

He crossed the ford, now barely two inches deep and followed the track they had taken to Coombe Bay the previous afternoon, and it was only when the spire of the parish church showed above the corn that he realised why he was riding this way. His memory of the Lovell girl was no more than a vague impression of dark curls growing close to a small, neat head, and the swell of a sturdy figure under the blue riding habit, yet this was enough to persuade him, now that he was alone, that the girl was linked to his ultimate decision and somehow the conclusion did not seem illogical or facetious. By the time he was

78

half-way down the village street, and passing the gardens of the Georgian houses, he had ceased to make excuses for himself and looked eagerly across to the wooded slope that enclosed the village on the east, searching for the house where Rudd had said she and her father lived, overlooking the harbour. He could see a couple of detached houses, each half-hidden in trees and facing due south but there was no sign that anyone was astir, although from somewhere in the yards behind the cottages he could hear the scrape of boots on cobbles and the metallic clank of a pail.

There was more activity down by the waterfront. Fishermen were at work hauling a boat down to the water's edge and far out across the bay he could see two or three other small craft, pulling into the sun. Gulls flew squawking from the harbour wall when he edged his horse down the slipway, and along the beach to the hillocks beyond highwater mark, but the long, curving shore was deserted. As he climbed the hummocks to a sandy plateau above the tideline he made another effort to concentrate his thoughts on what he would say to Rudd at breakfast, or what he should write to Zorndorff that evening. He had a sensitive man's horror of appearing ridiculous in public and an awareness of his unfitness for responsibilities of this kind. Rudd had warned him that he would have a monopoly of responsibility in this small, tight community, made up of such unpredictable people as the sly Tamer Potter, uncompromising Derwent, and the voluble Arabella Codsall, their families and their hired hands. How many were there for heaven's sake—thirty, fifty, a hundred? And who knew what currents of jealousy and rancour lay in wait for him under their smiles of welcome and deferential greetings? Of the families he had met, only one, the Pitts of Hermitage, seemed uncomplicated, whereas the Potters and Codsalls might present all manner of problems to an inexperienced young man savouring his first taste of authority. He sat astride the patient grey, his eyes squinting into the sun so that it was not until the horse threw up his head and whinnied that he was aware of movement below and to his right, where the white sand stretched as far as the distant land-slip.

She came out of the west at full gallop, pounding along the flat within yards of the sea, the bay's hoof-thrusts sending up little spurts of sand, the rider pitched forward in the jockey's huddle that Yeomanry riding-masters had been at pains to eliminate from the seats of recruits. She was wearing a white blouse and a grey riding skirt and she was hatless, thus breaking another riding-school rule in her mad-cap gallop along the water's edge. As he saw her she set the horse at a drift-log and sailed over it and then, without checking her stride she swung left, heading directly for the hummocks on which he stood, whirling in a flurry of sand and breasting the incline at such a pace that it seemed to Craddock she would sweep past him on to the sand-hills beyond. He tightened his rein, thinking that the grey might bolt in pursuit, but suddenly she brought the horse up short, rearing it back like an Arab executing a mounted salute and he saw then, from his position twenty feet above, that she was smiling and had recognised him before he had seen her approach along the beach.

She called, in a loud, clear voice, "Mr. Paul Craddock, I believe!" and he raised his hat as the grey sidled forward and descended to the beach.

"I saw you half-a-mile away," she said, with her tight, slightly ironic smile. "That's a good horse you have! When you get his fat down and corn him up he'll carry twice your weight all day! Where's Rudd?"

"Still asleep in bed," Paul said, "or he was when I left him."

Was it his fancy that a change of expression registered a little of her suspicion when she realised he was alone? He felt unsure of everything about this hard, compact parcel of energy but she continued to look straight at him, as though his presence here on a public beach early in the morning required an explanation. He knew then that this was the sign he had been awaiting, that, not-withstanding his uncertainty and fear of ridicule he would this very day be master of Shallowford, and Grace Lovell's landlord to boot. He said, gravely, "I'm buying the estate. I'm taking over Shallowford," and was surprised by the firmness of his voice. "Will you be attending the sale?"

She stared at him, not resentfully as in the nursery, or ironically, as when she had whirled to the foot of the hillock but with a frank curiosity, as though he had been a curious object left on the beach by the tide.

"You've been a farmer?" she asked at length, dropping her glance to his breeches and military boots.

"No," he admitted, "I don't know a thing about farming. I've been overseas nearly three years and after that I was in hospital but from what I hear the Lovells weren't farmers either!"

She laughed at this, throwing back her head and squaring her shoulders. He said, "I'm sorry, I shouldn't have said that. You were a relation I believe?"

"No," she said, "not really and anyway it's true. Neither Sir George, nor Hubert, nor my Ralph cared a row of beans about what went on here, so long as rents were paid, but I suppose you'll be buying it for the hunting?"

"By no means," Paul said, "though I shall hunt, providing I have time."

She looked genuinely surprised at this. "Why shouldn't you have the time? If you can afford to buy Shallowford you must have all the time in the world."

He said, convincing himself rather than her, "I'm partially disabled, but at twenty-three I don't care to look forward to a lifetime of idleness. I suppose that sounds pompous but I don't apologise. Months on your back gives a man a chance to think and there should be a better use for capital than to make more money, and dissipate the interest cutting a fashionable dash. I believe I might be using mine on a place as old and potentially fruitful as this valley and I think I'd enjoy doing it."

It was strange, he thought, that he could speak so freely to her, whereas he had been unable to clarify his thoughts to experienced men of the world, like Zorndorff and Rudd, both people who wished him well. It occurred to him that this might be because she was of his generation and then his mind fastened on her words "my Ralph" and this, he thought, might be the key to her brooding presence in the nursery, implying as it did that she too was confused and, to an extent, dissatisfied with her life. She interrupted his conjecturing with, "How badly are you disabled, Mr. Craddock?"

"Enough to deny me the chance of doing what I wanted to do, take a permanent commission. I had a bullet through the knee joint. It's healed now, and in time I shall be ninety-five per cent fit, but it was enough to get me thrown aside as a crock!"

"You're bitter about that?"

"No," he admitted, truthfully, "I'm not bitter, or not any longer." He returned her steady gaze and asked, "Are *you* bitter? About Ralph Lovell getting killed?"

The question disconcerted her. He saw that at once, for she looked past him and seemed to be considering whether to protest at his curiosity.

"I don't know what Rudd's told you about Ralph," she said, "but whatever it was it was prejudiced. Rudd hated the Lovells and I imagine he had good reasons for hating them."

"Yes he did," Paul told her, "and I happen to know those reasons, Miss Lovell, for he made a clean breast of them as soon as I arrived."

She seemed surprised at this, so he went on, before she could comment, "They never let him forget an incident that led to his resigning his commission, but I've been under fire myself, and if Ralph Lovell had survived I daresay he would have found it easy to understand Rudd when he came home. I like Mr. Rudd and I mean to keep him on as agent."

"I see; and have you got any plans for your tenants?" she asked, slyly. "I'm one, you know, at least my father and stepmother are; we live up there," and she pointed with her crop.

"Well I won't put up the rent, if that's what you're hinting at," Paul said and she laughed so that Paul thought it was a long time since he had heard a more musical note. Her laughter had resonance and sounded as free as the birdsong he had heard at the window an hour before.

"Look here, Mr. Craddock," she said, "I'd like you to know that I honestly wish you luck, and also that I'm sorry I was very rude back at the house the other night. I ought to be grateful to you really, I'd gone there to eat another helping of nostalgic pie. Your appearance gave me something else to think about."

"You were unhappy over Ralph Lovell's being killed? That's nothing to apologise for, is it?"

"Ralph was killed a long time ago," she said, "and I haven't had your chance to come to terms with the future. I've been feeling altogether too sorry for myself and it really doesn't do to start living in the past at my age. You'll be attending the sale, of course?"

"Yes," he said eagerly, "I shall bid for some of the things I might need up there. Furniture, fittings and tack especially. I daresay Rudd will advise me now that I've finally made up my mind."

"You mean he doesn't know?"

"That's right," Paul said, "I really came here this morning to decide. You just happen to be the first to hear, Miss Lovell," and he smiled.

The hand holding her crop shot up to her mouth and her lip touched the ivory handle, so that she suddenly looked like a child, puzzled by an unexpected turn of events. Then he saw the two bright spots appear on her cheeks once again and before he could say another word she clapped her heels to the flanks of the bay and dashed past him to the top of the sandhill. The grey whipped around, almost unseating Paul so that he was obliged to concentrate on the horse for a moment; then, looking up, he saw her again, sitting her horse in the precise spot where he had been when he had watched her gallop along the water's edge. She was smiling down at him like a child who had confounded her elders by a piece of showing-off and as he pulled the grey around she lifted her hand in a salute and swinging round galloped over the crest of the hill and out of sight in a few seconds.

Rudd received the news calmly enough until Paul added that he would like him to remain as agent on a three-year contract at a starting salary of three hundred a year. Then the agent's phlegm deserted him and he got up, standing by the open window with his face turned away and his hands clasped behind his back.

"You don't have to do that," he said gruffly, "you could manage very well on your own after a year."

"I should be an idiot not to take advantage of your experience," Paul told him. "You would be doing me a favour by staying."

At that Rudd swung round and said earnestly, "Well then, I accept, and I must say it's damned generous of you, Mr. Craddock! I won't pretend that I should find it a big wrench to leave here. As I said, I haven't been all that happy but I've always loved the place. There's been indifference here, and plenty of sloth too, but I still think the place could respond to a little care and imagination. You know what they say about a woman who is loved? She takes on self-confidence and beauty, and I've always thought this could happen here. Anyway, I'll promise you two things. I'll give you honest advice, and my heart will be in the job!"

"Well that should do for a start," said Paul and they shook hands on the bargain, spending the morning touring the Home Farm, which seemed to Paul well administered by Tom Honeyman, a plodding, bald-headed man, whose enthusiasm was reserved for Southdown sheep, for he was descended (or claimed to be) from the Newbury farmer who once won a thousand guineas from the local squire by making a hunting coat from wool sheared from a pair of Southdowns that same day. Honeyman was a widower, with grown children, all farming outside the estate boundaries, and managed the farm with a cowman, three or four boys, and two biblical looking shepherds, known as Matt and Luke, who were twins and, so Rudd informed Paul, unable to read or write. Later they went up to the house to select items of furniture that might be bought in at ten per cent above the reserve price. This seemed to Paul a very arbitrary way of doing business, for the sale had been advertised for the following day, and it occurred to him that bidders might be coming some distance to buy lots that they would now find withdrawn, but Rudd pooh-poohed his doubts. "It was laid down in the conditions of sale that anything the purchaser of the estate wanted he was to have," he told Paul. "The executors are more interested in selling the estate than disposing of the bits and pieces, and anyway, a lot of the stuff here is either worn out or second rate." Paul discovered, on closer inspection, that this was so. Most of the furniture was heavy mid-Victorian pieces whereas the carpets were badly worn, except in the main bedrooms which did not appear to have been used much. He had an opportunity, on going round with Rudd, to get better bearings on the house and found it longer and narrower than he had imagined, with a spacious drawing-room, and a dining-room respectively east and west of the entrance hall, a smaller and very cheerful library, stocked with over a thousand books leading out of the drawing-room, a billiard-room adjoining the dining-room, and a warren of passages and pantries about the huge, Elizabethan kitchen that still had its great hearth, and antediluvian cooking implements. Kitchen and domestic quarters lay behind the east wing and opened upon a wide, cobbled yard, enclosed by stables and coach house. The woods here began at the end of the kitchen garden, which rose steeply, making the back of the house rather sunless, except in the late afternoon. Behind the garden, which was in good order and enclosed by a mellow brick wall, was an orchard and Rudd said that in springtime this was full of daffodils and narcissi, and that later bluebells grew there so thickly that the ground was a blue mist. Paul asked him if he was fond of gardening and he said no but had an interest in wild flowers, which he was usually reluctant to admit. "For a countryman to confess to a liking for wild flowers is tantamount to him saying he opposes blood sports," he said with a chuckle.

They went up the backstairs and along the rearward passage to the staff sleeping quarters. Evidence of neglect and decay were everywhere, plaster and paper peeling from walls and at one place, on the east wall, a wide crack in the ceiling and a hole in the roof of the attic through which they could see the sky. Here the tiny bedrooms, some half-dozen of them, were airless boxes containing little besides an iron cot or two, a truckle bed and a few stools. Rudd told him that when Sir George had been in residence he kept a full staff of servants, sometimes as many as a dozen variously employed as kitchen hands, parlourmaids and grooms, apart from the resident house-keeper and three gardeners, but that when the house was empty all but the gardeners and Mrs. Handcock, the housekeeper, were paid off, "like a crew engaged for a single voyage". When Paul asked if this had not caused distress in the area Rudd said that it had, particularly in winter, but that regular work in the Sorrel Valley had never been plentiful and the family had not had difficulty in recruiting casual labor whenever they came down for a hunting season, or the period preceding or following the London season. "They wasted money they begrudged putting into the estate," he said. "I've known young Hubert pay out two hundred guineas for a hunt supper here but they paid atrocious wages, spending what they saved on any number of fads, like the old man's passion for photography. He had a dark-room off the library and his paraphernalia is still there, together with hundreds of photographs he took and developed. You can see what needs spending on the house before you start on the farms but I can find you a good local builder and if we get his estimate right away I daresay he'll move in and live here until the job's done. He can subcontract for the painting and plumbing and we shall need Vicary, the Coombe Bay stonemason. After the sale we can make a plan as to what's necessary and what, if anything, you would like knocked down or built on."

There was no bathroom—the Lovells seemed to have washed in wooden tubs—but the three main bedrooms at the front of the house were in better repair than the reception-rooms on the ground floor. Two of these bed-rooms looked over the paddocks and ford, and a string of smaller guest-rooms, ending in the nursery, faced west.

Paul noticed that the scrap screen and the rocking horse were labelled Lots 250 and 251, and he wondered if Grace Lovell would bid for them. In the largest bedroom was a huge four-poster and two or three pieces of late eighteenth-century furniture, including a serpentine chest of drawers, a military chest converted into a wardrobe, and two or three rosewood wig-stands which he said he would buy, together with about twenty lots in the guest-rooms and the rooms downstairs. He also marked down the library furniture and books, promising himself some pleasant winter evenings in what seemed to him the cosiest room in the house. The windows here looked over Shallowford Woods and Coombe Bluff and there was a deep leather armchair promising solid comfort in front of a wide stone hearth. When the list was complete they made their way back to the lodge and Rudd totted up the cost of the items Paul had bought in, making a total of under four hundred pounds. This excluded the grey, the trap and the tack in the harness room, which came to another hundred and fifty, so that Paul told himself he had done a good day's business, particularly when Rudd explained that all the gardening tools were included in the overall purchase price. That night Paul told the agent the source of his legacy and something of Zorndorff's part in the adventure. He was frank about his means, thinking it unfair to both of them if Rudd, who would be responsible for the initial outlay, remained in the dark and was tempted to either cheesepare or overspend.

"Well," said Rudd, bracing himself as though to speak an unpleasant truth, "I promised you good advice and I'll give you some right away. Don't tell anyone else what you've just told me—the source of the money, that is, or your association with trade of any kind. You are simply a fortunate young man who has come into a legacy and if you're wise you'll leave it at that! There's nobody in the world so snobbish as the peasant with a straw in his mouth!" As he spoke they heard the hooves on the gravel of the drive and through the open window saw Rose and Claire Derwent trot past on their way up to the house. Rudd said, with a chuckle, "One thing more, Mr. Craddock!" and pointed with his pipe at the disappearing horsewomen—"Are you the marrying type? Or committed elsewhere?" and when Paul admitted that he had never seriously thought of marriage the agent added, "Then I'd best warn you of something else while I'm at it! Every filly hereabouts will be anticipating the hunting season by a couple of months or more! There go two who have already started cubbing, so to speak, so sit tight until they move on to draw the next covert!"

It seemed that every man, woman and child as far afield as Whinmouth, and the villages north of the railway line, had taken time off to attend Shallowford House sale. By ten o'clock, an hour before bidding was due to commence, paddocks and forecourt were the scene of a vast picnic, with everyone in their summer best and ranks of gigs, traps, waggonettes and saddle-horses tethered to palings behind the avenue chestnuts. Paul and Rudd made their way to the house through groups of respectful strangers, some of them people Paul remembered having met on his tour. He saw Tamer Potter already refreshing himself out of an enormous flagon of cider, with his three girls gossiping with young men in corduroys under the trees, and their brothers Sam and Smut talking to a man in velveteens, who looked as if he was lecturing them, for he kept making emphatic gestures as Sam looked sheepish and Smut listened with a broad grin on his sunburned face. "That's Melrose, Lord Gilroy's head keeper," Rudd told Paul, as they walked up the drive, "giving Smut Potter another of his final warnings! There's Arabella, with Martin in tow. I daresay she'll make him bid for one or two of the fancy lots. And there's Dr. O'Keefe," and Rudd pointed to a rather handsome old man, in a black frock coat leaning negligently against a tree, surveying the gathering with contempt. "And there's Lord Gilroy himself, out for an airing after his last spell of gout. He's a supercilious old rascal but I daresay he'll be civil enough and suspend judgment on you until somebody gets wind of your connection with a scrapyard! After that he'll cut you, but you can get along without Gilroy patronage—the Lovells did!"

"I'm a bit astonished by the grip the eighteenth century

still has on the area," Paul said when they had been admitted by the back door and had moved into one of the rooms facing the terrace where they could overlook the crowd in the paddocks and drive.

"What else did you expect?" Rudd said. "We only got our railway link four years ago, and I can remember *The Times* being read aloud in the bar of The Raven once a week! You've caught us at an intermediary stage—say about 1860, and I think this might be the source of some of your biggest headaches! You saw one or two reach for their forelocks at the farms but when they realised they were doing it instinctively they felt shamefaced, and that's a bad thing. Either a man freely acknowledges power of wealth and class, or he doesn't think of himself as anything but a free man, with a free man's privilege of telling the squire to treat him as one or go fishing! Take that mob out there, flirting, guzzling and skylarking around the waggons. Not one in fifty has any intention of bidding for anything here. With one or two exceptions they couldn't afford to pay for it if it was knocked down to them, but does that stop them making a fête out of the sale? Why bless you, Sir George Lovell in his heyday would have had his keeper herd them the far side of the ford but today there they are and not a blush between them, except when Parson Bull buttonholes sermon-dodgers and threatens to name slackers publicly from the pulpit! There he is now, giving Arthur Pitts the edge of his tongue," and Paul saw a massively built clergyman, with a great mop of white hair, hectoring a downcast-looking Arthur, who stood with his wife Martha in the forecourt awaiting the auctioneer's signal to unlock the front door.

"What kind of man is Bull?" Paul enquired. "I daresay I shall have to attend church as soon as I settle in," and Rudd chuckled and said that even Sir George Lovell had been circumspect in his dealings with Bull, who was probably the last buttress of the eighteenth century in the Valley, for he hunted three times a week, swore freely in public and usually called for a tot of brandy before dispensing communion wine to his flock. "Willoughby, the Nonconformist, once challenged him outside The Raven, accusing him of setting a bad example to his parishioners," he said, "but Bull only shouted, 'If you meet a man carrying a lantern on a dark night don't question his character, you dissenting knave! Just be grateful for the light he's shedding, in the hope that it will keep your erring feet clear of hell!' He's a hard man is Bull, but he's respected. He's a real man, you see, and they prefer that to someone who hands out the Gentle Jesus brand of Christianity!"

The auctioneer asked Rudd if it was time to open the doors and when Rudd said it was Paul withdrew and watched the bidding, almost all the lots on the ground floor being knocked down to a dealer from Whinmouth, rumoured to be bidding on Lord Gilroy's behalf, or to one of the auctioneer's staff acting for absent clients. He recognized Claire Derwent's blonde head under the rostrum and she saw him and smiled, nudging her sister Rose and then looking quickly away. Arabella Codsall bought a mirror and one or two figurines, and in addition to greeting the Pitts and Tamer Potter, Paul acknowledged the polite greetings of Willoughby, his shy daughter Elinor, and the grim-faced Edward Derwent, who never once took his eyes off the auctioneer but offered no bids, either by word or gesture. After a time Paul's leg began to ache so he drifted into the library and thence into the adjoining room that Sir George had used as a photographer's studio. The window was still draped with black cloth and when he had ripped it down, and opened the window, he saw a jumble of faded photographs, hypo baths and fixing frames left on the benches by the late owner. The pictures gave him a closer insight into the family than he had obtained from reading the *Illustrated London News*. He decided that George Lovell was no ordinary amateur but a technician with imagination and finesse, for there were some cleverly posed groups under the chestnuts, and several excellent pictures of horses and of meets in the forecourt outside. There were also souvenir pictures of fancy-dress balls of more than twenty years ago, dated and signed on the back in Sir George's spidery handwriting—*Shallowford Christmas Rout, 1882,* and *Harvest Ball, 1883,* large photographs showing groups of Robin Hoods, Dick Turpins and fairy-tale characters. It all seemed to belong to an age as far away as Waterloo, or before then, when choleric squires dispensed lavish hospitality and drunk themselves insensible after gruelling days in the hunting field. Looking at them Paul thought of what Rudd had said regarding the transitional stage at Shallowford, and its time lag, reflecting that he would be the person responsible for quickening the tempo but he also wondered if good intentions and an injection of capital would be enough to drag this self-contained little community into the twentieth century? Did the people of the Sorrel Valley acknowledge the Age of Progress, that everybody in London talked about? Had they ever devoted a moment's thought to airships, and electric lighting, to motors, phonographs, and higher education? And even if they had, would any of these things add anything important to their lives?

He was returning yellowing photographs to the shelf where he had found them when he saw the brass-bound Bible, a ponderous volume on the one shelf free of litter. He pulled it out, wondering why its clasp was secured by a small brass padlock, and it occurred to him that a Bible of this size and weight might contain a family tree, or perhaps a record of Lovell births and deaths over the century. The little padlock presented no difficulties and he prised it open with his penknife, turning to a flyleaf which was disappointingly blank. Then, opening the book at random, he almost dropped it with astonishment, for it was not a bible at all but an album of near-pornographic photographs, most of them obviously the work of Sir George, for they were identical in tone, mounting and finish to the groups he had just laid aside.

He turned the pages curiously, glancing at twenty or more portraits of show-girls in various stages of undress and a variety of obscene poses. Some of them wore tights, others were draped in what looked like clusters of spangled tassels. The subjects were all plump, rather overblown girls, with great sturdy thighs, mountainous breasts and very ample behinds. Most of them were smirking into the camera, so that Paul found their poses grotesquely comic, as though the photographer, by housing them between the covers of a Bible, was playing a secret practical joke on society. There was nothing particularly shocking about the first half of the album. The girls were clearly the type who habitually posed for these kind of pictures, and their self-satisfied smiles and negligent poses indicated that they were not in the least ashamed of earning an honest half-guinea catering to their patron's eccentric tastes. But then the nature of the gallery changed abruptly and Paul recognised, with a sense of shock, one of the older Potter girls, photographed against a background of artificial foliage and looking, he thought, a little frightened and incredulous, as well she might for she was stark naked, her disordered hair masking part of her face as she stood with shoulders slightly hunched, as though poised to run. There were several other pictures of this girl but in subsequent photographs she seemed to have gained confidence, for in two she was grinning and standing with feet astride and her hands on her hips. There were also photographs of a younger girl whom Paul did not recognize, a dark, wild-looking creature, who could not have been more than fifteen and had been permitted to retain an unlikely pair of drawers, frilled at the knee and very much beribboned, as though to heighten her forlorn appeal. She had been photographed standing in front of a full-length mirror and the result of the double reflection was somehow pathetic, as the camera had caught a pile of shabby discarded clothing in the bottom right-hand corner.

Paul stared at the pictures unbelievingly, wondering if chance had revealed to him a well-kept secret, or whether the whole Valley acknowledged George Lovell as a lustful old goat, whose secret pleasure was to coax young girls into this airless little room and bribe or frighten them into stripping and posing for his camera. The local pictures made him feel slightly sick and he pushed the window further open, wondering where he could hide the book until he had a chance to destroy it but as he moved a loose photograph fell to the floor and bending to retrieve it he saw that it was a study of another unidentifiable girl. This one, although naked, seemed to have clung to modesty of a sort, for she had turned her face away from the camera and used her hand as a screen. She was, thought Paul, an unwilling subject, but then he wondered, for a deliberate attempt had been made to pose her against the sylvan background and parody the pose of a surprised nymph. She was, he would judge, about the same age as the girl in the frilled drawers but better nourished, and possessing a more mature figure and a healthy skin. He was slipping the picture between the Bible covers when he heard a step in the library and for a moment he panicked, glaring round for somewhere to dispose of the wretched album. He had just thrust it alongside the festive groups when the door opened and Claire Derwent's blonde head appeared. She did not seem surprised to find him there alone and smiled, showing beautiful teeth.

"Why *there* you are, Mr. Craddock! Mr. Rudd said you were in the library. I wanted to ask you if my sister and I can help about horses. He told me the news and everyone is delighted! Mr. Rudd also told us you had bought the grey and we're pleased about that too, because Rose bred him from Misty, one of the best mares we ever had in the Valley."

Paul, thanking God that Claire Derwent had not been numbered among Sir George's local models, made a determined attempt to compose himself, feeling almost that she had surprised him enjoying the old satyr's picture gallery.

"It doesn't matter a bit if it isn't convenient now," Claire went on, mercifully oblivious of his confusion, "we could easily discuss it some other time, but if you need a good groom we happen to know of one who was a soldier like you, and has just come back seeking a post. We should also like you to know that we could come over and look after any horses if you had to go away again before you settled in. What I mean is, if we can help in any way you have only to ask, and father told me to say he'll do anything he can to help because he's just as pleased as we are that you're going to be Squire!"

He had recovered sufficiently to pay some attention to her now and it struck him again that she was an extraordinarily pretty woman, with her small, neat head, tidy corn-coloured hair dressed in coiled plaits, Dutch fashion, clear blue eyes and soft, red mouth. Her figure was good too, not straight and lithe like her sister's, but rather full, with small hands and feet, so that everything about her suggested neatness and vigorous health.

"It's very civil of you, Miss Derwent," he heard himself saying, "and I daresay I shall take advantage of your kindness. I'm very much taken with the grey and I expect, soon enough, I shall want a good cob for the trap, and maybe a second hunter. However, my first job is to try and get some kind of order into this chaos. The house needs a great deal of renovation, don't you think?"

She looked round the room with a woman's appraising eye for defects.

"Eph Morgan will sort it out in no time," she said, "he's the local builder Mr. Rudd will recommend and what he can't manage himself he'll find somebody to do. It's going to be wonderful to have Shallowford come alive again after all this time. This could be a wonderful home, Mr. Craddock, it only wants somebody like yourself to . . . well, to love it, and care for it! The Lovells were always coming and going, taking on people and getting rid of them, and really keen farmers like Daddy felt rather wretched about it all, you understand?"

"It's going to be different from now on," Paul promised and was surprised at his enthusiasm. "I'm going to like it here and I've no interest in town life. We could pull the place together in no time, providing every family is as co-operative as yours!" And then, because he noticed a gleam of triumph in her eyes, he felt he had said too much, and added, lamely, "I'd like to see how things are getting on out there if you'll excuse me, Miss Derwent, I only came in because it was so stuffy among the crowd in the big room."

"Oh, they're all upstairs now," she said gaily, "selling the stuff in the guest-rooms. We've come over in the wag-gonette and brought a picnic lunch. Would you care to join us when they break for luncheon? We're at the top of the drive and Daddy's got some rather good claret."

"That's kind of you," he said, "but I must ask Rudd if Mrs. Handcock is expecting us for lunch."

"Oh no she isn't," said Claire, "I've already asked Rudd and he said I was to ask you."

"Very well then, I should be delighted," said Paul, a

little taken aback by her persistence, and they moved out of the library to join the crowd on the landing, at the point where the passages branched.

He could hear the auctioneer's voice droning away at the far end of the corridor and the crowd made way for him in a way that suggested the news had already spread far and wide. He shed Claire on the way and here, looking over people's heads, he saw that the room was packed with spectators and that some of the lots from the bedrooms had been carried in to provide more selling space. Then, in her familiar corner by the window, he saw Grace Lovell, and beside her, looking as if association with the crowd distressed them, was a slim erect man about fifty, and a handsome, hard-faced woman, in her mid-thirties, who held a lilac parasol and whose features were rigid with concentration. He identified them at once as Grace Lovell's father and stepmother.

The auctioneer was selling Lot 250, the nursery screen, and before he was done with his patter Grace called "Ten shillings!", speaking so quickly that her mouth was closed again before Paul had realised she was bidding.

"Ten shillings!" repeated the auctioneer, as one of his assistants lifted the screen. "Any advance on ten shillings? A lot of painstaking work has gone into this! How about some of you young ladies and gentlemen thinking of getting married . . . ?", and there was a dutiful titter, in which the Lovells did not join.

"Fifteen!" said a woman standing in front of Paul and he recognised Arabella Codsall.

"One pound!" Grace called, before the auctioneer could invite an advance and Arabella, with a tut-tut of irritation, said, crossly, "One guinea, then!" and Paul caught a glimpse of Martin Codsall's peaked face at his wife's elbow.

The auctioneer glanced across to the silent trio by the window. "Come now, Miss Lovell, you'll not let it go for that. Shall I say twenty-two and six?"

Grace shook her head and Paul, seeing her glance drop, said, "Thirty shillings, Mr. Auctioneer!", and everyone in the room turned to stare. There was a pause and then, swiftly, the auctioneer brought down his gavel. "Sold to Mr. Craddock, and I'm delighted something else is staying where it belongs, sir! Well, ladies and gentlemen, that's all in here and we'll break for luncheon. The remaining lots, including all those outside, will be sold commencing two P.M. sharp!", and the crowd began to surge out into the corridor, pressing Paul back to the landing and downstairs to the hall where they streamed into the open.

Paul waited beside the big fireplace, watching Bruce Lovell and his wife descend the stairs, and pass into the forecourt. They did not see him and were engaged in a low and earnest conversation. When Grace did not follow he went up again and along the corridor to the nursery. She was still there, standing with her back to the door examining the screen with care. He said, "I didn't really want it, Miss Lovell, but I could see that you did and it didn't seem right to lose it to Arabella Codsall. It's yours if you want it and I can see that you do."

She turned slowly, regarding him with disconcerting gravity.

"Very well," she said, almost inaudibly, "I'll send the money for it tonight. I daresay my father can get someone to collect it tomorrow."

"I don't want paying for it," Paul said, "I'd like you to have it for old times' sake. You said you used to come here as a child and I daresay this room has happy memories for you. I'd be very glad if you would let me make you a present of it, Miss Lovell."

She continued to gaze fixedly at him and he decided that he wished she would sometimes make an effort to put him at ease. As if she could read his thoughts she suddenly dropped her glance and said, still very quietly, "Happy memories? I don't know why I wanted the screen, I probably wouldn't have looked at it when I got it home, but I helped to make it from scraps, cut up in the schoolroom. I was about seven or eight then, but it seems longer ago than that!" She seemed almost as though she was talking to herself but suddenly her head came up and she smiled, "It was a kind thought anyhow, Mr. Craddock, and I don't intend to be churlish again! I'll accept it as a gift—a going-away gift!", and she walked past him into the corridor and down the stairs, leaving him as baffled as he had been by her two previous dismissals.

CHAPTER FOUR

I

Zorndorff, enthroned on his high stool overlooking the yard, adjusted his half-moon spectacles and re-read Paul's eight-page letter with the undivided attention he gave to every document addressed to him, even trade brochures and invoices. He had read before that morning but hurriedly, to assess its factual worth. Now, with time on his hands, he dissected it, phrase by phrase.

It told of Paul's meeting with Rudd and the understanding they had arrived at during their ride over the moor; it described the scenery, house, farms, tenants, sale and the terms of his contract with Rudd. It even reported on the progress of his wound but it said nothing of Grace Lovell, or of the episode concerning the nursery screen. Zorndorff, however, had been prising undisclosed information from letters too long to miss the inference that there was a pretty girl somewhere between the lines and her presence intrigued him for he was aware of aspects of Craddock's character of which Paul himself was unaware and among them was a certain loss of confidence engendered by the shock of his wound, his long illness and the certainty that he now faced life with a permanent disability. It was because he was aware of these factors that Zorndorff had not been impressed by the young man's summary rejection of the scrap-iron business. To Craddock, as to any young man emerging from hospital with one leg shorter than the other, the world had a slightly sour taste and he would be ready to quarrel with everything until the period of adjustment had passed. The fact that a few days in the west had enabled him to mention his wound in passing satisfied the Croat that Paul had somehow succeeded in making that adjustment in a matter of days. Fresh air, soft scenery, and a visit to a few run-down farms, Zorndorff reasoned, would hardly have inspired a letter as jubilant as this; he wrote like a man in love and Zorndorff, who, despite preoccupation with business, had lived a full life, could appreciate the difference between the stimulus of a pretty landscape and that of a pretty woman. The only aspect of the letter that puzzled him was its postscript, obviously an afterthought. Paul had written: *"One other thing—I need a stable lad and remembered that urchin, the one who was so smart with that cart-horse. Would he care to exchange smoke for fresh air? Anyway, ask him and advance his fare if he'll come. He'll get full board and half-a-crown a week, together with expert training as a groom."*

Zorndorff had to think hard before he recalled the incident and when he did he smiled wryly, judging that a street-urchin of Ikey Palfrey's temperament would not willingly exchange the freedom of the streets for Gray's Elegy in a Country Churchyard. He blew down the speaking tube to Scotcher, the yard foreman, and instructed him to send Ikey Palfrey, Sophie Carrilovic's boy, to the office as soon as he came in with a load.

The boy appeared within half-an-hour and Zorndorff guessed correctly that he had been playing truant again, for the schools, closed in anticipation of the coronation ceremony, had reopened as soon as it was known that the King would not be crowned until August. The boy stood before Zorndorff in his rags, eyeing him furtively, as though sure of a command to return to school at once which would mean a thrashing. Ikey Palfrey cared very little for a routine thrashing but he resented very much enforced separation from his barrow, for that meant loss of income. He said, with mock humility, "Gaffer said you 'ad special collection for me, sir," and Zorndorff chuckled.

"Gaffer said nothing of the kind, boy. He told you I wanted a word with you, and it isn't for skipping school either. Why should I care a damn if you remain illiterate?"

The boy relaxed a little although he still looked ready to dart out of the door.

"Wot was it then?"

"It's this," Zorndorff said, and read the postscript aloud, watching the boy's bewildered expression. "You don't recall Mr. Craddock then?"

"Yerse I do," Ike said at once, " 'Ee got me a tanner, didn't he? I ain't likely to fergit that—earning a tanner, just fer savin' that bleedin' carter's head from being kicked in!"

The boy's nasal accent jarred Zorndorff's nerves and he found it difficult to believe that Sophie Carrilovic, a woman born and reared in Zagreb, could have produced a child who could so outrage a foreign tongue. He would wager that the boy could not speak one word of Croat but then, why should he? He was probably nine-tenths the son of that layabout Palfrey, whom Sophie had been obliged to marry in order to acquire British nationality.

"Very well, you remember him," Zorndorff said shortly, "but you don't know that he was Mr. Craddock's son, or that he was badly wounded in the war."

"No, I never knew that," Ike admitted, "but wot's the odds, Mister Zorndorff? What's that ter me?"

"Mr. Craddock seems to think you can be taught to handle horses," said Franz, now rather enjoying the interview.

"I c'n 'andle 'em nah, I don't need to be taught nothin' about 'orses," said Ike sharply but Zorndorff saw that he was impressed by the offer. " 'Arf-a-crahn an' all fahnd," he murmured. "Well, it don't sahnd bad, do it? Pervidin' you could pick up the odd bit o' scrap and flog it. Could you do that dahn there, Mr. Zorndorff?"

"I feel confident that you could do it anywhere," said Franz, "but I wouldn't like you to miss the main point. Mr. Craddock probably intends that you should learn a trade. You aren't likely to get that opportunity here if I know your parents, and as a stable lad on a big estate I daresay you would have a chance to ride real horses, not cart-horses. You might even become a jockey before you're finished!"

The boy's face shone. "Cor!" he said. "You ain't kiddin', Mr. Zorndorff? You wouldn't kid abaht a think like that? I alwus reckoned I could be a jockey, ser long as I don't grow no more. I'll take it, Mr. Zorndorff, if you'll 'ave a word wi' Mum, but don't let the ol' girl talk you aht of it, will yer?"

It was all arranged with the maximum despatch and

Franz Zorndorff, pondering the caprices of mankind, went along to Sophie Carrilovic's two-roomed dwelling that same afternoon, depriving her of her eldest son and partial support, comforting her with promises of a substitute, and despatching Ikey to buy himself a suit of corduroys and two flannel shirts in the Bermondsey Market.

The boy presented himself fully kitted and with undeclared small change in his pocket the following morning and Franz, after inspecting him, gave him a Gladstone bag to hold his scanty possessions, plus a sovereign for his travelling expenses. It was the sight of the coin that destroyed Ikey Palfrey's composure. As he stood looking down at it in the palm of his hand Zorndorff saw him for what he was, a grimy, raggletailed, undernourished little boy of ten or eleven, with the fear and cunning of the jungle lurking behind his eyes. He had seen thousands of such children during his lifetime both here and in Austria, but for some reason the sight of Ikey Palfrey touched him and he said gently, "You don't know what might come of this, Ike. Work hard and don't steal. Even if you're not caught you'll be likely to cause Mr. Craddock trouble. It was very strange that he should remember you, so make the most of it for I have a feeling that you won't regret what you're doing. There now, make yourself scarce, tell him I'll write and might even come and see you both one fine day."

The boy, thrown off guard by Zorndorff's tone, stuck a knuckle in his eye and then, with a long sniff, jerked himself erect and bestowed upon his employer a Cockney wink. Zorndorff, shamed by his emotions, frowned but he watched him march down the ramp and through the debris to the double gates of the yard and the boy must have realised that the Croat was watching for, when he reached the road, he suddenly turned and lifted his hand, a gesture that surprised Franz very much. "Now why the devil did he do that?" he asked himself aloud. "Was he simply acknowledging my part in the business, or was he saying good-bye to the only place in the world that ever gave him anything but hard knocks?" Then he put the boy out of mind and addressed himself to totting up a list of fractions with the speed of an adding machine.

Ikey Palfrey was not entirely unfamiliar with the country. Twice in the last few years he had been hop-picking in Kent, and on two occasions he had travelled as far as Leith Hill in Surrey, on Sunday School treats, but always, when he had passed outside the rings of brick and stone that enclosed his entire world he had done so in the raucous company of two score of his neighbours, so that the terrible emptiness of a landscape had gone more or less unnoticed, had seemed, indeed, less real than the green patches on railway posters.

Now, for the first time in his life he was alone in it, and long before the train stopped to change engines at Salisbury the defensive crust of his urban cockiness had cracked and fallen away, leaving him as vulnerable as a country-bred child turned loose in a populous city. He was, however, very far from being a weakling. He in no way resented the cruelty of the society into which he had been born but fought back, more or less successfully, with fists, hobnailed boots, artfulness and lies. These weapons, however, were no defence against the loneliness that enfolded him as he sat looking out of the window at miles and miles of fields, coppices and picture-book farms, all as alien to him as the upper reaches of the Amazon. How, he wondered, did one find one's way about in a place bereft of landmarks, where every field and hedge were identical and every patch of woodland cover for nameless enemies? What did people do with themselves by day in such a wilderness? And when night fell, and darkness pressed down like a thick wet sack, how could one sleep with a certainty of waking again? He was by no means an introspective child, and was incapable of rationalising his fears, but they were there just the same, multiplying with every clack of the wheels, and in the terrifying isolation of the frowsy third-class carriage they began to undermine his courage, so that he would have burst into tears had it not been for the coins in his trouser pocket. Zorndorff had given him a sovereign and the fare demanded of him at Waterloo had been half-a-sovereign; never having possessed this sum before he regarded it as a special talisman against evil, and when he was not looking at it he was holding it in his moist palms, together with the small

101

change left over from the sum given him to buy clothes. Ever since he could remember money had been a guarantee against oppression and everyday hazards of cold and hunger. He had enormous respect for coins, all kinds of coins. With a halfpenny one could buy a roasted potato on a frosty night; with a penny for a juicy meat pie one could not only avoid going to bed supperless but could exchange half the pie for a seat beside a night-watchman's brazier. These things were fundamentals and coins were the keys to them, so that even the nameless dread conjured up by the endless fields and woods must, he reasoned, be subordinate to so much wealth for today, by the mercy of God and his own prudence, he was worth thirteen shillings and sevenpence; in view of that there could not be much to worry about.

They had told him at Waterloo that the journey would take about six hours but as he had no means of knowing the time it seemed to pass very slowly. He had eaten his pies and sandwiches long ago, and had begged a mug of water from a porter at one of the stops, but now he was both hungry and thirsty, and also much agitated by the prospect of overshooting his stop and missing the junction where he had been told to change trains. His stomach cartwheeled with relief when the guard looked in and told him to get out at the next stop and there was only one other train at the branch siding so that he was able, to some degree, to compose himself during the brief journey to Sorrel Halt. But when he arrived there, and there was no one to meet him, he gave himself up for lost.

He sat down on a platform seat, staring out over the empty moor like the sole survivor of a shipwreck gazing over a waste of water. The great moor, yellow with drought, stretched away in the distance, and across it ran the single white ribbon of a road. The sun, blood-red and ominous, was setting over the woodlands on his left, but the minutes ticked by and still no one appeared. What, Ike asked himself, did one do in such circumstances? What could one do but pray?

He had no real faith in the power of prayer. Every morning, at Alexis Street Council School, there had been a brief religious service that included a gabbled prayer

102

and on the rare occasions when he attended Sunday School (in order to qualify for the annual treat) the bearded Superintendent prefaced and concluded his address with interminable appeals for Divine guidance and mercy. Ike had remained unimpressed by his appeals. They seemed to him to have even less meaning than the words of the hymns they chanted, yet who could say with certainty whether or not there existed above the bright blue sky an Omnipotent Sunday School Superintendent in a long white nightshirt who might be disposed to extricate a petitioner, providing he made his plea with eyes tightly closed and palms pressed together? He arranged himself in the conventional pose and murmured, swiftly, "Lord, get me aht of 'ere quick! *Make* Mr. Craddock show up! Amen," and when he opened his eyes, and saw a trap speeding down the ribbon of road, he was ripe for wholesale conversion, so much so that, in the act of grabbing his Gladstone bag and leaping on the seat to wave, he did not forget to comment on the despatch of Divine service, saying, breathlessly, "Lumme! It *worked!*"

Paul came driving out of the sunset in a fast trot and saw the small figure capering on the platform seat. He had misjudged the time it took to climb the long, winding hill from the Sorrel Valley and seeing relief shining in the child's pale face he was contrite, saying, "I'm sorry, kid, I took too long getting over the moor. It's six miles and rough going. Have you been waiting long?"

"No, sir," Ikey said politely, for his spirits had been uplifted by the remarkably swift answer to prayer which boded well for an easy solution to future problems, "No, Mister, I knew you'd show up sooner or later, I'd have hoofed it on me daisy-roots if I'd known which way ter go!", and he climbed up and settled himself, gazing round at the countryside with disdain and assurance. The trap, he thought, was a very smart rig, and the bay cob pulling it seemed exceptionally fat, for plump horses were not within his experience. "I think you're going to like it down here," Paul said. "I do myself, so much that I don't think I shall ever go back to London! The big house is the other side of the woods, and as you'll have to find your way about sooner or later I'll tell you the names of the places we pass on the way. But I expect you're hungry after that journey. Could you eat a pasty? A home-made one?"

"Could a duck swim, Mr. Craddock!" said Ikey, and for the next five minutes was silent whilst accounting for the largest and tastiest pasty he had ever seen or heard described and one, he would judge, that would set anybody back twopence in Berstein's pieshop, in the Old Kent Road.

As they jogged on over the moor Paul outlined what he had in mind for the boy, an apprenticeship in caring for horses and harness under Chivers, the middle-aged groom the Derwents had sent him. He had arranged, he said, for Chivers to teach him the rudiments of horsemanship and tack-room work, and added, "You may find the speech of the people down here difficult to understand at first, but don't forget that they won't understand you either! Very few of them have ever been within a hundred miles of London, do you understand?"

"Yes, sir," said Ikey dutifully but privately considered the warning unnecessary, for although he seemed to have travelled a thousand miles since eight o'clock that morning he had not crossed a sea and was therefore still within the confines of the British Isles, where everyone spoke English. As they breasted the slope of the moor, crossed the main highway and dropped down on to the river road, the boy stole a cautious look at his companion, seeing a lean, thoughtful face, with a flicker of kindness in the grey eyes and determination in the small, jutting chin. Ike was well versed in the art of gauging character by a study of adult faces and voices, and concluded at once that here was a soft touch, provided he didn't overstep the mark. His hunger temporarily satisfied by Mrs. Handcock's enormous pasty he said, with infinite humility:

"I done a bit o' trap-driving, Mr. Craddock, sir. Would you like me to take the ribbons fer a bit? Just ter make a change for yer?"

"If you like," Paul said, "but take her gently, I only bought her yesterday and she might have one or two tricks I don't know about," and they exchanged seats, Ikey clicking his tongue in the fashion of all the best London cabbies. The cob seemed to understand for it broke into a steady trot and Paul, his shyness making way for a kind of conspiratorial affection for the urchin, said, "I know your surname is Palfrey. What is your Christian name?"

The boy grinned, shamefacedly. "Me proper name's 'Percy'," he said, "but I 'ates it! I mean anyone would, wouldn't they? Everyone back 'ome called me Ikey."

"Why?"

"I dunno why, Mr. Craddock, sir."

"Very well," Paul said, "it's 'Ikey' from now on," and he wondered if the name had been suggested by the boy's long, slightly curved nose, unusual in a boy from the South Bank where, Paul recalled, every other urchin's nose was snub.

II

Paul Craddock was to remember the long, blazing summer of 1902 as one of the happiest and busiest of his life. From early July, until the leaves of the avenue chestnuts began to fall, he was called upon to face an endless variety of problems, and to suffer not a few frustrations, but his spirits remained as unclouded as the weather. It was a joy to watch his home growing up around him under the ceaseless sawing and hammering of Eph Morgan's shock brigade, and to feel the pulse of a domain that seemed to him, admittedly a prejudiced witness, to be stirring after years of hibernation. He was fortunate during all this time, to have two such sponsors as Rudd and Mrs. Handcock, the resident housekeeper, for both made no secret of their liking for him, were ready to go to any lengths to help him adjust himself to the rhythm of country life, and also to mediate between a rank amateur and the people of the Valley. He was thus able to meet all the tenantry and their employees during this period, as well as most of the professional craftsmen and the few private residents in and about Coombe Bay, but he soon realised that conquest of the community as a whole was not something he could take for granted, simply because he had acquired Shallowford by a banker's draft. By August, when he had been living at the lodge for seven weeks, the Shallowford folk had sorted themselves into three groups. There were those like Rose and Claire Derwent, and Farmer Willoughby who openly proclaimed their relief that the estate was in the hands of an earnest if inexperienced young man; those like Arabella Codsall and Tamer Potter, who were somewhat fussed by his enthusiasm, and grumbled in private about city gentlemen who were prone to run before they could walk; and a third group of neutrals, like the Irish Doctor O'Keefe, Parson Bull, the head gardener, Horace Handcock, and some of the small tradesmen in Coombe Bay with whom Paul found it difficult to establish a close personal contact.

Some goodwill had to be purchased, as when Paul took Rudd's advice and gave Sam Potter the post of estate forester with a cottage at the far end of Shallowford Mere. Sam was grateful for both accommodation and post. He had lately married, and his wife Joannie was pregnant, and with winter coming on life promised to be bleak in the crowded family dell. Rudd reasoned that, with brother Sam drawing regular pay from the enemy's purse, brother Smut's poaching might be confined to robbing other people's coverts, east and west of Shallowford. Paul also won over the dour Edward Derwent, by buying in a small cliff pasture on the extreme eastern border and incorporating it into the High Coombe domain without an increase in rent, but in any case his relations with the Derwent clan, as with the amiable Pitts family, at Hermitage, were fairly cordial from the very beginning. Rose Derwent found him a good groom and a sturdy cob for his trap and her pretty sister Claire gave him plenty of frank advice regarding his approaches to the women of the Valley. "You have to pay each and every one of them the compliment of pretending they are equals of the men," she told him, when he came to her grumbling of Arabella Codsall's importunities one day. "It's a pure fiction, of course, except in Arabella's case, but it's Heads-I-Win-Tails-You-Lose for you because the women are flattered and their menfolk regard your approach as proof that they have married wives with good sense!" There and then Paul decided that Claire Derwent herself had more sense in her head than one could reasonably expect to find in a pretty girl of nineteen, but he was very careful not to discriminate between her and her sister Rose, for he soon discovered that Rose had a very warm heart, would go out of her way to help anyone and nursed no jealousy whatever in respect to her handsome sister.

In the immediate area of the big house Mrs. Handcock was his major-domo. Her immense weight did very little to reduce her mobility and she bustled breathlessly to and from her quarters in the domestic wing ministering to him and Rudd and engaging a troop of local girls to take service at Shallowford as soon as the renovations were finished. At first Paul had the greatest difficulty in understanding Mrs. Handcock's brogue, the broadest in the Valley not excluding Tamer Potter's, and would shake his head when she pounded into the parlour to ask if he would be available "to-zee-thicky-Lowry-maid-us-was-thinking-o'-taakin'-on-till-us-zees-'ow-'er-shaaapes!"

In the meantime the house was nearing the step of habitability, for Eph Morgan, the Welsh expatriate from Coombe Bay, had moved in the day after the sale and had since recruited a horde of local craftsmen on a sub-contract basis, setting them re-roofing, re-plastering, and papering according to the demands of Rudd's survey. The agent acted as architect but paid Paul the compliment of consulting him on important details. A bathroom was added, a passage cut through from kitchen to dining-room to ensure that meals were no longer served cold, joists in several floors were ripped out and replaced, every room upstairs was re-papered with a cheerful floral pattern, new storage water tanks were installed in the loft, and Sir George Lovell's dark-room was fitted up as an estate office. Paul spent a great deal of his time watching the builders at work and Ephraim Morgan, their sponsor, intrigued him. He was a very small man, hardly more than five feet in height, but with a huge, round head that gave him the appearance of an intelligent gnome. He had first come into the district as a railway engineer and had decided, when the line was built, that he could earn a better living in Devon than in his native Wales. Yet, like all Welshmen, he cherished a fiery patriotism for the Principality and was a great admirer of Lloyd George, concerning whom he would deliver long, rhapsodic speeches in his sing-song voice while his men stood around grinning and sometimes throwing in a sly comment as fuel to the Welshman's fire. Eph Morgan had two principal hates, The Brummagers (represented by his arch-enemy Joe Chamberlain) and The Brewers, whom he declared the mainstay of the Tory Party and he saw his hero Lloyd George as a dauntless St. George ambushing both from morning to night. Paul gathered, however, that Morgan was an exception as regards his interest in radical politics, for all the farmers, and most of their hired men, were tepid Conservatives, who had followed the Lovell lead at the polling booth for generations without devoting a thought to topical issues like Irish Home Rule, Welsh Disestablishment, or the legacies of the South African War like the concentration camp scandal and the importation of Chinese labour into the mines. They were content to plod peacefully along the well-beaten paths of rural forefathers, looking to the gentry to govern and to the owner of the big house to keep their premises in repair, promote country sports and occasional social activities like the annual harvest supper and Empire Day celebrations. Notwithstanding the activities of prominent local dissenters like Farmer Willoughby, of Deepdene, and Eph Morgan, the established church had the local community well in hand. Parson Bull was not only feared but genuinely respected in the district. Rudd introduced them after Matins one Sunday morning, and Bull struck Paul as a man at least a century behind the times. He treated all his parishioners, rich and poor, with impatience and showed little traditional deference to his patron, the Squire. Rudd said that Bull's consuming interest was hunting and that he was an ecclesiastical parody of Surtees' Jorrocks, inasmuch as he hibernated in the summer and came alive again when cubbing began, in the last week of September. Then, Rudd promised, Paul would see the real Parson Bull astride an enormous seventeen-hand skewbald, roaring his way across country and threatening whiplash and hellfire to anyone who blocked his approach to a jumpable fence. "He's a frightful old tyrant, and makes nonsense of the Sermon on the Mount," he said, "but he's so Old English that one can't help paying him grudging respect. You've got half the gift of his living but that won't mellow his approach to you, as you probably noticed. They say that even the Bishop goes in fear of him and he's scared so many curates into resigning that now he doesn't have one but simply goes through the motions of taking a monthly service in outlying churches over the river."

Doctor O'Keefe, on whom Paul called for a routine check of his wound, was equally offhand, and the reek of whisky in his surgery went some way towards explaining the speed with which the doctor drove his gig around the district. He asked Paul one or two questions about the war, glared at his knee, then warned him that "he would have his hands full with a damned shambles like Shallowford", but they struck no sparks, and Paul left feeling the doctor lacked the saving grace of Parson Bull, who was at any rate a rumbustious character. Rudd said that O'Keefe had not always been surly and uncommunicative but had become misanthropic after his wife's death from tuberculosis some years ago. He had always been very fond of Irish whisky ("the landlord of The Raven kept a special stock for him") and had turned to the bottle for solace. His wife had been a beautiful woman and the story was that they had been very attached to one another. "They've got a daughter somewhere," Rudd added, "a bonny girl she was, who ran off soon after her mother's death and is nursing or teaching up the country. If she had stayed she might have pulled the doctor through but it isn't a job I should have relished, and I daresay she'll keep clear of him until he floats into the grave."

When the morning temperatures cooled, and the period of drought was followed by a spell of soft rain and south-westerly winds, Paul rode far afield every day, sometimes alone but more often in the company of Claire Derwent, who showed him the maze of leafy rides between Coome Bluff and the northern edge of Shallowford Woods and all the short cuts to the Dell, Hermitage, Four Winds and bracken slopes of Blackberry Moor. Together they rode over to visit Lord Gilroy, in his elegant home, Heronslea, beyond the smaller, parallel River Teazel. Gilroy, stiffly polite, gave them tea in thin Rockingham china and threatened to send the local agent over to Shallowford in order to gather Paul into the local Conservative fold. He did not deign to ask Paul his politics, assuming, no doubt, that he was eager to ". . . stop the damned tide of Radicalism set in motion by that unspeakable bounder, Lloyd George", a politician, his Lordship declared, who should have been strung up on the occasion of his pro-Boer rally, in Birmingham during the war! Paul judged it tactful to make no comment upon this and after an hour or so they left, riding south to the sea, then east along the curving beach to Coombe Bay.

Paul had made one or two expeditions in this direction already but always unaccompanied, for although his thoughts constantly returned to Grace Lovell, and to their three improbable meetings, there was no one in whom he could confide regarding his infatuation. Rudd, he knew, would go out of his way to dissuade him from anything but a formal association with the family and on the one or two occasions he had mentioned her name the agent had abruptly changed the subject. It was clear that he carried his dislike of the family as far as the cadet branch still living on Shallowford property, for he once referred to Bruce Lovell as "a man who could borrow from a Hebrew pawnbroker and later have the man charged as a receiver of stolen goods!" Neither did Paul care to raise the subject of Grace Lovell to Claire Derwent, although their association had been completely circumspect. He decided that he would like to keep it that way, for she was a merry and informative companion, who seemed to enjoy showing him off to scattered local families, and although she looked undeniably attractive with her corn-coloured curls peeping beneath a hard hat and her pink cheeks glowing with health, she did not stir him in the way that Grace Lovell had when they had met on that first occasion in the nursery, or when she had accepted his gift of the screen at the sale. The screen had been collected the following day and since then he had not even glimpsed her although, on two occasions, he rode slowly past her house in the early morning, and at various times had ridden the grey, now named Snowdrop, along the tideline of the Bay.

The grey's name derived from a remark of Mrs. Handcock's, greeting him as he rode down from Priory Wood with, "I zeed 'ee cummin', you an' that gurt beast o' yours! Just like a man zitting atop a gurt bunch o' snowdrops!" and thereafter Paul discarded the grey's Irish name, which was unpronounceable, and settled for "Snowdrop".

So the summer days slipped by, until Eph Morgan announced that renovations were finished, and Mr. Craddock might write to the upholsterers in Paxtonbury for soft furnishings he and Rudd had ordered on their one expedition to the city. The day before they were due to arrive Claire turned up at the house on foot dressed, for once, in blouse, skirt and white, straw hat, announcing that her horse had gone lame and asking if she could help arrange the furniture that was coming.

Paul told her the vans were not due until late that afternoon. It did not occur to him at the time to wonder how she had managed to walk the four miles from High Coombe to Shallowford, on a sultry day and arrive looking as fresh as a spring daffodil. She seemed so disappointed that Paul, telling her that she was welcome to ride Snowdrop home and return him the following day, suggested they take a picnic lunch to Shallowford Woods, returning before tea to receive the vans. Claire brightened up at this and said it was a wonderful idea, providing Paul's leg was strong enough to carry him that far over rough ground.

"Hang it, Claire, I'm not a cripple," he said indignantly. "The hospital surgeon told me to walk as much as I could and since I've been down here I've never been further than the lodge on foot. I'll get Mrs. Handcock to pack up some pasties and tea and sugar. We can make a fire and boil tea if we take my army canteen with us."

They set out in high spirits, following the narrow path along the left bank of the river and skirting the shoulder of the Coombe to the edge of the woods, seeing no one except Hazel, youngest of the Potter children, said to be queer in the head and much given to talking to herself. She was doing it now, staring up at an isolated oak in the meadow and watching something half-way up the trunk. She did not notice their approach and they were thus privileged to overhear one of her impromptu poems.

111

"I-zee-you-bobtail, a-patterin'-along thicky-bark," she sang. "Youm grey, and a varmint they zay! But I loves 'ee! I loves 'ee bettern'n the red, 'cause youm like me, chaased be everyone, baint 'ee?" but at this point Hazel must have heard their approach over the turf, for she swung round and took to her heels, speeding across the field towards the Coombe and covering the ground as fast as Matabele children Paul had watched in the kraals.

"She's an odd little thing," Paul said. "I don't remember seeing her before. Does she live about here?"

Claire told him that she was Hazel Potter, an afterthought on the part of Tamer and Meg, and was reckoned half-witted on account of her tendency to spend her days roaming the fields and woods, sometimes holding conversations with trees, birds and animals.

"Well, I don't consider that convincing evidence of lunacy," he said. "She's a rather beautiful child and moves as fast as a greyhound. Doesn't she go to school?"

Claire said that she was enrolled at Mary Willoughby's little school but was absent more often than not, for the Potters could not be induced to make her attend regularly but she was clearly not interested in the subject and seemed preoccupied with thoughts of her own, so after watching the grey squirrel dart along the branch of the big oak and disappear into shadows cast by the leaves, he followed into the woods, wading through waist-high bracken to a ride that led down to the shore of the mere opposite the pagoda.

Despite his boast he found his leg tiring and was glad to sit and let Claire gather sticks for the fire. She had thrown aside her wide straw hat while he sat under a willow by the shore, admiring the grace with which she moved to and fro in the scrub, every now and again bending swiftly to add to her armful of sticks. She was, he thought, a very supple creature, with a figure shaped by healthy ancestors, years of hard exercise, and, he suspected, very little farm drudgery. Everything about her was neat, cool and somehow deliberate. She walked with a slight sway, like a tall flower in the wind, so that again he thought of a daffodil growing by a lake and he was glad now that chance had given him an opportunity of seeing her in feminine clothes. On all their previous expeditions she had appeared at the house in a brown riding habit and dull colours, he decided, did not flatter her as much as the cotton blouse and well-cut grey skirt she was wearing today. The water of the mere was very still and he could see the white ruin of the Burmese pagoda hiding in pines on the islet. The air was full of the hum of insects and far across the little lake the reeds stirred, affording him a fleeting glimpse of waterfowl— wild duck, teal or widgeon he supposed, making a mental note to ask Rudd if they ever shot down here.

She came back to him still looking pensive and not much inclined to gossip, so they lit a fire and made tea in his battered canteen, afterwards disposing of Mrs. Handcock's pasties and talking lazily of one thing and another. He admitted then that his leg ached badly and she asked him about his wound. To satisfy her morbid curiosity he rolled up his trouser leg and showed her the bluish depression, where the Mauser bullet had entered, and the hollow where, after chipping the bone, it had emerged in the bulge of the calf. She studied it with concern, saying that until now she had been unable to relate all the papers had written of the war with actual physical suffering. Down here, she said, it had all seemed like something out of a history book happening to people in another age. Then she became embarrassingly silent again, sitting back, her weight resting on her hands and looking out over the water, so that after watching her slyly for a few moments he surrendered to an impulse that had returned to him since he had watched her gathering sticks. Leaning forward he kissed her on the mouth, not as any young man might claim a kiss from a pretty girl but more as a jocular attempt to re-establish contact between them. To his embarrassment she offered neither protest nor encouragement but continued to smile, saying, with the utmost self-possession "Well, what now, Wicked Squire?" and incongruously he thought of George Lovell's album and the question he had asked himself on the day of the sale when she had surprised him with the mock Bible under his arm.

"You wouldn't know a wicked squire if you met one,"

113

he said but at this she laughed and said, lightly, "Don't believe it, Paul! We had one here for years!"

He looked at her curiously then for her remark implied that Sir George's weaknesses were general knowledge in the Valley. "How much do you really know of him, Claire?"

"Oh, that he couldn't be trusted a yard with a girl over fourteen and his son Ralph wasn't much better! Everybody round here accepted that—after all, they had to, for people with that kind of money can behave pretty much as they like, can't they?"

It struck him then and for the first time, that there must be a great difference between country-bred girls like Claire Derwent and their social counterparts in the suburbs, for she, it appeared, could discuss this kind of thing with a man without embarrassment or coyness. More than that; Lovell's eccentricities seemed hardly to interest her.

"You mean you know about his . . . well . . . his photography, a rather unusual kind of photography?"

She looked at him frankly. "Why of course! Everybody did. But who told you about it? Was it John Rudd?"

He told her how he had found the album by chance, admitting shamefacedly that he had been looking through it on the day of the sale, when she had come into the library with her invitation to lunch and at this she gave a little yelp of laughter.

"Oh dear! How awful for you! What did you do with his famous collection?"

"I burned it," he growled, "what the devil else could I do with it?" but she still seemed determined to treat the thing as a great joke.

"I imagine most young men would have kept it for their own amusement and do stop looking so shocked, Paul! Do you think a girl can grow up in a place like this without knowing about things like that?"

"Did he ever ask you to pose for him?"

"No he didn't but he certainly would have if I'd given him half a chance! He did start pawing me in our barn one day and I dodged into the open and fled. But I didn't see anything very unusual in it at the time. Rose

114

was a bit shocked, and thought I ought to tell father; I didn't though, because I thought it was—well—just silly. What I mean is, the Valley girls who did go into that messy little room of his and let him take pictures of them with their clothes off weren't enticed there. They did it with their eyes wide open and for what they could get out of it! I daresay the elder Potter girls' pictures were in that album, weren't they?"

Then, half-consciously, he noticed something else about her, that she was no longer smiling her slightly superior smile but was looking at him boldly as though assessing his mental confusion and perhaps weighing her advantage and his vulnerability; her eyes, watchful as a cat's, never wavered, so that he felt more than ever confused and began to bluster.

"Oh, I daresay you think me a greenhorn!" he began, but that was all he said for suddenly she was lying full-length beside him with his face held between her hands and was kissing him not as he had kissed her a moment since, but in a fashion no one had kissed him before. He was not, however, really aware that the initiative had been hers alone for it had all happened in a matter of seconds. One moment they had been sparring with words, the next embracing with a recklessness that swept away all traces of the restraint that had governed every moment of their relationship up to that time. He thought, fleetingly, of all that possession of her here in the summer woods might entail, a complete surrender of dignity for her and for him God alone knew how many obligations but the check was momentary. The softness of her mouth and the scent of her hair banished the last of his scruples and almost at once he began to assert his mastery, bearing down on her with his full weight, and fumbling at the fastenings of her blouse in his eagerness to use her as she so clearly intended to be used. There was no flicker of tenderness in his handling of her. She might have been the half-caste girl he had purchased for a few sweaty moments in the Cape Town brothel, for when the blouse buttons resisted him he dragged at her skirt and continued to press brutally on her mouth. It was as he sought to extend his grip on her clothes that she somehow ex-

115

tricated herself, taking advantage of the bank and throwing herself sideways so that suddenly she was clear of him altogether and standing between the willow and the water's edge, with her face turned away and her hands busy with her blouse that had broken free of the waistband of the skirt. Watching her from the crest of the bank he suddenly felt very foolish and very deflated, and his shame was not less intense because it was fused with exasperation. He rose slowly to his feet and when she had finished tucking in her blouse, and was lifting her hands to her disordered hair, he began to mumble excuses. They emerged as half-finished sentences, without conviction and without much sense but almost as swiftly as she had left him she was beside him again, and her voice had an almost pitiful earnestness as she said, shaking her head so that pins fell in a shower, *"Don't,* Paul! Don't apologise! Just listen to me, so that we have a chance of starting again, of starting differently!" and when he stared at her uncomprehendingly, "Don't you see? I meant it to happen! Don't you *see,* you idiot?"

He said slowly, "What the devil do you mean, *you* meant it to happen? I know you didn't mind my kissing you but . . ." She made a gesture and looked so distracted that he stopped, giving them both a moment to compose themselves. It was she who benefited from the pause, for suddenly she was calm again, and said, turning away, "It's just that I lied about the horse. Flash isn't lame. I dressed for the part and then got a lift as far as the lodge in Willoughby's trap. I knew very well that stuff wouldn't be coming until evening and that you would suggest coming here, or somewhere like here. *Now* do you understand?"

"Getting me out here was one thing," he mumbled, still greedy for a major share of the blame, "but don't try and tell me you hoped . . ."

She turned, interrupting him again, and this time she looked angry and exasperated, as though she was prepared to pound the truth into his head.

"Paul Craddock!" she said. "You've got to realise you had no part in it, do you understand? None that you could help that is, so do stop trying to be gallant, and face up

116

to what I'm saying, because if you don't it'll come to you sooner or later, and then it'll seem far worse than it is! Will you listen? Will you stop pretending?"

"Well?"

She came a little closer to him, shaking her hair free and sitting on a stump a yard or so away. "Any man would have acted as you did given the opportunity, any man who was a man, that is! *That's* what I'm trying to make clear to you, and if you think back a little and put two and two together you'll see me for what I am, or what I almost was! I'll tell you again since I have to—I meant something like this to happen, it's what usually hapens, it's how most marriages about here begin! The girl baits a trap in the grass and the man walks into it."

He baulked at this, moving swiftly across to her and saying, explosively, "For God's sake stop talking like that, Claire! You'll be damned sorry for it tomorrow!"

"I'm sorry for it now," she said, "about as sorry as I can be. The one thing I'm glad about is that I had enough honesty left in me somewhere to bring me up short at the last moment! Even that I can't take much credit for; if you had been just a little less clumsy I'd have gone through with it all right, and what would either of us gained by frankness afterwards? You would have resented me for the rest of your life I daresay, whereas now—well, at least we can go on being civil to one another!" She got up, brushing the shreds of bracken from her skirt. "Let's get the things and go home."

They gathered up dixie and basket and began the climb up the ride to the edge of the wood but it was not until they were clear of the trees that he spoke again. "Look here, Claire, we could pretend it never happened, couldn't we? Nobody else knows about it! Just the two of us!", and she stopped, looking at him intently, her head slightly on one side.

"Don't deceive yourself over that," she said. "Every busybody in the Valley knows about it! Oh, not that I hatched a silly schoolgirl plot, got you out here and encouraged you to seduce me, but the fact that I had it very much in mind! I could almost hear them as we rode around the estate together—'Claire Derwent is quick off the mark, isn't she? Claire isn't a girl to let grass grow under her feet!' " She gazed around, looking back at the woods, then forward across to Coombe Bluff and the sea. "Sometimes I hate this place and everybody in it! Including myself!", and she walked on so quickly that the effort of catching her up brought a sharp twinge to his wound.

CHAPTER FIVE

I

THE yellow-eyed herring-gull who, in mild weather is the scavenger of Coombe Bay fishermen, will fly inland as soon as the autumn gales blow from the south-west and the route he uses whilst awaiting better weather never varies.

He lies inland over the Bluff, crossing in two minutes a cliff that an active man cannot scale in under an hour and heads for Deepdene Farm to see if there are any pickings to be had from the Willoughbys. Then he flies low over High Coombe, veering north-west along the edge of the wind, croaking his way over Shallowford Woods and the mere, and on across the orchard of the big house to Priory Wood and the outbuildings of Hermitage, where he sometimes swoops to steal pig food from the troughs of Arthur Pitts and his son, Henry. Henry usually sees gulls and takes pot shots at them with his rifle, so this heads them into the wind, or almost so, for they fly on south-west by west across the Sorrel to Four Winds and if there is nothing to be had there on again over the moor to the Teazel, and so out of the Shallowford domain altogether.

The herring-gulls are greedy, cunning, inquisitive birds, with little sense of family but they are matchless aeronauts, cresting the strongest gusts and sometimes making pinpoint landings on chimneys and stable roofs to see and hear what is going on in the estate. If they could write diaries and read thoughts it would be possible to know everything that was happening hereabouts for they miss nothing, are witnesses to every trivial incident, and are so common that nobody notices them until they swoop to steal.

It was such a gull that saw Sam Potter and his pregnant wife Joannie loading their few things on to the family cart and setting out for their new home in Shallowford Woods, on the last day of September 1902. The first of the autumn gales had arrived ahead of time and the elms in the Potter Dell were creaking under strong, Channel gusts, with leaves that were still only half yellow floating down on the smoking camp fire over which the rest of the Potters sat trying to look as if Sam's departure caused them more than the minimum concern. Tamer, as usual, sat removed from his family, on the steps of the ramshackle farmhouse and Meg was off somewhere along the coast selling mats and baskets that the girls had made when the Potters decided that it would be courting sun-stroke to work in the fields, but the girls were all there —Pansy, Cissie, Violet and Hazel—talking and giggling among themselves and so was Smut, the poacher, helping brother Sam to stack the waggon with furniture that most families in the Valley would have discarded long ago.

Sam, his big, vacuous face wreathed in smiles and his stiff, carroty hair standing up like a forest of rusty pikes, was glad to be off, but no more so than his wife, for although her time was still two months away she was already enormous and there was little cheer in waddling about a leaking, draughty house where there was nowhere to sit and her gnawing hunger remained largely unsatis-fied. She had inspected the little cottage in the woods and was very grateful for this chance to make a home of her own, with Sam drawing regular money at last. Climbing on to the box seat of the waggon she heard her husband warn Smut to confine his expeditions to the west of the estate, well beyond the limits of Shallowford Woods. He sounded apologetic but firm.

"Dornee come my way, Smut," he said gently, for Sam

was a gentle man, "dornee come out-a-long! Just you stay down-a-long or up-a-long, zee?"

To the Potters, indeed to everyone in the Coombe, "out-a-long" meant east, "down-a-long" meant south, and "up-a-long" indicated Priory Wood and Codsall land over the river to the west. Sam reasoned, no doubt, that as a woodsman living on the eastern border of the estate he could not be held responsible for the loss of game, chickens or geese beyond a three-mile radius of his cottage.

"Dornee fret," Smut reassured him, "I'll leave that zide to you, Sam! Anyways, I'll be across the Teazel mos' nights in and about ole Gilroy's coverts. Good luck to 'ee, an' you too, Joannie! If that li'l tacker o' yours be a boy you c'n call 'un Fred after me, for no one yerabouts uses me real bliddy naame, do 'em?"

That was the extent of the Potters' farewells to the eldest of the family and soon after, as the lurking gull rose and flapped inland, the waggon moved off up the steep track and across the meadow where Hazel watched squirrels in the big, isolated oak.

The gull, who should have known better than to waste time looking for scraps in the Dell, rode a gust over the elms and crossed the neglected stubble fields into Deepdene land where the children were in school chanting out spellings like two rows of besmocked choristers and Elinor Willoughby was talking to her hens in the neatly-fenced yard, north of the schoolhouse.

The gull hovered, hoping she would leave so that he could beat in with flapping wings, frighten the strutting cockerel, and grab a beakful of meal, but Elinor did not go away for this morning she had a great deal on her mind and there was no one but the hens in whom she could confide. Her father, the solemn Edwin, who thought of all love as the love of God, had never given a thought to the yearnings of his daughter or her lover, Will Codsall, over the river, whereas Elinor was far too shy to consult her spinster Aunt Mary on such matters as courtship and marriage, so she told her story to the hens who were obliged to listen if they wanted their morning corn.

" 'Tiz cruel," Elinor told the complacent Rhode Island

Reds under her feet, " tiz cruel, and there baint a particle o' sense to it! I'd make Will a good wife, for I loves 'un as much as he loves me, so why shouldnen us go to Parson Bull an' put up banns, same as anybody else? I wish that mother o' Will's dead, that I do!" and she flung a handful of grain at the nearest bird as though she had been a feathered Arabella Codsall.

The gull heard nothing of all this. He was far too busy watching the scattering grain and had been far out on the sandbanks fishing all last evening, when Will Codsall and Elinor Willoughby had walked hand in hand along the rutted lane east of the woods discussing their dismal situation.

Will had confessed that his mother's nagging was driving him out of his mind, and that she returned to the subject of Elinor Willoughby every mealtime and often in between meals.

"Mazed about us, she be," he muttered, "fair mazed! To hear her prattle you might think you, your father and your Aunt Mary were wasters, like they Potters, yonder! Says I should vind a maid who could bring a dowry to the farm, same as she did, just as if money grew on trees like flamin' plums, and could be gathered all seasons of the year! I said to her, 'Listen here, Mother, *listen,* will 'ee, an' stop yammerin' for a minute for the love o' Christ! They Willoughbys is decent folk, as good as any family about here, so doan talk about my Elinor as though 'er was hard up for a man, because 'er baint, bein' the prettiest maid in the Valley'."

The indirect compliment pleased Elinor so much that she made light of her future mother-in-law's opposition. Now that dusk had fallen she lost her shyness in his presence and slyly plucked his sleeve as they passed the five-barred gate dividing Deepdene lane from the common pasture that separated the Coombe and the woods.

"Dornee fret about it, Will dear," she said, "it'll come right in the end," and she put up her face to be kissed which was thoughtless of her, for the discussion of his mother, followed by the gentle pressure of Elinor's body, fired Will with impatience to be separated from the one and have the other beside him all night. So he kissed her

121

in a way that startled her, indicating that he might not brook further delays.

He said, gloweringly, "There's talk of a new farm Young Squire's trying to buy, a plaace up behind Hermitage on the edge o' the moor. It's rough land, and not much of it but there's no knowing what us might make of it. For two pins I'd call and ask if us could lease it and they could get along at Four Winds as best they could! The farmhouse is half a ruin, and the outbuildings are cob, with the water running down the walls but it'd be better than nothing mebbe! What do 'ee zay, Elinor? Would 'ee live in a plaace like that, providin' I fixed it up for 'ee?"

"Ay, I would that," Elinor told him fervently, and thought fleetingly of the new Mr. Craddock and all his money and of his junketings about the estate since last June, but before she could speculate on their chances Will, making the most of his time, kissed her again in a way that made her knees buckle and she said, although . not very convincingly, "No, Will! Not now, Will, please!" as his big hand slid over her shoulder, across her tight bodice and then below the waist to fondle her little buttocks.

The gull, caring nothing at all for lovers' problems, decided that Elinor would stay in the yard all the morning so he flew off across the slopes of Deepdene to two small fields adjoining the cliff path, where Edward Derwent was leaning on a stile considering what use could be made of his new land and also what had prompted that unpredictable young fellow Craddock to incorporate it into High Coombe without raising the rent. There must, he reasoned, be a hidden motive for such an unrewarding act on the new Squire's part, for Derwent himself had never done anything without a profit motive. He pondered the possibility of Craddock's intention to sell High Coombe, and ask a higher price for a slightly enlarged farm but decided that this was unlikely for two small fields would not merit the addition of twenty-five pounds to the purchase price. It then occurred to him that Craddock might have made him the free gift of the fields at the suggestion of his daughter Claire, and this led to serious contemplation of Claire's involvement with the young fellow and whether it was within the bounds of credibility that he might have a real live squire for a son-in-law. The possibility, remote as it was, warmed his heart. The fellow obviously had a great deal of money (made in scrap iron it was rumoured) and was, on the whole, a likeable chap, as far as a city-bred man could be likeable. Perhaps it was not so improbable; perhaps Claire would steer the Derwents into a lawyer's office where the new Squire, enslaved by his bride's beauty, would hand over the entire acreage of High Coombe for a nominal sum! As he thought of this, and of Claire's golden hair and blue eyes, his stern face relaxed until it was about half-way towards smiling and he reflected that Claire was growing more like her dead mother every day and that between them, they must have been very clever to breed a young chit pretty enough to monopolise the attention of a rich scrap-merchant turned land-owner. Then his pessimism caught up with him and he thought of the recent change in Claire, and her solemn face at the breakfast table that morning, and also of her silent withdrawal into herself of late which was very uncharacteristic of his younger daughter. If she was in love, he decided, then so much the better, for that meant that his hopes had at least some foundation and if she was not, and there was no more in this association than a bit of flirting on Craddock's part, then she was probably sickening for something and would doubtless get over it as quickly as she had recovered from chickenpox and measles in her childhood. At this point his practical mind reverted to the use of the new fields. Barley, oats or wheat? He wasn't sure yet, he would have to sleep on it.

The gull decided that there was no profit in hovering over Derwent's unploughed fields and whirled into the wind, coasting along its warm, wet currents to the window-sill of the Derwent parlour, beyond which, through small panes of glass, he could see the fair head of Claire Derwent bent over a letter she was writing. The envelope beside her was already addressed to "Paul Craddock,

123

Esquire, Shallowford House", and the letter was by way of being a distress rocket, fired from a trim vessel adrift on a sea of uncertainty.

Four weeks had now passed since the picnic in the woods and she had not so much as glimpsed him as he rode up and down the Valley, but gossip kept her abreast of his affairs and she knew that the big house was finished and occupied, and that all manner of other changes were in the planning stage. Many times during the month she had called herself a reckless, impulsive idiot, not so much for rushing her fences as for reining back at the last moment, for although, in the early days of their friendship, she had been attracted to him as Squire Craddock, of Shallowford, a wealthy and amiable young man (who would, she supposed, have to marry someone sooner or later), the few moments in his arms beside the mere had wrought a dramatic change in her daydreams. She would now, she told herself, welcome his reappearance at High Coombe in any role, and his prophecy that she would live to regret her frankness had been miserably accurate, for it surely was this alone that condemned her to sit here inactive for as long as he cared to keep her waiting. Going back over the events of the momentous afternoon by the mere, Claire concluded that she had made three tactical mistakes in as many minutes. She had been far too forward, far too backward and ultimately, far too honest.

At the end of the fourth week she came to realise that her only hope lay in an entirely new approach, and although by no means so devious a young woman as she imagined herself to be, the plan she finally adopted had the hall-mark of first-class strategy in any kind of warfare; it was simple, direct and preserved an avenue of dignified retreat. She decided to write advising him to give a combined coronation supper-dance and house-warming for the estate tenantry and their dependants, reasoning that even a young man who had held her in his arms would have some difficulty in interpreting this as anything more than a piece of friendly, patriotic advice. If he liked the idea then he could hardly fail to ask for further advice; if he rejected it good manners alone would compel a reply.

The composition of the letter cost her a good deal of

thought and effort. Four drafts went into the waste-paper basket (each was torn into fifty pieces and scrambled) and she finally settled for a simply-worded note, pointing out the obvious advantages of such a gesture at this stage of his settling-in period. She addressed him as "Dear Mr. Craddock" and signed herself, "Your sincere well-wisher, Claire Derwent". Then she gave the letter to one of her father's farmboys who passed Shallowford House on his way home every evening, telling him that if Mr. Craddock should make him late when he called for a reply in the morning she would present his excuses to her father, a stickler for good time-keeping. The boy went off tipless, for Claire had no money in her reticule. Edward Derwent did not believe in women having money. It made them uppity and inclined to answer back.

The gull ignored the offal in the private trough of Sarah, the Derwent's prize sow. It looked tempting and accessible from twenty feet above the sty but Sarah had a savage nature and was notoriously averse to sharing rations with uninvited callers. The gull's new line of flight took it north-west across Shallowford Woods and there was nothing to be had in or about the mere, so it passed on, skirting the chimney pots of the big house, sailing into the cobbled yard and cocking an eye at Ikey Palfrey, polishing harness outside the tack-room and whistling the appropriate song from *H.M.S. Pinafore*.

Ikey always whistled at his work nowadays. He liked catchy tunes and he liked his new situation. He had a warm place to sleep, more than enough to eat, a chance to ride real horses at least twice a week and he had formed a deep but unspoken attachment for the "ex-Yeomanry gent" who, for some reason that was still a mystery to Ikey, had winkled him from the scrapyard and set him down in a great country house with, as Ikey might have expressed it, "all the trimmings".

Ikey had long since lost his fear of the countryside and soon replaced his familiar Thames-side landmarks with local ones, like the red, sandstone peak of Coombe Bluff, the steep green incline of Priory Wood, the lanes with broken gates and isolated trees, and the spire of Coombe Bay parish church in the distance. He got along very well

125

with "the local Swedes" although, as Paul had prophesied, he had initial difficulty with their dialect. By now, however, he could not only understand the Devon brogue but could speak it like a native. Sometimes, to amuse the motherly Mrs. Handcock, he would exchange nasal Cockney for the broadest Westcountry burr, interchanging words and phrases and reducing her to a quivering mass of flesh by his expert drollery. He took a careful note of everything and forgot nothing. Chivers, the rather old-maidish groom whom Paul had taken on, spoke very well of him, and said he had a natural seat and good hands, but most of Ikey's thoughts when he was alone were concerned, in one way or another, with his hero, Paul Craddock. To the boy it still seemed incredible that a man in Paul's exalted position, virtually a king ruling a subject race, should treat him almost as an equal and sometimes, when he rode into the yard to hand over the grey, stay and chat with him about London. As a Cockney Ikey cherished his independence and this easy condescension on the Squire's part was the mark of true greatness.

Gulls do not have the weaknesses of magpies and the glitter of Ikey's polished harness made no appeal to the bird. Soon it flapped over the steep roof and into the forecourt, where the Squire himself was sitting on the balustrade of the terrace munching a pasty as he studied a map that fluttered in the strong gusts blowing from the sea. Rudd, the agent, was beside him but neither man seemed aware of the fact that this was not the best place to study a map measuring three feet by two but they persisted, talking to one another in earnest tones as the gull edged warily along the balustrade towards the plate on which lay the Squire's half-eaten pasty. Here were pickings to be snatched from men who deserved to lose them and as soon as it was confident the snatch could be carried out with safety the gull swooped and was gone, Rudd shouting an oath and Paul throwing back his head to laugh at the bird's impudence. Then he forgot about the gull and returned to the map, which was one of the reasons why Claire had been left without word of him.

There were other reasons, the chief being that Paul felt that the next approach should come from her. As the

126

memory of the frolic in Shallowford Woods receded it became no more than an embarrassing moment that he preferred to forget, along with all the self-righteous nonsense she had talked trying to explain it away. If she said she had set out to compromise him in order that he would marry her he was prepared to believe her but he was not, at the moment, in the mood to consider marrying anyone, being far too deeply engrossed in his work and in Shallowford. He had discovered that he loved the house now that it was warm, habitable and purged of its gloomy Lovell associations. He liked his big, sunny bedroom and the high-ceilinged reception-rooms, where his few pieces of furniture looked very much at home but best of all he liked his snug, red-curtained library, with its shelves of leather-bound books smelling of comfort, leisure and repose and here he spent his evenings with John Rudd for company, learning about crops and soil and livestock and exchanging stories of African wars separated by half a generation. He liked his staff, who were polite without being servile, and well-trained without being officious. His wound troubled him hardly at all and there was so much to do and so much to learn in this new world that there was always an overspill of jobs awaiting his attention. He thought about Claire now and again but by no means as often as she thought about him. He also pondered, at a somewhat deeper level, Grace Lovell, who had disappeared as completely as if she had emigrated to Australia. Sometimes he thought of them together, comparing their dissimilar natures, the one buoyant and frank, the other withdrawn and secretive. Then, about three weeks ago, Rudd had come in with news of the death of old Hardcastle, the moorside freeholder whose widow was prepared to sell the smallholding, so they went over and measured out the sixty-odd acres, and inspected the ruinous premises and the resultant negotiations had occupied nearly a week, during which time he had not thought of Grace or Claire at all.

"How does it compare with our calculations, John?" Paul asked and Rudd replied, "It's an acre or two out in the east and north. These old estate maps are mostly guesswork. When we get time we ought to resurvey the entire Valley and bring the property in line with the national ordnance maps. I could do it myself, with a bit of help from you."

"You see now why I talked you into a three-year contract," said Paul grinning. "Very well, but it's a job for spring or summer, I wouldn't care to footslog over the fields from now on. Let's go into the office and trace the adjustments."

They tramped inside out of the wind and Mrs. Handcock brought them their morning beer. Sir George Lovell would have had difficulty in recognising his former darkroom for it was freshly painted in green, fitted with a small fireplace, a drawing board and had two walls of new shelves and cupboards, together with a large safe for estate documents. The two men settled down over the parchment absorbed and content.

Half a pasty had by no means satisfied the gull's hunger and after disposing of the titbit at the summit of one of the avenue gateposts it took off again, heading due north on the edge of the wind. Its flight led over Priory Wood and on to the plateau of Hermitage Farm, where the Pitts family were discussing new Squire's recent acquisition of the Hardcastle smallholding just north of their boundary. The gull saw nothing of them, for they were all inside the house but as it was not interested in unploughed land it flew on over the Hermitage fields seeking a worm, or an antagonist less formidable than the Derwents' prize sow. A small piece of luck came its way. Earlier that day young Henry Pitts, carrying two swill buckets to his sties, had staggered in a strong gust of wind and spilled a pool of swill on the path. A few other gulls were already there and the lone bird joined them, ignoring their clamour.

Inside the big kitchen old Arthur Pitts was discussing his son's proposal to apply to new Squire for permission to absorb the Hardcastle smallholding into their acreage, offering an increase of thirty pounds a year in rent, but the older man would have none of it. His main interest had always been in market gardening and he had but a poor opinion of old Hardcastle's skill as a farmer.

"Us have got as much as us can handle now," he told

his son, "and any money I lay out is going to be for a hot-house over by the hives. You can make a dam' sight more on early veg than on grazing sheep or fattening beef on that bit o' rough land!"

Young Henry had respect for his father's professional opinions, having seen Hermitage grow from a parcel of land not much larger than the Hardcastle holding into the second-best farm in the Valley.

"Arr," he said, gulping a pint of Martha's steaming cocoa, "it was on'y a notion I had, but what'll young Squire do with the plaace, now 'er's got his claws into it?"

"He'll make it pay," said Arthur, sagely, "that's what he'll do with it! For dornt none of you yerabouts under-estimate that young feller-me-lad! 'Er knows nowt about farming as yet, but he's not like most lads with money at the back of him! He's willin' to listen an' willin' to learn, and John Rudd'll be better'n a father to him! What did you think of him, Mother?"

"A praper young man, when he's worked through his fancy ideas," said Martha, and young Henry, finishing his cocoa, winked at his father over the rim of his mug. They were a happy, well-adjusted trio and the keynote of life in the Hermitage kitchen had always been tolerance.

"There's one change he'll have to make soon if he really zettles isself in the gurt, empty house," Martha went on, gathering plates and crashing them into the vast tub she used for washing-up.

"Ar, an' what's that, Mother?" Arthur demanded, well knowing the answer.

"A wife, an' one who knows her bizness," said Martha, and she sighed for it was always a matter of regret to her that Henry, now twenty-four, was still a bachelor and seemed likely to remain one. She would have welcomed a buxom daughter to share her enormous kitchen and she sometimes hungered for grandchildren.

Henry might have taken her point and advanced a time-honoured defence based on a preference for his mother's cooking but at that moment the gulls outside began a furious quarrel over the shrinking remains of the swill and shouting "They dratted gulls again!" he grabbed his rook-rifle and, loading as he ran, charged into the

129

yard and fired into the squabbling group but he aimed to scare, not to kill. He was not only a warm-hearted young man but a superstitious one and he knew that every time a seagull died a sailor was drowned, their souls being interchangeable.

The gulls rose in a screaming cloud, circled and flew south in convoy. They read the weather signs and knew that within an hour the wind would abate and they could resume fishing on the beach, where food was plentiful. As they beat into the wind they flew over the Codsall homestead, their quarrel forgotten but as they passed it was taken up in the kitchen of Four Winds, where the smouldering resentment of Will Codsall had finally flared up, and he and his mother faced one another over the long oak table, with poor Martin caught between the hammer of his son's frustration and the anvil of his wife's furious obstinacy.

"You c'n take it or leave it, Mother," Will was shouting, "and that's the last you'll yer from me on the subject! Either me and my Elinor put up the banns on Sunday, an' fix a day this side o' Michaelmas, or I march out o' here and won't wait until Michaelmas to do it, neither!"

"Neither! Neither!" sang Arabella, in her high whining voice, "you're already beginning to talk like her! Would anyone ever know you were something a bit better than the yokels who swarm in this Valley? It's a wonderful catch for her I daresay, but what'll she bring with her apart from bad blood? It isn't as if you were kept from the girls, as all the young men were in my day! There was that nice, refined Miss Agate as I asked here to tea in the summer, daughter of a solicitor if you please, who spoke up like a lady, and had a decent education!"

"Aye," said Will, grimly, "and a face like one of our bliddy Friesian cows and she wouldn't ha' taaken a second look at us Valley folk if her mother coulder found her a man back in Whinmouth!"

"You're coarse-minded too," Arabella shrieked, "and it makes me shudder to think what kind of children you and that Willoughby girl would raise between you!"

"Couldn't we have Willoughby over and talk to him?" suggested Martin—courageously for him, for he knew very well the remark would direct the tide of his wife's scorn from son to father.

"No, we couldn't!" snapped Arabella, "for I won't give houseroom to one o' them Nonconformist Radicals! What are you thinking of, both of you? During the war that man Willoughby prayed in public for the Boers didn't he, and was pelted for doing it! Have him up here for a talk? What about might I ask? Our eldest boy and his chit of a daughter getting wed before Christmas and from then on we should be related! *Related!* To a Coombe family if you please! What have I ever done to deserve this? Haven't I been a good wife and mother to you all? Hasn't this farm been stocked on my father's money? Don't anyone realise how I should feel to see everything I've worked for pass to the daughter of a psalm-singing smallholder, scratching a living out of his chapel collection plate and a few moulting hens?"

Martin Codsall considered this, wondering how far it was from the truth for the Willoughbys, although poor, had never been regarded as anything other than harmless, respectable people and the bitterness of his wife's prejudice against them puzzled him. It might, he reflected, be a pleasant change to hear another woman's voice raised in the kitchen, and personally he had nothing whatever against his son marrying into a Coombe family, so long as it wasn't to a Potter. He would have preferred it to be a pretty girl like Claire Derwent, who had made his mouth water when he watched her waltzing at the Victory Ball in the Whinmouth Assembly Rooms last May, but Will would be of age in a month and could marry whom he pleased, so where was the sense in making such an issue of it? He said, again in a low voice, "I don't want to lose our Will, Mother, I couldn't get along without him. It would mean taking on another man and another boy, and veeding 'em both, six days a week!" He thought this appeal to her pocket might make her think twice but he was wrong, for Will's revolt plucked at the taproots of her authority and in a way she was enjoying the dispute that must end in Will's unconditional surrender. She glanced at the white-faced Sydney, listening to every word and snapped, "Eat up your pie, and sit up straight, Sydney!" Then, like a boxer flexing his muscles before advancing to the centre of the ring, "If Will was so inconsiderate as to run contrary to my wishes I wouldn't receive him into the house again, or his wife either! 'Either' you'll notice, not *'neither'!*" and as though this was her final word on the subject she dabbed her lips with the napkin and cut into another portion of shepherd's pie.

There was a silence, Martin and Sydney looking down at their plates, Arabella looking past them at a brass warming pan over the fireplace. Then two sharp sounds were heard simultaneously, the scrape of Will's chair and the warning rattle of Arabella's cuckoo clock, which always made this sound a second before its doors flew open and the bird bobbed out to cry the hour.

"That's all I wanted to be sure of, Mother," Will said, "I'll be goin' along now, and don't *neither* of you come making a scene over at Deepdene when I'm zettled in! If you do I'll come back and do mischief!"

Arabella dropped her knife and fork and half rose to her feet as Martin stretched out his hand, as though to detain Will by force. Sydney remained quite still, masticating his mouthful of pie the requisite thirty-two times before swallowing.

"You go and I'll harness the trap and come straight over to fetch you back!" shouted Arabella. "I'll make such a fool of you you'll be the laughing stock of the Valley. You an' that girl too!"

Will stood facing her and Martin, looking up, noticed that the muscles of his son's jaw were twitching, and that his big hands, resting on the back of his chair, were trembling. Some instinct warned him that this was a real and final crisis and he jumped to his feet just as the cuckoo appeared at the double doors of the clock. Simultaneously Will's hands left the chair and reached across the table, grasping the heavy crock in which stood the remains of the shepherd's pie. It flew across the room and struck the doors of the clock in the act of closing, splintering them with a crash that sent the Codsalls' spaniel Nell scurrying for the back door. The crock itself, together with all that remained of the pie, ricochetted from the wall, fell on the table and then disintegrated, spattering Sydney with china, mashed potato and gravy, and shattering half the dishes. Sydney screamed and Arabella, after a single outraged yell, burst into a noisy flood of tears. Martin said nothing. He had been Arabella's husband for twenty-one years and therefore considered himself married to her cuckoo clock, a wedding present from the staff of her father's shop. There were no words to express the dreadful finality of such an act. But Will said one more thing as he turned at the door to the hall on his way out. "That's to show I baint bluffing, Mother!" he said. "I'll come back here, and do the same for every stick o' furniture in this house if you show your face at Deepdene arter I'm gone!"

They heard him stump upstairs and drag open a chest of drawers but after that there was silence except for Arabella's sobs and Sydney's intermittent sniffs but the horror of being abandoned by even such a silent ally as his son gave Martin a last spurt of courage.

"Well," he said, "I hope you're satisfied, Mother! I do 'ope you're satisfied!", and he left them to their mourning.

On their flight down to the beaches the gulls passed low over the two chalet-style houses standing in an acre apiece on the ridge above the harbour. The western one, "Channel View", was the home of Captain Bruce Lovell, his wife Celia (née Winterbourne, of Winterbourne Chase, Derbyshire) and Bruce's daughter, Grace, by his first wife. No vulgar quarrel was in progress here but there was enough tension under the roof to charge a searchlight battery.

Bruce Lovell's second marriage had not been as disastrous as his first, which had ended in his wife's suicide in a Madras reservoir. Celia was a well-bred, handsome woman, who seldom raised her voice, preferring to correct her husband's many failings by more indirect means, such as sentencing him, every now and again, to terms of banishment in the country, or keeping him short of money at the height of the flat season. Bruce was undergoing punishment now and had been, ever since his disastrous losses at Ascot, and an involvement with a little milliner in Camden Town, but his sentence was almost up and he was now watching the calendar like a new boy approaching the end of his first term at a particularly dull boarding school.

Celia had promised him that they would return to town on the tenth of October and he knew her well enough to accept the fact that no social obligations or pleas on his part would induce her to forward the date by twenty-four hours. They had now been at "Channel View" since the end of June, "a three-months' stretch" as he would tell his cronies at the Club, and it seemed to him a heavy penalty for backing an also-ran in the Royal Hunt Cup, and then seeking mild consolation in a rough and tumble with an amateur tart in Camden Town. He was, however, philosophical, so long as his philosophy could be practised in comfort, and life had taught him that a spree was usually followed by a flick of the whip by those controlling the purse strings. This was the pattern of life for a gentleman without private means of his own and he had followed it uncomplainingly as a cavalry subaltern, a tea-merchant, a stage-door Johnny, a remittance man, a tout, and finally as the husband of the elegant Celia Winterbourne. She paid up but she made him suffer and he was suffering now, by God, from the agonising pangs of country life by the sea. He hated the country. Ennui engulfed him as soon as he saw a ploughed field or a wood and prolonged residence in the country reared inside him a kind of octopus whose tentacles explored his vitals, his greying temples and finally every cell of his brain, so that instead of screaming he yawned until his jaws ached and even the sporting page of *The Times* could arouse in him no more than a candle glimmer of professional interest. Celia knew he was nearing breaking-point and wished now that she had fixed the date for their return a week earlier but the Winterbournes had not made a fortune in pots of boot blacking without showing firmness at factory bench and fireside, so she set her face against a surrender that revision of the departure date would imply, hanging on and watching his long, yammering yawns with a certain satisfaction. It was some consolation for having been obliged to ask her father for an advance in order to pay his bookmaker and for having to listen to an unspeakably coarse private detective's report on what had transpired in a basement flat in Camden Town.

Celia had not minded Bruce's infidelity as much as the smell of the detective's beery breath, or the fact that he wore heavy brown boots with a navy blue suit. She was that kind of woman; little things pleased or irritated her. Bruce's sun-tan, when they first met in Madeira, had been a little thing and so had his discovery that freesia was her favourite flower. Little things both, but enough to encourage her to share her life with a man whose sole qualification for a husband was that he looked a gentleman and could even behave like one in public.

What occupied Celia's thoughts just now, however, was not Bruce's breaking-strain, which she could assess out of the corner of her eye but the circumstances surrounding the new Squire's interest in her unpredictable stepdaughter Grace, Bruce's daughter by his unfortunate first wife. When Celia became the second Mrs. Lovell, Grace had been seventeen and had spent the greater part of the year at a convent in the Lake District. At that time Celia had nothing against the girl and had set out to do her best on Grace's behalf, arranging a season for her and casting about for suitable escorts, one of whom might ultimately relieve her of the responsibility of a half-grown stepdaughter, but Grace had been unresponsive. There had been a succession of sulks and tantrums, leading, now that Grace was of age, to a wary truce between them. Bruce played no part in this, giving his daughter less thought than a promising colt entered for next year's Derby.

In some ways Celia respected the girl, for at least she had a natural dress sense, caused her very little concern by cultivating unsuitable friendships and was an accomplished horsewoman who could have made herself a national reputation in this field. But Grace's disposition as a whole was baffling, for she was very difficult to type and this made it impossible to plan her future. The Winterbournes had been a very sociable family and Celia, in her youth, had met every conceivable type of young socialite at Winterbourne Chase. She experienced gawky girls, sulky girls, listless girls, dutifully innocuous girls and girls whose homesickness for the gutter led them to consort with grooms and bootboys. Among her friends were women who could be classified as Spartans, blue-stockings, religious maniacs, women who dieted themselves into a decline, and those who over-ate and acquired a matron's figure before they lost their virginity. She supposed that she understood the frustrations of every woman of her own class between the age of thirteen and forty but she had yet to make real contact with Grace, whose personality seemed to Celia a wild tangle of contradictions. That the girl had a good brain she had no doubt. She had heard her converse on equal terms with elderly men, and on subjects well outside the range of a convent-educated girl —Darwinism, the Oxford Movement and Universal Suffrage to name only three, but at Celia's "At Homes" she sat as mute as a mummy, and everyone left thinking her insufferably dull. Some days she looked pretty and on other days she was almost plain, her strange pallor without its lustre, her hair bundled any old how and always short of pins. Usually she had good manners but there were occasions when she behaved like an adolescent bore, anxious to attract attention to herself. She interested men, all kinds of men, but she never showed the least sign of wanting to exploit her conquests and often she seemed to Celia frigid and, what was far worse, aggressively so. In fact, regarding her stepdaughter, Celia was certain of only one thing. The girl hated her father and took no pains to hide it. Perhaps it was this, which, in a sense, was something shared between stepmother and stepdaughter, that encouraged Celia to persist in her efforts to help the child but so far her efforts had gone unrewarded. Grace Lovell continued to walk and ride in a strange world of her own; it seemed to Celia, a friendly, cheerful extrovert, to be a very arid, profitless world.

The incident of the screen intrigued her. She had heard a good deal of gossip about the young man who had appeared from nowhere and swallowed the Shallowford white elephant at a gulp. It was rumoured that his money derived from guns or scrap metal, and Celia, who, to do her justice, was still unconvinced that her own income stemmed entirely from boot polish, fervently hoped that it was the former, for whilst there was a certain dignity in shot and shell there was surely none in old iron. She had been very curious to see the young man for herself and that was why she had nagged Bruce into taking them to the sale but once there, gaped at by every hobbledehoy in the Valley, and inhaling their body odours at close quarters, Celia would have left at once had not Grace insisted on staying to bid for two items of furniture in the nursery. Celia had humoured her because she thought the girl might feel nostalgic regarding her past association with Ralph Lovell, the rackety son of that old rascal Sir George, and when Bruce wanted to go home and asked what purpose there could be in lumbering the house with Ralph Lovell's playthings, Celia told him sharply to hold his tongue and squeezed Grace's unresponsive hand, standing beside her whilst a vulgar farm wife had bid more than the things were worth. Then the curious thing had happened. The lean-faced young man who had bought the estate had topped the bidding and presented the nursery screen to Grace, when, as far as Celia was aware, he and Grace had not even met.

Discreet questioning on Celia's part provided half the answer. Grace said, off-handedly, that she had encountered Craddock whilst riding on the sandhills one morning, but this was enough to set Celia's thoughts in motion along strictly circumscribed lines. Ever since her own nursery days she had been accustomed to think and talk about suitable marriages for this relative or that playmate. She said nothing to Bruce at first, allowing the possibility of bringing these two young people together to mature, but day by day she held the possibility up to the light, searching for possible flaws and blemishes. She discovered none, or none that mattered nearly so much as getting Grace off her hands, in order that she could devote all her time to moulding Bruce into someone for whom it was not necessary to apologise to one's friends.

Only when she was quite ready did she fire her first range-finding shot, aiming it at the neat crease of Bruce's *Times,* behind which he was taking cover after dinner one evening. Grace was not in the house at the time, having gone on a short duty visit to Celia's sister in Derbyshire, so they had an opportunity to explore the possibility at leisure.

"When," said Celia, suddenly, "would it be convenient to call upon Mr. Craddock?", and Bruce, half-lowering his paper, replied, "Why in God's name should we want to call upon the fellow?"

"Well, for one thing he *is* our landlord," said Celia pleasantly, and Bruce, lowering the paper with a sigh, replied, "My dear; in the course of a life of movement, I must have had a hundred landlords, exclusive of one-night stays. I do not recall visiting any of them socially. Besides, they say the fellow's money comes from a bone-yard."

"From munitions," Celia corrected, as Bruce raised his paper.

"A mere matter of processing," he said. "From what little I saw of him he struck me as a common little tyke."

"Perhaps," Celia conceded, "but the fact remains that he is very comfortably off, and has also been showing interest in Grace."

She knew her man. The paper came down again and this time it stayed down. Bruce Lovell was a snob but he never let his prejudices make a fool of him. All the same, he was not yet ready to surrender unconditionally. He said, thoughtfully, "Is that so? Well, I must say it surprises me, but notwithstanding his money I wouldn't care to make a friend of the fellow."

"No," said Celia, with smiling malice, "I don't suppose you would, Bruce. You've never put yourself out to make a friend of your daughter, but even you must see that, things being what they are, it might prove a good opportunity to ensure the girl's future. You recall the terms of my settlement no doubt."

How could he forget them? In the event of her death Celia's money passed directly to her younger sister, and although Celia was the least likely person in his world to reduce him to penury by drowning herself in a reservoir like his first wife, there remained the routine hazards of sickness and accident. He reflected glumly how securely his fortunes would have been buttressed against disaster

138

by Grace's marriage to young Ralph Lovell, for although Ralph had been a younger son the Lovells had never been known to leave money to female relatives.

"Ah," he murmured, "that was a frightful thing, young Ralph getting himself killed in South Africa. He would have made Grace an excellent husband."

"Rubbish," said Celia, emphatically. "Ralph was a young blackguard and would have made her miserable but I daresay she had made up her mind his money was worth it. However, we are talking of the future, not the past. As I said, the new Squire has already met Grace, and there was that little matter of the screen upstairs. It may have been no more than a polite gesture. On the other hand it may have some meaning, for I have a feeling she didn't tell me the complete truth about it. They have probably met not once, casually, but several times, and for my part I think it ought to be encouraged."

"My dear," said Bruce, suddenly feeling cheerful, "I have never quarrelled with your judgment regarding really important matters. I'll have a word with Grace when she returns home tomorrow."

"The day after tomorrow," said Celia, and without another word left him to go up to Grace's room and examine the screen in detail, moving round it much as a conscientious detective might inspect the luggage of a suspect in the hope of finding an overlooked clue.

II

The naïve formality of Claire's note suggesting a combined coronation supper and a house-warming amused Paul but it was not until he and Rudd were having their night-cap before the study fire that he read into it anything more than a mild rebuke for his neglect of her.

"Claire Derwent seems to have a good idea here, John," he said. They had recently taken to addressing one another by Christian names and although Rudd had demurred a little, thinking it might encourage familiarity among tenants and staff, it had lessened the age gap between them and generally oiled their relationship. He read the note aloud, glad now that Claire had been discreet in her phraseology, for he knew that Rudd would strongly disapprove of what had occurred in Shallowford Woods.

"It's a better idea than she realises," he said, "but the object behind it is clear, of course. That girl is out to get you and I knew it the day I introduced you to her, but I don't see why we should hold that against her. Nothing wrong in aiming high, if you come into the field as well equipped as she is."

"You think a tenants' supper-dance would be a success? After all, I hardly know most of them. Mightn't it seem a bit pompous and patriarchal on my part?"

"It might in some circumstances but you have a cast-iron excuse in the coronation. There have already been countless local junketings, so why shouldn't we have one at Shallowford?"

He got up, sucking his pipe and stood with his back to the fire. "It's a damned good idea," he said finally, "for it can set the tone for what you want to do down here! They'll love it, every man jack of 'em and it's a pity I can't be here to see you through. However, I've a notion Claire Derwent will take over very efficiently."

"Why can't you be here?" asked Paul, surprised, and Rudd said, "Because I've given my word to attend the Spithead Review. It's my boy, Roderick. He's gunnery officer on the *Crecy* and I promised a long time ago. I haven't seen him in more than three years, he's been on the China station."

"I never even knew you had a son," exclaimed Paul, and Rudd replied with a shrug, "Oh, I told you more than enough of my life-story the day you arrived here! I was married soon after I got my first lieutenancy but Jean died, giving birth to the boy. I was overseas at the time and he was brought up by my sister and her husband and is closer to them than to me. But he's done well, or so I'm told. He doesn't write much, and I suppose his aunt persuaded him to insist on my attending the Review."

Something of the man's acute loneliness and the prickliness it had fostered over the years revealed itself to Paul, helping him to gauge the satisfaction John Rudd had derived from their comradeship, dating from that first conversation on Blackberry Moor. He said eagerly, "Couldn't we have our soirée later in the year when you're home again?" but Rudd said, "No, it wouldn't be the same. All the sparkle would go out of a 'do' like that if it was held after the national uproar had died down. Take my advice, and drop a line tonight to Claire Derwent telling her the idea has my blessing. Then ask her over and rough out some kind of plan. You'll need all kinds of things in the way of decorations, souvenir programmes and suchlike, and that girl obviously has the interests of you and the estate very much at heart. Leave all the catering arrangements to Mrs. Handcock, she'll be beside herself with bustle, and Claire can put you in touch with the local musicians. Mary Willoughby plays the piano well and the shepherd twins at the Home Farm are first-rate fiddlers."

"I'll do that," Paul said, his enthusiasm growing, "but I wish you could be here."

"So do I," Rudd said with a smile, "if only to see the girls scramble for you. By the way, *can* you dance with that leg?"

"I'll have a damned good try, if only in honour of King Teddy," Paul said, and after Rudd had gone home he sat at the library table and composed two letters to Claire Derwent, each covering a single page and respectively numbered "one" and "two".

The first was couched in terms that parodied her letter. "Dear Miss Derwent," it ran, "Your note arrived by runner this a.m. Have consulted my estate agent and he approves suggestion in principle. Perhaps, at your convenience, you would call, in order that we might discuss preliminary arrangements for staging some local festivities of a patriotic nature. Sincerely, P. Craddock."

The second letter was an attempt to revive their comfortable relationship: "My dear Claire, What a marvellous idea tucked away in a stuffy little letter! Rudd thinks your notion is just what is needed to play me in and is tremendously enthusiastic, as I am myself. Come on over, you silly girl, and we'll discuss what needs doing. I've missed you very much, but honestly I've been inundated

141

with work and John Rudd keeps me at it day and night! Affectionately, Paul."

He gave both letters to the Derwent farmboy when he called next morning and instructed him to present them in rotation. Then he went whistling about his work, riding over to the Home Farm to discuss the introduction of a new strain of Southdown sheep, afterwards crossing Priory Wood to consult one of Henry Pitts' hired men regarding the construction of a new boundary fence between Hermitage Farm and the new sixty-acre smallholding, acquired from Mrs. Hardcastle. He was back at the house shortly before the lunch hour and was delighted to see Ikey Palfrey watering Claire's bay in the yard.

"Miss Derwent rode in about 'alf an 'our ago, sir," Ikey told him. "She's in the kitchen with Mrs. Handcock."

"Good," said Paul, handing Snowdrop's reins to the boy and watching him lead the horse into the stable, "Do you dance, Ikey? I don't mean 'Knees Up Mother Brown' but real dancing, waltzing and suchlike."

"Lumme, *no, sir, Mr. Craddock!* Why would I want to do a thing like that?"

"Oh, you never know, Ikey," said Paul and left him, with his mouth agape, and went chuckling up the yard steps to the kitchen.

CHAPTER SIX

I

THE soirée organisers soon resolved themselves into a committee of five, with Claire Derwent as an enthusiastic chairwoman. Rudd stood back and gave advice, and Mrs. Handcock made herself responsible for a buffet-supper that promised to give everyone who attended indigestion. Ikey Palfrey ran all the errands and Paul, enjoying every moment of the upheaval, spent most of his time seconding Claire, who added fresh touches every hour they spent together.

It was a happy time for Claire Derwent and her inspiration flowered under Paul's patronage. It was she who discovered how to enlarge the dancing space, recalling that the dining-room and adjoining billiard-room were still connected by a sliding door that had been sealed and papered over. Paul sent for Eph Morgan, the builder, and had him re-open the rooms and build a dais for the musicians at the western end. The billiard-table and heavy furniture were carried away and there seemed to be ample space for The Lancers. Claire also made out an invitation list, the cards displaying pictures of the King and Queen and sat for hours at the library table listing names, checking and rechecking to make sure that nobody in the Valley was overlooked. "Those with young children will just have to draw lots and set up a baby farm for the night," she said. "That way most of the mothers will be able to attend. I make the total of certainties one hundred and fourteen, allowing for child-minders and sickness. Altogether you'll need to write out a hundred and twenty-five invitations."

"Can't they be printed?" he asked, and Claire said they certainly could not because the whole idea of this party was to establish personal contact between the new Squire and everyone between sea and railway line, and therefore letters in his own handwriting were essential. "I'll get Ikey to take a note to the Whinmouth stationers," she said, "and while we're at it we might as well start the decorations. We've only got ten days and we need every moment of them."

In fact it occupied the pair of them exclusively, for two or three days later Rudd left for Portsmouth, and Mrs. Handcock grew very testy under the strain of ordering and preparing huge quantities of food and drink, so that Claire and Paul were left to decorate the huge room unaided by anyone except Ikey. Two huge cardboard ovals, together with the gilded legend *"God bless our King and Queen"*, were brought in to dress the walls, so that the two rooms were soon transformed into a vast green cave, lit by strings of Japanese lanterns and hung about with

Christmas-tree decorations. The hall beyond became a kind of antechamber, for here Claire (who seemed to have ready access to the most improbable stage properties) hung pictures of Canadian forests, Australian deserts and Indian temples, together with the flags of all the nations, including some who would have disclaimed the suzerainty of Edward VII and Queen Alexandra.

The whole house was turned upside down and soon presented a more disorderly appearance than during its renovation period. Guest-rooms were prepared for those staying overnight, two cloakrooms contrived out of butler's pantry and estate office, washing facilities provided at key points off the main corridor and a dozen trestle tables hired for the kitchen staff, who were promised a Christmas party of their own to compensate them for their labours the night of the ball. For Paul had now begun to look upon it not as a supper-dance but a ball, hardly less important than the recent county event in Paxtonbury. Under Claire's driving force he saw the event mushroom from a local soirée, with a tinkling piano and a couple of amateur fiddlers, into the most important social event in the history of the Valley, and it pleased him to think that it might prove an evening that people like the Potters, the Willoughbys and the Pitts would remember all their lives.

As his excitement increased so he came to take more and more pleasure in Claire's company but although they were often alone after Rudd had left, and Ikey was usually out on one of Claire's missions, there was never a repetition of their mutual recklessness in Shallowford Woods and this not because Claire was always in a brisk, businesslike mood, but because of his shyness in her presence, that increased alongside admiration for her ingenuity and her skill in getting the last ounce out of over-worked maids and outside staff, like the head gardener, Horace Handcock, the old-maidish groom, Chivers, and particularly the stable lad, Ikey.

Only on one occasion, when he was helping her down a ladder, did their relationship enlarge slightly beyond that of a brother and sister, organising a family party and that was when, in the act of steadying her, he held her by the waist rather longer than was necessary and kissed her lightly on the cheek. She did not acknowledge the salute but neither did she say, as he half expected her to, "Now then, we've no time for that kind of thing!" or some such evasive remark. She merely stood still at the foot of the ladder and said, carelessly, "Thank you, sir!" and then, to his annoyance, Horace Handcock came stamping in with another great bunch of evergreens and they sidled apart.

It was after twilight when she arrived home that night and Rose was anxiously awaiting her at the top of the lane with a lantern. She had driven the trap at a slow walk, for she wanted an opportunity to summarise the events of the last few days, before being obliged to gossip with her father, sister and stepmother, all of whom were showing the liveliest interest in the event.

She had entered upon the task of organising the soirée with enthusiasm but caution. It was obvious from Paul's second note that he had dismissed or forgotten all that silly talk in the wood, although she rather hoped he remembered the moment that preceded it. That he enjoyed her company she now had no doubt but he seemed, in some mysterious way, to have retreated into a kind of boisterous adolescence during their separation. It surprised her the more because, in matters that did not concern her such as the daily issue of orders to Home Farm and estate workers, he seemed at the same time to have enlarged himself and she could see that, even without Rudd's presence to guide him, he had grasped the essentials of administration. He gave his orders in a confident voice and she could have wished that, on occasions, he would employ this tone and manner with her, but he did not, and his deference was the one small cloud on Claire Derwent's horizon during this season and one to which she gave considerable thought during her journey home to High Coombe that evening. "Maybe I'm being too bossy," she told herself, as the trap wheels slipped on the loose surface of the High Coombe ascent. "Maybe I should get him to make suggestions and applaud them, no matter how impractical they are!" and then the memory of his hands about her waist and his light-hearted kiss returned to her and she thought again of the hectic moment beside the mere, so

145

that it was fortunate for both of them that the cob knew its way home for it got little or no guidance from the rein.

Paul Craddock too was reflecting on the trivial incident that same evening, as he sat studying the invitation list whilst Mrs. Handcock prepared his supper. Under the incentive of her presence, he decided, the incident in Shallowford Woods had, to some extent, resurrected itself, and with it the distant tinkling of an alarm bell. He would need very little encouragement, he admitted, to whisk her off somewhere on a prefabricated excuse and begin the same kind of thing all over again but there was a very obvious disadvantage in this. The girl had already frankly admitted that she had marriage in mind and at the moment, enjoying the unexpected delights of the past few months, he had no desire to "settle" as they said; furthermore he was by no means certain that he was in love with the girl. He wished then that he had had more experience with women. What use was the ludicrous incident with the saucy Cherry in the barn, or his calf-love for the girl Daphne, or, indeed, the few minutes in the Cape Town brothel, in teaching him how to proceed with a purposeful and bewitching creature like Claire Derwent? He thought hard about the matter most of the evening when he should have been addressing invitations but the only certainties that emerged were that she was a very pretty girl and that he had no intention at all of being rushed into marriage by anyone. Later that night he found some comfort browsing through one of the big leather-bound books taken from a lower shelf. It was a rather windy account of Queen Victoria's youth, and he was a little amused by the admission she had made to Lord Melbourne when she declared that she was very satisfied with her situation and had no wish to marry for two or three years. That, he thought, was precisely how he felt himself. He would marry, almost certainly, when Shallowford was under his hand but not before. The challenge was there and he wanted to meet it, so that a wife and family could wait on events. It was fortunate for Paul's peace of mind, perhaps that he put the book aside and drove himself back to his homework, and thus did not

146

read the pages concerning Victoria's ultimate surrender to dear Albert.

Claire was over again early next day, the last but one before the ball and, as it happened, Paul came forward with a splendid suggestion, without any prompting on her part. When the ballroom had received the last of its finishing touches, and they stood back to review their work, he said, suddenly, "What we need now, Claire, is something to cap it all! Something spectacular, like fireworks!" and then, catching her hand, "That's exactly it! Where could we get ten pounds' worth of fireworks? And why the devil didn't we think of it before?"

"They've been selling them for weeks in Whinmouth," she told him, "but if we want as many as that we should have to go to Paxtonbury, right away. Suppose we both go now, in the trap? We can be back by teatime if we take your cob, for my old Nobby would drag his feet all the way home!"

He was tempted; he had only paid one visit to Paxtonbury and the prospect of the long ride there and back, with Claire on the box beside him, appealed to him but he remembered then that he had not answered a business letter in ten days, and baulked at the prospect of Rudd returning to find the office tray full of headaches.

"I can't go, Claire," he told her, "there's a desk spilling over in the office, and some of the matters have to be attended to before the ball unless I'm to look a helpless, undecisive ass when Rudd comes home. You and Ikey drive into Paxtonbury and I'll wait tea for you. Then Chivers can take you home after dark. We ought to have fireworks, with a set-piece of the King and Queen if you can get one."

She promised to do her best and drove off at once, taking the delighted Ikey for company. Paul watched them leave, spending the next three hours in the office, wrestling with correspondence from seedsmen, county agricultural advisers, dairy contractors, insurance rates and ideas spawned by their observations during rides about the estate during the last three months. He had a bite of lunch and pushed on in the afternoon, so absorbed that he did not notice the sky darkening over the avenue chestnuts or the first slash of rain on the window. It was not until he saw old Handcock run along the rose-garden hedge in search of shelter that he realised that it was now pelting down, and that Claire and Ikey would have a very uncomfortable journey home, charged as they were with the responsibility of keeping the fireworks dry. He went across the hall to warn Mrs. Handcock to have a hot meal ready for them but as he turned for the kitchen archway the front door bell jangled so he retraced his steps, opening the heavy door and peering into the grey murk of the porch. A small bedraggled figure was standing there, holding the handlebars of a bicycle but for a moment he failed to recognise her. Then, as she raised her hand to her dark curls to push them aside he saw that it was Grace Lovell and he hurried out to relieve her of the machine, propping it against the wall. She said, breathlessly, "I'm sorry, I only wanted shelter until it slacks off a little. I was on my way home but the ford is deeper than it looked. The water will go down directly the rain stops, it always does this time of year."

"Well, for heaven's sake come in and dry yourself first," he said, surprised at his delight in her unexpected appearance. "Leave the bike there and I'll get Mrs. Handcock to give you tea. You'll catch your death of cold for it isn't like getting wet on a horse. A horse keeps your blood circulating."

"I've never caught a cold in my life, Mr. Craddock," she said, but she stepped into the hall and he saw to his astonishment that she was wearing one of the new bicycling outfits, a costume that was a shapeless mass of pleats and pockets. He left her spreading her hands before the library fire and told a maid to bring tea and muffins at once. Then he put bellows to the coals and lit the table lamp, aware that she was watching him with the disconcerting concentration he now expected of her. Today, however, there was a difference for her scrutiny did not make him feel inadequate but rather the opposite, as though she was a child who had come in out of the rain expecting a scolding. She looked rather childish, he thought, in that absurd costume, and he decided that he heartily agreed with the people who were currently writing

148

letters to *The Times* complaining that the bicycling craze had robbed young women of feminine appeal.

"I didn't know you were a bicyclist," he said, as the girl came in with the tray and left again, averting her glance from the steaming figure by the fire.

"Oh, it makes a change," she said, listlessly, and then, chafing her hands and looking at the pyramid of sealed envelopes on the table, "Are all those letters invitations for the supper-dance?"

He was surprised by her directness and stopped in the act of pouring. "Why yes," he said, "as a matter of fact they are and there's one there for you, and for Mr. and Mrs. Lovell. You can take it now if you like."

"Who will be coming?"

"Just about everybody," he said, laughing, "at least I hope so. Do you think your father and Mrs. Lovell will accept?"

"Yes, they will," she said.

"You've been discussing it then?"

"Everybody's been discussing it."

He was pleased without knowing why and she went on, "My father can't actually attend. He's going to London tomorrow, but Celia, my stepmother, will, you can be sure of that!"

She said this almost as a threat and it occurred to him again what an odd young woman she was, for she seemed always to carry on a discussion from out of range, to be standing just inside the boundary of good manners so that it was like talking to a precocious child, in the presence of strangers.

He said, handing her tea muffins, "I trust you'll be coming too, Miss Lovell."

She looked round the room carefully, inspecting the evergreen decorations before saying, this time with a tired smile, "Yes, I will, Mr. Craddock, for Celia, my stepmother, would be annoyed if I didn't. Anyway, I'd like to come now that I've seen all the trouble you've taken. Everybody ought to back you up, for nobody did anything like this for the Valley people in the old days."

"Don't give me the credit," he said. "All the organising

149

has been the work of Miss Derwent, of High Coombe. She's been working on it a fortnight."

"Rose Derwent?"

"No, Claire Derwent, her sister. She'll be here in a moment I hope. The poor girl has driven into Paxtonbury for fireworks."

She nodded, sipping her tea and nibbling her muffin. She ate and drank, he thought, like a fastidious kitten and as he watched her, trying to think of something affable to say, the mystery that had surrounded her from the occasion of their first meeting returned to him, so that suddenly a break-through of some kind became a matter of importance to him.

"You keep coming back here, Miss Lovell," he said, "and always under improbable circumstances. Yet it seems to me as if being here makes you unhappy, and talking to me makes you angry—not with me exactly but—well, with yourself! Isn't there anything I can do to make you take me for granted? Almost everyone else is beginning to."

She listened with little change of expression but her pallor intensified a little, and her jawline moved as the small chin hardened. Her inflexibility made him uncomfortable so that he reached for her teacup, saying, "I'm sorry, it's bad manners on my part to say that when we hardly know one another. It's just that—well—we don't seem to make much progress, do we? Let me give you another cup of tea."

When he had refilled the cup and handed it to her he was surprised to see that she looked far more at ease than he felt.

"I don't blame you a bit, Mr. Craddock. The fact is, all the Lovells are odd, and I'm odder than most! Don't apologise for your breach of manners, I should do that, not you. You're wrong about something, however, I don't resent you being here. I did before I met you but I don't now. You'll make a better job of Shallowford than they did, anyone can see that with half an eye, if only because you're an optimist. Coming here doesn't make me unhappy either. I expected it to but it didn't, or not after that second time, when you bought the screen. I suppose I'm curious

150

and that's understandable. I once thought I should be running the house."

"Were you in love with Ralph Lovell?"

"No, never."

"But he was with you?"

"I'm afraid not, and he didn't ever pretend to be, but don't ask me to explain the mystique of dynastic marriages, or 'arrangements'. It has to do with money I suppose, but there's more to it than that. Ralph and I grew up with the thing more or less settled."

"But didn't you even like the man?" he persisted, but before she could reply they both heard the rattle of wheels on the gravel outside and then the heavy creak of the door and a ring of laughter followed by Ikey's explosive "Cor! What a carry-on!"

Her expression changed at once and she said, pulling on her gloves, "I must go now, the rain's stopped," and when he protested, saying it was only Claire Derwent and the stable lad returning with the fireworks she brushed aside his courtesies and hurried into the hall.

"I can get Chivers to drive you back, and take the bicycle in the trap," he argued, but she shook her head and opened the door.

"No, I've got a lamp and it's all downhill. Thank you for everything, Mr. Craddock, and I'll see you on the night. Post the invitation and I'll warn Celia it's coming. Good-bye, and thank you!" and in a swirl of skirts she was gone, yanking the machine round, hoisting herself on to the pedal and thence into the saddle without even stopping to light the lamp on the handlebars.

He called good-bye when she was half-way across the forecourt, noting that she seemed equally at home on a bicycle as riding side-saddle on a horse and then Claire, her skirt splashed with red mud, came through the kitchen arch and he saw that despite her wetting she was in high spirits and grabbing his hands said, "We got soaked, both of us! Just look! But we got the most wonderful fireworks you've ever seen and I wrapped them in an oilskin as soon as the rain came down. Ikey's unpacking them now and putting them in the still-room. Is there any of your tea left, while Mrs. Handcock makes fresh?"

He felt a little bewildered; the contrast between them was so great. "I've had a visitor," he said, taking her into the study and removing the fireguard so that she could enjoy the full benefit of the heat. "Someone else came in out of the storm, and had to be warmed inside and dried off outside."

"Oh, who was that?"

"Grave Lovell, the girl who was to have married Ralph."

"Her? What on earth did she want?"

He was too preoccupied to notice that the laughter left her eyes, or that her voice now had an edge.

"I told you, she came in out of the storm, she was riding a bicycle and wearing one of those awful cycling costumes. I gave her tea and muffins, it was the least I could do, wasn't it?"

"Yes, I suppose it was," she admitted doubtfully, and then, "Didn't you bid for something for her at the sale?"

"A nursery screen she seemed to want. She was mooning over it the night I first arrived here. Do you know her? She seems to know you and Rose."

"I know her father is a bad hat, and she gets on better with her stepmother than with her father. What did you talk about besides me?"

He did not miss the reproof this time but met it good-humouredly.

"She implied that you were the Belle of Sorrel Valley, and I said I had heard as much but thought it rather undignified for the Squire to compete with all the other chawbacons in the Valley! I said you were employed here as an apprentice parlourmaid, but had agreed to help out as an interior decorator for the party. She said—" but by now she was mollified and flaring her skirts to the blaze, said, laughing, "I don't believe either of you mentioned me! She was probably too busy telling you you'd never make a go of this place. That was what everyone of them except me believed when you came." Then, changing the subject very pointedly, "That cob Rose sold you is a corker! He didn't drop below a trot all the way from Teazel Bridge, and I didn't have to flick the whip once!"

Over her shoulder he saw her reflection in the fireplace

152

mirror. In the bright lamplight her cheeks glowed and her eyes shone with health. He put his hands on her shoulders and pulled so that her weight rested on him lightly and he could kiss the damp coil of hair above her ear.

"You look prettier than ever when you're soaked through," he said. "I was an ass to send Ikey. If I'd have driven we could have stopped somewhere, until the rain eased off," and he would have turned her and kissed her lips if, at that moment, they had not heard the rattle of crockery outside as Mrs. Handcock bustled in, barging the door open with her enormous hips and exclaiming, "Mazed you be! Sixteen mile there, sixteen mile back, an' all ter vetch a bundle o' Roman candles! You too, Mr. Craddock, surely youm old enough to know better! That Palfrey varmint coming into my kitchen drippin' wet, an' Miss Claire here like to catch her death!" She swept the corner of the table clear and set down the tray with a crash. "There, get a hot drink inside 'ee and then strip they wet things off an' give 'em to me to dry!" And so the moment passed, and Claire began to chatter gaily about the fireworks, the storm and the wonderful paces of the new cob but he was not really listening finding that his mind, unaccountably, was elsewhere, following a small figure in a bicycling costume down the long hill into Coombe Bay, up the harbour slope to an ugly Victorian villa and into a room where the screen might remind her of him. And Claire, although she continued to chatter of fireworks, was half aware of the fact.

II

At ten minutes to midnight, on a clear September night, the Shallowford House Coronation Supper-Dance and Soirée had run about half its course. Dancing had been promised until dawn to those who intended to stay, but already, four hours after the opening Paul Jones, the party had lost the brittle civilities that had bedevilled its first hour or so.

The sluggish start had been no fault of the musicians. Mary Willoughby at the piano, and the two biblical shepherds, Matt and Luke, as fiddlers, had played with gusto from the moment Paul made a formal round of the ballroom, hall and terrace and coaxed self-conscious couples on to the floor. Now, after a noisy set of Lancers, the Boston Two-Step, two waltzes and a break for ices, the atmosphere had thawed a great deal and Claire had made up her mind that the event was building into a spectacular success. A second Paul Jones was a riot, even Mrs. Codsall joining the ring to be caught by a grinning and half-tipsy Tamer Potter, who swung her round the floor at such a speed that she had no chance to escape nor breath to protest.

From the forecourt the din rose like a waterspout, soaring into the night sky and making every roosting bird in the Home Farm coverts fidget. Standing half-way down the drive the tinkle of piano and the scrape of violins were puny, intermittent sounds all but submerged in the roar of voices and crash of feet, in sudden shrieks of laughter and the long rolling clatter of crockery, as Mrs. Handcock and her sweating team plunged mugs and ice-cream plates into vats of near-boiling water.

Almost everybody in the Valley was now inside the house or, in extreme cases (like that of seventeen-year-old Violet Potter), in the shrubberies surrounding the house, but Claire had badly underestimated the final tally of guests, for labourers' wives from the Gilroy Estate had been recruited as Sorrel Valley baby-minders. The only family so far unrepresented was the Bruce Lovells, of Coombe Bay, who had sent a message to say they would be late. Paul was too busy and far too elated to miss them, and Claire privately hoped they would not appear after all, for she had not quite forgotten Paul's vacant look after Grace Lovell had cycled home the night she had returned with the fireworks. It was not a serious worry, however. She too had her hands full, supervising the staff, the refreshments and even the run on the cloakrooms, and reintroducing Paul to late arrivals, whispering their names to him when they were still out of earshot.

The Potters had arrived *en masse* in a farm cart, every single one of them, including the pregnant Joannie (who spared the company's blushes by staying to help in the

154

kitchen) and Hazel, the youngest Potter girl, who found herself a seat high up on a pedestal shorn of its bust and moved well back against the billiard racks. From here she could look down on the throng with her large, wonder-struck eyes, unnoticed by anyone except Ikey Palfrey, who, in his uncomfortably stiff collar prescribed by Chivers, the groom, had spotted her perch and staring up at her, shouted, "You look like a statcher up there, kid!" a remark, which, although made with friendly intent, caused Hazel to shoot out her tongue and put her thumb to her nose, a gesture that made Ikey slightly homesick for Bermondsey.

All the Derwents, together with their staff, were present, as were the four Willoughbys and the four Codsalls, with their hired hands. Three waggonettes had driven over from Coombe Bay, bringing many of the tradesmen and all the artisans, including Eph Morgan, who was already engaged in disputation with Derwent's foreman, Gregory, concern-ing the advantages of free trade over tariff reform. They could hardly hear one another but were enjoying them-selves, for Gregory was the honorary treasurer of the Whinmouth Conservatives and Unionist Association and considered it his duty to engage the Radical, even at a coronation ball.

Parson Bull looked in for an hour or so but left early, despite generous brandies. The vicar was a little confused by an event that, so far as he could recall, had no pre-cedent in Valley history. He supposed there was nothing basically wrong with farmers and their hired hands mak-ing brief holiday once in a while, and there was, of course, a loyal excuse to be found in the coronation but at the back of his mind he found new Squire's common touch disconcerting and he was not easily disconcerted. Anyone else, he thought, as he drove off, could have been scolded in public for encouraging so much dangerous familiarity inside the walls of the manor but it was difficult to chal-lenge a man who held the gift of part of his own living in his hand, and that in coronation year, so all he said to Paul on leaving was, "Well, don't let 'em drink too much, Craddock! If you do you'll regret it for there's no holding one of 'em once they're well liquored!" The admonition annoyed Claire who said, tartly, "That's rich, coming from him, a sponge in a dog-collar!", and she flounced off to confer with Mrs. Handcock on the supper relays.

Paul, primed in advance, chose a fresh partner every time and steadily worked his way through a rota of Mrs. Codsall, who was in rare good humour, Rose Derwent, who found it difficult to allow herself to be led after breaking so many horses, Meg Potter, the stern-faced gypsy, who marched round the room like a Hanoverian Grenadier, and the shy, eager Elinor Willoughby, who blushed scarlet when he took her hand, and mumbled replies to all his polite remarks. After that he joined Eph Morgan's set for the Lancers, and when it was over, perspiring from his enormous exertions, he sought out Claire and dragged her on to the floor for the Military One-Step. "I've earned more than this tame dance," he said, swinging her round in a final flourish and she replied, breathlessly. "We're not going home yet, are we?" and he left her to announce that, after the statue dance (which carried a prize), there would be first supper for those who were not remaining until morning and after that fireworks in the paddock, and finally a second supper for the bitter-enders. There was a good deal of ooing and aahing at this, and when the orchestra climbed down about forty of the middle-aged guests pushed their way into the hall, where a buffet supper was laid for them on trestle tables reaching from the hall door to the porch. After a hasty swig of lemonade the tireless trio returned to play supper music but the piano and fiddles were soon swamped in the roar of conversation and the rattle and clash of plates, cups, spoons and forks.

Mrs. Arabella Codsall was holding court below the big fireplace. Words flowed from her with her usual spontaneity but her tone was comparatively honeyed for her subject was the new Squire, and she wanted it known that, so far, she wholly approved of him and all his works. There were some present, she qualified, that Mr. Craddock might well have overlooked when compiling the invitation list. Nobody, for instance, would have missed that scoundrel Potter and his draggle-tailed brood but she supposed that dear King Edward, God bless him, had been called to rule over even such as these and she was ready to forgive a new man's difficulty in assessing the Potters and the Willoughbys for what they were. Martin Codsall, much embarrassed, whispered, "Shush, Mother!" but as Arabella's audience consisted of Martha Pitts, and the din was so great that even she heard less than half the words uttered, the warning was unnecessary.

Arabella Codsall's good humour was due, in the main, to the absence of her errant son Will but had she been privileged to see round corners it is doubtful whether any amount of cider cup would have prevented a shift in the wind. At that moment Will Codsall and Elinor Willoughby were face to face in the shadow of a stone buttress on the east wing, as far as they could get from the ballroom without breaking cover, and Elinor was having some difficulty in preventing a scene that would have anticipated the promised fireworks display.

"Dornee, think I'd *like* 'ee to cum inzide, an' 'ave 'ee swing me round, Will?" she said earnestly, "but where's the zense in it? Your mother'll up an' leave an' new Squire will want to know why, and where will us be then?"

"Dammit woman, she knows I'm livin' over your plaace, don' 'er?" demanded Will. "Us 'ave made sure us can't get married 'til January, when I'm twenty-one, unless us goes to court and if us does that the whole Valley'll know anyways!"

"I daresay," Elinor said shrewdly, "but let 'em get to know in dribs and drabs, not all at once with us bang in the middle of it! No, Will, us've talked it over with father, and he's promised to marry us in chapel on your birthday, so do 'ee let well alone an' go along home to baid, like you promised me!"

The distant music, and the softness of her body under the little gingham dress she wore, tested his resolution but he abandoned his protests and kissed her almost reverently on both eyes and the tip of her nose. Then, with a desolate, "Oh, Will . . . !", she left him but he did not return home, as he had promised. Instead he continued to skulk within earshot of the party, scowling at the rustlings and gigglings that emerged from the rhododendron walk where Pansy Potter was sporting with a young fisherman from Coombe Bay—"Having her turn"—as she put it, for the

Potter girls, although enjoying far more personal freedom than any of their contemporaries, realised that Tamer would disapprove of a family exodus from the ballroom and had agreed to take the air one at a time. Violet and Cissie were now back in the house and Pansy would be returning shortly in order to let Cissie take another stroll, perhaps with the same young man. The Potter girls were practical Communists. They shared men much as they shared rabbit pie, helping themselves to wedges whenever they felt like it.

As it happened Tamer had not missed them. He was in the yard with Sam, enjoying real beer from his own cask that he had brought along in the cart and offloaded into an outhouse. Tamer distrusted other people's liquor and on occasions such as this liked to top off every now and again with a brew on which he could rely. He was also glad of the opportunity to have a chat with Sam, always his favourite, and father and son were discoursing on the local changes that had been wrought since the end of the summer drought.

"Be'm proper mazed do 'ee think, Sam?" Tamer asked, nodding towards the house. "Is 'er goin' to keep this up, or will us vind us all have to pay for it, bimeby?" He found it difficult to believe that benevolence, on the scale practised by new Squire, could endure unless it was buttressed by an increase of rents all round but Sam reassured him. "Dornee worry about Mr. Craddock, Father! He's got religion, I reckon, on'y it don't show like it do in looneys like ol' Willoughby, who won't part with a bushel of maize unless voum prepared to pay in prayers an' hymns! No, he's different, for he don't want nothin' back for it, if you get my meaning! Think on this now—he rides up to my cottage a week ago and asks after Joannie, saying our tacker will be the first born to a tenant zince he took over. Brought along a bag o' seed for the patch and told her she was to have all the milk an' eggs she liked from the Home Farm, until we was zettled in, and had goats an' vowls set up at the back! Now could a man zay fairer than that? And him a gentleman, already paying for the roof over our heads?"

"No," said Tamer, impressed but not wholly convinced,

158

"I don't reckon he could, but to be on the zafe zide you'd best ask him to stand in as godfather when Joannie's nipper shows up! That way mebbe you'll get free milk an' eggs for the rest of your life!"

Sam nodded, admiring his father's far-sightedness. "Reckon I'll do that, Father," he said, "and now me an' Joannie had best get back along. Us can't bump along over they ol' tracks, with her zo near her time," and he carried Tamer's cask back to the outhouse and camouflaged it with straw.

Meg Potter sat with her back against the cue-rack, under the spot where Hazel squatted on her pedestal. Her expression was inscrutable, so that it was difficult to tell whether or not she was enjoying the spectacle of the dancers or despising their enthusiasm for the polka. The tactics of her elder daughters to mask their constant comings and goings had not fooled her for a moment but she was not concerned with their reputations or whether their repeated disappearances into the shrubberies resulted, nine months hence, in the appearance of yet another mouth to feed in the Dell. She took an extraordinarily broad view of life, all life, not simply that part of it prescribed by changing codes of social behaviour, for although she had left her tribe at sixteen to settle as the wife of a squatter, she was still very much a gypsy, with a gypsy's contempt for settled living. As long as the girls provided enough pence for necessities it was all she asked of them, or of her husband and sons. She was loyal to their clan but she did not love or respect them as individuals. All her respect was reserved for her second son Smut, who alone had inherited the spirit of her ancestors and was ready to challenge authority in every form and remain wholly free, not partially so, like her husband and the others. Smut had always been the exception. He looked like a gypsy, with his crow-black hair, swarthy complexion, and his curious, bouncy walk, as though wherever he trod he anticipated the snap of a mantrap. Mantraps were against the law now or so they said but Meg didn't believe it. A man like Lord Gilroy probably sowed them in his coverts just as he was known to have issued orders to his keepers to shoot poachers on

159

sight, but these hazards did not keep Meg awake at night, when Smut was out across the Teazel. She had faith in his skill and speed, in his ability to hear and interpret any movement in any patch of undergrowth and judge the thickness of shadows, and the distance of sounds. Smut could smell a Gilroy keeper at seventy yards, and move over the ground at night faster than any fox and almost as silently. So she sat erect, watching her favourite child casting his spell over Margy Voysey, the Coombe Bay butcher's daughter, reflecting that he was a rare boy for his work, for even on a gala night such as this his mind was on his markets. She wondered if Smut would ever marry and decided that if he did he might do worse than pick someone like Margy, who could at least provide a legitimate outlet for his game. She watched him take the dumpy butcher's daughter by the hand and lead her gallantly on to the floor, and then she fell to a contemplation of ballroom dancing in general. It was not really dancing at all, she decided, just a sweaty clasping and a prancing about, like a lot of fox cubs at play. She could remember real dancing, in the light of pine torches and great, blazing fires, on the occasion of gypsy weddings long ago and for a moment she regretted the passage of the years. Then Smut and his partner swept by and her eyes glowed with pride; Smut was worth all the hard work and loss of freedom of the last two decades.

Claire Derwent carried her glass of lemonade to a corner of the backstairs where she could remain detached from the throng but stay within reach of it. She wanted a few moments alone in order to savour her triumph, for it was clear by now that the party—*her* party as she thought of it—was a triumph. She had been worried by its sluggish start, assured that an anticlimax would dowse her in ignominy, and undo all the good work that had been achieved since the moment of her inspiration three weeks ago. But there was nothing to worry about now; Paul was launched as Lord of the Valley and it was she who had, so to speak, broken the champagne bottle. Every day since he had answered her letter she had been growing more indispensable to him and now it was obviously a pleasure to him to seek her advice. She was equally sure that she was deeply in love with him, there could be no doubt as regards that, either. Of all people in the Sorrel Valley she alone understood his potential, and luck, encouraged by her initiative, had chosen her as his impresario, so she sat on, enjoying her moment of solitude and wondering if he would come seeking her during the supper interval. Fireworks were due in twenty minutes so perhaps he could then spare a few minutes from his obligations as host to stand close to her in the dark, watching the first rockets soar over the avenue chestnuts.

Paul did not appear but her sister Rose found her, elbows on knees and glass in hand, and because there was a deep affection between them Rose recognised the satisfaction in Claire's eyes, saying generously, "It really *is* a success, Claire! Everybody says so, even Father!" and then, cautiously, "I *do* hope Mr. Craddock appreciates all you've done! I don't suppose you've had time to talk to one another tonight."

"We had one dance," Claire said, so dreamily that Rose laughed, "I expect he'll stand with me to watch the fireworks. Do you think you can get Father and Liz to leave soon? After all, you'll be staying, so he oughtn't to mind, with so many people about the house,"

"Oh, he's on your side all right," Rose said, and then, fearful of probing too deeply, "Has . . . has he *said* anything, Claire? After all, you've been over here a great deal lately."

This time it was Claire who laughed. "Oh, there's always been somebody else around for a party this size doesn't organise itself! No, he hasn't actually said anything but does he have to? I mean, at this stage?"

"I'm afraid I wouldn't know," said Rose and Claire, because she was feeling more elated and secure than she ever remembered, threw her arms round her sister's neck and kissed her, exclaiming, "Dear Rose! I'm so lucky to have you! And someone will show up for you, just see if he doesn't! I'll tell you what, if—when—anything does happen, I'll persuade Paul to fill the house with chunky, hard-riding, sporty men, the kind who always have taken more notice of you than me. We'll select our victim and stalk him and he won't stand an earthly against three of us!"

"Oh rubbish!" said Rose, sincerely, "I'm quite content to stay single but you wouldn't be! I only hope Paul Craddock has the sense to appreciate you before somebody else grabs you! Come on, he'll be looking everywhere for you, and the fireworks are due to start any minute."

They went downstairs hand in hand and met Paul coming up. Claire shouted, "Paul dear!" but Rose, perhaps because she had ridden so many half-broken colts was immediately struck by the exuberance of his stride, so that a prick of uncertainty punctuated her serenity. His expression was old too; the tolerant might have called it radiant, the more sophisticated fatuous. He said, without any attempt to conceal his excitement, "They've arrived! They're *here!*", and when Rose asked who had arrived he caught Claire by the hand and said, "The Lovells! Grace and her stepmother! They're downstairs drinking hot cocoa! They drove over in an open gig!", but by now Claire's serene expression had clouded and the shock was considerable as she read into his voice and manner a great deal more than Rose. She withdrew her hand from his and said quietly, "I'm sorry! We've run out of glasses Paul!" and scuttled away, running back upstairs and down the corridor, as though making for the room they had converted into an extra cloakroom. He looked after her so blankly that Rose, in a sudden rage, wanted to strike him across the face. His insensitivity maddened her and she could have cheerfully flung him down the stairs. Instead she excused herself and hurried after Claire, so that he thought, briefly, "They've had a tiff over something," and went downstairs again, joining the group standing round the open fire, listening respectfully to Celia Lovell's praise of the decorations.

III

He never discovered how close Grace and Celia came to not making an appearance at all. Two of his tenants could have told him as much but neither of these was actually present when the Lovell gig stopped in the forecourt

162

and Paul, warned by Mrs. Codsall, came running to help them down, direct the driver round to the yard and ask Mrs. Handcock for hot drinks for the late arrivals.

The first person to see the Lovell gig *en route* was Edward Willoughby, who was walking along the river road on his way from Deepdene. Willoughby had politely declined his invitation, for he disapproved of strong drink and also, although to a somewhat lesser degree, of dancing and non-sacred music. But there was nothing in the Bible against fireworks so he let his daughter Elinor persuade him to walk over in time to see the display. It was a fine clear night and he enjoyed his walk, seeing no one until he emerged from the Coombe track and joined the river road, where it ran towards the ford. It was here, under a mile from Shallowford, that the Lovells overtook him and then, to his surprise the gig pulled up a hundred yards further on and made as if to turn.

Will Codsall saw it about the same time from the far side of the ford, where he was enjoying his sulk while awaiting the fireworks and the seeming indecision of the driver puzzled him. He stood in the shadow of the gate, watching, and the murmur of women's voices raised in argument reached him.

The gig had stopped because Grace Lovell had called over the rail to the hired driver and then Celia had countermanded the order, and Grace had repeated hers, so that the man swore softly under his breath and halted while they made up their minds which way they wanted to go. Both women found it embarrassing to state their case in the presence of a part-time coachman but there was no alternative, short of getting out and continuing the dispute on foot.

"Grace, please don't be so tiresome!" Celia hissed, "we're almost there, and we've simply got to go! We told Mr. Craddock we should attend and it would be extremely rude of us not to at this stage, do you hear?"

Grace said nothing, being more inhibited by the coachman's presence than was Celia, so that after a moment, with a cautionary nudge of the kind administered to a wilful child, Celia told the driver to get started again, and the gig rattled over the ford and began to breast the slope of

163

the drive. Neither passenger spoke another word until Paul greeted them at the forecourt and then Celia, an expert social liar, said sweetly, "We do apologise for arriving so late, Mr. Craddock! We had the *greatest* difficulty hiring transport," and Paul said, handing her down, "I'm delighted you got here in time for the fireworks but you must be cold! Let Mrs. Handcock get you hot drinks!"

They went into the hall, where their appearance caused a little stir among the supper guests, for apart from Parson Bull quality had been noticeably absent from the ball. Mrs. Codsall bridled, and dropped half a curtsy, while all the younger women stared enviously at Grace Lovell's gown, a many flounced affair of scarlet silk that whispered as she walked across to the fire and spread her hands to the blaze.

"Oh, but she's beautiful!" Elinor Willoughby said to Pansy Potter, who was gaping at the late arrivals and Pansy, her big red hands smoothing the serge of her stained, grey frock, murmured, "Ah, 'er is an' all! Like a princess, an' Mrs. Lovell along of 'er," which expressed, fairly adequately, the opinion of every woman present who watched their entry.

The Shallowford House firework display began with a single rocket that soared over the chestnuts and fell, a far-off ember, on the Home Farm stubble three parts of a mile away. It ended with a large and rather smudgy set-piece of Queen Alexandra, Claire having been told by the dealer in Paxtonbury that all the set-pieces of the royal pair had been sold out long ago.

Between the rocket and the set-piece some thirty-five minutes elapsed, a split second in eternity and only about a sixteenth of the time spent by most guests at Shallowford that night, yet this was enough to mould the destinies of fourteen men and women who stood among the hundred and twenty spectators.

Out here in the open, with the undersides of the chestnut leaves exposed in the lurid glow of Roman candles and the dark mass of Shallowford Woods rising behind the rose garden, the company seemed small and subdued. In the house there had been barely room enough to hold them and they had drawn courage from one another, performing prodigies of chaff and buffoonery, but out here they were awed and hushed, because the harsh glare of an exploding firework is not natural light, like that of sun, moon, or even lamp oil but has a talismanic quality that can betray the future to those who follow its path across the sky and watch it die. There were some who neglected to do this on the night of the Shallowford soirée, in late September, 1902, and each of them paid forfeit. It was not, after all, a very spectacular firework display, so perhaps its yield in heart's-ease or heartbreak was out of proportion to the ten pounds Claire had paid for the rockets, Roman candles and rip-raps, but fireworks are unpredictable. They did their work and burned themselves out; what happened as a direct result of those on the ground was no concern of the men who made and sold them.

Perhaps the golden rain had the most to answer for in emotional by-products. Horace Handcock, cannoneer extraordinary, had planted a row of six to follow the initial discharge of his battery of sixpenny rockets and cries of delight greeted the first shower of green and crimson balls, erupting over the chestnuts and hanging suspended for a moment before drifting down and out of sight behind the trees. In the light of the shower of green balls Smut Potter made up his mind to remain a bachelor, while Walt Pascoe, a Coombe Bay bricklayer whose body and brain had been thrown in a ferment by the Potter sisters, made his choice, but these were only the results of the first discharge. As the second shower burst Edward Derwent came close to breaking his wife's heart, whereas Paul Craddock had a clear thirty seconds to study Grace Lovell's profile, not long but long enough to fall so madly in love with it that there was no hope of disguising the fact from anyone, certainly not Derwent or his daughter Claire, both of whom were watching Paul intently. At the third discharge, when both crimson and balls shot up and floated down, Mrs. Codsall saw the spare figure of Preacher Willoughby on the far side of the little square, and beside him, arms linked, her son Will and Willoughby's daughter, Elinor. She waited until the fourth discharge to make quite sure and then, with a squeal of rage, thumped Martin Codsall between the shoulders and roared, "So he's here after all! Look over *there!*" and Martin, following in the direction of her stabbing finger, caught a glimpse of Will and Elinor as the last laggard ball drifted behind the trees.

Of these few only Smut acknowledged his debt to the fireworks at the time. He had emerged from the steamy ballroom half-disposed to invest in the future and supply himself at one stroke with a dullish wife and a helpful father-in-law. For some time now he had been improving his relationship with Tom Voysey, Margy's father, possibly the one father in the Valley who would welcome such a wastrel into his family. The Potters, notwithstanding hearty appetites, had rarely been able to eat all Smut brought home from the Gilroy and Shallowford coverts. Sometimes there was a glut in the Dell, so that Smut had sought an outlet for his spoils in Coombe Bay and Tom, of late, had been buying his poached game at about half its market value. Smut, however, did not really poach for money but mainly to keep the family fed, and also for the hell of it, so he was happy to dump hare, pheasant, trout, conies and even venison in Tom Voysey's scullery behind the shop and go home with a half-sovereign in his pocket, knowing full well that Voysey's profit at Whinmouth weekly market would approach four hundred per cent. It had occurred to him lately, however, that if he became Voysey's son-in-law, as well as Voysey's main source of supply, he might in time become rich enough to buy his mother the painted caravan she had always coveted and give his sisters shop dresses, and himself green velveteens, a moleskin waistcoat and perhaps a good gun into the bargain. He was not ambitious but he had a strong sense of family loyalty, and to demonstrate it was almost prepared to marry a girl with two heads. Margy Voysey had one head but it was large, seemingly almost round and crowned by a topknot of mouse-coloured hair. More hair sprouted from a large mole on her receding chin but, as if to compensate for this, she had no eyebrows and lack of them gave her a permanently surprised look, so that sometimes Smut thought that her decapitated head, set alongside those displayed in her father's window, would have fooled all but the keen-sighted. He had remarked on this several times but it had not impressed him, one way or the other. Margy was Tom Voysey's only child and what she looked like had not seemed to matter at all until those revealing green balls in the sky exposed her face at close quarters. He made up his mind on the spot; Meg must continue to inhabit the leaking farmhouse, and the girls continue to wear rags, until he could hit on an alternative solution to comfort them. The gun he possessed was good enough for another season, and he would remain content with Voysey's half-sovereign. There were premiums that were too stiff for an insured future and marriage to a greenish-tinted pig's head was one of them. Mumbling, "Just thought o' something I got to do, Margy," he relinquished her hand, dodged out of the crowd and vanished into the starry night.

Edward Derwent had been his crusty, pessimistic self when he arrived at Shallowford that evening. Rose, his daughter, and Liz, his twittering second wife, had done their best to persuade him that something momentous was happening—that Claire's capture of a real live Squire was imminent but he refused to believe that anything so fortuitous could happen to him, a man who had seen the wife he worshipped lifted from a ditch with a broken neck. Even as a young man he had never been sanguine about life and it had taken him years to accept the fact that Molly Rodgers had married him, a penniless smallholder, and borne him children. When Molly was killed, early in the first run of the 1890 season, he had been overwhelmed but not surprised. Something of this nature had surely been lying in wait for him for years, and the only aspect of the tragedy that did surprise him was that it had taken some ten years to catch up with him.

He got over it in time and his doubting nature had helped, as had his capacity for long days of monotonous toil in the fields but when the shadow of his wife's death had passed another took its place. Buried down here, with no more than two hundred acres, he decided that it was hopeless to try and build a really prosperous farm to dower his two daughters and it worried him to contemplate what would become of them when he died. Rose, he imagined, could make some sort of a living out of her liveries but Claire, although a fair horsewoman, had no real flair for farming or the rearing of livestock and unless she married well who would provide for her? It was useless to tell him, as Rose often did, that Claire was even prettier than her mother, and that the odds against her becoming an old maid were about ten thousand to one. Derwent only countered by saying that, in this depopulated little backwater, there was no man Claire was likely to want to marry and who, so far, had come courting either one of them? So, in the main, he ignored their silly tittle-tattle claiming that Claire's constant attendance at the manor was a sure sign the new Squire was taken up with her; he did not believe it, it was far too good to be true.

Then, with his own eyes and ears, he had seen and heard acknowledgements of his daughter's influence at the big house, for as tenants arrived to pay their respects to the young man, Derwent noticed that he redirected their compliments to Claire and even received guests with his arm resting on her shoulder, and this evidence was reinforced by Craddock's cheerful, "Well, Mr. Derwent, my thanks for the loan of your daughter! Everything you see is her work, all I've done is carry out her orders, isn't that a fact, Rose?" And Rose had loyally agreed that the whole idea had been Claire's, after which Claire bustled away to introduce Squire to latecomers, for all the world as though she was already mistress of Shallowford.

Derwent was a slow-thinking man and continued thinking to some purpose, until past midnight, when everyone trooped into the paddock to watch the fireworks, and his thoughts, for once, were heart-warming, so that he sensed the spread of a satisfied glow deep in his belly that was not wholly due to rum punch and at length his rare feeling of well-being demanded physical expression. Hesitantly, as a man unpractised in familiarities, his arm stole round the waist of his wife Liz and he pressed her to him so that she almost cried out with astonishment and delight for it was the first public acknowledgement he had made of her in five years of marriage, the first acknowledgement at all discounting his lusty embraces in bed. She thought, for a moment, that he must be far gone in drink, and then she was ashamed of the thought, reasoning that perhaps she had misjudged him after all and perhaps the glorious conviviality of the occasion had wrought a miracle in him. She revelled in this illusion for two minutes and then Handcock discharged another shower of green and crimson balls, and the glare lit up the paddock like a searchlight, so that everyone there might have been standing under strong lamplight, and this was the biggest betrayal of all, for it showed both Claire and her father the face of Paul Craddock, who was looking down on Grace Lovell, standing close beside him. In that moment father and daughter conceded complete and utter defeat.

IV

Claire had been coaxed from the cloakroom by Rose and they had gone out into the paddock as the first rocket soared; she saw Paul standing in the angle of the box hedge, talking to Mrs. Lovell, and at once made up her mind to edge round towards them during an interval of darkness, but unluckily, before the rocket dipped, her father saw her and called, "Well, Claire, this is a rare night for Shallowford! The Lovells never came up with anything of this kind at either of the Jubilees!" and his voice was so jovial that she hesitated in spite of herself, puzzled by his rare amiability and pondering its source. Then, as the golden rain went up, she noticed that he had his arm round Liz's waist, and in the light of the rockets they both looked so spoony that Claire's spirits lifted and she wanted to laugh but did not for it pleased her to see them standing like lovers, with faces turned to the sky. She kept her mind on Paul, however, and when the volley of golden rain erupted she looked quickly in his direction and then wished very much that she hadn't, for he was still there, no more than ten yards away but was no longer talking to Mrs. Lovell. He was looking directly down at Grace Lovell and his expression was even more fatuously captive than that of poor Liz, and as Claire stared, almost choking with humiliation and dismay, Grace Lovell's chin tilted so that she seemed to be returning his rapturous gaze and for several seconds, as the glare in the sky faded, they continued to look into one another's eyes at a range of no more than twenty inches. As soon as it was dark again she fled, pulling back from the enclosure so quickly that Rose called, "What is it, Claire?" but she could not talk, even to Rose, hurrying back to her seat on the backstairs with tears of disappointment streaming down her cheeks and a throat so dry and constricted that she could hardly get her breath. She sat here alone for the remainder of the display, oblivious of the winking flashes of reflected light, and the thunder and crackle of explosions over the paddock.

Derwent had not missed the exchange of looks between Paul and Grace, and it brought him up with a severe jolt. He knew then, and instantly, that his original estimate of this affair had been more accurate than the family's and that Paul Craddock, for all their prattle, was not the least bit interested in his daughter, except perhaps in the way a lazy curate courts an earnest spinster who rushes to arrange flowers in the church, and polish the brasswork of the altar rails. It was all a lot of damned nonsense, he decided, dreamed up by silly womenfolk in their idle moments, and as the certainty of this laid hold on him he suddenly felt enraged with himself for being so gullible. He loosed hold of his wife, Liz, so abruptly that she staggered, and thrust both hands into his breeches pockets, as though to make sure he would never again surrender to a sentimental impulse. Fireworks continued to explode all around but he paid no attention to them. He was too busy assuring himself that he must take immediate steps to prevent his daughter being further exploited. "Damn the fellow!" he muttered. "Who the devil does he think he is, keeping a girl of mine dancing attendance on him for the better part of a month, when she ought to have been at work in the dairy?" He wondered, briefly, if the association had progressed beyond the mutual hanging up of a few paper chains and evergreen sprigs but decided this was unlikely. Surely a daughter of his would have more pride than to let a callow townee make a real fool of her.

170

He looked round as though to assure himself of the fact but Claire was not to be seen, so he switched his thoughts to the only source of comfort that presented itself—the prospect of persuading Craddock by any means, fair or outrageously foul, to sell High Coombe and thus make the Derwents independent of young men with too much money who came prancing down here to play at being farmers.

The flash that had sent Claire back to the house, revived her father's habitual pessimism and put a term to his wife's illusions, went flickering down the years to the end of time. Claire had gone, having seen enough, and Smut Potter had gone, having seen more than enough; Arabella Codsall was to leave as soon as she could tear herself from the engaging spectacle of a smouldering Queen Alexandra, and Paul Craddock, adrift on a sea of romantic speculation, was not thinking of fireworks any more. One golden rain beneficiary remained until the final discharge and this was Walt Pascoe, the bricklayer who had, that same night, spent fifteen minutes in the rhododendrons with Violet Potter, and about the same time with her sister, Pansy. He had not had an opportunity to sample Cissie, the third Potter girl, for Cissie was being squired by Bert Tidmarsh, a close friend of Walt's who was known to be very handy with his fists. This, as it turned out, was fortunate, for if Cissie had been added to Walt's immediate worries his problem might have proved insoluble.

The trouble was all three were as alike as peas in a pod and not only in appearance but in speech, gait and even courting technique. They both giggled and wriggled when he passed his hands over them and they both said "Dornee, Walt!" when he was quite certain they would have been very indignant if he had heeded their protests, for this was by no means his first brush with them. On several previous occasions he had skylarked with the Potter girls in coppice and hayfield, but that, he reflected sadly, was before his mother died, when he had every intention of remaining single. Tonight things had changed and he looked into a cheerless future, one of preparing his own meals before he went to work, and again when he returned, of making his own bed and keeping the cottage clean, of doing his own mending and firelighting and hearth-sweeping and generally leading the devil of a life as a bachelor. He had buried his mother in June and the loneliness of the cottage was getting on his nerves, especially at night. He had made up his mind that, sooner or later, he would have to share his life with someone, for he was a very amiable young man with a lively sense of humour but although, at first sight, it seemed that Violet would make him just as comfortable as Pansy, or vice versa, he was reluctant to make a hasty decision on a matter as final as marriage. Every time a rocket exploded he compared their upturned faces, noting their cheerful snub noses, their freckles, their thick chestnut hair and their strong, white teeth, and as he wrestled with his problem he did a sort of double-entry balance sheet of their merits and demerits, in so far as he was able on the strength of samples taken that evening. Violet, he noted, had drenched herself in some kind of rosewater scent, certainly home-made scent, and whilst it was pleasant and provocative it suggested that she might have something to hide. On the other hand Pansy used no scent, or none he could detect, but she had been slightly less accommodating than her sister in the rhododendrons whereas her sister Violet had surrendered to his embrace with apparent eagerness. On the other hand perhaps this was unfair, for he had sampled Violet first and now that he thought about it Pansy had proved harder to win, which surely implied superior virtue on her part. He was still undecided when the last Roman candle burned itself out and the darkness was only moderated by the glow of the set-piece. Then, with one sister on either side of him, Pansy made up his mind for him, almost as if she was guiding him towards the best prize in a lucky dip. Her hand moved up until it lay on his shoulder and then, as though caressing a cat, it moved slowly across his chest and down to his loins, a gesture that indicated two certainties. She had found him pleasing and had the kind of need for him that a man who worked hard all day and brought home regular money on Saturday ought to look for when choosing a wife.

The caress was casual and probably absent-minded yet it made him tingle from head to foot for it was as though she regarded him as a prize bull that had just been awarded the county accolade and he was ready to burst with manly pride. He said, hoarsely, "Come over yer, Panse! I got zummat to zay to 'ee midear!", and they withdrew from the enclosure just as Queen Alexandra's right eye went out in a spiral of smoke and a long, satisfied, "Ahhh!" rose from the spectators.

It would be untrue to say that Paul Craddock's mind did not return to Claire Derwent this night, or that he spent every moment of the next few hours in a cloud. He continued to go through the motions of host to a shrinking company but he would have found it hard to say with any accuracy who had left and who had remained for the dawn stirrup cup. He danced with Grace twice, one waltz and one polka, but they exchanged little conversation, a few conventional remarks from him about the way people of the Sorrel Valley had received him, a comment from her praising his initiative and the prodigality of his hospitality but even then he did not think directly of Claire. It was much later, about three o'clock in the morning, that he wondered vaguely whether it was time to serve more ices, and learning that Mrs. Handcock had gone to bed, excused himself, went in search of Claire and was rather puzzled at not finding her or any member of her family.

There were then about thirty of the younger guests on the floor, the girls still full or zest but the men a little unsteady with all the refreshment they had taken between dances. The heroic orchestra was flagging but it continued to play, the twins, Matt and Luke, standing one on each side of Mary Willoughby, who had been relieved from time to time by Crisp, the Coombe Bay organist. Unable to find any of the Derwents, Paul went into the yard to see if their waggonette had gone and here he ran into Gregory, the High Coombe foreman, supping the dregs of Tamer Potter's cask in the outhouse. Gregory was drunk and Paul had to shake him before he could get any sense out of the fellow.

"Where is Mr. Derwent and his family?" he shouted in Gregory's ear. "When did they leave?" The man, recognising the Squire, made a supreme effort to collect his wits.

"They'm gone off 'ome, Mr. Craddock, long zince!" he

mumbled, shaking his head violently in an effort to stop the roaring in his ears.

Paul thought it odd that they had left without saying good-bye, for he had understood both Rose and Claire were staying the night to help clear up in the morning but it occurred to him that Derwent might have objected to them staying so he returned to the ballroom and whilst Grace was dancing with Crisp, the organist, he sat out with Celia, eating an ice-cream. Mrs. Lovell was very gracious, saying that she and Grace much appreciated being invited and adding that dear Edward would certainly make a splendid King and keep the Kaiser in his place. She went on to say that she hoped he would be very happy at Shallowford and that she, for her part, was gratified that the estate had been bought by someone young, for under the Lovells it had been the resort of dull, middle-aged gentlemen, and had never had much to offer the young people in the district. "I have often thought," she said, laying an elegant gloved hand on his arm, "that this could be a happy house, full of noise and laughter and people who really cared for the land, and the families living on it," to which Paul, much encouraged, replied that he agreed whole-heartedly but was already finding his lack of experience a handicap. "There's John Rudd, of course," he admitted, "but a man ought not to put himself entirely in the hands of an agent, should he?"

"I should think not, indeed," Celia replied with an expert flutter of her fan, as though to shoo John Rudd from the place where important decisions were made, "but I should be flattered if you felt free to ask my advice about anything—well, anything social, you understand? After all, I grew up on a country estate—a much larger one of course but administered along the same lines and I believe I could be of service to you from time to time. We rejoin my husband in London the day after tomorrow, but we shall be back again shortly."

"I'm very obliged for the offer, Mrs. Lovell," Paul said, sincerely, "and I shall certainly take advantage of it."

"Well then, that's settled," she said, with a maternal smile and Paul thought how very gracious she was and what a pity it was she was the wife of a rake like Bruce

Lovell, rumoured throughout the Valley "to have led 'er a praper ole dance".

Grace returned to them then, her smooth, pale cheeks flushed with the heat and exercise and Mr. Crisp, the organist, bowed himself out, after she had declined his offer to bring her an ice.

"I've been telling Mr. Craddock that he is very welcome to seek our advice about Shallowford, my dear," Celia said and Grace murmured, "He seems to be managing very well on his own, Mother!" after which she remained silent but although Paul observed that her foot tapped to the rhythm of the music and asked her if she would care to dance again, she said, "No thank you, Mr. Craddock," without looking at him but then, to his delight she added, "It's very stuffy in here! Could we take a breath of air, do you think?", and Paul leaped to his feet, expecting Celia to reach for her shawl for he could not believe that so formal a person would countenance an unchaperoned walk on the terrace at three in the morning. She made no movement, however, but smiled saying, "I haven't thawed out after watching the fireworks. Please take her on the terrace Mr. Craddock, but see that you have your cape, Grace dear!", and they passed through the hall to the terrace, turning left along the walk under the library windows.

It was a mild night for late September and a very still one now that the roar from the house had been greatly reduced in volume. The starlight was brilliant and they could make out the blur of Shallowford Woods but the glimpse stirred in him no memory of Claire. As she stopped where the terrace ended at the steps he said, "I'm very glad you were able to come, Miss Lovell. I was talking to your stepmother and she seems very pleased I've taken over here."

The girl turned, so quickly and so unexpectedly that she seemed almost to spin round and he saw, in the light shed by the library lamps, that her face had the same look of exasperation as on the occasion they first met.

"Of course she's pleased," she said sharply, "and why not? She sees you as a quite unexpected means of getting me off her hands. Surely you must have realised that by now?"

175

Her candour made him gasp but for all that he was no longer intimidated by her for it occurred to him that her attitude offered a short cut to a courtship that had promised to be tedious.

He said, "Very well, Miss Lovell, I'll accept that, but if you can say precisely what's on your mind whenever we meet I ought to have the same freedom. If you aren't prepared to grant it we'll go inside at once!" and he waited, watching her consider the challenge. She met it with the same disconcerting frankness.

"I really don't know why I have to behave this way with you," she said. "Manners aren't my strongest point but they really aren't as bad as they must appear to you. I suppose it's because, while I can't help admiring your enterprise and honesty, it makes me very angry to see people like Celia exploiting it. So here comes one more apology! You get one every time we meet."

"I'm not looking for your apologies," he said. "I'd far sooner say what's in *my* mind for a change. It might upset you, but it would save both of us a good deal of sparring and the rest of the Valley a great deal of speculations!"

Her rather bothered expression gave place to curiosity so that she looked at him sharply from under her brows, like a sleek little spaniel uncertain of whether a pat or a cuff was coming her way.

"All right, Mr. Craddock," she said, at length, "you can be as blunt as you like, and afterwards I'll tell Celia I'm tired and we'll all go home to bed!"

He did not feel much like laughing but he almost laughed at this. It was an aspect of her he had not suspected and somehow made her seem about fourteen.

"Then to be absolutely honest I'm rather flattered by what you say was in Mrs. Lovell's mind and also by her going out of her way to let me know she approves of me! I've only got your word for it, mind you, but I hope it is so all the same."

"That's odd," she said. "If I were a man in your place I should find it very degrading!"

"Well I don't," he said, "and I think I've got a good enough reason. After all, you came close to being the wife of the Squire so why should canvassing his successor seem so outrageous?"

She was smiling now and obviously had herself well in hand.

"You're a very extraordinary person, Mr. Craddock! You appear straightforward, sometimes almost naïve, but you aren't really! In fact, you're a far more complicated person than you pretend to be!"

"Well," he replied, "that being so or not I'm still sufficiently broadminded not to resent local people like your stepmother trying their damnedest to marry me off! I suppose she regards it as her duty, like any other mamma, but I wouldn't like her to fall into the error of imagining I'm a substitute for a person like Ralph Lovell. I know absolutely nothing about the life or the needs of the people about here. I took this place on impulse so, without beating about the bush, I'll ask you on impulse to think seriously of your stepmother's intentions! I don't find them presumptuous or even embarrassing. As a matter of fact I find them exhilarating!"

He heard her catch her breath and the fact that she did not whip round on him, as he half-expected her to, gave him a moment to control the tension building inside him. Seeing that she made no kind of reply he went on, "I can say this not only because you obviously prefer candour but because I think I know rather more about you than you imagine, and I didn't learn it all from Valley gossip!"

She was standing with her back to him, her hands resting on the balustrade, seemingly neither astonished nor embarrassed by what he had said but considering it in a mood that was at once defensive and offensive.

"Whatever you know can't be much more than guess-work," she replied, at length. "People usually make guesses about me—it's all they can do. I'm an exceptionally private person!"

"Yes," he said, "you are but you can't hide everything. You can't hide the fact that you find your present life pointless and the future very uncertain. I have a special qualification for recognising that much about you!"

"And what qualification would that be?"

He hesitated. He was now so deeply committed that

prudence, politeness even, seemed a worthless currency between them. "All my life I've been a very lonely person. I suppose I should have remained one if I hadn't taken the plunge last June and staked everything I had on this place. Well, it was a gamble but it seems to me to have an even chance of coming off. Ever since my first evening here I've wanted very badly to talk to you like this but it didn't seem possible without going through the rigmarole of calling and leaving cards. The point is, we've been lucky and found a short cut, so why don't we use it? It isn't reasonable to expect you to back your instinct as heavily as I'm prepared to back mine but you could tell me now if you are prepared to consider marriage."

Suddenly he ran out of words, or words that did not sound fatuous. She faced him then, and he would not have been surprised if she had laughed in his face but she was not even smiling but looking at him with a kind of wonder.

"My father lives by and for gambling," she said, "but he would never gamble on odds of this kind. What makes you want to take such a chance with your life?"

What indeed, he thought, regarding the loveliness of her skin and then, as though it was transparent, he could see her vulnerability and it stirred in him the same kind of compassion as that roused by the sight of the urchin Ikey in the boneyard but far deeper, and far more compelling. Yet all he said was, "You have a special kind of beauty for me but it's not simply that. I honestly think I could make you happy. After all, you would have married Ralph Lovell without love, on his side or yours!"

"Neither one of us had anything to lose. Why should you risk your happiness, or whatever you think you might achieve, for someone who is—well, bad luck to everyone?"

"That's nonsense," he said calmly, "a person's luck is usually regulated by the amount of confidence they have in themselves."

"I doubt it," she said, "but even if it is so I've never had a very high opinion of myself, Paul. That doesn't mean, however, that I haven't been flattered by your proposal— if it is a proposal!", and suddenly she smiled her small, secret smile.

"It's a proposal," he said stubbornly. "All I'm asking is that you should think about it whilst you're away in London."

"I shall certainly do that," she said, emphatically, and then again, "Yes, I shall certainly do that! There'll be very little else to think about."

"When will you be back?"

"Some time before Christmas. Celia likes my father to hunt in December. He'd sooner back horses than ride them but Celia calls the tune in our ménage."

There seemed very little more to be said so he took her arm and led her back to the pool of light outside the main entrance.

"Then we'd best go in now," he said, "or Mrs. Lovell will be wondering what I've done with you."

"She could compose herself, whatever it was," Grace said lightly, and stopping at the porch, asked, "You said —'a special kind of beauty'?"

"Yes; for me."

She considered this gravely as though conceding that he might have a point. "And you never proposed to anyone before?"

"No," he said, laughing, "never, I'm afraid."

"Well," she said, "it was all very nicely managed," and as though rewarding an industrious little boy she placed her hands on his shoulders, stood on her toes and kissed his cheek, softly and swiftly. It was more of a salute than a kiss, something about half-way between mistletoe mischief and a benediction.

White light from beyond Coombe Bluff came stealing across the stubble field moving steadily west and north, as though unsure of what it might find in the paddocks separated by the line of chestnuts in the drive. It touched the charred stubs of Roman candles and the rocket sticks, still sagging beside the bamboos alongside the box hedge and then moved along the façade of the house. Everyone had gone. The ruts in the forecourt gravel were the only evidence that, an hour or so earlier, the diehards had wheeled and stamped here and shouted their hoarse goodbyes. Only one guest remained, Gregory, the Derwent foreman, who was sound asleep in the outhouse, beside Tamer Potter's empty beer cask. Ikey, and the gardener's boy Gappy Saunders, were snoring in their loft over the stable and even Walt Pascoe, now officially affianced to Pansy Potter, was walking home along the river road, congratulating himself on the final solution of his dilemma, for Pansy's final words to him, as they parted at the foot of the Dell ascent, had been, "I'll make 'ee comfortable, Walt! You can depend on it, midear!", which seemed to him as honest a pledge as had ever been made in the Valley.

The Derwents were asleep, all four of them, even Claire, worn out with weeping, and so were all the Willoughbys, with Elinor satisfied with Will's declaration, "Us'll see Squire about that freehold zoon us have slept on it!" Arabella Codsall had grumbled herself and Martin to sleep and Martha Pitts, who had returned home to the Hermitage after the fireworks, was already stirring in her sleep, as her fierce Plymouth Rock cockerel greeted dawn from the sty wall. Only one person was wide awake in the Valley and the wooded slopes enclosing it and he stood in the recessed window of the big Shallowford bedroom, in his shirt and dress trousers, looking south over the winding road that led across the ford to the Codsall fields, and the slender spire of Coombe Bay parish church. He was not thinking of the soirée as a whole but of its penultimate moment, when the Lovell gig had swept round the curve of the drive and Grace Lovell had looked back, lifting her hand as the fussy little equipage passed behind the line of chestnuts. There had been finality in the gesture, as though she had closed the first chapter of their association the moment of parting, but he was not uneasy, just tremulous and expectant. There would be other chapters, many of them and all, he reasoned, would have more conclusive endings.

The white light became whiter and stronger over the Coombe, until the grey line of Shallowford Woods turned to green and russet where autumn was already thinning the oaks beyond Hazel Potter's squirrel tree. Somewhere out there a single blackbird piped up and the Channel breeze, an unfailing escort for dawn in the Valley, came soughing over the stubble and shook down a dozen leaves from the red creeper underneath the window. Their soft undersides, Paul thought, were like the texture of her skin where it was taut under her small, pointed chin. It was a pleasant thought on which to draw the curtain. Before the breeze had lifted the last of the leaves from verge to terrace he too was asleep.

CHAPTER SEVEN

I

LOOKING back on the half year between his arrival at Sorrel Halt and his first Christmas at Shallowford, Paul came to view it as his probationary period, a first term at prep school. It had the same doubts and uncertainties, the same discoveries and testing strain on patience, fortitude and nerve. The coronation supper-dance was the climax but until then, until the moment of Grace Lovell's wave from the disappearing gig, he had been tutored every step of the way. Throughout the early weeks Rudd had been there to hold his hand and when Rudd went away there had been Claire Derwent making light of his cares of office. It was when the tumult of the soirée was done and rhythm was restored to the big house that he was aware of the loneliness of power, for Rudd wrote saying he had slipped down a companion ladder attending a sherry party aboard a frigate and had cracked two ribs, an injury likely to immobilise him for another month, and Claire Derwent had disappeared from his life abruptly and completely. He sent Ikey over to High Coombe with a second message (the first having gone unanswered) and learned that she had left home a day or so after the ball and was likely to be away some time. The note returned by Rose was noncommittal. It did not say where she had gone, or why, and its vagueness sent Paul grumbling to Mrs. Handcock, complaining that the hunting season was upon them and that he had looked forward to some good sport with Gilroy's Teazel and Sorrel Vale pack of hounds but everybody seemed to have decamped, Rudd to Portsmouth, Grace Lovell to London and Claire Derwent, who should have known better, to heaven knew where. Mrs. Handcock was sympathetic. "Ah, theym a rare trapsey ole lot, Mr. Craddock," she told him. "It warn't so in my young days. Us never stirred from the Vale, except mebbe to go once a year to Paxtonbury Market Fair or on a Sunday School treat, to Whinmouth. Now everyone rushes upalong and downalong to no purpose and if you ask me it all started wi' they pedally machines." Mrs. Handcock abominated the bicycle, refusing even to call it by its proper name for to her it signified the new era of restlessness in the Valley, promising an outcrop of reprehensible habits among the workshy, whom she said were multiplying with every local marriage. "No good'll come of 'em, mark my words, sir!" she would say, standing before him with hands on her enormous hips and sweat glistening on her forehead (for she was cook, as well as housekeeper at Shallowford). "No good'll be gleaned from they whizzing gurt things! A man's got two legs, baint 'ee, an' when theym too tired to carry un he's got four, waiting for un in the stable! Zo where be the reason fer a blight o' pedally machines about the plaace? Theym bad enough fer the men but the maids have taaken to riding 'em, showin' all they've got? I'd zee my daughter dade bevore I allowed her to zit 'er rump on one!"

This was a safe threat for, although Mrs. Handcock had been married for many years to the squat, bow-legged gardener, Horace, they were childless and she found consolation in a grotesque exaggerated respect for her spouse, to whom she ascribed mysterious oracular powers. Most of her opinions stemmed from Horace, who rarely declaimed in public but hoarded his gems until he could bestow them upon Mrs. Handcock, in the privacy of the housekeeper's two rooms in the east wing. Paul alleviated his loneliness during the autumn days encouraging Mrs. Handcock to recount some of her husband's gloomier prophecies and was thus regaled with all manner of terrifying forecasts upon subjects as diverse as Kaiser Wilhelm's navy, submarine warfare, the future of the House of Lords, Irish Home Rule, women's suffrage and, of course, the main threat to the social system, the pedally machine. He grew very fond of the stout, talkative old body and she spoiled him outrageously, the more so as Rudd, whom she revered almost as much as her husband, had been obliged to abandon him after such a brief apprenticeship.

During these days Paul began to take a more personal interest in his protegé, Ikey Palfrey, for he was impressed by the boy's willingness and also by his considerable powers of mimicry, and cockney sense of humour. Sometimes, when he was waiting for Snowdrop in the yard, he would encourage Ikey to vary his Devon and London dockside repertoire, with caricatures of Lord Gilroy, or Parson Bull, and even the solemn Chivers, who condemned ribaldry at the expense of the gentry. It struck him that Ikey Palfrey possessed unsuspected gifts of observation, and Paul wondered if the boy was not wasted in a provincial squire's stable, and would benefit from such education as the Vale could provide. Accordingly, a week or so after the ball, he sent him to Mary Willoughby's school and the result was a permanent alteration in Ikey's routine. In the mornings he rode the house cob over to Deepdene, and in the afternoons and evenings resumed his work in the tackroom. Paul thought that Chivers, the groom, would disapprove but Ikey's charm had already enlisted the goodwill of his superior and when, as upon hunting days, there was much to do, Chivers would rise an hour earlier and go to bed an hour later, in order to make sure that Ikey did not miss his schooling.

Ikey himself accepted the change reluctantly, considering himself finished with droning schoolmasters, free with the cane and the casual cuff, and now regarded himself a wage-earning adult but after a day or so under the mild Mary Willoughby he reversed this opinion and thereafter he went willingly, enjoying the morning canter over Coombe Bluff, and along the edge of Shallowford Woods. Mary instilled into him an interest in lyrical poetry, in geography and in military history and loaned him books to take home and read in the light of a lantern in his hay-loft. At first they were adventure books by authors like Ballantyne, Marryat and Henty but after she had loaned him *The Count of Monte Cristo* he became a very earnest reader and went on to tackle Dickens, Defoe and Scott, so that he could often be seen, to the astonishment of his loft-mate, Gappy Saunders, oiling saddles and polishing bits, with a book propped up in front of him on the tack-room table.

Until the third week in November, when hunting was in full swing, life was uneventful on the estate but towards the end of the month there was a flare-up in the smoulder-ing Codsall-Willoughby feud, which erupted with unpleas-ant suddenness one dismal morning when the Valley was draped in mist, and the ford ran high with the rush of streams draining into it from Blackberry Moor, Coombe Bluff and Priory Wood.

Paul was at work on his draft plan for the rebuilding of the Priory homestead, hoping to have the work in hand by the time Rudd came home, when Mrs. Handcock ushered a shuffling Will Codsall into the office, introducing him with a sense of outrage for she had told him Squire was busy but he had demanded his rights as a tenant. The young man was dripping wet, having walked over from Deepdene Farm without a coat and his heavy hobnailed boots left a trail of mud on the way through the kitchen and hall to the office. Paul saw that he was agitated and told Mrs. Handcock to bring in a towel, a day jacket and a mug of cocoa, and the housekeeper retired, muttering "Youm var too zoft with 'em!" but towel, jacket and cocoa soon arrived and when Will had drunk his cocoa and changed his coat he told Paul the reason for his urgency.

"Me'n Elinor Willoughby are getting wed come Satur-day, but tiz like there'll be a rare ole bust-up at chapel," he said. "I reckon Mother'll show up, shouting her objec-tions, and Mr. Willoughby, who'll be marryin' us, is in two minds whether to go through with it! Elinor, she's back at Deepdene, crying her eyes out, and me, well I reckon I bin druv too far and that's a fact, Squire!"

He then recounted the story of his mother's implacable opposition to the marriage, leading up to his dramatic exit from Four Winds, after smashing Arabella's cuckoo clock. To Paul, who had managed to steer clear of Arabella Codsall except for his first visit to Four Winds, it seemed no more than a storm in a teacup and after pointing out that until Will was twenty-one his mother had a legal right to oppose the marriage, he asked if the couple could postpone the wedding until he was of age.

"Ah, that's what I reckoned on doing," Will said glumly, "'til I had more'n I could stomach an' run out on her! But now us is in a right fix, for Deepdene won't keep another mouth through winter and I reckon on havin' to go abroad to find work. I can't take my Elinor along, unless us is man an' wife, an' 'er won't hear of me going backalong until I got me foot in a door somewhere!"

Paul had lived long enough in the Valley to differentiate between literal and local meanings of the word "abroad". To Will Codsall "abroad" meant anywhere outside a thirty-mile radius of Shallowford and to Elinor "backalong" was as final and desperate a removal as emigration overseas. Paul glanced at the plan of the Priory freehold lying on his desk and a solution at once suggested itself.

"Suppose I put you in the Priory freehold, Will?" he said. "Do you think you could make a go of it? It's no more than sixty acres, hardly enough to support a mixed farm like your father's, or even the Willoughby's but it would give you independence and I daresay you and Elinor could improve it."

The young man's eyes shone. "Well, sir, I had it in mind to come asking for that," he said joyfully, "but us heard you meant to lump it in with the Pitts' holding, at Hermitage."

"So I did," Paul admitted, "but the Pitts aren't greedy people, and yours is a special case. I'm planning to get Eph Morgan over there to rebuild the farmhouse and byres."

"Good God, Maister, you don't want to squander money like that!" Will told him. "Me an' my Elinor could do it ourselves, if us had the use of the Home Farm sawmill and a trifle for nails, cement and suchlike."

Paul was touched; it seemed to him a wonderful thing that, in this mechanical age, there were still young couples

185

eager to build homesteads with their own hands and Will's offer clinched the matter in his mind.

"Go there as soon as you've told Elinor," he said, "and then come back and tell me what you think you could do with the place. I'll write to the solicitors and get them to draw up a lease. The land is half derelict so I won't take a rent for the first four quarters. After that we'll fix a rental you can afford to pay."

Paul thought Will Codsall would have fallen on his knees and kissed his hand. His big ruddy face glowed and he seemed unable to decide what to do with his enormous hands, first clasping them, then chafing them, and finally stuffling them in his breeches pockets, as though to keep them from shaming him. Nothing would deter him from going out into the rain then and there, in order to hasten back to Deepdene to tell Elinor the good news so Paul let him borrow the cob, telling him to ride over to Priory and leave it in the yard on his way back. He also promised to see Honeyman at the Home Farm about timber and the use of the sawmill and then watched a jubilant Will take the short cut to the river across the small paddock, and disappear in a flurry of rain in the direction of the Coombe.

"Well, there's something achieved at all events," he said to Mrs. Handcock, when she served his lunch, reminding her of Elinor's reputation in the Valley for breeding a good strain of poultry but the housekeeper had reservations. "I doan't doubt but they'll maake a go of it," she said, "providing they'm left be that is, but that Arabella Codsall, 'er won't let it go at that, you can depend on it! Us'll have a proper spuddle bevore us is done, you see if I baint right, sir!"

Her suspicions were soon justified. After breakfast the next day she announced the arrival of Arabella and Martin Codsall, showing them in, Paul thought, with a grim satisfaction, as proof of her powers of prophecy.

Arabella opened on a disconcertingly mild note, whining that spiteful rumours were abroad in the Valley alleging Squire's championship of her son but that she, as one sensible to the Squire's good heart, had refused to believe that he was a man to drive a wedge between mother and son.

Paul listened to this with impatience, feeling sorry for old Martin Codsall, whose embarrassment was obvious and at last Martin interrupted with "Squire don't want to listen to all that rigmarole, Mother! Stick to the point, and ask 'un if there's any question of our Will takin' that bit o' freehold upalong."

Paul said, "Will's been here, Mrs. Codsall, and I've granted him a lease on Priory," whereupon Arabella, turning red in the face, burst out, "Then he's more underhanded than I could have believed, Mr. Craddock! Everyone in the Valley knows that land rightfully belongs to the Hermitage holding, and that when Hardcastle died it would go back to the Pitts!"

"That was the intention, Mrs. Codsall," Paul said, patiently, "but after hearing Will's intention to marry I thought it fair to give him a place of his own. Honeyman says he'll make a first-class farmer if we give him encouragement."

The word "encouragement" lit a fuse in Arabella's brain.

"Encouragement!" she blustered, "you think that wicked boy *needs* encouragement? Or her either, that chit who's bewitched him, along of her ranting father? Do you know what Will did the day he walked out on me an' his dad at Four Winds?"

"Yes," said Paul, trying hard not to smile, "he threw a shepherd's pie at your cuckoo clock!"

"Is that any way to carry on in front of his own mother and father?" demanded Arabella. "You give him that tenancy, Mr. Craddock, and you'll rue the day! A boy that wilful won't make a success of anything—farm, marriage or what all!"

"Suppose I didn't," argued Paul, somewhat ruffled by her attempt to browbeat him, "how would he earn his living? Deepdene can't support two families and he'd have to leave the Valley and work as a hired hand."

Martin made his first real contribution to the discussion, and it seemed to Paul that for once he spoke without reference to his wife's prejudice.

"He's no call to go hiring himself to anyone outside the

Valley," he growled. "He's our firstborn, an' Four Winds'll come to him in the course o' time. He can come home any time he's a mind to."

"With Elinor?" Paul asked and there was a pause, during which both of them looked at Arabella.

"Yes," she said finally, "with her, if he won't come alone. They can set up in one of the cottages, and we'll make the best of it, so long as they're married in church that is! I won't have a son of mine bedding his woman on the strength of a chapel wedding!"

For a moment Paul considered. It was obvious that Martin, irrespective of his wife, longed to have Will restored to him and as the elder of the Codsall boys his inheritance of the lease was protocol in the Valley but Paul doubted the wisdom of settling a truculent boy like Will, and a spirited girl like Elinor, on Codsall land, within close range of Arabella's tongue. He wished then that Rudd, or Claire were at hand to advise him, for instinct warned him that an incident like this could poison his relationship with the tenantry. Then he recalled Will Codsall's shining eyes and his heartfelt gratitude on the previous day and it occurred to him that Sydney Codsall, his younger brother, was his mother's favourite, so that Will might not inherit Four Winds after all. He said, bluntly, "It wouldn't work, Mrs. Codsall. Will's almost of age, and from what I've seen of him he'll be happier left to himself. He can still have Priory if he wants it but I'll see that he knows about your offer to return home."

"You'll advise him to?" This was from Martin, whose face, in contrast to that of his wife, had paled under the stress of the interview. "I'll tell him," Paul promised, "but he and Elinor must make their own decision."

"Well, I wouldn't have believed it!" said Arabella. "I just wouldn't have believed it!", and she marched towards the library door as Paul rose, saying "The boy's got his own way to make in the world, Mrs. Codsall. There's no sense in alienating him by making such a silly to-do over whom he marries. There are worse families hereabouts than the Willoughbys."

"Yes," she said, turning at the door and looking more

venomous than he could have believed possible, "there *are* worse, Mr. Craddock, but I can only name one—the Potters! Maybe you would have helped him to drag us down to *their* level, if he'd taken a fancy to one of they harlots in the Dell!"

Her implacability was like a wall of ice and to overcome her monstrous prejudice, to touch her in any way, one would have to chip away at frozen blocks of pride, ignorance and pretension, accumulated over the years since she had been a child over her father's shop. He saw that he was unequal to the task but his failure saddened him, for he recognised her now as an enemy and he doubted if he could afford an enemy as formidable as the wife of the best farmer in the Valley. He tried once again.

"Don't you see I must do what I think is right, Mrs. Codsall—right for Will, and for the Willoughbys, as well as for you? Will doesn't really want to go his own way but your way wouldn't lead to anything but more trouble."

She gave him a final bleak look and was gone but Martin remained a moment, lifting his shoulders and spreading his hands in a gesture of despair.

"Can't you do anything with her at all?" Paul asked, and Martin, looking at him unblinkingly, said, "No, Squire, I can't an' never could! Nor can't anyone hereabouts! I've always been one for peace, for turning the other cheek as the Good Book says, but after twenty years of it I've come to realise that baint right way to go about it! Holy Writ can make mistakes, like the rest of us! You might spend your life sowing Christian seed but the harvest on my land'll be tares just the same!"

He went out after his wife and the chill of the room was not solely the result of the steady drip of rain from the verandah. Paul stood looking after them, trying to persuade himself that what had happened was a trivial incident, and would seem even more trivial in retrospect but he knew, deep in his heart, that this was not so and that Martin's tares would be much in evidence before the year was past. The certainty of this made him more angry with himself than with Arabella. Old Squire Lovell, he thought, would have managed it so much better.

189

He remained despondent all day, although Will Codsall's high spirits when he called to say he would have the Priory farmhouse habitable in a matter of weeks, confirmed Paul in the rightness of his decision. Then, for a time, he forgot the Codsalls, for Ikey came in with news that the carrier serving the triangle between Whinmouth, Coombe Bay and Sorrel Halt had left a sealed wicker basket addressed to *P. Craddock, Shallowford House,* and that it contained some kind of animal, advertising its discomfort by scratching and whimpering. He followed Ikey into the yard and helped Chivers cut the fastenings. At the bottom of the crate, crouched and abject, was a half-grown puppy, with a label attached to its collar. On the label, in a neat feminine hand, was written, *"She has a defect in one eye and was condemned. No good for gun but rather appealing, don't you think?"* and then the angular initials, "G.L.".

He examined the dog carefully, finding it a well-bred golden Labrador bitch, and Chivers, inspecting the eyes, confirmed that there was indeed a slight defect but that otherwise the animal was very healthy although he doubted if it could be trained for the gun. Paul carried the puppy back into the house, setting it down before the library fire. He was touched not only by Grace's kindness towards the little reject but also by this proof that he had remained in her mind although it puzzled him somewhat to reflect that she should go to the trouble of sending a puppy all the way from London when she had not bothered to write a postcard. He sat on for a spell toying with names. "Grace" suggested itself but donor and dog had little in common. The pup was a shrinking little creature, already absorbing the warmth of the fire, and was clearly without a trace of Grace Lovell's prickly self-containment.

There was a meet the following day at Heronslea, Gilroy's place beyond the Teazel and because it was the first of the season within easy travelling distance the Valley contributed more than half the field. On his way down the river road Paul overtook a local cavalcade, consisting of Tamer Potter on a sturdy cob, Edward Derwent and Rose, riding two of the most mettlesome horses in the Valley and several farmers from further along the coast, some of whom Paul knew by sight. Rose was polite but distant but Derwent confined his greeting to a nod and a touch of his hat. Claire, Rose told him, was still away in Kent, but when Paul pressed her for details she seemed disinclined to gossip and he put this down to the fact that she was riding an untried gelding and had her hands full for, on reaching the crossing where Arthur and Henry Pitts came cantering down from Hermitage, the big horse threw up its head and screamed, siding towards the river and only returning to the road in response to Rose's urgent whispers and firm, gentle pressures. Paul admired both her skill and nerve but secretly relished the fact that he was riding a horse as docile and well-mannered as Snowdrop, whom he could ride on a loose rein. Arthur Pitts was in his customary good humour and gave his blessing on Will Codsall's tenancy of the adjoining freehold.

"He's a good lad, and I'm all for seeing him start on his own," he said. "Me and Henry have as much as us can manage, Mr. Craddock, so dornee give another thought to what you had in mind about tacking they acres on to our boundary! That boy of Arabella's needs to be out of range of his mother's tongue and Willoughby's li'l maid will make un a praper wife, mark my words! There baint a girl between Sorrel and the county border as can rear better chicken, nor make better clotted crame!"

Paul thanked him and wished heartily that all his tenants had the amiability of the Pitts family. Skirting the Codsall farmstead they headed west over the shallow Teazel to Heronslea Woods, picking their way through the extensive larch covers to the big white house, where old Gilroy and his son were standing on the broad steps under the portico watching the butler serve stirrup cup but otherwise remaining aloof. Gilroy had given up hunting some years before and his son confined himself to attending one or two lawn meets and the big Boxing Day event. Gilroy's chief whip, the virtual master of the pack, took charge of field operations, and at eleven o'clock they moved off to draw Folly Wood, behind the house, where they found at once and dashed off on a north-easterly line, across Blackberry Moor and over the railway.

There were several checks and Paul had leisure to enjoy the unfamiliar stretch of country and watch the antics of such of the field as he knew personally. Parson Bull lived up to his reputation as a thruster, pounding along on a barrel-chested piebald and cursing everyone who got in his way. He represented, thought Paul, a Christianity that was as dead as the Plantagenets and watching him plunge through a gap on the heels of the chief whip, it struck him that Bull had no business to be drawing an annual stipend for preaching the Sermon on the Mount, for anyone less meek would be difficult to find in the shire. Then a joyful shout from Henry Pitts made him qualify his verdict, for Henry, drawing level with Paul on an upslope, shouted, "Keep Passon in view, Mr. Craddock! If us loses us'll never be in at the kill!", and Paul thought that whatever Bull's demerits he had at least won the respect of his parishioners to a man. Rose Derwent, giving the gelding his head, was away up in front and Derwent, who rode just as fearlessly, was not far behind. Tamer Potter panted along in the rear, and was soon left behind but Paul managed to keep up with the middle section of the field, a group that included the two Pitts, young Gilroy (who rode as though he was indifferent as to the outcome of the day) and several of the farmers along the coast.

They killed about a mile beyond the railway and found again an hour later but this time the field moved off so quickly, and became so scattered in the broken country north of Shallowford Woods, that Paul soon found himself alone and decided to call it a day. He took a bearing on the red knob of Coombe Bluff and following a stream that flowed south, pushed on through the woods until he saw the gleam of the mere below. He was skirting the eastern arm of the pool, within sight of Sam Potter's cottage, when Sam ran out and hailed him, waving his arms in a way that implied a certain amount of urgency, so Paul put Snowdrop at the ditch separating them and cantered into the clearing, where Sam came running, his brown face glowing with excitement, his huge boots crashing through the dead bracken stalks.

" 'Er's arrived, Mr. Craddock!" he bellowed, when he was still fifty yards distant, " 'er come sudden, two or dree hours since, and 'er's the prettiest li'l maid in the Valley!"

Paul looked for the doctor's gig and not seeing it said, "Well, I'm delighted, Sam! Is Doctor O'Keefe with your wife now?"

"Lord bless us no, he baint showed up yet!" Sam said, striding along with one hand on Snowdrop's leathers, "Joannie told me her time was come first light so I had the choice o' leavin' her, or waitin' until Aaron Stokes come up to the mere for his withies. Zoon as I zeed him I sent him off for doctor, but that warn't till noon! It don't signify tho', fer I managed well enough, and Joannie seems comfortable. Will 'ee . . . will 'ee go up, an' taake a look at 'er, Squire? I tell 'ee, 'er's the prettiest maid in the Valley!"

"You mean you delivered the child yourself?" Paul asked, incredulously and Sam shrugged his shoulders, grinning. "Well, there warn't no choice, was there? I fetched calves an' foals often enough, and there baint all that difference, Maister!"

Paul climbed the stairs with some misgivings and peeped into the bedroom, the one upstairs room of the cottage. Joan Potter, wan but triumphant, was sitting up in bed feeding the child and when she saw him she blushed, saying softly, "Why ever didn 'e call up first, Sam? Squire's a bachelor, and whatever will 'ee think of us?"

Paul said, "Well—er—congratulations, both of you! I didn't realise babies could arrive without a doctor but you seem to have managed all right. What are you going to call it—her?"

"Well," said Sam, "I was thinking us ought to leave that to you, Squire, seein' you'm the first bar us to zet eyes on the tacker! Baint her a pretty maid? *Baint* her, tho'?", and he plucked aside the shawl to reveal a brick-red face crowned by a clownish patch of black hair. " 'Er's the spit of her Gran! Dark as a Gyppo, and likely as full o' mischief! Now *you* have the naming of her, Mr. Craddock, for us was goin' to call her after you, saving your presence, if 'er'd been a boy, warn't us, Joannie?"

His wife confirmed this, admitting that she had been

193

disappointed at first but was now reconciled to the child's sex, "because Sam be as plaised as a mongrel wi' two tails and us can have a bushel o' boys laater on!"

Admiring their comforting directness and cordiality Paul thought how wise John Rudd had been to advise him that Sam, the pick of the Potter litter, was a man who would respond to trust.

"Very well," he said, "since 'Paul' is out how about 'Pauline'?" and Sam, scratching his head said, "*Be* there such a name for a maid, Squire? Then, so be it, 'Pauline Potter'! Damme they zeems to run together, dorn 'em? Arr, Pauline it is, and now you must wet the baby's head, Squire, and praise to God you was the first along to do it, for I reckoned it'd be old Aaron Stokes and he be one o' they bliddy Temperance loonies!"

Paul said good-bye to Joannie and followed Sam down to the kitchen, where Sam filled two pewter tankards with rough cider from a barrel under the sink. The brew was in the Potter tradition, about twice as potent as the cider Paul had drunk at The Raven and when he had emptied his mug he took from his pocket a five-shilling piece that he had carried as a good luck charm through the last year of his service in the Transvaal.

"Here, Sam," he said, "keep it for Pauline or buy her something with it if you'd rather. It was given to me in Pretoria, and although it didn't bring me much luck in the field I was too superstitious to spend it before I was wounded," and he pressed the coin into Sam's hand. Sam was overwhelmed. "Damn it," he said, "I'll bore un through, an' the maid can have it for a necklace. From Pretoria, you said, sir? Would 'er be Kruger coinage, with the old Queen's head on it?"

"No," said Paul, laughing, "it's English money. They paid us in crown pieces over there; they weren't so easily lost as smaller coins. If you want a real souvenir I'll give you a Boer testament, printed in Afrikaans, with a bullet-hole through it. I'll be off now, before the doctor comes. If you need anything for the baby, blankets or a cot, let me know, and we'll see what Mrs. Handcock can find in the attics."

"You done more'n enough getting me an' Joannie out

194

o' the Dell," Sam said, solemnly, "and I'll maake it up to 'ee one way or another, sir. Things are good hereabouts an' like to get better, downalong and upalong and it's all your doin' I reckon, you an' Mr. Rudd's."

"Is that what most of them say, Sam?" Paul asked, feeling very encouraged.

"Arr, it be," Sam confirmed, "leastaways, them as matters. Good-bye, and God bless 'ee, Mr. Craddock!" and he held the stirrup as Paul swung himself into the saddle.

It was dusk in the wood as he put Snowdrop at the long slope to the meadow, where he and Claire had surprised Hazel Potter talking to the squirrel, and as he went along he began to do a sum in his head, balancing the credit and debit of his account to date as Squire of Shallowford. On the credit side was an obviously happy and well-housed Sam Potter, and a liberated Will Codsall, to which could be added, perhaps, the coronation supper-ball, but on the debit side the Derwents had clearly taken the huff over something and there was also Arabella Codsall, who would not easily forgive his championship of Will and Elinor. At the foot of this balance-sheet, however, was Sam's heart-warming pronouncement, "Things are good hereabouts an' like to get better . . ." Well, he hoped they would get better as time went along and he could translate all he felt for the woods and fields and farms of the Valley into action but from this point his thoughts enlarged themselves into a more general contemplation of the future.

At the top of the slope he reined in to give Snowdrop a breather, sitting with his legs free of the stirrups and looking down through the straggle of woods to the mere. The basin was full of violet dusk and the great clump of oaks, immediately below, still showed traces of summer, like dowagers clinging to the rags of finery. All the other trees, except the evergreens, had surrendered to autumn and away to the west, where the woods ran down to Home Farm pastures, the beeches stood like huge, bronze mushrooms, marching through a shallow sea of green. Most of the hedgerow flowers were gone but here and there, as a pledge of spring, was a stray campion and on the very edge of the wood a few foxgloves, still standing sentinel with bells ready to ring. As always, unless the wind was in the north, he could smell the sea here, and its tang reminded him of ventures past so that he could isolate his purpose as never before.

What was his true purpose in the Valley? What was he trying to do with and for the scattered families, enclosed by the sea, the railway line, and Gilroy's boundary in the west? Had he elected himself judge, jury and custodian of their lives over the next half-century? Or was his role rather that of referee? Or, again, was he simply a landlord, with the power to pull on the rein or bestow occasional bonuses?

Did ownership of the soil that sustained these people give him the right to plot their destinies? And if not, then who would? Perhaps his true responsibility was confined to his pocket and even to Zorndorff's, so long as he kept the scrapyard revenue in reserve; or perhaps, by coddling them too much, he would sap their initiative. Was his a conception of Imperialism in miniature? Did the investors in Britain's overseas possessions think along these lines, when they poured in their capital, hogged all the lucrative posts, and talked of the white man's burden over their whiskies and sodas in jungle clearings and delta warehouses? How much imperial outlay and effort was inspired by benevolence and how much by the profit motive, or the sweets of personal power? Surely there was a parallel here, for had he not enjoyed the power he wielded within the Shallowford boundaries? And might it not, as he grew older and more cynical, corrupt him? The Lovells, presumably, had been corrupted by it, for what had any one of them been prepared to contribute to the Valley? A harvest supper once a year and an undertaking to do outside repairs on half-derelict property but only so long as local forelocks were stretched.

His mind explored the margins of his suzerainty but soon, under the spell of the creeping dusk, it lost its way in irrelevances so that he shelved the answers to these questions, promising himself that he would seek them again in the long winter evenings ahead. In the event, he did not wait as long. Riding into the yard, and giving Snowdrop's bridle to young Ikey, he was told that he had had a visitor, a Mr. James Grenfell, from Paxtonbury, who had left a card saying he would be visiting Coombe Bay this day week, and would call again to pay his respects to the new master of Shallowford.

Paul was intrigued by the tacit irony of the note and after a traditional hunting tea of boiled eggs and toast, he took the trouble to sort through a pile of back numbers of the county press, certain in his mind that James Grenfell was someone of local consequence. He ran him down in the caption of a picture, illustrating the opening of a church bazaar, a slight, rather delicately built man in his late thirties or early forties, with a very earnest expression that gave his face a slightly fanatical look as he stood on the edge of a garlanded platform, presenting prizes. He found the report on another page and learned that James (Jimmy) Grenfell was the Liberal candidate for the Paxtonbury constituency (a division that included the Sorrel Valley, as well as the Gilroy estate adjoining) that was at present represented by Lieutenant-Colonel Hilton-Price, an amiable nominee of the Conservative and Unionist Party, and this caused Paul to wonder if his chance remark at Mary Willoughby's school, advertising sympathy with the defeated Boers, might have led Grenfell to anticipate support for the Liberals. He was glad then that he had been out when Grenfell called, for he was far too undecided as yet to commit himself but, in another way, the candidate's call flattered him so that he questioned Mrs. Handcock on local politics when she came in to clear away the tea things.

"What happens here when there is a general election, Mrs. Handcock?"

"Well," she admitted, "nothing much, as I knows of! Blue goes in, and Yellow maakes a praper ol' song an' dance about it! Us 'ave never been aught but Blue yerabouts, Mr. Craddock. My father voted for Lieutenant-Colonel Hilton-Price's father all his life but I never troubled myself with 'em one way or the other."

"How about your husband? Does he vote for the Conservatives?"

"Lord no," she said, "whatever would people like us want with either one of 'em? We both got more'n enough

197

to do without draping they ole rosettes about us an' marchin' up an' down chanting they silly ole ditties."

"What ditties?"

"Oh, giddon, you must have heard 'em! They as begin *'Vote, vote, vote for Colonel Hilton, kick old Grenfell out the door . . .'*, and suchlike ole rubbage!"

"But Mr. Grenfell has never managed to get his foot inside the door, has he?"

"Well, no," she said, "and a good thing too when a body comes to think of it, for us could 'ardly do with a nobody like 'ee standing for Parlyment, tho' they zay his father did, only up-country tho', among the chimbleys! My Horace says he ought to be locked up, along o' that rascal Lloyd George, for encouraging they Irish the way he does! Paxtonbury be church folk you see, on account o' the cathedral!"

"Now what the devil has church got to do with Grenfell's politics?" he demanded, smiling, but she looked at him severely, replying, "Now what call has an educated gentleman like you to be askin' that of an ignorant old body like me? You must know that Blue be church an' Yellow be chapel, zame as it be all over the country! If you baint teasing me, as I think you be, Mr. Craddock, you'd best go to Parson Bull for the answer! He'd lose no time putting 'ee right!" and she waddled out, to the whisper of starch and the rattle of outraged crockery.

About a week later, on returning home early one bitter afternoon, Paul was met by a flustered Mrs. Handcock on the steps of the kitchen. He had taken to using the back door and Mrs. Handcock, a stickler for the domestic proprieties, had complained of this more than once but today she greeted him with "You'll just have to go in by the front, Mr. Craddock! *He's* there in the library, waitin' for 'ee! And a fine to-do this be, I mus' say, marchin' up to the front door, ringing the bell, and zaying as he'll wait when I tell him youm about your business!"

"Who?" asked Paul forgetting Grenfell's promise to call again, and she said, *"Him!* That little wisp of a body, 'Jimmy Gren' Something-or-other but he might have been Colonel Hilton-Price himself for the airs about him! You'd best show him the door, Mr. Craddock, before there's a praper upset yerabouts!"

"Good Lord," protested Paul, "why should there be? Can't a Liberal candidate call on me as openly as a Unionist? Don't be so damned prejudiced! He might talk your husband into using his vote before he's done!" but Mrs. Handcock was so horrified by this possibility that she shut the door in his face and left him no alternative but to walk round to the forecourt and come in by the main door.

He found James Grenfell examining books in the library and although he was polite and affable Paul thought his greeting was spiced with a certain irony. The newspaper picture had not done him justice, for although he was of insignificant build, and looked far from robust, his brown, deepset eyes held in them a kindness and humour that could be seen as soon as he smiled.

"Ah, Mr. Craddock, at last!" he said. "I shan't keep you long, but I thought I must call again, on my way over to Coombe Bay. Tuesday is my Coombe Bay day, you see, when I call on Ephraim Morgan, my chairman in the Valley. He did some work for you I believe, so I have the advantage of knowing rather more about you than you know about me!" Paul murmured something polite and Grenfell went on, "Morgan is a bit of a hothead but I really don't know how I should fare in this political desert without him! When I first came here I couldn't count on a single vote south of the railway line. Now I'm certain of at least fifty! But I believe you are numbered among The Great Uncommitted, Mr. Craddock?"

"Yes, I am," said Paul, a little breathlessly, for the man's assurance was formidable. "I've never had a chance to vote; I was overseas on my twenty-first birthday and in hospital during the last election."

"Very well, Mr. Craddock, then let's put you at ease straight away. I'm not here to solicit, I came because I was curious! My intelligence service is the strongest part of my organisation (the weakest being finances) so I've already heard them speak of you."

"To my credit or otherwise?" Paul asked, smiling, for he found the little man engagingly original.

"Both," Grenfell said, "but somewhat loaded in your favour!"

"Look here," said Paul on impulse, "why don't you stay for lunch? What time are you due in Coombe Bay?"

Grenfell said, with genuine humility, "You'd really like me to stay?"

"I would indeed," Paul said. "I'm getting tired of my own company. Rudd, my agent, is laid up with an injury in Portsmouth, and the two other friends I've made since I settled in are also away. I haven't talked anything but pigs, crops, poultry and sheep in weeks."

Somewhat to his surprise Grenfell hesitated. "I don't know," he said, slowly, "maybe I oughtn't to take advantage of you. They said you were a friendly chap but I didn't expect this civility."

"It seems to me an ordinary enough civility," Paul said rather huffily but the little man lifted a protesting hand and said, smiling, "Look here, Mr. Craddock, don't take offence I beg of you. The fact is, entertaining me might easily damage your relationships with certain influential people round here. Ordinarily I wouldn't give a damn, but as you've admitted, you're uncommitted."

"And I daresay I shall remain so," Paul said, "but what the devil has that to do with inviting a casual visitor to have a bite to eat and a glass of sherry?"

"Nothing whatever," said Grenfell, chuckling, "I'd be delighted to stay and if I begin riding one of my hobby horses just cut in and cap it with experiences in the Transvaal."

Paul told the girl Thirza to inform Mrs. Handcock that the visitor was staying for luncheon and then, as they drank sherry, they fell to discussing the recent peace-treaty terms which Paul knew in outline but Grenfell, he soon realised, knew in great detail. When lunch arrived, served by a blank-faced Mrs. Handcock, Paul told his visitor something of the reaction among rank and file volunteers concerning the herding of Boer families into camps that had been sited without regard to water supplies or sanitary facilities. He found Grenfell a good listener and went on to tell him of the change in the attitude of most of the civilian-soldiers after actual contact with the Boers, speaking without regard to the hovering Mrs. Handcock, whom he guessed was saving every tidbit of the conversation for the oracular Horace. When she left them to their cheese and coffee Grenfell said, with a laugh, "I presume the excellent Mrs. Handcock is an enemy camp-follower?", and Paul recounted his housekeeper's simplification of politics, adding that her husband Horace had never yet used his vote.

"Ah, that's a real trouble in places like this," Grenfell said. "Most of them are so out of touch that nobody can make them accept their responsibilities as democrats. Even when the Tories bundle them into carriages, and haul 'em off to the poll, they haven't the least idea what earns them the free ride, although most of 'em put a cross for the man who pays the fare out of a sense of fair play. I wonder what the Chartists would think about it all, or going further back, men like Hampden, and old John Ball? Sometimes I'd like to call a party truce for five years—the life of a Parliament, say—so that both parties could drive home the fact that the most important single gain of the British people over the centuries was the Reform Bill, and the Redistribution Act that followed it."

"How would you personally go about it?" Paul asked, and Grenfell's eyes blazed as he said, "Why, by real blood-and-thunder methods! By the use of magic lantern slides, showing how much blood was shed by Englishmen from the fifteenth century onwards! By lecture on incidents like Peterloo and the Tolpuddle Martyrs! By borrowing the techniques of the halfpenny press, to drive the lesson home in all kinds of ways—plays, pageants, debates and the use of every mechanical gadget on the market! Then, when everybody had been pricked in one spot or another, we'd have an election and the result would astonish us all! Maybe they wouldn't have one or other of us, or the Fabians either, because people would see the main issues more clearly and not let themselves be fobbed off with party propaganda."

"What are the main issues?" Paul asked and Grenfell suddenly stopped crumbling his bread and placing both hands on the table looked across at his host: "There are only two that concern me," he said. "One is tolerance and the

201

other has been written into the first paragraph of every political tract of the last four hundred years—that men are born equal, and should enjoy equality of opportunity! Everything worth a farthing in politics is rooted in those principles."

The sparkle left his eyes and he smiled his winning smile as he stood up and extended his hand. "You failed to keep your promise, Mr. Craddock! You agreed to stop me if I began preaching. However, it has been delightful meeting you, delightful and . . . yes, I must say it, extremely encouraging!"

"I don't promise to vote for you," Paul said and Grenfell replied, "I told you—I didn't come here to solicit!"

Paul ordered Grenfell's trap to be brought to the front and when it was bowling away down the drive, with the little man crouched on the high seat flourishing his whip in farewell, he thought it was a long time since he had enjoyed such pleasant company at his table.

III

Will Codsall and Elinor Willoughby were married very quietly at the Congregationist Meeting House, in Coombe Bay, on the first day of December, when the seasons were still delicately poised between autumn and winter and the Sorrel Valley was awaiting the north-east wind to strip the last leaf from the Priory thickets and for the blue water between beach and sandbars to turn its wind-whipped winter grey. It was a day of strong gusts and the threat of sleet, no day for a wedding, or for anything more than the fitting of draught board to cottage doors and a cursing of finches who had weakened the thatch in nesting forays throughout spring.

Paul and Mrs. Handcock drove over to Coombe Bay and took their places in the back pew of the whitewashed chapel, Mrs. Handcock gathering her coat about her, as though close contact with so many dissenters was a physical hazard. She was here at the insistence of Squire, reinforced by her dislike of the groom's mother who, or so Squire had warned her, had advertised her intention of causing a riot. Paul himself would have preferred John Rudd as a buffer between himself and Arabella but Rudd's ribs were slow to mend and he had now postponed his return until New Year.

Word must have gone round that there was likely to be free entertainment at the meeting house, for during the interval between the arrival of Will (buttoned into tight blue serge and wearing a three-inch collar that kept his chin at a sharp angle) and that of the bride, every pew filled with Valley folk, each of whom entered quietly and cautiously, as though expecting the roof to collapse at any moment. The Potter girls were there and with them Walt Pascoe, who would be a bridegroom himself in the New Year. Rose Derwent tiptoed in and bowed her head, just as if this was a real church, and Farmer Willoughby's minister from Whinmouth a real priest. Paul smiled across at Rose but she did not return his smile and he wondered briefly about Claire, and her interminable stay in Kent but not for long, for he was far too apprehensive and his fears were not entirely allayed by having posted Ikey Palfrey at the head of the village street to warn him of the approach of the enemy. Arthur and Martha Pitts arrived late, causing everyone to look fearfully over their shoulders, and then came Willoughby's hired hand, who had obviously been detached as scout by the bridegroom, for he sidled up to the waiting groom and shook his head, indicating that so far there was no sign of Arabella. At this Will's chin shot up another point or two, and he ran his forefinger round the inside of his collar, sighing so loudly that some of the girls began to giggle. His embarrassment, however, did something to relieve the tension in the chapel, so Paul leaned towards the housekeeper and whispered, "Maybe she's thought better of it!" but Mrs. Handcock said nothing. She was wishing herself anywhere but here, abetting a young man whose kindheartedness was likely to be exploited to the prejudice of good order and discipline in the Valley.

She forgot her misgivings, however, when a stir at the rear of the church heralded the arrival of the bride and Elinor entered on her father's arm, a little wisp of a thing, in a white muslin gown, with a Honiton lace veil embroidered with true lover's knots held in place by an evergreen wreath. Edwin Willoughby looked very solemn as the two walked the length of the aisle and Will, nudged by his groomsman, jumped up with a clatter of boots and looked around helplessly, as though expecting to be told what to do next. Help was at hand for Elinor, half lifting her veil, smiled at him reassuringly and it was her smile that touched Mrs. Handcock as it did every other woman in the church. She looked so fragile, so pretty and yet so confident of her destiny.

After that the ceremony went off very smoothly, responses being uttered in voices that contained an element of defiance, and when the couple walked down the aisle to the chapel door, where they were showered with clammy handfuls of confetti by the Coombe Bay folk waiting outside, there was a general sense of anti-climax. Paul kissed Elinor on the cheek and shook hands with a beaming Will, who seemed almost dazed with relief that nothing had occurred to shame him or spoil the occasion for Elinor. There was no reception; the couple simply drove back to Deepdene in a hired Coombe Bay gig and the bride's father followed in his trap and everybody stood about in the wind until Paul, sensing that something was expected of him, issued a general invitation to everyone to join him at The Raven and drink the young couple's health in beer or cider. Mrs. Handcock whispered urgently, "Now, dornee indulge 'em, Mr. Craddock!" but she came along nevertheless and drank tea with Minnie Flowers, the landlord's wife, in the kitchen, whilst Paul entertained the groomsman, Walt Pascoe and a dozen others in the bar. It was Walt, feeling half initiated in the mysteries of bridal rites, who expressed general disappointment with the ceremony when he said, cheerfully, "Well, here's your health, Squire, but 'twas all a bit of damp squib, wasn't 'er? I would ha' wagered half-a-sovereign to sixpence old Arabella would ha' sailed in and set about poor old Will with her umbrella, but 'er must have been tied to a chair last minute by Martin!" This was received as a great joke, Martin Codsall being recognised as the most hagridden husband in the Valley, yet there was a grain of truth in Walt's guess after all. Arabella had certainly intended making good her threat and it was Martin who had, in fact, prevented her.

Word had reached Arabella that the wedding was timed for 2 P.M. and at one o'clock she came into the kitchen dressed in her high-buttoned best with elastic-sided boots and a huge fruit hat, a kind of horned cornucopia made of hard, black straw and glutted with plums and grapes and cherries, that swung like so many coloured bells when she turned her head. Martin, also in his Sunday clothes, awaited her, having spent the entire morning in earnest attempts to dissuade her from disgracing the family. Arabella knew Martin well but not so well as she imagined, or she might have noted his unnaturally high colour, as though the wretchedness of providing a public spectacle and destroying the last bridge between him and his first-born was already bringing blushes to his cheeks. He was unusually neat and tidy too, even for churchgoing, his greying hair damped down and his gold pin and boots twinkling in the firelight. He remained silent when Arabella consulted her bodice watch, saying that it was time to go if they were to arrive at the chapel in good time, but as they seated themselves in the high-slung trap he made a final appeal to her dignity, saying, "Then youm still bent on every layabout in the Valley laughing their silly heads off over us, Mother?", but all she replied was, "The sooner we get there the sooner it'll be over an' done with!"

"But damme," he protested, "it won't do a particle of good to any one of us! Do 'ee think this kind o' caper will fetch our Will back?"

"No, I don't," she said calmly, "but it'll make a fool of 'im an' shame her and that's all I care about at this stage!"

It was all he cared about too, and it tilted him into mutiny. She had not noticed that Flick, their sedate and ageing pony, was not harnessed to the trap or that Cobber, a recently acquired cob of doubtful sobriety, had taken Flick's place between the shafts. He was surprised that she had not commented upon this when they came out and even had an excuse on the tip of his tongue but he put her poor observation down to the cloud of spite that had settled on her brain. Saying no more he cracked

205

the whip as the trap moved off down the track to the bridge at a spanking pace, the measured gavotte of Arabella's cherries and plums changing to a brisk polka and then a reckless can-can, as the cob lengthened its stride and bumped over the ruts at twelve miles per hour. "At this rate," thought Martin, grimly, "us'll be in Coombe Bay in under the half-hour, providin' we'm *going* to Coombe Bay this afternoon!"

The first indication that Arabella had of his treachery was when the trap shot across the plank bridge and swung left instead of right, taking the river road that ran under the slope of Priory Wood. She was so astonished that for a few moments she could find no words to comment and this, for Arabella Codsall, implied a very great degree of astonishment indeed. Then it occurred to her that Martin must be so emotionally disturbed that he had forgotten his way to the coast, so she shrieked, "Fool! Pull him up, and turn him round!", but instead of obeying Martin lifted his whip and brought it slashing down across the cob's haunches, and the cob, already going at a rolling canter, threw up its head and moved from canter to gallop, almost pitching Arabella over the seat rail and causing her to let out a sustained scream that startled every bird in the Valley. She realised then that he had gone mad, for only madness could explain open revolt and she realised too, with a coolness that did her credit in the circumstances, that if they continued in this direction at this pace they would soon pass a point where it would be impossible to retrace their steps in time for the wedding. The thought submerged her fears so that she made a wild grab at the reins, but madness upon madness, Martin switched them to his right hand and fended her off with the butt end of the whip, so that she suddenly abandoned all thought of the wedding in the certainty that he was bent on oversetting the trap and killing her and himself. She began to plead, holding tight to the rail with one hand and keeping her fruit hat from flying away with the other. The hat, in fact, was beginning to disintegrate, and cherries were already cascading into her lap. A plum, or a large grape, also worked itself loose but this went unnoticed, striking her shoulder and shooting into the back of the trap among some sacks.

The cob was now at stretched gallop, and on the uneven surface of the road the trap was bumping from side to side like a hay trailer, coupled to a recklessly driven waggon. Martin concentrated on preventing the hubs of the wheels touching the bank on one side or the flood posts on the other but Arabella had nothing to do but hang on and scream and this she did, shriek upon shriek issuing from her mouth in an almost continuous sound that sent every river bird wheeling from the reeds and caused a curious buzzard, watching from an elevation of three hundred feet, to back up against the wind current until it could decide what was happening on the ribbon of road below.

Then, as the cob saw the freedom of the moor before him, he shot off along the upland track that was not even as well surfaced as the river road and suddenly, to cap all, a shower of sleet came down, driving into their faces and tearing Arabella's hat from her grasp, so that she stopped screaming and began to plead but all Martin did was to lay on with his whip and the cob, that had been enjoying the outcry until now, panicked and swerved, shooting off into heather and then back again but without varying its frightful pace across the moor.

It was when they came to a gradient where neither whip, shouts, nor rattle could induce the blown cob to maintain its pace that the trap slowed to an uncertain walk but Arabella hardly noticed the change. She was sobbing and breathless, her unpinned hair obscuring her vision, her lovely fruit hat a sodden bundle half-a-mile back along the road, her mind tormented by the prospect of living out the remainder of her days with a lunatic husband. The sleet still came at them like a shower of spears but he paid no heed to it, sitting hunched over the footboard, reins and whip in hand, eyes fixed on the crest of the moor ahead.

"Well, Mother," he said at length, "I reckon that does it! Us couldn't get to chapel in time now if us went there behind racehorses so put up your hair and make the best of it! Us'll take it easy going backalong!"

She stopped wheezing then and glared at him through a matted screen of hair, for clearly he was not mad after all.

207

Incredibly he had done this terrible thing deliberately, a crafty, premeditated manœuvre, aimed at cheating her of her revenge. She said, softly and murderously, "I'll make you pay for this, Martin Codsall! As God is me judge, I'll make you pay!" but her threat did not disturb him unduly for he reflected, whilst turning the trap and heading back to the river road, that he had already paid all he had or was likely to have and what profit was there in plaguing a bankrupt?

Barely a mile from the spot on the edge of the moor, where Martin Codsall had turned the trap earlier in the day, his son and daughter-in-law were using the fading light to make the Priory farmhouse habitable. It was not really a farmhouse at all but a largish cottage, still half a ruin. Will and Elinor, helped by the biblical twins, Matt and Luke, had retimbered and rethatched the roof, and had also given the whole place a thorough scouring but their main efforts had been directed to the outhouses, for, as Will had put it on the day he had first taken Elinor there, "Us can only live in one room at a time and us must have somewhere for the livestock when the weather zets in." Now, on their owners' wedding night, a fat sow and her litter were snug in the small sty and two dozen saddlebacks were snoring in the big sty, while Gertie, the Alderney, old Willoughby's wedding gift, occupied a byre that was rather more comfortable than the farm kitchen where some of the broken windows were plugged with cardboard. Bride and groom made light of discomfort, however, for it seemed to them a very wonderful thing to be alone in a house of their own and as soon as they had changed they borrowed Willoughby's trap and drove over the moor in the teeth of the storm, stabling the horse in the ramshackle stable and lighting a roaring fire from sawn timber left over from the repairs. By the time it was dark and the lamp was lit, the kitchen began to look like a home although there was nothing on the stone floor but a rush mat and only a single wooden chair beside the open hearth, where Elinor had set a rickety table and the milking stool left behind by the Hardcastles. Fortunately Hardcastle's widow had also bequeathed them other pieces that had not been considered worth the trouble of hauling away after the funeral. Upstairs, in the now rainproof main bedroom, was a rusty iron bedstead, already neatly made with Elinor's hoarded linen, a chest of drawers warped by damp and a cracked sheet of backed glass for use as a mirror. In the scullery was a built-in dresser, with a few chipped cups and plates which would do for the time being for all their savings, including the Squire's sovereign wedding gift, had been laid out on pigs and winter feed.

About six o'clock Elinor called Will from the stairs, where he was replacing rotted boards and she might have been married years rather than hours judged by the casual way she summoned him to his meal and sat him on the only chair whilst she took the stool and began to ladle generous helpings of thick vegetable stew into which he dipped bread she had baked that same morning. They ate in silence and while they were occupied in everyday habits —eating, firemending, washing up under the scullery pump—they were neither shy nor withdrawn. It was only later, when Elinor carried the stone hot-water bottle upstairs to air the lavender-scented linen she had brought as her portion, that the fearful wonder of the situation touched her and she took the opportunity, whilst he was finishing off his carpentry, of slipping out of her clothes and pausing for a moment in front of the cracked mirror to study herself in the light of the candle. She was not sure that she liked what she saw, a small, girlish body, with honey-colored plaits almost as thick as her wrists screening her small, hard breasts. "Well," she mused, "I wonder if he'll like me now he's got me?" and then, doubtfully but not altogether apprehensively, "and I wonder if he'll use me roughly, as he tried to often enough in the old days?" She already thought of their courtship as "the old days", belonging to the distant past but she no longer feared Mrs. Codsall's sourness or persecution. She was done with Four Winds and so, praise God, was Will! The few words, spoken by the red-haired preacher from Whinmouth, had banished Mrs. Codsall and all her works so that nobody, not even King Edward himself could separate them now and the certainty of this warmed her belly and thighs, reaching to the tips of her little toes on the bare boards at

209

the foot of the bed. She pushed the stone water bottle to "his side" and stood holding her long flannel nightdress against herself, fearful and expectant, yet somehow safe and rooted. Then she put the candle down on the box beside the bed and unlatched the door, calling to him as he knelt, hammering in the light of a storm-lamp hooked to the banister.

"Will," she said, "I'm going to bade now, unless you'll be wanting anything more."

"No, midear," he called back, "I'll damp the vire and come on up. Tiz a botchy ole job in this kind o' light!"

The mildness of his voice reassured her, banishing the last of her fears and she went back into the bedroom, folded her nightgown and placed it under his pillow, for he had told her some time ago that he liked to "sleep high" and the only pillows they had were two ratty old cushions, loaned by Aunt Mary. Then she got into bed and inhaled the lavender scent, reaching out and touching the space where he would lie and finding it well-warmed by the bottle. He came in holding the storm lantern high and looked down on her with a great broad smile, the first she had seen on his face that day.

"Ah, youm lovely, Elinor," he said, "and I dorn know what I done to deserve 'ee!"

"Youm a lovely gurt thing yourself, Will," she told him, "and never let no one tell you different! Make haste man and blow thicky candle out!"

IV

Winter entered the Valley, like a white nun, austerely beautiful but pitiless, glorifying in mortification of the flesh and calling upon men to face realities.

Young Henry Pitts, of Hermitage, saw winter not as a nun, however, but as a malevolent clown who got under his feet and threw him headlong on the steep path to the sties, who clothed his Guernseys in their breath and sent them mincing over iced ruts to frozen pools, who sealed the very gate latches with ice and threatened his winter corn, sown with so much effort in early autumn. For the snow reached Hermitage first, moving in from the north-east and the heavy flakes floated rather than fell, each being set down gently and individually by a wind that had carried them all the way from the Russian steppes. Then, having frozen the imperishable grin on Henry's rubbery face, winter moved south-west, scattering diamonds across the Codsall stubble, slowing the Sorrel current, sealing its oxbow and stiffening its rushes, until it plucked at Martin Codsall's long nose as he stood cursing the clumsiness of his new cowman and declaring that Will had emptied udders in half the time taken by his replacement. Then the frost doubled to strike the Home Farm, silencing the saw-mill and reminding the shepherd twins, Matt and Luke, that the lambing season was not far off and if snow fell now it might go hard with them in February. Down at the foot of the Coombe the snow lay lightly but the wind was just as keen and Meg and her thinly clad daughters shiv-ered in their leaking kitchen and wash-house. Only Tamer, with over sixteen stone of blubber to protect him, could sneer at the sky and waddle across his turnip fields won-dering who would do his spring sowing now that Squire had deprived him of Sam.

Higher up the Dell, where soon nobody could distin-guish between Potter's broken fences and the tiny hedge-rows of Farmer Willoughby, drifts began to pile where the timber was sparse and Willoughby's hired man, plodding about Elinor's business in the henhouses, won-dered glumly why the birds resented Elinor's abdica-tion so much that they had gone into a mass moult. Mary still kept her school, for the Valley children were a hardy lot and as long as the river road was open continued to ride or walk to their morning les-sons. There was a warm stove in the schoolroom and a long row of hooks over it to dry mittens and gaiters, and always, sharp at ten-thirty, cocoa for every scholar, even those banished to corners and wearing dunces' caps.

On the bleak upland of Derwent's holding tempers were sharper than the frost, for Edward Derwent sorely missed Claire and Rose was worried about her horses, realising there could be no hunting this side of New Year. Even at exercise the snow balled under shoes and brought animals down, so that they spent most of their time in loose boxes, eating the season's profits.

Perhaps the only two souls in the entire Valley to welcome the snow were Ikey Palfrey and Hazel Potter, the one because here in the country it was a novel experience, the other because it gave her an excuse to play truant every day.

Ikey had seen snow before, of course, but never snow like this, pure, unsullied and dazzling white, crisp, powdery and untrodden by man or beast. When snow fell on Bermondsey it never lay more than an hour but was soon slush under the pressure of boots, hooves and cartwheels. Under a mantle of snow every Thames-side factory looked like a prison and every dwelling was seen as the squat, defeated hovel it really was but down here, especially when the sun shone, the long slope between the big house and Shallowford Woods turned coral and rose-pink and every branch of every tree became a crystal chandelier. The birds grew tame, not merely sparrows and thrushes that always haunted the scrapyard but all kinds of birds, some of which he had never seen at close quarters, great tits and blue tits, crested wrens, greenfinches, bullfinches and dozens of perky robins, who perched on the harness pegs and ate crumbs from his hand. Then there were gloriously long slides in the drive and snowball fights with Gappy, the gardener's boy, when Chivers was safely out of the way but Ikey liked best his lonely tramps along the edge of the woods and up the west face of the Coombe to school, for here, in a silent, winter world, he could indulge his extravagant fancies and there was no one in sight to break the spell.

He saw himself in many disguises and by no means always against a background of snow and ice but sometimes crossing waterless deserts and mountain ranges and sometimes rafting across the Pacific or shifting for himself (and possibly Squire Craddock) on a coral island, like Jack, Ralph and Peterkin, in Ballantyne's book. During those tramps to and from Deepdene he was everyone he had ever met in Mary Willoughby's library—Robinson Crusoe, Monte Cristo, D'Artagnan, Sherlock Holmes, Jim Hawkins and David Balfour on the run from redcoats. Anyone watching him making his way across the meadow to Hazel Potter's squirrel tree, or along the southern edge of Shallowford Woods, might have thought him pursued by Furies. Every now and then he looked fearfully over his shoulder and darted for cover to emerge, bent double, to dash across the snow firing as he ran until he reached a bank where, it seemed, yet another ambush awaited him which he evaded by changing direction and disappearing into a ditch.

He was so engaged one overcast morning on his way home from Deepdene after Mary Willoughby had dismissed school an hour before time because Derwent had told her there would be another fall by mid-afternoon. Ikey usually went part way home with Sydney Codsall and children of a Codsall labourer, but they were an unadventurous group and preferred to take the track down the Dell and through the Potter holding to the river road, whereas Ikey liked the steep slopes of the Bluff, where he could toboggan down to the thick gorse that grew along the edge of the Coombe and then, by a frozen brook and two stiles, enter the meadows bordering Shallowford Woods.

It was very cold but he moved swiftly and kept his blood circulating so that when he reached the woods he felt pleasantly warm and was tempted by a faint gleam of sunshine to use his extra hour's freedom by pushing through brittle briars to the top of the escarpment, overlooking the mere. He had not thought of the mere as being a solid oval of ice, with its mysterious, pagoda-crowned island as the sole break in its surface but now it occurred to him that he might be able to cross over and inspect the ruin, which was something he had been wanting to do for some time. He went on down to the margin and tested the ice but it was not strong enough to bear his weight so he moved round the lake to its far side to explore a part of the woods that was new to him. A tangle of evergreens grew here, close-set larch and dwarf pine, stockaded about with overgrown laurels and rhododendrons and it was here that he flushed a hare, who bounded from under his feet and dashed into the wood with Ikey in hot pursuit. He soon lost sight of the hare but found instead some deer tracks and followed them for about a mile along a narrow twisting path that split and split again, until he lost the tracks at a spot where a pine had fallen across the path barring further progress.

He had been so intent upon the chase that he had not noticed snow had begun to fall but when he turned back, seeking the mere, it drove into his face so harshly that he could hardly see his way and although he reasoned that it could not be more than two o'clock the wood seemed terrifyingly dark and gloomy. His outward tracks were now obliterated and soon he realised that he must have taken a wrong turning, for he blundered on and on in growing desperation without being able to break free of the tangled undergrowth or come within sight of the lake. Snow whirled down on him more and more thickly and in spite of his exertions he began to feel numb, particularly in the foot that got wet testing the ice. He tried to console himself with the thought that this was a real adventure but it was little comfort. His courage ebbed with every step and soon he realised he was wholly lost and likely to stay lost unless he could find help or shelter. He held on as long as he could, and perhaps a little longer, setting his teeth and slashing with numbed hands at the clawing briars and laurel branches but at last, as he entered a tiny clearing, the storm, the thicket and the paralysing cold defeated him and he uttered a wild shout of despair that issued from him involuntarily like a soul quitting a body.

The sound of his own voice encouraged him a little and he shouted again but when there was no answer he suddenly burst into tears and sat down on a log, thrusting his knuckles into his eyes and howling with terror and misery. He was still in this unheroic posture when he heard the crunch of feet and looking up, wildly hopeful, saw Hazel Potter standing gazing down at him in silent wonder, one hand pulling at her lip, the other swinging a small tin attached to her wrist by a string.

He recognised her at once as the child who had sat crosslegged on the pedestal at the coronation supper-ball and the horrid embarrassment of being caught by a girl in the act of blubbering made him glare as though she had been a predatory animal on the prowl.

214

"What are you doing here?" he blustered, but she did not seem to resent his aggressive manner and continued to pluck her lip and swing her tin, which Ikey now identified as a home-made handwarmer of the kind he had often used in winter in the scrapyard.

"Youm lost, baint 'ee?" Hazel said at last, and the corners of her mouth puckered as though she could easily have laughed at his dilemma.

It was useless to deny the fact so he said, loftily, "Yerse, I am, I never bin this side o' the woods and was caught in the storm. Tracking deer!" he added, impressively.

This interested her. "You was gonner kill 'em?"

"No," he said modestly, "I ain't got a gun an' Squire won't have 'em killed. I was tracking 'em, to see where they went."

"Ah, they went downalong," she said authoritatively, "they always do in the snow. Henry Pitts puts feed out for 'em but they don't stay, they come back, soon as they've eaten an' move over to the spruce where there's plenty o' bark to bite on! Most everything lives this side o' the mere—foxes, hares, an' badgers too, tho' there's a set 'longside my squirrel tree, upalong."

She talked as an expert, as someone privy to all the secrets of the wood and he had a strong impression that she thought of foxes and badgers not as creatures but as family units, inhabiting farms and living within prescribed borders, just like the Potters, the Codsalls and the Willoughbys. He had never heard the word "set" before in this sense and would have liked to ask about it but not wishing to display his ignorance he said, "Can you show me the way aht? I'm late 'ome, and I got work waiting in the tack-room."

She smiled then, and he noticed that her rather vacant face underwent a remarkable change when her mouth widened, exposing strong, white teeth. It was as though the smile was something she used for switching identities— from a dullwitted waif to a woodsprite in a homespun skirt of undyed sheep's wool and long gaiters of rabbit skin, tucked into patched, lace-up boots. One of the boots gaped like the mouth of a fish and exposed pink toes. He was enormously impressed by her yet was careful not to

215

show it for although she clearly knew her way, which he did not, she was still only a girl and also a Potter and therefore of no account. She looked, he thought, only half human in her outlandish clothes, with a mop of matted red-gold hair and green eyes but as she continued to smile at him and her pink tongue emerged to moisten her lips, he had the impression that here in the woods she was a kind of queen and that all the creatures would come running to her whistle, that she could have told you everything in the wood that was good to eat and every berry that was poisonous, that there would be nothing that went on here that she did not know about and this gave her a purely local omnipotence exceeding even the Squire's. She said, carelessly, "You'd ha' died o' the cauld, Boy, if I hadn't 'eard 'ee squawk! You shoulder kept walking 'till you dropped an' even then you should ha' crawled! Youm praaper mazed to zit yourself down in the snow. Coom, I'll tak' 'ee backalong!", and without giving him an opportunity to justify himself in any way she took him by the hand and led him into what looked like a low tunnel cut through the thickest part of the laurels.

What astonished him more than her anticipation of every twist and turn in this maze of undergrowth was her body temperature. The hand that clutched his was as warm as if it had just been withdrawn from a fur glove, and he reasoned that her feet must be just as warm for how else could she endure to walk through thick snow with a gaping hole in her boot? She not only knew exactly which rabbit run to follow and which to reject but also the strength and thickness of every obstruction. Without leaving hold of his hand for a moment she twisted this way and that, pushing through a tangle of branches without a second's hesitation, so that presently they came out on the side of the lake that ran directly past the island with the pagoda. He said gruffly, when he had recovered from his astonishment, "Orlright, I know me way from here," but she did not relinquish his hand but began hauling him up the slope to the crest of the escarpment where, in the gathering dusk, he saw the welcome yellow glow of the Big House lights.

"I'll leave 'ee here, Boy," she said, "but dornee stray

that zide again 'till the snow's gone." She looked up at the sky and sniffed. " 'Er won't be long now; us've zeen the worst of it."

His respect for her grew and grew, whittling away at his male arrogance and making it seem mean and ungracious, so that he admitted, hesitantly, "I was lost orlright, an' I dunno what I'd have done if you hadn't bobbed up. What's your name? Mine's Ikey, I'm stable boy down there."

"Yes, I know. I've overlooked 'ee often enough," she said lightly. "I'm Hazel, and they zay I'm mazed, I'm not tho', but I let 'em think it's so, for that way I go where I plaises," and with this astonishing confession she turned away and seemed on the point of vanishing into the dusk but he called urgently, "Where can I find yer if I want to go that side of the mere again?", and she replied, pausing in her stride, "Come down by the Niggerman's Church and whistle. Whistle loud and I'll come to 'ee," and she put her fingers in her mouth and blew, producing a long, low and very piercing sound like the summons of a London cabby. Then, before he could ask her to teach him this engaging trick, or identify the "Niggerman's Church" as the old pagoda, she had disappeared, moving so silently that he could not have sworn whether she went back down the slope or east along the path towards the Coombe.

He stood there looking into the darkness where she had vanished and thought how far from mazed she was but how completely she fooled everyone in the Valley. Then he wondered if he should tell Chivers or Mrs. Handcock of his adventure, of how, without Hazel Potter, he might have died down there in the wood but he decided not for this would be an admission of personal inadequacy and might also mean future prohibitions. At least, this was what he told himself but the truth was he was reluctant to share with others the knowledge that Hazel Potter was really a princess, masquerading as a half-witted waif, or that God who had once before come to his aid in a moment of despair obviously had a special interest in his welfare. Why else should He have directed her to him, barely fifteen minutes before daylight faded?

He brushed the dead leaves from his coat and went on down the slope towards the pool of orange light.

CHAPTER EIGHT

I

HAZEL POTTER knew her weather signs. The wind veered round to the south-west before Christmas and the snow was washed from the banked lanes by driving rain, so that after a spell there was hardly a trace of it save for pockets of slush under the trees.

Paul went about his business cheerfully enough, making his rounds two or three times a week, discussing spring sowing with unhurried men like Arthur Pitts and Honeyman, and pigs with Will Codsall, whose ramshackle holding was now gradually assuming a patterned neatness like Four Winds and High Coombe. Paul did not think of Grace Lovell much during the day but at night, when he was sitting before the library fire, loneliness sometimes stole upon him and the technical books on soil, shorthorns and land drainage, prescribed as evening reading by John Rudd lay undigested on his knees as he pictured the dark, compact figure of Grace in the leather armchair opposite, her eyes bent over some sewing or gazing abstractedly into the red glow of the Home Farm apple logs blazing in the hearth.

It was, he admitted to himself, a very improbable picture but his thoughts of her were always in this pleasant frame for after an interval of seven weeks, with no word from her except the scribbled message on the label of the puppy's collar, his memories of her arranged themselves in thicknesses, laid one upon the other like dockets in his office tray.

First there was the overall impression of mystery that her presence brought to him, with the certainty that somehow she belonged here in this house and by this fireside and this conviction was as strong and unreasoning as that which had possessed him concerning the estate as a whole

on the day he had first ridden down from the moor alongside John Rudd. He could not say why this should be so;
she had done little or nothing to confirm it but it persisted just the same, matching his possessive pleasure in
the meadows, woods and leafy lanes between the Sorrel
and the Bluff, the railway line and the silver of Coombe
Bay. Then, adding a pinch of spice to her sense of belonging here, was the physical impact she made upon him—
her neatness, her containment, her cool, ivory skin seen
against blue-black side curls and straight fringe, her dark,
contracting brows arching over eyes the colour of dog
violets in Priory Wood, her long cheekbones and firm little
chin with the large dimple but above all, her presence as
a whole, that seemed to him to promise so much to a man
who could break through the defences she had erected
against an invasion of her intense privacy and self-isola-
tion. Was he such a man? He doubted it but doubts did
not deny him reveries and flights of fancy, so that sometimes the sudden fall of the heavy book from his knees
would drag him from an exotic dream in which he was
mastering her in silent places about the house, while she,
for her part, was submitting to his domination. The absurdity of these imaginings was sometimes brought home
to him when he recollected that a proposal of marriage on
his part had yielded no more than a vague promise to
"think about it", but then, for comfort, he would look
down at her dog and reflect that she must have thought of
him as a man of compassion, gauche and unsophisticated
perhaps, yet more eligible than the roystering Ralph
Lovell, or any of the men she met in her father's rootless
set, and this would launch him into fresh fields of speculation regarding the life she led in London, and what kept
her there all this time, and if there was a lover in the
background. He wondered too how much she knew about
the source of his money and whether, indeed, such knowledge would disqualify him in her eyes, or those of her
stepmother. It was then that the absurdity of his spon-
taneous proposal came down upon him with a rush, so
that he told himself that he really had no wish to be taken
seriously and that, for both their sakes, it would be better
if they could look upon his impulsive advances as a flirta-

tion, approximately in the same category as that he and Claire Derwent had shared before it went sour and she ran away to hide in Kent.

As the days passed it was this aspect of their relationship that began to gain ground at the expense of all the other daydreams. After all, he told himself, what did he know of the girl, and how much could one listen to instinct in matters as final as this? He had met her five times during a period of six months and on two of those occasions their conversation was such as might have passed between people in the street. He was sure, for instance, that a man like Franz Zorndorff would regard his infatuation as hopelessly immature, a park bandstand romance between adolescents, whereas John Rudd would have even stronger feelings about it, for he made no bones about including her family in his blanket of detestation of all the Lovells. And yet, behind all these misgivings was a curious inevitability of Grace Lovell as Mistress of Shallowford that could not be separated from his own identification with the estate and assumption of personal responsibility for all the people of the Valley. He had no clear idea of what he would tell either Rudd or Zorndorff about her, or what indeed he would say to Grace or Celia Lovell if either one of them took him at his word. He only knew that somewhere and somehow their paths would converge and that until they did real ownership of the Valley would elude him.

His thoughts were in this confused state when, a day or so before Christmas, a batch of letters arrived by a single post. He extracted all the seed catalogues, trade agricultural leaflets, bills and conveyances and carried the rest into his office, locking the door against interruptions.

The first was his fortnightly letter from Uncle Franz, to whom he had written in detail regarding his efforts to enlarge the estate to the north and east by the acquisition of the Priory freehold, now renamed Periwinkle Farm by Elinor and Codsall, and the cliff fields incorporated in High Coombe. Zorndorff had taken to addressing him as "My Dear Squire", using the form of address with restrained irony but he approved Paul's ready acceptance of a money draft from scrapyard profits, despite Paul's disclaimer which Zorndorff, it seemed, refused to take seriously. The Croat's letter was concise, businesslike and affectionate but there remained the hint of mockery in outwardly innocent phrases, as though, now that he had launched his "nephew", he could pretend that he was indulging the whim of an enthusiastic boy who would soon realise that the estate was all a bit of a joke between them, and could be wound up in the course of time. There was a footnote to the letter which seemed to Paul to underline this, for Zorndorff wrote: "If, by spring, you are persuaded that you have bitten off more than you can chew, don't despair, my dear boy! By pure chance you are batting on a safe wicket! Land values have jumped twenty per cent since the peace and we might even net a profit on your improvements!"

Paul smiled at this, made some notes in the margin and put the letter aside, opening a breezier one from John Rudd, who said he was up and about again and had been advised by his doctor to get as much exercise as possible in order that the cracked ribs could mend themselves. He added that he would be home again on New Year's Day, after seeing his boy Roderick off at Chatham.

The two letters in feminine handwriting Paul left until last and now opened a stiff envelope containing a very large Christmas card, with slapdash scrawl on the back. It was, he was relieved to discover, from Claire Derwent who had obviously emerged from her interminable sulk, for she wrote:

My dear Paul,

You must think me a presumptuous little fool! Perhaps Rose has told you why I went off without even saying good-bye, but the truth is, on the day after our party, I was so bored, restless and miserable, and everything seemed such a dreadful anticlimax that I just had to do something desperately different! The chance of a visit to cousins here (which I had previously declined) seemed one way out but I didn't know then, of course, that it would become permanent. Well, it has! I'm opening a tea shop in partnership with my Cousin Marion at a place called Penshurst

*that you may or may not have heard of because it's a
famous Elizabethan house owned by the De Lisle
family (Sir Philip Sydney and all that) and lots of
London visitors come here in the summer so it ought
to be fun as well as profitable! I shall miss the Valley,
of course, but not so much as you'd imagine, for the
countryside here is just as pretty and Kent, remember,
is the Garden of England! I do know (and how could
I fail to know) what a little fool I made of myself as
regards you. I was to blame from the beginning and
hope you won't hold it against me for the rest of my
life. I can only put it down to the dullness of life at
High Coombe until you arrived to brighten things up
a bit but now I've had lots of time to think it over
and, like I say, it makes me blush to think of the way
I behaved to someone who was such a good friend
and had plenty of worries of his own! I do most sincerely wish you all the luck in the world, Paul, and
I know you'll do well down there, "bringing all
they ole 'puddenades' bang up-to-date, midear!" and
heaven knows they need it! Keep at it, and bless you,*

Yours affectionately,
Claire Derwent.

The friendliness of her letter touched him deeply for he
began to see how he had encouraged her more than she
cared to admit and also that she had almost certainly been
taken to task by her father and packed off home from the
party with a flea in her ear. Her letter mellowed him so
that he could think of her now with warmth and laughter
and he reflected that a letter as frank and cheerful as this
might do something to sweeten his relationship with Rose,
whom he admired, and Edward Derwent, whom he respected. Ever since Claire had taken the huff relations between Shallowford House and High Coombe had been
very cool and Paul realised that he could not afford to
incur the enmity of both the Codsalls and the Derwents
within six months of moving in. So, before answering
Claire's letter, he wrote a note to Rose telling her that

he had heard from Claire and was writing to wish her luck with her tea-shop venture.

He then opened his fourth letter, to find that it was a brief note from Celia Lovell, stating that they would be returning to Coombe Bay shortly and inviting him to call for tea, at 4 P.M. on December 31st. That was all. No hint that Grace had confided in her, no enquiries concerning their conversation regarding the estate, just that they were coming home and he was invited for tea on the last day of the old year. Re-reading the letter in an effort to learn something of Celia Lovell's character he thought of her as someone who never put pen to paper without recognising the possibility that she might be called upon to justify it in a court of common pleas.

After lunch the rain stopped and a watery sun came out, so he told Ikey to prepare the dog-cart and put a loose halter on Snowdrop, so that he might drive into Coombe Bay for shoeing the grey and the cob. As an afterthought he took Grace's retriever pup, perched on the box beside him. She was a gawky, lovable little bitch, with a pathetic eagerness to make friends with everybody and Paul lavished upon her a special affection of which she took shameless advantage, calling her "Goneaway" because of her ever-hopeful but always unsuccessful pursuit of game flushed from the thickets during her walks. She lolloped at his heels as he rode about the estate, sometimes following him so closely that her face was masked by a film of liquid mud thrown up by Snowdrop's hooves. Paul had come to agree with Chivers, the groom, that she was untrainable as a gun dog but he went on trying, calling her to heel when she was half-way down a rabbit hole, or scrabbling at a molehill, and thus a curious rhythm was established between man and dog that varied according to the time of day. Whenever Paul thought anyone else was present he used a stern voice but when he and Goneaway were alone in the study, all pretence of trainer and trainee was abandoned and the bitch leapt on to chairs, dragged bones under rugs and invariably positioned herself where she could monopolise the heat of the fire.

The Coombe Bay smith, a squat, mild-mannered man called Abe Tozer, promised to shoe the horses within the hour, so Paul, taking Goneaway, walked up the east side of the slope overlooking the harbour, where stood Lovell's rented house, shuttered and silent. He was a little disappointed at this, and almost decided to call at the lodge and ask if the family was expected before Christmas, but thought better of it and walked on to the sandhills above the beach.

A high sea was running but the tide was out and beyond the empty beach he could see rollers throwing up a fine spray that travelled on the wind as far as the ridge. Beyond the bar, a mile out to sea, was a grey tumult of water and the horizon beyond Nun's Island and Whinmouth Head was empty and desolate, with the threat of more rain to come. He had walked perhaps a half-mile along the little plateau when the dog, barking furiously, dashed down the slope to the beach and began to worry the legs of a solitary figure who was so close to the water that Paul realised he was drenched by every wave. He called Goneaway to heel but the dog, as usual, took no notice of him, so he ran down the sandy slope to offer an apology. When he was half-way across the beach he stopped, recognising that the stationary figure was in fact Martin Codsall. The man was impervious to the dog or, indeed, to anything but the breakers crashing on the bar far out to sea.

He called, "Give the dog a cuff, Codsall!" but Martin seemed not to hear and made no movement of any sort but continued to stand in the overspill staring fixedly out to sea, as though fascinated by something happening beyond the bar. When he came up with him Paul was startled to see that his expression was blank and that his weather-beaten face was as unresponsive as the rest of his body. He noticed also that Codsall seemed very inadequately dressed for a wet day in late December, having nothing on his back but an old jacket, a collarless shirt with a pair of tattered trousers stuffed into topboots. Goneaway soon lost interest in him and scampered off to tease a stranded crab but Paul, taking Martin by the arm, shook him, asking, "What is it, Codsall? What do you see out there?", but still Codsall gave no sign that he was being adressed and Paul noticed that he was trembling, either from the cold or the rigidity of his posture. Just then a ninth wave drenched

224

them both and Paul swore, jerking the man higher up the beach and here Codsall gave a long shudder, seeming to emerge from a trance. Paul saw then that the fellow was suffering from some kind of self-hypnosis and his mind returned to some of the cases of epilepsy he had seen in hospital. He said, leading Codsall away from the water, "Come on, old man, let's get back and dry off," and they walked arm in arm back along the beach, Codsall stumbling sometimes and leaning more than half his weight on Paul.

It was only when they were ascending the slipway near the boat-shelter that he seemed to be aware of what was happening, for suddenly he withdrew his arm, stared at Paul for a moment, and said, hoarsely, "I thought I seed something out there! Out beyond the bar! A ship it was, but 'er's sunk now, I reckon," and he looked distractedly over his shoulder at the empty bay and stumbled slightly, throwing himself sideways, so that Paul had to brace himself to prevent his falling flat on his face. As this happened, however, he caught a strong whiff of Codsall's breath and was at once reassured for it reeked of cider and he came to the conclusion that Martin was blind drunk. It was strange, he thought, that he had never heard Martin Codsall described as a heavy drinker or, indeed, given to excess of any kind but as he watched him on their way up the street it was clear that Martin had been drinking very heavily indeed for his gait was dangerously uncertain and his speech so slurred that Paul abandoned all attempts to reason with him, hoisting him into the back of the dog-cart whilst he paid the smith and saw the cob harnessed to the shafts and Snowdrop tethered behind. The smith did not seem surprised at the piece of flotsam Paul had brought in from the beach. "Ah, Marty Codsall has been swilling like a good 'un lately," he said, grinning. "In the bar of The Raven most days he is and when he's had all Minnie Flowers will draw for him he wanders off along the beach, babbling about ships and suchlike! Catch his death o' cold he will, if he don't wrap up more and get the horrors too if he don't ease off a point or two, sir! Be you zeein' to him, or shall I?"

225

"I'll take him home myself," Paul told him, and then, "Does Arabella know that he's soaking it up like this?"

Tozer chuckled, saying, "Well, beggin' your pardon, Squire, if 'er don't it'd be the first bit o' tittle-tattles her's missed in a lifetime!", and Paul, reasoning this must be so, said no more, lifting Goneaway into the trap and driving off along the four-mile river track to the ford.

Once or twice during the journey he glanced over his shoulder at Codsall, who now sat slumped with his back to him, staring down the way they were travelling. Apart from heaving a long, gasping sigh now and again he remained silent. He seems drunk, Paul thought, but he doesn't look drunk, just completely bemused, and then it occurred to him that perhaps Martin was ill and wondered whether he should call at Doctor O'Keefe's before taking him home. He decided against, however, for it was now getting dark and Codsall was obviously suffering from the cold, so Paul drove him as far as the yard of Four Winds, resolving to leave him there for he had no wish to tangle with Arabella again and began to feel rather sorry for the farmer when he thought of the reception he was likely to get from his wife. They crossed the plank bridge and went up the rutted lane to where a square of light glowed beyond the yard rick and here Paul dumped his passenger on one of the Codsall labourers, who emerged from the long row of byres housing the Codsall Friesians.

"Master's had a drop too much," he told the man. "Sober him up in the barn!" Then, as he began to turn the dog-cart, a strange thing happened. Martin Codsall seemed to shed his helplessness in a flash and suddenly hoisted himself to full height, his features losing their vacuity as they contracted into a kind of mask that suggested scheming servility or deep cunning.

"Obliged to 'ee for the lift, Squire," he said, clearly and distinctly, as though his slurred speech had been part of a practical joke. "I'll go along in to me supper, and thank 'ee, zir, thank 'ee kindly." Then, spinning round on the man, he shouted angrily, "Dornee waste no time on me, Ben! Get to tending the cattle, you bliddy layabout! Go on, before I kicks your arse through the barn door!", and having succeeded in astonishing Paul beyond measure, and

226

effectively cowed the grinning farmhand, Codsall touched his forelock and marched steadily across the yard and in through the kitchen door.

Paul would have liked to question Ben on his master but the man had disappeared so he drove off down the lane, wondering if Codsall's heavy drinking had any connection with the recent abdication of his son Will, or with his wife's persistent nagging about the marriage. If it had, he decided, there was very little that he or anyone else could do about it. So long as the Four Winds rent was paid on quarter-day, and the farm continued to yield more than all the Coombe farms put together, it was none of his business yet he continued to think about the incident all the evening and went so far as to discuss it with Mrs. Handcock, who opposed his suggestion to call in O'Keefe on such a pretext. "The Codsalls 'ave all got a mazed streak in 'em," she declared, "but mostly it dorn amount to more than silliness. Marty's father, old Amyas Codsall, was a praper ole miser most of his life and then he got religion an' give three-parts of his money to missionaries in Zululand, or some such plaace. And *his* father, Sam, was mazed too! He once stood a whole night in Paxtonbury market-plaace in midwinter, just to watch somebody hanged outside the gaol! No, zir, like I'm always atelling of 'ee, dornee bother with all their upsets! They won't thank 'ee for it! Like as not Arabella'll traapse about the Valley zaying youm persecutin' 'em!" That clinched it as far as Paul was concerned and soon he forgot the incident altogether, to recall it a year later, when he had reason to blame both himself and his housekeeper for not taking a more sustained interest in the current trials of Martin Codsall.

II

The Reverend Bull sent a message over on Christmas Eve saying he "confidently expected Squire to attend Seven Carol Service that evening" and had "marked him down" to read one of the lessons. This was Bull's way with parishioners. He never suggested or invited he "confidently

227

expected". He never made requests, he simply "marked people down". Paul had already succumbed to the rector's tactics and sometimes even defended him against the attacks of his new friend, James Grenfell. The Liberal candidate admitted that he could not stomach the man and regarded him as a self-indulgent reactionary, using his cloth to patch a dying feudalism in the Valley, but Paul was growing tolerant of Sorrel Valley eccentricities and argued that a man of Bull's disposition at least projected the Church as something positive, a creed that men and women who lived with their noses in soil could understand and that Bull was an improvement on some of the professional hearties he had encountered in South Africa. He told the parson's messenger that he would attend the service and that he would bring along a contingent of Home Farm and indoor staff for the occasion. In the event Honeyman harnessed a couple of horses to the waggonette and they all rattled off to church with Mrs. Handcock, two of the maids, Ikey Palfrey, Chivers and the biblical shepherds, Matt and Luke, who seemed to Paul reincarnations of the originals in the popular carol. He himself rode over in the wake of the waggon for it was a clear, crisp night, lit by stars, and Snowdrop was familiar with the well-beaten track across the stubble fields and down the long slope to the village.

The little parish church was practically full and when he took his place at the lectern, sandwiching a passage from St. Matthew between "Once in Royal David's City" and "The Holly and the Ivy", Paul had some difficulty in restraining a smile on noting the incongruous assembly in the pews. The Potter clan was represented by Pansy and her swain, Walt Pascoe. She had persuaded him that attendance now might divert Parson Bull's wrath when they were married here in the New Year, for Parson Bull castigated loving couples at a marriage ceremony if they were known to have restricted church attendance to weddings, funerals and christenings. Arabella Codsall and her younger son Sydney were there, but neither Martin nor Will, the latter having defected to his wife's denomination since marriage. Edward Derwent and his wife were present, with their daughter Rose, and so were all the three Pitts. The remainder of the congregation was made up of Valley farm labourers and their womenfolk and a majority of Coombe Bay villagers, exclusive of the little fishing fraternity, who were chapelgoers to a man.

They sang lustily and prayed devoutly and when it was all over and they dispersed in the churchyard, there was a babel of gossip, a noisy exchange of Christmas greetings and a good deal of kissing and giggling among canting tombstones. Paul had left Snowdrop at the smithy's and was leading him out, preparatory to mounting, when Ikey came up with a message that someone was waiting to speak to Squire by the rear lych-gate and that he was asked to go round by the church wall on foot. Somewhat mystified by this cryptic message Paul asked Ikey who it was but Ikey could not say. The message, he said, had been relayed to him by one of the choirboys.

"Very well," Paul told him resignedly, for he was cold and hungry, "put the grey in the forge and tell Honeyman to drive on home," and he went down the steep lane beside the church wall to the rear part of the churchyard, now cut off from the light of the church lamps by a belt of yews.

As he approached the gate there was a movement beside the buttress and Grace Lovell's voice came out of the darkness. "Well, Paul," she said, "this rendezvous should appeal to an incurable romantic!", and she gave him her small, gloved hand.

He was more astonished and delighted than he could say. It had never occurred to him that the message had come from her and he had assumed it was from one of the dissenting members of the parish who were invariably treated as trespassers by Bull.

He said, excitedly, "I had no idea you were home! I thought if you were you would be sure to attend the service!" but she told him they had driven over from Whinmouth only that day and that Bruce, her father, was now in Biarritz and likely to remain there until spring. Then she said, more urgently, "Let's not waste time, Paul! I've only a few minutes and Celia would explode if she knew I was here alone. I wanted to see you before you called. You got Celia's letter?"

"Yes," he said, "and I replied to it saying I should be very happy to come."

"She didn't have the decency to tell me that," Grace said, "but it doesn't matter now."

He could not see her in the deep shadow but he could smell her perfume and it came to him like the scent of summer hedgerows. He still held her gloved hand and she let him hold it, so that they stood there, levelled by the lych-gate step and her nearness stirred him even more deeply than when they last stood together on the terrace at Shallowford.

"What is it, Grace?" he asked. "Would you prefer that I didn't accept Celia's invitation next week?"

"No," she said but doubtfully, as though by no means certain about this, "you'll have to come, I suppose, because she won't let go of you now if she can help it! But there is something you can do before you see her; you can tell me the truth. As far as you know it yourself, that is!"

"The truth about what?" he asked.

"About how serious you were on the night of the ball. Oh, you needn't protest, and you don't have to sound a gallant fanfare for my daring to doubt your sincerity! I daresay you thought yourself in earnest at the time but it was a heady occasion. You were probably full of cider-cup and feeling very sure of yourself that evening!"

She stopped suddenly and he could hear her rapid breathing. "Do you want me to go on, Paul? Can we talk to one another honestly and openly?"

"Yes," he said, feeling deflated, "you had best say what's on your mind, Grace."

"Well," she went on, "things came to a head while we were in London. My father brought home a fat prize one night, and they both expected me to agree to marry it almost at once! You needn't know anything about him, except that he was going bald, was well over forty, likely to become a Member of Parliament, and very comfortably off! Naturally I wasn't forthcoming and there was a great deal of unpleasantness, not only about Basil Holbeach, but . . . well . . . about many other things! It was then that I told Celia about you. I didn't want to but I needed her support, and I got it. Celia is mad to get me off her hands but she is neither as cynical nor as money-grubbing as my father, and neither is she more than an average snob. Besides,"—there was laughter in her voice now—"you made a very good impression on her! She thinks you're going to succeed down here and because her money originates from blacking she doesn't care about your scrapyard!"

It was the first time she had referred to the scrapyard although he had long since decided that she must be aware of it, as were most people in the Valley by now.

"Tell me where these developments lead us," he said, "and how you could be stupid enough to persuade yourself I was in liquor when I asked you to marry me! That seems to me to be the only thing that matters."

"Yes, it is, Paul," she said, choosing her words carefully now, "and that's why I wanted to talk to you before you faced Celia's batteries. I know what she'll say and how she'll approach the matter. She'll say 'Grace is a little wild and a little wilful' but that she's still very young, and will steady down the moment she has a husband and babies!"

"She's probably right at that," Paul said good-humouredly but in the darkness he sensed her impatient gesture, as she withdrew her hand from his. "She doesn't mean it that way," Grace insisted. "She means I should enjoy being the lady of the manor down here, organising soirées like the one Claire Derwent arranged for you, doling out blankets and logs to the poor at Christmas time, visiting the sick and trotting dutifully about the country behind Gilroy's pack of hounds! Because she's Celia she's convinced that this is the only destiny for the provincial girl of good family!"

"Well I'm not so sure that it isn't," he protested, "or could be if you didn't make it sound so damned dull!" and was surprised when she laid her hand on his arm and said emphatically, "Perhaps it is, Paul! For some provincial girls, but I've always known it wasn't my destiny, even when I was engaged to Ralph Lovell! A woman brought up to do that sort of thing, as I was, might achieve it without much trouble, providing she was in love with the man she married."

"Very well," he said, gruffly, "you aren't obliged to say any more, Grace, and in spite of everything I'd like you to

231

know that I honestly appreciate your frankness and when I meet Celia I hope I can be equally candid."

"Oh stop being so *young,* Paul," she burst out impatiently. "How many marriages of this kind, between people with money, are love matches? Not one in fifty and only then between a cow-like couple who do what they're told because it's so much less trouble! Of course I don't love you! How could I? Or you me, if you're really honest with yourself! I daresay you could learn to, and it's possible that I might learn to, but at the moment you're attracted to me by two factors; you imagine marriage to me would give you social security and you probably think it might be nice to have me in bed! Well, that isn't so original—a lot of men have been that much in love with me, but it doesn't mean we know each other, or could distil a particle of mutual happiness or usefulness from a permanent association!"

"Good God!" he said, "you make everything sound like a political tract! I think of you as the most exciting girl I've ever met, and I'm more attracted to you every time I see you, or hear you speak, or touch your hand! I can't reduce love to a kind of formula, like you seem to want to! I'm prepared to take something on trust and leave something to chance, the same as I did when I spent everything I had on this place! Everyone who falls in love and gets married takes risks. What about young Will Codsall and Elinor Willoughby? He turned his back on the best farm in the Valley to marry Elinor and she faced up to a mother-in-law with a disposition as sour as Krueger's! Can't you ever give your instincts a chance?"

She was not, it seemed, impressed by his arguments, or by the emphasis with which he presented them but she paid him the compliment of taking them more seriously than she had taken his proposal.

"I obeyed my instincts coming here and giving you the opportunity of unsaying what you said the last time we met," she said calmly. "I've got far more respect for you than for most men I've met so far, and there are things about you that I admire, Paul. But I don't love you, and I don't even know you sufficiently well to know whether I could love you. I've always had a contempt for the tradi-

232

tional responses of women on these occasions, particularly
when faced with the chance to make what they call a good
match! I'm not really interested in being the Lady of Shallowford. I think I might have bigger fish to fry, if English-
women as a whole ever break out of the seraglio!
Good-bye, Paul!"

"But in heaven's name we haven't begun to decide . . ."
he protested.

"There's time enough," she said, "and I daren't stay
longer. If I'm missed, or seen here it will make things ten
times more complicated for me than they are! Good night
and a Merry Christmas!", and before he could stop her
she had bobbed forward and kissed him lightly on the
cheek and vanished. He called "Grace!" softly but there
was no answer, only the scuffle of her shoes on the gravel
of the path that emerged lower down the High Street, opposite the hill leading to her home.

III

Celia received him in her boudoir, a small room off the
draughty landing that overlooked the bay. It was, he had
decided by then, a gloomy, badly-planned house, over-
stuffed with heavy mahogany furniture that contrasted with
Celia's fashionable clothes and hard good looks demanding an altogether lighter setting. She must have noticed his
appraisal for she said, deprecatingly, "It's your furniture,
Mr. Craddock! We rent it just as it is—antimacassars,
stuffed elks-heads, and all! If I made you an offer for the
place I should throw everything out but I wouldn't buy the
house anyway, the only thing I like about it is its site,"
and she pointed to the view of the harbour framed in the
sash window.

"I hope you won't be too disappointed at having tea
with me instead of Grace," she went on. "When I dropped
a hint that she paid a call in Whinmouth I expected tantrums but there weren't any. You never can be quite sure
of Grace and she seemed to prefer you and I to meet
alone at . . . er . . . at this stage! Does that surprise you?"

233

"No," he said, "I don't think she could surprise me, Mrs. Lovell."

Celia laughed, pleasantly and genuinely he thought, telling himself that there was something individual and very engaging about Celia Lovell as she sat pouring tea from a silver pot after boiling the kettle on a little silver spirit stove. There were muffins in a silver dish and cakes on a silver cakestand. Everything she used was expensive and delicately made, and all her movements were precise, as though she assessed in advance the exact amount of effort needed to lift a plate or pinch a knob of sugar with tongs. Then, when he was comfortably settled, she came straight to the point.

"Grace told me that you proposed mariage to her last October," she said, in a reasonable but businesslike tone. "I must admit to being surprised, as no doubt she was herself, but I was also delighted. I'm like her in one respect. I dislike fiddle-faddle and I'm glad to see that you don't seem to have much use for it, Mr. Craddock! I take it that she asked time to consider but has not written to you since?"

"That is so, Mrs. Lovell," replied Paul, feeling like a friendly witness being cross-examined by a sharp-witted barrister.

"Well now," she went on, kindly but expansively, "I should like you to know at once that I consider it very suitable! Very suitable *indeed!* In fact I think she would be a very silly girl not to accept!" She gave him a sidelong look, adding, "Upon my word, *I* should accept, Mr. Craddock!" leaving him in no doubt but that she spoke in earnest.

Paul said nothing for there seemed so little to say. After a pause, during which they both sipped tea, she continued, "In the circumstances, Mr. Craddock, I cannot but feel that you should know the full facts. The truth is, in some ways Grace has been causing both her father and myself a great deal of anxiety, but perhaps she told you something of this?"

It was a trap but he saw it in time. Celia obviously suspected that they had met since the family's return and

234

he said, smiling, "No, Mrs. Lovell, although I have gathered she is rather uncertain about her future."

"She has no need to be, I assure you," Celia replied, quite sharply, "for Grace isn't a gel who lacks admiration. Her father would have encouraged her to accept another proposal, from a gentleman in possession of considerable means but he was a good deal older than Grace and I'm not at all in favour of marriages between people of different generations, notwithstanding settlements. It was then that she came to me for advice."

It was all, he thought, like something from an early nineteenth-century novel, with mamma using a set formula for the occasion, and in the light of what he already knew it was difficult for him to feel that Celia Lovell was free from hypocrisy. He said, slowly, "You said you don't like fiddle-faddle, Mrs. Lovell, so I gather from that you would prefer us to be frank with one another. Would you mind telling me *how* Grace has caused you and Mr. Lovell anxiety? Was it a love affair?"

"Oh no, certainly not," she said, seeming alarmed. "No, Mr. Craddock, it wasn't that! As a matter of fact Grace never has been attracted by younger men and, to be perfectly honest, I don't think she was as upset by Ralph Lovell's death as she ought to have been! Or if she was then she didn't show it! No, no, it was something quite different and it began when we were last in town and still remains a source of well . . . a rather strained atmosphere between Grace and her father. I imagine you must have heard about these dreadful suffragists?"

"The National Union of Women's Suffrage? Why yes, hasn't everyone? Is Grace a member?"

"I really couldn't say," Celia replied, obviously shocked by his implied tolerance, "all I know is that she has been associating with them, has even attended their public meetings! That we found distressing enough but the original group, although faddist and, to my mind, quite ridiculous, was at least constitutional! Recently there has been a breakaway movement led by a very provocative woman called Pankhurst and her two daughters, but perhaps you have read of them in the newspapers?"

Paul had but had not paid particular note of the cleavage. There had been brief reports in copies of the *Westminster Gazette*, that arrived in the Valley a day or two late and described lively scenes at political meetings and demonstrations. He recalled an instance of a woman climbing on to a roof at a Unionist meeting and being removed by firemen and policemen but even in his conversations with Grenfell, the subejct of votes for women had never come under discussion and he was suprised to find that Celia Lovell took it seriously.

"It sounds quite harmless," he said evasively and was relieved to see Celia smile.

"I'm sure it is, so far as Grace is concerned," she admitted, "but her father took a very serious view of her involvement in this kind of thing and I must say I don't blame him! After all, a girl who makes an exhibition of herself is hardly likely to make a good marriage and that is what I want for Grace more than anything else. Being a stepmother carries exceptional responsibilities, Mr. Craddock."

"Yes," said Paul, "I can understand that, but it seems to me . . ."

"*Do* let me give you some more tea, Mr. Craddock!" she said, and he had the impression that this was to give her time to think as a barrister might drop papers when his witness was facing an awkward question. She poured tea and handed him the cakestand. When they were settled again she said, mildly, "*Do* go on, Mr. Craddock, and I hope you feel that you can confide in me. I most earnestly want to help in any way I can."

"I'm sure you do, Mrs. Lovell," he said, sensing that he had now got the measure of her, "but in the case of a girl like Grace I can't help feeling that the best way to help is to do nothing. I believe myself to be in love with her, and I'm sure that, in time, I could make her very happy here. However, I haven't any fatuous illusions about her being in love with me at this moment, and in this day and age surely a girl as intelligent as Grace should be allowed to make her own decisions."

She was now regarding him with admiration and he almost blushed for her, so artless were her tactics in contrast to those employed over the first cup of tea. He noticed something else too and it disturbed him a little, a glaze of ruthlessness in the alert, brown eyes and also the frank sensuality of the mouth. "By God," he thought, "I'll wager she can be worse than Arabella Codsall when she's roused! No wonder Bruce is keeping out of the way in Biarritz!" But again he was confident of handling her and the knowledge pleased and excited him, for he found his natural diffidence slipping away and he felt more assured than he recalled feeling in the presence of a woman. "Where is Grace now, Mrs. Lovell?" he asked and she replied, "I'm expecting her any moment, I thought we could have our little talk and then . . . well . . . I can find something to do and you could talk to her before you left. For that matter you could stay for dinner if you liked and . . ."

"No!" he said and stood up so abruptly that for a moment she looked at a loss. "I don't think that would be a good idea, Mrs. Lovell. It seems to me that it might . . . well . . . stampede Grace one way or the other! I think it would be wiser if I left before she returned, although I don't mind if you tell her about this discussion. There's no hurry, however, I'm not likely to fall in love again at short notice."

He said this as a joke but it was only after a moment's deliberation with herself that she could accept it as such. Then she was her assured self again, laying a long, elegant hand on his arm. "Do you know, I think I underestimated you, Mr. Craddock! I always thought of you as a kind, mildly ambitious young man but I also thought you had a great deal to learn about women."

"I have, indeed," said Paul, smiling, "and I daresay it will take me a lifetime."

"Nonsense!" she said, now almost caressing his hand, "you already understand Grace better than the rest of us. I don't suppose she is half as complex as we imagine and I'm sure that the time will come when she will look back on this votes for women nonsense and laugh about it! There now, let me show you downstairs, and when Grace comes I'll tell her I've been flirting with you, and that you would like her to ride over to Shallowford tomorrow."

"On a horse, not on a bicycle," said Paul, and Celia, again looking at him with approval, said, "We really do

237

think alike, Mr. Craddock! And it's been a pleasure to talk to you! I can only repeat what I said, I think she's a very lucky girl!", and she swept out in front of Paul and along the passage to the head of the staircase.

Paul was admiring the skill with which she handled her voluminous lilac skirt, and the effect of a wan shaft of sunlight on her light brown hair, when the front door opened and Grace walked into the hall. She was wearing the bicycling costume she had worn when she called at the house to shelter and looked, Paul thought, even more windblown than on that occasion. Her defeated expression touched him so that he cursed Celia Lovell for not whisking him out of the house before she returned. They stood in embarrassed silence for a moment and it would have been hard to say which of them was the more dismayed. Then Celia flashed one of her brittle smiles, saying, "Mr. Craddock was just leaving, Grace dear. I tried to get him to stay to dinner but he can't, he's very busy it seems. You are sure you won't change your mind, Mr. Craddock?"

"No, if you'll forgive me," he lied, "I've got a great deal to do before Mr. Rudd comes back tomorrow," and he saw Grace's chin come up sharply, as though Rudd's return was an added cause for depression but she said nothing, continuing to stare at the tiles on the floor and fidget with her shapeless hat. Mrs. Lovell said, with a brightness that Paul now found irritating, "Would you like to ride over to Shallowford tomorrow? May Mr. Craddock expect you?"

It was like listening to an unimaginative mother encouraging a stupidly bashful child and suddenly he felt desperately sorry for the small, dejected figure, standing so irresolutely in her hideous costume.

"Come if you want to, Grace, and come on your bicycle if you like," he said. "You'll always be welcome and I'll tell Mrs. Handcock to make you comfortable in the library if I'm out. I'm usually there until about eleven and always after tea. I could drive you home in the trap," and he was rewarded by a look of gratitude and an almost inaudible "Thank you, Paul" as Grace sidestepped Celia and walked quickly through a curtained aperture at the rear of the hall. As he opened the front door to let himself out Mrs.

Lovell seemed about to say something more but he cut her short, this time almost brutally.

"I don't want Grace harried, Mrs. Lovell! Please remember that, and tell Mr. Lovell the same!"

She made no reply to this but her lips parted and once again he had a strong impression that beneath her good breeding and natural amiability, she was as hard and ruthless as a professional whore. He went out into the gathering dusk and along to the yard of The Raven where he had left the trap. Looking back over his shoulder he saw a light in the upstairs room and he thought, "That must be her bedroom, and I'll wager she's up there crying, and even if I marry the girl I doubt if I shall ever discover why."

IV

Paul Craddock would have won his wager. Grace was weeping but not, as he had half-imagined, face downwards on her bed, shoulders shaking with sobs for she had never wept in this fashion, not even when the Ayah told her that the Memsahib was dead and she was facing the eternity of childhood with the man whose pale, protruberant eyes had never looked on her without impatience or contempt. When Grace Lovell wept, which was seldom, the tears flowed sparingly and never for more than a moment so that presently she studied herself in the dressing-table mirror impatient with what she saw and wondering how an uncomplicated man like Paul Craddock could hoodwink himself into imagining that she would make a good wife for a young man who was already close on a century out of date. Yet she conceded obstinacy that put him outside her experience. Her father was obstinate but only as regards matters related to his own comfort. Ralph Lovell had been obstinate in a different way, setting his face against the acceptance of any responsibility, even that of keeping sober in mixed company. Ralph's father, old Sir George, had been very obstinate indeed in persuading young females to take off their clothes and stand in front of his camera but neither could match the quiet obstinacy of this limping Cockney, with his nasal accent and dedication to a pastoral way of life that belonged in the reign of George IV.

Her tears ceased to flow and her features composed themselves into their habitual, vaguely mutinous expression, an expression that had defeated all but the most determined assaults upon her privacy. Up here, temporarily out of range of Celia's flashing smile and merciless solicitude, Grace did her thinking for when she was in the open her mind had a habit of shooting off at a tangent every few minutes. Sooner or later, probably sooner she thought, Celia would corner Paul Craddock, and persuade him to press his advantage. It had been touch and go whether Celia had declared in favour of the egregious Basil Holbeach and now that she had quarrelled with Bruce on his account her need to secure the substitute was imperative. Perhaps the important thing to consider was, did Paul Craddock possess any "advantage"? He was well off—not nearly so rich as Holbeach but surely comfortable if he could find thousands of pounds for a run-down estate and then pour more money into its rehabilitation. Not that his means concerned Grace. Money was important to Celia and absolutely essential to her father, but meant little to her for she had never possessed any and had not even had indirect access to small change until her father's second marriage. She found that she was able to think about Paul Craddock with detachment in a way that she had never been able to review any of the men her father or Celia had introduced into her life, after news of Ralph's death in the Transvaal had reached them. He was healthy and whole, except for that damage to his leg, which did not seem to trouble him much and he was obviously very kindhearted. He thought her beautiful and had even confessed to excitement every time he approached her and the boyishness of this admission made her smile into the mirror, for the poor man was obviously besotted if he introduced considerations of this sort into a marriage of the kind Celia had in mind for him. He was probably the most genuinely disinterested suitor to present himself but did this make him worth the sacrifice of individuality? For all his kindness, and boyish enthusiasm, marriage to him

240

would surely entail such a sacrifice, for clearly his idealism would never expand into wider, more adult fields and she could expect little from him but a humdrum life bounded by the sea, the main railway line, and the estate boundaries east and west, with possibly a monthly visit to Paxtonbury, which he would consider a rare treat. The prospect dismayed her almost as much as marriage to Basil Holbeach, soon to join the nameless ranks of Conservative and Unionist backbenchers at Westminster, a man who would lock his wife in her bedroom if he caught her reading a pamphlet of Mrs. Pankhurst's endeavours. Yet, unlike Basil or any of his predecessors, there was something appealing about Paul Craddock and what that something was she found it hard to decide. In a way it was a kind of sound, that seemed to reach him from a dead century, when Merrie England was an actuality and she fell to wondering about his background, and the strange impulses that had encouraged him to turn his back on opportunities that usually presented themselves to young men with fortunes. Even Ralph Lovell, lout as he was, with no other thought in his head beyond horses, wenching and whisky, had adventured further afield than Paul, whereas Ralph's father, the old satyr who pinched little girls' bottoms and photographed them in the nude, had had interests that sometimes brought him in touch with men of modern ideas.

She tried to imagine how a man with such an archaic dream would acquit himself as a lover. He would probably be courteous, considerate or accommodating according to her moods. If she held her face stiff when he kissed her good night he would go to sleep and awake next morning without resentment. He could be roused, no doubt, whenever she felt inclined and the inevitable result would be several nicely-spaced children, growing up like a row of cabbages and receiving formal education according to their sex. It was not a pleasing prospect but what was the alternative? A regular shuttle to and from this hideous house to Cadogan Square, and back again; wrangles with her father over her activities in London and tiresome importuning on Celia's part to capture the inevitable husband or, if not, to tread the social mill of her At Homes and the

241

musical soirées, where young men prattled endlessly of pictures and tepid novels, and bombazined old hags chattered scandal, deferring to smug-faced husbands on every issue that really mattered. There must in the name of God be a compromise between these two fates and for the hundredth time in the last few months she thought of flight. But flight to where or to whom? With sixpence in her reticule? The prospect was even more absurd than marriage.

And then, as her mind shied at the years ahead, her strong sense of fair play reminded her that it would be a shabby trick to use a man as vulnerable as Paul Craddock as a harbour where she could never anchor herself for long. He might be a fool, might even be addressing himself to the task of putting the clock back, but at least he was honest, warm-hearted and relatively harmless and deserved a wife who would expect no more of him than he had to offer. It was thinking along these lines that she made her decision and having made it felt carefree again. Tomorrow morning, she promised herself, she would ride over to Shallowford House and tell Paul Craddock, frankly and kindly, exactly why she could not marry him and afterwards acquaint Celia with her decision and direct her attentions elsewhere.

Downstairs the gong sounded for dinner and she changed into a green dinner frock without bothering to do more than wash her hands and tie a ribbon under her curls. She felt more than equal to Celia tonight, reflecting that she might even enjoy leading her partway up the garden path.

By ten o'clock on New Year's Day Grace Lovell was approaching the ford and as she walked her mare Roxy across the path-fields she was satisfied that her speech was word perfect. About half-a-mile from the crossing, however, a yellow dog-cart flashed past, going in the opposite direction and driven hard by a round-shouldered little man in an ulster and a billycock hat. She recognised him as Grenfell, the local Radical candidate, who had entered the field against Hilton-Price, Paxtonbury's Unionist M.P., and although she had almost as great a contempt for Liberals as for their political rivals, she wished him well if only for

242

having the courage to plant a Radical standard on such Philistine soil. She soon dismissed him, however, readdressing herself to the business in hand, and it was only when she was crossing the river that she remembered him for ahead of her, on the point of turning into Shallowford drive, was another gig with two men on the box, and she recognised them as well. The driver was Lord Gilroy and his passenger, a thickset man about fifty, was Cribb, the local Unionist agent, a man whose job, so they said, was a sinecure, for how could anyone but a Conservative win Paxtonbury, one of the safest seats in the British Isles? There was nothing odd about Gilroy and his agent paying a call upon the Squire of Shallowford on New Year's Day but the circumstances began to seem unusual when she realised that their visit followed Grenfell's by less than ten minutes and suddenly Grace forgot about her speech in an attempt to draw conclusions from this coincidence. Had Grenfell just come from Shallowford? He must have done, for this track led nowhere else, except to the railway halt and no train stopped at Sorrel Halt until after midday. There was clearly significance in Gilroy's visit too, or why should he be accompanied by Cribb? Were both parties competing for Paul Craddock's support? And if so, could there be the least possibility of the brash young man challenging local mandarins as powerful as Gilroy and the Hilton-Prices?

She gave the gig time to increase its lead and dawdled in the area of the ford for a few minutes. Paul could not receive her until they had gone and if they remained indefinitely she decided to postpone her call and keep Celia on tenterhooks for another twenty-four hours. The prospect of this did not displease her, and she rode round the paddock and entered the yard from the east, leaving Roxy with a perky little boy, who ran forward to take the reins. Gilroy's gig was in the forecourt, the horse tethered to a ring on a lamp socket and she could hear the murmur of voices coming through the library window. The garden door of what used to be old Sir George's studio was unlocked and by opening it, and standing in the angle made by the terrace, she could hear very clearly what was being said in the next room. If she hesitated a moment from taking her stand here it was because she was debating whether anything Gilroy and Cribb might have to say merited her attention, for Grace Lovell had no misgivings about eavesdropping. In her guerrilla war with her father and stepmother it had proved an indispensable means of survival. So she stood there, listening intently and so changed the course of her life.

V

Paul was map-tracing in the office when Thirza Tremlett, the parlourmaid, came in with the news that Lord Gilroy and Mr. Raymond Cribb were in the drawing-room on the other side of the hall. Thirza, the nearest approach Shallowford House possessed to a butler, was in what Mrs. Handcock would have described as "a rare ole tizzy", for the arrival of two such visitors in the forenoon frightened her and she came in flushed and out of breath. Paul himself was surprised, particularly as James Grenfell had only just left, and it occurred to him that the visitors might even have passed one another at the ford, so he was not entirely unprepared for the bleak look on his Lordship's face when Thirza ushered them into the library and fled. Cribb, however, was affable and quickly introduced himself, grasping Paul's hand with excessive firmness and apologising for having allowed six months to elapse before paying his call.

"Stopped by here a good deal in old Sir George's time," he said breezily, "but then, he was our local president before his Lordship stepped into the breach!" He went on talking about nothing in particular and Paul gained the impression that he was awaiting a cue from Gilroy but the dry old stick said nothing at all, seemingly less interested in Paul than in the room, for his eyes roved from book shelves to fireplace, then through the garden door to the office table where the estate maps were spread.

"Made a good many changes here," he remarked, gruffly, as though he resented not having been consulted. "Place didn't change at all in Lovell's time. Or his father's time either come to that!"

244

Paul murmured that the house and grounds had badly needed attention when he arrived in June and offered to show them round but when Cribb looked to Gilroy for a lead the old man waved a thin hand and said, rather impatiently, "No time today! Some other time! Might as well come straight to the point, Cribb. Nothing gained by beating about the damned bush!", and he moved over to the fire and spread his hands to the blaze.

"His Lordship refers, I think, to some idle gossip that has reached him regarding your political sympathies," said Cribb, and Paul was surprised at his directness as though he was an employer rebuking an assistant who had just bungled a sale. He went on in a slightly more genial tone. "No more than rumour, of course, but it doesn't do to let these things go unchallenged, Craddock. After all, we've got to stick together, particularly now that the Government is making such heavy weather. Wouldn't you say so?", and he flexed his massive blue jowels, so that it seemed to Paul that he was looking at two purple puddings divided by the broad peninsula of Cribb's nose.

Paul's first reaction to this challenge was astonishment. It seemed to him impossible that two men of their years could be so sure of themselves on another's hearthrug. Then, in the wake of his astonishment, resentment rose in his throat and irritation changed to anger when Gilroy, without even looking at him, said in his thin, rustling voice, "They tell me that little rat of a Radical has been courting you, Craddock! Won't do, you know! Best show the rascal the door straight away! Don't stand on politeness with scum of that kind! Give 'em an inch and they take an ell!"

Amazement at the man's insufferable arrogance held Paul's anger in check for a moment and he said, vaguely, "Rascal? Ruffian? . . . I can only suppose you must be referring to Mr. James Grenfell. He's just been here. He looks in almost every week when he's over this way," and Gilroy said, with a glare, "The devil he does! Then it's true then?" but without the least indication that he was aware of Paul's resentment.

"Yes he does," Paul said, sullenly, "and I'm bound to say that I find him not only extremely civil but excep-

245

tionally good company! Moreover, I can't help feeling that he wouldn't speak of either of you gentlemen as you have spoken of him!"

He felt much better after he had said this and regained control of himself, a process made easier by the startled look that crossed Cribb's face and the blankness of Gilroy's expression. Cribb said, in a much more conciliatory tone, "Oh come now, Craddock, you aren't going to tell his Lordship that you vote for those damned Radicals?"

"I haven't had an opportunity to vote at all yet," Paul said cheerfully, "but after this extraordinary interview I shall think about doing so at the next election!" whereupon Gilroy made a move for the door saying, in a voice scarcely above a whisper, "Come, Cribb!", but the agent was less impulsive and stood his ground, saying firmly, "No, your Lordship! Wait a moment, I beg of you! Our job is to win votes, not throw them at Grenfell's feet!", and he turned back to Paul with a smile that came close to a grimace and said, "I take it you are uncommitted, Craddock? Well, and why not? You're still a youngster and you've been out of the country throughout the war. There's no cause for a quarrel, my Lord, I daresay Mr. Craddock will learn as he goes along, and we ought, as neighbours, to give him the chance before we jump to conclusions."

Gilroy paused, seemingly undecided and Cribb readdressed himself to Paul with a great show of frankness. "Listen here, young man, I admit to being—well—a little shocked when I heard that Grenfell was a regular visitor here, and I daresay it seems presumptuous to have us pounce on you like this but you're a stranger in the district so you can't be expected to see through a wily bird like Grenfell. He's a good talker and I don't underestimate him in the way some of the party do but surely you must see that it can't be in your true interests as a landowner to get mixed up with that kind of rag, tag and bobtail! After all, if Grenfell and his kind had their way there wouldn't be any landowners!"

"Good God, man!" said Paul, "Grenfell isn't a Barcelona anarchist, or a Russian nihilist! He represents a respectable democratic party and what right have you or

246

Lord Gilroy to call here and virtually order me to show him the door?"

"We're wasting our time," Gilroy said, quietly, "the fellow is obviously a damned Radical! I suspected it from the first, when I saw what a drubbing he had given the old place!", and he would have walked into the hall had not Cribb, very flustered now, seized his arm and protested, "That isn't the way to canvass, my Lord! Believe me, I'm an old hand and there's never anything gained by turning your back on a constituent! Craddock must see for himself the harm done by adopting this we're-all-Englishmen-together attitude!", and he turned back to Paul and said, "You're open to reason, I take it? You haven't actually promised Grenfell political support in the constituency?"

Paul said, deliberately, "No, Mr. Cribb, I haven't. As a matter of fact he's never asked for it."

"He wouldn't," said Cribb savagely, "that's his way! Now listen to me, young man . . .", but Paul, plunging both hands in his breeches pockets, said, "No, Mr. Cribb, *you* listen to *me!* Before I came down here I never gave a thought to politics, except to wonder sometimes, when I saw what was happening to the Boers, how our treatment of them could be justified but I've learned a good deal about politics this morning, and I don't like what I've learned! You say this isn't the way to canvass votes and by God, you're right! I can't imagine a more hamfisted way of going about it! Grenfell, as I said, hasn't canvassed me in several visits here but neither has he treated me like a stupid child or a recently liberated serf! I'm not clear in my own mind what the Conservative Unionist Party stand for, or even what the Liberal Party stand for but you've made me eager to find out! I can see that your party lacks two things—tact and good manners, neither of which have been in evidence since you walked in that door!"

He moved above the fireplace to pull the bellrope but Gilroy cheated him by stamping out of the room before he could ring. Cribb remained, however, and seemed to be bouncing with rage, so that Paul, again seizing the advantage, said, "I'm sorry it had to happen like this, Cribb. I don't think you or I would have lost our tempers if you

247

had come alone. But what else would you expect a man to do when complete strangers walk into his house and quarrel with his choice of friends?"

Cribb was clearly a man of mettle and apparently possessed a very keen sense of duty, for he somehow mastered his rage and said, in a high-pitched voice, "You're committing social suicide here, Craddock! Good God, man, why won't you let someone experienced in these matters help you?" and Paul, scarcely knowing why, felt rather sorry for him as he said, "I don't want to seem ungracious but this is supposed to be a democratic country and we're supposed to have outgrown political pressures on the individual! Why didn't you come here like Grenfell, and make some attempt to get to know me before blackmailing me into joining a party?"

"Because it never occurred to me that you needed anyone to teach you common sense!" snapped Cribb. "A man doesn't buy an estate of thirteen hundred acres without being prepared to defend it! You should have learned that much fighting Kruger!"

He must have decided at this point that any further argument would involve him in loss of face for he picked up his hat and crossed the room but because Gilroy had slammed the door he had to fumble with the handle and while thus engaged, with Paul watching him, they heard a step on the stone floor of the office, and both turned as Grace Lovell walked into the room.

They saw that she was smiling a little sourly, as she said, with studied casualness, "I'm sorry to interrupt, but I just couldn't let you go without knowing I approve of every word my fiancé said, Mr. Cribb! You Unionists really are insufferable bullies, and I do hope we can make it hot for you down here! Shall I show Mr. Cribb out, Paul dear?"

Paul dear remained rooted, his back to the fire, but Cribb, now in a fighting mood, snarled, "I only hope your father feels the same way about it, Miss Lovell! And Mrs. Lovell also, both very good friends of mine, as you no doubt know!", and to Paul, "Good-day, Craddock! If it's war you want you won't find us as easy to beat as Boers!

248

We have their kind of staying power and a great deal more money!"

"Oh, but they weren't all that easy to beat," Grace said, "as you would have found out if you had been in the field like Mr. Craddock!", but it is doubtful whether Cribb heard her for he was already outside the room and a moment later they heard the front door slam and then the crunch of the gig's wheels on the gravel.

They remained silent for a moment, Grace standing leaning against the door, her head cocked slightly to one side and her little crooked smile giving her the look of a clever, impudent child, who has just scored a point over grown-ups. Finally Paul said, breathlessly, "That was very sporting of you, Grace, but you didn't have to burn your boats in order to rub salt into the smart! You realise Cribb will spread the news up and down the Valley in a matter of hours, and you'll look pretty foolish if you have to back down on it!"

"Well," she said, cheerfully, walking across to the fire and giving the sullen log a kick with her boot, "I don't know how you feel about it but I haven't any intention of 'backing down' as you say! As for you, you had your chance in the churchyard on Christmas Eve and didn't take it!"

"You meant what you said? It wasn't said simply to confound that bully?"

"I meant it," she said coolly, "but it was a rather different tale from the one I rode here to tell you."

"You mean that you were listening all the time, and it helped you to change your mind about us?"

"I haven't been very clever, have I?" she said, "I'm giving away too much and too quickly!" Then, facing him, "It's the first time I've ever *seen* you, Paul, can't you understand that? I thought of you as someone pleasant, kind, and well-meaning but I didn't know you were a rebel and I certainly didn't give you credit for that much nerve! I loathe people like Gilroy and Cribb, and everything they stand for, but until ten minutes ago I assumed you were only a watered-down version of them! Well, you aren't, quite obviously you aren't, and it makes a big difference! I'm not in love with you and it wouldn't be honest of me to pretend I was but we've got more in common than either of us imagined and that's a better basis for marriage than story-book slush!"

He crossed to the fireplace and lifted her hand, looking at it thoughtfully and noting the regularity of the long tapering fingers that somehow gave the hand strength as well as delicacy. "I don't know," he said, "without 'story-book slush' marriage must be a very dull institution, too dull to have lasted as long as it has. Maybe it emerges if the marriage is any good but I suppose it's much the same as any other endeavour—its success depends on what people are prepared to put into it. All I know for certain is that I'm willing to trust my instincts but I don't think you are, not really, and that's why it might be wiser to see a lot more of each other and be damned to what Cribb and Gilroy broadcast up and down the Valley!"

She looked at him steadily, without withdrawing her hand. "That's not how you were talking to them," she said, "it's more how I should have imagined you talked if someone had told me about what happened."

"The two things aren't the same," he said.

"Oh, but they are, because both are a calculated risk! You took one without a second thought but now you buck at taking another! You asked me to marry you and I said I'd think about it. Well, I have thought about it, and I'd be very happy to, so to the devil with hanging fire until all the fun's gone out of it! If we are going to marry let's do it without orange blossom and stale jokes!"

"You would be prepared to marry soon?"

"Today, Paul."

"We can't cheat Celia and the gossips out of everything. Half the Valley would regard marriage at Easter as indecent!"

"It's no concern of Celia's," she said seriously, "or of anyone else's in the Valley and that's important to me, Paul. This is one thing I'm not obliged to share with anyone but you." It did not seem preposterous that she should carry her passion for privacy into marriage and he found that he was beginning, at last, to be able to anticipate her approximate line of thought.

"Very well, Grace," he said, "and you would probably

like to be married away from here, in front of a couple of impersonal witnesses?"

"Yes," she said, "I should like that very much if it could be managed."

"It shall be managed," he said, grimly, "for all I want is a chance to prove how right it could be for both of us. We could get a special licence but that would require your father's permission and Celia would have to be won over. Could that be done, do you suppose?"

"All Celia wants is to get me off her hands. I can leave father to her. I don't imagine he'll be bothered to attend."

He began to understand something of the source of her bitterness, although he could not quite rid himself of a suspicion that she enjoyed over-dramatising a situation.

"All right then, that's how it will be! I'll ride back with you this afternoon and talk to Celia and if you'll stay for lunch I'll take her up on that dinner invitation I declined yesterday." Then, because her expression remained serious, he tried laughing at her. "I must say you don't look much like a girl who has just accepted a gentleman's proposal!" he said, taking her face between his hands and kissing her gently on the mouth. Her lips were no more than submissive, so that he thought of Claire Derwent's lips as he said, "You really *are* sure, Grace? We aren't under any obligation at all to rush things. I told Celia yesterday that I wouldn't have you hustled!"

She took her time answering this, looking at him steadily, so that he saw her in sharper focus, wondering a little at her composure but baffled as ever by her remoteness. He marked other, equally familiar things about her, the clipped fringe, blue-black against her pale forehead, the ivory lustre of the skin stretching along the jawline to the deep cleft of her chin and one other feature that he had forgotten, dimples, starved of laughter, on either side of her wide mouth. She said, at length, "You have been good to me, Paul, and I know you mean always to be good. Well, you won't find one aspect of me wanting, and I'll prove it!" and suddenly she threw her arms about his neck and returned his kiss in a way that drove all doubts from his mind, so that nothing existed for him beyond her lips or the strong pressure of her body that seemed almost to

251

clamour for him. When she drew back he was filled with a yearning for her that demanded immediate release and catching up her hand he pressed it to his lips and said, breathlessly, "I'll tell them, Grace! I'll tell them you're staying, dearest!" and rushed from the room as though he intended proclaiming his triumph from the housetops but when he bore down on Thirza Tremlett, dusting an engraving in the hall, he checked himself and said, gruffly, "Tell Mrs. Handcock Miss Lovell is staying to luncheon and ask Chivers to saddle Snowdrop and bring both horses round to the front door at two o'clock sharp!"

Through the open door Grace saw that the girl was startled by his eruption and wondered idly if she too had been engaged in eavesdropping but the possibility did not concern her overmuch. Half the Valley would know about it by now and she wondered, smiling one of her small, crooked smiles, what they would make of it, and whether they would credit her with a technique superior to Claire Derwent, the hot favorite in the Shallowford matrimonial stakes throughout the summer.

VI

No one could say how the news spread to every corner of the Valley in such a short space of time. Things usually did, of course, but not quite so rapidly as on this occasion. Perhaps the news was blown back on the Sorrel by the indoor staff at Heronslea, who heard Lord Gilroy and Cribb discussing it over luncheon, or perhaps Thirza Tremlett, the housemaid, had been keyhole peeping after all; or maybe Ikey Palfrey, an exceptionally observant lad, noticed the way Paul looked at Grace when he helped her mount in the forecourt, and told Gappy, the gardener's boy, "It's 'er, like I said!", for Gappy, living on the Coombe side of the estate, had offered to wager on Claire Derwent. At all events, it soon got about and was common in the kitchens and barns.

Elinor Codsall heard it from Matt the shepherd that same afternoon and Matt must have got it from the wind gossip of Priory Wood pines for he had been out along since first light and nowhere near the Big House. Elinor told Will as soon as he came into the kitchen and kicked off his boots and Will, for once, showed an interest in Valley tittle-tattle, exclaiming, "Well, I'm bliddy glad to hear it, midear! It'll ha' been lonesome for un in that gurt ole place, especially o' nights, eh?" and he winked, half-expecting her to blush, but twenty-eight successive nights beside Will had used up Elinor's blushes and all she said was, "Oh, giddon with 'ee! Come and zit down, man, I've made treacle pudding for 'ee!"

Martha Pitts heard it from the Bagman, who got it from one of the gardeners, Horace Handcock perhaps, who heard most things long before everybody else and Martha too was delighted. She had a great regard for the young city man who seemed so anxious to be a good landlord and had been hoping that the Big House would soon have a mistress to take some of the work off his hands. She told Arthur and Henry as soon as they came in at dusk and Henry said, "Well, damme, who'd ha' thowt it? The Lovell girl, you zav, who was to have been wed to that waster, Ralph Lovell?" His mother thought this a good opportunity to drive home a lesson on the subject of his bachelorhood and said, crossly, "Aye, and tiz time you thought about getting wed, boy! Baint the maids round here good enough for 'ee?" to which Henry replied, with a wink at his father, "The maids is well enough as maids, Mother! Tiz when they cease to be maids they shows their true colours!" and went on to talk about more serious matters, like the overflowing brook on the north slope of the wood.

Arabella Codsall learned it from one of the dairy-maids and it says something for the impression it made on her that she received the news in silence. There were times, these days, when Arabella retreated into silence, a change in her that disconcerted everyone at Four Winds. This is not to say she was mute. She still spoke approximately three times as many words each day as most people on the farm, but seemed to have ceased to expect replies to trigger off renewed outbursts and resorted to the long muttered monologue, which family and staff could safely ignore. She had two repetitive themes nowadays, one directed at Martin, and the other at her younger son, Sydney. Martin's began, "Well on the road to ruin we are, you, me, the boy, the farm, everything about us and I'm sure I don't know what I've done to merit it . . . !", whereas the monologue addressed to Sydney was more cautionary than abusive, beginning, "You see the fruits of the lusts of the flesh, Sydney! Take heed of a man like your brother Will, who can turn his back on bottom land like this and banish himself," and so on, a lamentation to which Sydney, ever a thoughtful, silent boy, would listen with rapidly blinking eyes, as his mother heaved herself about the big kitchen, going about her work with the joyless movements of a bond slave. But although Arabella made no comment on the new Squire's intention to marry she thought with sour satisfaction of his choice, for Bruce Lovell's reputation in the Valley was a scandalous one and it followed that his blood would bring tribulation to the deceitful young man at the Big House who had played his part in reducing her domestic audience to two.

News of the engagement reached the Potter Dell at dusk and Tamer Potter, lifting his nose, scented deprivation and strictures in the rumour. He had been relieved when the estate had been taken over by a bachelor, whom he sensed would regard him and his brood as characters and had done nothing since Paul's arrival to check the march of dock and nettle across Lower Coombe fields. Now, perhaps, changes might be on the way, for it was not improbable that a man with a wife to support would see him for what he was, a cunning and indolent old loafer, and urge him on pain of eviction to plough fields that had long lain fallow, or engage in the back-breaking labour of hedging and ditching. For his part he wished the young fool up at the Big House would remain single and count his blessings.

Farmer Willoughby, of Deepdene, heard the news with satisfaction. His gospel was love and Mr. Craddock's championship of Elinor had established him in Willoughby's heart as a patron of love. He knew nothing of the Lovell girl, whom the Squire was now said to be marrying but was sure that such an upstanding young man would choose wisely and he wished both of them well, even in the matter of procreation which, strictly speaking, did not feature in Farmer Willoughby's conception of love.

Edward Derwent was told the news at supper that night. His wife Liz should have known better than to broach the subject just as her husband was sitting down to a large helping of cold duck. She succeeded in demolishing his appetite with a single sentence for his eyebrows came together like the prongs of a badger trap and growling that here was another piece of women's tittle-tattle, he turned to Rose for corroboration. Rose confirmed the news. Alone among the Valley folk she was not much surprised by it for Claire had told her where the Squire's interests lay on the night of the fireworks. Now she wondered, a little wretchedly, whether she should relay the news to Claire, in Kent, but Derwent, satisfied that there must be something in it after all, left his food untouched and stumped off to the yard, lighting his pipe and leaning against the oak pillars of the byre to contemplate his cow stalls with masochistic gloom. He found himself wishing that he had never set eyes on the young fool up at the Big House. It was a tiresome and troublesome business to be levered out of one's comfortable pessimism only to discover that he had been right after all and would live and die as a tenant, without graduating to the status of freeholder for surely this was certain now. Marriage implied continuity and a married squire meant a squire with heirs to consider. In addition to that it was now painfully apparent that any heirs Craddock produced would not have Derwent blood in their veins, as he had once been led to believe possible. It would have been better, he reflected bitterly, if the estate had jogged along in its old pre-war muddle for all that recent changes brought to High Coombe was two cliff fields and the loss of his favourite daughter, currently wasting her time in a tea shop on the other side of England. Ordinarily he would not have cared two straws whom Craddock married but it was hard to have glimpsed such a bright prospect and then see it vanish, together with his eligible daughter. Standing there in the January fog, puffing clouds of strong tobacco smoke at his blameless cows, Edward Derwent silently cursed Paul Craddock, his bride-to-be, and all his works.

Sam Potter heard the news from Aaron Stokes gathering reeds for thatching and Sam threw down his axe and ran at once to his cottage to tell Joannie. Sam was delighted. Ever since he had become a father himself he wished all men to be blessed with children, and neither had he forgotten young Squire's generosity and lack of condescension when he had called at the cottage on the day little Pauline was born. He got out the crown piece Paul had given him on that occasion and swung it from the string to which it had been attached through a hole, drilled in Queen Victoria's diadem. Joannie, a practical soul, said it was fortunate Pauline's arrival had preceded the Squire's marriage for had it not the christening gift might have been bestowed on one of his own children but Sam laughed at this, pointing out that young Squire possessed more crown pieces than he could spend in a lifetime, and that when an heir did make its appearance there would be junketings on an unprecedented scale and free beer for everyone in the Valley. He then replaced the medallion in its box on the mantelshelf, gave a gleeful imitation of his child's gurgle and returned to work in the wood.

Mrs. Handcock, who surely should have been one of the first to hear, was, in fact, one of the last, learning it from own husband, Horace, when he was lying flat on his back in their double bed and she was struggling to free herself of the lips of her vast, whalebone corset. The act of undressing always occupied Mrs. Handcock upwards of half-an-hour and during this period it was Horace's custom to comment on life and the British Empire, with occasional snippets of local gossip gleaned from heaven knew where. His awareness of all that happened, or was about to happen in the Valley, was a source of reverent astonishment to his wife, and contributed in no small measure to her respect for him. He looked small and insignificant when he was in bed, with nothing but his bald head and side-whiskers showing above the coverlet but it was at these times that he was inclined to be more than usually oracular, staring up at the ceiling and giving her full benefit of his wisdom and logic. She still had nine hooks to free when he said, as casually as if he had been discussing compost, "You'll have heard, no doubt, that Squire'll be marrying Bruce Lovell's girl before the daffodils be out?" and she gave two yelps, one of surprise, and the other as her fingers slipped and she nipped a fold of flesh. He turned his mild gaze on her; "You mean you *haven't* heard? You've been on top of un and baint put two and two together?"

"I've heard no such thing," she said indignantly, "but I should ha' said if 'er was marrying anyone it would ha' been the Derwent maid!"

"Then youm behindhand, considerably so," he told her. "Squire'll wed the Lovell maid before you've time to bake a cake, and that's a fact, so you may as well make up your mind to it!" He did not need to look at her to know that his news had shocked her or that already, as she stood half-undressed, wrestling with her corset, she was boiling with uncertainty and resentment. This was understandable, he thought, for she was only a woman and therefore a fool, quite incapable of reasoning. Moreover, it pleased him that he had been the first to bring her the news for he was probably the only man in the world who could stem her panic.

"Now dornee get in one of your ole tizzies, midear," he said, mildly, "for there baint a need! Taken all round tiz well for us tiz the Lovell maid an' not the Derwent maid, because the Lovell maid, being a lady born, will be less likely to chase 'ee round than a varmer's daughter brought up to work with her hands! Let your mind dwell on that for a spell and mebbe you'll zee the zense in it!"

"But it won't be the same, Horace," she wailed, tearing at the last obstinate hook, "I've done for 'un ever zince he set foot in the Valley, and he's no more'n a baby to be taking a wife and unsetting things like this!" and she hurled the corset from her and burst into tears.

"Babies grow up, and gets interested in young wimmin," said Horace, unmoved, "so thank your lucky stars he's found someone who knows the plaace and no cottoned on one o' them townees who would have brought her own housekeeper, along with her trousseau! Now put on your nightgown before you gets your death o' cold woman, and take it from me we'm lucky it's turned out as it has. The Lovell maid won't be one to count the linen,

257

nor look too closely at the tradesmen's bills, I can tell 'ee that! You've had the ordering of the plaace all this time and you'll have it yet, zo blow the bliddy candle out and go to sleep!"

As always she was able to retreat under the mantle of his profundity and before she slept the worse of her alarms were stilled. She had been very happy mothering Paul, and before Paul, the widower Rudd, and before Rudd the tetchy Sir George on the rare occasions he was in residence but Horace was right, of course. A mistress had to appear sooner or later, and it might, as he said, have been worse, for at least Grace Lovell, a lady born, would be likely to leave the ordering of the house to servants. Then another, happier thought comforted her. There would soon be children about the house and she would like that very much and she smiled to herself in the darkness, listening to Horace's heavy breathing as she recalled the width of the Lovell maid's hips, in an attempt to estimate her child-bearing capacity.

The news reached Meg Potter when she was gathering herbs for her winter rheumatism cure. The Bagman, who had informed Martha Pitts, told her and passed on his way, leaving her to look for further enlightenment in the cards. Meg carried her cards everywhere, using them as a sailor uses a compass, or a stranger a signpost at crossroads. She now spread them on a beech stump, cutting, shuffling and recutting and three times out of five the face card that turned up was the Queen of Spades, Lady of Sorrow. This puzzled her, for she had gone to her cards on the day Paul Craddock first rode into the Dell and what they had told her had been very encouraging but today the turn up alternated between the Lady of Sorrow and the Knave of Diamonds, whom she recognised as her son Smut and no matter how often she reshuffled the result was the same. At last she gave it up, accepting the inevitable with the stoicism she brought to every turning-point in her life. There would be trouble in the Valley and soon and it would involve the Lovell maid and Smut, in the proportion of about five to two. She went back to herb collecting, wishing it could have been otherwise.

Meg Potter had her cards and everyone else in the Valley had self-interest to guide them but John Rudd, the only one among them to hear the news direct from Paul, had no guide beyond a persistent niggle under his strapped-up ribs and the niggle told him approximately the same story as the cards told Meg. He could not have said why this should be so. He was a man who usually rationalised his prejudices and he reminded himself that, whereas everybody knew Bruce Lovell was a bad hat, nobody knew much about his daughter, except that her mother had drowned herself in a reservoir in India, years ago. He listened, sucking on his pipe, to Paul's account of all that had taken place in the Valley during his absence, and could find it in him to admire the boy for his stand against Arabella Codsall and Lord Gilroy, but when Paul asked him outright what, if anything, he had against Grace Lovell he had to choose between his niggle and his affection. He could not admit to a young man in love that he suspected a streak of madness in his darling's veins or that for a woman to drown herself on account of a Lovell implied a fatal lack of balance on the female side. He had nothing but rumour and conjecture to reinforce his arguments, nothing more than a vague impression that Grace Lovell was bad luck. And now, as he stood leaning on the fence rails of the paddock watching the moon rise over the Bluff, he knew that he had deceived himself when he had assumed that Craddock's arrival here, and the enthusiasm he brought with him, meant a permanent anchorage for himself. There could never be a safe anchorage with a Lovell in the Big House. As the soft, white light touched the shallows at the ford, John Rudd said to himself, impatiently, "Now who the hell am I to pour cold water on the boy? What gives me the right to advise him on a matter like this? He's in love with a pretty face and a pretty figure and if he brings the same enthusiasm to his marriage as he's brought to the Valley I daresay he'll prove me a superstitious old fool!" And hoisting himself from the rail he knocked out his pipe and went across to the lodge to bed.

CHAPTER NINE

I

A MARRIAGE between strangers is an uncharted journey; Will Codsall knew his Elinor and Walt Pascoe his Pansy, before marrying them. Within certain limits, they knew what they could expect of them as cooks, housekeepers and bedfellows, and their brides were equally well primed, so that such surprises as they encountered had no power to astound them as Paul Craddock was astounded and delighted by Grace Lovell.

The 8 A.M. ceremony at Paxtonbury Parish church was so short and simple that Paul had some difficulty in realising that he was indeed married when they said good-bye to Celia and John Rudd after breakfast at The Mitre. There was no one else present to shake by the hand or kiss; no rice, no confetti, no jokes, no old shoes tied under the carriage that took them to the junction and thence, by the Cornish express, to London, where they stayed one night before travelling to Dover and catching the cross-Channel packet for Boulogne.

Paul had asked her where she would like to spend the honeymoon and she had told him Paris, a city she had never visited although she was a seasoned Continental traveller and had stayed in several Belgian spas, sailed down the Rhine on a paddle steamer and spent several weeks beside the Swiss lakes. That was the first of his surprises but there were many more and they continued to explode at irregular intervals, like the green and crimson rockets on the night of the soirée.

He discovered, for instance, that she could speak fluent French, whereas he was obliged to grope for half-forgotten phrases from school text-books, and perhaps, if he had not been so much in love, her accomplishment would have dismayed him a little. As it was he listened with awe as she exchanged banter with porters, ticket collectors and the concierge at the sedate hotel which she had found for him off the Avenue des Capucines. Another source of amazement was her apparent familiarity with Parisian history. She took him to all kinds of out-of-the-way places connected with characters he had met in fiction or in encyclopedias, and talked freely of people like Madame Roland, Catherine de Medici and Marguerite of Navarre. She hustled him off to an obscure little museum to show him the proclamation Robespierre had been signing when the Thermidorians burst in and put a term to the Terror. She told him whimsical ghost stories as they walked the gravelled paths of the Petit Trianon and was even able to identify many of Napoleon's marshals from busts that seemed to him identical as they looked down from niches in the old Palais Royale. She seemed to enjoy guiding him as though he had been an adolescent son instead of her husband, so that, during their sightseeing tours he trailed dutifully behind her feeling no shame on this account but rather a surge of pride that sometimes made him almost drunk with exhilaration. To give expression to his pride he spent freely, buying her a present every day. Sometimes it was a confection that caught his eye in a milliner's window, sometimes a dress that she declared, laughing, she could never wear within fifty miles of the Sorrel Valley and sometimes a mere trifle like a book, trinket or even a posy of spring flowers. So it happened that by day the initiative was hers but when they were alone in their first-storey room above the rattle of the traffic she deliberately abdicated and became a bride again who, while not in any way shy or withdrawn, allowed the initiative to pass back to him. Yet here again she had the power to surprise him, for he had not yet forgotten her kiss and the promise that accompanied it on the day she had helped to rout Cribb and although he meant to implement his pledge never to hustle her this soon proved beyond his power. He had, on embarking on this adventure, been only too aware of his inexperience but in some indefinable way she gave him a measure of confidence so that, to some extent, neither one of them suffered the disenchantment that might have attended the essays of two people who had grown to maturity in an age when discussion of sex was taboo. It did cross his mind during that first week, however, that her intellectual curiosity might have led her to seek and find some printed source of enlightenment, for she seemed to know very well how best to accommodate him and it was only in retrospect that he wondered whether she had acquired this awareness in the arms of the roystering Ralph Lovell, reputedly an expert wencher. When he falteringly touched on the subject, however, she answered him with her usual frankness, saying that Ralph had certainly done his best to anticipate marriage but that she had had no difficulty in thwarting him for, like all the Lovells, he was an arch snob and drew a nice distinction between women of her class and village girls like the Potters. On this he let the matter drop, not liking to contemplate just how many liberties had been extended to Ralph or to any other man. He was far too grateful for the patience and generosity she was prepared to extend to him and came to accept her accessibility as a physical manfestation of her exceptional candour. This was impressed upon him one afternoon about a week after their marriage when he had occasion to go into the bathroom of the little suite for his razor. The door was ajar and he called, "Can I come in?" and she said, laughing, "Why not? You're my husband aren't you?" and he went in to find her naked, with her tumble of blue-black hair reaching to her shapely buttocks as she stood before a mirror using her brush with long, sweeping strokes. She did not seem in any way embarrassed and went on brushing while he stared at her in wonder. He had never seen her more than half undressed and had thought of her as a rather sturdy little person, with muscles moulded by plenty of exercise but now he could marvel at the classic proportions of her limbs which, against all probability, contrived to give an impression of strength as well as infinite grace and softness. Nor, until this moment, had he appreciated the luxuriance of her hair that trapped the afternoon light in its bluish depths, or of the slenderness of her waist and the neatness of her feet. He said, gently, "But you're quite perfect, Grace! As perfect as a woman could be!" and she replied, in the

262

assured tone of a wife of years rather than days, "It's nice to be told so!" and went on with her brushing.

Her manner of answering reminded him poignantly that, for all her recent submissiveness, she had never admitted to loving him but had only contracted to try and it seemed to him very strange that a beautiful young woman could stand before him stark naked and yet continue to hold on to her spiritual independence. He said, "I'll make you happy, Grace. That means more to me than anything."

She was rather too quick, he thought, with her reply, for suddenly she stopped her brushing and said, "More than the estate? More than that Valley of yours?"

"Whatever we do in the Valley we'll do together," he said, without finding her question irrelevant and forgetting his razor he swept her off her feet and carried her back to the bedroom.

So the days and nights passed, with the leadership shared equally but one day she gave him a brief inkling of what seemed to him her contempt for the dominion of men.

She had taken him, guide-book in hand, to a little lodging house on the Left Bank, telling him that it was here that the girl assassin, Charlotte Corday, had stayed on the night she came to Paris to kill Marat. She seemed to have a very high regard for Charlotte Corday and to know facts concerning her that were not printed in the guide-book. She told him of the girl's indignation at the way the revolution had degenerated into an orgy of cruelty and bloodshed, and of Charlotte's determination to kill the man whom she identified as the chief author of the Terror, describing, with a certain relish, how she had bought the butcher's knife that she used on her victim. Paul said, jokingly, "She must have been a cold-blooded little devil!" but Grace snapped, "Cold-blooded? No, she wasn't that! Fearless and resolute, if you like, but not cold-blooded! The cold-blooded stayed home and talked of achieving something. She went out and did it, while all the men of her party were content to posture on the rostrum!" and as she said this he thought for a moment of Celia's warning concerning Grace's flirtation with the suffragists and wondered if she identified Charlotte Corday with the Pankhursts. She had never discussed modern politics with him and once or twice when he had mentioned Grenfell and his Liberals, she steered the conversation back to less controversial subjects but that same evening she opened the door on another unfamiliar word, conjuring two tickets for the ballet from a fellow guest at the hotel, and taking him, protesting complete ignorance, to the Opera, where *Giselle* was being presented by the Imperial Russian Ballet.

Until then he had always thought of ballet as no more than an eccentric form of dancing, but he tried to look as though he was prepared to enjoy it for her sake. It was not until he had stolen several glances at her during the performance that the magic began to work upon his prejudice and make his ignorance seem boorish. When the interval arrived he readily admitted this and was rewarded by a flash of enthusiasm in her eyes and an impulsive grasp of her hand as she said, "I was afraid you'd be bored and make nothing of it! This is an essential part of life, Paul! It makes up for so much ugliness, cruelty and stupidity! Will you promise me something? If the Ballet comes to London in the autumn may we travel up and stay for it? Will we get a chance to see something outside the Sorrel Valley every so often? Often enough to stop us growing cabbages for heads?"

He would have promised her the moon at that moment and replied, "Why certainly, darling, you can go to London any time you wish!" and then, recalling her enigmatic remark in the bathroom, "Is *that* what frightens you about Shallowford? The thought of being buried alive, and growing dull, like one of the farmer's daughters?"

"No," she said, "not really, but you must have hated the city very much to have gone there in the first place. They say you only visited Paxtonbury once, until we were married there!"

"Well, I suppose I do hate cities," he admitted, "particularly London, but my real reason for buying Shallowford wasn't as simple as that. I couldn't stand the thought of an office career and with my knee the field was very limited. Then, after I was committed, I soon grew to love every blade of grass in the place but I suppose it really began with the dream."

She showed interest at once. "What dream?"

"Oh, I can't tell you here and anyway it's time to go back."

"Will you tell me tonight?"

"Yes, but it will probably bore you. Other people's dream always bore me."

She held him to his promise and when they were in bed he told her as much as he could recall of the conflict between the static hosts on the hospital ceiling and the compensating view of the country beyond the ward window that had seemed, at the time, to play such a vital part in his recovery. He could not tell whether she was impressed or dismissed the story as an unremarkable symptom of fever and drugs and would have been very surprised to know that she lay awake long after he slept, or that his story helped to convince her that he was by no means the amiable simpleton she had first supposed him to be. She lay there wondering if, even now, he understood that she had married him as cold-bloodedly as any fortune hunter and in retracing her steps over their various encounters she realised that already her conscience troubled her somewhat for surely his apparent need of her could no longer be dismissed as the self-delusion all men used to disguise their clamour for access to a woman's body and the incidental acquisition of a woman servitor. His approach, she thought, already indicated something more substantial than that and it would be folly not to admit it, for although his physical enjoyment for her was uncomplicated he already respected her as a person and not as a bedmate or a brood mare for children to perpetuate his name. For this, in the main, was how she had thought of him in the brief interval between her unconditional surrender and marriage but it was not, unfortunately for her peace of mind, how she thought of him now. He was, she admitted, far more imaginative than she had supposed, possessing also a certain originality and infinitely more patience than most young men, and even if his eyes were still fixed on contemptibly small horizons his vision might, she thought, expand if she could teach him to look beyond Coombe Bluff. She made a half-playful attempt to separate the Paul Craddock of Shallowford from the Paul Craddock now sleeping beside her. The one she thought of as little more

265

than a gawky, earnest, ignorant boy who had served and suffered in a war but learned little or nothing about people and their overriding greed and self-interest. He could still suffer fools gladly, so much so that he accepted rascals like Tamer Potter and cranks like Edwin Willoughby as personal responsibilities. He liked to think of himself as a benevolent patron, administering a tiny kingdom of rustics when, in fact, he was no more than a lucky young ass, aping the country gentleman and lagging a century behind the times. He had probably never heard of people like Keir Hardie and his forlorn little working-man's party, or the vanguard of women prepared to sacrifice everything in an attempt to have a voice in their own destinies. Yet, and she was obliged to admit it, there existed, deep in this long, lump of a man, a spark of idealism that was never completely submerged by douches of sentimental claptrap or obscured by muddled thinking, and now and then she had glimpsed it. There was something even more rare—a male gentleness that she had never experienced in any other man. Intrigued by now, she lit the night light, turning carefully on her elbow and looking down on him as he slept. He was not, she decided, particularly good looking, with his long, craggy face, strong features and stiff, unruly hair almost as dark as her own. If they did have children they would probably have faces as long as a horse and complexions as swarthy as Spaniards. She rested on her elbow a long time, studying him calmly and objectively, noting his look of innocence that was offset by the unexpected firmness of the jaw and the fastidiousness of the long, thin nose. It was a face, she thought, that could have belonged to a ruthless or even a cruel person who would want his way with men and women yet she knew by now that there was no spark of cruelty in him and very little ruthlessness as far as she was concerned. She was aware too that she could, if she wished, manipulate him easily enough, either by appealing to his old-fashioned sense of chivalry or by the more direct method of throwing her arms and legs about him, and yet, was she capable of making him turn his back on his dream, so that they could advance as man and wife into the twentieth century? She looked at his jawline again. Perhaps, in time, when he

266

grew a little but not yet, possibly not until she had borne him a child or two. A month ago this conclusion would have depressed her but tonight it only made her smile. She said, half aloud, as she playfully drew a lock of her hair across his cheek, "Well, Squire, we shall see! And anyway, I've been luckier than I deserve!" and she kissed his forehead, blew out the light, turned over and chuckled. It was a long time since Grace Lovell had indulged in a chuckle.

II

It was after their return to London, when they were being lunched by an attentive Uncle Franz, at Romano's, that she surprised him again, this time by demanding to be taken to the scrapyard to see the actual source of all the war profits that had been diverted to Shallowford. Paul, once he had recovered from his surprise, said, "Now what the devil can interest you down there? I promised myself I'd never go near the stinking place again!", but she replied, watching Zorndorff, "That's a very arrogant promise, Paul, and could only have validity if you had renounced your interest in what it yields! As long as you use its income you've got as much responsibility for it as you have for the farms in the Valley!" and Uncle Franz said the lady certainly had a point and soon twinkled Paul out of his sulks, ordering a four-wheeler to take them along the route Paul had taken on his first day out of hospital.

As they went along, weaving through the traffic, Paul noticed that Grace had made a singular impression on the old Croat and because he had a groom's intense pride in his bride her conquest warmed him, for although old Franz was a Continental, and could therefore be expected to pay court to any pretty young woman, he knew his man sufficiently well to appreciate the difference between a genuine interest and conventional gallantry. They were talking now of motor-cars, one or two of which could be seen dodging about between the cabs and drays that flowed along the congested highway.

"I should have thought, Uncle Franz," Grace was saying, "that a merchant prince like you would have acquired a motor long ago! After the initial outlay upkeep must be far less than a carriage."

Paul, who privately thought of this as nonsense, winked at Uncle Franz but the old boy obviously took her seriously, for he said, "Oh, they'll have all the horses off the road eventually. Only a stick-in-the-mud like your husband will insist on keeping horses, but you're in error, my dear young lady, as regards the economics of the contraption. They cost more in oil than a horse eats in corn and you can't engage a trained chauffeur at the wage you pay a coachman. I daresay I shall experiment with one in a year or so, when they have got over their teething troubles, for it never does to rush in and buy mechanical devices until they have settled down. They tell me new developments are being made every week and a great deal of money has been sunk in promotion!"

They went on to talk of other topics, land development this side of the Thames, the prospect of a general election, and of Paris, which Zorndorff had not visited since he passed through it as a refugee. Paul noticed too that the Croat had also made a deep impression upon Grace, for she coaxed him to tell her something of his impressions of England, and how he had managed to make such a success of life in a land where he had arrived without knowing a word of the language. Paul could see that Zorndorff was flattered but he was only half listening, for the familiar reek of the streets made him homesick for the Valley and as they traversed the Old Kent Road, and passed the tanyard and Peek Frean's factory, he found himself comparing the dinginess and squalor around him to the charm of the French capital and wondered how Londoners could be so chauvinistic about their sprawl. Then, as they turned in at the gates of the yard and looked again on the jumble of desolation that filled the rectangle between the street and the backs of houses, he thought of the smell of the wind over Blackberry Moor and was impatient to be gone.

"I still feel damned ashamed of drawing money from the place!" he said, but his protest seemed to amuse her and she said, glancing at Franz, "How strange! Uncle Franz wallows in it, don't you, Uncle?"

"No, but I haven't a conscience about it," said the Croat, "and I imagine I tolerate it because it is alive."

"Would you say the Sorrel Valley is dead then?" demanded Paul but Grace was far too interested in the scene around her to take him up on this and began to bombard Zorndorff with questions regarding the collection, assortment and disposal of scrap, the prices it fetched and the use to which it was put when melted down. It baffled Paul that she could be so absorbed in such a dull subject when she had never so much as asked a single question about crops or cattle, so he left them to it, stepping out on to the platform above the weighbridge and gazing down at the yard, hating it all the more for the debt he owed it and would always owe it.

The last time he had been here it was in summer drought, when the debris had festered in the humid air but now, under a March sky, the vast array of odds and ends seemed to huddle together in the wind and the whole area had a pinched, dejected look. The scavengers looked pinched too as they pottered among the garbage and the rattle of their hobnailed boots came up to him like the chink of fetters. He was still there, glowering at his benefactor, when he felt her arm slip through his and her hand squeeze his wrist and at her touch his ill-humour left him. "I'm sorry to be so damned sour about it, Grace. I know I owe it money, and probably always will but I can't help it. The damned place disgusts me. Uncle Franz says my mother was a countrywoman and maybe that explains a good deal."

"Uncle Franz has just been telling me that," she said, "and it *is* a depressing spectacle, but don't you ever feel you could do something to improve it and with it the conditions these people work under? I think that's what would have recommended itself to me before I took on fresh responsibilities," and then she laughed, adding, "I'm sorry, Paul! That sounds mealymouthed!"

"No, it doesn't," he said, "but it shows a lack of understanding of the Cockney temperament! They don't recoil from the squalor, they feel safe in it and wouldn't give you a thank you for more than an hour or so in the country, or

269

by the sea. If you don't believe me ask Ikey Palfrey when we get home."

"Who is Ikey Palfrey?" she wanted to know and he told her he was the stable-boy who had taken care of her horse on the occasions she had ridden over to Shallowford, and because she was interested he went on to describe the incident of the frightened cart-horse, and how he had felt impelled to give the boy a chance of growing up in clean air. "Ikey is the exception that proves the rule," he added, "but then, his mother was a peasant too, a relative of Franz's."

"How does Ikey like it down there?" she asked and he told her the boy was doing well and attending Mary Willoughby's little school in the morning. "He's a very sharp kid and everybody's fond of him," he added and might have gone on to describe Ikey's cheekiness and powers of mimicry had she not stood back regarding him with a puzzled smile, saying "But don't you *see?* That's exactly what I meant! I just talked about it but you've already done something practical! You know, you're a very unpredictable person and sometimes bewilderingly human! I think I'm rather fond of you, really!" and she stood on tiptoe and kissed him on the cheek just as Franz, rubbing his hands, emerged from the office and said, "Get the man back to his mangolds and let me attend to the business of supporting him!"

III

For some time now Paul had been playing a private joke on himself but had kept it a close secret, even from Grace and John Rudd, for he would have half-agreed with them that his estate diary was evidence of gross sentimentality on his part. When he was alone in his office, usually after breakfast, he unlocked a drawer and took out the Bible-covers that old George Lovell had used to camouflage his collection of photographs. Paul had long since disposed of the pictures but the covers he had laid aside and now it amused him to use the same bindings for his diary. He could hardly have been more secretive about it had the old goat's harem still smirked from between the leather-backed boards.

In the diary he wrote down the daily trivia of estate happenings and the first entry read: *"June 26th, 1902. Met at Sorrel Halt by John Rudd, and rode to Shallowford,"* and the second, dated two days later, *"Bought Shallowford Estate and the grey, Snowdrop,"* and so on, brief and often unrelated entries, recording such minor items as the birth of Sam Potter's daughter, the purchase of the Priory freehold, the marriage of Will Codsall and Elinor Willoughby, his first meeting with James Grenfell and a page devoted to his coronation supper-ball. So far there was nothing written there concerning his wife but the day after his return home he wrote: *"March 7, 1903. Married Grace Lovell, my very dear wife!"* and when he re-read this entry a week or so later, he was somewhat embarrassed by it, as though he now saw himself as a patriarchal squire taking care that posterity would take heed of him and his chattels. He did not erase it, however, but made no further entries until the last week of April, when he wrote, *"Grace began work on the lily pond in the rose garden: Horace Handcock thinks it practical."*

The entry set him thinking and his thoughts ran through pleasant country. It was remarkable, he reflected, how quickly she had settled, winning the friendship of indoor and outdoor staff and sometimes, as in the case of Handcock, the head gardener, enlisting a personal champion. She had dropped enough hints during the honeymoon to give him cause to worry, leaving him in little doubt but that she would only live permanently in the Valley on sufferance and would have much preferred to travel and winter in London. Yet, within hours of their return she had found a small field of creative energy in the house and grounds and had at once set about banishing the bachelor atmosphere of the place so that within a month Shallowford was a home rather than a headquarters. She made no sweeping changes but made her impact everywhere and without fuss. She was careful not to antagonise Mrs. Handcock or the maids, particularly the parlourmaid, Thirza Tremlett, known to be prickly. She had a trick of persuading Mrs. Handcock and even Thirza that

271

various improvements had originated with them and thus it was that a gay, patterned wallpaper found its way on the featureless walls of guest-rooms, along the length of the corridor at the rear of the house and, to Horace Handcock's amazement, on the walls of the housekeeper's rooms in the east wing. By a partial replacement of furniture, carpets and curtains, the main bedroom lost its austerity and the bleak dining-room, which Paul had abandoned to its original browns and greys, began to borrow something from the solid comfort of the library. This room she left alone, declaring it was his but she took a very active interest in the garden, persuading Horace to dispose of most of the overgrown shrubs that cluttered the lawns. Daffodils and narcissi that this time of year spread a yellow and white carpet from the stable-yard to the edge of Priory Wood, now reappeared all over the house, standing in earthenware crocks Grace had found abandoned in a disused stable.

It was this old stable that gave her the idea for the lily pond in what had once been a well-stocked rose garden, between the corner of the paddock and the river. Horace had declared that "they ole arbours need a good ole zetto", by which he meant the rotting arches and trellis work should be replaced but Grace pointed out that the natural dip in the ground lent itself to the making of a sunken ornamental pond and water could be piped from the river if a culvert was deepened. The rose garden could then be laid out with flags taken from the old stable, and the pond, when complete, stocked with goldfish and bordered by great clumps of iris. Horace and his boy Gappy (occasionally assisted by Ikey to whom Grace had taken a liking) set to work at once and the pond was now ready for water. Grace did her stint arranging flags and Honeyman, of the Home Farm, sent over the Timberlake boys from the sawmill with a supply of freshly cut poles, so that soon this section of the garden was transformed.

She was equally successful as a hostess and they gave one or two little dinners, entertaining James Grenfell, Celia, and finally Parson Bull and his desiccated wife, Kate. Grace seemed to like Grenfell, although she crossed swords with him on several issues, including the political integrity of right-wing Liberals. Celia, for her part, was impressed by her stepdaughter's relaxed command of the house, easy relationship with such entrenched characters as the housekeeper and parlourmaid but, above all, by her seeming contentment. The dinner with Parson Bull and his wife went off far more successfuly than Paul could have hoped, for neither he nor Grace had much time for the rector, and Mrs. Bull was a nonentity, with even less to say for herself than the second Mrs. Derwent. Bull, however, was more genial than usual, partly because he had an eye for a pretty woman and when the ladies had retired congratulated Paul on his stand against Lord Gilroy, whom Bull dismissed as "a bloodless old stick", going on to describe Gilroy's heir as a "sack of potatoes strapped to a saddle". Bull, certainly no Radical, nonetheless declared it was high time somebody put a spoke in the wheel of the agent Cribb, who was for ever trying to hog the proceeds of local social events and divert money that belonged to the church into the local Conservative coffers. Paul asked Bull if he thought Grenfell had any chance of winning the seat and was surprised when the parson said he would probably triumph in the election after next, for the present member, Colonel Hilton-Price, was rarely seen in the area and the Liberals would soon sweep the country. Before they rejoined the ladies Bull made a direct reference to Grace, congratulating Paul on marrying "such a decorative and mettlesome gel", and one who could "sit a horse better than any filly between New Cover and Barnaby Clump"! Bull had his own names for Valley landmarks and seldom used those printed on an ordance map, referring to uplands, bottoms and coverts according to how they presented themselves to a field in full cry. Thus the western part of Shallowford Woods was "that damned hairy place, where you poke about all day!" and the plateau of Blackerry Moor "that stretch where a fox covers the ground with its neck in splints!" One way and another it was a reassuring evening, although Paul felt very sorry for Grace, left to make heavy weather with Kate.

It was a day or so after this that Paul, working in the office with the garden door open, heard sounds of activity coming from the rose garden, so presently, when Ikey had brought Snowdrop round for him to ride over and see the Potters about the loan of a cart-horse, he led the horse along the terrace and looked over the box hedge at the group working in the excavation beyond. Grace was there with Handcock, old Timberlake the sawyer, the boy Gappy and the dog Goneaway, the latter behaving as though the operation had been put in hand to entertain her. Grace looked up cheerfully when he called, wiping her forehead with the back of her hand. Her cheeks, he noted, had lost a good deal of their pallor and in the strong sunlight seemed to him almost as pink as the gardener's. She called "Gappy! Get that dog out of here! As fast as we dig out the idiot fills it in! If you're going out, Paul, take her along with you, please!" and Paul, laughing, whistled Goneaway over as Horace said, with quiet pride, "Us is gettin' along vamously, Squire! Us'll 'ave the watter in 'er be the weekend!" Paul left them to it but as he was climbing into the saddle Timberlake, who knew all about the cart-horse, said, "Dornee let that ole blackguard Tamer Potter talk 'ee into making 'er permanent, Squire! 'E'll try, mak' no mistake!" and Paul wondered at the changes Grace had subtly introduced into the place for before his marriage he had not been able to extract two words from the sawyer, who had stood about fidgeting and tongue-tied whenever he had called at the Home Farm and watched him at work.

He went on down to the ford and along the river road, pondering Parson Bull's comment that he was lucky to have found such a wife so quickly and he thought, as he turned up the steep lane to the Dell, "I'm lucky all right, but so are the staff and I believe they know it!" and because he was in such a good humour he listened with amusement to Tamer's catalogue of woes and his doubts as to whether the loan of a single horse would enable him to keep the wheels turning. "Tiz all on account o' me being zo shorthanded, Squire," he explained, "an' beggin' your pardon, zir, 'twas you who tempted away my Sam! Now my maid has gone an' wed that young Pascoe zo I'm obliged to attend to everything myself!" Paul reminded him that he still had two daughters to look after livestock and another son to help him work under two hundred acres, whereas Willoughby, higher up, managed with a part-time man and a boy.

"Ah," said Tamer, who had been ready for this, "but Willoughby's lad be a boy broken to varming, baint 'ee, whereas my Smut'll never do a handsturn about the plaace, an' my ole woman aids an' abets'n!"

The sun was shining for the first time in a month so Paul, reluctant to waste time arguing with the old rascal, said, "Well, you've got the horse and I'll ask Honeyman to lend you a man one day a week, providing you pay him. We all want to see you make something of this holding, Tamer, it's been a liability for too long," but Tamer was proof against this sort of talk and all he replied was, "Mebbe you'll be proud of us bevore us 'ave vinished hereabouts," but privately cursed the day when the new owner of Shallowford had taken a wife to hustle him into persecuting tenants. "Meg!" he bellowed, "come on out an' pay your respects to the Squire, will 'ee, you lazy slut?", and he turned his back on Paul to flush the survivors of his brood from the farmhouse. Meg Potter came out slowly and behind her the two girls, Cissie and Violet, but Smut was nowhere to be found. "Do 'ee know where that Smut be to?" roared Tamer, who always enjoyed exercising his largely fictitious authority over his family but Meg said no, she did not know, although she was well aware that Smut Potter, at that precise moment, was overlooking the Heronslea partridge coverts, five miles to the east and that his presence there was a reconnaissance pending a descent upon a fat buck that had been using the covert lately. She gave a bob to the Squire, however, as he rode up the track towards Deepdene. He was entitled to that, she thought, seeing how much tiresomeness lay in wait for him but she said nothing of this to Tamer or the girls, returning at once to her ruinous kitchen to finish brewing her winter rheumatism cure. The sweet-smelling concoction seethed in a huge iron pot, and a long row of medicine bottles, taken by stealth from Doctor O'Keefe's dispensary over the years, stood waiting to receive it but as it was not yet on the boil there was time for a quick look into the future. She took out her cards and fell to shuffling and cutting them and out came not the Lady of

Sorrow, as she had expected, but the Knave of Diamonds. Its appearance disconcerted her for it indicated that Smut's future was even more uncertain than the Squire's. It occurred to her then that she should warn Smut to leave the buck until it crossed into the safer territory of Shallowford Woods. Sam Potter, her firstborn, might have abandoned the tribe, but she knew he would never come between Smut and his livelihood.

IV

Spring, so Arthur Pitts told him, had been cruising offshore for long enough, but within days of Paul's return home it made up its mind, dropped anchor south of the sandbars and fired its green barrage over the Valley. The effect was salutary. The river went down overnight and all the Sorrel creeks and oxbows dried out. The banners of May appeared in all the hedgerows between Timberlake's sawmill and Codsall bridge. April showers still fell but were shot through with sunshine, so that the Teazel watershed was seen through a silver gauze and up and down the Valley there was bustle and expectancy. Henry Pitts sang as he herded his cows down to the water meadows and even Sydney Codsall, with a mind full of syntax and relativity, stopped his bicycle on the way to school one morning just to watch a ladybird on a sprig of cowparsley. A week or so later all the dwarf elms and beech hedges along the western edge of Hermitage Wood were full of nesting thrushes, blackbirds, tits and finches, and the vixens on the landslips further south were out all night hunting up food for their cubs.

There were plenty of other signs that the long, wet winter was done and that everything in the valley was bent on renewing itself. Over at Periwinkle Elinor Codsall, last year just a wisp of a girl, now dragged a thickening body across the uneven flags of the kitchen and in the woods north of the mere Joannie Potter, also pregnant, was wondering how, come the autumn, she would squeeze another crib into the cottage bedroom. Down in Coombe Bay were others with like problems, among them Pansy Pascoe. Pansy, once a carefree Potter, looked with distaste at her swollen body, envying her husbandless sisters who were not tied to a kitchen and one hungry male but the sudden warmth of the sun drove her out into the garden where, as she raised her snub nose to the sky, her spirits lifted and she set about peeling a mound of potatoes for Walt's supper.

Only Smut Potter, lying full-length in the bracken over-looking Heronslea, cursed the sun, for its sparkle com-plicated his scrutiny of the ground below where he sus-pected the fat buck he had earlier marked down was punishing the bark of the Norwegian pines Gilroy's forester had planted there. Smut had a customer for that buck and he meant to kill while the moon was up. He lay quite still, his eyes fixed unwinkingly on a patch of shadow under the trees, but it was not until the sun clouded over that he identified the movements down there as the chaffering of deer and gave a short grunt of satisfaction. "There 'er be!" he said aloud, "and I'll 'ave un tonight, sure as fate!" and he made a final eyesweep of the approach, memorising contours, gorse patches and places where the heaviest shadows would lie after moon-rise. Then, crawling backwards on all fours, he worked his way down to a cleft where a stream ran down through a small coombe to the Sorrel. In less than five minutes he was hidden by the trees that grew on the steep sides of the goyle.

He had moved quickly and cautiously but somebody had observed him from the opposite ridge, a man not as well versed in exploiting cover as Smut but one who had the advantage of binoculars, borrowed for the purpose of keeping Potter in view. Nick Buller, Gilroy's head game-keeper, had suffered a great deal on Smut's account and once or twice had come close to being sacked for failing to catch him. Recently, however, his luck had turned. A Paxtonbury butcher, who sometimes bought surplus veni-son from Heronslea when the herds were whittled down, had been heard to boast in The Mitre at Paxtonbury, that he could buy cheaper than Gilroy was prepared to sell and the outlay of a few shillings on Buller's part had traced his source of supply to the Dell. Buller was not such a fool as to hope that he could catch a poacher as wily as Potter in the actual act of taking deer but he thought he stood a good chance of being close on hand when the buck was killed, after which he could follow Smut to the Dell and confront him with a policeman while in the act of conveying the kill to Paxtonbury. He had made his plans accordingly but it was essential to know precisely where Smut would strike, and this explained Buller's presence on the hillside with binoculars. He returned to Heronslea in a happy frame of mind. If Smut Potter was out tonight he was as good as nailed.

If Buller had been allowed to follow this plan things might well have turned out as he had hoped. Smut would have been trailed at a safe distance and stopped by the police *en route* to the butchers but Gilroy's agent, Harry Kitchens, had more ambitious ideas. He argued that if Buller had marked the spot so accurately it would be a very simple matter to take Smut in the act and pay something off the score before he was brought before the Bench at Whinmouth Petty Sessions. Now Kitchens had been waiting for a chance to smash his fist into Potter's face as repayment for all the nagging he had endured on his account and he said, on receiving Buller's report, "Right! Get Scratton and Bostock and lay up both sides of the goyle before sunset. He'll come in by the goyle for there's cover all the way from the boundary. Meantime I'll take young Glover and we'll wait on the west side. We can have five minutes with Potter yourself, Buller, but leave something for me. Then we'll lock what's left in the stable and hand it over to the magistrates in a sack in the morning!"

Meg Potter passed her warning to Smut but he only laughed at her. He was fond of his mother but took small account of her fortune-telling. All his life he had put his trust in his fieldcraft, his highly developed powers of sight and hearing and, in the last instance, his expert marksmanship, so why should he worry about the prattle of a greasy pack of cards? He cleaned his gun, smeared his face and hands with half-burned embers from the fire and left the Dell soon after dusk. It was a long haul in the trap to Paxtonbury and he wanted to be there by dawn, so that he could enter the butcher's yard before Beefy Bickley's staff arrived. He would then top off a good night's work with bacon and eggs at The Mitre, pay a brief social call on a lonely woman whose sailor husband had been so inconsiderate as to sign on for an Australian run, and be back in the Dell by mid-afternoon. Smut never wasted much time in bed. A siesta would follow and he would be out again as soon as it was dark, this time moving east instead of west. But it all turned out very differently and neither as Smut, Kitchens or Buller planned. Perhaps Meg, in the interests of the Valley, should have passed her warning to all concerned.

He killed the buck with a single shot, stalking upwind at a speed of about a yard a minute. The last sound the buck heard, the first to warn it of danger, was the soft snick of Smut's hammer. Then it was twitching at the foot of the tree and Smut, moving expertly and rapidly, bound forepaws and hindpaws, twisted a stick under the cords and braced himself to hoist it on to his shoulders. It was at that moment, when he was still bent double, that the first of the ambush party moved in.

Smut had passed within yards of Buller on his way out of the goyle but Buller did not possess the patience to play longstop for the agent. The moment he heard the gun he came plunging down the slope and would have fallen on Smut had he not misjudged his distance and overshot him as the poacher crouched above the buck. The butt of his slung gun struck Smut a glancing blow on the elbow, jarring it so sharply that he cried out in pain. Then, as he heard a confused shouting he realised that men were closing in from all sides and Buller had him fast by the ankle, bellowing for assistance at the top of his voice. For a split second, as he heard the others crashing through the undergrowth at the head of the goyle, Smut lost his head and swung his gun in an arc, the butt striking Buller's jaw with shattering force and causing him to utter a single agonised howl as he rolled sideways in the scrub. By then Agent Kitchens and young Glover were almost upon them and two more of Gilroy's men were crashing through briars between Smut and the goyle, so that instinct told him he must run due north towards the moor, unless he was to be caught and half killed on the spot.

He dropped his gun and broke out of the circle with only a yard to spare, Bostock colliding with Glover as the latter dashed up from the west and the pair of them rolling on top of Buller as Kitchens, nearer the edge of the covert, bellowed, "Head him off to the right! Up to the moor!", and went blundering over the tangled ground in close pursuit. Glover followed but the others remained bent over the unconscious Buller and Bostock cried, "Strike a light, Tom, for Chrissake! He's killed un, I reckon!", and in the flare of a match they looked down on the keeper, his face a mask of blood, his feet across the body of the trussed buck and his gun snapped off at the stock where it had struck the roots of a pine.

It took Smut less than two minutes to lose his two pursuers. He was calmer now and ran with his head rather than his legs, doubling north-east, then north-west and once, for twenty or more strides, backtracking towards the cursing agent, now breasting the slope like an elephant pursuing a hare. After a hundred yards or so he gave it up and found his way back to the plantation where his raging temper was cooled by the shock of seeing Nick Buller, his head on Bostock's knees, as the other man, Scratton, kept repeating, dolorously, "He's done for un! He's done for un!" But Buller, although badly injured about his face, was far from dead and after they had lit the lantern he was able to sit up and gesture feebly, although he could not swallow the brandy Kitchens offered him from his flask. Working clumsily they bound his bloody chaps with strips of flannel shirt so that he sat with his back to the tree like a corpse ready for burial. Glover was sent on ahead to rouse the Big House and despatch a messenger to Whinmouth for the doctor and somehow, between them, they managed to carry Buller down to Long Covert and then across the paddock to his cottage. It was a tedious, troublesome journey and every step of the way Kitchens swore that somebody would pay a heavy price for their pains, as well as Buller's.

As soon as Smut was sure he had lost his pursuers he walked south-east, in a wide sweep that led him to the northern tip of Priory Wood and here, in a little glade, he sat down to ponder his situation. He was not at all sure that he had not killed that idiot Buller and now that he had won clear for a spell he had great difficulty in controlling a tide of panic and keeping his mind clear for his next moves for now it seemed his life might depend on them. He cursed himself for not throwing his gun aside the moment he felt his ankle grabbed and using his fists to persuade Buller to release his hold. That might have earned him six months for assault but nothing more, not the gallows, or penal servitude, and when these two alternatives presented themselves Smut's body, already bathed in sweat, began to shake from head to foot so that he had to hold himself rigid like a man clinging to a cliff. Presently, however, he began to regain self-control and the habit of logical thought that had extricated him from so many scrapes in the past. His first impulse was to put as many miles as possible between himself and Heronslea before daylight but he soon realised that he could not travel much beyond the county border before dawn and had neither food nor money to lie up, and move on the following night until he was clear of the district. He realised also that he could not go back to the Dell, for Kitchens would be sure to go there before reporting. He could take temporary refuge with Sam, in Shallowford Woods, but after calling at Low Coombe the police would probably make straight for the cottage and yet, a temporary hideout was essential if he was to get word to Meg and through her means to win clear. Smut knew every hideout between the Whin estuary and the county border and considered each, discarding one or another for different reasons and finally deciding on one that had the advantage of being within range of Meg but affording the most security. It was a cave formed by a fallen beech on the western shore of the mere and its main advantage lay in the fact that he could approach it wading along the shallows and through the running water of a rivulet, which meant that he would be safe from tracker dogs as well as men. It was an insignificant looking place and he felt sure he could remain here indefinitely, providing he could contact a member of the clan and get a supply of food floated downstream. He had found it some months ago whilst otter hunting and had occasionally slept there, warm and dry on a bed of bracken. To reach it before daylight he had to risk breaking into the open fields but he kept clear of paths and entered the western edge of Shallowford Woods with time in hand, passing within a few hundred yards of Sam's cottage on his way round the shore. He hesitated here, wondering whether it would be worth the risk to rouse Sam, beg some food and tell him where he was hiding but he decided against it, for rousing Sam meant rousing Joannie and Joannie was not, strictly speaking, a member of the clan. So he moved on, wading across the shallows and striking the stream a quarter-mile above its outfall. He followed it down to the great sprawling mass of the beech and then through the network of roots without leaving a single footmark in the silt. Once inside he felt secure and relaxed, his come-day-go-day philosophy returning to still the tumult of fear in his heart but under this protective belt self-righteousness began to assert itself, so that soon, although sorry for Buller and sorrier still for himself, he began to see himself not as a man wanted for violent assault or perhaps murder but as a persecuted minority who had cleverly evaded an ambush prepared by those who denied him the right to live by his wits. A little comforted by these reflections he smoked a cautious pipe and curled himself up in the dry bracken to sleep. Ten thousand men could walk shoulder to shoulder from Heronslea to the county border and back again, but they would not find him here, snug, warm and within hailing distance of the first Potter to use the path to Sam's cottage. He would be hungry, perhaps, but that was no hardship; he and all his kin had been hungry often enough in the past.

V

They came down the road like a plantation posse, four mounted, with slung shotguns, two on foot leading dogs, as though flushing a dangerous beast into the open. Rudd, meeting them on his way up to help Honeyman plant a windbreak in the water meadows, stared at them in amazement. They looked so theatrical that he could not imagine for one instant what they sought, or why they looked so grim about it, so he called to Kitchens, the agent, "What's going on, Harry?" and the agent flung back, "You know what's going on, John!" Rudd, irritated by his tone, caught his horse by the bridle and said, "Now, why in hell should I ask you what's going on if I knew what's going on?" and then Kitchens looked slightly confused as the party surrounded Rudd. "Well, maybe you don't, John," he said, "maybe nobody has told you yet but we mean business, I can tell you that. Last night we almost caught Smut Potter, after he had killed a buck. He showed fight and Nick Buller is badly hurt. He had his face smashed in with a gun butt and they've taken him to hospital. We're looking for Smut now, so if you know where he is you'd best say, and save everyone a lot of trouble. My chaps aren't in the mood to fool around!"

John Rudd's jaw dropped. "Great God!" he said. "Isn't this a matter for the police?"

"Yes, it is," Kitchens told him, "but you know how that lazy devil Price goes about his business. The Whinmouth police were told early this morning but by the time they get over here Smut will be miles away. We thought we'd flush him out and we're on our way up to the Coombe right now. Come on, lads," and he kicked his horse.

"Wait a minute!" Rudd cried, running alongside. "You don't imagine Smut will be waiting for you in the Dell, do you?"

"We've got to start somewhere and we can begin with that gypsy mother of his. She'll know something and she'll either tell us or face a charge of compounding a felony."

Rudd said, "Listen here, Harry, Low Coombe is one of our farms and if you're going up there to raise hell I'm going with you!", and he ran back into the farm buildings and threw a saddle over Honeyman's pony, Squirrel. By the time he had the bridle on and was mounted, however, Gilroy's men were half-a-mile down the road and he had to gallop to catch them up. He had meant to send a message up to the house to inform Paul but there was no time and when he followed them into the Dell Kitchens was already hectoring Old Tamer and one of the girls. Presently Meg, the other girl and the Potters' simple child, Hazel, came out and they all stood in a tight circle, like partridges roosting in the open, with Gilroy men posted round them like sentinels. Rudd pushed his way through to them.

"Smut's in real trouble this time," he told Tamer, shortly, "so if you do know where he is you had best tell me. I'll undertake to hand him over to Police Sergeant Price. They won't dare maul him in my presence!"

Meg said, sullenly, "We dorn know where he be, Mr. Rudd, but if us did, do you think us'd tell 'ee?"

"If you hide him you'll be in gaol yourself before you know it, the whole tribe of you!" Kitchens growled, but Meg only spat on the ground and said, "Aw, the devil take you all!", and walked calmly back to her farm followed by the two elder girls.

Rudd saw the veins swell in Kitchens' temples and heard the men muttering behind him. He said, ignoring Tamer, "You'd better follow me to Sam Potter's cottage in the woods. He might know something!" and Kitchens said, "All right, John, but don't try any tricks. These chaps are after blood and so would you be if you'd seen Buller's face last night!", and they rode out of the Dell with John Rudd leading, crossing the side of the hill and the big meadow and descending the long wooded slope to the mere.

"Listen here, Harry," John said, as they went along, "this is a ridiculous business and you know it! What'll happen if we run into Smut? They'll manhandle him and I shall be a witness, so you'll soon be joining Smut in the dock! You'd far better leave it to the police and Mr. Craddock."

"Craddock?" said Kitchens, with a short laugh. "Craddock's a Radical isn't he? I wouldn't put it past him to be thinking Smut Potter had every right to that buck!"

"Then you don't know Craddock!" John said, shortly. "I'll answer for him. There's no harm in calling on Sam
284

Potter but after that I'll see you all off our land and for your own sakes as much as Potter's! This isn't Czarist Russia and we aren't living in the Middle Ages!"

Kitchens seemed worried at this and dropped back to hold a brief consultation with his men, while Rudd dismounted and entered the cottage to find Sam and his wife at breakfast. He told them what had happened and asked if they could tell him where Smut might have gone.

"Lord bless you, no, I can't," Sam said, looking startled and unhappy, "he might be in any one o' a hundred plaaces, Mr. Rudd, and they'll have the works o' the world ter catch un, now he's won clear! Mashed in Nick Buller's face, you say? And with a gun? Well, an' what was they up to for such a thing to happen? Maybe Smut was on'y standin' up fer hisself, like anybody would?"

"He was poaching deer," Rudd said, "and they had every right to take him."

"Aye," Sam said, slowly, "but it depends on how they went about it, dorn it?"

"Perhaps, but if you find out where he is tell me or the Squire before you tell them, understand?"

"Aye," Sam said, readily, "I'll do that, Mr. Rudd. Smut? Well, he's wild all right, but he baint vi'lent, and you can tell 'em zo from me!"

Kitchens seemed in a somewhat more reasonable frame of mind when he rejoined them. Perhaps the hopelessness of flushing Smut Potter into the open had occurred to him, or perhaps he felt unequal to controlling the Gilroy keepers in their present mood. At all events he agreed to return to Shallowford and make a formal report to the Squire and sent the men home with a warning to be careful how they handled Smut if they were lucky enough to find him. They rode off still muttering and growling and Rudd had the impression that this business, coming on top of Paul's personal quarrel with Lord Gilroy, would be likely to widen the rift to a feud and that it was all very childish and unnecessary. He had always got along very well with Kitchens.

"I'll give you a piece of advice, Harry," he said, as they approached the house, "don't try and browbeat that young man. He isn't nearly as green as he looks and he's still very new to our kind of problems. It was Gilroy's manner that drove him into the Liberal camp." Kitchens said, sourly, "I'm sick of the whole business, John! Smut Potter is a waster, of course, but every landowner has poaching problems, and it needn't have come to this. But Gilroy means to make an issue of it and when Potter is laid by the heels he'll be for it! It won't make for peace and quiet hereabouts, I'm thinking!"

When they handed over their horses to Ikey in the yard they saw that Paul was already aware of what had happened, for the police sergeant's trap was there and Chivers, the groom, said he was in the office with the Squire now. "Has anything serious happened, sir?" he wanted to know but Rudd grunted, "Serious enough!" and left it at that.

They found Paul and the police sergeant in the library with Grace, whose presence disconcerted Kitchens, and when Rudd explained that they had been to the Dell and Sam Potter's but had drawn a blank the sergeant said, "Buller has a fractured jaw and two teeth through his tongue but there's no question of him not making a recovery. I saw his Lordship before I came over, and he seems to think it should be a charge of attempted murder. It's not for me to decide, of course, but my inspector will want to know the full facts, even if we do take our time catching him. He has a record, you know."

Grace said, unexpectedly, "Yes he has. Two spells of fourteen days for trespassing in pursuit of conies!" and everyone looked at her.

"That's so, ma'am," said Kitchens, "but this is surely a far more serious matter."

"I don't see that it has to be," Grace said, ignoring Paul's glance. "As far as I can see there were five or six of you on the spot and we have yet to hear Potter's version."

"No doubt we shall, when we catch him!" said the sergeant pacifically but Grace shrugged and said, "Will we? I doubt it! If I was facing half-a-dozen Gilroy witnesses ready to swear my life away, I think I should stay out of reach as long as possible!"

Kitchens said, "I was present when it happened, Mrs.

Craddock. Buller jumped on him just as he was lifting the buck and when we came up our man was unconscious on the ground."

"Then you weren't actually present, were you?" she said, "and I also hear Buller's gun was snapped off at the stock."

Paul said, crisply, "Leave this to me, Grace! John and myself will sort it out."

"Oh, you'll sort it out I don't doubt," said Grace, thrusting both hands into the pockets of her overall, "but neither you, nor John Rudd, nor the sergeant here will be able to ensure that Potter gets a fair trial, with Lord Gilroy pressing the charges. Why don't we all admit it?"

The policeman looked miserably embarrassed and Paul said, "Listen, Grace . . ." but she turned and walked out of the room and Rudd noticed that her manner of exit had the effect of hardening Kitchens' mouth. Paul said, half-apologetically, "My wife and I crossed swords with Lord Gilroy on another matter, Sergeant, but that need have no bearing on this. If I get word of Potter I'll do my utmost to bring him in without further trouble, you can rely on that!"

"I'm sure I can, sir," Price said, in a tone that made Rudd doubt it.

There seemed nothing else to say so, after both the sergeant and Kitchens had refused a drink, they all left. Rudd said slowly, "That wasn't very wise of her, Paul. Maybe you'd best tell me what you feel about it, personally."

"She has a point, John. It might be difficult to get an unprejudiced hearing in the circumstances, but we could get Smut a good lawyer to take care of that, couldn't we?"

"You'd want to do that?"

"Why yes, of course I would, and so would Grace. He's one of our people, poacher or not, isn't he?" And then, ruefully, "I don't seem to be able to put a foot right in Gilroy's direction, do I?"

"What has it to do with you? Smut Potter is jumped by Gilroy's keepers in the act of taking game. He hits out and lands himself in this kind of mess. Damn it, man,

287

you can't be responsible for the behaviour of every Tom Fool in the Valley, can you?"

"No," said Paul, "I don't suppose I can, John, but I have an uneasy suspicion I'm partly responsible for the viciousness with which Gilroy is pressing charges. Battery and assault is one thing, attempted murder quite another. A man can go to prison for ten years or more for that, can't he?"

"Not in these circumstances," John said, "so stop worrying about it. If Smut keeps hidden for a while and Buller picks up, I daresay everybody's temper will soon cool."

"You really think that, John?" and he sounded, Rudd thought, pathetically eager to be reassured. "Yes, I do!" Rudd went on. "After all, it sounds bad to begin with, a man surprised in the act of committing a felony using a gun to resist arrest but what does it amount to really? A scuffle in the bushes after dark. If Smut had fired a shot it might be different but he didn't and all I can say is it's a great pity he didn't use his fists. A good solicitor ought to be able to get him off with six months. Poaching is a national sport about here and has been since the time of William Rufus."

"Well, I hope you're right," said Paul, "I'd better find Grace and tell her. She's very worried about it."

"You do that," said John, but to himself, as Paul went on to the terrace, he murmured, "You'll get little comfort there, my lad! She's raised Kitchens' hackles just as I'd managed to lower them and every word she said will be stable gossip at Heronslea in an hour!" Grumpily he stumped out across the water meadows, reflecting that he could cheerfully wring Smut Potter's neck himself for landing them all in such a desperately embarrassing situation.

It was not until Paul was alone with Grace after supper that he was able to pursue the matter. He said, "It would have been better for everybody if you hadn't said that in front of Kitchens, Grace, and if he or Gilroy come here again I'd feel a lot happier if you kept out of it!"

She did not resent this rebuke, seeming to have expected it. "I'm not likely to seek either of them out," she said, and then, looking steadily at him, "but that doesn't mean I'm sorry for what I said! Somebody had to say it."

He flushed, saying sharply, "Why? Why couldn't you let things take their course? Or at least leave this kind of thing to me?"

"That's what you're upset about, isn't it?"

It was the closest they had yet come to an open quarrel and Paul wanted, above all, to be as honest as she always was. He said, flatly, "Yes, I suppose it is, Grace. No man likes his wife to do his talking for him and I think you made me look a fool."

"Well," she said, "I'm sincerely sorry about that but it had to be said all the same. You still don't know what you're up against down here and sometimes I don't think you ever will! If the Gilroys could lay hands on Potter now he would appear in court on a stretcher but that isn't what's so important. They'd pull every string within reach to get him gaoled for half a lifetime and partly to teach you your place! If I did speak out of turn this morning it was in your interests as well as Potter's."

"I think you're exaggerating," he argued but he felt uneasy all the same. "Anyway, if I locate him I'll make sure the police get to him first."

"I don't doubt that you would," she replied, still speaking very calmly, "but that wouldn't stop him getting a savage sentence!"

"Damn it, Grace, don't let's overlook his liability," he said, feeling cornered. "He bashed a man's face in and the chap is still in hospital."

"What do you imagine they would have done to Smut if they had laid hands on him? When I was a little girl here a Whinmouth poacher was peppered with a shotgun and left to bleed to death in Gilroy coverts. The verdict at the inquest was 'Accidental Death' but everybody knew who was responsible."

"I've still got to do what I think is right," he said. "I happen to believe in civilised conduct."

"Yes, I know," she said in the same tone, "and that's why you should have stayed in a city," and she left him to his own gloomy company.

They did not refer to it again until they were going to

bed. The implication that he was unqualified for his responsibilities rankled with him but he was too unsure of himself to make an issue of it.

"We don't have to quarrel over this, Grace," he said, when he blew out the lamp and was getting into bed beside her.

"No we don't, Paul," she said, "because, luckily for all of us, the issue has resolved itself already. Smut Potter is clear away by now and they'll have to take it out of the next poor devil they catch contravening the Ten Commandments and the landed gentry's Enclosure Acts! Good night, Paul," and she turned away. He lay awake a long time listening to the night sounds of Priory Wood and the muted hunting clamour of the river banks, dismayed by this unforeseeable rift that had opened between them but wondering, with the detached part of his mind, how much of his land and Gilroy's across the Teazel had once been common pasture, available to everyone in the Valley.

Grace was wrong in her estimate of Smut's margin of safety. At the moment, and every night until Midsummer's Eve, he was no more than two miles away, and far less as the heron flew from the river to the edge of Shallowford Mere. When the Valley worked he slept and when the Valley slept he was at one with the foxes in the glades further east and the otters fishing under the logs near his hideout.

He could have been gone by now, up the country, over to Ireland, to America even, for Meg had begun scraping money together the moment Hazel brought news of his whereabouts, and by now she had somehow accumulated enough to spirit him out of reach of everybody, providing he travelled by night. But to her dismay he was still there, lying all day in his holt under the fallen beech and drifting about the woods all night, living on what he trapped and the food that Hazel floated down to him according to instructions given the day after he had gone into hiding. None of them had actually seen him, for even when he first made contact with Hazel he remained out of sight in the foliage that grew down to the water's edge and told her how to keep in touch with him by using the stream that flowed past the mouth of his lair. She had obyed his instructions to the letter so that now he had most things a man could need, a blanket, a stewpot, tobacco and trap wires, with bread, salt and a stub of blacklead on which he could scrawl messages.

Yet it was not comfort that kept him here or fear of the Gilroy keepers and police, nor even the news that Nick Buller was now out of hospital, with a lopsided jaw and a slight impediment in his speech, caused by the passage of two teeth through his tongue. He was still there because he could not bring himself to turn his back on the fields and woods that had enclosed him all his life or separate himself from his kin in the Dell. He knew every bush and tree in the thirty-odd square miles about the Coombe but never once, not even for a day, had he travelled further afield, or wanted to and now that he was faced with the prospect of leaving it all and perhaps never coming back his resolution faltered and he hung on, waiting for some miraculous turn of fortune that would make everything the same as it had been before that unlucky incident in Heronslea plantation. He had never been called upon to make a decision as final as this, that would shatter the rhythm of his life and throw him among strangers, an act that would, in a sense, not only deprive him of his means of livelihood but compel him to come to terms with people who worked from dawn to dusk, lived in brick houses, raised families and paid rates and taxes. And so it was, in the end, that the decision had to be made for him by others, after news of his whereabouts leaked outside the clan.

Discovery of his hideout came through Ikey Palfrey, whose wits, always keen, had been whetted to a very sharp edge by his association with Hazel Potter, after she had found him lost in the snow. He had seen her several times a week since then and she had revealed to him most of her secrets of the wood but although he was an apt pupil, and learned all she had to teach him at remarkable speed for a boy reared in a city, he remained in awe of her, regarding her as someone paying a brief visit from another planet. He marvelled at her strength and agility, at her ability to imitate bird calls and animal noises, from a moorhen skimming across the mere to draw an intruder from her nest, to the steady scrunch of a badger's claws enlarging a set. There was nothing, it seemed, that she did not know about the woods and the countryside, about the weather and the whereabouts of plants and insect colonies. She showed him, at one time or another, each species in the wood at work and at play and about these things she could invent orations that seemed to him (familiar now with all Mary Willoughby's favourite ballads) an almost miraculous deluge of sounds, part monologue, and part chant, and delivered in a mixture of broad Devon and gypsy argot that contained words he had never heard uttered before. Her appearance bewitched him too, for it had little in common with that of any of the children who sat at lessons in Deepdene schoolroom. She was invariably dirty and unkempt but somehow strikingly beautiful, with eyes that seemed to change colour according to the strength of sunlight, with long, supple limbs, half-naked now that it was summer, and a great mop of tangled hair sometimes chestnut and other times bleached the colour of ripe barley. Her teeth intrigued him, so white that they shone like the underside of a cloud when she laughed at him, as she did when he stumbled or lagged behind her long, skipping strides. But the association was not quite so one-sided as it might have been, for slowly, as their friendship ripened, she began to show more interest in his background and ask him to tell her about "thicky gurt, smelly plaace", from which he had, by a miracle, escaped. And because this was all he had to offer at that time he was glad to tell her, painting heroic pictures of his struggles in the metropolis, where he had often seen carriages bowling along without horses, and had once cheered Queen Vicky in a carriage surrounded by her lifeguards.

All that spring, whenever he could escape from school or his work, he sought her out at their meeting place opposite the old pagoda which she continued to call "The Niggerman's Church", and together they ranged the woods and slopes as far as the railway line (but never over it) and the long curving shore of Coombe Bay. For him she was a kind of priestess and he told no one of his association with her; for her it was a taste of dominion over another soul, in whom she sensed a kind of worship that warmed her like June sunshine, so that it piqued her to sacrifice his company in the interests of clan loyalty, and to observe him waiting for her by the mere when she was on her way to or from her brother's hideout.

One still evening, when she was descending the long wooded slope carrying a sack containing a supply of tobacco and fresh vegetables, she weakened and called to him, saying that she was on her way to "a beastie in a caave, yonder", and dumb with curiosity he had followed her, not knowing in the least what kind of pet she had hidden in the wood but guessing it was this that had kept her from him all these long sunny days. It was only when she emptied the sack and poked among the bushes beside the swift-flowing stream that flowed into the western margin of the mere, that he realised her beastie was a man and could be none other than her fugitive brother, Smut, and at once his heart sank, for he now saw himself faced with a choice of loyalties, to her, who trusted him, and to his other idol, Squire Craddock, who was rumoured to have quarrelled with his wife and with Lord Gilroy on Smut Potter's account. For the moment, however, he was too interested to worry over what he should do with the information but watched her fasten a carefully-wrapped parcel to a small, raised plank, attached to a long coil of parcel string and set this little raft adrift on the current, paying out the string until it was taut. The plank sailed out of sight through a clump of harts tongue ferns and when, after an interval she began to wind in, it reappeared without its parcel. He said, goggling, *"It's Smut, ain't it? He's holed up down there?"*, and she smiled and laid a finger to her lips, saying, "Arr, that's zo! Us dorm mind *you* knowin' for youm different. Come on, us'll go an' zee they badgers, shall us?" But he was not interested in badgers now, or anything else she could show him, and as soon as he could he escaped pleading extra chores at the stable and here entered upon a terrible battle with his conscience for it seemed to him that he was obliged to betray one of them, the girl who had shared

293

her terrible secret with him, or the man who had given him the keys to this new world.

He lay tossing and turning in his hayloft all that night and in the morning, red-eyed and yawning, he made his decision. It would have been different, he told himself, if Smut had been hiding in neutral territory but his presence here, inside the estate boundaries, involved the Squire in the poacher's crime, and the police had not yet ceased to search for him east of the river. Ikey was not unfamiliar with the police, regarding them with an inherited distrust. Police always meant trouble for someone and police here meant bad trouble for the Squire; it was therefore in his master's interest that he get rid of them and once Smut's whereabouts were known Squire would manage that one way or the other.

He went through the kitchen and taking advantage of Mrs. Handcock's back slipped into the hall and thence to the library. Paul was at work in his office and Ikey braced himself to cross the room and tap on the closed glass door but as he did so he heard a step behind him and swung round to face Mrs. Craddock and for a moment he faltered, looking furtive and guilty. Then his expression cleared, for he knew Grace Craddock shared the Squire's interest in him and it occurred to him that the Squire would be certain in any case to pass information regarding Smut's whereabouts to his wife. He said, before she could ask him what he was doing, "I know where Smut Potter is, Ma'am! I was comin' to tell Squire."

He was startled by the expression of alarm that crossed her face and by the nervous manner in which she slammed the library door, leaning against it, with her hands behind her.

"You've seen him?"

"No, I ain't seen him, Ma'am, but I know where he is orlright. He's 'iding aht, the far side of the mere." He decided to skirt Hazel's involvement and the fact that his knowledge was shared by the Potter tribe as a whole. They could find that out for themselves if they wished. His responsibility ended with passing on the fact that the fugitive was still here, on the estate.

"You're quite sure of this, Ikey?"

"Yes, Ma'am."

"You could take us there?"

"I wouldn't need to, Ma'am, it's opposite the little island, in a kind of cave under a fallen tree."

She stood thinking for a moment and then, it seemed to him with an effort, said, "Very well, wait a minute will you?" and went into the office, closing the door.

He heard the rise and fall of their voices and presently both came out, Paul looking bewildered. "Go and fetch Mr. Rudd, Ikey," Grace said, "but don't mention this to a soul, you understand?"

"No, Ma'am."

He went out, shutting the door softly. Without exactly understanding why he realised that his news had shocked them and he had a sense of becoming involved in events that could bring trouble and discord and was already regretting having told them. He found Rudd at the lodge eating breakfast and the agent received the news phlegmatically. "I always had a notion he hadn't run far," was all he said and told Ikey to go back to his work and keep his counsel, even from the groom.

When Rudd entered the library a few minutes later he was at once aware of the tension in the room but for all that he went straight to the point. "The best thing we can do is to urge Potter to surrender to us tonight," he said, "then we might be able to persuade him to give himself up to Sergeant Price first thing tomorrow."

"That's what I've been saying, John, but Grace is very much against it."

"What does she suggest?" he asked, as though Grace was not present, and she snapped, "That we send Ikey to tell him to clear out and take his chance as soon as it's dark! Are we to play thieftakers for the Gilroys?"

"To send Ikey would involve the boy," Rudd said, quietly. "If it came out, as it well might, he could be taken in charge himself and I'm not sure it wouldn't lay your husband open to being an accessory."

She did not seem impressed by this but smiled her tight little smile.

"Why should it come out?"

295

"Don't forget, there's a warrant out for Potter, Mrs. Craddock."

"For attempted murder?"

"For malicious wounding and that carries a severe penalty."

She was silent for a moment and Rudd felt desperately sorry for Paul, who opened his mouth to say something but closed it again. Presently she looked up, first at Rudd, then at Paul, and when she spoke her voice sounded flat and defeated.

"No matter what I say you're both determined to give him up, aren't you? It's the law, isn't it? It's safe, for everyone but Smut Potter!"

"Damn it, you're twisting the facts, Grace," Paul burst out. "I wouldn't 'give him up' as you say, and neither would John. We want him to give himself up, in his own interests!"

"His own interests? Three to five years in a stinking gaol!"

"He won't get three to five years," Paul said, "he'll more likely get six months and less if the case is dealt with summarily, as one of poaching and common assault."

"Can you guarantee he'll be so charged?" she asked, and Rudd said no, they couldn't, but if he came in voluntarily his chances were far better than if he was arrested out of the district and committed for trial at the Assizes.

"I said in his own interests and that's precisely what I meant!" Paul argued. "Any other way, what are his prospects? He goes in fear of arrest every day of his life and can never show his face here again! I don't think he'd want that, not when he understands all it means and the fact that he's stayed so near home all this time proves as much, doesn't it?"

"It might prove he hasn't any money," she said.

"And you'd have me send him money?" Paul said.

"Yes," she said deliberately, "I would and if you wouldn't I would."

"Well I'm damned if I'll let you and that's final," he said, and Rudd thought, "Maybe he's beginning to learn how to handle her! Well, good luck to him, but this is no place for me," and he made as if to go but she called sharply, "Don't leave, John! That wouldn't be very brave of you!", and he stopped, his neck reddening, and said, "Surely this is something you have to settle between yourselves, Mrs. Craddock?"

"Fundamentally, yes," she said, "but not simply as regards Potter's fate. There will be other issues like this and Paul needs your advice as much as mine. You'd better say exactly what's in your mind."

"Very well," he said, turning back, "what's in my mind is clear. I think Paul is complicating the issue and you're sentimentalising it! Potter caused a man a serious injury while that man was doing a job he was paid to do. It doesn't matter to me who that man was, or who was paying him. The law is there to protect every one of us and Potter, who derides the law, got himself into this mess and must now take his chance with the magistrates! We'll do all we can to get him off lightly and I think Paul is right to want to provide him with a lawyer but beyond that I wouldn't go an inch, not for my own sake, or the sake of good relations hereabouts."

She said, looking at Paul now, "Well, there's your answer! You'd best do as John says, Paul."

He looked at her appealingly. "But you still don't agree with us, do you? You still think it a shabby trick on our part to deny him a sporting chance?"

"He's had one sporting chance and if it were left to me I'd give him another, that's all!", and left the room.

Rudd said, as her steps had ceased to sound in the hall, "It's a pity you told her, Paul."

"I didn't," he said, "but I'm glad she knows. Better this way than have her thinking we said nothing until it was all over."

"Does she know where he's hiding?"

"Yes, Ikey told her. Are you suggesting I should lock her up?"

"You might do worse," Rudd said, trying but failing to make it a joke. "I'll take a stroll there right away and tell Potter to come here after dark, shall I?"

"Yes, and tell him I'll leave the garden door of the office open." He paused and the agent saw that he was still not wholly convinced and that Grace's attitude had shaken him badly.

"You're doing right, Paul," he said, "and I believe you know that in your heart."

"Yes," he said, "I know it, John, but it's hard on both of us to have to face this situation so soon. It was working out, John, in spite of your misgivings and you did have them, didn't you?"

"Yes," Rudd said, "I did and it is a pity because I was beginning to lose them, Paul. I should like you to believe that," and because he felt his presence only increased the man's unhappiness he went out, turning east along the terrace in the direction of the woods.

VI

Smut's case came before Mr. Justice Scratton-Forbes, at the Devon Quarter Sessions in mid-July after he had appeared before the Petty Sessional Court at Whinmouth, where a procession of witnesses went into the box to testify against him. Kitchens had promised Rudd he would do his best to limit the charge to one of assault whilst trespassing in pursuit of game, but either Kitchens was a broken reed, or the authorities were otherwise inclined, for in the end Smut was charged with wounding so as to cause actual bodily harm and only the original charge of attempted murder was withdrawn. Yet Paul did not give up hope that something might be done to improve the situation when the trial opened. It was only when he saw the judge, a dry, withered nut of a man, that he realised that Grace had been right after all and Smut's chances of leniency were slim. There was so much to be said on one side and hardly anything on the other and the same procession of Gilroy witnesses, five in all, swore to Potter's murderous assault upon a man seeking to restrain him from carrying away the buck. The inevitable distortion of facts made Paul feel slightly sick, for it was soon clear the Gilroy team had been carefully rehearsed, and although the barrister he hired for the defence did his best to present another aspect of the case, arguing that Smut acted in panic when about to be assaulted by armed men, the story sounded lame in the dock, where Smut cut a pathetic figure, far removed from the spry young rebel Valley folk recalled. A month of soul-searching in his cave, followed by another month's confinement awaiting trial, had cut him down to a bewildered young man with frightened eyes and the tan fading from his cheeks, clearly at a loss to know what was going on around him. Under his barrister's probing he told the truth in so far as he knew it and the testy little prosecutor did little to shake him, so that for Paul at least a true picture of the incident began to emerge at last—that of a man gripped by fear and fighting back with the first weapon that came to hand before taking refuge in flight. The picture was confirmed when Rudd leaned towards Paul and whispered, "He's right, Paul! They're after his blood! If things had turned out otherwise it would be Kitchens and his mob in that dock!"

The case excited a great deal of local interest and during the period the jury were out Paul saw Meg Potter and went across to her, against Rudd's advice.

"I should like to say how sorry I am about this business," he said, "and that I won't hold it against Smut if he comes back to the Valley," and she replied, to his astonishment, "It was in the cards and the only way he could have run contrary to 'em was to run faster! He couldn't bring himself to do that, Squire. There's less gypsy in him than I reckoned on. A real gypsy would ha' run and kept on running, but the Potters baint gypsies, except mebbe my youngest girl, Hazel. They others, they're their father's seed, although time was when I thought differently o' Smut!", and she walked away with her slow, stately gait, without waiting for the verdict. It was as though, by allowing himself to be netted, Smut had sacrificed her sympathy.

The verdict, as foreseen by everyone, was guilty and Mr. Justice Scratton-Forbes settled down to indulge himself in a little homily before pronouncing sentence. Dry and crisply righteous phrases issued from his lips like a shower of darts . . . "malice in your heart" . . . "despoiling property with the heedlessness of a savage" . . . "must be taught a severe and lasting lesson . . ."; the sentence was five years' penal servitude so that the limit of Grace's prophecy had been achieved.

Paul, and Rudd too, were appalled. Paul had resigned himself to eighteen calendar months and the agent would have been relieved to have seen the poacher go down for two years, but five seemed to them a savage and unwarranted penalty and others presumably shared their view for there was a murmur of indignation in the court that was instantly repressed by the ushers. Paul said, as they sought the castle yard, "Until now I never really believed there was one law for the rich and another for the poor, John!" and Rudd replied. "Well, perhaps we ought not to be shocked. Scratton-Forbes is a big landowner himself and we ought to have pressed for a trial outside the county. At the worst he would have got away with three years."

He glanced at Paul shrewdly, knowing that the young man's mind was not entirely monopolised by the memory of Smut Potter's blanched face, as he had stumbled from the dock with a policeman at each elbow but was trying to adjust itself to the prospect of facing his wife waiting at home. He said, slowly, "I still think you did right persuading him to come in, Paul, and this doesn't really change things, you know. The law is far from perfect, but it's the only law we've got and without it where would any one of us be? You've got to make your wife understand that, for if you don't then what you're trying to achieve back there won't amount to much. Would you care to see Smut before he's sent off? I expect it could be arranged."

"Yes," Paul told him, gruffly, "I owe the poor devil that," and Rudd went back into court, leaving Paul to look down on the city basking in the afternoon sunshine. John's reassurance regarding the rightness of his decision brought him no comfort. There was, he realised, a direct link here between his decision to coax Potter out of hiding and his own tenuous relationship with Grace, who seemed only to respect him as long as he was waving a rebel banner under the noses of authority. She would, he felt sure, back him every inch of the way if he resolved himself into a kind of Sorrel Valley Robin Hood, contemptuous of even such social reforms as those advocated by progressives like Grenfell. She was really, he reflected, a kind of anarchist who welcomed turmoil but he had no wish to live like that. He favoured steady, ordered, constitutional progress, where tolerance and education for the underprivileged promised hope of justice and stability but she had no faith at all in this dream. Her sympathies were with people like the Pankhursts, still raising hell up and down the country and it was on this cleavage that their relationship, so fragile from the beginning, seemed likely to founder, for what was that she had said when he told her Smut Potter had agreed to give himself up? "I was badly wrong about you, Paul. You aren't a rebel at all and could never be! That scene with Gilroy and Cribb was just a flash in the pan. Perhaps you knew I was listening and hoped to make an impression!" He thought it a bitter thing to have said and realised now that she regretted it but they had been strangers to one another ever since, with Grace resisting all his attempts to put this stupid business into its correct perspective and stop her using it as a looking-glass held in front of his character.

John came back and said they could spend a few minutes with Potter. He looked around for Meg but she was not to be seen, so they followed the police sergeant down a long, gas-lit corridor under the court and were shown into a waiting-room where Smut sat with his hands on his knees, wearing the same dazed expression as he had worn throughout the trial. His pale, blue eyes kindled when he saw Rudd, whose approach to him had always been that of a jocular schoolmaster, dealing with a wilful but not unlikable scholar. "Well, it was a lot more'n I reckoned, Mr. Rudd," he said. "It was like I tried to explain, they'd ha' done fer me if I hadn't got one in first! *You* believe that, dornee, Mr. Rudd?"

"Yes, I believe it but it's too late to think about that now, Smut! Mr. Craddock is here to say you can come back to the Valley when it's all over."

The eagerness of the young man's expression as Rudd said this touched Paul more deeply than anything he had witnessed in court. He said quickly, "That's true, Smut, and I've told your mother the same. I'll find a place for

301

you somewhere and perhaps give you a job like Sam's, where you could use your skill with the gun and all you know of the Valley."

A flicker of humour crossed Potter's face. "Me, a game-keeper? That'll zet the boys laughing all right, Squire, but I'd like to come back some time. I'd like that, Mr. Craddock, Squire, and it's good o' you to tell me. It'll give me something to think on where I'm going."

"You'll get time off if you watch your step, Smut," Rudd said and Paul envied the ease of the agent's approach.

"Yessir, they told me that," Smut said, and then, hesitantly, "Do you reckon one o' you gentlemen could spare the time to look in an' give me news once in a while? I'd like to know what's goin' on back there and letters baint no gude. I never could read much mor'n me own name!"

"I'll come and see you," said Paul, and felt better for saying it. "Good-bye and good luck for now, Smut, and don't worry about the family. I'll see they're left alone in the Coombe."

They shook hands and went out, walking into the hot sunshine of the castle yard and down the hill to the livery stable where they had left the trap. As it was being brought out, and Rudd was already on the seat, Paul felt his arm jogged and turning looked into the face of James Grenfell. "I heard about it," he said, "and it was a damned shame in the circumstances! It won't do Gilroy any good about here, if that's any comfort."

"It's no comfort," Paul told him, "but I tell you one thing, Grenfell. From now on, I'm your man! I'd like to help to break the crust around here and I think I can promise Rudd and my wife, too, will back me up."

"Well, we can certainly do with your help," Grenfell said, and then, with a smile, "But it won't always be this way, you know! It's going to change sooner than you think!", and he nodded and went on down the steep street, a small, insignificant figure among the lumbering farmers and draymen discussing the trial outside The Mitre.

It was in her heart to be sorry for him in the days that followed the eclipse of Smut Potter but she found it difficult to forgive pedantry on his part, and on John Rudd's, that had resulted in a man being shut behind bars for five years, and yet, she realised how humiliated he was in being proved so wrong so quickly.

The shadow of Smut Potter seemed to linger in the Valley and harvest prospects, which had looked so good, were cut back by heavy summer storms that left wheat and barley in disarray and put everyone's temper on edge. The semi-estrangement between them persisted because he seemed almost to nurse his defeat like a sulky boy but in the end it was his sulkiness that encouraged her to find a way of breaking the tension in the house. It was odd and a little pitiful, to see him fling himself into a frenzy of work alongside Honeyman's Home Farm team, to come home tired and skulk in the library, trying to lose himself in pamphlets James Grenfell had sent him, as though he sought there a means of reversing Smut Potter's sentence by social upheaval. Then a way out of the ridiculous impasse presented itself, for the certainty that she was now carrying his child persuaded her that two adults could not, after all, spend an entire summer brooding about a man in gaol.

Her own feelings about her pregnancy surprised her. She would have thought that it would compensate her for the life she had chosen to lead here in this wilderness, where every man, woman and child was a slave to the march of the seasons and men half-killed one another over the ownership of a buck, but this was not the case. A child, she reasoned, would be one more anchor, final proof of submission to men and their chattels and the only satisfaction she derived from the prospect was a conviction that, all things being equal, it was likely to inherit a world that was changing at speed and where ideas were likely to blow up under the noses of people like Gilroy.

About a fortnight after the trial she got up from the breakfast table and followed him into the office, where he looked up from a heavy leather book in which he was writing. She recognised the book with a start and for a moment was so astonished that she could only stare at it and her anxiety increased when he closed it hurriedly and seemed to wish it out of the way. She said, forgetting why she had come, "That was Lovell's Bible! But it wasn't a Bible! He kept pictures of girls in it!"

He looked, she thought, very embarrassed at this, so that the thought of him sitting here, seeking compensation for her withdrawal in contemplation of old Sir George's picture gallery made her want to laugh. He looked so shocked, however, that she bit her lip as he said, "You know about that? You saw them?"

"Yes, I saw them," she told him. "I imagine most people who were allowed in here were shown them. He wasn't ashamed of having them."

"He must have been a disgusting old reprobate!" he growled and then, rather pompously she thought, "Did you ever tell your father the kind of man he really was?"

"No," she said, "because he was quite harmless. He never molested his models, he was quite content to gloat over them, as you seemed to be doing!"

He flushed at this but then, perhaps because she was now smiling, he laughed and opening the book showed her that there was nothing between the covers but manuscript pages of cartridge paper, the first of them covered with his neat entries.

"It's my estate diary," he told her, "a kind of record of what happens. I destroyed the pictures the day I found them but I didn't do it as a puritanical gesture. It seemed to me the wrong people might have got hold of them and I recognised two of the Potter girls."

"Oh? Anyone else?"

"No, not even Arabella Codsall!"

He laughed, less at his little joke than with relief at being once again on joking terms with her, and she joined in gratefully enough, reflecting that it would have shocked him into speechlessness to hear all she could tell of this little room, once so dim and stuffy, now so functional. It seemed a lifetime ago when she had stood over there where his map-rack stood, posed against an improbable background of stage woods and ferns, with that old rascal Lovell, headless under his black cloth, his sibilant voice muffled and his elbows jutting as he crouched over his tripod. That was the first time, when he had persuaded her to be photographed as a faun and had loaned her a

304

costume from a trunk of props he kept. At thirteen she had been flattered and, a year or so later, amused when he posed her as The Boy David, for a photographic competition, or so he told her, and then again as Juliet on a rustic balcony. She had not much minded his pattings and pawings, or even his sudden appearance round the end of the screen when she was half-dressed. It was some time after that, when she found out how her mother came to die, that she posed for him from entirely different motives, a thrust at the world of men, especially her father, a sneer at all their shoddiness and cruelty. She wondered what had happened to those particular pictures. Obviously they had not gone in the book and neither, it would seem, had any of the more innocent ones, or Paul would surely have remembered them. Perhaps George had kept the nudes for his pocket book and sniggered over them among cronies at his club. She recalled then that she had hoped her father might see one of them and realise how whole-heartedly she despised him, and what venomous ways women had of proclaiming contempt.

He broke into her reverie. "You came here to tell me something, Grace. Or was it to hear me admit how right you were about Potter?"

She forced her mind back to him, saying, "No, it wasn't that at all. Something quite different and rather more cheerful! To the devil with Smut Potter and Gilroy. I came to tell you I'm going to have a child in the New Year!" and she waited for him to exclaim, or to do whatever expectant fathers did when they heard this kind of news. He did not whoop or coo or do any of the things she thought conventional. He simply took her hand, looked down at it for a moment and said, quietly, "I was wondering when you would tell me. I thought— 'If she holds out much longer I daresay I shall hear it from one of the maids'!"

"But I really did believe you hadn't the least idea, Paul! I don't know why, but I did!"

"Well, I may be a bit slow on the uptake but I happen to look at you quite often," he said, smiling, and she was glad then that she had used this means of restoring the atmosphere of the early weeks of their marriage.

She said, suddenly, "It's a lovely day, Paul. Why don't we call a truce and take a walk up through Priory and on to Shallowford Woods? It's surely time we did!"

He seemed pleased with the suggestion but said, "That's all of six miles. Do you think you should walk that far?" and she laughed, heartily this time. "Good heavens, Paul, the baby isn't due until January! It'll do us both good and when we get back we shall be too tired to argue the pros and cons of poor old Smut and his troubles."

He picked up the book, selecting a key from his ring. "Very well then," he said, "there's nothing here that can't wait!", but as he was putting the diary in his desk she said, "What exactly *do* you write in The Book From Which There's No Rubbing Out? Is it very private?"

He opened it at random and pointed to an entry, dated March 7th, *"Married Grace Lovell, my very dear wife,"* and she thought, "Dear God! He doesn't belong to this century at all! Yet maybe a lot of us could do with his directness and simplicity!", and she kissed him impulsively and went upstairs to get a sun bonnet and a pair of walking shoes.

They passed one of the biblical shepherds (Grace could never tell one from the other) preparing a sheep dip in the hollow near the sawmill and climbed the slope of Priory Wood to the spur where they could look down on Hermitage and away, on the very crest of the moor, the white smudge that was Will Codsall's little place, Periwinkle Farm. Up here, backs to the firs, stood great ranks of foxgloves, some of them as tall as grenadiers and each with its cluster of mottled bells at a regulation angle to the sturdy, green stems. The Sorrel below looked as lazy and heat-drowsed as everything else in the Valley and only one or two of Henry Pitts' big red Devons ambled along the shade of the hedge searching sanctuary from the flies. The sky was cloudless but what little breeze there was still carried the faintest tang of the sea and sounds travelled easily too, for over a distance of three miles they could hear the clank of the Four Winds' pump and the dry rattle of a trap on the moor road. He told her this was his favourite spot on the estate for up here there was a sense of permanence and in clear weather like today the Valley had the promise of eternal fruitfulness so that one could discount days of sleet and snow when nothing thrived about here or could keep warm or find food. She did not say what lay deep in her mind, that it was fair enough but empty for all but those wanting refuge from new ideas and new thoughts.

They crossed the extremity of the Hermitage holding to the deep rutted lane that led down to the north-westerly tongue of Shallowford Woods and then by a stile into the cool depths of the big beech grove and finally to the edge of the mere where the Lovells' ruinous boathouse still stood, with its half-rotted pier and punt. They used to fish here as children, she told him, Hubert, the elder boy, Ralph and herself and on summer days had sometimes bathed from the old punt, with the boys' tutor, then a much persecuted undergraduate, now a canon. He asked her what kind of man was Hubert, the heir, and she said very stuffy and dominated by his livelier brother. "It seems curious that all those years of growing up here should have ended in a couple of skirmishes in Africa," she said, "and then you should come running from the same battle-fields to step into their shoes. Why don't we punt over to the islet and take a look at the pagoda? That old tub can still float and I don't suppose you have ever been there, have you?"

He admitted that he had not, so they freed the punt and poled it through the reedy shallows, approaching the islet from the bank directly opposite Smut Potter's hide-out. The island was no more than thirty yards broad and perhaps twice as long and the pagoda, a tiered structure roofed with shingles, stood in the centre, its lower half screened by firs and clumps of evergreen. She told him she had not been here for more than five years but did not add that the act of setting foot here gave her an extraordinary sensation of recapturing her adolescence, yet her mood must have communicated itself to him for when they sat side by side on a fern-grown terrace he suddenly turned her face to his and kissed her on the mouth and when she returned his kiss with an eagerness that surprised them both, she said, as his hand sought her breast, "You want me? Well, why not?" and although

307

gratified by the invitation he was mildly shocked when she carelessly unhooked her skirt, slipped out of her single undergarment and motioned him nearer the pagoda where the ferns grew shoulder-high.

There had never been an occasion like this. From the outset she had been dutiful, complaisant even, but she had never once matched his excitement or, indeed, appeared to have more in mind than a wish to accommodate him. She matched it now but what surprised him as much was the deliberate and almost ritualistic manner in which she went about it, restraining him until she had removed the last of her clothes which she then used to make a bed among the ferns before embracing him with a kind of zestful gaiety. Only when the fire had gone from him, and she was lying still and contemplative in his arms, did he reflect upon the distance they had travelled since she had walked into his office that morning with her flag of truce and then the humour of it struck him and he laughed, saying, "Well, I can't think of a better way of signing a peace treaty!" and set about helping her to dress. At the same time he glanced, a little apprehensively at the mereside track opposite, remembering that it was often used at this time of day by Sam Potter and Aaron Stokes, the reed-cutter. Nothing stirred over there and when he met her eyes again he realised that she too was enjoying the comic element of the reconciliation and pleasant absurdity of man and wife making love in such improbable circumstances.

"Was anyone over there?" she asked, and when he told her no, "It's just as well! Otherwise it would soon be all over the Valley that history was repeating itself and new Squire had got a love nest in the woods!"

"Squire could easily build one," he said, grinning, "it would certainly seem to recommend itself!" and steadied her as she stepped into her clothes. She laughed at this, the first wholly natural laugh he had ever won from her. It struck him as even more rewarding than her embraces.

CHAPTER TEN

I

On the night of January 3rd, 1904, when the hands of the grandfather clock were ticking their unsteady way to midnight, Paul sat before the dying fire in the library listening for renewed sounds from the room above but hearing none or none that he could identify, as he had identified them in the late afternoon. Only the brusque voice of Daladier, the peppery little French obstetrician Celia had introduced as a reinforcement for the baffled O'Keefe, kept him from yet another restless prowl into the hall and up the stairs, to listen outside the room where Grace's labour had now entered its fourteenth hour. An hour or so ago the specialist had caught him there for the second time and sharply ordered him downstairs and Paul had gone, growling a protest to soothe his raw nerves and had taken refuge in whisky, half emptying the decanter with as little effect upon him as though it had contained barley water. The silence upstairs, together with the steady, harsh movement of the clock and awareness of his own helplessness made him sweat and fidget, and every moment that passed seemed to him to increase the chances of news arriving that the child had been born dead and that the mother was not expected to recover from her ordeal.

He tried, desperately, to think of other things, to occupy himself in office work, or a book, or more drinking, anything that would cocoon his imagination from what was happening up there, but every alternative thought seemed ridiculously trivial and the only escape route to his fears lay in contemplation of the specialist's blunt appraisal of the situation, delivered about four o'clock that afternoon, soon after his arrival.

He had made no bones about it being touch and go, for Grace, the child, or possibly both. It depended, he

309

said, on a number of imponderables, some of which he tried to reduce to layman's language but Paul's mind was so blanketed by fright that he had not even tried to absorb the watered-down medical terms. All he did understand was that the labour was indefinitely prolonged and that it was something to do with the baby's position in the womb and the suspense of waiting, after O'Keefe had come down about seven o'clock to help himself to a drink, was unbearable and had now continued, almost unbroken, for five hours. Listening intently Paul heard a few indistinct bumps, as of furniture being moved, then the rumble of conversation and once a long, low-pitched cry that made his blood freeze but after that hardly any sounds at all, except the maddening, metallic tick of the big clock, a far-off cough or two and the steady whoosh of the wind and the slash of rain against the windows.

The storm outside made it worse, for not only did its uproar drown sounds that he might have interpreted as progressive but brought with it a sense of onrushing doom that dispersed everything but fear. It also obliged him to endure his vigil alone, for Celia had promised to be here after tea and was not likely to appear now for the ford would be shoulder-deep after such a downpour. The staff had been sent to bed two hours ago, Mrs. Handcock having to be practically pushed from the room. He was very fond of the old soul but she had no stomach for this kind of crisis and the sight of her sitting there, puffing out her red cheeks and beginning sentences she could not finish, had maddened him. Rudd's presence would have been a comfort but Rudd was miles away, having driven off before luncheon to attend a farm sale in a village beyond Paxtonbury, with a promise to bring back an almost new threshing machine for a tenth its real price and although the subject had interested Paul a good deal the previous evening, he now thought of a threshing machine as of less significance than a feather in his wife's pillow.

Earlier in the evening he had, by degrees, succeeded in getting himself under control by looking round the room, itemising the changes Grace had wrought in it in less than a year's custodianship. He noted the glittering Sheffield plate candelabra, the warm red and gold wallpaper, the heavy velvet curtains with their tall pelmet, the rearrangement of the books, formerly shelved any-old-how, now neatly organised into sections. He was able to think of, and to appreciate, each of these things objectively and from them assess her value as a wife and a friend but this encouraged him to make a deeper survey of their marriage, remembering some of the other things she had brought to him and these too he began to itemise, like a man making an inventory of salvaged possessions after finding himself alone on a desert island. He could appreciate now, after ten months as her husband, his previous callowness and ignorance. She had opened so many doors that he could not even count them. She had shown him, by example, how to strike a workable balance between familiarity and authority with staff, how to distinguish between good and indifferent wine, how to nurse a sick horse, how to make a garden grow, how to buy clothes and even how to conduct a public meeting, although she cared nothing at all for his wholehearted conversion to the Liberal creed and had refused to accompany him to a fund-raising ball in Paxtonbury. In one field alone, the management of the estate, she had left him alone. The submission of advice regarding Smut Potter's fate had been her single excursion in this sphere and she had learned her lesson, and so, perhaps, had he and there now existed between them an unspoken pact that such advice as he needed must be sought from John Rudd. There remained between them, however, the personal honesty that had characterised their association from the beginning. She accepted his possession of her as a woman if not as an individual, for her preoccupation with privacy did not extend to her body. She had once said something to him in this respect that he was never to forget, for it made a deep impression on him at the time. It was when he had expressed his appreciation of her generosity and she had replied, calmly, "When I begin to be dutiful you can turn me out. You know the convention in the West—men have orgasms, women have babies! Well, it was never intended to be that way between man and woman and if I had believed as much I would have

311

gone out of my way to remain a virgin. The only way a marriage can hope to succeed is by yielding mutual satisfaction. Even then it can founder but without a physical basis it doesn't stand a chance. If it is there, or it develops quickly, then even incompatible people like us can get along."

Now, he reflected, as a direct result of her affection, she was in agony and perhaps at the point of death but he could do nothing whatever to help her and the awareness of helplessness made him grind his teeth and kick the dying fire with the toe of his riding boot that he had forgotten to draw off when he returned from High Coombe and Mrs. Handcock had told him, in her quaint, old-fashioned way, "Mrs. Craddock, poor dear, 'as been brought to baid!" adding that O'Keefe had been sent for, his mother-in-law notified and that he had best "zit down an eat a gude meal fer the three of 'em!"

That had been nearly twelve hours ago and since then there had been nothing but the arrival, wet through, of Celia's French specialist, indeterminate thumps on the floor, the rumble of voices and that one, low-pitched moan. He had just made up his mind to risk the doctor's wrath by a return upstairs when he heard a sharp rapping on the glass of the French doors opening on to the terrace. He thought at first that part of the trellis had come down in the gale but then the rapping was repeated and he pulled aside the curtains, fumbling with the stiff catch. When he got the window open the force of the storm almost wrenched it from his hand and a very bedraggled Ikey staggered into the room, holding a storm lantern tied to a short length of ash, Paul closed the doors and redrew the curtains and turning saw the boy crouching over the fire, rain streaming from his peaked cap and a look on his face that Paul remembered seeing on the faces of troopers awaiting the order to advance across open country in the face of Boer marksmen. He said, gruffly, "Well, what is it, Ikey? Why didn't you come in the proper way?" and Ikey replied, his voice shaking with excitement, "I couldn't make nobody hear sir, I on'y just got back and tried Mr. Rudd's lodge first, but it was the same there, the wind's making such a racket!"

Paul remembered then that Ikey had taken the cob to the Coombe Bay forge for shoeing and had been told to summon Celia while he was in the village, but Celia would not come now as it was already after midnight. Where had he been all this time? The boy said, in the same shaking voice, "Something funny's bin happening over at Four Winds, sir! I follered Farmer Codsall along the beach, then back over the dunes. He saw me and tried to do for me with his shotgun!", and held out the tails of his coat and Paul saw that they were shredded, as with buckshot. He said, urgently, "Go on, Ikey, tell me exactly what happened!"

"Well, I first see him when I was mounting the cob to get on 'ome, sir. He was drunk as usual, an' weaving about, so seein' he had his gun with him I thought— well, I thought I'd better keep him in view till I made sure he was clear o' the village."

"That was the sensible thing to do; then what?"

"Well, it was getting dimpsy by then so I follered him along the beach. He went right into the water once an' didn't seem to notice me, for I kep' back beyond the tideline but then he come out an' went over the dunes and I still follered, thinking he hadn't got a proper butcher's— proper *look* at me, but he must 'ave! When I crossed into the first field he let fly with both barrels and on'y just missed me!"

"Good God!" said Paul, forgetting everything else for the moment, "why didn't you get help in the village?"

"Well, I reckoned I ought to 'ave, sir, but I didn't want to let him out o' view, not knowing what he might get up to, once he'd reloaded. I skipped back out o' range pretty smart but he seemed to forget about me an' went off across the fields. It was pitch dark be then but I chanced he'd gone on home an' follered, tying the cob to the farm gate when I got to his yard. Then . . . well, then . . ." and suddenly the boy's face crumpled and he began to sob, so that Paul, acting instinctively, poured a measure of whisky into his glass and said, "Drink this, Ikey! Then tell me what happened at Four Winds."

The boy gulped down the spirits and it set him coughing but it steadied him for he was able to continue in a level tone. "I couldn't see nothing at first, it was so dark, but after a bit I heard a lot o' thumping and screaming from upstairs an' then, all of a sudden, the winder o' the end room crashed open an' all the glass blew out, an' out come the boy on to the sill an' made a jump for it, not into the yard but right across to the roof o' the barn opposite! I could see him jump in the light coming from 'is winder an' he landed orlright but was stuck twenty feet up till I found a ladder an' fetched him down. He was in 'is nightshirt an 'awful scared. I tried to get 'im to show me the way to the foreman's cottage but 'e couldn't, he just started carrying on something awful, an' I couldn't make no sense of it, except that old Codsall had come for 'im an' 'is mum like a madman an' that's what made 'im jump for it!"

"Where is young Codsall now? What did you do with him?"

"I brought him back here," Ikey said, "and when I got to the loft I woke Gappy, an' we give 'im a good rub down an' put 'im in Gappy's bed, which was warmlike. I told Gappy to make cocoa for 'im, fer 'e was perished when he got here, 'im in his nightshirt an' all! But you don't want to worry about 'im, sir. Gappy'll take care of 'im. It's just that—well—I reckon someone ought to go over to Four Winds right away, sir!"

Paul began to think logically for the courage of the boy steadied him. He said quickly, "Throw some chips on that fire, Ikey, and warm yourself. Mrs. Craddock is having her baby and nothing is going right for her but I'll have to go to Four Winds at once. I daresay we shall need the police and help from elsewhere!" He thought of waking Horace Handcock but Handcock couldn't sit a horse and wouldn't even go close to one and apart from him there were only the doctors and the girls. He swallowed another tot and went into the hall, up the stairs and along the corridor to the bedroom, rapping gently on the door.

O'Keefe's flushed face appeared instantly and from inside came a whiff of stale air and ether. He got a glimpse of the room, with the lamp beside the four-poster throwing its light on Grace's tumbled hair but saw nothing more, except the fire roaring up the chimney and an array of instruments on the table near the window. He said, urgently, "How are things going?" and reading impatience and irritation in the Irishman's face, added, "It's not nerves on my part, Doctor! Something bad has happened at Four Winds. Codsall seems to have gone off his head and he tried to kill my stable-boy! I shall have to go, no matter what happens here. Are you making progress?"

"Yes we are," O'Keefe said, and Paul felt a tremor of relief, "but it'll be about half an hour. It was a breech birth, if you know what that is but the worst is over and they'll both do well enough with luck! What's this about Codsall? You say he's gone crazy?"

"It seems so," Paul said, "can you be spared?"

"No," said O'Keefe, "not unless you want to run a very grave risk, Craddock!"

Paul made his decision. Whatever had happened at Four Winds wasn't worth the risk of mounting the old man behind Snowdrop and racing through a storm. If the boy Sydney had been left behind it would be different but Ikey, gallant kid, had whisked him out of harm's way and Arabella and the staff must look to themselves. He said briefly, "Well, I shall have to go, I can do nothing here and I may be useful over there. If my wife asks for me tell her I've had to see to storm damage at the Home Farm."

"Yes, of course," O'Keefe said soberly, "you get off right away and I'll come over as soon as it's light. Good luck, Craddock!"

"There's one other thing," Paul said hurriedly, "wake Mrs. Handcock, the housekeeper, and tell her to have a good fire and hot drinks ready. As soon as it's light, or before if possible, send Handcock to rouse Honeyman and send the two shepherds to Four Winds right away!"

"I'll do that!" said the Irishman. "Mother of God, the trials we're called upon to face!" and at once withdrew, closing the door.

Paul returned to the library where Ikey now had a bright fire blazing. The boy's cheeks were flushed but he seemed to have himself well under control. He said, "Saddle up Snowdrop, Ikey, I'm going there right away."

"Who'll be going with you, sir?"

"Nobody for there's nobody to go! I can't waste time

315

making a detour to Home Farm, I'll have to cut across the corner of the wood and head straight for the bridge. How was the water level when you came over?"

"About up to the planks, sir!" Ikey told him, and then, obstinately, "If you're on your own, sir, I'm coming with you! Young Codsall's orlright an' that drink you give me put noo life in me, sir!" and he grinned.

"Do you think you can stick another trip over there, Ikey?"

"With you along o' me I can," the boy said and Paul put his arm across the child's shoulder.

"I won't forget this, Ikey, you've done splendidly! None of the men could have managed any better. Have you got a dry coat and boots?"

"I c'n take Gappy's, sir. The cob's fresh enough and I'll 'ave Snowdrop ready in a trice!" and he shot out of the room giving Paul the impression that he welcomed the adventure now that he could share it with someone. Ten minutes later, with Paul riding ahead and carrying the lantern, they were picking their way along the edge of Priory Wood and round its western boundary, probing for the track that led down to the river road. The rain had slackened somewhat but the force of the gale tried to tear them from their saddles and twice Snowdrop stumbled, almost pitching his rider to the ground. Above the roar of the wind Paul heard a pine crash in the wood behind and again his thoughts returned to the steadfastness of the boy, splashing along in his wake. There was no chance to call to him. All he could do was to hold the swinging lantern high and trust Ikey to follow the light. If it went out they were finished. At last, after what seemed to Paul about an hour, they struck the park wall, groping their way along it to the gate that breached it opposite Codsall bridge. The boy was still in his wake and came alongside to take Snowdrop's bridle while he dismounted to wrestle with the stiff gate. It came open at last and they were out on the road, where it was less dark but they had now lost the protection of the wall and the wind made the horses restless. There were, he recalled, some white flood posts at the bridge-head and as soon as he saw them he dismounted again and led the grey forward, shouting at the

316

top of his voice for the boy to follow. The roar of the current vied with the shriek of the wind and the river level was dangerously high, lapping the planks to a depth of nearly a foot. Paul slopped across, however, remounted and followed the path that led down to the farm, trusting in the grey's sight more than his own and in this way they soon reached the first of the Four Winds' outbuildings, a great bulk of a barn, in total darkness. Here, in the angle of the building, they could talk again. Paul said, breathlessly, "Well, we made it, Ikey! We'll put the horses inside and go round the back, the front door is sure to be locked," and he groped along the face of the barn until he found the fastening, bracing his shoulder against the door to prevent it crashing back on the horses.

The barn faced east so the wind here lost some of its force and together they managed to lead Snowdrop and the cob inside. The first thing they saw, in the dim light of the lantern, was a shotgun resting against a small bale of hay and then, as Paul broke it to see if was loaded, he heard the boy utter a cry and turning, holding the lantern high, he saw a pair of rubber boots swinging four feet clear of the ground.

"It's 'em!" Ikey cried, his teeth chattering, "it's Farmer Codsall!" and Paul dropped the gun and crossed the barn to where Martin Codsall swung in the strong draught from the door, suspended from a cross-beam on a length of baling cord.

They could see little more than his outline for the barn was large and its recesses beyond the range of the lantern's rays. Paul thought, fighting the shock, "Well, it's best I suppose but it's terrible that the boy had to see it!" and he took him by the arm and said, "Don't look, Ikey, let's go outside!"

He heard the boy retch and felt him shudder violently, so that his first thought, that of climbing the ladder and cutting Codsall down, was forgotten in concern for the child. He hustled him into the open, shutting the door in the teeth of the wind. "There's nothing to be feared from him," he told the boy, "but we'd best go in and see if Mrs. Codsall's safe and then rouse Eveleigh, the foreman, and send someone for the police," and he took the boy's hand,

317

groping his way across the yard to the Dutch barn and, moving between barn and farmhouse, to the gate that opened on the kitchen garden. He remembered the geography of the place with great clarity and found the back door at once. It was open and they went in, setting the lantern on the table and lighting a table lamp with a faggot from the fire still glowing red in the fierce chimney draught. Paul said, "Wait here, boy! I'll take a look upstairs!" and feeling Ikey would be better with something to occupy his mind, "Blow up the fire and boil a kettle. There's sure to be cocoa somewhere about and we could both do with a hot drink. Go on, get busy!" and he lit one of the candles on the mantelshelf and went through the kitchen to the wide staircase.

Winter gales both tormented and stimulated Martin Codsall. As soon as the winds freshened in the south-west, and the Channel spray whipped across the dunes, he would sniff the air like a retriever and presently, as the elms began to creak, he would wander off, telling no one where he was going and make his way to the shore to watch the breakers crash and cream along the flat sand. The power of them fascinated him and the inevitability of their spill gave him confidence in the sureness and certainty of nature, as though here was the one thing upon which he could rely utterly, the rush and swirl of green-grey water, foaming round his feet and tossing its flotsam high up on the beach. Sometimes, but not always, he would fortify himself against the thrill of the spectacle by drinking a few pints of rough cider and a dash of rum at The Raven but lately the landlord had been reluctant to serve him and when he entered the bar other customers drew together, so that he knew very well they were telling each other he was off his head. He would strain his ears to catch the drift of their conversation but they were not always talking about him, it seemed, for on the third day of the New Year, when he was sitting in the sawdust bar settle, he heard them reopen the topic of Smut Potter's assault on Keeper Buller back in the summer. The Potter-Buller incident interested Martin almost as much as the curl of the breakers in the bay. He had kept all the newspaper ac-

318

counts of the trial and paid particular attention to Buller's injuries for to him they were the highlight of the whole incident. They said that when they carried Buller back to Heronslea his face was a mask of blood and Martin wished very much that he had been there to see it, for it was not often that a man got a chance to witness such a sight. He fell to wondering sometimes how much blood a man had inside him. Some more than others, he would think. Arabella, with her high colour and overweight, would have a great deal, but young Sydney, pale and slight, not very much, hardly worth the shedding. It was on this particular day, when he heard them talking of Buller, that his obsession with blood and with the breakers fused so that he had a sudden revelation. After leaving the pub he wandered far along the shore, noticing that the waves had changed colour. They were no longer grey-green but bright crimson, the colour of blood and he took even more pleasure in them than usual, standing with water washing about his knees and the spray beating in his face, watching and watching the curl and crash of the great crimson waves, oblivious of discomfort and the growing force of the gale.

It was only when he glanced over his shoulder to follow the rush of a particularly big wave that he saw the boy on the brown cob, standing back against the dunes and watching him intently. Codsall was aware, however, that it was not really a boy on a cob but the Devil, masquerading as a boy, and mounted on a horse that could move in any direction without its feet touching the ground. Fortunately he had brought along shotgun and cartridges, hoping to get a shot at a partridge or two if there were any in the stubble fields and standing there in the water Martin felt more than equal to a mounted devil disguised as a boy. He pretended to take no notice but turned his back on the water and climbed the dunes as far as his first field, where there was a stile set in a gap between clumps of elderberry. Here he loaded his gun and waited and sure enough the little devil came on at a walk, presenting a fine target against the skyline of the dunes. When he was twenty yards off Martin fired both barrels and saw the devil's skirts fly out, saw him reel in the saddle and slump forward, the cob wheeling and tearing back the way he had come. That disposed of the boy and he could now carry on with his main task which was to discover just how much blood Arabella had, and whether it was enough to make a really big wave like one of those he had just seen break on the sand.

He did not go straight home but wandered slowly along the river bank, making sure that he really had scared the devil out of range, for he was not such a fool as to suppose that a devil could be laid low with buckshot. One needed a silver bullet for work of that kind, and sooner or later the boy would get over his fright and follow on, perhaps in some other guise, as a labourer, or a buzzard, or even a harmless little creature like a vole. He saw nothing, however, and when it grew dark he was in the vicinity of the farm but even then he did not go in but continued to skulk in the spinney near the river, sheltering as best he could from the slashing rain and terrible wind that came out of the west. One thing worried him a little. His coat was so wet that his spare cartridges were damp and probably useless, so he threw them away, promising himself to get more as soon as the kitchen lights went out and he could enter the house without being seen. He saw his hired men trudge off across the fields and later, his foreman Eveleigh go down the lane to his cottage but even then he waited and it must have been close on nine before he crossed the yard and tried the front door. It was locked but he knew he could get in through the buttery window which had a broken catch and on his way round he looked into the big barn and lit one of the storm lanterns. It was here that he had another inspiration for immediately under the lantern, wedged in a bale of hay, was a hay knife more than two feet in length and freshly whetted, as he could tell after running his thumb along the edge. He gave up all thought of finding fresh cartridges and laying the gun aside picked up the knife. He was wet to the skin but hot and sweating rather than cold. He felt stronger and happier than he had felt for months and he stayed snug in the barn until he was sure that Arabella, Sydney and the two maids were in bed and asleep. The force of the gale shook the wooden building to its foundations but he enjoyed the uproar for to be alone in it made him feel superior to everyone. At last he got up and went out into the storm, not forgetting to latch the barn door. He tried the back door and was surprised to find it open and the kitchen fire still bright. He stood there listening and heard Arabella, or someone else, moving about upstairs and that made him glance at the clock, noting that it was still only half-past nine. Suddenly he could wait no longer. He opened the kitchen door very quietly and went upstairs.

Arabella was half-undressed when he entered the bedroom. She was standing beside the bed, great folds of flesh straining at her corsets and her hair screwed into a cluster of ringlets, as though she had been a girl of fifteen instead of a fat woman of fifty. He had never realised how fat she was, with breasts like huge pink cushions and thighs that were like saplings stripped of bark. She turned when she heard him enter and when she saw him standing there, wet through, and with the hay knife in his right hand, she began to gobble like a turkey, perhaps, he thought, to scare him off but he made no move, for a man who had disposed of the devil was unlikely to be intimidated by Arabella Codsall. So they faced one another for what seemed to him a long time, he regarding her with mild pleasure and Arabella with her pale blue eyes almost popping from her head and her turkeycock cheeks getting more turkeylike every second. He had never seen her look at him like this before, without contempt or exasperation but without fear too, for her expression was one of the blankest astonishment, as though he was not a man at all but a freak of nature like a midnight sun. She seemed to be trying to say something, for her lips moved but no sound issued from her and it seemed to him that both of them had been turned to pillars of salt like Lot's wife fleeing from the cities of the damned. Then, with a single, well-aimed kick, she upended the little table on which the candle stood and plunged them into total darkness and at the same time she began to scream so that her voice rose above the continuous roar of the storm. She began to run, too, although in what direction he could not have said except that it could not have been towards the door for he had his back to it. Then a little of his calm left him and he advanced into the room, groping with his free hand and after a few

321

moments of blind man's buff they collided and he took hold of her by the hair, striking outward and downward, twice and then, standing back a pace, a dozen times but without being sure that he was hitting anything except the bedpost, or the pile of her discarded clothes on the armchair. Then she seemed to melt away and her screaming ceased and he despaired of finding the candle among the wreckage of the room but it did not matter for he realised at once that he had failed in his essential purpose. He had not seen a wave of blood after all and disappointment choked him so that he flung down the knife, turned and began to grope for the door.

It opened before he got there and he saw Sydney was standing just outside in his long, white nightshirt, with a candlestick raised above his head. Martin rushed upon the boy with relief meaning him no harm at all but Sydney, uttering a single shriek, flung down his candle and fled. A moment later there was a loud crash of glass and Martin forgot about Sydney in his efforts to find the second candle and light it from matches he kept in his waistcoat pocket. He had some difficulty in lighting it for the matches were damp and his hands trembled violently. He managed it at last, however, and turned across the doorway to survey his work. There was blood enough in all conscience but it was not curling over in a wave, as he had imagined it would, whereas the untidy bundle that had been Arabella, although it looked rather like a large piece of flotsam, was not floating as surely it should have been. His sense of failure began to drag at him, like a cart being drawn up a steep hill and presently he understood the truth. Now, having made such a muddle of things, the devil would get him after all so he had best use what time there was to make away with himself in his own fashion. He clumped down to the kitchen, across the small yard to the barn and then up the ladder to the loft where he knew that baling cord was kept in a barrel. He found a length and in less than five minutes was out of reach of the devil in any guise. He hanged himself expertly, without even bothering to relight the storm lantern and see where to anchor the rope.

Paul came slowly downstairs and found Ikey had already made the cocoa for the kettle had been on the boil and the cocoa was on the long table, together with sugar and a can of milk. For a few seconds, pausing outside the bedroom door, Paul had been sure that he was going to faint, but the sight of the boy pottering about in the kitchen was like looking through a window on a sane, workaday world, where folk went about everyday tasks and children of thirteen were sometimes capable of tremendous exertions and matchless courage. He said, hoarsely, "We'll go for the foreman, Ikey. Don't bother with the drinks!" and he grabbed the boy and almost pushed him out of the house and into the blessed open air, stumbling over the slippery cobbles and down the muddy lane that led to the foreman's cottage a hundred yards away. All the time he held Ikey's hand tightly but for his own comfort more than Ikey's and together they staggered through the slush until the lantern, which he had picked up instinctively in his flight, revealed the outline of the squat, thatched dwelling under the bank. Paul hammered on the door, shouting into the wind and when no one answered he fell to kicking the door with all his strength until a voice above called, "What's to do? Who is it?" and Paul shouted, "It's Craddock, the Squire! Open up! There's been bad trouble at the farm!" and a moment later the door was unlocked to reveal Eveleigh, the foreman, his flannel nightgown stuffed into his corduroys and a bemused expression on his narrow, intelligent face. They went into the kitchen and Mrs. Eveleigh called down from the top of the stairs, "What is it, Norman?" and Eveleigh told her to come down and blow up the fire and make sure that the children stayed in bed.

Inside the little kitchen Paul's senses again began to swim and it required a stiff tot of Eveleigh's rum to steady him. Mrs. Eveleigh, a pleasant-voiced, ginger-haired woman, bustled about getting hot drinks and it was not until she put a mug in his hand that Paul said, "Martin Codsall is dead, Eveleigh! He's just made away with himself!" But he made no mention of the bundle upstairs, waiting until Ikey's eyes were lowered over his cocoa before jerking his head to indicate that they should get the boy out of the room. Eveleigh seemed an exceptionally quick-witted man. He said, briefly, "Pop the boy in with young Gil, Marian. He's chilled through and we can send him back in the morning, when he's got a good breakfast inside him!" and Ikey went off without another word. Eveleigh said, sombrely, "Did the lad see it?"

"He saw Martin hanging from a beam in the barn," Paul told him, "but thank God he saw nothing worse!"

"Arabella? And their boy, Sydney?"

"Only Arabella. Ikey was there earlier and got Sydney away. Arabella is lying in the bedroom."

Eveleigh looked thoughtful and Paul, who had always respected the man, could not help admiring his remarkable self-control and complete lack of blather. The foreman said, finally, "Well, I can't say I'm surprised but I never thought it would run to murder. How did he go about it?"

"With a hay knife," Paul said, "it's still up there and nothing will induce me to go back, Eveleigh. In any case, everything had better be left as it is until the police get here. It's a miracle the boy escaped," and he told briefly of Codsall's attempt on Ikey's life with the gun and how Sydney had jumped from the window.

"It might easily have been my missus and my kids," Eveleigh said, soberly. "Doctor O'Keefe should have put the old fool away months ago!" Then, glancing at Paul under his dark brows, "Do you think you could help me take The Gaffer down, sir?"

"Yes," Paul said, "I think I could manage that after another glass of rum!" and Eveleigh poured him a measure and went into the scullery to get his rubber boots and mackintosh. He called upstairs, "I'm going up there now, Marian! Better dress and start breakfast," and Paul marvelled at his matter-of-fact tone and phlegm. "How many children have you?" he asked and Eveleigh told him six, four girls and two boys, the eldest of them eleven. "Gaffer was a hard man to work for," he said, as they trudged up the lane, "but his son Will would have made things all right. She was the main trouble, of course; she never could get to grips with a farm. A man oughtn't to go looking for a wife outside the place where he was born and raised!"

It was only then that Paul remembered Grace and the child she was struggling to bring into the world. It seemed to him incredible that he could have completely forgotten her during the last two hours but it was so. All his nervous energy had been expended getting here through the storm and after that the sight of Codsall, and the shambles in the bedroom, had wiped everything from his mind. He said, "Mrs. Craddock is having her first child tonight, Eveleigh. There were serious complications and I had to leave before it was born," and he thought the man glanced at him sympathetically although he could not be sure. The storm was subsiding rapidly now and the comparative silence, after the uproar, was uncanny, as though everything in the Valley had been smashed down and beaten flat like Arabella. Eveleigh flung the barn door wide and there was just light enough to see the two horses, munching hay beyond the partition and, over to the left alongside the loft ladder, the thick-set figure of Martin Codsall gyrating in the draught.

"God's mercy!" Eveleigh said, softly, "how did he manage it? Did he leave a lantern burning?"

"No," Paul told him, "it was pitch dark when we came in. He must have gone about the whole business in the dark!" and he thought "That's curious! Eveleigh's first thought was the danger of fire! He's a good farmer and deserves something better than this," and he found himself drawing strength from the man's stillness as he respectfully directed Paul to climb the ladder and cut the cord, while he enfolded Martin's body in his strong, wiry arms and gently lowered it to the floor. Codsall did not look much like a man who had hanged himself. His eyes were closed and his mouth tight shut. He looked almost as calm as someone who had died in their sleep. "He must have done it soon after the boy left here," Eveleigh said, "for he's stone cold, poor old devil!" Paul noticed that the soles of Codsall's boots were caked with blood and turned away, so that Eveleigh said gently, "You go on home, sir, and see to your wife. I can manage here, me an' the missus

325

will take care of your stable-lad. He must be a spunky kid to ha' done all he did."

Paul, ashamed of his weakness, said, "What about informing the police?" and Eveleigh told him that Ben and Gerry would be here in an hour and he would send one of them to Whinmouth and meantime keep everyone out of the house. "You might send one of Honeyman's men over, sir," he suggested, "we shall need help one way and another," and Paul recalled then that Honeyman would have been informed by now and would probably arrive before the labourers. "Now you'd best get off, sir!" Eveleigh said, impatiently, as though he would prefer to handle things alone. "I'm mortal sorry about it, Mr. Craddock, and somehow I feel it's partly my fault not keeping an eye on him. Still, a man has so much to do, things being what they have been about here lately."

Paul thanked him and led Snowdrop out of the barn, leaving the cob for Ikey. It was almost light now and the temperature was surprisingly mild for January. He rode out of the farm gate half resolving never to enter it again but as he forded the river, and rode along the road under the wood he thought more anxiously of Grace than of Four Winds. Half-way up the drive he overtook the forlorn figure of Horace Handcock, the gardener, swathed in an immense overcoat and splashed to the waist with the red mud of the paddock. Paul reined in at once and asked him if Honeyman had been alerted.

Handcock's red face emerged reluctantly from the folds of his coat but he brightened when he recognised the horseman.

"Aye, I've done that! He's on his way now, along with Matt but there's good news for 'ee, zir! It's a boy, and Doctor O'Keefe told Mrs. Handcock they're both doing well! May I be the first to wish 'ee good luck, zir?"

"Yes, you may indeed," Paul said, thankfully, "and I'm sorry we had to get you out in the middle of the night! Mrs. Craddock is bearing up?"

"The missus has been in to her and 'er's taken broth," Handcock told him, gleefully. "It all happened minutes bevore I zet out. Seven pound odd he be zo they zay an' bawling like a young calf when I left, zir!"

A great wave of gratitude engulfed Paul and he began to feel lightheaded, as though all the whisky he had swallowed earlier in the evening and the rum poured him by Eveleigh, were mounting to his brain. He thought, "There's good and bad here and it's all mixed up! Martin Codsall runs amok with a hay knife, children leap from windows in their nightshirts, a man hangs himself in a barn but then, as counterweights, I've come up against Ikey's guts, Eveleigh's steadiness and this little character's goodwill!" And suddenly he felt braced and optimistic, riding into the yard where everyone was astir, and there was an air of bustle about the house. Mrs. Handcock beamed at him from the top of the kitchen steps and Chivers, the groom, took Snowdrop's bridle with an air of deference, as though the arrival of an heir improved the status of the father. He found O'Keefe supping tea in the kitchen and was at once reminded of Four Winds but he did not have the heart to wipe the smile from the housekeeper's face by telling what had occurred. Instead he said, "May I go up and see her now?" and the doctor said he could and that the specialist had agreed to accompany him to Four Winds as soon as he had washed and packed his bag. "Well, there's little enough you can do over there, except certify!" Paul told him as soon as Mrs. Handcock was out of earshot and the doctor shrugged and lit his pipe. As a practitioner of nearly fifty years' experience he was proof against the shock of violent death.

Paul went up the stairs hesitantly, a little shy at the prospect of seeing her. Thirza, the parlourmaid, wearing the mantle of nurse as though she had been created a baroness, slipped out of the room as he entered and said smugly, " 'E's a praaper li'l tacker, Mr. Craddock, but 'er's had a turrible bad time, I can tell 'ee!"

He saw that Grace, although propped up, was asleep and stole across the big room to the window where the cot stood in the angle of the wall made by the bay. The baby's eyes were open and he looked back at Paul with a kind of shrewd interest. Newborn babies, Paul recalled, were usually brick-red, as bald as coots, and generally regarded as ugly by all but their mothers, but this child was neither red nor bald. His skin was as pale as his mother's and his hair as dark as Grace's but the tufts looked as though they had been stuck on his pate by a practical joker. Paul lowered his finger gently, letting it slide along the baby's cheek and the child opened his mouth like a day-old thrush.

He was still standing there, back to the bed, when he heard a movement from the bed and turning saw that she was not asleep after all but looking directly at him. He tiptoed over, aware of the filth on his boots and the clamminess of his clothes, noting that she looked exhausted but very composed. Her skin glowed and her two large dimples played hide and seek in the lamplight. He said, quickly, "I can't kiss you, Grace. I'm filthy. I never stopped to wash but came straight up thinking you were asleep!" He tried to say something conventional, to ask how she felt or whether she was pleased the child was a boy, but the sharp memory of Arabella's bedroom confused him and he dropped his gaze, waiting for her to speak. She said, calmly, "You had to go out somewhere?" and he told her something had happened during the storm at Four Winds but that it was attended to now.

"It must have been important," she said but without irony and he answered that it had been important and that was why he had no choice but to go. "The baby is a lovely child," he said, trying to steer her away from Four Winds, "but it was terrible to have to go through all that, Grace! I was downstairs most of yesterday and felt absolutely useless."

She smiled faintly, "Well, I imagine you were, Paul, but that's a husband's prerogative. You're pleased it's a boy, I suppose?"

"I didn't care what it was," he said truthfully. "All day yesterday I don't think I gave the baby a thought as anything except a source of your pain and my fear. I'm glad now, though, and happier still that it's behind you. You'd best sleep, dear. I'll get a bath and change and if you're awake I'll come up after luncheon." He wished that he could bend over her and kiss her but he checked the impulse, moving towards the door. He had his hand on the knob when she called, "Paul!" and he turned, looking at her anxiously.

"What is it, dear?"

"What did happen at Four Winds?"

"I'll tell you about it later."

"But I want to know, Paul. I want to know why you're in such a mess, and why you're so upset. I don't like people treating me as if I was a sick child and you should know that by now!"

He knew it well enough and cursed himself for not stopping to wash and change and compose himself a little before blundering in here. He said "Martin Codsall went off his head and took a shot at Ikey on the Dunes."

"Ikey was hurt?"

"No, but Martin—well . . . he killed himself and we've sent for the police."

She nodded, slowly, "Thank you for telling me, Paul. I knew it must be something grim. So you've had a bad time, as well?"

"It wasn't very pleasant," he mumbled, "but go to sleep and don't worry about it!"

"Tell Thirza I'm hungry," she said suddenly, "and do impress upon everybody not to creep about the house as if I was in a decline! I'm not, you know, Daladier said I managed it pretty well, considering it was a breech birth."

"I'm sure you did," he said and suddenly vertigo assailed him again so that he gripped the door-knob with all his force and glanced over his shoulder to see if she had noticed. Luckily she was looking towards the window and it relieved him to see that her expression, seen in profile, was serene and even a little smug. He thought, savagely, "I suppose Codsall never meant much to her and why should he? But this Arabella business will have to be kept from her for a day or so and I'll punch anyone's head who blabs about it!" The moment of faintness passed and he was able to go out, closing the door softly. He went along to the guest room they had prepared for him and peeled off his wet clothes, throwing them in a heap. He gave himself a vigorous towelling but he was too spent to bother with a bath and climbed into bed not expecting to sleep but soon he was snoring and they let him lie until late afternoon.

His first thought, on waking, was not of Grace or Ara-

329

bella but of Will Codsall, whom he supposed must have been told by now. He wondered how he would take it and whether he would blame himself for his desertion of a year ago, thinking, "If he does, then that wife of his will soon drag it out of him," and it occurred to him that Will might want to return to Four Winds and this would mean finding another tenant for Periwinkle. At once he remembered Eveleigh and his six children, surely the safest bet in the Valley. He lay there wondering at himself for worrying about estate routine when, a few yards away, was his wife and son, and thought, "If the child was born soon after I left last night he entered the world just as Martin left," and the notion of a simultaneous birth and death remained with him as he took his bath and went along to the big bedroom, opening the door an inch to see if she was asleep. She was awake and was combing out her hair and it seemed to him a very striking thing that she could be so engaged when, only twenty-four hours ago, she had been battling for her life and the child's, or so it had seemed to him waiting below. He took the brush from her, imitating the long, sweeping strokes that he had first observed her make in their bedroom in Paris.

"I've been thinking about names," she said. "Have you any particular preference?"

"None at all," he said, "as a matter of fact I expected a girl."

"I didn't," she told him, "not for a moment. I always knew it was a boy all right. An athlete too, I wouldn't wonder, judging by the way he kicked out! It was probably his restlessness that caused the trouble."

She sounded calm and relaxed and he remembered reading somewhere that this was a common reaction after an aggravating labour. "I quite like your name," she went on, "but it's a nuisance to have two Pauls about one house. What was your father called?"

"Saul," he told her, grinning, "so that's out of the question!"

"There are too many biblical names around here already," she said.

"Joshuas, Samuels, Jacobs and Micahs, and most of the popular ones get shortened, all the Bills and Bobs and

Walts and Dicks! No, I want him to have a two-syllable name that nobody lops. Who is your favourite historical character?"

"Oliver Cromwell," he said, "and I don't see him as 'Oliver', do you? There's another man who always intrigued me, however—Simon de Montfort!"

"That's it!" she exclaimed, " 'Simon'! It's clean and uncompromising like a . . . like a blade!"

"All right then, 'Simon' it is and I don't know whether we can take that noise for his approval."

The baby had begun to whimper but before Paul could pick him up Thirza had rushed in, all rustling skirts and galvanised efficiency and looking sternly at Paul said, "It's time for his feed, sir!" but when Grace held out her arms and Paul seemed in no hurry to go the girl looked so embarrassed that Grace laughed and said, "Oh, don't be so stuffy, Thirza! How do you think I got the baby anyway?" and without more ado slipped her nightdress from her shoulder and gave the child her breast. Thirza left the room in three strides, Grace's laughter following her down the corridor as Paul said, "Every convention in the book is a kind of hurdle you have to jump, isn't it?" and she replied, "Most of them, so you can tell me the truth about Codsall!"

He was unprepared for this and growled, "What idiot has been telling you things while I was asleep?"

"No one mentioned it," she said, "but I should be witless if I didn't know something was being kept from me! What really happened over there?"

He sighed, reflecting that it was never any use trying to cushion her against facts for every time he attempted it she made a fool of him.

"It was a ghastly business; Codsall killed his wife with a hay knife but if you want all the gory details you can read them in the newspaper after the inquest." He added, however, the story of Ikey's part in the tragedy and said how well the boy had acquitted himself, and this seemed to interest her as much as the murder. "We shall have to do something for that boy," she said, "and we ought to do it at once!" and when Paul pointed out that Ikey was perfectly happy as a stable-lad she said, impatiently, "I daresay, but he won't be later on! The time to start on him is now, while he's young enough to do as he's told."

"What can we do for him we aren't already doing?"

"We can send him to a proper school where he'll get a real education," she said, emphatically, and it was useless to suggest that Ikey might be unhappy at a school where his outlook and Cockney accent would put him at a disadvantage for her agile mind was already grooming the boy for a career and at last Paul had to admit that her plan had possibilities, for she reasoned that if Ikey could mimic anyone on the estate he could also learn to speak and behave conventionally, particularly if Paul made demands on him. He grumbled, "Why saddle me with the responsibility? It was your idea, not mine!"

"He worships the ground you walk on," she said, "he always has and always will. Why do you suppose he tracked Codsall like that and then insisted on going back to the farm? Everyone has to have a hero and you happen to be Ikey's, whether you like it or not, so talk it over with him and if he backs down because going away to school would mean parting from you then I'll have a talk with him!"

"You're always in such a damned hurry," he said, laughing, but she replied, seriously, "Yes, I am, Paul, and I always will be while things like that business at Four Winds and others like the Potter case occur so needlessly!"

He could see very little connection between the poaching incident, Codsall's craziness and his stable-boy's education but reflecting that this was no time to argue with her promised to speak to Ikey after the inquest at Whinmouth, the next day. She seemed satisfied with this and handed him Simon to return to his cot. He cradled the child for a moment and she watched him, her eyes alight with secret amusement. It was curious, she thought, that women produced children but never sentimentalised over them in the manner of men. She was glad about the child but more for his sake than her own. She felt no sense of achievement, as Celia and all the other sentimental old bodies had promised, no more than relief that it now had an existence of its own and that she could retreat into her own privacy. Then, away at the back of her mind and hardly as a conscious thought at all, she wondered if it was this kind of prejudice that set her apart from other women and whether, indeed, she had any real right to a man's protection and love.

III

The inquest produced no surprises. It was a survey of known facts, volunteered by a short procession of witnesses, beginning with Doctor O'Keefe, who said he had treated Martin Codsall over the last year for headaches and had cautioned him on the probable results of his excessive drinking. He also mentioned the strain of eccentricity in previous Codsalls he had known, notably Martin's father, and when he was talking of this Paul glanced at Will Codsall, who was sitting on the witnesses' bench between his wife Elinor and the stolid Eveleigh but Will did not seem to resent this implication but merely blinked and absentmindedly scratched his chin so that Paul thought, "Nobody ever asks the important questions or digs for the real facts, like Arabella's eternal nagging or Martin's terrible sense of inferiority, engendered by years and years of denigration." He gave his own evidence briefly, as did Eveleigh, and was glad when the Coroner complimented Ikey on his dogged pursuit of the deceased and his prompt rescue of the hysterical Sydney. It was over and done with inside an hour and outside the little court Will Codsall told Paul that the funeral would be at Coombe Bay parish church the next day, murderer and victim being buried in the same family grave, despite a rumour that Parson Bull would prohibit it. His family, he said, had been churchwardens at Coombe Bay for more than a century and having regard to Martin's mental illness Parson Bull agreed to stretch a point. Elinor stood by tight-lipped while they talked, only joining in when Paul asked Will if he would like to return to Four Winds as master.

"No," she snapped, " 'er woulden, an' you can taake that as vinal, Squire! Thankee all the zame but tiz 'No'!

333

Four Winds be a bad plaace an' us is better off where us be, at Periwinkle!"

Paul agreed but noticing that Will looked shifty thought it right to press the point somewhat.

"There's no comparison between Four Winds and Periwinkle as farms, Elinor," he said. "One is well established and close on 350 acres, the other a mere sixty, enclosed by Pitts' land and the moor."

"It's no odds," she said stubbornly, "us want none of it, do us Will?"

"No, I reckon not," Will said slowly, "we'm zettled enough, Mr. Craddock," and Paul pondered the tendency of Codsall males to let their women speak on their behalf as Elinor added, "As to what that old vool in there said about the family being mazed, I don't reckon nothing to that! Will baint mazed, nor my little Mark neither! A man's what he maakes of himself to my mind, or what his woman maakes of 'un!"

"I daresay you're right about that, Elinor," said Paul, and thought how much luckier Will had been in his wife than Martin. "Stay on at Periwinkle and good luck to you both! Will you be taking young Sydney to live with you now?"

Elinor glanced at Will. It was plain that she did not relish the prospect but she said slowly, "I reckon that'd be our duty, Squire, providing he wants to come, but he'll never maake a varmer, he's too zet on book-larnin'. Maybe whoever moved into Four Winds would board him. He don't eat much and he's at school most o' the time."

"Then leave Sydney to me," Paul said and went across to the black-browed foreman, Eveleigh, who was adjusting the harness of his pony and deliberately avoiding involvement in the conference.

"Suppose I transferred the tenancy of Four Winds to you, Eveleigh?" he asked and the man's head came up so sharply that the pony shied. To cover his agitation Eveleigh shouted, "Quiet, damn you! Stand still, boy!" and glanced across at Will and Elinor, now on the point of moving off.

"That wouldn't be right, would it, sir?" he asked, "not with Will 'avin' to make do on sixty acres o' rough land?"

"Will doesn't want the farm," Paul told him, "I've just offered it to him. He'll have the contents, of course and some of the stock no doubt, for Martin probably left a will but he's only got sixty acres and I daresay you could come to some arrangement with him and buy stock over a period? Or perhaps you could split the Friesian herd between you. The point is, how would you feel about running Four Winds?"

Eveleigh considered, making the decision of a lifetime. Finally he said, "I could make it the best farm for miles around but I've got nothing put by. How could I, wi' six kids and the pittance Codsall paid me? I couldn't run it alone, and I couldn't pay the hired men a week's wages. It isn't Will I'd have to come to terms with, but you, Squire. It'd be five years before you saw money come back but by then my boys an' girls would be old enough to lend a hand so I wouldn't need hired help. I'd say it was you who had to make the decision, Mr. Craddock!"

Paul remembered the man's steadfastness and the gentleness he had displayed lowering Martin's body. He recalled too, the relationship between Eveleigh and his wife, and the way she had hustled Ikey into bed with one of her own boys. He said, "I'd take a chance on you both, Eveleigh! The place is yours if you want it and I'll get Rudd to draw up a new agreement. You can have it rent free for three years and I'll undertake to pay the two men until you see something back from your harvest. Did Martin sell all his milk locally?"

"We do right now," Eveleigh said eagerly, "but my missus is a wonderful hand with the churn. I've always thought we could send butter an' cheese up the railway line to the cities if we got things on a proper footing. There's money in that if you can cut out the middlemen." And then, his dark eyes glowing, "You'll not regret it, Squire! You give me this chance and I'll make something of it, you can rely on that!"

"I'm sure I can," Paul said, and wondered briefly what Rudd would say when he heard he had struck the best farm in the Valley from the rent roll for three years.

335

Then he thought, "To hell with John! Grace would agree and it's time I made some of my own decisions!" To Eveleigh he said, "You'd best go back now and get things moving. Come over and see me on Sunday morning."

Eveleigh nodded, too moved to say more. He climbed into his trap and drove off after Will Codsall just as Rudd came out of the courthouse looking more than usually gloomy. "I always seem to be missing when anything serious happens around here," he said glumly, "but it looks as if you and that stable-boy managed as well as anyone could have done. However, I can take over from here so get back to your wife and baby and take it easy for a day or two." He did not give expression to the thought that crossed his mind as he mentioned Grace, or how events seemed to be justifying his nagging suspicion that, in some way, Grace had revived the bad luck of the Valley simply by being who she was, a hangover of the Lovell tradition. There had been the quarrel with Gilroy, then the Smut Potter affair, and now this, a murder and a suicide, all within a matter of a year. And there was more to come he wouldn't wonder!

He went back to confer with the Coroner and the Police Inspector, while Paul mounted the trap Ikey had brought round and the two set off along the coastal cart road towards Coombe Bay. Ikey, to his delight, was allowed to drive and they were soon clear of the town and breasting the long hump of the red cliff that enclosed Whinmouth on the east. They were walking the horse down the next hill into Teazel Coombe when Paul said, "Mrs. Craddock and I have been discussing your future, Ikey. She thinks you should go to school, a real school, you understand?"

The boy looked startled. "You mean, away to school, sir?" and when Paul told him this was so he burst out, "But I like it fine where I am, an' what I'm doing, sir! I don't want no more upsets. This ain't because o' what 'appened at Four Winds, is it, sir? I did right the Coroner said, and so did you when we was doing of it!"

"Of course you did right," Paul said, "but both Mrs. Craddock and I feel that the way you've shaped since you've been here and the progress you've made at Miss

336

Willoughby's school entitles you to a real education. You can't get higher than Chivers if you stay a stable-lad, and you can never earn more than a pound or two a week. How old are you?"

"I couldn't say for sure," the boy said, "but I reckon I'm thirteen, or near enough. My Mum told me I was eleven when I first come 'ere but what would it mean, sir, going away and being put to a big school? Would it mean . . . well . . . that I grew into a gent, like you, sir?"

Paul chuckled. "By no means," he said, "for I'm only half a gentleman, Ikey. I bought my place here with money made from the scrapyard, and I didn't even make that myself, it was all earned by my father and Mr. Zorndorff. No, that isn't the point, at least Mrs. Craddock wouldn't think it was. She says that you've got a naturally quick brain and if you put your mind to it you could learn to speak properly and stand a far better chance of getting on in the world. Apart from that a good education is a fine thing in itself. I didn't have one and I've missed it, I can tell you! You can never really catch up, you only think you can."

The boy glanced at him curiously. "There's nothing you can't do, sir," he said, "so I don't see what . . . well . . . I don't see what the way a bloke talks has to do with it!"

"It has, believe me," said Paul feelingly, "in England it's the most important thing of all. I don't know why it should be but it is. Your accent, and mine, for that matter, would hold us back all our lives so long as we stayed at home. It wouldn't hinder us in America or the Colonies but here it's a kind of password. But I'm not the person to give you the best advice about this, go and have a word with Mrs. Craddock when you get home?" and when Ikey still hesitated, "You like Mrs. Craddock, don't you? You'd trust her, the same as you would me?"

Ikey said reverently, "I think she's the most beautiful person I ever see, sir. She's like . . . like a picksher in a book. I'd talk to her about it, sir, but I'd tell her same as I told you, that I'm 'appy enough as I am!"

They left it at that and Ikey saw Grace but the result was as Paul had expected. She converted him to her point

337

of view in half-an-hour. He at once sought Paul in the stables and said, grinning shamefacedly, "Mrs. Craddock reckons I could board out a bit with a schoolmaster she knows in Paxtonbury, sir, so I'm orf tomorrer! Then I got to try fer one o' them nobs' school, I dunno where exactly, but I 'ope it's 'andy!" That was all; the guardianship of Ikey Palfrey had passed from man to wife.

Paul learned the details later, when Grace was up and about again. The staff, he noticed, now treated her with increased respect, as though, by producing a male heir, she had accomplished a very singular feat indeed and although he was amused by this he was dismayed by her curious lack of interest in Simon, whom she cheerfully abandoned to Thirza, now promoted from palourmaid to Nannie. Grace breast-fed the baby, O'Keefe telling Paul that she had made an excellent recovery, far more rapid than he had anticipated, for the difficulties of the breech birth had evidently rattled the old man. Daladier, the specialist, came over once or twice to re-examine her and Celia accompanied him. Grace was convinced that the French surgeon was Celia's lover, for Bruce, her father, remained abroad. The notion of her forty-five-year-old stepmother enjoying a Continental lover amused Grace but in a strange way it seemed to bring them closer together so that Paul thought, "I suppose it's because she finds this one more example of flying in the face of convention, or is it just another score off her father?"

Rudd, to Paul's surprise, unequivocally endorsed the new tenancy of Four Winds, declaring that Eveleigh was far more likely to make a success of the farm than Will Codsall. After Eveleigh had settled in Paul rode over once or twice and was impressed with the transformation of the place. Its air of explosive gloom had gone and the ghosts of Martin and Arabella seemed to have been laid by the teeming, tumbling Eveleigh brood, four flaxen-haired little girls, all lively and pretty and two stolid boys. Marian Eveleigh more than fulfilled her husband's promise in the buttery and the results of her industry were soon going up the line to London markets, where her butter and tinned yellow cream was reputed to appear on the tables of famous restaurants. The two elder girls were

338

initiated into the art and might have increased the dairy output if Eveleigh had not been a stickler for their regular attendance at Mary Willoughby's school. He had, Paul noticed, a great respect for the value of education and later on, when he would have been glad of his eldest boy's help about the farm, he preferred to see him canter off on the Four Winds' lively pony and ride the eight-mile round trip between Deepdene and Four Winds every weekday.

The weather that spring was mild and crops were forward. Up at Periwinkle, on the edge of the moor, Elinor Codsall was busy building up a strong strain of poultry that promised to improve on the hens she had left behind at her father's farm. She favoured a sturdy crossbreed, Rhode Island Red and Light Sussex and she too availed herself of city markets made available by the railway. Paul sometimes met her at Sorrel Halt unloading crates of eggs in the siding and noticed that she was pregnant again. He thought, "That was one of the best things I ever did, promote that marriage! How Will would cope without her I can't imagine," and he looked upon Periwinkle as one of his successes. Elinor made no secret of her relief that Four Winds, with its fine Friesian herd, had passed into other hands. "If Will had gone backalong," she told Paul, "I'd ha' lost him! 'Tiz as well for us things happened as they did and young Sydney is better along of all they Eveleigh children. Mebbe it'll taake him out of himself for he's got too much of his mother about him, whereas my Will has no particle of 'er, Glory be!"

Henry Pitts, at Hermitage, was courting at last, to his mother's satisfaction and his jolly father's amusement. He had been taken in hand, with little impetus on his part, by a grenadier of a girl, full-bosomed and red-haired, who was employed as dairymaid at one of the Gilroy farms and occasionally, when Paul was riding along the lanes of an evening, he would pass them walking slowly and in step, with Henry's arm tucked firmly under the girl's, so that he looked like an amiable prisoner being exercised by an affectionate wardress. As he passed them and Henry gave him a good evening Paul reflected that the women of the Valley were more vital and purposeful than its men and seemed also to have a clearer conception of what was important and what was not and that in most cases it was they who made the decisions. There was Elinor Codsall and her Will, Henry and his tall red-head, Martha and the easy-going Arthur Pitts, Mary Willoughby and her preacher brother, and, to some extent, Eveleigh's wife Marian, now keeping the pot boiling through the difficult period of the take-over. He wondered briefly if Valley folk thought the same of him and regarded Grace as the originator of policy at the big house but thought this unlikely, for Grace's interest in the estate was purely personal, like her patronage of Ikey Palfrey. He wished sometimes that she would show a more active interest in the estate and not continue to regard it, as he was sure she did, as a tiresome hobby on the part of a boyish husband. Their relationship as man and wife remained tranquil enough but he failed utterly to interest her in his political activities and so did James Grenfell, for all his persuasive charm. Paul had been a witness to their last skirmish, when Grenfell, arriving at Shallowford with news that a bye-election was a probability in the constituency in the summer, admitted that, whilst favouring the principle of the woman's vote, he thought it should await the settlement of more important issues, such as tariff reform, the bridling of the House of Lords, the Irish question, and a mass of badly-needed social legislation on subjects as divergent as shop-assistants' hours and pensions for the aged. He could not regard women's suffrage as a major issue; for Grace it dwarfed every other.

"You Liberals will never get your major reforms through without enlisting the support of every intelligent woman in the country," she declared. "You prattle about social reform until your platforms disappear behind a cloud of gas but you don't really believe in it, not you, not Lloyd George, not that cold fish Asquith, or Oh-So-Courteous Mr. Grey! The right of women to have a say in the kind of society in which they live ought to be self-evident! We produce the children you need to play 'Snap' with the German Kaiser but you still relegate us to the kitchen and nursery! Well, it won't do, James, and I'm hanged if you'll get my support until you stand up in

340

Paxtonbury Drill Hall and admit that a woman is no longer a second-class citizen! If a male cretin can vote, why deny the same right to a qualified woman doctor?" It seemed to Paul that she had a point, but James only laughed and replied, "When a modern political party aims at rebuilding the entire fabric of that nation, my dear, it has to select priorities and deal with reforms one at a time. It dare not risk hard-won gains on a highly controversial domestic issue. You'll get your vote all right but you'll have to wait until you're thirty-odd instead of twenty-odd!" and Grace had snapped, "It's too long to wait, James!" and had retired to her rose garden in one of her withdrawn moods, not mentioning the subject again until Paul was getting into bed when she said, astounding him with her guile, "Why don't you work on the local committee to persuade Grenfell to stand down and put you up instead? I'd work hard for you, providing, of course, you stood for women's suffrage. After a trial run or two we'd get to Westminster!"

"But I haven't the slightest desire to get to Westminster!" he protested and she replied, with a sigh that troubled him, "No, Paul, I'd forgotten that!" and dropped the subject.

After that they had kept off the subject of politics and the spring days passed pleasantly enough. One day, to his genuine pleasure, Claire Derwent appeared at the last hunt of the season and contrary to expectations he found that he could talk and joke with her without embarrassment. They seemed, in fact, to slip into the easy, unexacting relationship of the earliest days of their friendship, when she had ridden beside him all over the Valley and introduced him to people he now addressed by nickname. She was a little less plump, he thought, but her figure, if anything, was the better for it and she looked very fit for a girl who, according to her own account, spent most of her time indoors and had not sat a horse since leaving the Valley. She made no reference to the abruptness with which she had decamped after the Coronation soirée, or to the fact, now clearly established in Paul's mind, that she had felt certain he would propose to her but she still seemed interested in everything that was happening in

341

the Valley and congratulated him warmly on the birth of his son, Simon.

"Why don't you come over and see the place again, Claire?" he said. "You ought to meet Grace and I'm sure you'll like one another. She's a great gardener and has made all kind of changes outside, although she won't even give advice on the administrative side. Come over to tea and bring Rose?" and Claire said that she would be happy to visit them the day before she went back to her teashop in Penshurst to prepare for the summer influx of visitors.

"I can't imagine you pottering about a teashop, Claire," he said, as they rode part-way home together, "you're an open-air girl and that's a city job," and she had glanced at him, a little sharply he thought, and said, "I'd sooner do that than spend my life as an unpaid servant for father!"

"Well, I don't suppose it will be for long," he said lightly, "you'll be married very soon for sure."

"Maybe," she said, and left it at that, but she redeemed her promise and she and Rose arrived in the Derwent's yellow dog-cart the following Saturday, both dressed in their best and Claire looking very smart in a diagonally-striped blue and white silk dress, with a huge picture hat of matching straw, openwork mittens instead of gloves and a long-handled parasol of saxe-blue silk.

Handing her down from the box Paul thought it was going to be a rather trying occasion but it proved exactly the opposite. As he had predicted she and Grace seemed to find a good deal to talk about and abandoned him to Rose, who lured him into the yard on the pretext of talking shop with Chivers the groom and then set to work to sell him a cob and exchange the old Lovell trap for a smarter equipage. He was easy game for this, having already made up his mind to buy a more modern dray before Grace, with her modern notions, persuaded him to get a motor, still foreign to the Valley but sometimes seen in the steep streets of Paxtonbury. When they had more or less clinched the deal he asked Rose outright if she thought Claire was happy away from home and Rose said she was as happy as most girls who could never settle for anything short of a husband and babies. Paul half expected her to make some reference to the general belief that he had jilted her but she did not and he was grateful. She praised Grace, saying that she thought her "quite lovely", and adding that she was popular among the tenants and then they returned to find Grace and Claire in the drawing-room after her inspection of the baby. Claire paid him the usual compliments and they left, declaring that they had enjoyed the visit enormously, and that Paul and Grace must come to High Coombe and not wait until Claire came home again, for that might not be until Christmas-time.

As the yellow trap passed out of view behind the curve of the chestnuts Grace said, "She's still madly in love with you, Paul, but perhaps you don't need telling that."

He was shocked and angry, not so much by the statement but by the blandness with which it was uttered, as though this had been a subject of debate between them and that it was now time to concede her the winner and pay the bet. He growled back, "That's a damned silly thing to say! And not a very kind thing, either!" and stumped off into the library, leaving her smiling on the porch steps. A moment later, however, she opened the door softly and came in and he saw that she was quite unruffled by his touchiness.

"It wasn't such a silly remark," she said, after a pause, "and I didn't mean it maliciously! There are all kinds of things wrong with me, Paul, but I'm not catty about other women."

"All right then," he said, resignedly, "let's regard it as bad guesswork. I don't think she ever was in love with me, in fact, I know she wasn't! She may have been a bit infatuated when she was nineteen but it was never more than a flirtation on my part or on hers, no matter what you might have heard to the contrary!"

"I've heard nothing about it," she said, in the same reasonable tone, "I was just using my eyes. Her sister knows it's true and I daresay old Edward Derwent was disappointed too; that would account for his grumpiness! You didn't see her as I did, holding your Simon just now.

She's not only in love with you but unselfishly so, and that's rare!"

He said, sullenly, "All women look that way holding babies! And he isn't just 'my Simon', Grace, he's yours as well!" but then, sensing that this might lead to a discussion that provoked one of her dismal withdrawals, added, "As a matter of fact she behaved rather badly at the time. Rose knows that and is still ashamed for her. She made the running and when it was obvious to her that I was in love with you she flounced out of the Valley and has never returned until now! It was more pique than anything else, as she frankly admitted in a letter to me!"

"Have you still got the letter?"

"I don't keep Claire Derwent's letters tied up with chocolate-box ribbon," he said. "Why should I?"

"Oh, I don't know—as a scalp, perhaps. Do you keep mine?"

"You've never written me one," he told her and she laughed, in a way that encouraged him to treat the whole thing more lightly than he was disposed to do.

"No, that's right, I never have! But there really wasn't time, was there and we've never been parted since then!" She came across and perched herself on the edge of the table close to his chair, her skirts rustling pleasantly. "Come on Paul, admit it! Don't you find me a little cloying? Like David Copperfield's Dora?"

"No," he said, "you're much more like Agnes, the practical one!" but she had coaxed him out of his sulk so that they were able to discuss the Derwents objectively, Grace saying that Claire had done herself a good turn without knowing it by fleeing the Valley. She was now living less than an hour's journey from London and could therefore enjoy the best of two worlds. Suddenly she added, "As soon as she sat down, holding her knees close together and sitting half sideways as I handed her tea, she reminded me very vividly of someone and I couldn't think who but now I think I've got it! Wait a minute . . ." and she went over to the lowest shelf of the bookcase where there were several bulky volumes of coloured reproductions of famous masters, returning to him with a book called *Famous Paintings of the Western World* that Paul had never opened.

"Here it is," she said triumphantly, "and I was right! There's your Claire, three centuries ago!" and she laid the book open at an illustration of Rubens' "Bathsheba receiving King David's letter", a picture described as "one of the master's most enchanting later works, a fiery love song and a poem in praise of sensual beauty". Paul looked at the reproduction with interest, seeing a handsome, full-breasted girl sitting with bare knees pressed together and her body turned half-left as she received the letter from a Negro page. Grace's memory had been remarkably accurate, for the girl, listed as Helène Fourment, whom the painter had married when she was sixteen, was Claire Derwent in almost every particular. She had the same rounded face, the same air of mild provocation and the identical attentive pose, for it seemed to Paul that this Bathsheba might have been checking her shopping list rather than receiving the advances of a royal seducer. He studied the picture with interest, struck by its superb composition, by the way the painter had directed light on the carelessly bent arm, the soft, drooping fingers and the chubby knees. Grace, watching him closely, said, "Well? And what has she got for you Paul?"

"Detachment more than anything else," he said, but Grace shook her head violently and said, "Oh no! It isn't that! It's a kind of *fruitfulness,* a ripeness that he's captured. A man could enjoy that girl very much but without ever getting emotionally involved. She would have children very easily, I'd swear to that!"

"Well," he said, closing the book, "I daresay you're right but there's something missing for my taste."

"What is it?"

"There's no 'secret' about her and I suppose that's what initially attracted me to you! Besides," he went on, more jocularly, "I'm partial to brunettes and always have been," and he told her something about the girl whose surname he had forgotten and the fourteen-year-old hoyden who had scared him so badly in the stables as a boy, reflecting that both had been dark, rather sallow girls.

345

It was good to be able to talk to one's wife like this and he thought, "If I had married Claire Derwent I daresay we should have made a go at it, but it would have lacked adventure!" He said aloud, "Let's go and look at your garden, Grace. Horace tells me it's almost finished," and they went out through the French doors and along the terrace to the corner of Little Paddock.

Great clumps of daffodils and narcissi were growing on the grassy bank dividing field and the path that led to the rose garden. There had been none about here last spring and he remembered now that she had planted more than a thousand bulbs hereabouts and more on both sides of the drive. It struck him as odd that a woman as self-contained as her, someone who worried about imponderables like women's suffrage, should expend so much energy on a garden, for surely the Pankhursts and their supporters would deride anything not brought to their notice by a pamphlet. As always when they were alone out here, with the great house silhouetted against an evening sky and blackbirds piping in the thickets, a glow of possession and satisfied memories stole over him, embracing not only the scene, and the long vista of woods and fields to the south and east, but her also and when they stopped at the stone wall she and Horace Handcock had built he slipped his arm round her waist and said, "I shall never want anything more than this and a man ought to think himself lucky to have found all he needed at twenty-five! Does that saddle me with a sluggish imagination?"

"No," she said, "not necessarily but it's a fortunate state of mind, Paul, and uncommon enough to be valued I think."

"Well then, I appreciate it to the full," he admitted and he bent to kiss the lobe of her ear.

CHAPTER ELEVEN

I

IT came stuttering down from the moor like a lean, lamed hen, moving in short, uncertain flutters, pursued by a rolling cloud of white dust and because of its erratic progress the cloud occasionally overtook it and loitered just ahead until it emerged into clean air with an undertone of *bub-bub-bub* and an overtone like the bleat of a deprived ewe.

Henry Pitts was the first man in the Valley to see it, abandoning his plough to run wide-eyed across two acres of downslope where he could stand on the crest of the moor and look down on the road it travelled. It was the first horseless carriage he had ever seen for he rarely travelled as far as Paxtonbury and had never really believed the stories his drinking companions told them in the bar of The Raven. Yet here it was, careering along the track that led from the moor to the river road, a real and unmistakable horseless carriage, propelled by noisy magic and steered by a stranger in heavy goggles, a peaked cap and a long white coat, like the cloak of a French horseman in "The Squares at Waterloo", the only picture on the walls of Hermitage Farm.

Henry stood on the bank with mouth agape, telling himself that seeing was believing yet not fully acknowledging what he saw as fact, for the thing was now moving at the speed of a galloping horse and the dust streaked behind it like the wake of a ship. Its wheels, Henry reasoned, must be made of iron, for they struck the uneven surfaces with murderous force and several times the driver would have been thrown out had he not clung to a wheel perched on the end of a long vertical rod rising from between his knees. Henry thought it a very clumsy device for this purpose, reasoning that something

347

fixed and square would have afforded a better grip but while he was standing there the squat vehicle reached the junction of track and cartroad and suddenly stopped, its trailing cloud of dust again rolling down on it until Henry thought it had been an illusion and feared for his reason. It was still there, however, for when he ran down from the bank and advanced along the track the dust cloud had settled and the thing could be seen clearly for what it was, a kind of foreshortened brougham, with spoked wheels like exceptionally heavy bicycle wheels and rims swathed in thick bands of rubber. He saw now that the wheel to which the man had been clinging was obviously used for guiding because, just as Henry approached, the goggled man began to haul at it so that the front wheels moved around in a half-circle. There were, in addition, all manner of levers and appurtenances attached to the rigid brass frame, a pair of fishy-eyed lamps, another thick iron rod fitted with a handgrip and a bulb that looked to Henry like a hunting horn with a cricket ball attached to it. The young man smiled encouragingly when he saw Henry make his cautious approach and shouted above the *bub-bub-bub* of the little monster's voice, waving his arms as if urging Henry to come nearer but Henry stopped a good ten yards away and continued to stare, knuckling the dust from his eyes and trying to make up his mind which way to run should the thing explode in his face. So must his ancestors have approached a local pit in this same Valley when word came that a strange and ferocious beast had been trapped therein.

"*Hi!*" the young man continued to shout, "*Hi,* there! Am I right for Shallowford? Do I turn right or left?" and then, gauging the extent of Henry's uncertainty, he made some adjustment so that the shattering *bub-bub-bubbing* stopped and the thing stood as silent and unoffending as a dog-cart.

Henry said slowly, "Gordamme, maister, I never zeed such a thing! Never in my bliddy life!" and advanced a step or two as the young man climbed down, stripped off his goggles and turned on him a pair of laughing blue eyes under sandy, upsweeping brows. He was, thought Henry,

348

a very cheerful-looking fellow and Henry's trepidation put a twinkle in the eyes as he said, "You mean that I'm a pioneer? The very first?" and he was clearly delighted for he went on, "Now that's one up for Diana because she's nearly seven now! It'll be something for her to remember in her old age, won't it, Di?" and he patted the casing at the front of the contraption just as though it was a horse. Henry was now half persuaded that he was dealing with an amiable lunatic but, remembering Martin Codsall, reflected that even amiable madmen were subject to violence so he continued to keep his distance and said, "Youm almost at Shallowford, zir! Baint no more'n a mile along the river till you strike the lodge!" Then, but still moving with caution, he sidled nearer, reaching out to touch the casing, finding it very hot and withdrawing his hand as though it had been bitten.

" 'Er's *seven,* you said?"

"Yes," replied the young man, "she's a Benz, you see, a German model, copied from one of the early Rileys. I only bought her yesterday. She's not half bad on a good road but this stretch almost did for her."

"Where . . . where've 'ee come from, maister?" Henry asked and he would not have been much surprised had the young man told him from the moon.

"Plymouth," he said, "I started about noon. Not bad, is it?"

"Not bad!" Henry echoed, "forty-five mile in dree hours? It's a bliddy miracle, maister! Dornee mind risking your neck?"

"Good God, there's no danger!" the man said laughing. "Not half as much as riding a young mare across country!"

"Jasus!" said Henry, fervently, "you gimme the mare, maister! Be 'ee callin' on Squire Craddock?"

"On my father," said the sailor, "John Rudd, the agent. Do you know him?"

"Arr, that I do," Henry said, losing a little of his awe. "So you be Maister Rudd's on'y son? The Naval gent?"

"That's me!" said the motorist cheerfully. "I've just finished a short cruise and I've got a long leave, so I'm

349

off all around England. If Diana lets me down I'll sell her and buy a Wolseley. Mind you, there's a lot to be said for this model. They have a mechanically-operated inlet valve and you don't get so much trouble with fuel intake. She's ten horse, you know, and can do thirty-five on the straight and flat!"

He might have been talking High Dutch as far as Henry was concerned and must have realised as much, for suddenly he hopped on to the seat, fiddled with levers, hopped out again holding a crooked piece of iron and ran round to the front where he seemed to tease the contraption's secret parts with his uncouth weapon. Suddenly there was a series of shot-gun explosions causing Henry to leap for the cover of the ditch but when he peeped out again the staccato *bub-bub-bubbing* had recommenced and a cloud of bluish smoke was pouring from Diana's hindquarters. With a wave the young man was off again down the river road, the noise of his progress stampeding Eveleigh's Friesians half-way across the water meadow.

"Gordamme!" Henry said softly, "to think I should live to zee a bliddy dog-cart driven by smoke!" and as he returned to his plough, realising that he would now have to treat his drinking companions' stories with more respect, for Willis, the wheelwright, had told him only a week ago that he had seen one of these same carriages climb Cathedral Hill in Paxtonbury at a speed twice as fast as a man could run.

One or two of the Home Farm workers saw the Benz turn into the main gates of the big house and pull up at the lodge, but either they were more sophisticated than Henry Pitts or they lacked his curiosity for they merely stopped work to see what would happen when the driver turned his back on the contraption. Then, calling encouragement to one another they edged nearer, watching the young man in the white coat hammer on the lodge door. Nobody answered, for nobody was there, but when he returned to the drive he saw what his wardroom companions would describe as "a fetching little filly" bending double over the controls in such a way as to expose a pair of exceptionally neat calves. He coughed twice, expecting her to bob up blushing, but she remained absorbed, her head half under the steering rod so that, in her light summer dress, he had an unlooked-for opportunity of appreciating what he would have described as "her upholstery", all the way from ankles to shapely little bottom. At length he had to admit to himself that he was taking a mean advantage and said, "Excuse me, Miss! I'm looking for my father, John Rudd. Do you know if he's around?"

The girl straightened up slowly and he noticed, with surprise, that she had oil on her fingers. He noticed also that her front view was even more attractive than her back view, that she had dark, close-growing curls, a pretty, heart-shaped face, deep blue eyes, a short, regular nose, and something he always looked for in a girl, two large dimples, not counting one in the cleft of her chin. He thought, "My God! What a little peach!" but he had good manners and instantly whipped off cap and goggles, giving her a quarterdeck bow, of the kind he used when the captain brought ladies aboard and he was under orders to make himself sociable.

She smiled, a slow, friendly smile and said, "Mr. Rudd is up at the house I believe. Are you Roddy, John's son?" and he stood to attention, looking rather ridiculous in his long, shapeless coat and said, "Yes, Miss! I'm on leave and I thought I'd look him up before setting off on a motor tour. I seem to have caused a bit of a sensation in the Valley. A chap back there told me they'd never seen a motor here before but that can't be true, can it?"

"Yes, it's true," she said and he noted her low, almost masculine voice and thought, "By George, I wish the skipper had invited somebody like this aboard during one of his blasted chit-chat parties!" But she was to surprise him further for she said, pointing to the motor, "It's a Benz, isn't it? The model the Germans copied? I've never seen one before but I've ridden in a Panhard and a Daimler. One of the original Daimlers it was, assembled in Wolverhampton. Does she boil on hills? Do you have to wait for her to cool off every now and again?"

"Why no," he said, eagerly, "she's not a bad little crock at all! I tackled a one-in-five on my way across Dartmoor this morning. Had to take it quietly, of course,

351

and nurse her, but she only stalled once. The main thing is to find even ground. She's apt to move in jerks on rough surfaces, like the moor road back there. I say, would you like a lift up to the house?"

"Indeed I would," Grace said, laughing at his enthusiasm, "but perhaps I'd better introduce myself. I'm not a 'Miss', I'm a 'Mrs.'—Mrs. Craddock, the Squire's wife. I expect your father has told you about me."

"No, he hasn't," he said, disappointment clouding his good-looking face, "but I do beg your pardon and I'm delighted to meet you, Mrs. Craddock! You don't often encounter a lady who doesn't think of a motor as an infernal machine, liable to blow the curious to smithereens! Where did you ride in a Panhard? They're the best, so far, but the whole industry is in a state of flux and Panhard won't lead for long. Wolseley has something very lively coming up, I hear, and now that His Majesty has taken to motoring I wouldn't wonder if they aren't all the rage in a year or so!"

"I'm sure they will be," she said, as he handed her into the passenger seat, "and I wish I could persuade my husband to buy one but he's just bought a brougham, so I'm afraid it's unlikely."

She watched him start up and the Benz coughed its way up the steep drive. Conversation was impossible while they were in motion but they arrived in the forecourt without incident, just as Rudd came out on to the terrace and saw his son handing Grace Craddock down from her perch.

"Good God!" he exclaimed, "what the devil are you doing here in that thing?" and Grace explained, noting that for all Rudd's scorn he was nonetheless pleased to see Roddy.

They all three took tea in the library, Rudd explaining that Paul would not be back until late that night, for the long-awaited bye-election had just been announced and he had driven to Paxtonbury to sponsor James Grenfell, in the Drill Hall. "I daresay he'll try and talk you into campaigning for him," John said. "Grenfell might like a modern approach and display a poster on a motor 'Keep abreast with the Liberals' or something like that."

"Good Lord, I couldn't allow that!" Roddy said, with genuine alarm, "we chaps aren't allowed to side with either party, although we're naturally expected to vote Tory! Will you be helping your husband in the campaign, Mrs. Craddock?"

"No, I'm afraid I won't," declared Grace, "I'm every bit as opposed to the Establishment as he is but I don't think the Liberals offer anything better. I'm a Suffragist, you see."

He was surprised more than shocked, although a trace of shock showed on his face. He said, "You surely don't mean you're one of Mrs. Pankhurst's women?"

"Well, not yet," Grace told him, laughing, "but certainly would be if I lived in town. I attended a few meetings in London, before I was married and I still get all the literature through the post, I even subscribe five guineas a year to the cause."

Roddy said, gaily, "Well, jolly good luck to you, Mrs. Craddock! Those politicians need a shake-up! I think you'll get the vote, if you keep tormenting them!" But John Rudd, who knew his son rather better than the latter was aware, was thinking, "Now why did he say that? He doesn't believe in women's votes any more than I do," and he smiled, thinking it amusing that a boy who had never had a serious thought in his head should be so obviously smitten by Grace Lovell, for he was still unable to think of her as Grace Craddock, any more than he could adjust himself to other changes of names in the Valley. He said, rising, "Well, I've work to do. We shan't see much of your husband for the next month! He can hardly wait to take a crack at Gilroy's nominee and I can't help feeling that Grenfell chap stands a chance this time," but when he proposed that Roddy should ask Mrs. Craddock to make him up a bed at the lodge Grace said, "Why does he have to do that? The spare bedroom there is like a cupboard and our guest rooms are hardly ever used!" and without waiting for his assent she went to find the housekeeper.

"Were you surprised to find that Paul Craddock was married, Roddy?" Rudd asked and when his son admitted that he was, he added, "Well, the truth is I've never liked

353

our Mrs. Craddock until lately and I suppose that was simply because she was a Lovell. I'm ready to admit, however, that I was prejudiced. It's been a much better match than I hoped."

"She was interested in the motor," Roddy said. "Imagine that! A woman like her, getting oil all over her hands!"

"Oh, she's very much in favour of the new century," John said, "but the Squire isn't and never will be! However, he's a good chap, and you'll like him. He's made a big difference to my life, I can tell you. It's the first time I've ever felt needed and I'm beginning to like it!"

Roddy looked at him with affection. They had seen very little of one another but the boy was not unaware of the source of his father's surliness, or the difference in him since Shallowford had changed hands. He said, as proof of their new relationship, "Look here, Gov'nor, I hope you've put that silly business about the Prince Imperial behind you! It's ancient history now and nobody my age has ever heard of the damned Frog! There was no future in the Army anyway and you were lucky to get clear of it. The Navy is the only thing that counts, the Army is just a glorified polo club."

John said, slowly, "Yes, Roddy, I have put that drumming-out business behind me but I only succeeded in doing it since the change-over here. As I say, I feel I've found a purpose in life after more than twenty years and it was Craddock who helped me find it. He's become a kind of son to me, you understand, and not only because of what I owe him but because I believe in what he's trying to do down here."

"What exactly is he trying to do?" Roddy asked, innocently. "I hear he has plenty of money and can't imagine why he doesn't want to cut a dash with it! Most fellows of his age would."

"I daresay," Rudd said defensively, "but Craddock isn't that kind of man. He's an anachronism maybe, but he's a sincere one and the country has to be nursed into the twentieth century, as well as the cities. Will you stop a day or two?"

"I'd like to," Roddy said but without adding that it was the prospect of driving the fetching Mrs. Craddock about the district and not an interest in a rural renaissance that attracted him.

II

Paul was enjoying the campaign more than he anticipated and this not solely because he was much encouraged by the local support Grenfell was getting. In spite of the Candidate's careful priming Paul mounted his first public platform with a shrinking sensation in his stomach but he soon realised that he was not expected to juggle with political issues but to act as a buffer between the Candidate and Tory hecklers, who followed them everywhere and did their utmost to prevent Grenfell getting a hearing. Soon he found himself looking forward to engagements, for James proved himself adroit at handling the opposition and, as Jorrocks might have put it, the campaign had all the excitement of war and only half the danger. The adoption meeting was an unqualified success. Several small landowners from the area north of Paxtonbury came forward with support and subscriptions and as they drove about the constituency Paul realised that they could count on the Nonconformist vote to a man, as well as on a proportion of the smaller tradesmen and professional men. Gradually, and with a wonderful display of patience, Grenfell mustered his array and by the first week of the campaign candidates were running neck-and-neck and local excitement was mounting. Lloyd George himself wired his promise to travel down for the eve-of-poll meeting, and after hearing the new Gilroy nominee speak, Paul's confidence in turning the tide grew with every meeting, so that he was caught up in the whirl of the battle, devoting every moment of his time and every ounce of his nervous energy, to presenting James Grenfell as the only fit and proper man to represent the constituency at Westminster.

The big farms provided their toughest opposition for the more successful farmers feared the entry of cheap food into the country and were thus fiercely Protectionist but among their labourers the Radicals made progress, although they had to work very carefully, for many of the men feared for their jobs if it became known that they would vote contrary to their employers' interests and this was especially so within Gilroy boundaries, where Grenfell was received like a poacher.

Paul's singlemindedness, and the enthusiasm that he could bring to the cause on account of his sincere admiration for Grenfell, kept him absent from home for the greater part of the month, so that he saw little of Grace and observed their unspoken pact not to involve her in a cause for which she lacked conviction. Sometimes, a little forlornly, he wished that James would openly espouse the cause of Women's Suffrage and bring Grace in but he did not, holding to his theory that, while universal franchise was bound to come, it was an issue that would cost precious votes and to some extent Paul agreed with him for whenever Women's Suffrage was raised at a meeting the issue was invariably greeted with derision. In the main they stuck doggedly to the major issues, Free Trade, Chinese labour in South Africa (where Paul's local knowledge was useful) and social legislation, including workmen's compensation in factories, better housing, public health and education. Now and then they touched on broader topics, like the Irish Question and the Kaiser's new fleet but these subjects had small appeal for countrymen who regarded the Irish as noisy clowns, the Germans as bandsmen and the Kaiser as a sausage-eating buffoon in an eagle-crested helmet. Germany's attempts to rival the British Navy was an even better joke than votes for women, for down here, within rumour reach of Devonport, most voters took a personal pride in Britain's ironclads and dressed their children in sailor suits with the names of dreadnoughts braided into the ribbon bands of their hats.

Paul had been introduced to young Rudd and privately considered him a rather shallow young man, preoccupied with explosive mechanical toys and moulded to a type by the traditions of the Senior Service. He lacked, he thought, John's steadiness and confused prejudices with judgments. The campaign had made Paul edgy and even Rudd, who had promised to vote for Grenfell, smiled at the Squire's lurch towards demagogery, but whereas Rudd was old enough to enjoy watching a young man get drunk on politics Grace was not, and Paul's obsession began to irritate her a little as the campaign moved to its climax.

"You really should try and keep a sense of proportion," she said to him one night, after he and Young Rudd had exchanged acrimonious views on the causes of the South African war. "After all, a Devon bye-election isn't the end of the world and Roddy is not only a guest but hardly more than a boy!"

"He's only a year younger than me, so it's high time somebody put him right on his facts!"

"He's had a Service upbringing," Grace argued, "and in my opinion he's weathered it very well! He isn't nearly as stuffy as most naval officers and at least he makes an effort to keep abreast of the times, which is more than I can say of you!"

He was outraged, if only momentarily, by her criticism. "Good God!" he said, "Roddy Rudd's political thought is lagging behind Palmerston's! He believes in sending gunboats to discipline natives! How can you say a thing like that?"

She said, with the moderation she always used when they disagreed, "He knows about motors and he's interested in flying, that's all I meant. There's nothing personal about it! I find him intelligent and he's been good company all the time you've been barnstorming. However, if you really dislike him, and want him to go, all you have to do is drop a hint to John!"

As usual when they approached an impasse Paul pulled back. Her championship of Roddy had pricked his self-esteem but he was hampered by the realisation that he had neglected her shamefully since the campaign had opened. "I don't dislike him," he said, "and I'm glad he's been fun for you but you must understand I've got to do all I can to help Jimmy Grenfell. He's got a terrific fight on his hands and every vote counts!"

"I don't quarrel with that in the least, Paul," she said, in the same quiet tone, "but please don't pretend that

357

you are making domestic sacrifices! I've never seen you enjoy anything so much!"

"Why does a thing have to become a drudgery before it qualifies as a virtue?" he demanded, asking the rhetorical question that millions of husbands had asked before him. "Damn it, that's the trouble with women . . ." but he stopped for she was now regarding him over her shoulder as she sat at her dressing-table mirror and he recognised her look at once. It recalled the Smut Potter issue and warned him that there was a boundary to their truce over which it might be unprofitable to stray. He said, grumpily, "You have to admit that it would be easier if man and wife could pull together on this kind of issue. After all, it is fundamental, isn't it?"

"No," she said, laying down her brush, "not in the least fundamental, Paul. If you haven't learned that after nearly eighteen months with me you can't have learned anything! *Your* kind of politics, Grenfell's and Gilroy's politics, aren't fundamental! That's what's wrong with them!"

"But yours are?" he countered. "The only fundamental issue in politics today is women's suffrage?"

"Now you're being very tiresome, Paul," she replied, wearily, but he was so nettled that he did not take her hint.

"Isn't that what you meant?"

"No," she said, very sharply now, "it isn't what I meant! Women's suffrage is very important to me but I concede that it isn't to you, or to your precious James Grenfell. There are plenty of fundamental issues but political parties dependent on a flow of wealth from one class or the other, aren't deeply concerned with them! Their impetus doesn't depend on a cause but on personal ambitions. That isn't true of you and it isn't true of Grenfell but it is true of all the other rabble rousers!" Then, with the edge of her voice blunted, "Do we have to prolong this stupid quarrel, Paul? It began over Roddy Rudd."

He had forgotten that and now that he thought about Rudd again, he realised that he had been rather boorish, and ought, perhaps, to be grateful to the young man for entertaining Grace while he devoted his attention to the campaign.

"I'm sorry, dear," he said, stooping and kissing her shoulder, "the fact is I'm overtired, and liable to fly off the handle. We're having to fight every step of the way and today was a bad day. We couldn't even get a hearing in Whinmouth."

She turned slowly on her stool and regarded him gravely.

"When is election day?" she asked and he told her on July 20th, about a fortnight from now.

"Do you remember a promise you made to me on our honeymoon, Paul? A promise you made the night we attended the ballet? You said that when the Company came to London we would go up to town for a few days."

He did not recall such a promise, although he did remember how much she had enjoyed the occasion. "Are they in London now?" he asked, knowing that he would have to refuse her and wondering how it could be gracefully achieved.

"No," she replied, to his relief, "but I hear they are to pay a two-night visit to Bristol soon. If they do, will you take me? No matter what?"

"Darling, of course I will," he said, happy to be out of it so cheaply and she replied, quietly, "Thank you, Paul, I should like that very much."

"As to Roddy," he said, "I admit I was a bit short with him, and as you say, he is a guest. I'll apologise to him in the morning!"

In the morning, however, one of Grenfell's runners arrived with sensational news. There had been a major split over policy in the local Tory Party and Sir Keith Cresswell, a wealthy manufacturer of agricultural machinery on the northern edge of the constituency, had declared for Free Trade, so that the balance was now tipped slightly in favour of the Radicals. In the excitement he forgot all about Roddy and all about the ballet, galloping off on Snowdrop to the Liberal headquarters, to be seen no more for three days for he was canvassing fifteen hours a day. To save journeys he slept at Grenfell's rooms in Cathedral Close each night.

That same day Roddy had an idea. It was fine and warm and he suggested that they should drive to a village near the Somerset border where a former shipmate of his, a young man who had recently come into money and left the Service, had just bought one of the latest models assembled by Charles Rolls, the man who had converted King Edward to motors.

"It should take us about three hours each way," he said, "and Branwell will give us lunch. He keeps a big place near Dulverton!"

Grace agreed to go and Roddy asked his father if he would accompany them but Rudd, with too much work on his hands, declined but promised to wait dinner for them. He watched them chug down the drive with Grace at the wheel, her wide straw hat tied on with a chiffon scarf and her body shrouded in a long white dustcoat, borrowed from Roddy. He thought, "I suppose I understand their enthusiasm for the honking, snorting little abortion! It's their world, one of machines and gadgets of one kind or another and Paul might as well invest in a motor, if only to keep her happy, for she seems to get plenty of fun out of Roddy's!" He made a mental note to suggest as much and this led him to a morose contemplation of Paul's entry into politics and the change it had wrought in him. It was only temporary, he hoped, for ordinarily the youngster was a tolerant, easy-going soul but the campaign had shattered the rhythm of the estate and this displeased him, for things had been progressing very well lately, particularly over at Four Winds, where the Eveleigh family were proving their worth. Life was quiet in the Coombe, too, now that Smut was out of the way and even Tamer seemed resigned to using hired labour and the equipment the estate had loaned him. It was years, John reflected, since Low Coombe fields had been properly ploughed and now the old rascal was said to be going in for sugar beet, as had Derwent, on his new cliff fields. Willoughby's lad was proving his mettle too, and so were Will and Elinor over at Periwinkle, whereas he had never seen the Home Farm so fruitful after its record lambing season and the introduction of a small Guernsey herd during the winter. It was a pity, he reflected, that Paul had to be absent now, when the promise of the Valley was so rich. Political issues were ephemeral but the land was always there, waiting to be loved, coaxed and cared for and he would have thought that Paul was old enough to get his values right. It did not occur to him, however, to give more than a casual thought to Roddy, driving off with an unchaperoned Grace, for he had never been able to take Roddy or his enthusiasms seriously. He was like his mother, who had romped through her short life without a thought beyond how pretty she looked and he wondered what she would have thought of her son and his obsession with mechanical toys. Then, remembering he was due at a sale across the county border, he forgot about Paul and the motorists and did not remember them again until a message reached him from Paul saying he would be away for the night and he was to tell Grace what had happened and how they now had a more than even chance of "giving old Gilroy a thrashing at the polls". He thought, "Much she'll care!" and ordered dinner for seven-thirty, returning to the lodge and sitting at his open window smoking as he watched the ford over which the Benz would come. Soon the heat went out of the day and the shadows of the chestnuts fell across the paddock but there was no sign of the motor. Grumpily, because he was both hungry and lonely, he trudged up to the house and ate a solitary meal. By nine o'clock he was irritated; by the time darkness had fallen he was worried and considering saddling up and riding along the river road down which they must come.

It would have availed him little. At that moment the Benz was stationary in a deep, leafy lane, fifteen miles north-west of Paxtonbury and about the same distance from the house where Roddy and Grace had lunched.

The outward journey had been made in record time, forty miles in one hour forty-five minutes, and after lunch Roddy's host had taken them for a drive in his Panhard, allowing Grace a turn at the wheel and encouraging her to coast over a flat stretch of moor at a speed just under forty miles per hour. They had returned about teatime and Roddy had persuaded Grace to stay for dinner, pointing out that the drive home would provide them with appetites for another at Shallowford. Branwell, his friend, had been so kind and hospitable that Grace did not like to refuse, so they made a latish start, taking a cross-country route aimed at the main road north of Paxtonbury. It was growing dusk when they stopped in the lane to light the big brass lamps and then, to Roddy's astonishment, the Benz refused to start. He swung her until he was wet with perspiration and had Grace hold one of the unscrewed lamps while he opened the bonnet and probed in the engine. It was no use. The Benz remained silent and Roddy said they would have to accept a humiliating tow from a cart-horse.

They set off together for the nearest farm but this proved all of three miles and when they got there the farmer, an unobliging fellow, declared that he had a market-day ahead of him and needed a fresh team for the twenty-mile journey to and from the city. He sent them on to another farm but they could get no response to their knocking and as it was now past eleven o'clock Grace said they had better return to the car and try in the opposite direction at dawn. She made very light of their dilemma, although Roddy was depressed by it and a little anxious about her reputation. When he mentioned this, however, she laughed and told him not to be stuffy, adding that both Paul and John would rejoice in the triumph of horse over motor.

Fortunately it was a fine night, with stars blazing and no breeze but under the trees, where they had left the Benz, it was pitch dark and they had to grope their way down the long lane towards the owlish glimmer of the lamps. All the way Roddy stammered apologies; he was an idiot, he ought to have set out before; he ought to have been capable of restarting the blasted car; she would think him a fine kind of escort to get her stranded in this ridiculous fashion, until at last she said, "Oh stop accusing yourself, Roddy! It's my fault as much as yours and anyway, I don't care that much! It's a long time since I had

362

any kind of adventure and if you want the truth I'm rather enjoying it!"

He was very thoughtful at this, interpreting it as meaning she found little joy in her life at Shallowford, or in marriage to that hectoring fellow Craddock who was such a crashing bore about politics. His experience with women, although fairly wide, did not include anyone like Grace who was calm, competent and beautiful but also so much wiser than any of the girls he had met voyaging round the Empire. She was essentially English but without the helplessness or the coyness of the average English country girl. She treated him as an equal but she did not try and flirt with him, as so many married women had done in the past and she was, moreover, genuinely interested in the really important things of life, such as petrol-driven engines and heavier-than-air machines. Looking back on the past two weeks it seemed to Roddy that they had known one another for years, that she was a kind of heaven-sent sister, but a sister who was able to disturb him in a way he had not yet been disturbed by a pretty woman. She had a stillness that he had not found in another human being, man or woman, and also a self-sufficiency that, in most girls, would have intimidated him but in her could be dissolved by a single light-hearted remark so that she was both attainable and unattainable. He could even marry a woman like that and decided that Craddock, who did not seem to appreciate her uniqueness, did not deserve his luck. He supposed she had married him for his money and yet as he continued to reflect on their relationship as man and wife, he could not help wondering whether Craddock would be capable of rousing her as he felt himself capable of doing, given the opportunity.

His musings had made him very thoughtful during their progress back to the car and it was only when they arrived there, and had made one more unsuccessful attempt to start the engine, that he realised the open Benz would afford inadequate shelter for the night and suggested sitting under the bank and lighting a fire to ward off the night chill. She said this was a good idea but that it had better be at a safe distance from the car. A hundred yards back they had passed a shelter of the kind used by sportsmen on a winter

363

shoot and she suggested they should return there and seek help at first light. He was just the slightest bit shocked by this suggestion but accepted it eagerly enough so they took the unscrewed lamp and retraced their steps to a three-sided shelter built on the edge of a wood above the level of the road. Here, in the glow of the lamp, they got a small fire going and in its light saw that the hide was carpeted with dry bracken. They went inside, sitting with their backs to the log wall and watching the fire flicker in the opening. She refused the loan of his coat, declaring that she was quite warm and when he suggested that she should try and sleep she said that she did not feel sleepy and would rather talk. As she said this she came a little closer to him, leaning some of her weight on his shoulder, so that he began to think benignly of the obstinate ignition of the Benz.

She had taken off her hat, tying her scarf about her neck and the scent of her hair mingled with the pleasant tang of resin and burning twigs, so that he found it very easy to convince himself that all she awaited was his seizure of the initiative. Yet the courage to take it eluded him and he wondered if he was losing his touch, as they talked of one thing and another and the scent of her hair stole upon him like incense, so that he found himself growing vague and leaving her questions unanswered. At last, when the fire had burned low, he made a rather clumsy essay to get things going. Turning, he tilted her chin and kissed her lips. He kissed them expertly, or so he thought, but the kiss did not seem to give him the licence he needed, so he kissed her again, this time extending his arm round her shoulder and slipping his hand under her breast. Gently she disengaged herself, saying, with laughter in her voice, "You can have my lips, Roddy, but no more! I'm very comfortable here and not inclined to spend the remainder of the night wrestling with you!"

He was very piqued at this, muttering, "I don't know what to make of you, Grace! You put a fellow in an intolerable situation!" and she laughed again, saying, "Come, be fair, Roddy! *I* didn't get us in this situation, I'm just making the best of it, so why don't you?"

"Because you obviously don't intend to let me," he said, his sense of humour reasserting itself.

"No, I don't, Roddy, but not for my sake, or even Paul's."

"Whose then?"

"For yours and your father's."

"Now where the devil does the Guv enter into it?"

"Because he's proud of you and very fond of Paul! In addition, he doesn't wholly approve of me although I believe he is beginning to!"

"Then he must be senile," Roddy said, "because any man between twenty and sixty ought to approve of you! I did, the moment I set eyes on you and now . . . well, now I'm very much in love with you, Grace!" He felt her shrink a little at this so he went on, hurriedly, "I know I don't stand any sort of chance and that you aren't in the least in love with me but you can't blame a chap wanting to make something of an opportunity like this! I've never met anyone the least bit like you before, Grace."

He waited, feeling that he had said enough and she was silent for some time. Finally she said, "You aren't in the least in love with me, Roddy! Paul is, but you aren't and I don't think you'll be capable of loving anyone until you're about thirty-five! *Then* you might, when you're had your fill of gadding about. You might even make someone a very charming husband!"

"How can you know that?" he demanded, irritably.

"How? I imagine because I've never been in love myself and that gives me a rather special kind of detachment. I made a misjudgment, Roddy, and my only excuse is that I didn't, as you probably imagine, marry Paul for money. I really did think myself capable of making a success of it and in a way I suppose I have, or still could! What I won't do, however, is to make a fool of him the conventional way, or console myself by imagining that I can still try elsewhere and involve somebody I like, such as you. You don't understand love, Roddy. You could make love to me here, and persuade yourself it was extra-physical, and as for me, well—I'm sensual enough to enjoy it more than you but what could it lead to but self-deception on your part and cheapness on mine? No, Roddy, my dear, we shall have to behave I'm afraid, whether we like it or not!" and she settled herself comfortably against his shoulder and half-closed her eyes, looking out at the dull glow of the fire and the blue blackness of the trees on the opposite bank.

Her bland summarisation had a finality that divorced this from any parallel situation in his past. He had never thought deeply about anything but her honesty appealed so strongly to his commonsense that he remained silent, and presently (incredibly when he looked back on the occasion) he dozed but she remained awake, half-aware of the night scuffles of hunters in the wood behind them and the blaze of stars in the gap of sky between the belts of trees. She thought, "He's just another Paul but he'll never suffer like Paul! All the men I met when I was capable of being hurt were so-called men of the world, who enjoyed putting the screw on women, but now that I have learned to give as good as I get all I meet are boys with men's bodies! There ought to be some kind of half-way house between these extremes but there isn't. One has to settle for one or the other. If Paul could see me now he would never believe how innocent Roddy was and would still be if I did let him take me in his arms but thank God he's kind enough not to exploit the situation." She found that she could think of Roddy Rudd objectively, as she had often thought of Paul in the last few months, and of how he would have behaved had she given him the chance. The speculation amused her a little, for Roddy, thinking himself such a ladies' man, would surely pride himself on a fancied technique but his love-making would probably lack Paul's masculine approach, which was something she had deliberately fostered knowing that Paul Craddock would always need an injection of confidence in everything he attempted. She half wished it was possible for a woman like herself to experiment with men. It would be interesting, she thought, to really know men, all kinds of men, and acquire knowledge in such a simple way. All they needed to persuade them that they were godlike was a little physical flattery and one could practise in gratifying them in this respect. The fire was a heap of red ash now and disengaging herself from the sleeping Roddy she moved to the entrance of the hut to replenish it, sitting there watching the sky pale and wondering what she should tell Paul and John Rudd of this escapade. Perhaps it would be better to lie and pretend they had spent the night with Roddy's friend, Branwell. He was an ex-sailor and could easily be persuaded to back the story, and thinking this she was relieved that she would not have to comfort Paul with real lies.

It was almost light when she heard the far-off jingle of harness and returned to the motor to see a startled carter horse had shied at the Benz blocking its path. The man was delighted to accept a half-sovereign for a tow to the main road and she left him attaching a drag rope to the motor. After washing herself in a brook and brushing the bracken fronds from her coat she woke the snoring Roddy.

"It's all arranged," she said, "a man is giving us a tow and you can probably get her started when we can get to a slope."

He sat up, rubbing his eyes, looking so bemused that she laughed.

IV

Paul, although reluctant to admit it, was beginning to be disenchanted with politics. He believed what he preached, and desired most earnestly to send Grenfell to Westminster, but his commonsense bucked at the racket and claptrap of the campaign and the ranting of half-intoxicated supporters of both candidates who swaggered about shouting their silly catch-phrases at one another. The business of government, he told himself, ought not to depend upon this kind of thing, upon the moods and impulses of leather-lunged yokels marching up and down with their banners and chanting doggerel like:

> Vote, vote, vote for Jimmy Gren-fellllll!
> Kick Verne-Jonesy out the door . . . !

but obviously it did so depend, and scenes like this were repeated all over the country at a General Election. Later, he supposed, all the Jimmy Grenfells and Verne-Joneses who had out-shouted and out-postured each other at the hustings forgot their rivalry in the genteel atmosphere of the House of Commons, where real policies were formulated in cold blood. The more strident the campaign became the less he could identify himself with it, and at last he was obliged to carry his misgivings to Grenfell who, as it happened, had a rational explanation on the tip of his tongue.

"It's simply the price one has to pay for the use of democratic machinery, Paul," he said. "Under an autocracy you could dispense with it. A man would become one of the legislators by reason of wealth or position in a particular locality but now that all adult males have the vote this farcical nonsense is inevitable! It's really quite harmless, you know, and it does jolt some of the more thoughtful into making an honest and deliberate choice. I've heard people like you ask why we need parties at all or why a man like me can't judge every issue on its merits but whenever you get more than a score of men together they tend to divide into groups thinking roughly along the same lines. Then, hey presto, you have a political party and all the trimmings!"

Half satisfied with this Paul went back to his canvassing and stumping, drawing comfort from his belief in James Grenfell's integrity, for Grenfell did indeed practise restraint, rarely resorting to platform tricks and it now looked as if his careful nursing of the constituency was bearing fruit, for he was said to be leading the Tory Bernard Verne-Jones by a short head and the odds were five to four in favour of a Liberal victory. Once or twice, in his movements about the country, Paul's path crossed that of Gilroy and on one occasion, on a Paxtonbury market-day, he saw the crusty old patrician drive his brougham through a milling crowd about Martyr's Cross, on the Cathedral Green. He could not help admiring the old man's bearing, as contemptuous as that of a French aristocrat in a tumbril. The crowd surrounding the carriage was part hostile and there was a good deal of catcalling and booing but the expression on Gilroy's face remained impassive. He might, thought Paul, be taking a drive across Blackberry Moor, or paying an afternoon call on a duchess. He sat erect, enclosed in his aloof, glacial cage that was proof against plaudits and insults. Grenfell, standing beside Paul, said admiringly, "Well Paul, there goes the last of eighteenth-century England! You want to take off your hat to it, don't you?"

It was that same day that Paul had his brief and rather mystifying conversation with Farmer Venn, pot-bellied supporter from a farm a mile or so north of the city, whom he had met in the early stages of the campaign. He was eating a sandwich lunch at The Mitre when Venn waddled in, his broad chest half-covered by a huge yellow rosette and he greeted Paul heartily as he ordered ale and pasties.

"A rare ole fix your good lady was in t'other mornin'," said Venn jovially. " 'Er an' that young shover o' yourn an' their ole motor! Crawling along behind Ned Parsons' cart they was, an' at two mile an hour all the way to Norton Edge bevore they managed to get 'er goin'! 'Twas news to me you'd got yourself one o' they ole stinkpots, Squire!"

"I hadn't heard of their breakdown," Paul said, so far only slightly puzzled, "but I haven't been home much lately. And it isn't my car, Venn, it belongs to my agent's son, a naval lieutenant. Where did you see them?"

"Coming up the hill, towards Norton Edge backalong," Ven told him. "Early on, it was, as I was comin' in to market, an' both lookin' pretty sorry for 'emselves! Tiz a rare come-down to be towed home by a grey mare when they'm all so pleased to talk about 'horse-power', baint it?"

Having heard nothing about the incident Paul's impulse was to question Venn further but then it seemed to him that this would make him look ridiculous in Venn's eyes and perhaps start a rumour about Grace's relationship with that young idiot, Roddy, so he drank his beer and hurried away but found it difficult to give his mind to the chairmanship of meetings during the afternoon and excused himself at teatime, telling Grenfell that he had an accumulation of work at home and wanted to clear it before preparing for the eve-of-poll meeting.

He learned, on arrival at the lodge, that Roddy had left for London earlier in the day but Rudd was evasive when he asked about the breakdown, saying, off-handedly, "Oh, I believe they had several about the country, Paul. Motors aren't all that reliable, you know, but I daresay we shall have to have one in the end!"

"Over Snowdrop's dead body!" Paul told him and sought out Grace, less disturbed by the realisation that she must have spent a night away from home without telling him than by Rudd's implied championship of the motor. He found her alone in the rose garden, absorbed in her work and when he walked round the lily pond she looked up saying, "Hullo! I didn't expect you until after midnight!"

"I decided to take an evening off," he said and wondered how a husband began asking the kind of questions he wanted to ask whilst leaving room to manœuvre. He said carefully, "A farmer came to me today with a silly story about you and Roddy having to be towed home one day last week," and found himself watching her eyes for signs of guilt. She gave a shrug and dusted earth from her gardening gloves.

"It wasn't a silly story, Paul, it was quite true. We were stranded overnight and a cart towed the Benz half-way to Paxtonbury."

He was startled and showed it. "When was this?" and she told him last Friday, the night he sent a message saying that he would be staying with Grenfell.

"Why on earth didn't you tell me about it?"

"Why? I suppose partly because I didn't have a real opportunity, and partly because I thought you might put a wrong construction on it, as you seem to be doing now."

"Is that unreasonable?"

"I think it is."

It was clear that she considered him ridiculous in the role of the outraged husband and was determined not to rise to the bait but he read in her impassivity an evasiveness that was not there. He said, shortly, "You can imagine what a fool I felt, having to stand in a public bar and hear about my own wife coming home with the milk! Doesn't that mean anything to you? Don't you care if I'm made to look as if I enjoy my wife gallivanting all over the country with a young idiot in a motor?"

She looked at him compassionately now but he was too angry and humiliated to notice it.

"Yes, I care, Paul," she said, quietly, "I care very much, but in this case my share of the blame is confined to not telling you about it and for that I apologise. Now I think we'd better go in."

He followed her along the flagstones and across the corner of the paddock to the terrace. When they were inside the library he said, petulantly, "Well, what *did* happen? Were you stranded at that friend of Roddy's? John told me you had paid a call there."

The white lie she had intended telling him changed colour with his attitude and now she felt under an obligation to tell him the insignificant truth.

"As a matter of fact we were stranded half-way between there and home," she said, "and spent the night in the open."

"Roddy and you?"

For a moment he was too outraged to speak. When he did the violence of his tone surprised her. "What do you mean *'in the open'*? How could he let such a thing happen? And how could you be a partner to it?"

"It wasn't Roddy's fault," she said wearily, "it was just bad luck. The car broke down miles from anywhere and we couldn't get help . . . We tried but there was no alternative."

"You were together in that damned motor all night?"

For the first time since he had challenged her, she could smile.

"No, not in the motor, Paul. We found somewhere a little more comfortable."

She had not said this with the intention of goading him but he reacted as if she had, taking her by the arm so that at once the smile left her eyes. "Please don't act like that, Paul!" and she wrenched herself free yet still contrived to give the impression that she was in control of herself. She said, more patiently, "Do we really have to go on with this, Paul? Are you interested in chapter and verse?"

"Yes I am," he shouted, "what husband wouldn't be?"

"Very well then. There was a pheasant hide close by that offered some kind of shelter. We lit a fire and stayed

371

there until it was light. Then a cart came along and pulled us on to the main road and on a hill Roddy managed to start the motor so we got home about breakfast time. It wasn't as romantic as it sounds, just the kind of thing that might happen to any pair of travellers. At least, I thought so at the time."

"And that's all?"

For the first time she seemed to resent his questions and her jaw hardened. "What am I supposed to read into that? That Roddy is my lover? Is that what you're trying to make me say?" He was so taken aback by this that it was plain to her he had no clear idea what he believed and again she felt compassion for him, although it astonished her to discover that a man could share her life for more than a year but learn so little that was important about her.

"Roddy wasn't my lover, then or at any time, but if you can't bring yourself to believe that there's nothing I can do about it, Paul. I'm sorry, but there it is," and she walked past him and out of the room.

He stood there cursing himself and her; himself for his hamfisted approach, her for allowing herself to be squired by a man whose incompetence involved women in compromising situations. For it was a compromising situation, as even she had tacitly admitted by withholding the facts from him, although he did not doubt her innocence for a moment. There was no reason, however, why anyone else should believe in it; Farmer Venn, for instance, or the carter who found them, or even John Rudd, whose evasiveness regarding the incident he now recalled. The thought of another man spending the night in a pheasant hide with his wife annoyed him but it did not frighten him, as it might have scared a man married to an unpredictable woman. For Grace was predictable, at least as regards fundamentals. She had always been candid with him, even when he would have secretly preferred her not to be and it was this that baffled him, the fact that, but for Venn's chance remark in the pub, he might never have discovered that she had spent a night in the woods with the type of man likely to boast about the experience. It was the thought of Roddy, and the ease with which he had cap-

372

tured and held her interest from the moment he came honking up the drive, that crystallised his resentment and it was not resentment against her for a single indiscretion but for their failure, after more than a year, to achieve harmony as individuals. She was his wife in bed and about the house and garden but beyond these narrow limits they shared nothing and while, for some men, this was enough to make a marriage work, for him it was not. Here he was, striving to make a way of life for both of them, while she continued, in her secret way, to deride him and the Roddy incident, so trivial in itself, emphasised the cleavage. He thought, wretchedly, "If this divergence continues there can be no real happiness for either of us! God knows, I've been patient but where has patience led me? To within a few inches of being cuckolded by a lady-killer who uses a blasted motor instead of a bouquet. I'll be damned if I give way again, the way I did over the Potter affair, the election, and everything else that gives purpose to my being here!" and he flung himself into the office and tried to cool his temper assaulting the accumulation of work in the desk-trays.

Yet, as a measure of calmness returned to him, he did not relent towards her or not in the real sense. When he went upstairs about eleven o'clock she was reading in bed and he was still inclined to deliver an unrehearsed ultimatum and would probably have done so had she not fore-stalled him by laying the book aside, looking across at him mildly, and saying, "It was very wrong of me not to have made a point of telling you, Paul. Will you believe me if I say I'm genuinely sorry about that?" and again he felt he had lost the initiative. He said, "Yes, of course I believe you. I realise you have far more dignity than to let a man like Rudd take advantage of you but that isn't the real issue, Grace!" He was standing at the foot of the bed, feet astride and hands behind his back, and for a moment it was all she could do to stop herself laughing at his un-conscious caricature of an outraged husband as depicted by Mrs. Braddon or Mrs. Henry Wood. The moment passed, however, for he went on, "It's your whole attitude to our life down here, to what I'm bent on doing and what I've set my heart on. I don't just mean the political aspect

373

but everything, the estate, the attempt to . . . well . . . to *create* something lasting and rewarding."

"I've never concealed the truth from you about that," she said. "You know very well I could never see it through your eyes, Paul."

"You could try!"

"I have tried, far harder than you imagine."

"You haven't tried hard enough, Grace! Take this election; you aren't committed to the Party but I am and as your husband I'm entitled to at least a pretence of support from you."

"I've never been the least good at pretending, Paul. That's something you should have learned by now."

"But damn it, lots of wives aren't deeply interested in what their husbands are doing but they make some kind of show. They stand beside them once in a while!"

She said, slowly, "I don't think it's much use prolonging this argument, Paul, at least, not in your present mood. Perhaps it won't seem so vital in the morning!" and she reached out an arm with the object of turning her bedside lamp out.

"Leave that light alone!" he snapped. "I tell you this *is* vital, Grace, and it won't seem less so in the morning! Are you prepared to discuss it or aren't you?"

He had never addressed her in this tone and she was more astonished than hurt, probing among the probable reasons for the loss of his sense of humour and the male tenderness that had been his most endearing characteristic. She was angry because hectoring always angered her yet she retained a very real regard for his sincerity and it was this that kept her temper in check. They faced one another in silence for a moment and it was as though each hesitated to push the quarrel further but then it seemed to her that so they might stand for ever, unless she made a gesture, something that, however inappropriate, would restore the delicate balance of their relationship. She said, "That ballet company, Paul, they are due in Bristol on Thursday for two nights so I wrote off for tickets. I think you badly need a change and I'm sure it would help us put this nonsense behind us before we start saying unforgivable things to one another. Will you take me, as you promised?"

It was probable that, had the approach been made earlier, he would have surrendered but he was under no illusions as to what surrender would mean. It would be the final acceptance of a measure of spiritual isolation down the years ahead and they were still young, and there were many years, too many to renounce all hopes of the full partnership on which he had set his heart. He said, miserably, "Thursday is eve-of-poll and Friday is polling day. I couldn't be away from here until Saturday but that doesn't mean you can't go, if you have to. It seems to me, however, that we could make a better start by you joining me on the platform at the rally on Thursday. You do what you think best, Grace," and he picked up his robe and walked out of the room, making his way along the corridor to the guestroom beyond the nursery. Simon's cot was visible through the half-open door with a night-light burning under a pink glass between cot and door. He hesitated outside but he did no more than glance inside. At that moment the child did not seem to belong to either of them.

V

The eve-of-poll rally was scheduled to open with a small-fry warm-up at seven-thirty. Paul, and several other local speakers, had undertaken to keep the audience occupied until nine o'clock, the earliest hour the candidate could be expected to arrive with the Great Man, for Lloyd George had wired that he would cover the last five miles of the journey by four-horse brake and act as chairman for Grenfell on the last stage of his eve-of-poll tour. The Tory Party had not succeeded in getting anyone of comparable weight into the West and Grenfell's foresight had baulked them of the opportunity to hold an equally big rally for he had booked the only large hall months ago and the opposition was reduced to an open-air gathering in the cattle market. Liberal luck was in flow during those last few days for the weather turned dull and showery, to the delight of the nine hundred ticket-holders queueing outside the Drill Hall hours before the doors were opened.

Paul, as chairman, welcomed the responsibility thrust upon him, for at least it kept thoughts of Grace at bay and when the meeting commenced and he faced the difficult task of controlling a restive audience (in addition to a few hecklers who had slipped in with forged tickets), his nervous energy was fully deployed. He had never addressed a meeting of this size or importance, certainly not without Grenfell's professional support. He was no more than adequate as public speaker but tonight he was better than he imagined for all that was needed was a summary of the candidate's achievement in local government, his fitness for wider horizons and the unique treat in store for everyone present—that of seeing and hearing the most celebrated firebrand in the country.

Paul himself had been looking forward to the occasion, for Lloyd George's brazen attacks upon the Boer War had made him a byword among the troops overseas and since then hardly a day had passed without examples of his wit, impudence and debating skill providing headlines for the newspapers. It was known, for instance, that he had attacked privilege in a hundred dynamic speeches, that he had hounded Joe Chamberlain up hill and down dale, had trounced the brewers financing the Tories, had even challenged the Lords and cocked a snook at Royalty, generally keeping the country in an uproar. Grenfell's success in getting such a lion to the remote province was the best card he could have played and as soon as news of the visit was made public the betting on a Liberal victory shortened from five-to-four to two-to-one.

The stewards, to Paul's relief, soon disposed of the scattered hecklers and the stop-gap speakers, inveighing against the sins of the Government and howling for Free Trade and Irish Home Rule, gave him a chance to scan faces in the hope of recognising Grace among the converted. It was just possible, he told himself, that she had taken advantage of his order to Chivers to bring the carriage and pair into town by the time the meeting began and, being Grace, she might have entered the hall by the speakers' door and taken her place among the anonymous at the back. They had not reopened the quarrel during the last few days but had said very little to one another during the brief intervals that he had been at home. He thought it possible that she might have gone to Bristol by herself but more likely remained at home, nursing her imagined grievances. At last he saw Chivers sidle in by the platform door and take his stand behind one of the side benches and then there was a stir at the back of the hall and a great shout went up as Grenfell marched down the centre aisle and behind him, hardly able to progress because of the hysterical surge on either side, came the Great Man himself, short, thick-set, smiling and apparently well satisfied with his reception. As he mounted the platform the audience threw off all restraint, rising to their feet and roaring a welcome so that Paul, after a formal handshake, indicated by gesture that it was useless to began a speech of introduction and that Grenfell must take over from here on. Grenfell was given an almost equally enthusiastic reception but wisely limited his speech to a simple statement of his intentions if returned the following day. Then, to the accompaniment of another prolonged roar, he ushered Lloyd George forward and the famous Welshman began to weave his spell about the hall, his first words compelling a hush that seemed frightening after such a din.

He began very quietly, his soft, persuasive voice seeming to reach out and caress the rows of upturned faces, as he spoke of the certain dawn of the Celtic revival, of the kinship of Welshmen and Westcountrymen, of the rising clamour for justice and security in a world of plenty that, for centuries past, had been reserved for the wealthy, the privileged and their nominees at Westminster. It was not a political address so much as an inspired fairy-tale, related by a man who not only knew every trick in the book but could use subtle inflexions and wide, graceful gestures to highlight the pathos of the story and point the way to the infinite possibilities that lay ahead for a race already the envy of every community in the world. His theme was The People, a majority poised to enter the ark of the covenant of Democracy. He extolled their patience, their courage and their determination to transform the social pattern of Britain but without—and here his voice gained

377

volume—without resort to pike and tumbril and without endangering gains won since the ancestors of all those present had sweated as villeins on acres stolen from The People! He said that there had been an awakening among some who had been their masters for so long and that a few of the unselfish landowners (such as their young chairman tonight) had already espoused the cause and were marching with them, and at this direct reference Paul found himself hoping very much that Grace was present, so that he missed a searing comment on the enclosures of common land that must have had local relevance for a growl of anger rose up and was instantly checked by one of the speaker's swift, heaven-pointing gestures. And then Lloyd George began to speak of the candidate, turning to smile paternally upon Grenfell, asserting that he and Grenfell had much in common for both, he understood, had known what it was to hoard their pennies to buy an education and that Grenfell was the type of man so badly needed in Westminster, a man of The People, with The People's interests at heart! By this time tomorrow, he went on, "as sure as the sun will set over these beautiful Westcountry uplands", they would have a champion in Westcountry whom they could trust to work selflessly and unstintingly in their interests, in their children's interests, and, above all, a man in step with the march of the twentieth century!

It was difficult to determine whether the speaker had intended to finish on this flourish for at these words the tension broke and suddenly everyone in the hall was on his feet, surging and swaying towards the platform, so that stewards, poised for such an emergency, had to rush in from all sides to head off a dangerous stampede. Paul slipped down to floor level to help and almost at once was buffeted against Chivers, who clutched at him as if he was a lifebelt and the two of them were swept involuntarily on through the exit that had been flung open to ease the pressure inside the building. Chivers said breathlessly, "God Almighty, sir, I never saw aught like this bevore! Nor my old dad neither, notwithstanding his tales o' bygone elections! I brought the trap, not the carriage, sir.

The new cob would have dragged her feet all the way back after two outings, I reckon!"

"You mean the carriage has been out today?" said Paul, breathless and rather irritated by the change. "How far did Mrs. Craddock drive?"

"Why to the station, upalong," the man said, "with her heavy luggage. I would have taken her in the trap but there wasn't room to stow the baggage, sir!"

The din from the hall beat across Paul's brain like breakers and in the wild confusion about him only a word or two registered so that he took Chivers by the arm and dragged him round to the rear of the hall, where the uproar was partially subdued. Bewilderment made him sound furious. "What happened, Chivers? Never mind about what's going on in there, just explain why you brought the trap instead of the brougham, as I ordered!"

Chivers peaked face stared up at him in the glow of the gas lamp above the platform entrance. The man's wits seemed lost in the noise and excitement.

"It's like I said, sir I had to use both cobs for the brougham and I didn't reckon they could stand the fifteen-mile trip here and back tonight, not after taking Mrs. Craddock up over the moor to the station! I know you give orders for the brougham, sir, but there wasn't room in the trap for Madam's luggage."

The gist of the groom's stuttered explanation filtered through to him. Grace had needed the brougham to convey luggage to Sorrel Halt and she would not have taken heavy luggage for a two-day trip to Bristol. The transport of her and her trunks in the brougham, instead of the trap, could only mean one thing. She had left home for a prolonged period.

The effort needed to absorb the shock was the more difficult inasmuch as he was prevented from advertising astonishment or alarm to Chivers, who seemed no more than puzzled by his master's failure to excuse his switch of vehicles. Paul said, quickly, "Mrs. Craddock must have changed her plans, she intended going on Saturday. She probably left a message with Mrs. Handcock." And then, sharply, "Bring the trap round here now. We shall be going home in a few minutes," and he climbed the steps

379

into the band-room behind the platform, shouldering his way through a crowd of party workers until he saw Grenfell standing talking to the treasurer. He said, briefly, "I must have a word with you at once, James!" and they edged into the scullery where the Women's League were brewing tea in huge urns and here they could hardly see one another for steam.

"I shall have to go home at once, James," Paul said. "I'm sorry but I can't avoid it. You can manage without me now, can't you?"

Grenfell, struck by his expression, said, "It's nothing serious I hope, Paul?" and Paul replied, "Serious to me, Jimmy! Grace has left home. We had a quarrel, partly over this business, but I never dreamed . . . well, I can't burden you with my domestic troubles at a moment like this, I just wanted you to know I couldn't stay and may not be able to get over tomorrow."

He was grateful for the man's serenity. Most people, he thought, would have plagued him with questions and offered a choice of fatuous possibilities but all Grenfell said was, "Of course, and please don't worry about me. It's decided now one way or the other and we've got all the transport we need for tomorrow. I'll get in touch with you the moment I can and I'm sorry, Paul, truly sorry."

He had no opportunity to say more for one of the local secretaries spotted him through the steam and shouted, "Hi, there, Jimmy! There's to be a torchlight procession! They're getting drag-ropes on the wain now!" and Paul thought, "What the devil am I doing here anyway? How childish it all seems, and how vulgar and noisy!" and he thrust his way into the cool night air, half-running down to the Close and standing at the junction of Angel and Resurrection Streets, until Chivers should appear with the trap. He was sweating and trembling and the dull roar coming from the Drill Hall was like the clash of gongs inside his head. He thought, savagely, "I must get hold of myself! I mustn't let Chivers see what's really happened! It would be all over the estate by morning and suppose there was nothing in it? Suppose she had just decided to take a trip to town and give this idiotic quarrel a chance to blow over or teach me a lesson?" Yet he knew that this was not so, that there was a measure of finality in what she had done and that it would take all his tact and persuasion and pleading to induce her to return on even the old terms. The certainty of this made him grind his teeth for he now saw himself humiliated as never before in the face of every man, woman and child in the Valley; a squire who had stepped into the shoes of the Lovells and had been deserted by his own wife, herself a Lovell.

The steady clip of the cob's shoes on the cobbles made him aware of Chivers' approach and he climbed on to the box, saying gruffly, "I'll drive and for God's sake let's get away from this pandemonium!" and Chivers glanced at him curiously. He was not a sensitive man but was puzzled to find the Squire in such an ill-humour after such a personal triumph. He said, respectfully, as they descended the hill outside the town, "They say Grenfell will win, sure enough, sir. If 'ee does it'll be your doing as much as his!"

"He'll win right enough," Paul grunted, "but tonight I've had enough of it, Chivers! Let's get on home, let's get clear of it!" and he whipped the cob into a trot as they breasted the level stretch that led on to the first fold of the moor.

CHAPTER TWELVE

I

ALL that autumn and the winter that followed there was a conspiracy of sympathy in the Valley. Nobody could have said how it communicated itself to Paul, or how and where it originated but it was there, perhaps the first bittersweet fruits of his stay among them. It was this, more than anything, that encouraged him to hold on.

He owed little enough to time or to the counsel of the more articulate of his friends, men like John Rudd, James

Grenfell or even Uncle Franz, who wrote several sympathetic letters before the one that brought Paul post-haste to London. It was as well, perhaps, that this letter did not arrive until spring, for by then the link between himself and the people of the Valley had helped him to climb to his feet again and take stock of the future. Without it he might have continued to brood until his thoughts festered and destroyed him.

It was strange, in view of his active role in the election, that he should have been one of the last to learn of James Grenfell's resounding victory at the polls. It was Mrs. Handcock who enlightened him long after he had arrived home to find no note and no message, nothing but half-empty wardrobes and a dressing-table swept clean of feminine clutter. She had gone, and that was all that could be said. Gone, God alone knew where, and although reason told him that this was monstrous and ridiculous, that it was the gesture of a hysterical woman and that she was not given to theatrical gestures, he was certain in his own mind that she would never come back and that threats and promises would leave her unmoved. For this was the sum total of the little she had taught him of herself.

It was pathetically plain that Mrs. Handcock had no idea of the finality of what had happened, was unaware that there had been more than a lovers' tiff between them. She bustled in with his breakfast the day after the election announcing, "Well, you won so I yer!" and when he replied with a noncommittal grunt she decided that he was disappointed with the statistics of the victory and waddled out again, seeking out Horace for further enlightenment. Horace, with his sensitive nose for scandal, guessed the source of Squire's ill-humour at once.

"Tiz about her running off, Ada," he confirmed, rubbing the nose that made him the Shallowford oracle, "tiz her doin' an' tiz taaken the 'eart out o' the boy! Mark my words, Ada, tiz a bigger up-and-a-downer than you give me to understand! They've had but a rare ole bust-up, and us baint heard the last of it!"

She soon realised that he was right. Day after day, as Paul lounged about the house, she noticed that he had been at the decanter during office hours, that the swing had gone from his step, and that when he addressed any member of the staff there was a hesitancy in voice and manner that belonged to his first uncertain days among them.

Then, after John Rudd had rushed off and reappeared a day or so later with his motor-mad son in tow, the alarming truth spread through kitchen, stable-yard and gardens, whence it crossed the paddocks to the Home Farm and into the Valley beyond, rumours that crept along belly to ground and the first of these was also the most obvious, involvement with the agent's son. Soon, however, there were fresh rumours, the most persistent being the refusal of Squire's wife to have another child and, when Horace Handcock pooh-poohed this, came whispers of a lover or lovers in London. Finally the Valley found itself discussing the most bizarre explanation of all—a bitter cleavage of political thought, brought to the surface by the triumph of the Valley Liberals.

It was natural that Paul should think of Roddy first and just as understandable that John Rudd should deny it and set about proving his point. Nothing would stop him hurrying off to Portsmouth and bringing his son back like a fugitive under escort. Roddy was scared, not by the threat of scandal but by his father's attitude for he had never seen him so truculent and vindictive but he had no trouble persuading him that he was innocent of any part in Grace Craddock's abdication, saying that during their drives she had never spoken disloyally of Paul and Rudd realised the boy himself was astonished by what had happened. For all that he insisted on Roddy confronting Paul and they met, the three of them, in the library, an hour after father and son had returned. By this time however Roddy was exasperated and said, indignantly, "I give you my word of honor, Mr. Craddock, I haven't set eyes on your wife since I left here! She hasn't written or communicated with me in any way and she doesn't even know my address." Then, seeing Paul and his father exchange glances, he added, sulkily, "Mrs. Craddock isn't the slightest bit interested in me if that is any consolation to you!"

It was not for Paul, feeling that he had been made to

look even more ridiculous by his agent's confrontation, had to apologise on Rudd's behalf and thank Roddy for coming right across country on such a fool's errand. He realised then that he had been a fool to suspect the boy. He was not the kind of man to hold Grace's interest for more than a day or so, and her temporary absorption with him had its origin more in the motor than its owner.

After Roddy had gone Rudd spoke very frankly. "I did what I could to warn you when this began," he declared, "and I say this even though I realise that to come between a man and his wife is unforgivable! She never did belong here, Paul, any more than the Lovells belonged! It was no more to her than a pleasant place to spend a summer's day and as to loyalty, as people like you understand it, no member of that family ever possessed any! It's not their fault, I suppose. At fifty I've come to realise people like you can't help their temperaments but if I was in your shoes, hard as it sounds, I should wipe the slate, boy! I wouldn't waste an hour looking for her!"

Paul took this harsh advice more impassively than Rudd had anticipated, saying, "That's easy enough to say, John, for you never trusted her, did you? As for me, I happen to be in love with her, although I fully appreciate all you say about the streak in the family. It's a kind of congenital amorality, an opting out of the ordinary rules that most of us take for granted. Old Sir George, that boy Ralph of his, Bruce Lovell, and now Grace prove as much. But there were times, many times, when I thought she was fond of me, or all events respected me."

"Well, I'll tell you something else," Rudd said, unhappily. "I never trusted her or her me but I was beginning to think I was prejudiced and although you may not believe it this gave me a good deal of satisfaction, if only for your sake! And she did respect you but in a way you might find it difficult to understand. I believe she could stand outside and see what you were trying to do down here and although nothing could convince her it was worth doing she could still admire the helping hand you gave people like Will Codsall and Elinor, Eveleigh and his family, and even Smut Potter, in spite of the friction he caused between you. However, people can admire an effort without wanting to take part in it. I've cleared Roddy and that's a personal relief to me!" and he left, feeling he had presumed enough.

John Rudd's logic yielded Paul small satisfaction, for his main purpose now seemed as sterile as Grace had always regarded it and his work no more than a dullish method of passing time and tiring himself physically. Grenfell's counsel brought him even less comfort than Rudd's. He drove over the night after the rally, when his place was at the polling booths, and was frank enough to confirm Paul's growing belief that this was an irrevocable decision on Grace's part.

"I don't think it has much to do with you personally, Paul," he said. "I believe there were far more complex reasons for her disassociating herself from what you're trying to achieve down here!"

"You're not going to tell me that women's votes are that important to her," Paul growled. "Damn it, a wife doesn't turn her back on home, husband and baby in order to march about with a banner and make a fool of herself at public meetings! Frankly, I'd prefer to hear she had left me for a lover and so would any man!"

"That's your trouble, Paul," Grenfell said seriously, "you try and rationalise every issue that presents itself. You can't do it with most political issues and you certainly can't with personal ones! Her preoccupation with the Women's Suffrage movement is a manifestation of what she feels about everything important to her, and I believe that goes for a good many of those gallant but misguided women! They want a *purpose*, Paul, like yours or mine and we have been denying them one ever since they lived in caves."

"But surely a home like this and a family is a purpose in itself?"

"It was and still is for most women but not for women like your wife! That's the price we are beginning to pay for universal education and men might find it a heavy one in the near future. It isn't *you* she is rejecting, Paul, but your whole way of life."

"You mean you suspected this might happen?"

"Not precisely this, but something less drastic perhaps."

"You said nothing!"

"Who the devil am I to criticise a man's wife to his face, Paul?"

"Yet you're now telling me, as kindly as you can, there's absolutely nothing I can do about it?"

Grenfell considered. Far more clearly than Paul he saw the wider issues confronting him and could view them free of bias. "Not at present but after an interval there may be; it would depend on all manner of things."

"What kind of things?"

"On what happens to her and to you. On how quickly the pair of you mature and on the changes in the world we live in, perhaps. She may not have the moral strength to struggle on alone. If she tried and failed, would you take her back on her own terms—freedom of action to go where she wished and to do what she liked? To make her own friends so long as she was loyal to you in the conventional sense?"

"No," he said, after a moment's hesitation, "I don't think I would, Jimmy. That isn't enough to stop a marriage like ours going sour. At least, not the kind of marriage I need so long as I stay here."

"I daresay you're right at that," said Grenfell, sighing. "God knows, your outlook as a landowner who puts human beings first and profit second is rare enough and a man needs peace in his own house to project it in this day and age! I'm desperately sorry about this, Paul, but not as sorry as I would have been if she had gone off with another man. All I can add to that is to tell you that I owe this seat to your loyalty and single-mindedness and I won't ever forget that! If ever you need me I should be more hurt than I can say if you didn't call on me!" and he shook hands warmly and left.

Good enough advice but it did little to help. To Paul, through the rest of the summer, the Valley seemed stale and profitless, and this in itself was strange because she had been such a quiet, unobtrusive person. Thirza, in her new role of Nannie, now took undisputed charge of Simon and was fiercely jealous even of Mrs. Handcock's

386

interference. Rudd saw to it that he had plenty of work and at length he taught himself to stop anticipating the post. It was now, he soon realised, known throughout the Valley why she had left him and that she was unlikely to return but at least, as time wore on, he could stop speculating on what they said to one another when he rode by, or passed on having spoken to one or other of them on a routine matter. It was during these daily excursions that he became conscious of their mute concern, although it was months before he was able to distinguish between sympathy and a conspiracy of embarrassed silence. Throughout the autumn and a cheerless Christmastide he wasted few words on them, saying what he had to say then riding off with a nod. Yet his sullenness and bitterness were contained and perhaps it was this that won their respect. Slowly, and imperceptibly, he was able to translate their curiosity into warmth, so that he became aware of a kinship with them that had not existed in his most sanguine days before his marriage, when he had thought of himself as a well-meaning, bungling amateur and hoped that they would make generous allowances for his inexperience. Something was reaching out to him from all of them and he noted and welcomed it in all parts of the Valley. It was there in the twinkle of Martha Pitts' brown eyes, when she insisted he stayed to a meal and ate a little of "Henry's gurt duck." It was recognisable in Eveleigh's stolid respect as he submitted his harvest figures and marshalled his little regiment of children to present homemade Christmas cards to "Young Squire". He found it in Elinor Codsall's voice, when she thanked him (as she did almost every time she saw him) for helping her rescue Will from Four Winds, and it was present in Sam Potter's determination to name his second daughter Grace, notwithstanding, as he explained to Joannie, that "Young Squire's missis 'as up an' left 'un, the poor, mazed crittur, not knowing a gude man when one be lyin' bezide 'er!" These subtle communications of their friendship would have gone unnoticed by anyone who had grown up among them but to Paul they were the first evidence that he was accepted, that his good intentions were recognised and that he was already regarded by them not as a brash young man with a bushel of fancy ideas but as the natural leader of the community. It was this realisation that encouraged him to look back and reconsider Grenfell's advice, and it was the same current of unspoken sympathy that enabled him to read Celia Lovell's startling letter objectively.

II

Celia's second letter arrived towards the end of January, more than six months after Grace had left. Her first, replying to his angry demands for news of his wife's whereabouts had merely annoyed him for he concluded from it that Celia was not much surprised by what had occurred and that it was not, in her view, an astonishing thing for her stepdaughter to have abandoned home, husband and a six-months-old child after an apparently trivial disagreement. The letter, moreover, expressed a neutrality that he would not have expected from her in view of her eagerness to arrange the marriage and he thought, bitterly, "Damn the woman! She might at least have said something sympathetic, even if she does make it very plain she won't accept the job of umpire!" He had not written again and was therefore surprised by a message from Coombe Bay one grey morning, informing him that she had returned to the Valley and would be glad if he would call as soon as convenient. He rode over that same afternoon but as he stood outside the door awaiting an answer to the bell his mind returned to the first occasion he had stood here, also in response to Celia's urgent invitation; it seemed to him more like fifty than two years ago. She received him graciously when the trim maid showed him up the narrow stair to her little boudoir, looking out across the restless winter sea but he was in no mood for polite preliminaries and said, bluntly, "I could make no sense at all of your first letter and can only suppose that you now regard the marriage as a mistake on everybody's part!"

She looked at him with her head on one side and then,

laughing heartily, took his hand in both of hers and kissed him on the cheek.

"Paul," she said, "you might have frightened Grace with that baronial approach but it doesn't impress me in the least! Sit down, unbutton your coat and tell me exactly what led up to it. More important still, tell me how you got along *before* it happened."

He was nonplussed by her heartiness but her charm began to reassert itself after a few moments so that he found himself thinking not so much of Grace or his own situation, but how she managed to look so young and attractive. He discovered too that he envied her assurance, reflecting that it was no wonder she had taken his news so lightly for there was so much experience behind her friendly brown eyes. He told her, without embroidery, of the passive period of their marriage and the sense of security it had given him, and then of their two quarrels, one over Smut Potter and the other over Roddy Rudd, and their exchange of ultimatums in respect of the rally and the visit to the ballet. She was a good listener and he saw that she did not miss a point but when he had finished, describing how Grace had packed her trunks and disappeared, she said, with a smile, "I daresay that's all very relevant, Paul, but if I'm to bring you together again I shall have to know a great deal more than that! How did Grace behave as a bride, before and after Simon was born?"

It crossed his mind then that she was using the occasion to satisfy a prurient curiosity and he recalled her more than maternal approaches to him when he had called upon her the first time, and again when they had parted after the wedding and she had drawn him aside and whispered, "Don't stand any nonsense from her, Paul! Remember the old proverb—'Thou goest to a woman? Do not forget the whip!' " Then, without understanding why, he knew that she was drawing him out for a purpose of her own, that she could tell him a great deal more if she chose but had not yet made up her mind to tell what she knew. The thought put him on his guard and he said off-handedly, "Grace was a perfect wife in the way most

389

young men look for one, although maybe 'wife' isn't the word you had in mind!"

She nodded, eagerly. "Now that's odd, but very interesting! It knocks the bottom out of a theory I had about her before you were married."

He said, impatiently, "Look here, Mrs. Lovell, I'm only interested in getting her to behave like a reasonable human being. I know she's bored down here and I'm willing to make allowances. The estate is running itself now and we could go to London occasionally and maybe visit the Continent. Damn it, I'd even buy one of those blasted motors she seems so keen on and have a telephone and electric dynamo installed, if those things are that important to her! The one thing I won't do is change my way of life and I don't think she has the right to demand that. If you know where she is—and I believe you do—you can tell her that! She made a bargain and I intend to hold her to that part of it!"

"I should have no patience with you if you didn't," Celia said, eyeing him carefully, "and the fact is, you happen to be right—I do know where she is, I saw her less than a week ago."

"She's abroad?"

"No, in London."

He got up with an air of exasperation but she motioned him to sit again, adding, "Don't rush me, Paul! I have to consider very carefully what to do, for I'm genuinely fond of you and would like nothing better than to restore her to you on your own terms. Her kind of nonsense would have been thrashed out of a young wife when I was a girl but times change and she happens to have a little money of her own, for which you can blame me. Then again, I suppose there is some kind of excuse for this silly revolt against men. She did watch her father drive her mother to suicide but perhaps you never heard about that?"

"I knew her mother drowned herself in India," Paul admitted, "but naturally I never discussed it with her."

"Perhaps you should have done, for it goes some way towards explaining her oddity. Bruce Lovell drove that poor woman to her death with his debts and women and rather special brand of cruelty. I ought to know, although I didn't hear of it until it was too late."

"You mean that Grace, seeing that happen, conceived a contempt for men? That this suffrage nonsense is a kind of revenge?"

"What other reason could there be for an intelligent girl like her trading security and comfort for a fad?"

He knew that he could never convince a woman of Celia's background that some people might consider themselves more deeply committed to a political principle than a trend in fashion, so all he said was, "I made a point never to quarrel with her political views. After all, she has as much right to hers as I have to mine."

"Quite," said Celia, "but yours haven't led to the police court!"

He sat up, alarmed and astounded. "Police court? When?"

"She would be in gaol right now if I hadn't read of her case in the papers and paid her fine, very much against her will. These women hate to be deprived of their martyrdom."

"Grace was actually charged in court? What the devil for?"

"Throwing a bag of flour at a Cabinet Minister or so I understand. It's all so futile! What would they do with the vote if they got it? March around in hideous clothes campaigning for one nincompoop or the other I imagine. But perhaps you, as a Radical, sympathise with them?"

"I've never been convinced," he said, "but I'm damned if I think that issue is worth my marriage! Besides, Grace's desertion hasn't all that much to do with votes for women. I realise now that it's more of a repudiation of our way of life down here, a kind of compulsion to see everything new as miraculous and everything old as fuel for a bonfire. In that respect we should never see eye to eye but it need not prevent us from leading a normal married life? Do you see any prospect of convincing her of that."

"Well, I suppose we could try," she said, sighing. "Would you be prepared to travel up to town and talk to her if I could arrange it?"

"Yes I would," he said eagerly, "I should be glad of the opportunity. I don't think I would have been but now —well, I've always regarded dignity as a rather negative virtue Mrs. Lovell and I threw mine away when I bought myself a leading position among people who had been farming land since the Conquest."

She gave him a long, affectionate glance and once again he was conscious of something frankly sensual in her contemplation. "You know, Paul," she said at length, "the thing I admire most about you is your lack of complacency! I think Grace is an absolute fool. You're a real man, and you'll be a big one hereabouts one of these days! Will you stay to supper?" and when he declined she looked very disappointed and said, with a lift of her elegant shoulders, "Oh very well, hurry home and stick your nose in your beloved dirt! I'll write the moment I can arrange something!"

She kissed him then, warmly on both cheeks, inclining her body towards him with rather more pressure than necessary and he recognised the perfume that Grace used. For a moment he was half-inclined to accept her invitation, and perhaps demonstrate his contempt for personal pride and she would have welcomed him, he was sure of that. The vague prospect of a reconciliation, however, caused him to recollect himself and he thanked her, turning for the door. Little, he reflected, had been achieved, but enough to make him feel more cheerful than he had felt for months.

III

January passed with a spell of mild, muggy weather and white, drenching mists came in from the sea, shrouding those parts of the estate free of timber. All along the Valley, except for brief periods about noon, the clouds remained dense and almost motionless. The mist muffled the continuous whine of the Home Farm saw and moon-faced cattle loomed out of the fog along the river road, their hooves making sounds like soggy corks being withdrawn from bottles as they squelched across the half-seen landscape. Paul had resumed the rhythm of his work by then and was drawing up plans for a communal marketing scheme that he had been pondering a year or more but with the arrival of hard frosts in late February, and flurries of snow and sleet beating in from the north-east, it was difficult for busy men like Arthur Pitts, Eveleigh and the Derwents to assemble and exchange views on prospects of pooling resources instead of competing for the Whinmouth and Paxtonbury markets. Travel along icebound roads was irksome and hunting, where they might have conferred in the field, was at a standstill. Celia kept in touch, writing once from the village and twice from London but apparently it was not proving easy to locate Grace, and although Paul thought of her frequently some of the ache had gone from his heart and he was able, for long periods during the day, to put her out of mind altogether. John Rudd took to spending his evenings in the library again and once James Grenfell, down from London, dined with them, talking of events that might have been happening on the moon for all they affected life in the Valley. He said that the Tsar's régime in Russia was tottering under the stresses of revolution at home and a disastrous dispute with the Japanese in the Far East. Grenfell, to Paul's amazement, backed the Japs to win the war that was on the point of breaking out but said he had scant sympathy with Russia, a nation that was the social equivalent of England about the time of the Wars of the Roses. The M.P. also discussed home affairs and prophesied an early general election, with a landslide victory for the Liberals but when Paul asked him if the cause of women's suffrage was likely to make progress under a radical government Grenfell said it would not, for no government could allow itself to be blackmailed and blackmail was the strategy of the militant group dominating the movement.

They sat talking until the small hours and Paul was grimly amused to note the subtle changes wrought by a few months in what Grenfell now called (rather self-consciously) "My Workshop". He was already a little thinner and a little greyer, Paul thought, but some of his tolerance had departed and Paul now thought it unlikely that he would suffer fools gladly. There was also a slight formalism in his manner and in his ways of pronouncing judgments, as though his opinions were unchallengeable statements of fact that no one in his senses could dispute. It was all barely noticeable but it went some way towards confirming Paul's distrust of professional politicians, who, once translated from candidate to Member, seemed to take on the pedagoguery of schoolmasters unable to distinguish between children and adults. Perhaps Grenfell himself was conscious of this for, on saying good-bye, he suddenly seemed less sure of himself as he said, hesitantly, "You've heard no more of Grace I suppose?" and when Paul told him there was still a possibility of a reconciliation he perked up at once exclaiming, "That's splendid! As for me, to be honest I'm sometimes very homesick for the Valley and I wonder she isn't! It can be disappointing up there at times. One begins hopefully enough but inside the House one sometimes has a curious sensation of having joined an all-party conspiracy against the people we're supposed to represent! However, I hope I'll outgrow this when we are a government and not an opposition," and he climbed into his trap and rattled away down the drive, leaving Paul with a conviction that Grenfell had found travelling more rewarding than arrival.

A day or so later, when the weather had mended somewhat, Meg Potter arrived sitting sidesaddle on the carthorse they had loaned Tamer, fording the swollen stream as unconcernedly as if it had been a brook. She told him that Tamer was laid up with sciatica, that she and the girls were busy with spring-sowing, and that she had heard Smut had been transferred to Paxtonbury gaol. "He's mentioned you in every scribble us've had," she said, "so he'd take it kindly if you could bring yourself to go up to that bad place, Squire." Paul said he would be glad to, for such visits as Smut had been allowed during the first two years of his sentence had been made by Meg herself. Twice Paul had loaned her the trap and she had driven right across Dartmoor and over the Tamar to Bodmin gaol, to spend a bare thirty minutes with her son, and Paul realised that she was relieved he was now back in Devon, for at least this was an earnest of his ultimate return to the Valley.

In a day or so Ikey Palfrey was due to start his first term at High Wood, a small public school in the north of the county, so Paul let him accompany him to Paxton-bury and wait with the trap whilst he approached the red-brick prison and presented his visitor's ticket. The vast bulk and silence of the ugly building oppressed him, and he wondered what on earth he could say to a man who had been locked up in such a place for more than a hundred weeks but when the wicket gate was opened and he was escorted to the waiting-room, curiosity conquered his distaste and he looked around with interest, watching a group of convicts at work in the courtyard with besoms and drain rods, and noting the blank faces of the other visitors who lined the bench like patients in a dentist's surgery. Eventually he was conducted to a low-ceilinged room furnished with a long table and divided down the middle by a wire mesh and after another delay a warder jangling keys at his belt entered, escorting a small, shrunken man in a mountebank's jacket and breeches of coarse canvas. For a moment Paul failed to recognise this clown-ish creature as the spry, suntanned poacher, with the insolent glance and soft, springy step, for Smut looked as if he had been confined in a small, sunless cupboard for weeks and hardly a trace of his natural ebullience sur-vived. There were still irregular areas of brown on his cheeks but they were mere blotches, emphasising the moist pallor of his skin, and only the light blue eyes that lit up on seeing Paul recalled the Smut Potter he had met his first day in the Valley.

Smut said, in an odd, jerky voice, "It was rare gude of 'ee to coom, Squire! Mother zed you would, tho' I didn't taake it as zo till I zeed 'ee zittin' there!"

"Well, at least you're back in the county and only a few miles from the Valley," Paul said, feeling uncertain of his own voice. "What kind of work do they give you, Smut?"

Potter winked and his mouth pretended to grin. "Well, tiz better'n downalong in Bodmin, Squire," he said, "where us is sewing they ole bags most o' the time. I'm a trusty now, you zee, an' I work in the gardin, zo tiz altogether diff'rent. A man can turn his face to the sky every so often an' smell the sea when wind's in the west! Oh, tiz well enough now, Squire, and they zay if I minds me P's and Q's I'll be gettin' more'n twelmonth off an' be back-along in just over the year. How be things in the Vale, Squire? Mother, 'er can't write, an' tiz six months zince I zeed her, that time she come over the moor to Bodmin."

"Things are going along very well," Paul told him, "especially in the Dell. Tamer and the two older girls have been raising sugar-beet and I'm going to have Eph Morgan mend the roof before you come home!"

"Arr," said Smut, absently, "youm gude to us varmints, Squire! Mebbe, if someone like you had been backalong when I was a tacker I wouldn't have taaken the wrong turn I did! Do 'ee ever zee that Gilroy keeper I drubbed?"

"Yes, I've seen him," Paul said, "and he's not even showing a scar. Gilroy's made him head keeper so you'd best stay our side of the Teazel when you do come out!"

"I'll do that right enough," Smut said earnestly, "for I woulden chance more time in a plaace like this, Squire! Tiz never worth it, an' they'll all tell 'ee the zame but mind you, most o' the ole rascals will be back in again zoon enough for they've no other means of earnin' a livin'!"

It was curious, Paul thought, how carefully Smut dis-associated himself from the ordinary convict and he wondered if he thought of himself as a felon, or rather as an honest poacher who had fallen on hard times.

"You really do intend to finish with poaching, Smut?" he asked and Smut made a throat-crossing gesture and swore that he did indeed, and that if the Squire had meant what he said about having him back in the Valley, he would prove that the Potters could be as industrious and law-abiding as anyone in the county. "Us'll maake the Dell show a profit, even if us has to harness ole Tamer to the plough!" he added.

"Very well," Paul said, smiling, "I'll remember that! As soon as you come home we'll go to work on the Dell. I'll talk to your brother Sam and maybe we can clear part of the thicket north of the Bluff and add twenty acres to the holding. By the way, I suppose you know Sam now has a girl and a boy, and that sister Pansy has one girl and a baby boy?"

"No, I never heard tell o' that," Smut said, with awe in his voice. "Lor bless us, to think on that! Four little tackers, in just over the two years! But then, we Potters is a rare tribe for breedin'. I dessay I've got a few around somewheres, tho' none o' the maids ever took me to court for 'em!"

It was this remark, uttered as the warder rose and brought the session to an end, that made the visit worthwhile, for in the final moment it seemed to Paul that the original Smut triumphed over the ingratiating penitent. He was hustled away and Paul went down the steps and through the wicket gate to the embankment, where Ikey trotted up and asked, in his ironed-out Paxtonbury accent, if Smut had had chains on his feet. "Good God, of course not!" Paul replied, but as he said this he thought, "But they still treat convicts like half-tamed beasts and dress them as buffoons. It's a pity they can't be spared a few shreds of human dignity," and was silent half the way home.

When the trap began to descend to the river, however, he cheered up, reflecting that he had left Smut something to think about and to hope for and then he glanced curiously at the boy sitting on the box beside him thinking, "Well, Grace and the *avant-garde* can sneer as much as they like but there is some point in my being here! Would the Lovells have given Smut Potter a second thought? And would this boy Ikey be getting a sporting chance? She might have originated the idea but she didn't stay and see it through!" and he went on to ponder the Eveleighs at Four Winds and Will and Elinor's success at Periwinkle and then smiled at himself for seeking personal reassurance in a balance-sheet of good works. "Are you scared of going to a real school?" he asked, suddenly, and to his surprise and slight embarrassment the boy gathered up the reins and brought the colt to a sudden halt. He turned and met Paul's enquiring gaze steadily and Paul realised, for the first time, how greatly he had matured in the last two or three years. His skin, once fish-belly pale, was brown and healthy, his eyes were clear and his hair neatly cut, so that there was about him an air of confidence altogether different from the perkiness of the scrapyard urchin.

"Yes, Mr. Craddock, sir," he said, "I'm scared all right but you don't have to worry, I won't let you down, sir! The tutor told me all the new boys got ragged and that I'm not to mind because it's an old English custom!"

He had lost, Paul noted, all traces of his thin Cockney accent and it came as rather a shock to realise that he had almost forgotten the poor little devil during his own troubles. The boy, he thought, could hold his own anywhere, for the toughness and resilience of the street Arab was still there under the looks and manners of a conventional lad on the point of exchanging prep. school for public school. He said, as though to excuse his recent neglect, "Well, I've had troubles of my own lately as you've probably heard and that's the reason why I appeared to lose interest in what you were doing over at the crammer's. You remember it was Mrs. Craddock's idea that you went in the first place?"

"Yes," the boy said, "I'm not likely to forget that, sir," and then more hesitantly, "Will she ever be coming back, sir?"

"I don't know, Ikey, probably not," he said gruffly, and Ikey, taking the hint, shook out the reins and they moved down from the moor to the swollen Sorrel in a rather embarrassed silence.

Wild daffodils and yellows iris showed on the margins of the half-flooded meadows and the blackbirds were noisy in the Hermitage thickets. The sun, which seemed to have been away visiting another solar system since autumn, had returned to play a spring game with the darting current and a bay hunter, out to grass on the Four Winds side of the stream, whinnied a casual greeting to the cob, before throwing up her heels and galloping madly across the levels. Paul said, "Tell me, Ikey, are you ever homesick for London now?" and the boy replied, "No, sir, never! I don't think I should ever want to go there again. This is my home now, sir."

"Me too," Paul said and the kinship that had been

398

born during their first ride down this road during the coronation summer, suddenly reasserted itself as he thought, "I must write to Uncle Franz and find out more about the boy. If there's a likelihood of Grace coming back, I'm damned if I won't think about adopting him officially for he is the only soul about here who shares my feeling for the Valley and that makes him a kind of heir!" They said no more until they were passing under the long park wall for each was absorbed in the familiarity of the scene, the swift river and wide stretch of meadows to the right, the sweep of Priory Wood to the left. Then Paul said, "There's something else, Ikey, I don't know whether your tutor mentioned it but at a school like High Wood they will expect you to have some kind of domestic background. Did he ever talk to you about that?"

"He did mention it, sir, but said it was a matter for you and Mrs. Craddock."

Paul considered. He was confident that Ikey would pass muster in all outward respects but he recalled his own limitations as an officer in the Yeomanry, reflecting that there was no accounting for the graduations of the English caste system and the snobberies it spawned but there it was and one either accepted it or withdrew from the game altogether.

"Do you ever write to your own parents, Ikey? Do you keep in touch with them?"

"No, sir, I don't," said the boy, unsentimentally.

"All right," said Paul, "then we shall have to do a bit of bluffing. Sooner or later the subject of your family is bound to crop up. Did you have any story in mind?"

The boy grinned, suddenly an urchin again, and said, "Well yes, sir! I was going to say my guv'nor was dead, and *my* mother was still living abroad. Could I say that you were . . . well . . . a kind of cousin, looking after me over here?"

"You can do better than that," Paul said, laughing, "you can tell them I'm your stepbrother and official British guardian. The word 'guardian' always seems to impress the snobs somehow. Would you like to do that?"

"I would, and thank you, sir."

"Well, then that's settled. When you leave on Tuesday

do you want me to take you to school, and see you settled in?"

"If it's all the same to you, no sir," Ikey said unexpectedly. "I'd sooner take the plunge on my own, sir."

Paul glanced at him, noting the set of the jaw and his mind returned to the child's gallantry and initiative on the night Codsall had hanged himself. "By God," he thought, "that snob school is lucky to get him, even though he might be the product of a drunken docker and a Hungarian emigrant!"

"Very well," he said, "that's something for you to decide but I'll drive you as far as Paxtonbury in the brougham. We must have the brougham for an occasion like that!"

"Thank you, sir," Ikey said, "I should like that, in case any of the High Wood chaps are going by the same train."

"Any of the High Wood chaps," thought Paul, grinning. "Damn it, he's half-way home already!" and they turned in at the gates and set the cob at the steep drive.

IV

As it turned out it was Chivers the groom, who drove Ikey to Paxtonbury in the brougham that warm spring day for Paul was already on his way to London. Celia's telegram arrived the night before, delivered by a perspiring telegraph boy who had cycled all the way from Whinmouth but it told Paul very little. "Essential you are in London early morning of the third," it said. "Will meet 10.40 A.M. from Paxtonbury, Love Celia." That was all and Paul had to make what he could of it, reshuffling his programme, saying good-bye to Ikey and catching the main-line at Sorrel Halt. Celia had a carriage waiting for him at Waterloo and he was at her town house in Devonshire Square by late afternoon finding that he was expected to stay the night, for Celia had arranged his meeting with Grace at seven-fifteen the following morning.

"Where and why so early?" he demanded but the Frenchman Daladier was present and he did not press the enquiry after Celia's warning glance. They ate dinner together, making polite conversation and afterwards the Frenchman, who seemed to live on the premises, wandered off into the billiard-room. As soon as they were alone she said, urgently, "Pierre knows nothing about the real reason for your coming and I don't want him involved, you understand? He's practising here now, and any kind of scandal would injure him. I won't have that happen, Paul!"

It was not, he reflected, the Celia who had received him at Coombe Bay in January, but a taut, nervous woman, manifestly irritated by the situation. He said, seeking to reassure her, "There's no reason why either of you should be involved. Just tell me what kind of arrangement you've made with Grace."

"I haven't made any arrangement with her," she said, sharply. "I haven't set eyes on the little fool since I paid her fine at the police court, a day or so before I saw you in Devon! The fact is . . . she's in Holloway Prison at this moment!"

"Holloway Prison? For suffragist offences? Good God, Celia, what the devil has she been up to now?"

Celia looked as if she was about to cry. "I've had the greatest trouble keeping it from him," she wailed, "he's a very perceptive man and I daresay he's guessed the truth but he's very tactful and hasn't brought it into the open." She looked at Paul defiantly and he noticed that she was vulnerable and beginning to look her age. There were wrinkles under her eyes that he had never noticed before and the skin of her neck was slack. Suddenly he felt sorry for her, sorry but at the same time grateful, for it was obvious that a decision to get him to London had involved her in risks she did not care to take and that her fear of involving her lover by public scandal was real. He said, "Look here, Mrs. Lovell, don't think I'm unappreciative of what you've done. Just give me the facts and then let me go to a hotel. I'll see you aren't involved in any way. After all, this is my responsibility, not yours. How long has Grace been in gaol? And what did she go there for this time?"

She said, only slightly reassured, "There is a very militant section of this suffragist movement led by that dread-

401

ful woman Pankhurst and her daughters. It seems that Grace is one of the most irresponsible of them, she and a woman from the North, called Kenny. You must have read about them in the papers?"

Paul said, shortly, "The last I read about them they were organising a petition to the Opposition leaders, to Campbell-Bannerman, I believe but Grenfell tells me they'll get even less change from him than from Balfour!"

"That's so," she said, "but they have begun to picket the big Liberal meetings in the provinces. Up in Manchester, a month or so ago, Grace and some others climbed into a loft over the platform of a hall when Churchill was speaking. They had banners that they let down when the meeting started and were thrown out neck and crop, as you would expect them to be."

"Well?"

"Most of them went meekly enough but Grace didn't. She hit a policeman with an umbrella and was later charged with resisting arrest. She was put on probation but would you believe it she did the same thing two days later down here and this time they sentenced her to a month without the option! She comes out early tomorrow. That's why I sent for you."

"Why didn't you send for me straight away?"

"What good would that have done? She had legal representation in court and he couldn't stop her going to prison!"

"I can't understand how I didn't hear about it," he said, "it must have been in all the papers."

"She was charged under a different name. She didn't use yours or her father's. She used her mother's name, 'Philimore', and I don't know what her grandfather, the canon, would have said about it if he had been living!"

"You've written to her?"

"Yes I have but she didn't even answer. I told her that I'd seen you and that you were anxious to talk things over, and asked if I should get in touch with you. Listen Paul . . ." she spoke with a kind of desperation, "if you like, you . . . you can bring her back here! I'll get Pierre to take me to the races and if you could keep her out of the way until midday, you are welcome to do that! All I

402

ask is for time to get Pierre away before she arrives. The French can be even more censorious about this kind of thing than the English, and I just won't face the risk of losing him, you understand? I've got a right to my happiness. God knows, I earned it, with Bruce Lovell!"

"Yes you did," he said, thinking of John Rudd's comment about the Lovell streak and the misery it introduced into the lives of everyone associated with them, "but I won't risk bringing her here. I'll take her straight home. It was very good of you to go to so much trouble and I'm not sure that either of us deserve it!"

"She doesn't," Celia said, "but I don't know why you should blame yourself! Millions of women would consider themselves lucky to have had her chance and I can't forgive myself for bullying you into marrying her."

He smiled at that. "Nobody had to bully me into marrying Grace Lovell," he said, "I made up my mind to marry her the first time I saw her. As to blame, I must have gone wrong somewhere or other or perhaps there wasn't a chance from the beginning. I've got Simon, and he's part of her, and in spite of what you think I've got some pleasant memories."

He kissed her for the first time as a friend and not a relative and it amused him to see the effect, for at once she shrugged off her despondency and said, "Let's join Pierre in a drink. If he asks after Grace say something pleasantly non-committal," and they went into the billiard-room where the big Frenchman was potting with what appeared to Paul to be the expertise of a professional. He was a heavy-jowled, phlegmatic man, more like a middle-class Englishman than a Frenchman and it was difficult to see what an elegant, fastidious woman like Celia found so engaging about him. Then it was obvious, for the surgeon put up his cue, took her hand and raised it deliberately to his lips and Celia smiled over his head and for a moment looked almost girlish. She said, "My son-in-law has to be away very early. Would you like a drink before he goes up, Pierre?" The surgeon looked at him very carefully, as though assessing his chance of surviving a tricky operation and Paul thought, "He knows quite well why I'm here but he's probably got hundreds of more important secrets in his head!" They drank brandy and soda together and Paul left them listening to a scratchy Mendelssohn recording on Celia's latest extravagance, an Edison Bell phonograph. The tinny (and to Paul, wholly unmusical) sounds penetrated as far as the first landing. It was not solely his instinctive recoil from mechanical contrivances that made him aware of the mockery of the song.

She came out of a little wicket-door that might have been the twin of the one by which Paul had entered Paxtonbury Gaol and it was of Smut Potter's shrunken frame and mountebank garb that he thought as he saw her stand uncertainly under the great stone gate, a pitiful little figure against a blank and grotesque background. Then, with a sob, he dodged between carts and cabs and ran across the shining wet surface of the road towards her, expecting to see her stiffen with surprise but she did not seem in any way agog at his presence but merely smiled, politely rather than joyfully, and said, with her customary containment, "I thought it would be you, Paul. Celia isn't very good at concealing things, is she? Have you got a cab?"

He told her a cab was waiting across the road and asked if she had had breakfast.

"A sort of breakfast," she said, casually. "Smut Potter might have kept it down but I couldn't!" and a sensation of pity and desolation engulfed him, so that for a moment he felt sick and dizzy and must have showed it, for she took his hand and piloted him across the road to the side-street where the cab waited. It was an old victoria and the interior smelt like a neglected tack-room. He called to the cabby, "Anywhere! Back to the West End," and they moved off at a trot, sitting isolated from one another, like a young couple having a tiff and waiting for each other to capitulate. After a few moments he had mastered himself sufficiently to look at her, deciding with relief that she did not seem to have changed much in the months that had passed since they had parted. If twenty-eight days in Holloway had marked her in any way there was no outward sign of it. Her skin had the same wax-like transparency, her hair was neatly if plainly dressed, and her eyes, reflecting the glint of morning sun after the dawn showers, were still hard and clear and blue.

He said at length, "I only heard you were there last night. I came up here expecting Celia to give me an address," and when she made no reply, "She promised to arrange a meeting between us as long ago as last January; I've been waiting to hear ever since."

She turned suddenly, swinging her small, compact body at right angles to him and looking at him with a kind of desperate resignation.

"I'm not coming back, Paul! You might as well know that at once! It was good for you to come, and I'm glad to see you, but I'm not coming back, for your sake as much as mine!"

It came as no real surprise but it had plenty of power to wound. "We can at least discuss it, can't we?" he muttered, fighting to keep the note of pleading from his voice.

"We can talk like civilised human beings, I suppose, but only until ten. After that I've got to report to H.Q."

"Report?" he said savagely. "What the devil do you mean, 'report'? Are you a private in some kind of army? Whoever you have to 'report' to can wait! We're still husband and wife and I've neither seen you nor heard of you in almost a year."

"Well, I'm sorry, Paul," she said quietly, "but I still have to report. And we *are* an army, fighting impossible odds. That's why every individual counts."

He could not trust himself to reply at once and they bowled along in silence for three of four minutes. Then he said, sourly, "I don't begin to understand you, Grace! Anyone can be absorbed in an abstract idea but not to the extent of throwing everything life has to offer on to the rubbish heap! You've got a home and a child, even if I count for nothing, and you'll never persuade me that you weren't happy down there most of the time! I'll concede the right of women to vote, I've never seriously challenged it but it can't be this important! Nothing can!"

"What about your own 'abstract idea', Paul?"

"Shallowford? That's entirely different! It doesn't hurt anyone and it doesn't make nonsense of other people's lives!"

"No, perhaps not," she said, as though debating the substance of a breakfast-table remark, "but it obsesses you just as much as mine obsesses me."

"You knew about Shallowford when you married me, Grace. It's true that I also knew you were interested in women's suffrage but whereas I made it perfectly clear what I had in mind you didn't! You didn't see fit to warn me that you wanted to spend your life between committee rooms and Holloway!"

It seemed that he had scored a point for she considered some time before replying. "That true enough, Paul, that's quite true and I suppose it puts me in the wrong. But it doesn't make any real difference who is right and who is wrong, not now that I've had a chance to look back over the past and forward into the future!" and to the cabby she called, "Take us to the Embankment and stop by Cleopatra's Needle!" and addressing Paul again, "I wonder if it's possible to make you understand? It was very wrong of me to marry you, I realise that of course, but I think it would be far more wrong to go on pretending to make the best of it, and prevent you from leading a useful life as well as me. No, Paul," as he opened his mouth to protest, "let me say what I have to. We haven't very long and we might never have another opportunity."

"But that's monstrous!" he burst out. "It makes me wonder if you understand what you're doing!"

She looked at him sharply. "You mean that I'm slightly insane? Like my mother?"

"No, I don't mean that, and don't keep twisting my words! You're as sane as anyone in London but you're allowing yourself to become the victim of a kind of mania. We could agree to differ, couldn't we? Millions of husbands and wives do, without tearing their lives up by the roots! You say you didn't love me but you give a good imitation of love sometimes!"

"Yes," she said, "I did and in that way I still could, Paul. But it doesn't stop me from despising your whole way of life."

"You never shared my way of life and I never insisted that you did!"

She said, with a final attempt at reasoning, "Suppose I

406

came back with you now? I should have a choice of playing nursemaid to a community with a medieval outlook, or accepting the role of a toy shut in a cupboard all day and taken out to be played with after dark! I know what would happen well enough, and so do you if you face up to it! You wouldn't be content to let me develop wider interests of my own, and anyway, even if you were, I couldn't do it down there, cut off from every new idea and everyone with a spark of intellectual curiosity. In the end you would retreat into a permanent sulk while I bore a child a year and pottered about in the rose garden between pregnancies! You think there is worthwhile work to be done in a place like Shallowford and maybe there is, for a man. But there's nothing there for me and could never be and that's why I decided to leave before we began to destroy one another, before it was too late for you to make a fresh start!"

The cab had stopped opposite the incongruous monument and they got out, Paul paying the man and following her to a seat facing the sluggish river. The sun shone brightly now and the Thames traffic was in full swing. Behind them trams sang back and forth along the Embankment and in front of them fussy little tugs towed strings of barges downstream, like ducks teachings ducklings to swim. Paul said, when a group of pedestrians had passed by, "How can you talk about a fresh start? We're man and wife, aren't we? We could only make a fresh start with each other but you won't even discuss it!"

"It isn't easy to discuss it, Paul," she said earnestly. "When I was back there, alone in that horrible little cell, I could separate everything in my mind and I did think of you a great deal and could see very clearly the differences in our points of view but now, seeing you so hurt and desolate . . ."

"Our points of view can't be all that different, Grace," he interrupted. "I remember you saying that if we were able to bring physical joy to one another everything else could fall into place."

"I said there was a *chance* of that happening, Paul. It took me eighteen months to appreciate the real sacrifices demanded of marriage! Don't you see, you're concerned

407

with the particular, and I'm concerned with the whole! Your outlook is honourable and useful enough but you're content with a tiny field—a few dull-witted villagers, a little bad housing, involving maybe a dozen families. I want to work for an entire change in the system and I can't even begin until women are admitted into the counsels of men! It isn't a fad, Paul, it's my reason for being alive!"

"Nobody can move mountains alone, Grace. You're got to begin somewhere and in a modest way."

"That's well enough for you, Paul, and I've always understood that, but can you imagine a Raphael happy to paint miniatures? That's what's been wrong with us from the beginning. When I married you I thought I could change you, that perhaps I could use your idealism and money to create something worthwhile and enduring! But I can't, and I never will! I see now that in trying to enlarge you, you will diminish me, until I go dry and sour inside. Neither one of us is to blame for this. You are new to patronage and see nothing contemptible in it but I grew up hating it, and determined to do battle with it! How could I do that if I was still part of it?"

She put her hand on his and looked at him with great earnestness. "You can get married again, Paul! You're the kind of man who desperately needs a wife but the right kind of wife. I'd make it easy for you!"

He looked at her with an expression of such incredulity that she made a hopeless gesture with her free hand, as though to reduce the width of the gulf opening between them. "I owe you that much, Paul! It was a selfish, stupid act on my part to marry you but to hold on to you, as a kind of long-term insurance, would be unforgiveable! Can't you see that this isn't really a personal issue? I'll never cease to think of you as kind and generous and honest but we don't make a pair. We never have, in spite of all the self-deception you've indulged in about me!"

It was a spiritual annulment of their marriage and the final dissolution of his hopes. He knew then, and with certainty, that he would never hold her again, that there would be no more embraces, no more companionship by the fireside and certainly no more children of the marriage,

408

nothing but a dry interchange of ideas that he only half understood and her insistence on reducing everything to words and phrases that belonged in pamphlets rather than hearts enraged him.

He stood up, brushing away her hand as though even her touch was repugnant and then he saw tears in her eyes and rejoiced that he had found a means to hurt her. He was surprised at the intensity of his feelings and his sudden move away from her, across to the embankment wall, was a recoil against the violence of feeling that urged him to strike her across the face, to beat her senseless, to fling her down on the pavement and jump on her. He understood then how Martin Codsall must have felt as he struck Arabella, and recalled Rudd's observation concerning the provocation under which some murders occur but the moment passed. By the time she was beside him again he was almost drained of emotion and conscious only of a sensation of inertia and drabness, that drained all the colour from life and set him apart from the passage of people and vehicles on the pavement and roadway behind. He stood there silently for a moment but at length managed to say, "Simon? I suppose you took Simon into account when you did your thinking back there in the cell?" She made no reply so he remained looking fixedly at the river until he realised that the touch on his elbow was heavier than hers and turning looked directly into the face of a middle-aged policeman, a man with a heavy walrus moustache and a look of professional concern in his eyes. "Are you all right, sir?" the man said and when Paul stared as though he had materialised from the base of the monument, added, half-apologetically, "I thought you looked a bit queer, sir."

With a tremendous effort Paul pulled himself together. His sense of humour was too far off to help but his sense of irony remained. He said, "I'm all right, officer. It hadn't occurred to me to jump in!" and then, "Did you . . . did you see which way the young lady went?"

"Yes, I did," said the man, looking relieved, "she boarded a tram, heading for the tunnel! Bit of a tiff, sir?" and he grinned and waited.

"You could call it that," Paul said, "but she's more accustomed to them than me it seems. She's a suffragette—and my wife!"

The policeman looked surprised and then amused. "You don't say, sir? Then do you mind my giving you a piece of advice? Don't go after her, just take it out in beer. Then, when you're braced up, take a dog-whip to her! If all you chaps did that we chaps would have a quieter time on the beat, sir!" and as though feeling that he had shown too much levity he suddenly straightened his face, nodded and continued slowly on his walk towards the Boadicea statue.

The encounter had the effect of steadying Paul somewhat, so that, for the first time since he had seen Grace leave the prison he was able to make some shift at viewing the situation objectively, putting aside thoughts of pursuit, compromise or following her to the headquarters of the suffragists and perhaps dragging her home by the hair. Yet he did not abandon all thoughts of violence, for his mind conjured for a moment with male licence of the past, when, as the policeman had hinted, a husband in his situation could have legally thrashed his wife in public and been applauded by the magistrates for setting a good example. But as he considered this, the ultimate sacrifice of dignity, the sheer hopelessness of the situation overwhelmed him and again he almost succumbed to a physical nausea and thought he might do worse than follow the policeman's advice as regards a drink, or several drinks. He crossed the road and passed under Charing Cross arches, turning in at the first public house in Villiers Street and ordering a double brandy. It was only after he had swallowed his second dram, and had nibbled at a beef sandwich, that the forces of resentment began to reassemble inside him, swelling until they embraced not only Grace and the suffragettes but all womankind and yet, as he continued to drink, his thoughts began to sort themselves into a less extravagant pattern. He knew that his immediate need was for companionship and thought first of Celia, then of Uncle Franz across the river, and finally of Grenfell, over at the House, but after a moment's thought he rejected all three. Celia would not be available, Zorndorff was too cynical and Grenfell might even sympathise with Grace, for he too was preoccupied with pamphlets, white papers and

410

codifications compiled from the raw material of human emotions. "God help me, I have to talk to someone," he said aloud and a cheerful voice beside him said, "Well, I've bin hoping you would, dearie! You wanter buy me a stout?"

He did not recall ever having seen a more obvious harlot plying in public. She was a study in bright mauve, mauve summer dress, with old-fashioned leg-o-mutton sleeves, mauve straw hat, openwork mauve mittens and it struck him at once that she was approximately Grace's age, with Grace's sturdy hips and shoulders and narrow waist. Her cheeks were heavily rouged and her lips gleamed with salve. She had on a pair of ear-rings made of some dull metal and a cheap coral necklace. Her hair, dark at the roots was dyed straw-blond and her eyebrows had been so mercilessly plucked that they had almost ceased to exist. He noticed all these things, misery sharpening his perceptions to an unusual degree and decided that her brittle smile was the saddest welcome he had ever been offered. He said, politely, "I'll buy you a stout; you can have as much stout as you can drink."

She laughed uncertainly, as though a little wary of him, but said, in her grating, Cockney voice, "Christ dearie, you wanner be careful wi' your invitations!" and to the impassive barman, "Fill 'er up, Fred!" as she coiled herself on the high stool next to him, throwing one leg over the other and exposing a few inches of booted calf.

"Whatever it is you don' wanner do mor'n damp it down, dearie," she said, gaily. "Too much too quick an' where are yer? Back where you was in no time at all with an 'angover as a bonus! You wanner take it nice an' steady like me," and she downed half her stout in a gulp and he asked the barman for another brandy. As he raised it to his lips he saw that the girl was now looking at him closely and that her brittle smile was gone. She said, "Well, just that one if you're really interested, dearie!" and finishing her stout stood up and adjusted her hat in the gilded mirror. He followed her out into the sunshine, she slipped her arm through his and they went slowly up the hill towards Charing Cross Station. Seven brandies on an empty stomach left his mind free to conjure with irrelevancies, the

411

warm colour of a pyramid of oranges on a coster's barrow, the gap-toothed grin of the vendor, the words "Latest on Far East War" on a billboard beside a newsvendor. The girl said, "My place is behind the Turkish Baths. Lot o' my gentlemen friends like to pop in after. Do you good it would, dearie, in your mood—quick game o' Mums and Dads then sweat it aht an' sleep it orf!"

She steered him into a narrow alley between two vast, slabsided buildings, then through a door and up two fights of uncarpeted stairs. At the top of the first flight an obese, bald-headed man was deeply absorbed in a newspaper, flaunting a heavy-type headline, "Japs Rout Tsar's Army at Mukden!" and Paul thought, "Now there's idiocy for you! What real interest could a bald-headed old whoremaster have in Mukden?" but the man did not look up as the girl ushered him into a small, sunless room that seemed full of stale steam. The bed was unmade, the single wickerwork chair pilled with litter and there was unwashed crockery on the bedside table. The impact of unrelieved squalor sobered him within seconds but the girl seemed disinclined to waste time. She reached behind her, unhooked her dress and let it fall, lifting her feet from the folds and stooping swiftly to unlace her boots. He watched her stupidly as she kicked them off, then picked up her dress and tossed it over the back of the chair, before making a half-hearted attempt to straighten the sheets. She wore no petticoat, only a punishingly tight corset and a pair of white, beribboned drawers the legs of which fell short of the top of her black stockings. He saw now that he had been misled by her padded shoulders and that although she had broad, fleshy hips that strained at the grubby rim of the corset the upper part of her body was very slender and her shoulders narrow and stooping. She said briskly, as she slipped off her drawers, "Are you one o' the altogether boys or will near-enough do?"

"How long have you been on the streets?" he asked suddenly, not because he was interested but because it was the first conversational gambit that occurred to him but she looked at him now with amused exasperation. "Oh Gawd!" she said, with mock despair, "you ain't one o' them nosey parkers are you?" and then, as though decid-

412

ing for herself that he was not, she said, "Let's say long enough to send you on yer way rejoicing, dearie! Well, is it the lot or not? Or would you like a cup o' cawfee first to clear yer pore head? No extra; all on the 'ouse!"

"No coffee but thank you, thank you very much," he said foolishly, and for some reason this pleased her and she said, "I like you! You're diff'rent! I dunno why, but you don' go with the girls neither, do you, or not all that much! You c'n alwus tell, mos'ly be the way they stand gawping, like you! Either that or they're in such a perishin' hurry! Tell you what," she put a finger in her mouth so that suddenly she no longer looked like a tart but a lewd parody of a little girl teasing an adult, "we'll 'ave our cawfee after an' jus' for you we'll 'ave the altogether, so as you c'n swank to yer pals after!" She swung round, putting her back to him. "You'll 'ave to un'ook me, tho'!"

He stared at her narrow back, noting the contrast between the slack hooks at the top of the corset and the terrible tautness of those sheathing her buttocks. The stench of stale steam filled his nostrils so that he found it difficult to breathe and his head seemed hardly to belong to him at all, yet it continued to record details with the accuracy of a man making an inventory. He noted that the closed window was half covered with peeling paper, that the paper had a fussy pattern and that the girl favoured mauve above every other colour, for even the ribbons on her discarded drawers matched her outdoor clothes. Then, as though these facts revealed to him the absurdity of his presence here, he said quickly, "I'm sorry, I'm going now! Here . . . " and fumbling in his pocket he found a sovereign, slammed it down on the bedside table and hurried from the room.

The girl was so astonished that he was half-way across the landing before she realised he had gone and then, darting as far as the threshold, she shouted, "Come on back, Soppy! I'm *clean* I tell yer, I'm *clean!*" but he went on blundering down the stairs two at a time, rushing past the old man and down the second flight to the passageway.

The clean air of the streets seemed as heady as the rush of a gale over Coombe Bluff and he gulped at it as if it was liquid. He went up Northumberland Avenue and into the Square, hurrying through the slow-moving traffic, across to St. Martin-in-the-Fields, then up Charing Cross Road as far as Leicester Square, where at last he slackened speed, crossing under Shakespeare's statue to a seat opposite the Empire. He sat down with a vast sense of relief, as though he had just escaped suffocation in a sulphurous tunnel.

Traffic flowed round the Square and people passed to and fro in front of him but he seemed to have lost the knack of recording inconsequential detail and the only thing that impinged upon him, apart from relief, was a hoarding, advertising "Pearson's Preserved Peas" fronting a building in the process of demolition. It struck him as being a very eye-catching advertisement, calculated to inspire almost anyone to have the utmost confidence in Pearson's Preserved Peas. It was a great splash of colour, a compound of greens, yellows and blues, depicting a sea and country landscape not altogether unlike that of the Vale south of the final bend in the Sorrel. He thought, "By God, I believe it *is* the Valley!" and then he realised that no corn was ever as golden as that and no sea as blue, not even on windless days in high summer. The illusion braced him and in a persistent way worked upon his fuddled brain, so that presently, when he had recovered his breath, his head began to clear and he was able to review the events of the day, from the moment he had issued from Celia's and hired the four-wheeler to his irrational flight from the sordid little room behind the Turkish Baths. He thought, "It can't all be due to too much brandy on an empty stomach. I must have had a kind of brainstorm!" and he wondered idly where Grace had gone after boarding the tram and then, by degrees, what he should do about her or himself, now, or later, or at any time in the future. He thought of hailing a cab and calling on Uncle Franz, or walking down to Westminster and sending in his card to Grenfell but a growing self-disgust prompted him to put both courses aside. What could either of them do beyond tendering advice? And what use was advice against an obstinacy like hers? Then he looked up at the hoarding again and this time it seemed to have a message for him, reminding him not solely of home but of all the people of the Valley, women and children who, he supposed, had come to rely upon him to some extent. He thought, "As long as I'm here I can't even think! I can always think down there so why don't I just go home, out of all this fume and clatter to people I need, even if hardly one among them really needs me?" Then, as he stood up, he thought of Ikey Palfrey, now launched upon his first full day at school and buttressed by his bogus kinship with the Squire of Shallowford, a boy with a manufactured background and a superimposed accent but with the courage of a hunted fox. The inevitable comparison between himself and Ikey made him shudder, so that self-pity ebbed from him. "Craddock," he said to himself, "that boy would make a baker's dozen of you at this moment! For God's sake pull yourself together and get out of here!" and he got up and began to walk swiftly down the hill towards the Strand, remembering that there was a train from Waterloo at midday and if he could get a cab at Charing Cross and promise the cabby double fare he might conceivably catch it.

V

It did not take Ikey long to realise that he was an exceptionally privileged new boy at High Wood for whereas all the other first-termers possessed but one background he had three. He had arrived at the school adequately supplied with academic qualifications, for the crammer had brought him up to prep school level with little trouble to either of them. High Wood, however, was not an establishment that set great store upon common factors, French verbs, and Latin declensions. It was a comparatively new foundation and was thus hard at work fashioning an image of itself calculated to persuade middle-class parents that they were getting Harrow and Winchester polish at half the cost and yet it was by no means a sham institution. The headmaster was a northerner and a realist who naturally made the most of the fact that his predecessor, High Wood's first headmaster, had actually sat at the feet of the great Arnold of Rugby. Outwardly the school had

a good start over most of the smaller public schools that
had sprung up all over the country in the last half-century
with the object of catering for sons of a newly-prosperous
industrial class, together with those of private gentlemen
with limited means. It was a vast, isolated group of buildings on the edge of the Exmoor plateau, six miles from
the nearest market town and endowed with more playing
fields than its two hundred and fifty boys could use. A
youngish staff was qualified to equip these boys with what
was advertised as "a comprehensive modern education"
and encouraged pupils to set their sights about half-way
between city counting houses and the outposts of the Empire, boys in short, whose fathers were prone to quote
Kipling without taking him too seriously. Unwittingly, in
his original conversation with the crammer as to where
Ikey would be most likely to succeed, Paul had made an
ideal choice. Had he aimed any higher even Ikey's wits
might have been severely taxed to maintain the charade
but here, among prosperous farmers' sons, and the sons of
merchants, doctors, dentists and clergymen who had
married a little money, he was given time to adjust himself. He was to take unique advantage of the opportunity.

He was made aware of his head start by his habit of
careful observation underlined by a personal experience
arising out of the mild system of bullying new boys, something High Wood had adopted as a matter of course in
the same way as it encouraged senior boys to wear fancy
waistcoats and walk arm in arm to chapel, or called its
Annual Speech Day "Speecher" and its nightly call-over
"Bill".

During his first term Ikey was assigned as fag to Juxton,
vice-captain of cricket and a notable "blood", with the
faintest shadow of a blonde moustache. Juxton was an
amiable oaf whose study was usually crowded with other
bloods and whilst going about his chores, whitening cricket
boots and making tea and toast, Ikey learned from their
conversation precisely what was done and what was not
done, what could be worn and what would brand a man
as an "Oick", a "Yob", or a "Swedebasher". There was,
in fact, a very great deal to learn in this field and a single
bad mistake on the part of a new boy might have taken a

good deal of living down but Ikey's acute observation, together with his unerring ear for accent stood him in good stead, so that he was soon Admirable Crichton to all the other first-year boys in the Lower School. He could tell you, for instance, at what angle one's cap should be worn at any stage up the school; how much familiarity it was safe to show certain masters and certain boys, and even such minutiae as exactly how long one should hold on to the second syllable of the Dervishlike howl of "High *Woooode"*, whilst applauding the inter-school cricket matches. He found it absurdly easy to absorb these essentials so that his quick eye and ear kept him clear of trouble with the seniors, who came to accept him as a deft hand with the toasting fork, a notable polisher of sporting equipment and a quiet but respectful scrag-end of humanity. With the Middle School, however (where dwelt the Flashmans, the Scaifes and the Beaumont-Greens), other tactics were required and it was here that Ikey's triple background gave him an enormous advantage over all the other little toads who arrived at the school from moderately prosperous homes and cheap prep schools. This was made clear to him at the first New Kids' Concert, half-way through his first term.

At stipulated intervals every newcomer to High Wood was required to mount the fifth form rostrum and divert his betters with songs or recitations and whereas most of the new boys, giving of their poor best, received nothing from the audience but a shower of books and inkwells, Ikey's imitation of a Cockney coster rendering "Knocked 'em in the Old Kent Road" won genuine applause. The audience was, in fact, stunned by what they naturally assumed to be a superb mastery of the Cockney dialect and when he obliged with an encore, giving them "Widdicombe Fair", as it might have been sung by Tamer Potter or Horace Handcock, he was at once acclaimed "A Turn" and thereafter treated with a degree of geniality by boys whose Sundays (Sunday was dedicated to the persecution of new boys) were long vistas of unutterable boredom.

It would have been fatal, of course, had he let it be known that the coster idiom was his native tongue, or that he had learned broad Devon whilst employed as a stable-boy on an estate only fifty miles away but he was far too astute to allow this secret to fall into enemy hands and preserved it jealously from all, including his cronies in the Upper Third. In fact he did the reverse, using his mastery of the two accents to imply that he was a man of the world, familiar not only with the music-halls, but the idiom of grooms and house-servants in the provinces. It was this, more than anything, that gave him not only stature among his peers but also a chance to bring his wider, overall strategy into play for in one way he was handicapped, the crammer not having had the time to teach him the important things about life at a minor public school. He was completely ignorant, for instance, of Rugby football, he could not swim, and his experience of cricket was limited to standing before chalked stumps on the scrapyard wall and hitting an underhand ball with a piece of plank. His prospects in the athletic field were no more promising. He discovered, for instance, that he had short, rather clumsy legs and was usually the last to arrive at the tape in a 100 or 220 yards junior house sprint. He knew that, somehow or other, he must make this deficiency good by the end of his second term, and perhaps he was fortunate in beginning his school life in the summer term, when cricket occupied the seniors and nobody took the junior events seriously.

He thought about his handicap a great deal, and at length arrived at a possible solution. If he could never expect to run fast then he might train himself to run a long way, for he was told that in the term ahead cross-country running took precedence over every other sport except Rugby football. Rugby, he felt, he might learn from a book and as a new boy he was unlikely to be called upon to play in even a Junior House match. He thought it best, therefore, to concentrate on long-distance running and during his first holidays, when his new status as gentleman freed him from chores in tack-room and stable-yard, he went into strict training, refusing all Mrs. Handcock's heavy pastry and going out over the stubble fields as far as Coombe Bay morning and evening in sandshoes (known at High Wood as "stinkers"), running shorts and vest. He had seven weeks in which to translate himself into a potential winner of marathons and here again he was lucky, for he soon made another discovery that he could never have found in a book. Early in his training, he discovered that a run across firm, springy turf was far less demanding than a run along the tideline of Coombe Bay and that to cover a mile on the beach was far more punishing than the same distance on the hard-packed track beside the Sorrel. It occurred to him then that if he trained on sand his calf muscles and wind would develop very rapidly so that he would have the edge on boys who did not have the luck to live beside the sea. Thereafter he merely jog-trotted to the beach, or sometimes rode the cob across the dunes and tethered him to a tide-post after which he ran as far as Nun's Head and back, using the landslip boulders as the equivalent of High Wood's hedges and ditches. By the time the autumn term arrived he was confident of giving a good account of himself in the first series of runs and so it proved, for at the first cross-country event he was the first junior boy into the quad and this set him apart in a way that might have gone to the head of a less wary athlete. Thereafter, in five successive runs, he scored a total of seventy-nine points, a record for a first-year boy. Nobody seemed to remember his dropped catches and gasping sprints of the previous term.

His efforts to master the mystique of Rugby football were not so successful, for he found the game complicated by rules against forward passing, by dropped kicks and the off-side prohibitions but his stamina, developed by his concentrated training, soon won him a place as a forward in the Junior Grenville pack and here he put into practise a trick of falling on the ball and letting the field storm over him, something he had marked down as worth remembering in *Tom Brown's Schooldays*.

Juxton, his fagmaster, developed an interest in him and the fact that Ikey privately considered Juxton a pompous fool did not prevent him taking full advantage of the great man's patronage, even to the extent of obliging study guests with song and dance, so that seniors came to refer to him as "That Palfrey kid, Jumbo Jaxton's fag, an amusin' little devil, who can run like a hare but doesn't put on side".

And so, after a couple of terms, the metamorphosis was almost complete and a boy who began earning his bread as a collector of old iron at the age of nine, and had subsequently shared a loft with the gardener's boy over a stable, was absorbed into the narrow, formalised life of boarding school without one of his contemporaries suspecting for a single moment that he was the victim of a bizarre practical joke. Yet there was a curious element in the transformation and this was Ikey's own appreciation of it, for not once did he cease to regard it as a social experiment practised upon a community not so much by himself but by Squire Craddock and there grew in Ikey a terribly urgent sense of obligation to Paul, a longing, so far unappeased, for the means to repay a little interest on the investment represented by himself. As the weeks passed, however, he could see less and less hope of achieving this for he was all too aware that the Squire had changed a very great deal during the last year and Ikey connected the change, as did everyone else in the Valley, with the inexplicable disappearance of the Squire's wife, said by some to have run off with a man in a motor, and by others to have gone raving mad so that she turned her back on hearth and home in order to chain herself to railings and throw soot at politicians. Ikey considered these theories separately but could make no sense of either, being reluctant to accept the view of Mrs. Handcock, who declared, "Missus 'as gone mazed, same as all they other suffragettes, an' Squire's well shut of 'er, the daaft baggage!" He was, in fact, persuaded to the contrary, it being clear that Squire was quite unable to put his wife out of mind and Ikey, having an affection for Grace Craddock, refused to believe that she could have lost her wits in the manner of Farmer Codsall. He was ready to admit, however, that her behaviour was eccentric and altogether outside his experience. He had been witness to many quarrels between man and wife in his childhood and remembered that they had all ended in a cuddle and a quart of beer and was therefore convinced—provided the means could be found of bringing the principals together—that all could be settled in minutes. In the meantime, concern over the Squire's despondency grew as the months passed and on the whole he was inclined to blame Mrs. Craddock the less, for a careful study of the Squire's demeanour during the Christmas holidays left him with the impression that Paul was almost enjoying his sulks and this made him wonder if, in some mysterious way, that man with the motor was at the back of it all. When, therefore, he learned that the agent's son was now cruising the China seas it struck him that something should be done before he came home again to charm Mrs. Craddock into committing further indiscretions in his motor and Ikey gave the matter the same careful consideration as he had given to the process of consolidating himself at High Wood. It was some time, however, before he hit on a plan to improve the situation.

Part of his duties in Juxton's study was to light the fire and Juxton, who read the sporting page of the *Daily Mail* every day, saved the political pages for this purpose. It was in this way that Ikey came to read a lengthy report dealing with suffragette activities in London and he put it aside to study in the latrines, the only place at High Wood where new boys could expect privacy. The article interested him far more than he thought it would. He had never dreamed that suffragettes had so much fun, or were regarded so seriously by the police. He read an account of various outrages committed by these extraordinary women and became excited when he found the name "Mrs. P. Craddock" bracketed alongside the name of "Grace Philimore". It worried him a little, this name "Philimore", for it might mean that Squire and his wife were already divorced and that she was now married to someone else but he soon discarded this possibility, reasoning that such a dreadful scandal would certainly have reached the Valley and become common gossip in the kitchens. It must mean, therefore, that Mrs. Craddock had two names, one as the Squire's wife and another as a suffragette. He read on to learn with some dismay that she had actually been to prison, just like old Smut Potter and was not wholly reassured when he gathered (lower down the column) that suffragettes were always going to prison, and were, in fact, more often to be found there than not. The value of the report, however, lay in the address of the movement's headquarters which he ringed in pencil before putting the clipping in his pocket book. It came to him then precisely what he must do to restore happiness to the Squire. Somehow or other he must travel up to London, find her, and bring her back with him, and although he realised that this might prove a very difficult undertaking he had faith in his lucky star, and more in his ability to tell such a harrowing story that she would have little choice but to accompany him home at once.

He spent the last week of term perfecting his story, toying with a variety of illnesses but finally settling upon a fiction that could not be verified by a call upon the doctor, or indeed exploded by Grace returning home to find Paul in excellent health. He would tell her bluntly that he had proof that Squire was considering suicide but he was too good an artist to draw directly upon the well-known circumstances of the Four Winds tragedy. He would simply tell her that, on one occasion, Paul had been dragged half dead from the Mere (and his rescuers sworn to secrecy) and that on a second occasion he himself had caught Paul's bridle just as he was putting Snowdrop at an impossible fence. He thought it almost certain that she would check these reports but he could probably delay this somewhat by warning her that Paul had also sworn him to secrecy, and that he alone was cognisant of the cloud that had settled on Squire's brain. The important thing was to bring them face to face and shock the Squire out of his unforgiving sulk. After that he was sure that God would wade in and help. After all, he would have done the spadework and how many times had it been proclaimed from pulpits that God helped those who helped themselves?

Having settled his approach he went to work on practicalities, realising that he would have to explain absence from home during the first two days of the holidays. He would also have to pay his own railway fare to London and as it was near the end of term, and his wealth amounted to tenpence, at least ten shillings would have to be raised for journey money. First, however, at the final Sunday letter-writing session, he wrote to Mrs. Handcock telling her that he had accepted an invitation to spend a couple of days with Rawlinson, his particular friend, who lived near Plymouth, adding that Rawlinson's father owned a car and had promised to drive him back to Shallowford. He did not post this letter but held it back until the final evening, in order to guard against a cross-check with the headmaster. Then he buttonholed Davis Minor and offered his tuck-box at the knockdown price of ten shillings. He selected Davis not simply because he was the Lower School miser but because he was also the only boy in the Third who did not possesss a tuck-box, his father being a faddist who disapproved of the tradition. He knew that Davis was secretly ashamed of this and when the boy, having inspected the tuck-box, offered seven-and-sixpence, Ikey closed his locker and said he would accept Martin's offer of nine-and-sixpence. Money changed hands at once, and Davis carried away the tuck-box in triumph, having decided to torment hungry companions throughout the following term by praising the fictitious delights of the contents.

All was now ready for a descent upon the suffragette headquarters, and when, during prep, on the last night of term, he was summoned to his housemaster's study Ikey obeyed the order promptly, anticipating that Mr. Ralston would issue him with his ticket to Paxtonbury and probably half-a-crown journey money, a sum that would bring expeditionary funds to thirteen shillings and fourpence halfpenny. There was, of course, the return fare to be considered, but he assumed that the erring (and by then penitent) Mrs. Craddock would pay for both tickets.

He knew that something was seriously wrong as soon as he saw Ralston's expression. He looked, Ikey thought, sympathetic and began, with a brave but false smile, "I'm afraid I've a bit of a disappointment for you, old chap!" At this form of address Ikey's stomach contracted but Ralston went on hurriedly. "You will have to stay over a week or two, Palfrey. I've just had a . . . well, a rather sensational message from your guardian's agent, a Mr. John Rudd . . ." and Ikey, suddenly feeling sick, said, "What's happened, sir? Is the Squire dead?" so that Ralston went on reassuringly, "Oh, it's not that bad, old man, it's well . . . something rather unusual, something I think you may well be proud to hear when you get over the shock! There was a shipwreck a few miles from your home and your guardian, along with a number of his tenants, was instrumental in saving several lives. The place has been turned into a hospital and everything is at sixes and sevens. Mr. Rudd telephoned to ask if we could keep you here for a day or so."

His bright smile did not deceive Ikey for an instant. This was only Ralston's second term as a housemaster and his first attempt at breaking bad news to a boy, so that he would have done well to have rehearsed his speech. Ikey said, quietly, "Is the Sq . . . is my guardian all right, sir?" and Ralston, unable to meet the boy's eye, replied with tell-tale hesitancy, that "Mr. Craddock had been knocked about a bit during rescue operations. He's getting the best attention and there's absolutely no need to worry," he added, "but for a week or so he needs rest and quiet, so I agreed that you could either stay on with us or, if we can arrange it, stay with a chum. Who is your particular chum? Is it Rawlinson or Hooper Two?"

"Rawlinson, sir," Ikey said but before Ralston had finished speaking he had made up his mind. The conclusion was obvious; if the Squire had been injured in such an improbable event as a shipwreck, it was obvious that God was already taking a hand in his plan, for now there was no need to cod Mrs. Craddock with stories of attempted suicide. All he had to do (and surely the need to act was more urgent than ever) was to go through with the main part of his scheme, that is, get to London, find her, and tell her Paul needed her desperately. If that did not bring her back by the first train then nothing would but, as he decided this, he was aware that certain difficulties had arisen to cancel out such unlooked-for advantages and that the Almighty was rather overdoing it. As things were it now looked as though he would remain a prisoner at school until Squire was in a fair way to making a recovery and this milked the urgency from his mission. He looked carefully at Ralston and decided that the housemaster was telling the truth, or most of the truth, and that Squire was neither dead nor dying. He said, quietly, "Thank you, sir, I'd sooner stay at school until I can go home. Will that be all, sir?" and Ralston beamed at him and said heartily, "Why of course old man, and I'm bound to say I admire your pluck! Would you like to spend the rest of the evening with Mrs. Ralston and take supper with us? Or would you rather go back to prep and keep this to ourselves until tomorrow?"

"I'll go back to prep, sir, I should like to write a letter home straight away!"

"Naturally, naturally," said Ralston, patting his shoulder. "I'll look in after dormitory bell tonight, just to cheer you up," and Ikey, muttering "Thank you, sir!", slipped from the room.

He knew that he must act at once. He must go to the bursar's office, find his ticket to Paxtonbury among the tickets drawn in advance and get clear of the school before the morning papers made him the centre of attraction and flight was impossible.

The bursar's office was unlocked and the tickets were in their marked envelopes on the desk. He soon found his own, pocketed ticket and half-crown, and hurried back to Big School, where reading prep was still in progress. He took out his letter, read it over, scribbled a brief postcript and then readdressed it. When supper bell rang he posted it on the way to the dining hall. It would be collected early in the morning and arrive at Shallowford the following afternoon. By then he would have been missed, and Ralston would be trying to get in touch with his home, but this would be difficult since there was still no telephone at Shallowford (Rudd must have telephoned from The Raven) and it would increase his already excellent start. For a moment or so Ikey felt almost sorry for Ralston but the moment passed after the housemaster came softly into the dormitory to whisper something to Geary, the dormitory prefect. Ikey saw Geary glance across at him and then say something back, so that when the housemaster came down the aisle between the beds he pretended to be asleep. He did not want to risk discovery of the fact that he was wearing his nightgown over shirt and rolled-up trousers. He would give them a couple of hours to settle down before slipping out and walking the six miles to Barrow Market. He would would have to walk fast if he was to reach there in time to stow away on the late goods train that crossed Barrow viaduct in the small hours every week-night. Ikey knew all about that goods train, even to the time of its arrival in Paxtonbury, having made it his business to find out from Gobber Christow, the school lamp-trimmer. Gobber's son was an engine-driver and drove it three times a week.

He lay still listening to the excited chatter and end-of-term laughter until silence bell and to the scrunch of Geary's feet as the perfect came up, undressed and got into bed. He waited for Geary's contented sigh, for his neighbour's high-pitched snore and finally the far-off clank of the earlier goods train crossing the viaduct, the rattle telling him it was now almost midnight. Ten minutes later he was out of bed and he had jacket and boots on before he remembered the prayer. He did not need reassurance of the kind he had sought long ago, when he had prayed for Squire Craddock's appearance at the railway station the day of his arrival in the Valley, but thought it might be just as well to buy some insurance on the Squire's health. He knelt by the bed and muttered, "Keep Squire in bed and everyone busy until I get back with Mrs. Craddock, Oh Lord!" In his unseemly haste to get started he forgot the obligatory Amen!

CHAPTER THIRTEEN

I

ON the afternoon of March 14th, 1906, Tamer Potter was also in communion with God, having decided that it was high time he made a survey of his private beach, in order to see what the Almighty had sent him in the way of a bonus to his conventional activities. He went through the cliff-top rabbit-run and down the dry gully to the tiny bay that he thought of as Flotsam Cove (although it was unnamed on the Ordnance maps) and there began a meticulous examination of the boulder-strewn margin between high- and low-water mark, commencing at the knob of sandstone in the east and working westwards as far as Coombe Bluff, where the overhang of the cliff had kept this tiny section of coastline out of reach of less knowledgeable beachcombers.

The Cove was not more than eighty yards across but the points enclosing it were never uncovered, not even at extreme ebb tide, so that nobody could walk here from Coombe Bay or from the area further along the coast. High tides surged almost to the foot of the cliff, all of two hundred feet high at this part, and the sole approach, save by boat, was by the Potter tunnel, discovered forty years ago by an inquisitive lurcher called Kitty that Tamer had owned as a boy. The tunnel was really a long, steep rabbit run, beginning below the cliff path and weaving a path through thick gorse to the head of an old water-course, dried up since the stream had dug itself a new channel. It was a tricky descent but safe enough for anyone knowing it as well as Tamer, who usually went down there about twice a year, once after the autumn gales and again in early spring, for these were the times of the year when he could expect a harvest from the gales and the cross-tides sweeping up Channel to meet the outfall of the Whin further west.

Flotsam Cove had brought Tamer several slices of luck in the past. Once he had salvaged a watertight box of Virginia tobacco, which had kept his pipe filled throughout three winters. Another time he had found a strongly-built dinghy which he had repaired and still used for inshore fishing. Then there had been an almost new buoy and an anchor, which he sold for a sovereign to Tom Williams, a Coombe Bay fisherman, and later still, after a week of gales, he had salvaged a thing that had been a man, still wearing sea-boots and a few rags of clothing. Tamer was not squeamish. He searched the corpse and found a leather bag containing a gold crucifix and two sovereigns. He pocketed them and reported the presence of the body to the proper authorities.

On this particular day the weather was wet and wild,

with an unseasonal south-westerly gale blowing itself out and a particularly dense sea fog creeping in from the west when the wind lost some of its force. It was warm, however, almost muggy, and Potter, who was a cold mortal, never minded rain so long as the temperature stayed round about fifty degrees. He buttoned his reefer and dragged his sixteen-stone-ten through the narrow tunnel to the gully where, with surprising agility for one so gross, he lowered himself to the beach and began his square search.

About five o'clock, when the weather was setting in really thick, he came across a park bench. It was an odd thing to find wedged between two knife-edge slabs of rock but a close inspection showed it to be in good condition, with its iron rails and back supports intact, the latter stamped with the letters "U.D.C." indicating that it had been washed out to sea when a storm lashed some esplanade. Tamer assessed its worth at about thirty shillings, providing he could prise it loose and get the girls or Sam to drag it up the cliff. In all cases of salvage it was Tamer who prospected and the family who supplied the muscle work. The Potters never called in auxiliaries, no matter how heavy the task, for this would have meant revealing the secret of the approach to the cove.

He worked away doggedly for half-an-hour and all the time the wind was dying and the sea fog getting thicker and thicker along the coast. After an hour or so he could not even see the long tongue of rock that split the cove into two parts, a kind of natural causeway that ran south for perhaps a hundred yards ending in a solitary bastion of sandstone that had resisted thousands of years of erosion and formed a tiny island shaped like a broad-bladed dagger embedded on a shelf of rock. At last he worked the bench free and stood upright, grunting with satisfaction and it was just then that he heard some confused and subdued shouting that seemed to come at him from all points of the compass. He located it, however, as soon as he had made allowances for the echo in that enclosed place, realising that its centre was the sandstone pinnacle about a cable's length from the beach. It was an eerie sound, a combination of human and metallic noises, a steady grinding and crashing, with overtones of voices raised in fear and punctuated by hoarse shouts and just once a long and piercing scream, almost certainly the scream of a woman.

Tamer was a very stolid man and not easily frightened by noises. Some people might have interpreted the shouts as the wails of long-drowned creatures revisiting the scene of a tragedy long ago, but Potter understood at once that, whoever was making them, was in danger of being drowned at that particular moment. He forgot all about the seat and climbed over the rocks to the causeway, thinking that he might edge along it in the face of the rising tide and get some notion of what was happening behind the thick, wet blanket of mist, but when he was less than ten yards from the beach he realised that to go further would be suicidal, for the sea was running high and there was nothing to grasp for support on that narrow, weed-covered rock. So he put his hands to his mouth and bellowed "Ahoy, there!" and at once a man's voice answered "Ahoy!" after which there was more confused shouting and several isolated shouts for help.

Even at that distance, and with the voices distorted by fog, Tamer knew that the poor devils stranded there were foreigners, for in the answering voices an accent was clearly noticeable. The presence of foreigners on the reef did not surprise him. He was familiar with the Whinmouth coastal trade, a coming and going of Dutch and German brigs, some of them operating under sail with a single auxiliary engine, that carried cargoes of apples, timber, cattle food, coal and coke. He thought, gloomily, "They'm in a rare ole fix, an' there's no 'ope for 'em in this sea while the tide goes on risin'! They'm stuck on that ole point for sure and although the sea's goin down it won't zettle till it ebbs and by then there'll be thirty voot o' water on that slab!" He hesitated a moment, his instinct to help at war with his strong reluctance to reveal a close family secret to coastguards, police and even local foreigners west of the Whin, but then he realised that he could not let a personal consideration prevent him from doing what he could for the poor wretches out there in the fog, so he shouted, "I'm a-goin' for 'elp! I'm a-goin' fer the lifeboat! 'Ang on, will 'ee, now?" and without waiting for an answer he hurried back to the beach and began the steep ascent of the gully.

By the time he was half-way up he was sobbing for breath and his heart was pounding at the cage of his ribs. He paused to strip off the reefer jacket and then continued climbing, moving from foothold to foothold until at last he struck the mouth of the rabbit run and went on up to the cliff-top on all fours.

When he reached the top he was convinced that he was dying. His eyes misted over and he fell on his knees, bowing his head to the grass but after a few minutes his vision cleared and although he could not see five yards through the fog and still knew precisely where he was, he was uncertain where to go for immediate help. He was kneeling there, wheezing and gasping, when he heard the chink of iron shoes and to his relief a mounted figure loomed out of the east, looking gigantic in the dense trailers of mist. Tamer at once recognised the horseman as Farmer Willoughby, his neighbour, returning no doubt from one of his evangelistic missions at one or other of the chapels along the coast, and well mounted on his strong, barrel-chested cob. Willoughby stared at the thick-set figure in mild surprise.

"Why Potter," he said reproachfully, "you shouldn't be out in this weather without a coat, man! Jump up behind and I'll take you across to the Dell," but Tamer, still very breathless, grabbed his stirrup leather and gasped, "Tiz a wreck! Down on the reef below! They'm out on that ole rock ledge an' if us dorn get 'em orf before high tide they'll drown, every man jack of 'em!"

Willoughby's gentle face crumpled with dismay and he said, "Dear Lord, are you sure?" and Tamer, who had some regard for the man but privately thought him quite daft, shouted, "Gordamme, o' course I'm sure! I bin talking to 'em, baint I?" and at once made a decision, based on the potentialities of himself and his neighbour. "Lookee," he said "stay yer to mark the spot and I'll take the cob and rouse Meg an' the girls! One of 'em can ride on into Coombe Bay and talk into that ole telephone at The Raven and another can roust out Squire an' Mr. Rudd. Us can't wait for the Whinmouth lifeboat nor the coastguard! Time they get 'ere the tide'll be full, and there's a big sea running! They'll be drowned, the whole bliddy lot of 'em! Stay right where you be an' when us hollers holler back, an' keep on hollering, do 'ee mind?"

In a situation like this Willoughby was ready to concede leadership to an erring brother. He had lived for so long in celestial regions that he felt helpless in the face of an urgent, earthly problem, so he dismounted and helped Tamer into the saddle and a moment later the latter's bulky figure had disappeared in the mist, leaving Willoughby to seek the counsel of God. No one in the Sorrel Valley could have done this as well as Edwin Willoughby, noted for his long, improvised prayers, which invariably contained a plea for distressed mariners. He stood there like a biblical prophet on the edge of the cliff and one might have thought, by the urgency of his voice and posture, that he was asking Providence to aid him in staying the flow of the tide immediately below.

II

Tamer reached the Dell less than ten minutes after leaving Willoughby and minutes after that the Potter household had dispersed, Violet mounting the cob and riding for Coombe Bay, Hazel running through Coombe Wood and across the meadow to warn the people at the Big House and Cissie (alone among the Potters without the gift of moving across country by instinct) along the track that led to Sam's cottage in the woods. Sam was a good man in an emergency and Tamer, sweating and wheezing in his stable as he searched for rope, cursed the authorities for depriving him of the services of Smut, who would have known just what to do and how to go about it. His wife Meg, however, was a good substitute. Once she understood the basic facts she wasted no time bothering him with questions but slung baskets each side of the cart-horse and helped him load them with coils of one-inch rope. She also had the forethought to drag out a hurdle that could be used for a stretcher, fastening it to Bessie's saddle by a length of cord. Once or twice, as they were getting ready to return to the cliffs, Tamer spared a thought to worry about himself, for the speed he had climbed the gully and the mad ride through the mist to the Dell, had left him dizzy and his heart continued to pump with the savage beat of a piston. He thought, savagely, "Damme, I'll 'ave another o' my ole turns if I doan't taake it easy but how can a man bide, when the water will be under the cliff in two hours and us 'aven't got down to 'em yet?" Meg noticed his distress and ran into the house, returning with a leather bottle on her girdle. "Here man," she said briefly, "take a swallow or two o' that," and he swallowed gratefully, feeling the potion warm his belly and put new vigour into his calves. A moment later they were off, Tamer riding the horse, and Meg following the sound of the dragging hurdle; only Potter could have found the still-praying Willoughby in under half-an-hour.

The Potter girls also accomplished their journeys in record time. Cissie reached Sam's cottage in forty minutes flat and was on her way back in another five, Sam accompanying her with more ropes. Violet entered Coombe Bay village like another Paul Revere, shouting the news right and left as she cantered down to The Raven, to tell her story to Abe Tozer, the shoeing smith, who then made his first ever telephone calls to the Whinmouth coastguard and local police. He told them as much as he knew and what was being done in the way of rescue, then ran down to the quayside cottages in the hope of getting Williams to launch his boat and go round by the Bluff to the Cove but Williams was appalled at the news. "That'll be the German boat," he said, "I seed her beating out o' Whinmouth about noon and if 'er's gone ashore no one'll get her off! As for going round under the Bluff, well, us c'n try, but tiz risky. The tide is beatin' inshore now an' not due to turn till near midnight. I'll talk to Ned Hockings an' us'll see what us can do! Meantime, get the landsmen together and go over the headland to see if you vind some way down to the beach."

"You can't never get to that beach from the top,"

Tozer protested. "There baint no way down and with the tide running how can any of us get into the bliddy Cove, save by boat?"

Williams said soberly, "Tamer Potter got there Abe! Tell him to show 'ee the way while I get a boat party together. Has anyone told Squire?"

"Aye," Tozer said, "Hazel Potter is there now. Well, good luck to 'ee, I'll do the best I can!" and he ran back to The Raven, where a party led by Eph Morgan, the builder, had already assembled. They set off across the headland at once and on the way somebody thought to call in and leave a message with Doctor O'Keefe, telling the old man to prepare for casualties. They were leaving the street for the path to the headland when Abe Tozer's boy, a notable hunter of gull's eggs, had another thought and doubled back, rejoining them later with his thirty-foot rope-ladder.

III

Paul at once recognised the shipwreck as yet another of these sudden crises he had been called upon to face at intervals during the last four years and yet, for the first time, there was a difference, for here was a challenge that involved not only him but every able-bodied man and woman in the Valley and it was because of this that he could meet it with more cool-headedness than when caught up in the Smut Potter scandal, or the fatal madness of Martin Codsall, or even the quarrel that caused the split of the Four Winds family. For here, at last, was something that demanded swift planning and resolute action, something akin to a junior officer's work in the field and whilst with one half of his mind he was issuing orders and making the decisions necessary to rally the manpower of the estate, at a deeper level of consciousness he was uplifted as he had not been for close on two years.

He was standing talking to Rudd in the stable-yard when Hazel Potter came panting out of the mist with news of shipwreck off Coombe Bluff, and at once Paul

433

acted entirely on his own initiative, without consulting his agent. His first impulse was to ride for the village but when Hazel said her sister was already on her way there he gave the child a moment to catch her breath and then questioned her patiently, whilst John called for Chivers and together they saddled Snowdrop, the agent's bay, the youngest of the cobs and the trap pony. Hazel, who soon recovered from her cross-country run from the Dell to Shallowford, could not tell them much, for Tamer had been badly blown when he came in with the news and had despatched his daughters in all directions without telling them more than the barest facts. In addition, Hazel Potter's brogue was the thickest in the Valley and sometimes almost unintelligible. Paul gathered, however, that Coombe Bay had been alerted, the coastguard and police almost certainly informed by telephone, that Sam Potter would soon be on the spot, and that under the Bluff were an unknown number of persons in imminent danger of drowning. He made his dispositions accordingly, despatching Chivers to summon all the available men and two carts to the Dell, instructing him to call at the Home Farm, Hermitage, and Four Winds, in that order, before riding to the edge of the moor to fetch Will Codsall. Chivers rode off at once on Rudd's bay and before setting out for the Dell, where he hoped Potter or his wife would have more detailed information, Paul told Mrs. Handcock to prepare guest rooms and make a cauldron of pea soup against the probability of visitors. He would have taken rope from the stables but the girl said, breathlessly, "Dornee bother, Squire! Pa will ha' taaken rorpe, Pa's got bushels o' rorpe!" so they cantered off unencumbered, Hazel leading the way through the mist as far as the junction of the Dell cart-track where Rudd pulled up and said, "I'd better check on the village, Paul. They'll send out a boat party no doubt!" but Paul replied, "Not until ebb tide, John! There's no power-driven boat in Coombe Bay and no one could pull round under Coombe Bluff against a flowing tide!" and as he said this he was surprised by his instinctive knowledge of local conditions. Later that night Rudd was to remember this and say to himself, "By God! And he has talked to me about throwing his hand in! He's been here less than four years but he knows the ebb and flow of the tides as well as Potter!" He said, "Lead on then, and we'll hope to God they had the sense to make straight for the headland and bring along tackle. All I hope is that she's struck well to the east, where we can climb down to the beach!"

They found the Potter farmhouse deserted, although the doors were open and the lamp was still burning in the kitchen and for a moment Paul was baffled. The mist was shredding a little here but visibility was still reduced to yards. The girl said, in a matter-of-fact voice, "They'm gone upalong! And they've taaken rorpe, like I told 'ee!"

It was this second reference to ropes that gave Paul a clue she was holding something back. In general with the rest of the Valley he had always regarded Hazel Potter as a halfwit, and partly because of this and partly because he was worried by the time factor, he seized her by the arm, shaking her impatiently.

"Do you *know* where the wreck is, Hazel?" he demanded. "Can't you tell us exactly where your father and mother have gone?" and the girl said sullenly, "Arr, us knaws! But he'll flay the hide offen me if I taakes 'ee there!"

"But you've got to take us, Hazel," he said. "People are out there, drowning at this moment!"

"Wait a minute, Paul," John said as he edged his cob alongside the pony. "Listen, Hazel, your father told you to take Squire to wherever he's gone, didn't he?"

"Arr," said the girl, hesitantly, "he did that, but tiz funny for he zed he'd flay the hide offen any one of us who chattered!"

"What the devil is she talking about?" Paul demanded irritably, but John readdressed himself earnestly to the girl. "I *know* about that, Hazel! Tamer knows a way to the Cove and you know a way to the Cove but the Squire will give your father the Cove if you take us there now, do you understand?"

"Will 'ee zo?" said Hazel, looking wonderingly at Paul, and Paul, only half comprehending, hastily endorsed the promise and at this Hazel seemed satisfied and said, "Well, get along then and I'll show 'ee the tunnel, an iffen 'er belts me for showing 'ee I'll run off to the woods till 'er's safe an' drunk again!", and she clapped her heels into the pony and trotted off up the steepest side of the Dell and over several Potter hedgerows to the level ground of the cliff-top.

Up here the visibility was better and they could hear the roar of the breakers under the Bluff. John said, "We're damned near the edge, Paul, take it easy and let the girl lead. I've always had my suspicions about Tamer's unwillingness to cultivate these fields and it takes a shipwreck to prove them justified!", but before Paul could answer Willoughby's bewhiskered face loomed out of the fog and he called in a high-pitched voice, "Praise God you've come, Squire! Potter and his wife went down nearly an hour since, leaving me to show others the way! It's yonder, through the gorse to the head of that dry gully and after that the Lord go with you, for it's more than a hundred feet and close on sheer!"

"Great God, that's suicide in this mist," Rudd exclaimed. "They've gone to their deaths!" but Willoughby said, civilly, "No, Mr. Rudd, sir, they took ropes and Meg Potter came back to tell me she would wait by the steepest part to help others down! She's there now, I believe, at the head of the gully!"

Paul peered over the belt of gorse but it was impossible to judge the angle of the cliff. Rudd said, "If you go, I'm coming with you, Paul!" but Paul, turning back to him, replied, "You damned well won't, John! You're over fifty and that's a young man's climb in the mist or in the clear! Wait here with Willoughby and send some of the young men down if they've got the stomach for it! As for the girl . . ." and he turned back to the thicket just in time to see Hazel's heels disappearing through a hole in the gorse and went after her, crawling on hands and knees along a tunnel less than two feet high until he could hear the voice of Meg Potter chiding her daughter from a perch about half-way down the cliff. A moment later he was beside them on a small platform of sandstone over which two ropes had been flung, the ends running back into the bushes.

Meg said, in a matter-of-fact tone, "Oh, tiz you,

Squire! Well, my man needs help below but if so you'd sooner bide here me and the maid'll go down. Thicky tide has about an hour to flow!"

"Have you made contact with the poor devils?" he asked and Meg said she believed not, apart from the initial exchange of shouts when Tamer first located them.

"I'll go down at once," Paul told her. "You and the girl stay here and guide the others," and he seized the ropes and lowered himself over the ledge, hanging by his hands until his feet found partial holds in the clefts each side of the gully.

It was, as Willoughby had said, almost sheer but the surface was rough and the descent was not as fearful as he had anticipated, although how anyone had ever managed it without the ropes he could not begin to think. Then, when he was part way down, a soft orange glow showed through the mist, and then another and a third, and he realised Tamer must be lighting fires along the beach and using fuel more inflammable than driftwood. As soon as his feet touched shingle he saw Potter's thick-set figure silhouetted between the cliff and the most easterly of his fires and smelled the sharp tang of burning pitch. Tamer called, "Who is it?" and he called back, "It's me, Tamer, Squire!" and Tamer came crunching over the loose shingle looking, Paul thought, preoccupied but by no means excited.

"Rudd's on top and others are coming down as soon as they get here," he told him. "Are they still alive out there?"

"Aye, they'm there," Tamer said. "But whether there's two or dree or a dozen I can't say in this bliddy ole fog! They'll do till the tide's full but if us don't get 'em off the ebb will taake 'em as far as Conger Rocks. I reckon they was comin' ashore from there in a boat when they capsized on the rocks yonder!" and he cupped his hands to his mouth and bellowed, "Ahoy there! Dornee move! Us is comin' for 'ee!" There was a faint answering hail and Tamer turned back to Paul. "It baint a particle o' gude waitin' for the lifeboat," he said. "Us'll have to taake a chance on it an' use my boat paid out on cable from the western zide o' the cove."

437

"You've got a boat down here?"

"Aye," said Tamer reluctantly, "but us can't use un till others get here. Then, wi one other along o' me, and a shore party holding us, I could let her drift downalong till us touches the rocks an' maybe bring off dree or fower of 'em."

They stood facing the sea for a moment, seeing nothing but the dense wreaths of mist and occasionally the cream-flecked crest of a wave as it crashed on to the shingle and beach debris. Paul said, finally, "Show me the boat," and Tamer led the way along the beach just as a rattle of stones higher up announced the arrival of the first newcomer at the foot of the descent.

IV

The alerting of the Valley beginning with Violet Potter's arrival in Coombe Bay, and carried inland by Paul's despatch of Chivers to rouse the farms, was not really a haphazard operation. It had about it a speed and precision absent from the war games of professional generals working with trained soldiers and this was because, basically, it was a tribal exercise, performed by men who had been dependent upon one another's goodwill all their lives. The impulse to unite in a common cause was in their blood and bone and although, in fact, twentieth-century apparatus had been employed to summon Whinmouth lifeboat and coastguard, these factors played no part in the attempt to rescue eight men and one woman, marooned on a shelf of rock eighty yards seaward of Tamer's Cove and invisible behind the veils of mist. The feat was achieved by the people of the Valley and was due not so much to the courage and ingenuity of a sixty-year-old gypsy farmer and his twenty-six-year-old landlord, or even to the men who controlled the boat from the beach, but to the tribal instinct that had assembled them on an inaccessible stretch of shore in a little over one hour from the moment Tamer had galloped into the Dell with news that men were needed and time was short.

The Whinmouth lifeboat crew spent the whole of that

wild night circling the hulk of the *Sulzbach* that was straddled on Conger Rocks, three miles south-east of the Cove but rescued nobody, for there was no one alive on the wreck. It was only when dawn came that they were able to recover two or three bodies from the sandbank inside the bar and cruise off-shore, watching Tom Williams' boats move in and pick up the stranded survivors, and such of their rescuers who preferred to return to Coombe Bay by sea rather than tackle the ascent of the gully after such a strenuous night. Then the lifeboat rounded the Bluff to put into the little harbour and its crew learned what had happened but by that time the story was known as far away as Paxtonbury.

The alarm had travelled the Valley in a wide circle, using the reverse route of gulls flying inshore when gales cut them off from their offshore feeding-grounds. The gulls always flew in on the wind, north-east from Coombe Bay to the Coombe farms, then west from Derwent's yard across the woods to the big house before passing Priory Wood to the Hermitage, and finally over the Sorrel to Four Winds and south to the coast. The cry for manpower took the opposite course, beginning at the Dell and moving via the big house across the river to Four Winds, then back again to Hermitage and Periwinkle Farms and finally over the woods to Derwent's farm at High Coombe. This clockwise circuit had an unlooked-for advantage. It meant that men like Hugh Derwent, and the younger Willoughby, were the last to learn of the shipwreck but they had less than half the distance to travel to the shelf below the rabbit run, where Meg Potter remained all night lowering gear and showing the more awkward among them how to descend the gully. This was why widely scattered units arrived more or less together just as dusk was setting in and the wind was getting up, dissolving some of the sea-fog but driving the full tide hard among the boulders of the cove.

The Coombe Bay party, seven or eight in all, were the first to cross the headland and grope their way down the cliff path to the spot where Rudd and Willoughby awaited them. They had between them more than a hundred yards of good rope and a small inflatable canvas raft of doubtful age. They also had Davy Tozer's rope ladder, which proved invaluable in replacing the last two lengths of Tamer's rope and thus adding forty feet of cable to the coil on the beach. Rudd took charge of the cliff-top team and nobody questioned his authority when he told them Squire Craddock was already on the beach. The younger men, like Davy Tozer and Walt Pascoe thought little enough of the descent but some of the others, Eph Morgan, the builder, and Rudd himself, could not have attempted it had not Tamer pioneered the climb. In the red glow of the flaming canisters those at the top could just make out Squire and Tamer working at something wedged in a cleft under the shoulder of the headland and at first supposed them to be trying artificial respiration on somebody washed ashore. Then, after Davy and Walt Pascoe had gone down and secured the ladder to the shelf, Hugh Derwent appeared out of the mist and after him young Willoughby and then, in ones and twos, Will Codsall, who had had the longest ride, Sam Potter, Arthur Pitts and Henry, and Old Honeyman, with the shepherd twins, Matt and Luke. Last of all came Eveleigh with his eldest boy Gil and his two hired men, Ben and Gerry. Rudd, now using Hazel Potter to maintain contact between cliff-top and Meg's shelf, sent the most active of them down to the beach as soon as they appeared and when he saw they had arrived safely he said to Willoughby, "You take over here, Edwin, and send a message when you get news of the boats. I'm going down myself." Willoughby did not try and dissuade him and would have followed had not Rudd forbidden it. A responsible man was needed at the top, for hope that the lifeboat would arrive offshore before high tide had now faded and Davy Tozer, who made nothing of the climb, had come up again with news that Potter had a skiff in the cove and they were about to attempt a direct rescue with a paid-out cable.

"When the coastguard arrives explain what's going on down there," Rudd told Willoughby, and sent Hazel back to the village with a written message for Tom Williams or his deputy. He scrawled it on an envelope in the light of a lantern, making no attempt to explain details. All he

440

wrote was, *"Shore party and possible survivors in cove just east of headland. Try and pick up at first light or soon as ebb begins. Rudd."* Then, after a moment's hesitation, he added, "Per pro Squire Craddock," without thinking that Tom Williams would be most unlikely to know the meaning of 'per pro'.

There had been one spluttering rocket from the end of the reef, so that it was clear that someone there was still alive but the drenching spray had already doused two of the tar canisters and only the most westerly still burned brightly. In the light of this the men worked methodically, knotting the assorted ropes until they had a cable about a hundred and thirty yards in length. Abe Tozer tested every knot and Tamer showed them where to anchor the shore end, looping it over and through a twisted snarl of iron buried in the shingle, itself a relic of a wreck on the Conger Rocks a generation ago. Then, with the skiff stern firmly lashed to the long rope they carried the boat over the boulders to a point where sand had piled up in a broad crevice and there was a chance of launching between breakers, for here the beach was partially protected by the isolated rock and the causeway connecting it to the shingle. The causeway itself was already under four feet of water.

Paul took no part in these operations. Tamer obviously knew the tides and rock formations like the back of his hand, and Abe Tozer made himself responsible for briefing the shore party, emphasising the doubtful quality of the cable.

"She'll hold so long as youm careful to pay out an inch at a time," he warned them. "Dornee be in no bliddy hurry or they'm all gonners, an' Squire too!" He said nothing about Tamer's prospects but the old fellow was not slow to remind him.

"Ay, and me along of 'im," he growled, and because this was the nearest thing to a joke uttered on the beach that night everyone laughed and Eph Morgan, in his singsong Welsh accent, said, "There's a brave thing you're doing, Tamerboy! The Lord go with both of you!"

It was now close on high tide and waves were breaking within twenty yards of the cliff wall. Glancing round the circle of faces Paul realised that there could hardly have been a more representative gathering of the Valley families. Not since his Coronation soirée had he seen so many of them in one place at one time. The Coombe Bay folk were represented by the two Tozers, Walt Pascoe and Eph Morgan, the Dell by Tamer and his son Sam. Young Willoughby was there from Deepdene, and so were the Derwents, father and son, from High Combe. Will Codsall and Eveleigh's team represented Periwinkle and Four Winds and although old Arthur Pitts had remained at the top with Willoughby and the Home Farm men, Henry Pitts was there to represent Hermitage and had, in fact, already quarrelled with Paul in an attempt to take his place in the boat. Paul counted them, without knowing that he did so and numbered fifteen and only when they were ranged each side of the skiff, waiting for the lull after a ninth wave, did he realise that his own presence brought the total to sixteen.

For a moment, on launching, the sea under the headland seemed almost calm and they made it in a single rush, Tamer at the oars, Paul sitting astern with his weight, in accordance with Tamer's instructions, pressed on the rudder bar, causing the skiff to swing south-east as the bows struck the first breaker and brought a drenching shower of spray into the boat. The rope went taut, then slack, then taut again, so that at first Paul thought they would be dragged back into the eddy and thrown at the feet of the shore party but the scour, sweeping round the extreme tip of the Bluff, caught them within seconds and glancing over his shoulder he could still see the beach in the glow of the tar beacon. Then the buffeting of the waves drove every thought but self-preservation from his head and they seemed to be spinning in wide circles, with Tamer grunting and wheezing in the bows and every now and again lifting his starboard oar clear of the water as he lashed away with his port blade to increase his sea room and hold a course for the rock.

Without the cable they would have been helpless, for the scour here had the force of a cataract and they seemed to be rushed towards the causeway at fantastic speed. The wink of the beach fire had been blotted out yet they could

442

see no sign of the big rock or of the men clinging to it. Paul saw that Tamer was back-paddling with all his might, doing what he could to check the onrush of the boat for each time the cable went slack they feared that the next jerk would rip the stern from the boat or tumble them both in a heap in the bows. The shore party, however, seemed to know their business. Soon the sickening jerks ceased as the cable remained taut and Tamer, glancing over his left shoulder, drew in his starboard oar and set to work solely with his port, so that in smoother water west of the break-water the sheer weight of the wet cable steadied them somewhat and when Tamer shouted "Hard up, Squire!" Paul found the boat answered to the rudder perfectly and they drove right in under the rock, Tamer breaking the force of the collision with the oar. Then a minor miracle occurred. At the very moment of arrival the mist parted and they must have been visible for a few seconds from the beach for Paul heard a faint cheer and was astonished by it. It seemed to him that they were now miles out to sea.

It was to this momentary break in the mist that the survivors on the rock owed their lives, for although the shore party might have been able to drag the boat within reach of the beach, they would have had to guess the moment to do so whereas now they could see enough to show them when to let the cable slacken and give Tamer an opportunity to make his own last-minute approach. He achieved it with a skill Paul would not have expected of an expert seaman, standing upright in the tossing boat and somehow steadying it between a platform of rock on one side and the unbroken wall of the pinnacle on the other. The first man fell on them as from the skies and it was only when there was a concerted movement on the platform that Paul saw where the survivors were huddled, wedged in a compact group under a concave slab of sandstone and covered, every few seconds, by vast sheets of water spouting through gaps in the pyramid of fallen rocks about there. It was astounding, he thought, that anyone could still remain on the shelf, for each big wave flushed it from end to end and even more astonishing that, in the tiny runnel where Tamer was holding the boat steady, the overspill cascading from the shelf did not capsize them. The second man reached the boat between two smaller waves and then came a young woman, with a great mop of dark hair, who managed it more skillfully, judging her moment and crawling crablike across the level surface before somersaulting into the bows. The survivors obviously had fight left in them for at once they set about baling with sea boots and it was time somebody did for the skiff, with five adults aboard, was shipping water in alarming quantities. Tamer, however, remained erect, arms widely spread and looking like an old prophet pronouncing a blessing as a half-naked boy with an injured leg was handed down. Then the mist closed in again and the men on shore began to haul, so that there was no chance of plucking anyone else from the shelf as they were bounced away, the keel scraping on the submerged causeway in its rush for the beach. They shipped so much that it was a miracle the boat bobbed up again as the next wave crested past and then, in a bound it seemed, they had grounded on shingle and the shore party were then hauling them in, dragging woman, boy and the two men from the boat and carrying them up the beach to the fire. Tamer, chest deep in the swell, still held on to the waterlogged boat, bellowing "Dornee mind 'em! Drag the boat clear, you bliddy vools, bevore 'er's smashed to tatters!", and enough of them heeded him to lift it clear and carry it along the tideline to the point where it had been launched fifteen minutes before. Eveleigh said, hoarsely, "How many more be there for God's sake?" and Paul told him four or five, as far as he could judge and they would have to return for them at once.

It was odd how every man seemed to find himself a task and needed little direction, either from Paul or Tamer. The little cove now seemed crowded with figures, all moving cumbersomely among the scattered boulders and crossing the dull glow of the fire. Paul noticed that the shephered twins and Meg Potter had now made the descent and came forward to carry the injured lad out of reach of the spray. The woman with the wild mop of hair walked alone, seemingly little the worse for her experience, and Paul left them to help Eveleigh and the others gather up the cable and follow the party with the boat back along the tideline to the western edge of the cove.

They had, perhaps, another fifteen minutes in hand, for the sandy runnel from which they had made the launching was now knee deep in water and although the mist was dispersing, the sea, even at this protected point, still ran high. They had upended the skiff and drained it before moving off but although it was no great weight it was very difficult to manœuvre over broken ground in semi-darkness, with yards of heavy rope trailing behind as they slipped and slithered on the bladder wrack and weed-covered limpet shells. When they regained the launching point Paul saw that Tamer was near the end of his strength and said, as the men positioned the boat and began coiling the cable, "Can you make another trip, Tamer?", to which Tamer replied, bluntly, "I got no choice, 'ave I? There baint one o' these lubbers knows the cove like me, nor that skiff neither! Suit yourself whether you come along, I reckon I could manage alone if I shipped the rudder and trusted to the skulls!" Paul said, briefly, "There's no time to argue. Line up each side and push us clear again!"

It was by no means so straightforward an operation as before. The fire had burned low and with water splashing all round them they got in one another's way, so that twice the keel fouled ledges of rock and hurled the boat back on the shingle. At the third attempt they won clear and the improved visibility helped Paul steer a more direct course for the rock while Tamer, shipping his starboard oar, used the other to prevent them swinging broadside on to the breakers. Almost at once, or so it seemed to Paul, they were running straight for the niche where the survivors crouched and immediately Tamer rose to brace his oar against the rock two men scrambled aboard, one using the spare oar to offset Tamer's pressure in an attempt to keep the boat comparatively steady. A second later a middle-aged seaman, whom Paul judged to be the captain, left the rock but rolled over the stern into the water shouting to the last castaway, a young man naked but for a pair of canvas trousers, to join him on the tow rope. Paul and the rescued men at once began to bale but

445

the moment Tamer withdrew his oar the shore party must have begun to haul for the boat shot stern first from its tiny haven, ploughing straight into the backwash of a spent breaker recoiling from the big rock. It was not a large wave compared to those breaking beyond the causeway, or even those falling on the beach eighty yards distant, but it was more than sufficient to capsize them into the trough. Paul, losing hold of the rudder bar, was pitched head over heels into the bows and for a moment he, Tamer and the two men amidships, tangled as the stern lifted under the suck of another backwash. Then he was flung clear and an oar, shooting past like a javelin, struck him a shattering blow on the temple. He felt the sharp sting of salt in the wound as the next wave crested over him but after that nothing but a confused buffeting as a tumult of water rolled him six feet under towards the breaker line.

They dragged them from the surf more dead than alive, Paul first, then the captain who kept his hold on the rope and made a lucky landing on sand at the launching point, and finally another man, who made a successful bid for his life by striking seaward, judging his moment to dive and finally landing in the arms of the shepherd twins as they stood waist deep in water to catch him. Minutes later a big wave tossed Tamer on to the ruins of the most easterly of his tar beacons. The other two sailors did not come ashore in the Cove. One was washed up a fortnight later on the Whinmouth bar, twelve miles to the West; the body of the other was never recovered.

They carried them beyond the shingle barrier and nobody had any comment to make at that time. After a few mouthfuls of spirit from Meg's leather bottle the captain recovered enough to tell them in precise English that there were no more survivors out on the rock and certainly no one alive on the wreck three miles out to sea but in any case further efforts were out of the question for the cable had parted, the boat was in splinters and both oars had been lost.

Rudd, as soon as he heard the news, came down the gully again and in the light of lanterns rigged on driftwood spars watched them at work on the survivors, himself kneeling to bandage the deep gash in Paul's temple. It was still bleeding freely and the rush of blood gave him hope. One of the sailors, who had been unconscious when brought ashore, responded to artificial respiration but Paul, although they worked on him for thirty minutes, yielded no more than a dribble of water. His pulse stil registered and he muttered a few incoherent words when they lifted him and laid him between the replenished fires, wrapped in dry blankets brought down by the tireless Davy Tozer, making his fourth ascent of the gully that night. Tamer Potter would never be revived and everyone realised that as they dragged him ashore. His jaw had been smashed to a pulp but no blood flowed from the wound and his body was so bloated that it was all they could do to lift him clear of the boulders and carry him up the beach. By then it was after eleven o'clock and they could expect help any time now, for the sea was going down rapidly and the tide was on the ebb. Tom Williams, who had made two unsuccessful attempts to round the Bluff, sent word by Hazel Potter that he would come in and land before it was light and that they were to keep big fires burning and mark the sand runnel with two rows of lanterns. Meg Potter made no outcry when Eveleigh told her that Tamer was dead but accompanied him along the shingle to the spot where he lay slightly apart from the others. Rudd went with her, the others standing back in a silent huddle. She looked down on the disfigured face for a moment and said, calmly and quietly, "Well, Mr. Rudd, 'er was a rare ole waster but 'er died a man's death come to last." She then took off the short, braided jacket she was wearing and covered his face, afterwards busying herself among the others and administering carefully regulated sips of her cordial.

Just before the boats arrived a group of them, wet, shivering and little realising what they had achieved, gathered round the body of Tamer, muttering among themselves, shamed by the corpse of a man whom all had regarded with varying degrees of contempt. Presently Ephraim Morgan, the only man among them born outside the Valley, said, "There's a name you give the poor chap

—'Tamer'. Was he christened so?" and Honeyman growled, "How would a man get a given name like 'Tamer', you old fool? When he was a boy living here-abouts a circus come to Whinmouth and he won a gold sovereign for staying five minutes in among they mangey ole lions! Seed him do it I did and his father gave him a belting for it, but he was Tamer Potter from then on. Anyone in the Valley could have told you that, I reckon."

They drifted away, moving among the survivors, who were sitting round the fire huddled in blankets. Pride was beginning to steal upon them and with it impatience for Williams and his boats to take them off this accursed stretch of beach. They stopped at the still figure of the Squire, watched over by a grim-faced Eveleigh and the silent Rudd. The bandages about his head showed white in the grey murk and once, as they watched, he groaned and moved his hands in a futile little gesture. Perhaps Edward Derwent voiced the general opinion when he said, "There's more to him than I supposed and it's a blessing, maybe, he came among us! Pray God he's not mortally injured," and he moved on to warm himself at one of the fires, remembering the time when he thought to have this man as son-in-law. It seemed a lifetime ago.

V

Grace, from her seat on the platform, first noticed the boy during the chairman's preamble and wondered at his presence. He was too far back for her to recognise him as the stable-boy whom Paul had rescued from a scrap-yard but she could assess his age at about fourteen and supposed him to be the son of someone in the audience. Then she forgot him until spotting him again, marching along the kerb in pace with the procession. This time she recognised him at once and wondered what on earth he could be doing there and whether Paul was somewhere in the crowd and using the boy as his emissary.

As she had predicted in Committee the park rally was proving a dismal failure. She belonged to the élite of the movement, who understood that the time had passed when

448

processions, banners and appeals to the public conscience produced any effect. With two prison sentences behind her she was stripped of democratic prejudices and contemptuous of rearward troops who still believed in persuasion by leaflet and argument. She was no longer a campaigner but a revolutionary, one of two or three hundred, whose bruises taught that a revolution demanded sacrifices of a kind that few spinsters, and even fewer wives, were prepared to make. She thought of the great majority of women marching behind her as emotional adolescents, ready enough to carry a banner, or perhaps bait a harassed bobby but untested by the ordeal of pain that the hard core of the movement now expected its initiates to seek out and suffer.

She had changed a great deal in the last year, changed physically, having lost close on two stone on Holloway diet but also psychologically, for she believed that she had at last won the battle against herself and had renounced all men, from Prime Minister Campbell-Bannerman down to that chubby-faced boy trotting along beside the vanguard and apparently searching for her in the ranks. It had been an uphill struggle this complete and utter renunciation and throughout it, every step of the way, she had envied the spinsters of the movement their virginity and their apparent physical repugnance of men as men, reflecting that it must be a very simple matter to renounce something one had never sought or enjoyed. She found the renunciation of the claims of motherhood (a subject some of the newcomers debated with the ecstasy of young nuns) a relatively simple matter for although she sometimes felt curious about her son she did not yearn for him, as she did for a man who could solace her and to whom she could bring solace. There were sleepless nights in Holloway when she read more into the occasional howls of women in the cell block than a desperate loneliness, or deprivation. They were keening perhaps, for their men, for some stupid, patronising, pompous overlord, who was probably sharing the bed of some other hapless slut but they keened nonetheless and their outcry set Grace Craddock's teeth on edge. Yet it was her prison spells that had won her the battle in the end, for there were men on the

449

staff of Holloway, as well as wardresses, a few of whom singled out suffragettes for special persecution. There were chaplains, doctors and visiting magistrates, men with bland, rubbery faces and well-nourished paunches; doctors who threatened forcible feeding, chaplains who talked about duty to God, which meant, of course, duty to men, and magistrates, who would cheerfully have reintroduced the horsewhip and the ducking stool had those methods of persuasion remained on the Statute Book. These occasional reminders of the sex had done more to stiffen her resolution than the bullying of the wardresses, with their harsh, morning cries of "Slops outside!" and their habit of standing by whirling a bunch of keys on a short chain whilst prisoners crammed spoonfuls of revolting grey porridge in their mouths. She could sometimes sympathise with the wardresses, some of whom were disconcerted by having to deal with educated women, but the men were like all men outside, ready with a smile, a pat or a pinch but only if wives, daughters and serving wenches were prepared to jump through hoops like a string of performing bitches. They were just as ready with their fists and their heavy-booted policemen to prevent any enlargement of a woman's role, or any claim by women to reshape society.

When the procession had been broken up, as she knew it would be the moment she saw the decoys march in with their Union Jack, she slipped away from the scrimmage and made across the park towards the Serpentine and it was here, away from the cheering, hysterical buffoons around the rostrum that she saw that the boy had followed her but was keeping his distance, like a cautious private detective. She sat down on the first available seat, watching him stop, edge forward uncertainly and finally touch his cap and grin in a rather rueful way, as though by no means sure of a welcome. She called, "All right, Ikey! What do you want?"

He came up quietly and sat down beside her. He was looking, she thought, travelworn and dishevelled, as though he had slept in his clothes. His wide Eton collar was a limp rag and his dark hair tousled. She noticed too that his boots were coated with dust and that under the dust

450

was a stiff layer of red, Devon clay. He said, with a more cheerful grin, "I had a job keeping track of you, Mrs. Craddock. I found the place easily enough but when you started marching there were so many ladies and they were all dressed the same."

His accent struck her as unfamiliar. The nasal Cockney twang had been extracted from it and yet, somehow, it was not yet a normal speaking voice. She said, briefly, "Is Mr. Craddock with you?", and he looked very surprised and said, "Good Lord, no, Mrs. Craddock! How could he be? Haven't you heard?"

"Heard what?"

"Why about the wreck, about this!", and he took a crumpled copy of the *Daily News* from his pocket and opened it. On the front page was a banner headline, the second feature of the edition. It said: *"Westcountry Wreck Drama; Villagers Save Seven Lives,"* and underneath, in smaller type, *"Gallant Rescues by Squire and Farmer; Five Believed Dead."* He let her read the story through without comment. It was a garbled, inaccurate version but its outline was factual. In the stop press, under the heading *"Wreck Drama",* was a three-line paragraph reporting that Squire Craddock had been critically injured getting the last of the German sailors ashore under the cliffs. She said, sharply, "How bad is he? Is he likely to die?", and Ikey admitted that he did not know for he had not come to her from Shallowford but from school, having run away early the previous morning. She looked at the newspaper again and saw that it was a day old. It did not surprise her that she should have missed the story. She seldom read anything but political news.

"Ikey, when did this happen? And why did you run away?"

"Three nights ago," he said. "My housemaster told me I was to stay on at school but I was coming to find you anyway—in the holidays that is! I knew the address of your headquarters, so I rode a goods train to Paxtonbury and then caught the main line train."

There were so many other questions she wanted to ask but she noticed now that his grin was forced and that behind it his features were drawn. She said, "Where did you sleep last night?"

"I found somewhere," he said defensively and she remembered then that he had once been a wharfside boy. "Have you eaten anything?"

"I had meat pie, early on."

She got up and took his hand. "Well, let's get something inside you and then you can talk. After that you can sleep at my lodgings while I tell them where you are. They'll be frantic and I expect the police are looking for you!"

They walked along to the Achilles statue and hailed a cab and in a Kensington teashop she watched him eat ravenously yet with punctilious attention to his table manners. When they were going up Sloane Street to her bed-sitting-room she said, "How do you feel now, Ikey?" and he grinned again, this time without effort and said, "I feel fine, Mrs. Craddock! Are we going back home now?"

"No," she said, "that is, you are, but not until you've had a good sleep. I've got to let them know you're safe and well, Ikey. If the Squire is as ill as they say they won't want a thing like this worrying him, will they?"

"No," said Ikey, mildly, "I hadn't thought of that. How will you do it?"

"I'll telephone the Whinmouth police," she said, "and ask them to take a message to Mr. Rudd. Then he can let the school know and after that you can take your time going back." He was about to protest at this but a yawn caught him unawares and while he was stifling it she said, "We can talk later, after I've done what I have to do." They climbed the stairs to her room overlooking the Square. It was simply but pleasantly furnished for her austerity did not extend to the deliberate sacrifice of comfort. Enough sacrifices of that kind were required in gaol. She made tea while he went behind the draw curtain to undress and when she took him a cup of tea he was sitting up in bed and blushed when she looked at his neatly folded clothes. She thought to herself, "Somebody is working hard on Ikey and I don't believe it's just Paul—he's changed a very great deal but the little ragamuffin is still there, under the straitjacket they're knitting for him!" She

452

sat on the end of the bed watching him and liking what she saw, and presently said, "Did you really run away with the idea of finding me and taking me back with you?"

"Yes, I did," he said, with another yawn, "it was the only way I could think of to help Squire," and he handed her the empty tea cup and snuggled down under the sheets. Before she had passed beyond the curtain he was asleep.

She chose a police station where she was not known and gave her real name. She took Ikey's paper along and showed it to a serious-looking sergeant, explaining who Ikey was and saying that she would like to get a message sent through to Whinmouth police station. She would have preferred to pass the information by telegram but this would have taken longer. As it was the sergeant, gravely interested, allowed her to speak to the Whinmouth sergeant and she asked him to telephone the landlord of The Raven and tell someone to ride over to Shallowford and report to Mr. Rudd that Ikey Palfrey was safe and would be coming home on the first train tomorrow. Then she asked for news of Paul and was told he was on the mend, although likely to be laid up for some weeks. The head wound, she learned, had caused severe concussion but more serious injuries included two broken ribs and a fractured arm. The serious-looking police sergeant at her elbow listened to every word, and when she had concluded the call he said, trying hard to sound nonchalant, "The er . . . gentlemen concerned in the rescue is your husband, ma'am?" and she said that was so and thanked him for his assistance but left without satisfying his curiosity. It was a long time since she had scored over a member of the Metropolitan police.

It was growing dusk when she climbed the stairs to her room again to find him still asleep. She made some vegetable soup and a ham salad, and set two places at her little table. Then she woke him, showing him where he could wash, and while he was splashing in the cubicle she told him what she had done and gave him the reassuring news from Shallowford. When they were sitting at table she said, "Very well, Ikey, now I'll listen," but suddenly he was tongue-tied. It had seemed so clear-cut when he had set out but now the purpose of his mission was getting

453

blurred, and his presence here, drinking her soup and eating her ham salad after sleeping in her bed was farcial, like an elaborate practical joke that had misfired. She said, trying to reassure him, "Whatever you say, Ikey, will remain between the two of us! After all, you must have had very strong reasons for doing such a silly thing, particularly when you already knew the Squire had been injured and the whole Valley would be in an uproar without you adding to it!"

"I don't properly understand it any more, ma'am," he admitted. "I thought I did but I don't. I suppose I just wanted to . . . well to *help* him! He's been jolly decent to me, and it seemed right to pay back somehow. You see, he was so different when you were there and even before you came but now, well, it isn't like it was, not for me and not for any of us! I reckoned that if you came back it would be all right again but I daresay it's none of my business, ma'am."

Suddenly she felt great compassion for him. If she could have been sure that it would not have embarrassed him horribly she would have flung her arms round him and kissed him for his confusion. The honesty that prompted it seemed to her one of the most genuinely touching things she had ever witnessed and for the first time in a very long period she could have wept without shame. She said, mastering herself, "I can't ever come back, Ikey, and I don't think the Squire wants me back, not unless I changed my whole life and I can't do that. Far too much has happened but I don't blame you for trying. I think it was a rather wonderful thing to do and you're quite right to look up to the Squire the way you do because he is a very good man and not simply because of what he did for you or what happened in Coombe Bay the other night. It's just that he and I have different work to do and neither of us could do it if we went on living together in Shallowford or anywhere like Shallowford." She paused, adding, "Do you understand anything of what I'm trying to tell you, Ikey?"

"No," he said, stubbornly, "I don't reckon I do, ma'am. Married people live together for always, don't they?"

She tried another approach. "What do you believe in

most, Ikey? I mean . . . what *idea?* What's terribly important to you, apart from Squire Craddock? Would it be your new school?"

He considered the question carefully, as though resolved to give as truthful an answer as his understanding of it permitted. "I suppose, England," he said finally, and then, doubtfully, "is that what you meant, Mrs. Craddock?"

"Yes," she said, "that's exactly what I mean and now see if you can follow me a little further. England is your country and it's very important to you. So it is to me and to the Squire, only we don't all have the same ideas of how to work for it, or make it a better place for everyone to live in."

His eyes never left hers as he said, "I can't see what that's got to do with you and Squire, ma'am."

"Oh yes you can, if you think, Ikey. You're very sharp! If you weren't you wouldn't have got the idea of coming to find me in the first place and even if you had you could never have found your way here alone. What I'm trying to say is this—the Squire and I don't live separate lives because we've quarrelled in the way that lots of married people quarrel. It's just that he wants the *old* kind of England and I want a very different one. When married people think as opposite as that they cease to get any pleasure out of one another's company."

"You mean you ran away just to join the suffragettes?" he asked, incredulously.

"Not exactly," she said, smiling, "but that was what decided me. I really left because there was no real place for me in the Valley and I believe Squire understands that now. If you give him time I don't think he'll continue to hold it against me!"

"Then why is he so miserable?" demanded Ikey and she said, quickly, "Because he's very lonely. You're away at school most of the time and Shallowford is a big empty house for a man to live in alone. Besides, I don't believe he is miserable all the time or not when he's out in the open. Maybe he'll marry again!"

"How could he do that when he's married to you?"

"People can get unmarried—divorced, and I've already gone into that, although he doesn't know about it yet. I suppose it must sound terribly complicated to you, Ikey, so you'll just have to take my word for it until you're older! It wouldn't be the slightest good my coming home simply because he was injured. You see, I believe in what I'm doing here, with all my heart and soul, just as much as Squire believes in what *he's* doing, and besides, I wouldn't want to live in the country again." She paused. "Have I made any kind of sense to you?"

"Yes, I reckon you have," he said, slowly, "but it doesn't help much, does it?"

"I believe *you* might help straighten things out," she said, "but you would have to give me your word of honour never to tell a soul, not even the Squire, that I had a hand in it!" and she paused, looking at him speculatively, scrutinising and ultimately sanctioning an idea that occurred to her with disconcerting suddenness. "Do you remember Farmer Derwent's daughter? Claire, the pretty one?"

"Yes, of course," he said, "she used to ride a lot with Squire. She was always over the big house before . . ." He was going to say "before you came" but checked himself, feeling this might annoy her and said instead, "before I started taking lessons in Paxtonbury."

"That's right," she said, "and since we seem to have so many secrets now, Ikey, I'll let you into another. If the Squire hadn't married me he would have almost certainly married Claire Derwent! It was me who stopped him marrying her but she's still very much in love with him."

"How do you know that?" he demanded, unequivocally.

"Well, I do know," she said, "and what's more I know where she is at the moment. She's running a tea-shop quite near here. She owns it but she also trains as a nurse. I met her by accident some time ago and we . . . well, we talked! It was before the news got around that I had run away and she thought I was up here on a visit. She's the one you ought to spirit back to Shallowford, not me."

A small bubble of mischief popped through the crust of his bewilderment and he said, with an engaging grin, "You mean, he might fall in love with her again and marry her?"

"Why did you say 'again'?" she said sharply and he

456

said, half-apologetically, "Well, they were laying odds on it when I was a stable-boy!"

"Who were?"

"All of them, Handcock the gardener, Chivers the groom, and the rest! Mrs. Handcock was sure Squire would marry Claire Derwent and I remember her and Thirza grumbling about it in the kitchen." He grinned again. "She clouted me for telling Chivers what they said!"

She noticed something new about him as he said this, that his loyalty was wholly Paul's. Her patience and cosseting had made no impression upon him, for he did not see her as an individual, or even as Paul's legal wife, but merely as a possible means of improving the humour of his hero, Squire Craddock. She realised something else—that she had grossly underestimated his intelligence and had been wrong to deal with him as one might deal with a child. He was not a child—in many ways he was far more mature than Paul and seemed almost to be mocking her as he said, "And how would I go about that, Mrs. Craddock?" His cold-bloodedness, his apparent readiness to regard her as something expendable was chastening.

"You came to me out of the blue so you'd better do the same to her, Ikey," she said and got up, with the intention of checking on Claire Derwent's address in the directory she used for canvassing. The initiative, however, had now passed to him. He seemed to be considering the matter with clinical detachment.

"That wouldn't do at all," he said finally, "not now you've told them where I am. If Miss Derwent got to know I'd been here first she wouldn't believe a word I said! No, that wouldn't work, or not with a lady!"

He seemed to imply that her sex was not so much tiresome as impossibly devious, and while this might have enraged her had he been a grown man she found herself admiring his easy familiarity with human weaknesses, so much so that she felt she had done her part by reminding him of Claire Derwent's existence and could safely leave the mechanics of intrigue to him. When she spoke again she was the pupil, he the instructor.

"What new mischief are you planning now, Ikey?"

"It would have to be done by a letter," he said slowly,

"and the letter would have to be posted in Shallowford. I could write it here tho', and you could read it. Then I could post it as soon as I get home and it would have a local postmark on it and she wouldn't suspect." He had clearly made up his mind on the essentials. "Could you lend me a sheet of paper and pen and ink, ma'am?"

She gave him some plain writing paper, a pen and a bottle of ink, and left him to himself while she cleared the supper things. All the time she was washing up and drying he was bent over his task, his pen scratching away, his tongue peeping from between his teeth in the effort of concentration. When she had finished she lit the gas fire and sat beside it, pretending to read but actually giving him her whole attention. At last he straightened up and handed her the paper, now covered with his half-formed schoolboy scrawl and signed *"Ikey Palfrey"* and in brackets, below the signature, *"the one you may remember as stableboy."* The naïveté of this afterthought made her smile but the letter itself was by no means naïve but a little masterpiece of special pleading. If she knew Claire Derwent as well as she thought she did the girl would find it irresistible. Ikey had written:

Dear Miss Derwent,

I got your address from the Xmas Card you sent Squire. You may think it rood of me to write like this but I take the chance because I love Squire and can't think of any other way to help. You will have hird all about how he and Tamer Potter rescued the German sailors, and how he got badly hurt and is still laid up, also how Mrs. Craddock run off a year ago and hasn't been seen since. Well Miss Derwent, now I come to the mane thing. I was in and out of his room before he began to come round from the whack on the head and he kept asking for you, not nowing it of course but calling out your name as if you was in the room. I asked Mrs. Handcock about it and she said maybe he was remembering all the good times you had when I used to saddle up for him and you rode in the woods I thought you might like to know about this so as you could call in and cheer him

458

*up a bit if you were down this way to see Miss Rose
or Farmer Derwent soon. I know he would like that
because he's been very low lately, nothing like he was
in the old days so again appollergising for writing and
hoping you are well as I am since Squire sent me to
school Respectfully, Ikey Palfrey.*

She read the letter through twice and handed it back to
him, together with Claire Derwent's latest address in Bayswater.

"Ikey," she said, "either you'll end up in gaol like Smut
Potter, or you'll be Prime Minister! I couldn't improve on
that in a thousand years. Now tell me about yourself, and
how you're getting on at that big school in North Devon."

CHAPTER FOURTEEN

I

IT was not until she was alone in the room that Claire
Derwent knew with certainty she had come home for good,
that never again would she willingly exchange this view
and these scents, for the asphalt of Bayswater or the genteel atmosphere of Tunbridge Wells. It was mid-April now
and in the afternoons the sunlight over the paddock was
the colour of buttermilk, with wide belts of river sedge
lying like strips of green velvet on either side of the stream,
and flocks of starched clouds, moving slowly down from
the Bluff casting patches of creeping shadow over the
stubble fields of Four Winds and the long slope dividing
the two rivers.

She stood by the big window a long time, occasionally
glancing at the man on the bed, unworried by his restlessness, for they had warned her that he would be feverish
for a day or so and the doctor had promised to look in
on the way back to the village to "make him a little more

comfortable". Claire had attended enough V.A.D. lectures at St. Thomas's to accept this phrase as a cliché that not even a lady doctor like O'Keefe's down-to-earth daughter could avoid using.

He looked, she thought, supremely uncomfortable, with his left arm awkwardly angled in its shiny metal splint, his body slumped in a position half-way between sitting and lying and his head turbaned in bandages, like the heads of wounded soldiers in illustrated magazines. He needed a shave too, and perhaps tomorrow they would allow her to shave him. That was something she had learned in the first series of lectures—"How to remove hair from the helpless"—and the memory of the sub-title made her smile, so that she had to chide herself for feeling so cheerful in a sick-room and turn again to look at the view, taking a brief mindseye ramble over the horizon where the Shallowford beeches formed the eastern frame for the landscape.

She had not realised how little thought she had given this place in the last few years. Once the first wave of homesickness had receded, and she had become absorbed in the teashop adventure, she had felt rather patronising about the Sorrel Valley and Sorrel Valley folk, thinking of them as a collection of raggle-tailed rustics without benefit of the urban delights of a fashionable spa and out of reach of the great city, where she had spent the final year of her exile. But now only three weeks since she had been lured home by that fantastic letter (penned by what was surely the Squire's most devoted tenant!) it was the people of the Spa and of the faceless homes along the Bayswater Road whom she thought of as underprivileged. What had any one of them to compare with this except a formal park or two, or a village already cluttered with honking, dust-trailing motors and enclosed by clusters of red-brick houses, where prosperous merchants were carica-tures of men like Craddock? Yet, she had only made the journey on impulse, and with no intention of doing more than pay a hasty call on her father and Rose, and per-haps, in response to that devoted stable-boy's plea, to congratulate the hero of the Valley on having put the

Sorrel Valley on the front pages of the newspapers for the first and probably the last time in history.

She had made her call and had returned to High Coombe shocked by his appearance and afterwards, with no real object in mind, she had hung on, waiting for the crisis of his attack of pneumonia, a not unexpected result of his incredible exertions on the night of the wreck. She found the rhythm of the big house shattered. People came and went, and the place seemed half full of foreigners, not foreigners who lived within half-a-day's ride of the Valley but real foreigners, who spoke a foreign tongue. Poor old John Rudd went about with an undertaker's face and Mrs. Handcock wept freely into her pastry. The only lively person about the place was two-and-a-half-year-old Simon, who soon made friends with her and clamoured to be taken for rides on the pommel of her saddle.

Then, like the false dawn of a new era, Doctor Maureen O'Keefe, the Coombe Bay physician's fully-qualified daughter, swept into the Valley, the first lady-doctor that any of them had heard of much less attended, with her mixture of sardonic humour, brisk efficiency and shrewd Irish charm that had succeeded in routing prejudice in less than a week. She had brought with her a sense of rapid change, fresh air and wide open windows, so that soon news began to spread that Squire Craddock was on the mend, and "thicky lady-doctor" had miraculously repaired his damaged ribs and set one of his fractures, using the big kitchen as an operating theatre. Even John Rudd was seen to perk up a little and Mrs. Handcock ceased her eternal snivelling. The boy Ikey lost his look of tragedy and optimism returned to the Valley in the wake of spring. Yet, although Doctor Maureen showed a certain interest in Claire's claim regarding a V.A.D. training at St. Thomas's it was not until after the second operation on Paul's arm that she accepted her offer as sick-room nurse, whilst she drove her gig about the Valley, bullying blushing labourers into peeling off their shirts and answering her questions about diet and cottage hygiene.

At any other time the invasion of a woman doctor in the Valley would have provided a pub topic for a month but so many things had been happening here of late that

Doctor O'Keefe's daughter was able to play herself in in a matter of days. Rumours rushed up and down the Valley like flights of starlings. The Squire was dying. The Squire was recovering. Old Tamer Potter was being buried in a common grave with seven German sailors. Old Tamer Potter was having a granite memorial tombstone all to himself paid for by the Kaiser. And then rumours that grew out of these rumours; young Palfrey, the stable-boy Squire was trying to turn into a gentleman, had run away, been caught and sent back by the police; Claire Derwent, who was once said to be marrying Squire, had been rushed down from London to nurse him as soon as it was known that Squire's wife, that mad Lovell girl, had been locked up yet again; Smut Potter, languishing in Paxtonbury gaol, was said to be due for early release, an official reward for his father's heroism, and finally, perhaps the most disquieting rumour of all, old John Rudd, a widower with a son old enough to drive motors and seduce wives, was said to be madly in love with the lady doctor and courting her, while her father was taking a cure in an alcoholic ward of Paxtonbury asylum! It was too much, too quickly served and the Valley was unable to digest it, so that soon it gave up trying, the weather being warm, spring well advanced and work waiting upon idle hands in field and byre.

Slowly the great springtide of speculation receded but the Valley families were never to forget their moment of high drama. In farms and cottages newspapers containing stories of the wreck, and the funerals that followed it, were carefully folded and laid away in chests of drawers, so that future generations could appreciate the national importance of the Sorrel Valley in years to come.

II

He saw her sitting sideways to the bed, an open book on her lap and the afternoon sun, flooding through the tall, mullioned windows, playing games with tendrils that had escaped from her golden "bun" and hung like tiny tongues of autumn bracken over her ears.

It took him a moment or two to realise who she was

462

for when he saw her sitting there, with her knees pressed together and her head bent low over the page, he at once associated her with a picture he had seen somewhere and the effort of establishing the link tired him, so that he closed his eyes again and went about disentangling the fabric of dreams from reality. Then, when he opened his eyes again, he remembered. The woman sitting beside the bed, knees pressed together, smooth, rounded face half-turned to the window and a book on her lap, was Bathsheba, reading the message from King David, yet also— and this was puzzling—she was Claire Derwent, late of High Coombe farm. He studied her very carefully, or as carefully as his damnably awkward posture would permit, trying to remember whether she had been there during his few lucid intervals when he had exchanged a word or two with John Rudd before being pulled this way and that by a strange woman said to be a doctor and the daughter of that drunken old Irishman, O'Keefe. He could not recall seeing Claire in the room then and this disturbed him, for it suggested that he was still dreaming and that Claire Derwent, or Bathsheba, belonged to the world of fantasy. Then she looked up and saw that he was awake, and her eyes lit up as she smiled in a way that somehow reassured him. She said softly, "Hullo, Paul! More yourself?", and reached out to take his pulse. This again struck him as odd, for it seemed extremely improbable that there should be two lady doctors in the Valley.

"What are you doing here?" he asked, "and why the devil am I still trussed up like this?" but this time her smile was professional as she said calmly, "Which question would you like answered first, Paul?" and because her voice and touch soothed him he smiled back, saying, carefully, "They were going to reset this damned arm. That's the last thing I remember. Is it done now? Is this why I'm still in a straitjacket?", and she told him that this was so, that "the lady doctor" would be in to look at him again soon and that meantime she had volunteered her services as nurse. "Semi-professionally," she added, with a touch of pride, "for I did V.A.D. training in London but I don't think you should talk much now. Suppose I get you a cup of tea?"

463

"I don't want a thing to eat," he said, "but I could do with some tea! I've got a mouth just like the bottom of old Honeyman's sawpit! Chloroform I imagine. Get tea Claire, but don't go away, because I want to know what's happened. I'm still very hazy."

"Of course you are," she said, "you've just come round from an anaesthetic but you'll be all right in the morning. I'll get tea now," and she rustled out of the room and hurried down the backstairs to the kitchen.

Without understanding why she felt elated, perhaps because his recognition of her, and his inclination to chat, gave substance to Maureen O'Keefe's assurances of a swift recovery. Mrs. Handcock read good news in her face and in the demand for a pot of strong tea. "Is 'er comin' round, then? Is 'er really on the mend, do 'ee think?" she asked and Claire told her that he was very definitely on the mend, and that she could pop in and have a word with him after the doctor had been. The bulletin transformed the housekeeper. She puffed out her cheeks with relief and waddled to and fro laying the tea-tray, saying, "Tiz been a turrible carry-on about yer, Miss Claire! A *turrible* carry-on! Right plaized to zee *you* back I be for mebbe you c'n maake 'un smile again! What with one thing and another us didden know 'ow 'twould end sometimes. My Horace has been in a rare ole tizzy about 'un, I can tell 'ee!"

"I can believe it, Mrs. Handcock," said Claire, and took the tray up the backstairs to the bedroom, cooling the first cup with plenty of milk in case he spilled it, then putting her arm round his shoulders to steady him as he lifted it to his mouth with his free hand.

He drank it gratefully and asked for another and hotter cup out while she was pouring he passed his hand over his chin and exclaimed, "Good God, I've got half-an-inch of stubble! Why the devil didn't somebody shave me before they brought you here?" and she laughed and said she would shave him herself if the doctor gave permission and then let him drink his second cup without help, remembering the stress laid upon such niceties in the lecture entitled "Convalescence!"

"All right," he said, when she had relieved him of the cup, "now you can tell me how you happen to be here

464

and something of what's going on. That woman doctor can't because she's a stranger here and as for John Rudd, he fusses like an old hen every time I ask him a straightforward question! All I get from him is 'Don't fret, Boy! Leave everything to me!' as if that helps a man to clear his head!"

"Well, he's right," she said, "for you have been rather ill you know. Apart from being badly knocked about you had pneumonia and pneumonia plus broken ribs can be very dangerous."

He grinned and she realised he was laughing at her readiness to dispense medical knowledge.

"So you sold that wretched tea-shop and took up nursing?"

"No," she said, "but I might. I was always interested in nursing and would have gone in for it years ago if Father hadn't sat on the idea. I enrolled for a V.A.D. course at St. Thomas's when I left Penshurst and opened a shop in London."

He remembered vaguely that she had taken new premises in Bayswater about a year ago and that news of this had reached him through Rose after the arrival of a Christmas card showing a sketch of her shop. It gratified him that he could remember such things and that his brain seemed to be working normally, and after being prompted to tell him more she explained that she had read of the wreck in the London newspapers and decided to come home and hear about it first-hand. She said nothing of Ikey's letter, deciding that it was not for her to tell him that her presence here was in fact due to the boy's statement that he had called out for her in a delirium. Then he asked her the date and seemed surprised when she told him that it was April 8th, nearly a month since the night of the wreck yet with this reminder she witnessed a mild puff of pride when he said, being careful to speak collectively, "We did a good job down there, didn't we? Seven out of the nine on that rock but it was more by luck than judgment! Poor Old Tamer was the real hero and I wish to God he'd lived to realise what he'd done, and have people respect him for once! Will you remind John Rudd to see that Meg and the girls don't want for anything until I can get about again?"

"You really can't start fretting over things until you're really well," she told him severely. "For heaven's sake let the Valley look after itself, Paul! It's been doing it for centuries you know!", and then she regretted having said this for it implied that his leadership was a non-essential, so she added, quickly, "That doesn't mean that everybody round here doesn't think a very great deal of you, Paul! I realised that the moment I talked with Father and you know how difficult he is to impress! He said the Valley people would never have achieved anything like that under a Lovell and that you've done a wonderful job here and this proves it."

He pondered this for a moment and she took the opportunity to draw the curtains. When she returned to the bed he was asleep and as she stood looking down at him it crossed her mind that he had the face of an Elizabethan, with a jawline and high cheekbones that were uncommon today, especially about here, where almost everyone had the squarish Anglo-Saxon cast of features or, where the Celtic strain predominated, a smoother, chubbier face. There were plenty of dark-skinned men in the Valley but their beards had a bluish gloss that his lacked. All in all, she reflected, he was a strange, alien man to want to make his life here where he had no roots yet his doggedness was making itself felt, even upon men as conservative as her father. He was like a wedge that had first attached itself to the soil of the Valley by its own weight and every blow strengthened its bite. There had been that awful Codsall business, then the dismal Smut Potter affair and the quarrel with Gilroy and finally the strange abdication of Grace Lovell but nothing seemed capable of dislodging him, not even the recurring scandals of his wife's gaol sentences. He absorbed all these setbacks, still clutching at his rather old-fashioned conception of duty. His outlook would have amazed his predecessors and was said to have exasperated his wife but this ought not to have surprised him—anyone could have told him that a well-bred woman like Grace Lovell would be incapable of seconding his arch ideas.

She stood there a long time and the memory of their

466

association returned to her like a windsong, pleasant but unsubstantial, without a clearly recollected beginning and with no promise of renewal. She had once thought of herself as madly in love with him but now she understood that her self-deception had grown out of the prospect of co-owning the acres on which she had been born and where she had spent such a happy childhood. She had forgiven herself all those clumsy schemes to capture him, supposing that any girl of her age and limited experience would have done her best to catch a husband who was rich, young and very amiable. Perhaps he was the real loser, for surely no one else in the Valley understood him as she did and had done from the moment when she had been able to evaluate his terrible earnestness. The thought interested her. Had Grace Lovell really been obsessed with the campaign to win votes for women or had she run off simply because she was bored to death by his obsession with chawbacons and their affairs? And wouldn't any intelligent, educated woman be bored with them if she had access, through his money, to a richer and fuller life? It was, she decided, unfair to ask herself this question, for she had never regarded herself as an educated woman and had been brought up to accept the authority and the willfulness of males as uncomplainingly as one faced up to a wet haymaking season, or a false spring half-way through January. A Valley wife did not necessarily have to embrace her man's enthusiasms; she either absorbed them or shrugged them off and went about the business of making a home and rearing children. Yet would it be as simple as this with Paul Craddock? Whoever married him would marry the estate and personal happiness with a man as obstinate as him could only be achieved by a fusion of interests that went beyond those of heart and nursery. It was not simply a matter of acreage either, of cob, thatch and husbandry. Whoever shared his life would be required to know the Christian names of every soul dwelling inside the magic circle, together with their needs, hopes, fears and capacity for skilled and unskilled work. It was something to which she had not given a thought when she made such a goose of herself beside the mere and in the days immediately before the Coronation soirée.

There was a scrunch on the gravel outside and she looked down from the window to see the doctor's gig cresting the drive. As she watched Doctor Maureen handed down by John Rudd, she thought, "Well, O'Keefe's clever daughter may know what's wrong with his body but I could do a better job on the real man, so I'm hanged if I give that teashop another thought until I've made him laugh again!"

III

No poet lived in the Valley so there was no one to idle along the banks of the Sorrel, or sit musing beside the mere that season and make some shift at capturing the magic of spring in the fields and bottoms, or the effect it had upon the men and women who lived there. Hazel Potter sensed what was happening because she communed with each successive season but Hazel had great difficulty in writing her name and her poetry either stayed in her head or was expressed through gibberish or the flash of her nut-brown arms and bare legs, as she ranged the woods, or crossed the moor as far as the railway line. Hazel saw the drifts of bluebells under the beeches west of the mere and the trailing clusters of primroses nestling in the steep banks of the back lanes between Hermitage plateau and the thickets of the Bluff. She heard the oratorios of the thrushes, blackbirds and finches in the birch woods and laurel clumps, and saw the voles slipping along the Sorrel flats between the straight, green stems of wild iris. She knew some of the otters by name and the badgers too, where they had their holts in the broken hillside north of the mere, and she often stood for an hour talking to darting squirrels in the oak on the meadow above the big house.

Tamer's death brought her no sorrow. She had never been afraid of him, as were the older girls, and her appraisal of death differed very materially from that of almost everyone else in the Valley. When the Valley folk heard Parson Bull intone at the graveside of the German sailors, using phrases like "man springeth up and is cut down like a flower", or "in the midst of life we are in death", they did not understand these warnings as Hazel understood them, regarding them as no more than extracts from the Prayer Book. Hazel, so accurately in tune with the rhythm of the Valley and with the cycle of life and death that involved every living thing in the Valley, accepted the phrases as plain statements of fact. Every creature, every leaf and every flower in the Valley lived its hour and died its death, sinking back into the earth again and reappearing in changed form next spring, or the spring after that. There was no profit in deploring this, or in wearing mourning and uprooting flowers to pile on pits at places where men and animals and even windfalls and the husks of horse chestnuts were recommitted to the earth. There they had been and there they went and that was that; there was no dividing line to be drawn between a pot-bellied old drunkard like Tamer Potter and, say, a hedgehog struck down by a hawk. It was the pattern of things and to question it or even think about it was futile. Yet this did not mean that Hazel Potter was deaf to the muted trumpet of spring, or that the throb of renewed life in the Valley aroused no response in her heart. Her step was lighter and her eye and ear sharper than when she trod these same paths in autumn or winter and her heart beat faster as she silently dogged the movements of Ikey Palfrey (whom she still thought of as "The Boy") in his lonely tramps through the coppices and bramble brakes behind the big house.

She had been surprised to see him again for they said that Squire had sent him away to a big school, and it must have been so for he had stopped coming down to the mere opposite the Niggerman's Church to wait for her. She did not resent this severance of their association, supposing him to have passed out of her orbit after being condemned to sit all day scratching among papers like a squirrel making a dray but sometimes she was curious to learn what had induced him to abandon the jolly life of a stable-boy for a wearisome life like the Squire's and whether, in fact, the change had been imposed upon him as a punishment, perhaps for stealing away and meeting her in the woods. Her curiosity encouraged her to keep a close watch on him and one morning she followed him across the bluebell orchard behind the house and through Priory Wood to the high-banked lane linking Hermitage land to the northern boundary of the Home Farm. When he turned east, as though making for Shallowford Woods, she stepped from behind a big ash and called so that he stopped in his tracks looking surprised and undecided. Then, when he saw her slide down the bank, he blushed and seemed on the point of running back the way he had come.

"Where've 'ee been, Boy?" she demanded. "An' why didden 'ee come upalong, like 'ee used to?"

His embarrassment left him as soon as he heard her voice but was replaced by a kind of wariness. He said, "I thought maybe you wouldn't be there, on account of your father being drowned," and at this she looked surprised, not so much by the remark but by the dramatic change in his voice, as though it had been dug out of him, put through a mangle and replaced, a lisping relic of the original.

"You spake diff'rent," she proclaimed, gleefully. "How cum you do that, Boy?"

He said, with dignity, "My voice has broken. All men's voices change when they are fourteen."

This seemed to interest her, as though it was one of the few processes of nature that had somehow escaped her notice.

"Is it zo?" she said. "I never heard tell of it bevore," and then, forgetting his voice, "Do 'ee want to zee the badgers, Boy?", and he conceded gravely that he would like to see them and they went up the lane, across the wood and round the edge of the mere to the hill near where she had found him in the snow.

They did not see any badgers but they saw many other things that interested him, a bullfinch's nest with three eggs, an otter diving near the island, a lame vixen at the entrance of an earth close to Smut's hideout, and soon a little of their effortless relationship returned so that he found himself slipping back into her brogue and wondering about her again. He asked her if her father's death had

470

made her as miserable as the Squire's illness was making him and was shocked by her seeming indifference.

"Giddon, no," she said, contemptuously. " 'Er's dade idden her? And 'er diden know a dandelion from a daisy!"

Unable to follow this logic he said, "Well, he was a hero down in the cove, Hazel!" and she replied, glumly, "Ar but 'er smashed our boat to tatters bringin' they foreigners off the rock!" The discovery that she valued the boat far above her father gave him another clue to her character. She had always intrigued him, with her astonishing knowledge of woodlore and her free communion with wild creatures, but now he saw her as the one person of his world who had achieved complete independence and it seemed to him a very wonderful thing, this ability to remove oneself at will from the ties of authority and wander over the Valley, impervious to social obligations and the weather. In a way he thought, she was a kind of queen with privileges denied men and women tied to chores and caught up in the rhythm of the seasons. She was beautiful too, with her great brown eyes, healthy, freckled skin and wild mass of chestnut hair that fell, free of all pins and ribbons, to her shoulders. Contemplating her, as they sat side by side on an old log beside the mere, he said, enviously, "You have a marvellous time, Hazel, doing exactly what you please! Why can't everyone do as they please, just the way you do?"

She gave him a shrewd, sidelong glance, her strong teeth flashing in a merry smile. "Mebbe tiz along o' they old books, Boy," she told him, "they'm all mazed about books. I dunno why. What can 'ee vind in 'em that baint starin' 'ee in the faace about here?" and she reached out and plucked a celandine growing in the bank behind them, holding it between a grubby finger and thumb and twirling it so that the moist gleam of its petals changed it from a flower to a golden ring. "Idden 'er pretty, now? Dorn 'ee think on that when youm in skuel, along o' they ole books?" It was a salutary object lesson and impressed him tremendously for somehow it revealed to him his own duality, part waif like her, part gentleman-in-the-making and for the moment the latter role seemed very sterile. He reached out, tentatively and touched her hair, finding it unexpectedly soft and glossy. She did not move or smile but sat quite still as the tangled tresses slipped through his fingers but when the impulse to touch her was spent, and he shyly withdrew his hand, she said, "Tiz soft, baint it?" and shook her head so that hair tumbled about her shoulders and then, with her head on one side, "Do 'ee think I'm beautiful, Boy?" He said, sadly, "Yes, you are beautiful, Hazel, and the best times I ever had have been out here with you but I'm going back to school tomorrow, so I shan't see you again until the summer holidays. Suppose . . . suppose I write you a letter from school?"

"No dornee," she said, laughing, "I coulden read un," but then a thought struck her and she added, "I could get Pansy to spell un out mebbe. 'Er's the best scollard of us."

"No," he said, hastily, "I wouldn't like that!" and suddenly feeling deflated he got up and began skimming pebbles into the mere, watching them break the surface all the way to the islet.

She sat on the log watching him, plagued by emotions that she did not understand and moved by impulses that were the first she had been unable to obey as soon as they were felt. The recollected touch of his hand as it passed over her hair made her shiver and this puzzled her greatly, for the sun was very warm on her bare neck and legs. She got up, puzzled and angry with herself, and went quietly up the slope through the close-set timber. When he tired of throwing stones and returned to the log she had disappeared behind the trees.

IV

The fingers of spring were probing everywhere in the Valley now and their licence was not restricted to the young and untrammelled. High on the long slope of Blackberry Moor, Elinor Codsall was aware of them that same morning, when the persistent twitter of birds awoke both her and Will at first light, and in yielding to him she casually conceived a third child, despite their plan to limit the family until they had enough capital to buy some portable hovers Will had coveted at the experimental poultry farm, north of Paxtonbury. He had thought at first that he could make hovers as good as these but the days were far too short and they could not afford hired help like the other farms in the Valley. As soon as he had done with her Will began to snore again, a gross indulgence on his part in view of the fact that it was time to rise and start work, so she prodded him, calling "Will! Will! Dornee drop off again! I'll brew tea an' us'll make an early start today!" He grunted and sat up, knuckling his eyes and then, in the soft light of dawn, grinned down at her fondly and possessively. "By God, Elinor," he declared, "youm prettier'n ever, midear! I reckon I could taake 'ee again if us had time," and although she said, "Giddon with your ole nonsense!" and slipped hurriedly out of bed in case he was tempted to waste more time, she was pleased with the compliment, reflecting that most men of Will's type, having been so recently indulged, would have grumbled at being dragged from sleep.

The sun almost shouted at Sam Potter, striding over the dyke-banks at the eastern end of the mere on his way to fell timber for a pheasant compound. He walked as though all his joints were fitted with small, steel springs, covering just over a yard at each stride, and as he loped along he sucked in great mouthfuls of sharp April air, sparing a thought for poor old Smut, now ending his third year behind bars and due, so they heard, for release on licence in the new year. He did not think of his father, Tamer, lying in Coombe Bay churchyard surrounded by such unlikely names as Ledermann, Schmitt and Kohlhoff, for it was not a morning to contemplate death and shipwreck. Instead he watched, with an admiring grin, a great dog-fox leap clear of the bracken and bound across the soft ground towards the badger sets. "Show a leg, you ole thief!" he shouted, "us'll be arter 'ee when the nights draw in!" Then, having selected a sapling, he swung his axe in a wide, slashing arc and the sound of the stroke rang through the woods, flushing out three moorhens and sending them skimming across the lake for their sanctuary on the islet.

The Codsalls and the Potters were habitual early risers but Arthur Pitts and his son Henry over at the Hermitage worked to a more leisurely schedule and ate enormous breakfasts before issuing out of doors. They were munching away now with their womenfolk moving to and fro from the stove, Martha and her great tawny daughter-in-law from over the Teazel, absorbed into the cheerful atmosphere of Hermitage kitchen and privately thanking her lucky stars that she had chosen the genial Henry for husband, instead of the bucktoothed kennelman at Heronslea. The Hermitage, she often reflected, was a home in the very best sense of the word and she now thought of herself as settled for life, although it sometimes puzzled her that Henry, with so much to offer in the way of good temper and security, had remained a bachelor for so long. She was not entirely convinced by Martha Pitts' explanation that "Henry was waitin' on Mrs. Right an' you be 'er, m'dear!"

Four Winds usually erupted about the time Will Codsall, at Periwinkle, was making his first rounds of the hen-roosts, and filling the hoppers while Elinor followed in his wake collecting the eggs. It was strange that a cautious and sober man like Norman Eveleigh and his practical wife, Marian, should have produced between them such a noisy, rollicking brood, or that they should suffer them to make so much noise as they trooped down the uncarpeted stairs to breakfast, spilling over one another in their eagerness to get to the table and squealing with laughter when Sydney Codsall (now regarded as one of the family) used one of his long, unintelligible words when making a simple request, like "Pass the marmalade!" Their father and mother had impressed upon them that they must show great kindness to Sydney, who had lost both father and mother and thus qualified as an orphan but they found it difficult to avoid teasing him, for he was so unlike any other boy in the Valley, so solemn, studious and unblinking behind his steel-rimmed spectacles that he sometimes seemed more like a little old man than a schoolboy.

Sydney ate sparingly, paying more attention to a book propped against the cruet than to the home-made bread and jam piled on the wooden platters. Marian had given him permission to read at meals for he was already recognised as an exceptionally clever boy, who would go far, although in what direction nobody had yet decided. The headmaster of the Whinmouth Secondary School was said to take a keen interest in him and had told Eveleigh that he was a boy to be encouraged. He was therefore absolved from any work on the farm and spent hours in a room upstairs that was not much bigger than a closet. Up here, although he worked methodically, he did not spend every moment of his isolation preparing lessons. Sometimes he gazed out of a little window at the sons and daughters of the new tenant of Four Winds as they moved to and fro about their regulated tasks in the yard and deep in his heart he despised them all as a gaggle of geese, boys and girls who would never amount to anything but hewers of wood and drawers of water. He had inherited his mother's hunger for gentility but even at fourteen he could see quite clearly where his mother had made her first and fatal mistake. She should never have married a clodhopper like his father, for the road to gentility lay not through labour but through attentive study and the accurate memorisation of cohorts of declensions and tables. The headmaster had told him that knowledge was power and power, sometime and in some undefined sphere, he was determined to possess. Then all those giggling, skylarking Eveleighs would work not for their father, a jumped-up farm foreman, but for him, Sydney Codsall, the real master of Four Winds and all the acres beyond. After breakfast he set out on his bicycle to pedal the nine miles to school. The sun was hot by then and the birds sang in chorus all the way to the bridge over the Teazel but spring had no message for Sydney. He did not even notice it, being fully occupied repeating to himself a list of irregular French verbs.

The warm spring weather and the tumult it provoked in the thickets and hedgerows of the Valley did have a very dramatic effect upon someone old enough and experienced enough to know better. This was John Rudd, rising fifty-three, and a widower for more than twenty years but age and experience had not prevented him from falling hopelessly in love with Maureen O'Keefe, M.D., and that at first sight, when she drove her gig over to the lodge a day or two after the shipwreck and told him, in her pleasant Irish accent, that she was "after taking Father's place for a spell".

From the moment she consented to take tea with him in his little parlour, and they had discovered in the city of Cork a topic of mutual nostalgia, he found her the most engaging young woman he had ever met and he continued to think of her as young after she had admitted to thirty-seven. It was her humour and frankness that engaged him during that first meeting, but later, after she had paid several visits to Paul, she rapidly enlarged her hold upon him so that he began to think of her small, puckish features as beautiful, and her sturdy, thickset figure as statuesque. Yet he was not such an old fool as to imagine that she was in the least attracted to him and would have been more than satisfied with her friendship, for she was the only "liberated" woman in his experience who did not make a tiresome fetish of emancipation. He was as astonished at the arrival of a qualified doctor in petticoats as every one else in the Valley for it was a phenomenon that he had neither encountered nor imagined but after watching her at work on Paul and other equally embarrassed males in the Valley, he had conceived an enormous admiration for her skill and her easy approach to cottagers that overcame their prejudices and won their confidence in the course of a single visit. She was obliged to rely on him a good deal that first month, for she was a complete stranger to the Valley and her close relationship with O'Keefe did not help, for the old man had been losing his grip lately and even patients who had suffered him half a lifetime were beginning to distrust his diagnoses and his rough and ready surgery. She was very frank, however, about her father's shortcomings, admitting that the old man was no longer fit to attend a sick cat and this, she said, was the real reason she was here, to save him making a mistake that would "blot his copy-book and mine, on account of our names being one below the other in the Medical Register"!

She soon packed him off to take his cure and had the

practice to herself. "Playing herself in", she called it, while she continued to search for a firm of practitioners who had not taken the pledge to stop the infiltration of women into the profession. One of the things that John Rudd most admired about her was her cheerful acceptance of male prejudice in the medical field, for in spite of it she preferred male doctors. "Women in authority," she told him once, "are usually hell-cats, like the matrons and nursing sisters I trained under before going on to take a degree in Dublin!" She was like her father in one respect. She drove everywhere and did everything at high speed and with enormous gusto but she enjoyed her work enormously and was very proud of having wrested her M.D. from the English. Although born in Ireland she had spent part of her childhood and some of her training period in Scotland, so that her accent was of a Celtic hybrid, half Country Kerry, half Lowland Scot. Her outlook and sense of humour, however, were all Irish and her long struggle to qualify had done nothing to moderate a natural ebullience. During her five years in Dublin she had lived, she told Rudd, on about fifteenpence a day, "doled out in three-penny bits" by the Scots uncle who took her in when Himself (Doctor O'Keefe) had made his one-way crossing to England thirty years before. John Rudd would have liked to have satisfied his curiosity as to why O'Keefe had come here in the first place but reserved the question until he could be sure it would not give offence.

Like so many Irish patriots Maureen O'Keefe could laugh at her enthusiasm for Home Rule and even sympathise with the English for having to contend with such an indigestible morsel as Ireland. Perhaps John Rudd's intimate knowledge of Ireland, and the fact that he had enjoyed many a day's hunting in the West, did something to draw them closer together at a time when the agent was depressed regarding the Squire's slow crawl back to health. She was a good talker but an even better listener and within a few days he had unburdened himself regarding his own situation and his relationship with Paul. This was touched off by a direct question she addressed to him after he had watched her encase Paul's ribs in plaster. Before he could congratulate her on what seemed to him a very dexterous display she said, as they drove off down the drive, "You love the man, do you not, John? Now would you be after wantin' to tell me why?" and he had replied, impressed by her discernment, "Yes, I love him and I'd be glad to tell you why if you have the patience to listen!"

"I have that," she said, whipping up the cob, "for it's no more than a trotting road here," and as they bowled along to Four Winds on their way to dress the septic hand of a labourer, he told her of his years under the Lovells and of Paul Craddock's sudden appearance in the Valley and how, over the last few years, they had made the estate their life. He told her too of the manner in which he had left the Army and settled in this remote corner admitting that until Craddock had come his entire existence had seemed profitless. Then, in response to her frank questions, he described the recurring crises they had shared culminating in Grace Craddock's flight and the night, just before her arrival, when they had seen the spirit of the Valley at work in the cove and Paul had twice risked his life to save seven lives. It was this incident that he saw as the first fruits of their partnership and it seemed to him a bitter thing that Paul was too ill to evaluate it. "If I could only get that across to him I swear he'd begin to mend," he declared but at that she laughed, saying she knew a better tonic for the boy and that luckily was at hand in unlimited supply. She said merrily that she had only drawn him out on the subject in order to confirm her diagnosis. "You'll not be put out by what I say, John? You'll not think me presumptuous for interfering?"

"You're the doctor," he said, "and any judgment you made would be based on good sense and a kind heart."

She stopped the trap, sucked in her cheeks in a way she had and let her body slump back on her hands. "Paul Craddock is as strong as an ox!" she said, "and there's no reason in the world why he shouldn't be up and about again in a fortnight, providing he looks ahead instead of brooding on what lies behind! Sure, he did a man's job of work there in the cove, but his physical hurts aren't important! There's more to it than that, John, the boy's pride is in ruins!"

"How could you know that?"

478

"I guessed it the moment I heard tell of the little baggage he married. It's a special balm the boy needs and you can't buy it by the pot at the pharmacy!"

"Baggage or not," said John glumly, "he's still in love with that madcap and neither you nor I can do a thing about it."

"You think not?" she said. "Then you've a thicker head than I suspected, John! I was five and a half years working for my degree and there was nothing in the lectures about broken hearts. Maybe there will be when there are more women in the field but there isn't yet! We still leave it all to the ladies of the circulating libraries, who make a very good living out of it I'm told. Do you pay no account to this other girl!—the one who rushed down from London the moment she heard of his plight?"

"Claire Derwent? Don't be misled by her—they're old friends and I daresay after reading the papers she . . ."

"If you think she came simply because he was laid up with broken ribs and pneumonia, John, you must have your nose so deep in the soil that you'll end up down a rabbit hole!"

"Oh, he was fond of her but mildly I'd say and before he married Grace. It never amounted to anything serious."

"It's taking a serious turn right now," she said, "and I mean to give it a push! Why do you suppose I engaged Miss Derwent, in preference to a real nurse from Paxtonbury? Did you think I was impressed by her having played nursing games at a V.A.D. lecture course?"

"Well, to tell the truth I was a bit sceptical," he admitted, chuckling, "for I made sure you would get a professional in for night work. After all, he can afford it and you can't be on the spot all the time."

"John," she said, with Irish mock solemnity, "I'll tell you something else about the patient and I'll risk shocking you! It's a little night work the boy needs, bless him, and given time and patience on both sides I think he'll get it!"

He laughed outright at this, one of the few honest guffaws since his garrison days in Ireland twenty-five years ago. "Maureen O'Keefe," he said, in a very fair imitation of her brogue, "as Almighty God's me witness it's a brazen, scheming hussy you are and I have it in mind to pass

479

your prescription to a medical council and plaised they'd be to get shut of ye!"

"You do that, m'boy," she replied, "and I'll argue the diagnosis before any number of them! Now will you not admit it's high time the country had more of us petticoat quacks? And what's so different about my prescription either? Sure, it's no more than the mixture as before!" and she cracked the whip and pulled the cob back on to the river road. It was a week before he learned how to look impassive when listening to Maureen's solemn and detailed instructions to "Nurse" Derwent, when she reported for night duty after the evening visits.

The situation in the sick-room linked agent and doctor in conspiracy for as Paul's wounds began to heal and he could move around a little John found himself studying the relationship between patient and nurse with an attention that sometimes made him nervous. It seemed to him that both Paul and Claire were very much on their guard, as though determined to keep their distance but when he mentioned this to Maureen she scolded him, saying that he would do well to keep away from the sick-room when Claire was on duty. If the girl got so much as an inkling what was expected of her she would be over the hills and far away in a flash. He took her advice and thereafter confined his visits to daylight hours but he went on worrying all the same and presently it occurred to him that the boy Ikey might be able to supply a clue regarding the latest situation between Paul and Grace. In the turmoil surrounding Ikey's return he had not exchanged more than a few gruff words with him, whereas Ikey had kept out of his way, probably anticipating a rebuke. John waylaid him one morning in the orchard and called, sharply, "Hi there! I want a word with you young feller-me-lad," and when the boy put on a virtuous expression, added, "You don't fool me! I haven't forgotten all that extra trouble you caused us skipping to London like that and I hope you get a hiding for it when you go back to school tomorrow!"

"I daresay I will, sir," the boy said, but so cheerfully that John at once suspected the boy was laughing at him.

"What in the name of God possessed you to do such

480

a thing?" he demanded. "You must have known we had enough trouble on our hands and that having you home only made work for everybody!"

"I know that," said the boy, enigmatically, "but it was something I had to do!" Then, more doggedly, "I can't tell you, sir! I'd like to but I can't! I promised, you see."

John said, coldly, "Will you tell me why you went to Mrs. Craddock? Did she send for you?"

"No, sir," he said, "it was all my idea. She was surprised to see me and sent me back the next day."

"How the devil did you know where to find her?"

"I read it in the newspaper, Mr. Rudd."

"You found her address in a paper?"

"No sir, just where those suffragettes met. I guessed she'd be there and—well, she was, sir."

Curiosity tormented him but his army training stopped him bullying the truth from the boy. He had heard cornered troopers use this stalling technique in the orderly room and had, in fact, used it himself when he was Ikey's age. The boy, he was sure, was not being evasive out of cussedness but from motives which he regarded as honourable, loyalty to a comrade perhaps, or maybe loyalty to Grace. He said, with a pretence of bad grace, "Very well, Ikey, I daresay the Squire will want to know all about it when he is better. After all, you're his responsibility, not mine!" and he walked back to the stableyard. When he looked over his shoulder, however, the boy was still standing where he had left him and his expression suggested a certain amount of distress and uncertainty. For no reason that he could think of the interview both puzzled and disturbed Rudd but when he saw Maureen's trap enter the yard he shrugged off his doubts muttering, "I daresay it's all trivial enough but how the devil is a boy to know that at his age?"

V

John Rudd was correct in surmising that his questions had upset Ikey. In fact, one way and another these holidays had been a disconsolate period apart from the hours

481

spent in Hazel Potter's company. The rush to London, the tracking down of Mrs. Craddock, the dramatic switch to Claire Derwent and the luring of her to Devon, had seemed achievements at the time and when Claire actually arrived he had enjoyed a moment of triumph. But since then events had slipped and slithered beyond his comprehension and the more he contemplated the adult world the more baffling and illogical it became, lacking the fixed loyalties that regulated the world of school and stable-yard. He suffered badly from lack of a confidant and, as the days passed, with Squire in the sick-room and Claire Derwent spending her nights at the big house, Ikey's elation began to moderate so that he passed from bewilderment to a permanent state of anxiety, seeing himself as the author of a plot that had gone awry and might ultimately touch off a domestic explosion involving everybody concerned and himself most of all. He could make nothing of the situation. The Squire, presumably, was still married to his wife, who had not only refused to visit him when he lay critically ill but had actually connived at the introduction of another woman into the house. It was this that ran counter to all Ikey's conceptions of human nature. He was familiar with sporadic domestic eruptions in the backstreets but wives south of the Thames, however resentful and vituperative they felt towards their husbands, stopped far short of encouraging rivals. They would, he reflected, be more likely to tear the clothes from their backs and claw out handfuls of hair, at which stage, in Ikey's experience, husbands usually intervened and tempers were cooled in the nearest four-ale bar. And there was another aspect of the affair that bewildered him. He would have thought that Claire Derwent, once installed, would have been sure to seek him out and question him very closely about that letter but not only had she failed to do this, she had gone out of her way to avoid him and had, in fact, not addressed a word to him since her arrival. He could get little reassurance from Mrs. Handcock or Thirza Trimlett regarding Squire's health and yet they were forever whispering together and he guessed that their furtive confidences concerned Claire Derwent's more or less permanent presence in the house. He would have

482

talked it over with Gappy, the gardener's boy and former room-mate over the stable, but since going away to school his relationship with Gappy had changed and Gappy now regarded him as one of the gentry, hardly less exalted than the Squire and had even taken to addressing him as "Young Sir", a form of address that made Ikey blush. After John Rudd's crusty interrogation he wandered away along the river bank towards Codsall Bridge, having considered but rejected the idea of seeking Hazel Potter's advice. With the best will in the world, he decided, Hazel could be of no assistance here and having decided this he again envied her her freedom and from this it was a short step to gloomy contemplation of his own changed status in the Valley and a conviction that it might be better for his peace of mind if, the moment the Squire was approachable, he applied for reinstatement as stable-boy. He drifted along the path beside the river, hands deep in pockets, forehead creased with melancholy, reflecting that here was a rotten end to a thoroughly rotten holiday.

He had always preferred the Sorrel banks to any other corner of the estate, except perhaps the green depths of the woods near the islet. Last term the English master had introduced him to a poem called "A Boy's Song," and the lea, described therein, seemed to Ikey to refer to this particular reach of the river. Recollection of the verses, however, only served to deepen his gloom for he had no Billy with whom to share his enthusiasm for the darting trout and the tremble of tree shadows over the pike pool. He stood leaning on the rail of the bridge staring down into the clear water like a man contemplating suicide and was so drenched in self-pity that he did not hear the whirr of the trap wheels or turn aside when hooves beat on the planking. The first indication he had of the presence of the lady-doctor was her hail of, "Hi, boy! *You*, boy!" and then he turned and flattened himself against the rail, supposing himself an obstruction to her passage. She did not advance, however, but stared down at him, her eyes glinting with amusement.

"You're from the big house, aren't you?" she asked,

and when he admitted that he was, "Aren't you a relative of Squire Craddock's?"

Now this was not a simple question to answer. At school the Squire was his stepbrother but he had never made such an impudent claim on home ground, so he said, evasively, "I'm Ikey Palfrey and I used to work yonder but now Squire sends me to school!"

"That's it," she said, triumphantly, "I knew you belonged! I don't forget faces that easily. Squire adopted you, didn't he?"

"He sends me to school," Ikey repeated obstinately, privately thinking her a very nosy woman and wishing she would stop pestering him.

"All right, have it your own way," she said cheerfully and then, to his dismay, she hoisted herself from the box, looped the reins round a post and joined him in contemplation of the water.

"Any fish down there?" she said casually.

"Trout," he told her, "and sometimes grayling but Squire won't let it off. Anyone can fish free so long as they work on the estate."

"Ah," she said, with an air of satisfaction, "the Squire's a sensible man. A good one to work for I'm told."

"Yes, he is," said Ikey, somewhat mollified, "the best! Anyone will tell you that, Doctor."

They remained side by side squinting down at the stream and presently he saw, or thought he saw, a chance to relieve at least one of his private anxieties. He said, bluntly, "Is he going to get better? *Really* better?"

"Why, of course he is! He'll be out and about as soon as we get the plaster off his ribs and his arm out of splints. He's through the worst of it."

He felt himself warming towards her, so much so that he was tempted to break the first seal of his confessional and said, "You . . . you heard about me running away to London when it happened? They all said it was a bad thing to do but I didn't mean to cause Mr. Rudd or anyone any trouble. I . . . I had an idea, that's all."

She said, with elaborate unconcern, "You did? Well then you must have a clear conscience so don't bother!" And then, even more casually, "What kind of idea?"

484

"A daft one it turned out," he said, beginning to suspect that he had already said too much.

They fell silent again and perhaps two minutes passed before she said, suddenly, "Look here, Ikey, if you want to get anything off your chest get it off and it won't go any further! If you don't then I'm not in the least worried. It's a fine spring day and a boy of your age ought to enjoy it! No dam' sense in taking troubles seriously at your age!"

The advice, and the fashion in which it was offered, levelled them in a way that astonished him for he might have been leaning on the rail alongside one of his Third Form cronies. This woman, whom everybody for miles around regarded as a freak, seemed far more approachable than, say, one of the prefects at school. He put a finger in his mouth and pulled at his lower lip, screwing up his face in an effort to assess her trustworthiness and then, as he recalled his miserable confusion of mind, he made a decision in her favour. "I can't explain how it all happened," he said, "but it was me that began it! Now I don't know whether I did right or wrong and that's a fact, Doctor!"

"All right," she said, equably, "suppose you explain and leave me to sort it out for you? Why *did* you run off to London, instead of staying at school until you were sent for?"

"I went to find Mrs. Craddock and tell her she ought to come home," he said.

He must have succeeded in astonishing her for she gasped and then chuckled, a rich chuckle, beginning deep in her throat so that he was prepared to share the joke to some extent.

"He was very low," he explained, grinning, "not like he was before she ran off. I got to thinking about it and then, before he got hurt rescuing those sailors, I thought I'd . . . well . . . get her back if I could. I would have managed it without anyone missing me if it hadn't been for Mr. Rudd ringing up and telling them to keep me at school for a week!"

She was regarding him now with admiration. "Glory to

485

God!" she said, "but you're a deep one and no mistake! How old are you, Ikey?"

"Fourteen," he said, wondering what his age had to do with it and she added, "So you put it to her, just like that? What on earth did she say?"

"She said she wasn't ever coming back."

"And then?"

He licked his lips having now arrived at the most improbable part of the business. "Well," he went on, reluctantly, "she was nice to me and we had a talk about things. She said the person who could really cheer him up wasn't her at all but Miss Derwent, the one who was daft about him when he first came here."

"I see," she said, "so all you did was to hop round the corner and enlist Miss Derwent as Comforter-in-Chief?"

"No," he said, "I wrote her a letter saying the Squire was calling out for her in his deliriousness!"

"In his deliriousness? But was he?"

"How should I know, I wasn't here then."

She annoyed him then by exploding with laughter and he added as though in extenuation, "Well, it worked! It worked a lot quicker than I thought it would! She was down here almost at once."

"I'll wager she was," said Maureen O'Keefe, standing with feet astride and hands on hips as she regarded him with the closest attention. "Well then, since it worked what are you so bothered about?"

"It doesn't seem right when he's not married to her but to Mrs. Craddock," he said and the genuine note of piety in his voice told her that it would be boorish to laugh at him again; instead she laid a hand on his shoulder, pulling him round facing her. "Look here, Ikey," she said, "I think you're marvellous, do you understand? You went right to the root of things, and didn't let the prospect of trouble for yourself stop you! Did they give you a hiding when they got you back?"

"No," he said gloomily, "but I daresay they will when I get back to school tomorrow. Not that that bothers me, for a walloping doesn't amount to much. What really worries me is . . . well . . . not knowing whether I did

486

right and whether . . . the Squire really *wants* Miss Derwent around all the time."

"You can set your mind at rest on that," she said. "You did Squire the best turn anyone could have done him and he does like having her around, take it from me! As to getting a thrashing from your housemaster for running away you can forget that too. I'll give you a note to take back and you'll hear no more about it."

"Look here, Doctor," he said, wriggling out of her grasp, "that won't do at all! I don't want anyone at school to know what I ran off for and I don't want anyone here to know, especially Squire! I wouldn't have told you if . . ."

"Don't be so stupid," she said, "do you think I'd split on a pal? Me? The person responsible for getting him well again? I won't breathe a word to anyone upon my honour!"

"Not even to Mr. Rudd?"

"Least of all to him," she said. "It'll be between you and me and for always!"

"Well, thanks," he said gratefully and then, "I don't reckon it would do for Miss Derwent to know Mrs. Craddock read the letter first!"

"*She* read it? Mrs. Craddock did?"

"Yes. I wrote it while she was there and took it back to Devon to post so as it would have the right postmark."

"Ikey," she said, "there's a word you wouldn't have heard yet that just about describes you so remember it and you can recognise yourself later on! You're Machiavellian! Remember that—*Mack-i-ah-vellian!*"

"What does it mean?" he asked and she said, gesticulating, "It's having an instinctive understanding of people and how their minds work and it's a priceless quality to possess, particularly if you ever think of going into business!"

"I'll not do that," he said, scornfully, "I'm going to join the cavalry!"

"Ah," she said, "then I'm afraid it won't be much use to you. Still, it's nice to have and I daresay it'll help you get along with the ladies!"

"I shan't ever marry either," he said, firmly, "it muddles things up so!"

"Well, it needn't," she said, "but while we're on the subject I'll let you into my secret. I think it very likely that Squire will marry Miss Derwent in the end. You see if I'm not right."

He stared at her in amazement. "How could he do that?" he said and then remembered what Grace Craddock had said about "getting unmarried", a remark he had not taken seriously at the time.

"Well," she said, "we won't go into it right now but it'll happen about this time next year, maybe. The thing is, if it does, what would you think about it?"

"I don't know," he said, slowly, "Miss Derwent and me always got along. She's a sport and I like her all right but I liked Mrs. Craddock. One time everyone up at the big house thought Squire and Miss Derwent would marry so I suppose it would work out all right!"

He began to wonder if, after all, there might be some kind of pattern to the strange behaviour of adults, even if it was so complex that it could not be related to everyday life. He said, "She'd *fit in* better I mean, she *belongs* and somehow Mrs. Craddock never did, did she? She was well . . . a *town* person!"

"You've hit the nail on the head again," she said and unlooping the cob's reins hoisted herself on to the box. "Would you like to finish the round with me, Ikey?"

"No," he told her, suddenly feeling a glorious sense of release, "I think I'll cross Hermitage and cut through the woods to the mere. We've got woods round the school but they're not like our woods, mostly just pine where nothing much grows."

She lifted her whip in respectful salute and rolled across the bridge towards Four Winds. He looked after her a moment and then ran across the road, scrambled up the bank and disappeared into the ash thickets on the river side of Hermitage Wood as she drove to Four Winds at a spanking speed. "Well," she said to herself as she clipped through the gate, "I came here thinking a country practice might be dull but I'm learning otherwise and that's for sure!"

He was aware of her less as a nurse and a personable young woman with a glowing complexion and corn-coloured hair, than as an agent whose presence completed a cycle of years, beginning with the long weeks of drought when he had first ridden about the Valley in her company, and ending in another spell of unbroken sunshine that followed the mild spring and promised a record crop providing sufficient rain fell by the first week of July. Thus, in a sense, she was impersonal, not a woman at all but a spirit of the Valley unexpectedly restored to him and bringing the promise of better times.

He did not remember her as a tranquil person. Spirited and joyous perhaps, and always eager for laughter but certainly not a woman who could communicate repose. Yet she was so now and sometimes he wondered what experience outside the Valley had changed her, calming her without making her moody and withdrawn. Her still-ness was now an essential part of her, like her watchful blue eyes and a head of hair that was sometimes gold, sometimes almost auburn and sometimes the bronze shade of the sea an hour or so before sunset. He would watch her for long minutes as she stood by the tall window, supposing him to be taking his afternoon nap although in fact he seldom did take it, but maintained the pretence of doing so for a fortnight or more in order that he could study her through half-closed eyes when she thought her-self unobserved. He would lie still and wonder about her, comparing her in a thousand ways to Grace and pondering questions that never suggested themselves during their brief conversations in the evenings. Privately he thought it odd that she should sit here at all through the short nights, for once he became accustomed to the awkward-ness of his posture caused by the splint and the plaster that itched so mercilessly, he felt he no longer needed a night nurse and wondered why the woman doctor John Rudd had introduced into the house insisted someone should watch him until splint and plaster were removed. He did not quarrel with the decision, however, because

Claire's presence gave him something to think about and he much preferred her to a stranger.

After a time her tranquillity communicated itself to him so that he found he was able to think of Grace, and Martin Codsall, and Smut, and poor old Tamer objectively, and was even able to regard the misgivings they aroused as a by-product of illness and high temperature, like the fantasies of his long spell in hospital. He got accustomed to her neat ways and patient method of hoisting him this way and that, and even to her shaving him each morning. Soon, in a sense, he began to enjoy his comparative helplessness for it was very pleasant to lie here with nothing to do but read and think abstract thoughts. The doctor told him that the plaster would have to remain at least a month and at first this had exasperated him for he had sharp memories of the boredom of sick-bed life, but soon he was more than resigned to it and Claire Derwent's presence reconciled him to inaction. It was Claire who encouraged him to pick up the threads of everyday life about the house and here she had the power to surprise him, first in the matter of her piano playing, then as the only person at Shallowford capable of overcoming young Simon's distaste of the sick-room.

He knew nothing of music and had been curious to learn who was playing the old upright piano in the drawing-room one evening, just before she came on duty. The piano had stood there since Lovell's day and nobody had played it since the Coronation soirée. When she admitted it was her and told him the instrument needed tuning, he was astonished. Nobody had ever told him that she could play.

"Who taught you?" he wanted to know and she said that her mother had given her elementary lessons but after her death she had taught herself to play by ear. Now she was able, in her own phrase, to tinkle up and down and pick out a tune providing the basic chords had stuck!

"It sounded pleasant enough from up here," he said. "Go down and play again and leave both doors open."

She seemed mildly embarrassed by the request but she went and the muted melodies of Strauss waltzes and popular student songs reached him from the stair-well. He said, when she returned, "That was delightful! I'll persuade Doctor O'Keefe to prescribe it night and morning!" and she said, laughing, "It wasn't really playing at all! You must have a dreadful ear, as bad as Simon's!"

"Have you played for Simon?"

Yes, she said, now and again when he was particularly tiresome but he was only interested in discords and the squeak of the pedals.

"How is the poor kid?" he asked and for a moment her tranquillity deserted her and she said, sharply, "He's playing Thirza Tremlett up. You ought to have him in here and talk to him, so that he knows you meant it."

"Ah come, he's only two and a half," Paul protested, "and besides, he won't come in here while I'm trussed up like this. We've tried it and he nearly screamed the place down!"

"That depends on the approach," she said. "He wouldn't make a fuss if I was here!"

"Very well," Paul said, "go and get him and I'll wager he kicks up the devil of a row!"

She went out at once and returned a few minutes later leading the child by the hand. He looked uneasy but subdued, staring at Paul with Grace's expression and a finger in his mouth. Paul thought, not for the first time, "He's all hers, there's hardly a trace of me about him. He's got her looks and her obstinacy but Claire seems to know how to manage him." Claire said, addressing the boy, "Well, there he is, Simon, and he isn't so frightening after all is he? He got hurt saving people from drowning and it isn't very kind to leave him on his own all day! He'd come and see you if you were hurt and had to stay in bed!"

The boy considered this, regarding the patient thoughtfully and presently he put out his hand and scratched the plaster where it showed under Paul's open nightshirt. Then, to Paul's surprise, he chuckled and said, "You could write on it! You could, couldn't you, Auntie Claire?"

"Yes, you could indeed," Claire said, picking up a pencil from the bedside table. "Draw something. It'll give Daddy something to look at when he's bored."

The boy took the pencil, sucked it a moment and then,

with neat, careful strokes, drew a crude sketch of a sailing boat. Paul laughed so heartily that his sore ribs gave a twinge and the laugh ended in a gasp, whereupon Claire lifted Simon down and said, "All right, run along now but don't forget to come in and say hello in the morning and good night when you go to bed! Go on, off with you!" and she patted his rump and shooed him out.

"Well I'll be damned," Paul said, "I've never seen him behave like that before! You must have a flair for children, Claire. I've hardly been able to approach the boy since Grace went."

"That's not wholly your fault," she said, "it's the fault of the women about the place. Thirza spoils him, so does Mrs. Handcock and so do all the maids and Chivers, the groom. A child getting that much attention is naturally going to bellow every time something doesn't please him. You'll have to look into the Simon situation when you're up and about again."

He knew that what she said was true, that the staff did spoil the child outrageously, particularly since Grace had left and also that Thirza, his nanny, had come to regard Simon as a personal possession but it was obvious that the child had respect for "Auntie" Claire.

"You've changed a great deal since you went away," he said.

"You've changed yourself," she told him cheerfully, "and not altogether for the better!"

"Well, at least you don't over indulge me in goo-goo invalid talk," he said, smiling. *"What* changes, particularly?"

She looked down at him coolly, perhaps considering whether or not he was prepared to digest home truths and apparently decided that he was, for she said, "What I liked about you when you first came here was your enthusiasm for people rather than ideas. You didn't settle here simply because you like unspoiled country but because you were lonely and found a couple of hundred ready-made friends. It was your warm approach to people like Rose, the Codsalls, the Pitts, and the Potters that gave you a flying start but if you don't watch out you'll lose all the headway you made! Then you'll stay here not because you want to but from force of habit and from lack of an alternative and I think that would be a shame."

"You really think I made headway then?"

"Good heavens, of course you did, tremendous headway!" she snapped, "and that remark only illustrates what I'm trying to say! You see setbacks of the kind anyone attempting anything new is bound to encounter as . . . well . . . as personal failures but what's so disappointing is that you are beginning to hug them to yourself like a hypochondriac! Why don't you try balancing them against your successes? There isn't a person about here who doesn't wish you well and that's very different from feeling sorry for you!" She stopped and he noticed to his surprise that she was blushing. "I'm sorry," she added, "it's really no concern of mine, is it? What would you like for supper tonight?"

"A straight talk," he said, writhing himself into a more upright position, "finish what you were going to say! I'm still cock of the roost round here but nobody talks to me any more, not even old John."

She sat down beside him, saying, "You're a natural optimist, Paul, but lately you've been hard at work converting yourself into a pessimist, just like my father! There isn't so much enthusiasm about that we can spare it, least of all in a place like this, while everyone in the big world outside is making money and mistaking it for progress! All right, you took a toss over Martin Codsall, and another over Smut Potter. Then your wife walked out on you and from what I hear you've been sulking ever since, or at least until the wreck. But things like that happen to everyone who lives anything but a fenced-in life. They shouldn't stop a man with your kind of enterprise, at least, not at your age! Perhaps you don't realise it but you've already made a name for yourself round here and not only because you fished seven people off that rock! Folk round here believe in you and believe in what you're trying to do, although some of them don't really understand it yet. My advice, for what it's worth, is that you should go right on doing it, not gloomily and doggedly, the way you have since Grace left but the way

493

you began, with a sense of fun and adventure, do you understand?"

"Yes," he said slowly, "that's easy to understand Claire but by God I badly needed someone to spell it out for me!" He was going on to defend himself by citing the loneliness of authority but before he could phrase it the sentiment seemed pretentious in the face of her outspokenness so he held his tongue and said: "I'll have supper now, Claire, and when Mrs. Handcock brings it up stay down there and play some more. I haven't much musical taste but your playing stimulates thought and maybe it's time I did some real thinking!"

She left him and went down to the kitchen and a few moments later he heard the tinkle of the untuned piano. She had, he thought, a very light touch, as though youth came out of the tops of her fingers coaxing melody from a battered old instrument that he would have thrown out long since if it had come to his notice. He thought, "She's a damned good sort to bother with me after all that's happened and I hope she doesn't take it into her head to fly off again as soon as I'm out of this blasted straitjacket!" The flesh under the plaster itched and in twisting to seek relief he noticed Simon's drawing. "She's right about the kid too," he mused, "and I won't wait until I'm up before doing something to sort that out. I'll get Mary Willoughby over and talk her into occupying the boy's mind with the alphabet or something and after that I'll draw up some kind of programme for him, for as long as they treat him like a baby he'll stay one!"

He was still reassuring himself along these lines when Mrs. Handcock waddled in with her rich bedside manner and said, referring to the music, "Tiz real pretty, baint it? 'Er's a rare maid an' no mistake!" and Paul smiled, knowing precisely what was in her mind, and what she and Thirza, and possibly everyone else about the house were speculating. Tonight the thought amused him and he said, in excellent imitation of her brogue, "Oh, giddon with 'ee Mrs. 'Ancock, I dorn reckon 'er be a maid no more! I yeard tell 'er got 'erself married to someone in London but ab'm got around to braaking the news to us yet!" and the look of pained astonishment on the house-keeper's face was ample reward for the twinges produced by his struggles to sit upright and balance the supper tray on his knees.

CHAPTER FIFTEEN

I

THE estate record book, enclosed between the Bible covers of Sir George's photograph album, had grown into an estate encyclopedia. Personal data, births, deaths and marriages were still entered in Paul's tall, sloping hand-writing on the left-hand pages but on the right was a summary compiled from hundreds of jottings of how each farm was stocked and what was grown on its acreage. It could tell you, for instance, how much fallow land Eve-leigh had at any one time, how many acres supported his Friesians and how many were devoted to wheat, barley, oats or root crops. It could correct Henry Pitts when the latter stated that his twelve-acre field had been given over to kale the year before last when, in fact, it had produced mangolds, or rye for green fodder. Paul set everything down there in black and white, season by season, year by year and daily access to this book had formed certain patterns in his mind, so that he thought of Periwinkle as a chicken farm, of Four Winds as the mainstay of the estate's dairy output, of Deepdene as the principal source of market-garden produce. Similarly, everyone on the estate had a mental tag. Sam Potter was the tree-feller, Edward Derwent was the best stockman in the Valley, and his daughter Rose, Shallowford's most accomplished horsewoman and breaker of horses. Yet, for all his pas-sion for detail, Paul was an easy-going landlord. He had let old Honeyman have his way about sheep and suffered the Potters to farm any way they liked, for away at the back of his mind, too remote to find expression even in casual shop-talk with John Rudd, was the outline of a collective scheme in which every tenant farmer, and many of their employees, became specialists operating within self-chosen and clearly-defined limits, a communal plan that would one day—perhaps a generation hence—establish the Valley as the most productive in the West. This was his dream but he was not yet fully aware of it; it was also the spring-board of his patriotism, for England beyond the Sorrel and railway line had little meaning for him, save as a kind of impersonal audience.

In four years he had still to show a credit balance and had not ceased to feed money into the estate but the amounts ploughed back grew smaller each year and by Lady Day, 1906, he was close to breaking even. He thus had cause to thank Franz Zorndorff for his insistence that he paid into Paul's account his share in scrapyard profits, for in the first two years, when so many implements had had to be replaced and several tied cottages rebuilt in addition to routine renovations on some of the farm-houses, he had drawn heavily upon his capital whereas the original income of the estate had shrunk, partly owing to his arrangement with Eveleigh at Four Winds but also by default on the part of the Potters. Now, however, John told him that they could anticipate a steady climb towards solvency, for Will Codsall was reclaiming land north-west of his borders, Derwent paid slightly more rent for additional acreage on the cliff, Eveleigh was making a spectacular success of Four Winds and two houses and several rebuilt cottages in Coombe Bay had been let on long leases at increased rentals.

The stock on every farm in the Valley had improved, even the Potters coming up with several fine litters of saddlebacks, that thrived under the oaks on the edge of the woods. Eveleigh boasted one of the best herds in the district and Will and Elinor Codsall had recently produced a sturdy cross between Light Sussex and White Leghorn and were said to be despatching forty dozen eggs a day. Honeyman's last lambing season had been a success owing a good deal to the exceptionally mild winter and over at Hermitage, where the Pitts clung to the mixed economy of their ancestors, the rent was never a day overdue. Old Willoughby kept few animals at Deepdene but because of improved transport his fruit and vegetables were finding a ready market in Paxtonbury and he was also sending cut blooms to Covent Garden during part of the year. All in all, Paul decided (once he was chipped out of his plaster and could move about more comfortably), prospects seemed very fair, especially if the fine weather lasted into July and there was occasional rain at night, as there had been throughout the summer.

During the long days of June he would stand in his office propped against the drawing-board (a position he found more comfortable than sitting) and thumb through his own and John Rudd's notes, occasionally turning aside to write a letter, or make a ledger entry but often filling the big white pages of his bible, for this was something that gave him a sense of achievement, his personal index to the circulation of the estate in terms of stock, crops, income and human beings. He noted, for instance, that his "population" had risen sharply during the last few years. When he took over there had been six farms supporting a hundred and two men, women and children, a tally that included some forty craftsmen and casual labourers, some of them part-time workers and almost a score of them women, wives or daughters of Coombe Valley men who were not employed on the estate. Mary Willoughby at that time had seventeen children on her roll call. Now there were seven farms, supporting one hundred and nine people and Mary had twenty-five children in her farmhouse schoolroom, for the fecundity of the Valley seemed to extend to the women living in it. Elinor Codsall had produced a girl and a boy and was now expecting a third child. Joannie Potter had two girls and a boy. Pansy Tozer had a girl and a boy and Henry Pitts' rawboned redhead had recently presented him with a great lumping boy, weighing ten-and-a-half pounds at birth. Over at Four Winds Marian Eveleigh dutifully produced an annual addition to the long family and there was also his own child, Simon, born in January, 1904. It was almost certain that Cissie and Violet Potter, still

497

officially unclaimed, had done their share out of wedlock but their efforts were not entered in the record.

There were, of course, more sombre entries in the book, one relating to the Four Winds tragedy, another to the death of old Tamer Potter, but deaths were lagging far behind births, for people seemed to live to incredible ages on this side of the Sorrel. There was one entry, dated March 20th, 1905, marking the hundredth birthday of old Floss Timber lake, the estate sawyer's grandmother, who had been born the year of Trafalgar. Paul sometimes called in on the old lady, who lived in a cottage close to the Home Farm and found her enjoying a clay-pipe and berating her long-suffering daughter, aged eighty, whom she continued to treat as a child in a pinafore. In Coombe Bay there were three nonagenarians and Arthur Pitts' father, who still lived at Hermitage but never left his room now, claimed to be as old as young Floss Timberlake. Arthur said this was nonsense for it made him out to be eighty, whereas records at the parish church showed that he was only sixty-nine.

Paul did not spend all his time in the office during the latter part of his convalescence for Maureen O'Keefe was no coddler of invalids and told him that by far the best way to heal his cracked ribs was to keep them at work, no matter how painful it proved and that, providing he was careful, he could ride Snowdrop at a walk. His arm was fully healed and apart from stiffness gave him no trouble at all but despite his eagerness to get about and take advantage of the long spell of fine weather he found that he tired very quickly after more than five weeks in bed and at first was subject to occasional spells of dizziness, so that on the doctor's instructions Claire Derwent acted as escort when he went afield on horseback or on foot. Her orders in this respect were so peremptory that John Rudd, that most cautious of suitors, went so far as to warn her one day when they watched Paul and Claire walk their horses down the drive and cross the ford to the river road, with the intention of going as far as the landslip at Nun's Head and taking a swim.

"Look here, old girl," he said (having progressed this

498

far in the last few weeks), "I'm not at all sure you ought to encourage that in the circumstances!"

"What? Forbid them a health-giving bathe on a day like this?" she said, innocently, but he replied, "You know damned well I'm not referring to the curative properties of salt water! You are determined to throw those two together willy-nilly and one ought to remember that he's still a married man and she has a reputation to protect!"

"Oh, stuff and nonsense," she burst out, "you talk just like one of those circulating library queens! Who gives a damn about reputations around here? She's good for him, any fool can see that, and as for his wife, is she likely to object?"

"She might. She might even have them spied on for grounds for divorce!" he argued but this was too much for Maureen, who exploded with laughter and was tempted to break faith with Ikey by explaining Grace's part in luring Claire back to the Valley. She checked herself in time, however, and said, "Well, you should be the last to come forward with that kind of pious notion, John Rudd! Everyone in the Valley is gossiping about you and I and heaven knows we give them all the ammunition they need!"

"Ah, that's different," he said, secretly delighted by her admission, "for I'm a widower and you're old enough to look to yourself in that respect! All the same," he added, as an afterthought, "we could easily put a stop to their gossip, Maureen!"

He had not meant to make such an informal proposal, not here, on a bright June morning, as they walked down the drive to where her cob was tethered. It had slipped past his tongue before he could stop it but now it was done he was relieved when she neither laughed at him nor so much as checked her stride but only said, calmly, "So you'd be after making an honest woman of me, John? You'd like us to be married, providing, of course, I decided to stay down here and give up all idea of joining a city practice?"

"I should like that very much, my dear," he said, "but you don't have to commit yourself to a country practice.

My contract with Paul Craddock has run out and we haven't got round to renewing it yet. I've got a little money, never having spent much down here and I daresay I could find part-time work wherever you went. I could do your accounts, too, and make sure you didn't work sixteen hours a day for nothing."

She stopped as they reached the gate of his lodge. "You would be prepared to leave here? To let Young Lochinvar manage by himself?"

"Why not? He's quite capable of doing so! For a town-bred man he's learned more of estate management in four years than the Lovells acquired in two generations. The point is he's genuinely interested and doesn't really need me now, or won't by this time next year."

"But John," she said, and he had never heard her speak so softly, "I'm well on the way to being an old maid and I'm also a freak, with far more dangerous ideas about women's rights than the laddie's wife! I'm not much to look at either and you know well enough my job would always come first."

"You're the most intelligent woman I've ever had the luck to meet," he said, "and as for being an old maid, you've no qualifications for the role! You're thirty-four —you told me that the first day we met—whereas I'm fifty-two but we're both fit and in our right minds. Incidentally, you're as handsome a woman as Claire Derwent in your way, so don't get to thinking otherwise!"

It was the first time he had ever seen her blush and it gave him confidence. He went on, lifting her hand from the iron knob of the gate, "Did I know anything of your character or qualifications that first day you took tea with me here, when I was desperate with worry about all that had happened down in the cove? I didn't care a straw what you were—an actuary, a governess or an Irish seamstress! You put me on an even keel in ten minutes and I said to myself, 'Now there's what they mean when they talk about Irish charm!' I could have proposed on the spot and that's the truth of the matter!"

The blush faded as she said, in a businesslike tone, "Come inside a minute, John!" and pulled him into the porch and then, without closing the door, into his untidy

500

parlour, with its bachelor jumble littering table, armchair and sofa. The impetus of his declaration had spent itself and he seemed bewildered. She said, bluntly, "Now what is it you're looking for, John? You've been twenty years a widower so how do you expect a dedicated woman like me to give you back two decades? Tell me true, John Rudd, wouldn't you be scared out of your wits if I took you up on this, put the city out of mind and agreed to marry you next week or the week after?"

"No," he said, deliberately, "that I wouldn't! A man doesn't have emotional impulses at my age and neither does a woman of your experience respond to them! I was deeply in love with my wife, but I don't expect to recapture that kind of feeling at my age. This is something quite different and I'm not going to dress it up in fancy language. I was lonely and crotchety during my time here with the Lovells, and I owe my fresh start to Paul Craddock. But when he married I was lonely again, and after his wife left him I was lonely and miserable into the bargain. Your coming here was a kind of miracle, a third start in middle age, which is something no man has a right to expect. I'd make you a good husband and I think we should suit one another. I'm interested in your work and I envy your self-confidence and high spirits, two things I've always lacked. However, if you think the idea is ridiculous, say so. You won't give offence to me and we can remain good friends and leave it at that!"

Her laugh seemed to fill the stuffy little room and momentarily he was disconcerted but then he saw that there was no derision in her merriment and that she looked younger and prettier than he would have thought possible.

"John," she said, taking his hands, "I like it so much better when you speak off the cuff and forget to rationalise! Sure I'll marry you, the moment you give the word but I'm not so long in the tooth as to seek nothing better in marriage than twilight companionship! You make it sound damned dull, so you do, and this is to prove there's a chance it might have its livelier moments!" and she gave him a resounding kiss on each cheek, after which she skipped over to the corner cupboard where he kept his drinks and poured a couple of stiff whiskies, bringing them back to him and raising her glass with the toast, "Here's to us, John, and bless you for everything but your modesty!"

II

The bay was as smooth and as flat as a silver platter and looked just like one from the top of the drowsy village street but when they had gone down the slipway and walked the horses along the tideline, the water lost its silver gloss and turned forget-me-not-blue inshore, with great belts of emerald-green under the sandbanks of the bar. Everything on the beach was lazy in the hot, morning sun. Gulls idled about the pools pecking listlesssly at their catches and two of Tom Williams' boats, a mile out to sea, were stationary specks and seemingly unmanned, which told Paul that Tom and his crews had dropped anchor, set their lines and gone to sleep until the sun should pass beyond the headland that marked the outfall of the Teazel.

There was not a soul about on the beach and when the horses reached the shade of the giant boulders, scattered like giant's marbles for more than a quarter-mile below the largest landslip, they were reluctant to leave it, so Paul found a tiny bay backed by steep rocks where there was a rock pool half-way up the beach. It was a pleasant place to linger so they unsaddled and let the horses potter about in the shallows, while Paul peeled off jacket and shirt and stretched beside the pool, luxuriating in the sun and saying this was something he had longed to do throughout his weeks of confinement.

She stood on the far side of the pool smiling at him and presently she called, "Are you a swimmer, Paul?" and he told her he was not but could thresh about in a calm sea and enjoy it, providing the water was lukewarm. "This pool has a Table Bay temperature," he told her, "so I'm having my dip right here. Do you swim?"

"Yes," she said, pensively, "Rose and I used to come here often when we were children. My mother could swim like a fish, and taught us when we were still toddlers. I

502

often wonder where she learned to swim as well as she did, for she wasn't a local girl. Father was always vain about her horsemanship but he thought sea-bathing un-ladylike and often told her so but she never let his old-fashioned notions worry her. She was an extraordinary woman in her way, Paul. All the older people in the Valley still remember her, some of them more vividly than Rose and I."

He recalled then the little Rudd had told him about the dashing first Mrs. Derwent and for the first time realised that Claire and her sister Rose must have been old enough to recall the day their mother had fallen to her death at a jump over the Heronslea border. He would have asked her more about it but it was neither a time nor place to probe disagreeable memories so he said, "Well, here goes! I'll paddle about as Doctor Maureen advised and then sun-bathe," and she took the hint and wandered further down the beach towards the horses while he slipped out of the rest of his clothes and lowered himself gently into the pool.

It was deliciously warm and the water soothed the sore belt of flesh where the plaster had been. Presently he struck out and crossed the pool, using a clumsy sidestroke and telling himself that he had been a fool to let four summers pass without once coming down here to swim. He had been splashing about for half-an-hour before she returned carrying a parcel wrapped in oilskin.

"What's that?" he called, "you didn't say we'd picnic. I was going to suggest lunch at The Raven on the way back."

"It isn't food, greedy," she told him, "it's only my bath-ing costume. It's a hideous thing and one might as well try and swim in a crinoline! You men don't know how lucky you are being able to bathe in a single costume. Just look at it!" and she held it up, a voluminous garment in heavy serge, with sleeves and wide ornamental frills ending in bloomers tied with ribbon just above the knee.

"Good God!" he exclaimed, laughing. "I've seen pic-tures of them in the newspapers but I didn't think people actually swam in them! Won't it drag you down?"

"I'll chance it. Will you be a perfect gentleman and watch the horses for a few minutes?"

"Not me," he said, "I'll wait and watch you go in and I wish I had old Sir George's camera! You'll look ravishing in that outfit!"

She made a face at him and went off behind the shoulder of the rock, emerging after an interval in the costume, with her hair crammed under a mob cap of the kind that Lovell's housemaids had worn but Paul had long since banished. It was odd, he thought, that she could enhance a costume as sexless as that, investing it with an element of comedy. The only parts of her exposed were face, shins, feet and hands, five pink and white patches relieving yards of navy-blue worsted. He said, regretfully, "They don't leave much to chance, do they? Do all the girls dress like that when they bathe from the machines at Folkestone and Margate?"

"More or less," she said, "but the men don't see them because usually they're shooed to the far end of the beach. Only the really go-ahead resorts allow mixed bathing and as for what I'm doing right now, I'd be drummed out of society altogether in any self-respecting Spa if it got about that I'd actually shared a rock pool with a man and him married into the bargain! Well, as you said, here goes!" and she poised herself on a rock three feet above the water and plunged, very expertly he thought considering her handicap but the dive did not astonish him so much as the pace at which she raced the length of the pool, turned, disappeared under water and swam back to him with a powerful over-arm stroke.

"By George, you make my efforts look silly!" he said admiringly as she went up and down again with a back stroke, climbed out and plopped herself breathlessly beside him.

"I was always a lot better than Rose," she said. "Mother made up her mind to produce the best horsewoman and the best swimmer in the county. She was only interested in bests and as far as Rose is concerned she succeeded but I don't think I could have learned to swim in this outfit. She used to let us swim in the nude. Nobody ever comes

504

here except an occasional beachcomber from Coombe Bay but of course we had to keep it from father."

"She sounds a great deal of fun," Paul said and then, throwing his towel over his shoulders, "Look here, if I promise not to play Peeping Tom would you like to take it off and have a real swim? I can see you're longing to!"

"All right," she said, doubtfully, "if I can trust you not to cheat. Go along the beach to where the landslip begins and stand guard. No one can come from the west because low tide doesn't clear the point and Tom Williams is way out of range."

"Perhaps he has a telescope," Paul said and she replied, "If he has good luck to him!"

He picked his way over the boulders to an empty stretch of sand and was still standing there, presenting a chivalrous back, when she called and he rejoined her to find her dressed with her great mass of golden hair tousled and loose about her shoulders. She said, "It was wonderful! I felt a little girl again and I could almost hear mother laughing at us! Lend me your towel and I'll try and do something with my hair. It'll have to dry before I can show my face in Coombe Bay or the truth will have run as far as the railway line by sunset!"

He said, handing her the towel, "Do we have to bother that much about gossip, Claire?" and she replied, without looking at him, "Yes Paul, I'm afraid we do! If we stopped caring there's an end to the fun we're having and the prospect of more in the future."

"You mean your father?" he said, remembering Edward Derwent's coolness towards him that had been maintained until the night of the wreck but she said, calmly, "No Paul, nothing whatever to do with Father! And nothing to do with anyone else in the Valley, except you and I, but me especially! I wouldn't care to go through that experience again and if I thought I was likely to I should go back to London tomorrow."

It was the first real indication he had had that she had suffered on his account, having always regarded her flight from the Valley as an exhibition of pique.

"I didn't mean to act shabbily, Claire," he said. "It honestly didn't take me long to realise that! In any case, I imagine you've since been hurt a great deal more, so let's forget about it and get lunch at The Raven."

She got up and went down the beach to collect the horses, leading them back to him where he stood beside the pool. The sun still shone but for him at least the sparkle had gone from the day. As she was saddling up, he said, "You only met Grace that once—the time you came over to tea. Didn't Rose write to you and fill in the blanks?"

"No," said Claire, sharply, "Rose did not! She isn't given to tittle-tattle! All I heard was that : . ." She stopped and addressed herself to tightening the girths so that he said, impatiently, "Well? What did you hear?"

"That you weren't getting along," she said, briefly, "but do let's stop discussing it, Paul."

"No," he said, suddenly exasperated with the conspiracy of silence regarding Grace and irritated that it should run all his personal relationships into cul-de-sacs where the mere mention of her was regarded as unmannerly. "I'm over it now and I haven't forgotten what you said about making a fresh start. How can I do that if everyone shies away from the subject the way John Rudd and Mrs. Handcock always do, the way you are doing right now? Grace isn't ever coming back so we can all stop pretending it didn't happen!"

"I'm not so sure we can," she said, regarding him steadily across her saddle. "Everyone here says you're still very much in love with her and that you'll never give her up!"

He was not much astonished by this, reasoning that he must have given this impression by his churlishness over the last two years but it struck him now that it was no longer true, that in the last few weeks most of the resentment and humiliation had been purged from him, although just how this had happened he did not understand. It was something to do with a shift in the centre of gravity, removing Grace as the dominant factor in his life and filling the vacuum with the Valley, and the people of the Valley and he supposed that this shift had been brought about by the wreck but it was clear that Claire's return had a share in it. "I was very much in love with her," he admitted, "but it seems to me that love can only stand up to a cer-

506

tain amount of battering, Claire. Grace walked out on her duties as wife and mother and I'm reconciled to the fact that I never will understand why. It's one thing to lose out to another man but quite another to be made a fool of by a political fad! I suppose the heart of the trouble is that Grace didn't simply turn her back on me and Simon but on our whole way of life down here. That being so there comes a time when a man has to accept what can't be altered!"

She had finished adjusting the girths now and was holding both horses by the bridles. She looked, he thought, very young with her damp hair tumbling about her shoulders but for the first time since her return she also looked resentful.

"I don't see way you have to involve me in it," she argued. "I won't have people thinking I'm waiting in the wings, waiting . . . well, for things to happen! I've already made a fool of myself twice over you, Paul Craddock, and there isn't going to be a third time, I promise you!" and with that she dropped Snowdrop's bridle, swung herself up and set off at a smart trot down the beach. He did not follow her at once but remained standing by the pool, smiling to himself. Perversely her flash of temper had overthrown the barrier their mutual wariness had raised and unaccountably he felt more lighthearted than at any time since that ridiculous quarrel with Grace over young Rudd and his motor. And this was not because he was flattered by her demonstration but because he was able, for the first time in years, to get his dilemma into perspective and view it objectively without self-pity or indignation. It was this glimpse of himself that opened up an entirely new vista on his marriage. He could see it now for what it was, no more than a compromise from the very beginning, an arrangement entered into with reservation on the part of a woman with her back to the wall. Surely there could be no such thing as a marriage conditioned by such strictures and anyone but an infatuated fool would have realised as much from the beginning. He had been too obsessed with her to weigh the cost against the probability of failure. He had temporised and gone on temporising, buying time with intermittent flashes of hope, like her interest in the garden and her ability to hypnotise credulous peasants, like Horace Handcock. There had never been a real marriage between them, no real fusion of interests and responsibilities, only the mutual appeasement of physical appetites, together with resignation on her part and hope deferred on his. Standing there on the rock, with the sun warming his body and Claire a solitary figure on the tideline, he saw this so clearly and unmistakably that he felt like proclaiming it at the top of his voice, for self-knowledge brought with it a sense of release that was immensely reassuring and uplifting. "Damn it," he said aloud, as he retrieved his clothes, flung them on, and swung himself on to Snowdrop, "a man ought to be guided by his head when he goes looking for a wife! If I'd had a ha'porth of sense I'd have finished what she started in Shallowford Woods years ago!" and forgetting Maureen O'Keefe's caution he clapped his heels into Snowdrop's flanks and pushed him into a canter, so that Claire, looking over her shoulder, stopped and swung her cob round as he came up with her.

"Get down," he said, curtly, "for I can't say what I've got to say to you jog-jogging along the beach!" and when she only stared at him, he jumped down, threw both sets of reins over his arm and half yanked her from the saddle, although the effort gave his ribs a twinge that made him grunt with pain.

"Listen to me . . ." she began and he guessed that she was on the point of reassuming her role of nurse.

"No, I won't," he said, "I've been 'listening' long enough and always to women of one sort or another! I don't give a damn what your father or the Valley think about it and I'm not interested in what happened four years ago, or two years ago, or two minutes ago! If I get a divorce will you marry me? And if you do will you guarantee to stay put and not run off and open a teashop at our first difference of opinion?"

"You're insufferable!" she said, trying to dodge between the horses but he caught her round the waist, dropped the reins and kissed her on the lips. It was a claim advanced with such determination that it threw her weight against the bay, who shied seawards and made off at a smart trot with reins trailing over the sand.

508

"Well?" he said, without relaxing his hold, "what else do I have to do to convince you?"

"You might ride after Rusty and take me somewhere a little more private!" she suggested, "for if anyone sees us from the cliff path I shall be packed off to Tunbridge Wells again within an hour of getting home!"

"I'll catch him but wait here!" he said, and dashed off after the bay. She stood watching him circle and head the horse off, hands pressed to her tousled hair, a slow, half-rueful smile puckering the corners of her mouth. How was she to know that her thoughts were identical to his when she said to herself, "Well, if we had pushed that first encounter in the woods to its logical conclusion we should have saved everybody a great deal of time, trouble and expense!"

III

Paul saw Zorndorff's motor standing in the yard when he rode in shortly before sunset, a shining, snub-nosed monster considerably more impressive than the first motor to descend the Valley under the inexpert guidance of young Rudd two years before. He was surprised, for he had not expected Franz to respond in person to his letter and had in fact resigned himself to making another journey to London.

He found the Croat already established in the library, with Mrs. Handcock fussing round him, impressed by his air of polite patronage and treating him as though he was a distinguished relative of the family, paying a duty call on Squire and his chawbacons. He was as neat and dapper as ever, in what he imagined to be "country clothes", a pair of salt-and-pepper knickerbockers, pleated Norfolk jacket, heavy brogues and brown worsted stockings; there was also a carnation in his buttonhole. He embraced Paul warmly, at once issuing orders for supper, as though this was one of his shooting lodges and Paul was a welcome but unexpected guest. Paul said, "I didn't expect you to come down here, Uncle Franz. I intended coming up to see you as soon as you had news from the solicitors," but

509

Franz replied, patting his shoulder, "Nonsense, my boy! I know you loathe London and I've been promising myself to pay you a visit for I don't know how long."

"For four years," Paul told him, smiling, "and it took a situation like this to get you here! How long do you intend staying?"

"Oh, I'm afraid I shall have to be off bright and early in the morning," the old man said and the regret in his voice was so counterfeit that Paul laughed but made no protest, realising that the country had the same effect upon Franz as urban sprawl had upon himself. It occurred to him also that this distate of open spaces might have helped to establish the contact between Franz and Grace and that had led to the casual postcript of Uncle Franz's last letter for he had written, *"Grace called at the yard and I took the unfortunate little pigeon out to dinner."* The use of the word "unfortunate" had irritated Paul at the time, implying as it did that Grace was the injured party but after reflection he had made allowances for Franz's kind heart and had obeyed an impulse to write him a frank letter expressing his wish to marry again and asking Franz to sound their London firm of solicitors on the prospect of a divorce. And now here he was in person, barely forty-eight hours after receiving the letter, yet for all his despatch he did not seem over-anxious to discuss the situation. It was not until after supper, when the glow of sunset filled the room and Franz had examined Paul's current bank statements, that he pushed the papers aside, removed his half-moon spectacles, and said, "Well, my boy, you've shown me your figures so I'll show you mine!" and had unlatched his briefcase giving Paul the impression that he was due for yet another lecture on the amount of money he had poured into the estate over the last few years. Instead Uncle Franz opened a buff folder and took from it the receipted bill of a hotel called The Golden Angel, at Windsor, handing it to Paul without comment. The bill related to a two-day stay at the hotel by a "Mr. and Mrs. James Monteith", and for a moment it meant nothing at all to him. Then he turned it over and found a piece of notepaper attached to it with a paper-clip. On the note, in

Grace's handwriting, was written, *"Will this do? If not let me know at once—Grace."*

He stared at the note curiously, conscious of the old man's eyes on him and said, without any attempt to hide his distaste, "Is this how one goes about it? Is this the legal way?" and Franz chuckled, replying, "Not strictly legal, Paul, but it serves. More than half the divorces granted nowadays are arrived at by similar means and you might consider yourself fortunate that Grace is willing to accommodate you without being paid for it! Most wives would value that evidence, at, say, a thousand guineas or a settlement but then, she's an eccentric girl, wouldn't you agree?"

The receipt, the note and its obvious implications moderated Paul's pleasure at seeing the old man again after so long an interval. He said, briefly, "I don't know much about this kind of thing but I was under the impression a divorce could be obtained on grounds of desertion."

"So it could," Franz said, "providing you and the lady you hope to marry are prepared to wait about five years, plus the time the suit will take to get heard. This is by far the quickest and cheapest way of going about it."

"And the most unsavoury," Paul said.

"That's for her to judge, isn't it?"

He said this with such a ferocious lift of his eyebrows, that Paul's sense of injustice was roused.

"Damn it Franz, am I to understand from that that you sympathise with her?"

"To some extent," the old man replied frankly, "but also with you, my boy, for now that I know her better it seems to me to have been an extraordinarily ill-considered affair on both sides! To my mind you are entirely incompatible and you aren't such a fool as not to have recognised that by now!"

A few months ago Paul might have argued the case with some heat but now he had enough philosophy to appreciate the old man's difficulties as go-between and also his obvious willingness to help in any way he could.

"There's no point in raking over the past, Uncle Franz," he said, "and I daresay it's sporting of you to involve yourself. If we did proceed along these lines would Grace and I have to meet again?"

"No," he said, "not necessarily. The fact that she sent me that bill means she wouldn't defend the case. You would have to attend, of course, but it isn't the ordeal most people imagine, it's becoming rather fashionable I'm told."

"Fashionable or not it's something I don't relish," said Paul. "Did you see her more than that one occasion when you took her to dinner?"

The old man twinkled. "Yes," he admitted, "I've seen her several times. As a matter of fact she came to me to discuss the possibilities of letting you go free before you wrote but I didn't take any action because I couldn't be sure you weren't anxious to have her back on any terms. As soon as you wrote I got in touch with her and that bill arrived by return of post."

Paul studied the bill again and asked, "Who is James Monteith?" and Franz, sighing, said, "You really do live in another age down here, Paul! He's no one in particular."

"He isn't someone Grace has taken up with?"

"Knowing her I should think it extremely unlikely. He's almost certainly a professional, someone to whom she paid money for the purpose of getting evidence."

"Good God!" Paul exclaimed, "I've heard of women employed in that respect but never men!"

"I still don't think you really understand the situation," Franz said, patiently. "In almost all these cases it's accepted that the man takes the initiative, on the assumption that he has less to lose than the woman, but as the law stands you would have to provide evidence of adultery and cruelty and refuse to have her back. Well, for your information, Grace won't hear of anything like that but not simply because she recognises you the injured party. She won't be under an obligation to a man, so as far as I can see it will have to be that evidence or a long wait. You would have to write inviting her back and she would have to reject the offer. It could drag on for years and she considers this would be most unfair on you. If I was in your shoes I should give me instructions to go right ahead on what you have there."

512

"Tell me honestly, Franz, does it make any kind of sense to you? I don't mean simply her approach to divorce but her entire attitude to life?"

"No," said Zorndorff, "not sense but there's a kind of glory in it."

"Glory?"

"Yes, glory. These women see themselves as a vanguard carving out a new social structure. There have always been minorities set on martyrdom. The early Christians were one and some people might even include the Lollards and Lutherans in the parade. The world usually begins by mocking them, then slams them behind bars and ends by canonising them! Today the fabric of society is changing at frightful speed and although the process has not been going for quite some time it's only recently that people are sitting up and taking notice."

"Then I suppose you class me with the minority who won't face up to change and takes refuge in a bolt-hole like this?"

"No," said Franz, "not altogether and neither, I think, does Grace. A man ought to follow his destiny and yours is clearly here doing what you believe yourself capable of doing. Take my advice my boy and let her have her own way about this and I tell you that not because I agree or disagree with her but because I happen to know it will ease her conscience. Believe me, she has one, and it's troubling her a good deal!"

He seemed to prefer to leave the matter there and went on to talk of more general matters, of the stimulating effect the dreadnought race with Germany was having upon the price of scrap iron, the increasing pressure building up under the new Liberal Government for an avalanche of social legislation, of matters that were common currency to him but to Paul were little more than London newspaper topics. They talked on into the small hours and when Paul had shown him to his room, and they stood together at the open window looking out over a paddock bathed in moonlight, Franz said, "Well, it doesn't look as if much has changed around here since the Tudors but it will, although I daresay it will last you out, or maybe

513

you'll be so set in your ways you won't even notice the differences."

Paul said stubbornly, "I'm not afraid of differences, Uncle Franz. My policy here involves change. What I am opposed to is dissolution."

"Ah, I daresay," he said, cheerfully, "and who isn't? Sometimes I think we're all heading for perdition but so long as we get a choice of route I'm satisfied. You stick to yours, Paul, and let Grace stick to hers! That's my advice, for what it's worth."

Paul said good night and went along to his own room, where Mrs. Handcock had lit the small lamp and shadows were playing hide-and-seek in the window draught. He sat on the bed and pulled off his tall boots that he wore almost exclusively in these days, for he was on horseback most working days. The strong Maxwell boots gave support to a leg still inclined to trouble him where the tendons surrounding his Transvaal wound had been strained during his buffeting in the cove. Tonight there was an ache in his heart as he thought, with a touch of nostalgia, "This room was her creation and whenever we were alone in it we were at peace. If I marry again I suppose Claire will make changes but a man doesn't slough off a woman as easily as all that, not when he's held her in his arms through long winter nights." He got up restlessly and padded over to the window, flinging it wide and sniffing the night air, heavy with the scent of the woods. "Franz talks of changes," he thought, "but I feel their presence myself tonight. So many things have changed since I spent my first night here; Martin Codsall and Arabella were alive then, and Tamer Potter, and poor old Smut was ranging the woods, poaching deer; Lord Gilroy's tame M.P. represented us at Westminster and now Grenfell's up there at my instance, making what he can of this clamour for change. Simon was born in this room and Grace spent her last night at Shallowford here, with me beside her, never dreaming what was in her mind. All this, in four years! I wonder what the next four will bring?"

Over in the chestnuts an owl hooted and from the rhododendrons nearer the house, came the sounds of a stealthy scuffle. He yawned, feeling detached from the past yet near enough to look back and savour its bitterness and sweetness. Then he thought of Claire, of her smooth oval face, pink and white freshness and the repose she seemed to have acquired during her exile and suddenly he felt more cheerful, flung off his clothes and climbed into bed. "Maybe I'll stop shaping things and let 'em happen in future," he told himself and on this compromise he slept.

IV

Paul's moment of self-revelation, and what came of it down by the landslip, released a spate of letter-writing up and down the Valley. The Sorrel people were shy of pen and ink. Some of them had never written a letter in their lives and a majority were content to scrawl greetings on Christmas cards once a year but events in the cove during the early spring, and their appearance on the front pages of newspapers, made the Valley folk aware of themselves as a clan. Some, with relatives in other parts of the West, followed up with news of events that grew out of the wreck, notably the Squire's intention to divorce his wife and marry Claire Derwent as soon as he was free.

Claire herself was not guiltless of rumour-spreading. Having written to her cousin and partner, arranging to sell her share of the business and stating that she was unlikely to return to London, she added an enigmatic post-script: *"Have been seeing a good deal of 'P'. There is talk of him divorcing his wife, who left him some time ago and has since been mixed up with the suffragettes."* What her cousin made of this is not certain but if she recalled Claire's four-year-old confidences on the subject of "P" she probably put two and two together.

Maureen O'Keefe wrote two letters in illegible scrawl (deliberately cultivated for writing prescriptions) to the only woman who had shared her medical course in Dublin, a glum, Hebridean girl, now junior partner in a Belfast practice where women doctors were just tolerated, providing they were good Protestants. Maureen succeeded in astonishing her friends by adding, after saying she was taking over her father's Westcountry practice, *". . . and I expect you will be even more surprised to learn I am to marry in September! I still can't believe it, especially when I (a) look in the mirror, and (b) check up on my birth certificate! I think you would like John—John Rudd that is, for in some ways he reminds me of you being dour, very solemn and wonderfully kind. He is fifty-two, a widower with a son in the Navy, and has been agent on this estate for years . . ."* She rattled on about Paul, Grace and even Claire Derwent, but mention of Claire reminded her of another letter she intended to write, so she cut short the Irish mail and began a slightly more legible letter to Ikey Palfrey.

"My dear Ikey," she wrote, chuckling again as she recalled the encounter by Codsall bridge, *"I think the time has come to keep you up to date but burn this as soon as you have read it, or we shall find ourselves on the carpet again! I took care not to breathe a word about your MACHIAVELLISM but I felt you should know that it worked out better than any of us could have hoped, for Squire, so I hear, is taking steps to get a divorce and there isn't the slightest doubt that if and when he does he will marry Miss Derwent, and jolly good luck to them! By the way, he's quite his old self again now. Today, when I was visiting in Coombe Bay, I watched him go past without him seeing me and he was whistling loud enough to loosen his front teeth. He's very fit and putting on weight and Mr. Rudd tells me he's just not the same man at all, so we can both take credit for that! Good luck to you, Ikey, and I do hope you're happy at school and are looking forward to the holidays. Affectionately, Maureen O'Keefe."*

Ikey read this letter in the Fives court, having first extracted the five-shilling postal order enclosed with it and fortified himself with two cream horns at the tuckshop. He was gratified by the news, although it seemed to him that the slightly crazy woman doctor must be pulling the longbow somewhat, for he still found it difficult to believe that people could change wives like horses. The information regarding Squire, however, was cheering and having obeyed her instructions, and carefully burned the letter, he occupied his Sunday letter-writing period composing a suitable reply. *"Dear Doctor O'Keefe,"* it ran, *"Many thanks for P.O. which is now spent and also for news. There are lots of things I should like to know more about but better not write them as you never know with letters do you. I am looking forward to coming home for summer half hols and entered in the under-fifteen mile sports day which is soon and I hope you and Squire will come up for it because I might win Cooper our running capt. thinks so. Good-bye and thanks again for the P.O. Respectfully, I. Palfrey."*

Maureen O'Keefe did not burn this letter. It amused her so much that she put it away in her souvenir box, alongside her degree and collection of trainee photographs.

Sam Potter, at the instance of his wife Joannie, wrote one of his very rare letters to Smut, who had completed his third year and was expected to be released on licence by autumn. Sam had accompanied his mother on a visit to the gaol immediately after Tamer's death and had decided that nothing would induce him to go there again but his wife thought he should tell Smut about the special headstone the German Mercantile Marine had erected over Tamer's grave. After a great deal of laborious pen-chewing and chair-squeaking as he writhed in the agonies of composition, he produced the following: *"Dear Smut, this is to let you no they Germans paid for a stone over Father and chipped out a lot of wot hapened on it—must have cost I don't no how much but you can read it when you get here—I can't rite it even if I could think on it. They say Squire is puttin aside his missus and there is tork he will take Ted Derwents dorter to church the pretty one I mene see you soon Sam."*

Smut was intrigued by this letter, although both items of news puzzled him for, although there were a number of Potters laid in Coombe Churchyard, none had attained the dignity of a headstone which, as he recalled, were luxuries reserved for freeholders and prosperous tradesmen. He was more mystified by Sam's reference to the Squire's possibility of taking a second wife, supposing that this privilege extended only to heathens and was against the law in England, even for a man as exalted as a Squire. His memories of Claire, however, were vivid for she had always been reckoned the most fetching girl in the Valley and he had suspected that she might one day make a good match, although not quite as good as this.

Something of Smut's natural exuberance had returned to him of late for they had recently put a card on the door of his cell, explaining that the legend thereon, *"E.D.R. 15. 10. 06"* meant *"Earliest date of release, Oct. 15th, 1906"*. If things continued to go smoothly he would be back in the Valley in less than three months but the nearness of his release date was not the sole reason for his cheerfulness. Since his shift back across the border into Devon, where he could smell the sea and, if the wind was in the right quarter, the scent of gorse blowing down from Blackberry Moor, some of the sting had departed from confinement behind stone walls and iron doors and under the encouragement of the officer in charge of trusties working in the prison grounds, he had found a new interest in growing flowers. Smut, although he had lived his life in the open, had always taken flowers for granted but he did so no longer for in here a small splash of colour riveted the eye and sometimes made a man catch his breath. All summer he laboured away tending geraniums, lobelia, calceolaria and marguerites and bit by bit, as he watched the results of his work, the occupation became the focal point of his existence so that he sometimes thought a little fearfully of the time when he would be separated from them and some other clumsy lout would have charge of them. He pondered this a good deal and wondered if it would be possible to make some kind of livelihood out of potting plants in the Coombe. If so, then he would prefer to devote himself to a job like this rather than share the casual husbandry of Meg and the girls, for here a man could see something in return for energy expended whereas nothing ever prospered under his hands in the Dell. He made up his mind to broach the subject to Chief Officer Phillips as soon as the opportunity presented itself.

In the meantime, however, unknown to Smut, a place was being prepared for him in the Valley, for the manner in which Tamer had died forged a personal bond between Paul and the shiftless tenants in Low Coombe. At harvesttime Paul rode across to the Dell and had a talk with Meg

518

on the family's future, after which he crossed the corner of the Bluff and descended the wooded slope to Sam Potter's cottage beside the mere.

He found Sam at his midday meal and Joannie, always flustered by a visitor, wiped a damp cloth across the jam-smeared face of his god-daughter Pauline, who held the distinction of being the first child born on the estate under the new régime. Paul always felt very much at home in Sam's cottage and accepted a brew of tea whilst Snowdrop was given a feed in the lean-to stable.

"I've been discussing with Meg what we can do about Smut," Paul told him. "He's due out in the autumn and I'm officially responsible for him until his full sentence expires. Do you think he'll go back on poaching?"

Sam said that he thought not but he was clearly worried by the possibility. Despite their temperamental differences the brothers had always been close and Sam's visit to the gaol had strengthened the link, for he found it difficult to imagine a worse fate than that of being locked inside a grey fortress for years on end. He said, reflectively, "Ah, tiz a real problem an' no mistake, Maister! Smut were never a varmer, no more'n any one of us, an' like as not he'll be praper rusty after being cooped up in that gurt ole plaace! God knows, Mother needs help over there, and I bin in two minds to ask 'ee to give Smut this job o' mine and let me move downalong, wi' Mother an' the girls. I'm no great shakes at varmin meself but I could best Tamer's efforts and maybe end up a credit to 'ee, Squire."

"It's more or less what I had in mind, Sam," Paul told him, "but you and Joannie have been happy here. How will you really feel about moving out and letting Smut take over as keeper and woodsman?"

Sam looked glum and said, with a glance at his wife, "I'll be honest with 'ee, Squire, us won't like it at all, will us Joannie? Us've maade a praper nest for ourselves here an' us don't fancy going downalong, an' bedding down in that old muddle! Still, us'd maake a better job of it than Smut and I zee no help for it if us is to give the varmint a fresh start!"

The same thought had already occurred to Paul. Sam had more than justified his faith when he had set him up here and it was asking much of Joannie to leave her clean, tidy home and share a kitchen with Meg and her sluttish daughters. He said, "I don't like the idea of uprooting you at all and maybe there's another way round it. Perhaps I could get your mother a permanent hired man and settle Smut somewhere on a patch of his own."

"Beggin' your pardon," Sam said, regretfully, "he'd never prosper on a patch of his own, Squire. 'Er's a good sort at heart but 'er's more shiftless than ever Tamer was. But if us dorn settle 'im somewheres you can be certain sure us is in trouble again, and neither me nor Joannie would like that seein' how good you been to us! No, us'll get packed up, I reckon, and Smut can move in here. Mebbe he'll marry an' zettle down an' if 'er does, then it will have been worth it. What do 'ee zay, Joannie?"

Joannie said, without looking up, "Aye, us have got to stand by the family and there's an end to it!"

As he rode back through the woods it occurred to Paul that there must be some good blood in the Potters somewhere for how else would they produce courage like Tamer's and loyalty like Sam's? He wished, however, that he could buy a few acres west of Four Winds or north of Priory, in order to give Smut a fresh start without disrupting the lives of his brother and sister-in-law.

V

The announcement that John Rudd and Maureen O'Keefe were to marry in September intrigued and amused the Valley but it surprised no one. John, although much respected, had never captured the affection of the Valley people and when it was known that he was openly courting the lady-doctor (who, although acknowledged a far more skilful healer than her father, was judged even more eccentric) people like old Honeyman and the shepherd twins told one another that here was someone who might succeed in shaking old John out of himself and maybe encourage him to take himself less seriously. For in some ways Rudd remained a symbol of the Lovell

520

régime and this despite the fact that he was known to be held in high regard by Squire Craddock.

Paul himself was not surprised by the news. It had been obvious from the first days of her sojourn among them that Maureen O'Keefe had bewitched the agent, who had trotted up and down the Valley behind her like a big collie, blind to the smirks and deaf to the innuendos of his beloved's patients. The Doctor made a great joke out of his subjection, sniping at her fiancé's dignity without mercy but in some mysterious way warming a place for him in the hearts of tenants and their dependents. As soon as John had proposed she drove up and down the Valley broadcasting the news like a town-crier and very soon, on a sunny September morning, the marriage was solemnised in the parish church. Every pew was crammed and the entire population of Coombe Bay, including freeholders who had no dealings with the groom, assembled in the churchyard to witness the event. The bride arrived in the Squire's waggonette, attended by a male cousin and the two Derwent girls as bridesmaids, for Maureen O'Keefe, declaring that she had never expected to be a bride, had announced that she intended making the most of the occasion and doing the Valley full justice.

Paul was already inside with the groom and much relieved to get him there, for John's natural phlegm had basely deserted him when Paul called at the lodge an hour before the ceremony. In the act of fastening his high collar the agent had dropped both hands and exclaimed, "Damn it, this is bloody ridiculous at my age! Why did I let her talk me into making a spectacle of myself? Why can't we slip out of the Valley and marry in the Paxtonbury Registry Office?" Paul had replied, laughing in spite of himself, "Look here, John, it's her day and you damned well do as you're told! As soon as you're properly dressed I'll get you a stiff drink and the moment Parson smells it he'll gabble through the service at top speed in order to get across to the house and drink his quota!"

After his favourite toddy John calmed down somewhat and as there was time to spare he sat on the edge of a chair puffing away at his pipe and ruminating on the present situation in terms of mild astonishment.

"Now who the devil would have thought of anything like this that day I waited for you to get off that London train, Paul? Did you know that I hated you before I set eyes on you? And I made sure the first thing you would do was send me packing! Damn it, it's like a crazy fairy-tale and this is a fitting climax I must say! Me, sitting here in a frock coat and a Come-to-Jesus collar, waiting for you to steer me down the aisle and be sniggered at by every yokel for miles around!"

"Well, it's improbable, I'll grant you that," Paul admitted, "but as for getting married in a registry office you thank your stars you didn't! I have no choice in the matter, for the Church won't marry a divorced man and that's a big disappointment for Claire, I can tell you. I daresay she'll be thinking of it today and I wouldn't wonder if she doesn't plague me to have a go at Parson Bull about it if we ever get around to marrying."

"Oh, you'll marry the girl all right," said John, "and if you ask me . . ." but Paul decided this was not the time to involve the nervous groom in his own problems and said quickly, "Will you have one more before we leave?"

"Yes I will," said John, "for God knows I need it," and then, glancing at his watch, called to Chivers who was waiting with the trap in the drive and asked if he thought the cob would make it comfortably in under the half-hour. Paul said, "Were you as jumpy as this on your first wedding-day, John?" and the remark must have steadied the older man for he smiled, relit his pipe and replied, "Do you know, I'm hanged if I can remember? I've been trying to ever since I woke up this morning but I can't, it's all too long ago—three years before you were born!"

"And that's strange too," Paul said, "for I seem to have known you all my life, John," and he poured himself another small drink to make up for the groom's excessively large one.

"There is one thing I would like to say," John said, suddenly, "and since we've still got five minutes I'll say it before we get caught up in the clamour awaiting us yonder. You aren't under any obligation to renew my contract. I told Maureen only the other day that you don't really need me any longer and you could save yourself three hundred a year and plough it back into the estate. I'd manage well enough, I've saved you know—and my first wife left me a little money. I wouldn't be idle either. I can always drive Maureen around and do her accounts."

"You'd prefer that?" Paul said, looking at him sharply, and John said, "Well no, I don't say I'd prefer it but . . ."

"Then don't make a fool of yourself on your wedding-day! I can afford three hundred a year and anyway you earn it and always have! I've got plans for next year, John, and you're included in them. It wouldn't be the same without you. You're the best friend I ever had and certainly the most honest!"

"Thank you, my boy," John said sincerely, "you couldn't have said anything more calculated to steady me!" and raising his glass, added, "I daresay there'll be a lot of gaff talked before the day is out, Paul, but this is my toast—to you and what you stand for in the Valley!" and as though fearful of seeming over-sentimental he tossed down the drink, cleared his throat, picked up his hat and gloves and marched out into the drive where Chivers helped him on to the box as though he had been a chronic invalid.

The gathering in the big marquee erected in the paddock was the most representative since the Coronation soirée four years before and many of those present recalled as much. There were over sixty official guests and about a hundred unofficial ones but after the first glass of champagne, and the cutting of a spectacular cake baked by Mrs. Handcock, the two categories intermingled for this was as much a Shallowford event as the wreck and the funeral of Tamer Potter that had followed it.

All the farmers, their families and employees were present and most of the estate and Coombe Bay crafts-men and fishermen, and when the honeymoon drag arrived from Whinmouth to convey the couple to Sorrel Halt everybody surged into the forecourt for the send-off. By this time, however, several casks of beer had been broached and many of the unofficial guests, together with several of the official ones like Henry Pitts, were in fine fettle. The bride's appearance on the porch steps was the signal for so much scuffling and shouting that the beribboned greys harnessed to the drag would have bolted had it not been for Sam Potter and young Willoughby, who hung on the reins and shouted for Paul and others to clear the drive. When this was done John stood up on the box and made a little speech, pointing out that the age of those gathered to wish them well covered a span of over a century and it was a point well taken. Among those on the verges were Marian Eveleigh's six-months-old baby and old Floss Timberlake, who disgraced her chapel-going daughter-in-law by reciting a traditional wedding toast that had not been heard in the Valley for three generations. As John concluded his speech of thanks she bellowed, for all to hear:

> Yer's to the hen who never refuses,
> An lets un tread whenever 'ee chooses!

a couplet that produced a frenzied "shhh!" from her family but laughter so immoderate from Henry Pitts that he came close to choking. Then the drag was off, trailing its strings of tin cans and old boots but the professional greys expected nothing less and were well in hand by the time John reined in at the lodge where Paul, Rose and Claire waited to remove the garbage. As Chivers (charged with bringing the vehicle back from the station) took his seat Paul said, "Well John, this isn't a day we'll forget in a hurry! Good luck, and all the happiness in the world!" but this did not satisfy Maureen, who thrust aside his proferred hand, threw her arms round his neck, and kissed him half-a-dozen times, after which she climbed back in the box and threw her bouquet at Claire who caught it so expertly that Paul was half-persuaded the gesture had been rehearsed. Then Chivers cracked the whip and the drag moved off at a bowling trot along the river road, best man and bridesmaids returning to preside over the meat tea provided for the invited guests. Rose was excited and talkative but Paul noticed that Claire seemed thoughtful and when, on reaching the house, she excused herself and went upstairs, he said, looking after her, "You don't think she's having second thoughts, Rose?"

"She's enjoying every moment of it," Rose replied, equably, "and she's perfectly reconciled to having a very quiet wedding if and when things are sorted out. However, there is one thing you could do and today seems a very good opportunity, for I've seen to it that father had plenty to drink. Could you . . . well . . . could you try and explain the situation to him? He's terribly old-fashioned, and neither Claire nor I have had the nerve to do it, although I daresay he's heard all kinds of rumours up and down the Valley."

"I don't mind telling him" Paul said, although by no means relishing the task, "but wouldn't it be better to wait until I'm actually free to remarry?"

"No," said Rose, "it would not! He'd far sooner hear it from you than from outsiders, so if I were in your place I'd get it over and done with right now. I know Claire would be very relieved if you did!"

He said, squeezing her hand. "Very well, I'll be guided by you, Rose. He's talking to Arthur Pitts now. Get Arthur out of the way and I'll bring him in here."

They went out on to the terrace and Arthur was skil-fully detached with news of a new snaffle Rose was using on the half-broken trap pony. Paul said, approaching Edward Derwent with a glass of champagne in his hand, "Do you think we might have a private word in the study, Mr. Derwent?" and was relieved to note that the farmer's stolid features assumed a slightly startled look as he fol-lowed Paul along the terrace and into the house, stand-ing with his feet planted well apart and looking as if he envied Paul his full glass.

"It's about Claire," Paul began. "Rose thought it proper that I should tell you precisely how things stand between us, if only to anticipate the gossips. You will have heard that I'm suing for a divorce?"

He was glad then that he had not waited to replenish Derwent's glass for he had him at a slight disadvantage, but then he suddenly felt sorry for him, reasoning that he must find it damnably embarrassing to be bearded by his landlord on the latter's home ground and added apologetically, "I'm assuming you had heard Claire and I hope to marry when I'm free?"

"Aye," Derwent said, or rather growled, "I heard that right enough and who hasn't? Well, she's twenty-three now and has usually gone her own way no matter what but there's limits, Squire, as to what a father is prepared to put up with! Notwithstanding you owning the land I farm I'd see you in hell before I let you drag my Claire's name through the Courts!"

His truculence, Paul thought, did him credit but it was plain that Rose's suspicions were well founded and that some of the more extravagant rumours must have reached him. He said, quietly, "There's absolutely no question of that, Derwent! I'm divorcing my wife, my wife isn't divorcing me. The lawyers are dealing with it now but it will take time, these things always do. What I should like you to know is that, if and when I'm free, Claire and I want to marry at once. Would you have any objections?"

Derwent frowned, biting his dark moustache and looking, Paul thought, less embarrassed than exasperated. Finally, however, and with what appeared to be considerable effort, he said, gruffly, "No, Squire, I wouldn't stand in your way and I don't mind saying why. Time was when I would have set my face against any girl of mine taking up with a man in your position, and him with a wife living into the bargain but most people about here realise Mrs. Craddock's capers were no fault o' yours, and most of us were right sorry about it at the time! I never held with divorce. If you make a mistake you bide by it, or you did in my time but times are changing and, as I said, she's not a girl and can earn her living independently! If she's set her heart on you I'll neither say nor do anything to turn her aside."

It was not, Paul thought, a particularly gracious answer but it was a more conciliatory one than he had anticipated and it amused him slightly to hear the unsmiling master of High Coombe dismiss Grace's desertion as "a caper". The man's unexpected tolerance, however, tempted him to press the subject further and he said, "Well, that satisfies me, Derwent, but I'm not sure it will satisfy Claire! She's always had respect and affection for you and she'll want your blessing! Would you give it to her?"

Since the day, more than four years past, when Rudd had first taken him over the bluff to High Coombe he had seen Edward Derwent in a variety of moods, all the way from brusque civility to downright truculence but he had never, until now, seen him humbled. Derwent's face, dark under its suntan, flushed as he stood looking down at his large, well-polished boots.

"Yes," he said at length, "I reckon I could do that for her mother would have given it soon enough," and then, meeting Paul's eyes defiantly, "The fact is, Squire, I was badly wrong about you and a man of principle oughtn't to mind admitting a bad judgment when it comes back on him, as mine did the night o' the wreck! They others about here, they'm flippety-gibbets for the most part—anyway for a pint o' cider as they say, but me—I'm not easily taken in and I don't mind admitting it always seemed to me you were a young man wi' too much money playing the fool at farming! Well, I was dam' well wrong, as I saw wi' my own eyes when you and Potter took that cockleshell to sea in the cove! If I don't admit a fault I'm under an obligation and that's something I don't care to be to any man, not excepting my landlord!" Paul murmured acknowledgement of this apology but Derwent went on, relentlessly, "Wait now, there's more to it than that! Before you came, and many times since, I wanted badly to be a freeholder but now I'm not so set on it, particularly as you want to marry my girl soon as you can! Maybe I'm too old and too set in my ways or maybe I'm content for my boy Hugh to take it up with you later, but seeing what you're bent on doing in the Valley I'm well content to let things remain as they be. From now on, whether or not you take my girl, I'm your man, Mr. Craddock!"

There had been many occasions since he had come to Shallowford when Paul had been heartened by individual recognition of his intentions. Arthur Pitts and Henry Pitts had always encouraged him, and so, in a more roundabout way, had John Rudd and old Honeyman. Eveleigh, and his wife Marian, had never ceased to show their appreciation of his faith in them whereas Sam Potter and Will Codsall had been his partisans from the beginning. But this blunt statement from the tight-lipped Edward Derwent was something different. It was the conversion of a man whom Paul had always recognised as the hard core of opposition to his policy and because of this it touched him far more deeply than the loyalty of men like Henry Pitts, or even a farmer like Eveleigh, who had plenty for which to thank him in the material sense. He reached out and clasped Derwent's hand and for the first time he felt he had gained a powerful ally, not as a prospective father-in-law but as a friend whose weight counted for something in the Valley.

They went back into the hall just as Claire came downstairs and called as though it had been she who had been kept waiting, "Oh, *there* you are, Paul! Really, we ought to be getting them seated. Some of them have a long way to go before dark!" and Edward Derwent looked at Paul with an expression that could not, under any circumstances, have been called mischievous or even sardonic, but somehow suggested an alliance between men who, from time to time, would be called upon to suffer jointly the maddening illogicality of wives and daughters.

CHAPTER SIXTEEN

I

LESS than an hour after sunrise, on the last morning of April, 1908, Claire slipped out of bed without waking Paul and went downstairs, through the big kitchen and across the stable-yard to climb the path that led through the orchard to the cart-track dividing kitchen garden from the first trees of Priory Wood.

She walked barefoot as she usually did on these early

morning expeditions, enjoying the sensation of the dew passing between her toes and savouring the smell of the long grass, and the great clumps of late primroses and early bluebells that grew all the way up the slope. Up here, looking down on the great sprawling house, was a favourite viewpoint, for here she could take out her life and prospects and examine them, as a craftsman might examine a half-finished piece of work; here, in the past twelve months, she had spent her most complacent moments.

Today, her wedding anniversary, was especially propitious and she was glad that Paul had been late to bed the previous night, having ridden across the Whin to look at a pair of cart-horses. He would sleep on, she decided, until about seven-thirty and the next ninety minutes were her own, for even Mrs. Handcock and Thirza would not stir for another half-four and Chivers, the groom, rarely appeared until eight.

The scent of wild flowers and pine sap came out of the woods on a westerly breeze and she sniffed it like a pointer, deciding that it was among the most evocative scents in the world, along with the smell of the sea and the whiff of autumn bonfires. It had stillness in it and promise, and so far most of its promises had been kept for she had wandered up here to listen to them in the very earliest days of her marriage and could look back on no more than a single disappointment, an early miscarriage more than six months ago but now forgotten in the certainty of a second pregnancy. For the last two months, ever since Maureen O'Keefe had confirmed that she would have another child at the end of August, she had been able to view her disappointment with detachment, reflecting that Maureen must have been talking sense when she had said that Claire had no one to blame for the miscarriage but herself. She had been too exuberant and too active, continuing to ride and swim, stay up late, overtire herself entertaining, and join Paul in all his political jaunts and market researches. She would not make the same mistakes this time, although she knew quite well why she had made them last summer. She had been so eager to be the kind of wife he wanted and needed, resolving to share all his enthusiasms and achievements and had laughed at Maureen's warnings until it was too late, but youth and natural vitality had limited her depression to a matter of weeks and ever since Christmas, by which time she suspected that she was pregnant again, she had been serene and cheerful, although this time she had been careful to follow Maureen's advice in every particular.

Apart from this one setback the year had passed happily and eventfully, with his plans slowly taking shape and the Valley expanding under his thrust and initiative. His touch was surer now and she gave herself a little credit for this, for he was always relaxed and seemed to find in her someone who could match his enthusiasm for the Valley. Yet there was far more to it than that. After the barest minimum period of adjustment, she had become wholly his, as much his as this wide, wooded valley and everything growing on it, as much a part of him as his secret dreams. She could laugh now at old wives' whispers of the indignities demanded of a woman given in marriage, and had, indeed, never taken their warnings very seriously, for she had been born and raised on a farm and a witness from earliest childhood of the farm cycle.

For all that marriage presented her with a variety of surprises and not the least of them had been his unexpected gentleness during their first few weeks together. Although far less inhibited than the average city girl of her generation Claire had experienced a certain amount of anxiety as regards the purely physical aspects of marriage and her doubts were centred on his previous marriage to a woman of a different *milieu* from her own. Grace Lovell had been accepted in the Valley as a "modern" woman, possessed, no doubt, of all kinds of mysterious "modern" ideas, some of which she may well have communicated to her husband and it was this that caused Claire to magnify her own ignorance. Her mother had died when she was nine and no one had taken her place, for Rose, and later Edward Derwent's second wife, Liz, were even less experienced than she was herself. She had read very little apart from the romantic lady novelists of the period and such information as they could supply on the subject of marriage stopped short at the altar. This was why, once the modest tumult of the wedding was over, Claire Derwent found her confidence at low ebb, particularly after they had arrived in Anglesey where she had elected to spend the honeymoon.

They took a suite in a hotel and it was here, in a matter of hours, that she was blessedly reassured, for she found him not merely tolerant and patient where tolerance and patience were not to be expected of a groom but able, in a way that was peculiarly his own, to spice his ardour with a humour that soon demolished such reservations as had survived her upbringing on a farm under the eye of a man of her father's temperament. With this shedding of false modesty on her part came other discoveries, chief among them a secret delight in his frank worship of her body. She had never thought of herself as more than pretty and even that in a somewhat countrified way, but he obviously thought of her as beautiful and under the stimulus of his glorification she learned to respond to him in a way that not only brought him gratification as a lover but stature and authority as a man, and to a degree that had eluded him since he first came to live among them. It pleased her enormously that she should have been able to achieve this so rapidly and so effectively that, on their return, even people like John Rudd noticed it but for all the accord and delight they found in each other's arms laughter was never quite banished by urgency. These lighter notes were struck, in the first instance, by his appetite for love which had mildly surprised her until she remembered that he was only four years her senior (which was something she had half-forgotten during his long illness) and also that he had been deprived of a woman for almost two years and had not, it seemed, consoled himself elsewhere after Grace's desertion. Sometimes, when he was asleep beside her and his arm lay across her breast, she would feel herself blushing at the memory of an encounter, of words that had escaped her and extravagances she had actively encouraged and sometimes half initiated but then her sense of humour would reassert itself and she would smile in the realisation that there was surely health and resilience in the sharing of so much ecstasy compounded with so much silent laughter.

She stood by the stile at the north end of the orchard watching the coral pink sky shedding its veils of light over the Bluff as the sun topped the eastern slope of the cliffs. The bluebells were already half out, spreading handfuls of pale blue dust between the older apple trees, and in hedges crowded by clusters of primroses, solitary campions, violets and periwinkles peeped, like shy neighbours in a street of extroverts. She thought, "God knows how scared I was, scared of comparisons, of him accepting me as a second-best, a good-intentioned hobbledehoy but there was nothing to be frightened of after all! All my instincts about him were accurate, for where there is kindness and courage anything is possible given goodwill on my part and that he always had in abundance!" And suddenly life and prospects seemed as smooth and round as her belly and the future as predictable as the seasons. With a song on her lips she went on down through the wet grass, stepping in her own footsteps and then round to the forecourt and in at the big door that they never locked since the night of the Codsall tragedy.

There was still no one astir and she went through the library and into the office to get the Bible-camouflaged estate record. His gesture in giving her this book to maintain had been one of the most rewarding in her life and she took great pains to justify it although, under her pen, it had become less of a record and more of a great, gossipy diary. She carried the book back to the library and sat facing the empty grate, and as her eye fell upon the bearskin hearthrug she laughed for this morning the rug had a special significance for her and for the child in her womb, conceived here on the blustery night they had both taken too much of Martin Pitts' punch at Hallowe'en and had rattled home by moonlight to find a great fire burning and the room more inviting than the bedroom overhead. She paused, after opening the book, to reflect on the moment, half in wonder and half in amusement, recalling his boisterousness and her own half-hearted protests about the possibility of prowling servants. A single kiss had driven all thought of them from her mind and there they had lain for an hour or more, with the room lit by the flicker of pungent-smelling apple logs and the familiar tide of gratified accomplishment sweeping over her, for although he was soon asleep, and the punch or the makeshift couch made him snore, she would never forget what he had replied when she had said, "We're behaving more like a pair of precocious adolescents than a respectable married couple!" He had said running his hand through her disordered hair, "Having you restores my adolescence, Claire! Every time I touch you, look at you even, I feel about seventeen, and surely it must be good for a man to have that kind of wife within reach!"

She remembered this now and it produced the satisfied glow she had experienced at the time, so that she no longer had patience with the book and put off writing an entry about his purchase of the cart-horses, flicking through the later pages and scanning items like *"Smut Potter's second hothouse erected"*, and *"Stream End block of four cottages, in Coombe Bay, bought and rethatched"*, until she arrived at blank pages and wondered what events would be recorded on them after the final one which read, *"April 22, 1908. Jem Pollock signed on as foreman, Low Coombe. Dell problem solved but in what a curious way! Squire's approval still conditional."* Then she closed the book, replaced it in the safe and went out to brew some tea, filling two china mugs and carrying them trayless to the main bedroom.

He was still asleep when she drew the curtains and she woke him by holding a braid of her hair and drawing it slowly across his face. He opened his eyes and looked bewildered for a moment and then, with a laugh she said, "I've been out! It's wonderful! Just like the early morning of the world up there in the orchard! Take it, it's freshly made"—and she gave him his tea, but as he sat up to drink it he noticed her bare feet.

"You ought to wear shoes out there, Claire! Maureen warned you to be more careful this time!"

"Not about getting dew on my feet," she said, and lifting her foot invited him to feel it, which he did, finding it unexpectedly warm.

533

"Well, I don't know," he grumbled, only half seriously, "if old Chivers saw you walking barefoot in the orchard at crack of dawn he'd probably tell old Horace Handcock you do it to elude my early morning demands on you!"

"He's only got to look at me to discover I didn't succeed!" she said and faced the full-length mirror on the clothes closet door, adding ruefully, "I'm enormous, Paul! About twice as big as I was last time. Is that a good sign, do you think?"

"It's probably a sign that you've badly miscalculated," he said grinning.

"Oh no it isn't. I'm not likely to make a mistake about that. As a matter of fact I've just been in the library remembering. You and your Hallowe'en parties! A fine climax to nibbling apples in a bowl and wearing turnip lanterns I must say!"

He put down his mug and clasped his hands behind his neck, regarding her humorously. "Come over here!" he ordered, and when she came a little closer but remained out of reach, "What were you doing when I opened my eyes just now? Were you pulling the bedclothes from me?"

"Nothing so heartless," she sad, kneeling on the bed so that her hair covered over his face. "Just this! Surely the most enchanting awakening a man can expect, even from such a doting wife as me!"

"Yes, it is," he said, seriously, gathering a double handful of tresses and kissing them, "but I'm hanged if I don't believe you've forgotten what day it is," and before she could indignantly deny the fact he threw aside his pillows and produced a small leather box, pressing the spring and showing her a beautifully wrought brooch, with a heavy gold circlet and a central star composed of one large and a score of much smaller diamonds, the whole being suspended on a thin gold chain. She showed the wild excitement of a child opening a Christmas stocking.

"Paul, it's lovely! I didn't expect anything, honestly I didn't! I didn't dream . . .", and then, as her hand reached for it, "Did you really buy those cart-horses yesterday? Is that really why you went all the way to Torhaven?" and he told her, chuckling, that it was indeed

534

and that the purchase had been an afterthought that occurred to him minutes before the quay curiosity shop had closed, that he had walked inside without an idea in his head and had seen the brooch on a blue velvet cushion, surrounded by a lot of trumpery jewellery.

She crossed to the mirror and fastened it to her blouse, jerking her head this way and that and cooing like a pigeon.

"Well, it's wonderful and I wouldn't have given you credit for such marvellous taste!" she said. "Look! Isn't it right? Isn't it *different?*"

He said, smiling, "No, it's you who are different, Claire! And you don't need jewellery to convince me!"

II

The Dell problem had indeed been solved and it was not flippancy on Claire's part that had prompted her to write "in a curious way—Squire's approval conditional" in the record book. The Dell had always been a nursery of Valley scandal but never more so than in the spring of 1908, some time after Smut came out of gaol on licence, having served three years, eight months of his five-year sentence. He at once astonished his welcome committee by declaring that he intended to become a horticulturist, specialising in hothouse and bedding-out-plants for sale in the city.

This ambition baffled everyone who had known him but in many other ways he was a parody of the Smut Potter they recalled as the terror of Shallowford and Heronslea coverts with his gun and traps. His impudent smile had gone and in its place was a sleepy, ingratiating grin; his stubby hair had streaks of grey and his loping, poacher's walk had shrunk to a careful shuffle. Instead of balancing himself on his toes, as of old when he had always seemed on the point of leaping for cover, he now stood with joints relaxed, as though awaiting the bark of command before he moved in any one direction. Yet one thing about him had not changed. He was still extremely obstinate and nothing could induce him to have a hand in uprooting Sam and his family from their cottage and taking Sam's place as woodsman and keeper. Yet, to their dismay, neither would he consent to having Tamer's lease transferred to him and settling himself on the derelict farm. He was done with poaching, he said, but also with pig-farming and crow-starving. All he wanted to do was to grow flowers in a green-house and if Squire Craddock, bless his warm heart, could see his way to dismantle and re-erect the dilapidated glass house now standing empty behind the Shallowford rose garden, then he would raise pot plants that had never been seen in the Valley and sell them as far afield as Paxtonbury. He knew he could do it if only he had a single quarter-acre under glass, and if Squire would not part with his greenhouse he would set to work, collect discarded panes from all over the Valley and build one on the long, sunny slope where the Potter land ran down to the river east of Coombe Bay.

The Potters went into conference with Paul and the upshot of their deliberations was that the project was just possible although Meg expressed private doubts as to Smut's staying power, saying he would be more likely to keep out of trouble if he went to work in the woods. It was Claire who finally won them over. She came out as an enthusiastic ally of the ex-poacher, reporting that Smut had obviously acquired an extraordinary amount of expertise in the prison gardens and not only knew the names of a wide variety of fashionable conservatory plants but could designate them in Latin! This piece of information convinced everybody that Smut was in earnest and for three days after Paul had given assent to his plan the Potter haywain trundled to and fro along the river road with its load of glass panes and metal frames to be reassembled on the southern slope known as Seafield, and subsequently repaired and repainted by a team of volunteers, including one of the Eveleigh boys who enlisted as an apprentice.

Old Willoughby, of Deepdene, himself interested in horticulture, gave Smut a good deal of useful advice and a supply of seeds and most of the other farmers chipped in with second-hand tools and supplies of manure, so that Smut was soon established and working sixteen hours a day, sleeping in a poacher's shelter built against the green-house boiler that had been hauled over the bluff on Timberlake's tree waggon, along with its complement of cast-iron pipes.

It was encouraging, Paul thought, to see the Valley folk rally round the rascal, giving their labour free and taking collective pride in the ungainly structure on the downslope of the Low Coombe boundary. When all was as ready as could be Claire presided at a half-humorous official opening, launching the enterprise with a bottle of Meg's hedgerow wine smashed against the boiler at the southern end of the house. Everyone, it seemed, was pleased to see Smut home again and all wished him well in his unlikely venture. His initiative, however, did nothing to solve the vexed future of the Potter farm as a whole. Meg had little interest in steady farming or animal husbandry and spent most of her time collecting ingredients for her elixirs, or making the mats and bas-kets she sold across the Teazel, whereas the girls, who could make a shift at looking after pigs and occasionally ploughed a few acres, were unsuitable as long-term tenants for they were now in their mid-twenties and unlikely to remain single indefinitely.

It was through their agency that the matter was settled, and although the manner in which this took place caused scandalised comment in the Valley, the arrangement drifted on until it was hallowed by time, and Big Jem Pollock was generally accepted as the master of the Dell, and in some ways proved a worthy successor to old Tamer.

Jem was not a farmhand, although he had worked on farms during his semi-vagabond life before appearing in the Valley with a travelling fair licenced to set up on Blackberry Moor each Whitweek. The fair billed him as *"Jem Pollock, the Goliath of Bideford"* and his act consisted of tying knots in iron bars, hauling struggling teams of yokels across the ring and driving six-inch nails into billets of wood with his bare fists. The fair was a seedy little attraction, with the usual collection of swings, roundabouts, giant-slides and catchpenny booths but it attracted a public from as far away as Paxtonbury in the north and Whinmouth in the west whereas the Valley folk always attended *en masse*. The Potter family, very much at home in this kind of atmosphere, invariably downed tools and attended every evening, the two girls, Cissie and Violet, acquiring trinkets and entertainment by means of their personal cunning. It was here that they encountered and passed under the spell of Jem Pollock, the Bideford Goliath, or it might be more accurate to say that it was they, a pair of slingless Davids, who brought Goliath low, for having arrived in the Valley with no intention other than making sport of panting locals at the end of a rope Jem remained there until attracted to the colours by Kitchener's arresting finger.

It happened on the final night of the fair. Jem had a barker and a tent to himself, and during the previous visits the Potter girls had watched spellbound as he bent over knotted bars, buried nails in tree-trunks with blows of his enormous fist and won frenzied cheers by marching round his patch of sawdust trailing six of the lustiest Heronslea estate workers on a tow rope. The Potter girls had always appreciated a man and were connoisseurs in this field, having, between them, sampled most of the available men living within walking distance of the Dell, but never before had they looked upon a man like Jem, whose calves were like half-grown pine trunks and whose biceps and magnificent torso reminded them of illustrations of the famous Sandow. But it was not his display of muscles that drew giggles from them so much as his working costume, consisting of a leopard-skin toga augmented by pink and excessively tight-fitting hose that left very little to the imagination and had spectators comparing him to Eveleigh's prize bull. Another unusual thing about the Bideford Goliath was his geniality and the vacant mildness of his expression as he performed in the ring. He had the innocent gaze of a timid girl and features that were delicate for one so huge and muscular. On his splendid limbs grew forests of short, golden hairs that glistened with sweat as he stood flexing his muscles between each act. He also lacked the vainglory of the professional giant and seemed to find nothing very remarkable in his extraordinary feats of strength, which was strange considering the effect they produced upon his audiences, particularly upon the ladies, who flocked to his tent in large numbers for every performance.

Meg Potter was on familiar terms with several of the showmen and it was over a bread-and-cheese supper in the acrobats' tent one night that the girls were introduced to Jem as a man rather than a performer. They found him so shy that they made little progress with him on that occasion, beyond extracting from him an admission that he was not forsworn to circus life and was, in fact, "looking about for a likely place to zettle" and perhaps set up as a smith or forester. On hearing this the girls sounded their mother on the possibility of engaging him as a permanent replacement for the hired hand, loaned to Low Coombe by Four Winds after Tamer's death. The prospect of having so magnificent a specimen of manhood within call day and night, was inviting from a variety of aspects, for the Potter girls hated their farm chores and Meg, looking on Goliath with an unprejudiced eye, agreed that he would more than earn his keep at Low Coombe and promptly offered him fifteen shillings a week, plus board and lodging. He promised to think it over and the girls saw that he did, following him about the fair every night and stupefying him with affection. On the last night of the fair he made up his mind and it was years before they learned what had tipped the balance. In a rare moment of expansion he told them saying, in his broad North Devon burr, "I zeed the pair of 'ee cum sliding down thicky giant slide showin' all 'ee had which was considerable!"

The Potter girls, although promiscuous were not harlots within the meaning of the word. It was simply that they delighted in the company and admiration of men and always had, ever since they were fourteen-year-olds but they did not consort with them from motives of personal gain alone and regarded anything material that emerged from encounters as a bonus to the simple pleasures derived from jolly companionship. They wandered among the world of men like children gathering wild flowers, each subject to furious, short-lived enthusiasms over one bloom or another and although, in the view of the Puritan, they possessed no moral sense whatever, they exercised discrimination and had learned something from their sister Pansy's dolorous experience of life pledged to one particular man. For poor Pansy, who had been so elated when she had secured Walt Pascoe as a husband, was now anchored to a cottage teeming with squalling children and seemed not to have any fun at all whereas Cissie and Violet were still gloriously free and valued their freedom far too much to form a permanent attachment. The establishment of Jem Pollock in the Dell would not, as Violet had pointed out, commit either of them in any way. As a hired hand, they reasoned, they could take him or leave him at will at the same time relieving Meg and themselves of the irksome responsibilities of work on the land. They found nothing distasteful in the prospect of sharing him, turn and turn about. They had shared all their lovers and sometimes extracted a good deal of amusement comparing notes. They had made their mistakes and there were two toddlers in the Dell to prove as much, but a child or two under their feet did not bother a Potter, for the Dell seemed always to have been teeming with children. So the fair moved on, leaving the Goliath of Bideford behind as man-of-all-work at Low Coombe, and soon the whisper ran along the Valley that the Potter girls had at last found a male capable of accommodating them and had established a cosy *ménage à trois* in the Dell. That, however, was before the story broke new ground and an unexpected sequel forced the true state of affairs into the open. This might never have happened if the girls had been able to adjust themselves to their new way of life, and their antics had not awakened a fierce possessiveness in the heart of their willing captive.

It happened about a month after Jem had moved in. He soon proved himself a sound investment from Meg's viewpoint for his willingness and strength, expertly applied to the rundown acres, transformed the farm almost overnight. He was more tireless than any cart-horse and under Meg's direction cleared all the brushwood and weeds from the southern-facing slopes, later ploughing three of the largest fields for winter wheat and planting kale in the more enclosed part of the Bluff. When this was done he cut timber and built several new sties, sinking a small well on the edge of the wood and also repairing the ten-year-old leaks in the farmhouse thatch. His stamina was amazing, for although he worked hard all day he seemed to need very little sleep, so long as his huge frame was nourished by cauldrons of Meg's savoury stew, enormous helpings of fresh vegetables and an average of three loaves of home-baked bread between sunrise and dusk. He ate about ten times as much as a normal labourer but even so he more than earned his board, and everyone in the Dell was delighted with him, blessing the day he had been detached from the Philistines. Then, one mild summer evening, he suddenly presented his bill and it was seen to be a formidable one for it included, in addition to about a basketful of food each day and fifteen shillings a week for beer and baccy, the personal freedom of the girls who were dismayed to find themselves more married than their sister Pansy in Coombe Bay.

He was returning to the Dell at dusk when he heard a ripple of laughter in the long grass on the eastern edge of the wood, close to the spot where he had dug his well. He recognised the sound as Violet's laugh and stolidly changed direction to plod to the top of the slope, where he almost fell over the girls and the two Timberlake boys. Jem was neither a talkative nor an explosive man, his tongue being the one organ of his body that wanted for exercise. After blinking down at the recumbent couples, who were unabashed by his presence, he gave a short grunt that some might have mistaken for the sigh of a man who finds a small task overlooked as he is about to climb into bed. He bent down, gathered a Timberlake under each arm and ambled on as far as the well where he paused for a moment, as though uncertain how to dispose of his double burden. The Timberlake boys, Dandy and Jerry, were not weaklings. Each of them measured around six foot and weighed around thirteen stone but when Jerry heaved himself round and struck the Bireford Goliath a heavy blow on the back of his head, he minded it no more than the impact of a descending beech nut. All it did, it seemed, was to remind him that he had yet to dispose of his rivals

541

and lumbering a few strides further up the hill he dropped both young men into the new well.

Cissie and Violet, screaming their protests and scrambling in pursuit, now made a concerted rush at him, their shrieks carrying far across the meadows and startling gulls on the rock ledges over the cove but the outcry was largely a reflex for the well was only nine feet deep and after floundering for a moment in thick, red mud the boys scrambled out and ran for the woods, without so much as a glance over their shoulder. The ease with which they had been transported from near heaven to the pit convinced them that counterattack would invite further humiliation and possibly grave personal injury, so they did not pause in their stride until they had circled the Bluff, crossed Shallowford meadow and reached the sanctuary of their father's saw-pit.

Bereft of their champions the two girls looked at Jem a little apprehensively, never having seen him in such a ponderously active mood but for a moment they were cruelly deceived by his apparent amiability as he poked about in the hedge and seemed disposed to begin some new task. When he took out his clasp knife, however, they looked anxiously at one another and Cissie said, sharply, "Put up that knife, you gurt fool! They're half-way home be now and us don't want real trouble!"

He made no reply but as he came back to them they saw what he had been doing. He had cut himself three or four pliant ash shoots and was binding them together with a piece of bast. Violet said, "What be at now for God's sake?" and he replied, mildly, "I'll show 'ee in a minute or so, midear," and swished his birch through the air in such a manner as to dispose of their doubts in the instant. Hitching their long skirts they turned and fled towards home almost as precipitately as the Timberlake boys but it was not until they reached the head of the winding path leading down to the Dell that they realised they were barefoot, having shed their brogues in the long grass before Jem arrived to spoil a pleasant evening with a display of uncharacteristic vindictiveness. Jem was close behind them and apparently in no hurry so that they could easily have out-distanced him had it not been for the tangle of briars and roots that grew over the path here. Cissie said, "We got to get our shoes, Jem . . ." but the remark ended in an agonised yelp as the birch landed its first blow and after that there was no more talk of shoes or anything else but a clamour that startled everything in the thicket as the girls made a rush down the steep path. Jem managed to keep just within range and every now and again landed a casual swipe on the nearest posterior, so that the sisters jostled with one another for the honour of leading the procession. Violet, who had been in the rear, overtook her sister about a third of the way down but here, where the trees grew thickly, it was difficult to see in the gathering dusk and she stumbled, Cissie falling over her, so that Jem, still administering leisurely swipes, stood over them as they rolled together in the nettles. Smut, who happened to be visiting the Dell, heard the uproar from the campfire and ran to see the cause. He was just in time to witness the climax and the spectacle, once he had recovered from his surprise, made him double up with laughter for the two girls came down the incline at a stumbling run and behind them came a fast-striding Jem, herding them along like a drover escorting a couple of frisky heifers to market. Thirty yards from the glade Violet made a grave tactical error. Thinking to increase her speed she whisked up her skirts waist high and Cissie at once followed suit but it was a sad mistake on their part, for as long as he could keep them moving Jem was not specially vindictive and seemed in no particular hurry. With two such tempting targets, however, he settled to his task and scored a bull's-eye on one or the other about every three yards. With renewed shrieks the girls dropped their skirts and settled for a good steady pace so they soon arrived, leaping this way and that like a pair of Chinese crackers, while Jem, his humour restored, came up with a broad, gap-toothed grin, as though proud of the brisk manner in which he had headed his cows for home.

The girls disappeared into the house and Meg, glancing after them, absorbed the situation at once. She did not join in Smut's uproarious laughter but her stern features relaxed sufficiently to register approval of the way in which affairs at the Dell had been set in order. She said, incuriously, "Was it they Timberlake boys?" and when he nodded, "Ah, then us'll see no more o' they, Jem! You did right, boy, and they'll be the better for it! 'Ave 'ee vinished with 'em now or be gonner give 'em a real tannin'?"

"Leave 'em be, Mother," he said, carelessly, "I skinned the arse off 'em all the way 'ome," and then, sniffing, "What's for supper?"

"Rabbit stew," she told him, "and I should eat yours, midear, an' tak' their into 'em later. They'll be busy now putting lard on one another's backsides I reckon."

This was, in fact, precisely what they were doing in the light of the kitchen lamp and after they had quietened a little Violet, the sharper of the two, grumbled "Well I doan 'ave to tell 'ee what this means do I?" and Cissie said no, she supposed not, and that it meant they were now Jem's exclusive property and that the sooner everyone in the Valley got to know it the fewer broken heads and whole skins there would be hereabouts. Silently, as they inspected one another's welts, they reviewed the prospect of lifelong bondage to the Bideford Goliath. It was, they felt, a sorry ending to a life of freedom but it had certain advantages that were expressed, perhaps, in Violet's summing up after they had peeped fearfully out-of-doors and watched their tormentor stolidly supping his stew by the fire. "Well," she said resignedly, "it could be worser I reckon! After all, there's only two of us but Jem makes six of any other man in the Valley!" And Cissie agreed, adding wistfully, "I can smell that stew from here, Vi! I wish I dare nip out an' get some but I darn't, dare you?"

"No," said Violet grimly, "I dasn't, fer I shan't zit comfortable for a week as it is! Us'll bide yer and be real nice when 'er brings some in, and if 'er comes in among us tonight dornee start that ole nonsense about you bein' a year older than me! Us'll cut cards for it now—ace high same as Mother decides!"

They cut the cards and Violet drew a queen to Cissie's eight and from that night on there was peace and modest prosperity in the Dell. It took a world war to upset the equilibrium established there by the Bideford Goliath.

On the day that Claire's twins were born old Parson Bull breathed his last and the double quota of news ran up the Valley like a heath fire.

Claire had not really believed Maureen O'Keefe when she had told her to prepare for two babies but Maureen had done some investigating into parish registers and discovered that, unknown to Claire, and even to Edward Derwent, there were twins on both sides of her family and that there might well be on Paul's for all she was aware. When she was half-convinced Claire began to worry but Maureen said, impatiently, "You can forget about last year's mishap for you know well enough what brought that about! You're a strong, healthy girl and the theory that twins are more difficult to bring into the world than one child is old wives' prattle! I'll undertake to deliver them if you do your part by taking things easily instead of gadding about after your husband as if you're afraid to let him out of sight!"

The event occurred on the second day of September with the minimum of alarms, although John Rudd had to be summoned as nursemaid to Paul, who spent the day walking about the house like a man awaiting a last-minute reprieve from the gallows. He had just descended from seeing her, and peering dutifully at the pink, bawling scraps in the cot, when Chivers asked for him and said word had arrived from the Rectory that Parson Bull had died after a long illness dating from a fall he had received in the hunting field more than a year ago. Paul was so relieved that Claire was safely through her ordeal, and so intrigued at becoming the father of twin boys (weighing, they told him, respectively a shade over six pounds apiece) that he could find little regret for the passing of the choleric old parson, although he had always half-admired the man as a genuine left-over from the eighteenth century; in any case, Bull had reached the age of seventy-eight, had been hunting at seventy-seven and was usually well ahead of the field. Paul wondered, as he sipped his brandy in the library, who would succeed him as rector and it was not until John reminded him that he was a patron of the living that he realised that this, in large measure, would depend on himself.

"However, there's no hurry," John said, "a locum will come over from Whinmouth until we've had a chance to look around. You don't know any parson who would be likely to fit in here with your policy, I suppose?"

Paul said he did not but supposed that he would get guidance on the subject from the Dean and Chapter at Paxtonbury.

"Oh, they'll have someone in mind, you can be sure of that," John said, "but if we have a candidate they'll have to consider him seriously. Bull was appointed by Sir George Lovell and must have been rector here all of forty years and it's odd the old battleaxe should have passed on today. Why don't you occupy your mind entering it in the record book while I go down and make sure that Maureen has a hot meal ready when she's finished upstairs? She'll have to go out again afterwards, she has three evening visits to make yet."

Paul was glad of the excuse to be alone, for his nerves were calmer now and after John had gone, and he sat listening to the indeterminate thumps from upstairs, his mind went back to the wild evening he had spent alone here the night Simon was born, when Ikey, dripping wet, had burst in with news of the Codsall tragedy. It occurred to him that the contrast between the occasions was symbolic of his two marriages for that night the world outside had gone mad, with volleying rain slashing at the windows and trees threshing in a full-south-westerly gale, whereas tonight the evening sun filled the landscape with soft, golden light and the curving rows of chestnuts were as still as trees painted on canvas. He took out the estate book and read the last few entries, noting how proudly and self-consciously Claire had written of his trial scheme to set up a shuttle service of carts moving on a planned route through the Valley to dispose of produce from points as far apart as Smut's greenhouse in the east and Eveleigh's dairy in the west. He saw that she had referred to the innovation by the name used for it, in the Valley—"Squire's Waggon Train", an offshoot, he supposed, of the recent visit of Buffalo Bill's Wild West Show to Paxtonbury, but although they made jokes about it it seemed to work satisfactorily and eliminate a great deal of duplicated labour. In the past each farmer had used his own transport to take his milk, eggs, vegetables and plants to the railway halt, or to collection points established by the Paxtonbury and Whinmouth wholesalers but now, with three light light carts and their teams in constant commission, they were relieved of this chore and their individual output had soared as the latest figures proved. He took his pen and wrote, at the head of a new page, *"September 2, 1908. The Rev. Horace Bull, Rector of Shallowford-cum-Coombe for forty years, died today, aged seventy-eight,"* and underneath, in his neatest writing, *"My dear wife, Claire, gave birth to twin boys, as yet unnamed. They were born at two in the afternoon and safely delivered by Doctor Maureen O'Keefe, M.D. All three reported to be doing well."* He smiled at the entry and was tempted to add to it a light-hearted comment, expressing his delight or astonishment but he decided against this, reflecting that as soon as she came downstairs Claire would rush to the book and fill in her own comments. If she took pleasure in writing of his waggon train how much more would she extract from describing the arrival of the twins? He put the record away and listened for fresh sounds but all seemed silent now, so he lit a cigar and went out on the terrace, turning to look up at the window which was wide open, Maureen being a stickler for well-aired sick-rooms. The doctor found him there and said, gently for her, "She's asleep now and there's not a thing to worry over, Paul. Congratulations if I haven't said it before. They're a couple of sturdy brats and should do well. By the way, she can nurse them—no reason at all why she shouldn't and she was happy to learn as much!" Paul said, "Did she have a bad time, Maureen? It seemed so quiet most of the time," and she answered, "It was just as straightforward as I expected, thank God, but you've got her to thank for it, not me! I always have thought the mental approach to birth is as important as the physical—given no complications of course and Claire wanted to bear you children more than anything else in the world. And why not? After all, she has everything now, bless her! She's a wonderful wife, Paul, but I don't have to tell you, do I, boy?", and she kissed him impulsively and went down the terrace steps to the lodge, now half a dwelling and half a surgery. He looked after her gratefully, not knowing how close she had just come to explaining how Claire Derwent had been reintroduced into his life as the direct result of an alliance between her predecessor and *That Boy*. She supposed she would tell him one day but right now he had enough to think about and all of it reassuring.

IV

There seemed no reason why the vacant living of Shallowford-cum-Coombe should concern Ikey Palfrey, yet it did and in more ways than one. Indirectly it was to teach him to box; years later it helped to change his entire cast of thought.

Ikey returned to school soon after the birth of the twins (by that time, and after interminable discussions, christened Andrew and Stephen) and found himself saddled with the melancholy task of chaperoning a new boy, Keith Horsey, fifteen-year-old son of the Reverend Edward Horsey, who had replaced Bull as rector of Shallowford-cum-Coombe.

The Reverend Horsey's appointment came about through a combination of chances but the most important factor, unknown to Squire Craddock until much later, had been the bishop's anxiety to hide a troublesome shepherd in a remote pasture, where his embarrassing social and political views would be likely to cause the minimum number of ripples in the diocese.

The newcomer was recommended to Paul as a Radical, and at the initial interview Paul found him a pleasant, scholarly little man, although somewhat too innocuous for his taste. After consultation with Rudd, however, it was decided to offer him the living on the theory that Bull's overbearing ways had isolated the substantial nonconformist minority in the Valley whereas it seemed likely that a man of Horsey's temperament would contribute to the spirit of teamwork Paul had worked hard to foster.

The new rector was short and slightly built, with myopic brown eyes and a few wisps of grey hair that made him look years older than in fact he was but he had a soft, persuasive voice and, as Paul was quick to realise, a very lively appreciation of the problems of the poor. He had been engaged in missionary work in China but his health failed under the strain and he had taken a curate's post in London's dockland. Here again, however, his physique proved unequal to the strain and he was given a curacy in a residential stronghold of the newly rich, in a Birmingham suburb where he soon alienated parishioners by pulpit attacks on conditions in local factories. From here he drifted south-west but it was apparent to his superiors that no Tory parish would keep him long and when Bull died, and the bishop recalled that the area south-east of Paxtonbury had just sent a Liberal M.P. to Westminster, he made a gift of Horsey to Paul. Horsey was quick to settle in, passing as harmless and establishing contact with dissenters like Farmer Willoughby and the Methodist fishermen of Coombe Bay and this he achieved without any noticeable falling-off of his official flock who had become accustomed to regarding the local pulpit as a source of entertainment.

A month after his arrival the Reverend Horsey made a request of the Squire, informing him that his only child, Keith, had gone to High Wood much later than most new boys. His education had been interrupted by illness and he would not have gone away to school at all had not the doctor prescribed upland air as the best medicine for the child. Horsey, however, was anxious about his son, fearing that his stammer and poor physique might invite persecution, and when he heard that the Squire had a relative established in the Upper School he asked Paul to write to Ikey and request him to keep an eye on the boy.

Paul complied without a second thought but Ikey received his letter with misgivings. The ragging of new boys, particularly well-grown ones, was traditional at High Wood and Ikey was now removed from the hurly-burly of Lower and Middle Schools, for he was almost seventeen and his progress up the school had been spectacular in the last year or so. He was not yet a "Blood" but was in a fair

549

way to becoming one after being awarded his running colours and a place in the pack of the House fifteen.

Ikey had never varied the original technique of his entry into public-school life via scrapyard and stable-yard. He never made the mistake of trusting to luck and was therefore never wholly offguard. From the moment of arrival he had but one object in mind—to do Squire Craddock credit and justify the faith reposed in him. His entire stock of nervous energy, plus his not inconsiderable powers of mimicry and assimilation, had been directed towards this end so that, four years later, he still had everyone at High Wood thoroughly hoodwinked. They thought of him, from the headmaster down to second-form urchin, as an accomplished eccentric and within certain limits eccentrics were encouraged. As a scholar he was reckoned capable of achieving far better results than he did in fact achieve, but in general deportment he was accepted as a gentleman and the son of a gentleman. He made friends easily, dressed casually but not too casually, employed the careless drawling, "g"-dropping speech that was *de rigueur* in the Upper School, was earmarked for a prefecture and a house-captaincy, and was permitted to despise all forms of sport except running in which field he was supreme, holding the under-fifteen and under-sixteen school records for the mile. Everybody at High Wood believed that Ikey Palfrey (rumoured to be the son of a Hungarian countess) could have excelled at cricket, football, shooting, swimming and even fives had he been so inclined but he continued to devote himself exclusively to cross-country and track events, never hurrying. It was even said to his credit that he could have lapped most of his competitors had he chosen but checked his stride in order to encourage them and this was, in fact, partially true, although Ikey himself never admitted it; it would have seemed to him putting on side and he set great store on modesty, at least outwardly.

Yet Ikey's performance as a Highwodian was not entirely a charade. As the terms passed he began to develop an almost mystic affection for the place, for its dove-grey stones, for the music of distant shouts rising from the playing fields, for the bells, the fads, the newish traditions but more particularly for the country beyond the ridge of beeches from which the school derived its name. Imperceptibly it grew on him like another skin, covering his two other personalities—the Ikey Palfrey of Bermondsey, and of the Shallowford stable-yard, so that his pretences were subconscious and there were times when he almost came to believe in the fiction of his relationship to the Squire. Paul's marriage to Claire, and the secret understanding this had developed between himself and the lady doctor, removed the source of anxiety that had clouded his first school year and as he increased in importance and felt more a part of the place, his life became serene and untroubled by anything more urgent than a housematch or an end-of-term examination.

And now, when he was poised for the final leap into the top echelon, when he looked like getting into the first fifteen and perhaps succeeding Henley-Jones as Captain of the House, the Squire was asking him to play nursemaid to a new kid, the son of the Shallowford parson and whereas Ikey's loyalty to Paul was absolute, and therefore any request amounted to a command, it was also an insufferable bore and Ikey hoped fervently that the wretched kid would not place too much reliance on a chap to steer him through his first, troublesome year. He was soon disillusioned. When, after some slumming in the Lower School Keith Horsey was unearthed and interrogated it did not take Ikey long to assess the new boy's vulnerability or the risks one would invite attempting to pilot such a drip through the Lower School rapids. To begin with he was as thin as a beanpole, with a tin-whistle voice and, to crown all, old-fashioned steel-rimmed spectacles and as if these were not sufficient handicaps, the whey-faced toad also possessed larger, nobbly knees and was clearly outgrowing his strength, for although very thin he was also tall and his height made him noticeable among the bullet-headed scruff who had joined the school as newcomers that year.

Yet it was not merely Keith Horsey's physical oddities that singled him out as a target for the second-year boys, all resolved to exact payment for their own sufferings in the past. He was also, it seemed, a brilliant scholar and proved as much by beginning his school life in the Upper Fourth, which was rather like an enlisted civilian starting an army career as a first lieutenant. Ikey found the new boy hiding in the latrines (where he himself had sought refuge a thousand years ago) and after ordering him out led him behind the sanatorium where they were unlikely to be overlooked.

"Squire told me to look you up," he mumbled, "your pater being the new rector at our place. The fact is, you're likely to get hell this term but if you don't let it bother you it'll soon ease off, the same as it does for all new kids." He stopped and ran his eye over the shambling figure. Having just finished *Nicholas Nickleby,* the set book for half-term exams, it occurred to him that the new boy was curiously like the wretched Smike and he added with a sigh, "Is there anything you are likely to shine at? Anything at all? Just to start working on?"

"Lllatin," said Keith hopefully, "I'm gggood at Latin!"

Ikey winced, not so much at the discovery of yet another handicap, but at the idiocy of the reply. The toad did not even know enough to understand that familiarity with Latin verbs was as good as a leper's bell among the Middle and Lower School riffraff. Just in time, however, he recalled his duty to the Squire and said, patiently, "No kid! Cramming don't count! I mean *sport*—games, football, *anything!*"

"I haven't played any games," admitted Keith blandly. "I was too anaemic they said. I didn't go to a Prep School you see but had a private tutor. Pater taught me too, he's a first-class classical scholar, you know."

"Well," said Ikey heavily, "you can keep that under your thatch to begin with! If I was in your shoes I should muff your first term exams and aim for somewhere near the bottom. If you got moved up at the end of your first term God help you, because I couldn't!"

They walked in silence for a moment, Keith relaxing in the patronage of this tremendous being, whom he knew to be one of the most popular boys in the school. He had had a wretched time so far but now, it seemed, the worst part was over, for surely nobody would dare to put him through the Sunday new kids' ritual when Palfrey was his champion. He said, pleasantly, "Do *you* lllike it here, PPPalfrey?"

"Yes, of course I like it," Ikey said irritably, and then, defensively, "why shouldn't I? It's the best school in the West, isn't it?"

"Pater said it was," admitted Keith doubtfully, "but I'm not so sure now. The classical standard isn't all that good, you know, and that Latin master made a shocking mistake on the board this morning."

Ikey's small stock of patience burned itself out and he stopped, swung round, took Keith by the shoulders and shook him so hard that the new boy's glasses slipped down his long nose.

"Listen here," he said savagely, "I told Squire I'd keep an eye on you and I will, but you've got to help! You've got to stop . . . *asking* for it! If Henley-Jones had heard you say what you've just said about the school he would have tanned your hide so hard that your arse would have looked like a ploughed field! You've got to . . . got to . . .", and he broke off, for the boy's chapfallen expression proclaimed the magnitude of his task. "You've just got to keep out of sight, that's all! Hide in the bog when the chaps aren't playing rugger and are milling about in the quad and passages! Keep out of *sight*, you understand? And don't try too hard at half-term tests—get things wrong on purpose . . . and well, play the fool in class, just to make some kind of a name for yourself!"

He could think of nothing else calculated to help the boy, deciding that he would have to give the matter more thought. He walked swiftly away, leaving Horsey standing under the beeches, with tears in his eyes and a sense of having somehow mislaid the key to the citadel.

Ikey did give the matter thought, indeed, he thought of little else during the next few days, during which time he took care to keep clear of his new responsibility. Then he had an inspiration; he would solve Keith's problem, and incidentally his own, by providing The Beanpole with a foolproof alibi, something that would not only explain why he was the kind of person he really was but also blunt and disarm his tormentors into the bargain. He buttonholed the new boy during morning break, pushed him into the band-room and carefully closed the door.

"Now look here, Horsey," he said, "I've thought of

something! All you have to do is back me up when anyone asks you. You got that stammer, and you had to wear those glasses, after being shipwrecked on the way from New Zealand! You were thirty days adrift in an open boat and were the sole survivor! When they picked you up your eyeballs were scorched and you couldn't remember who you were but now it's coming back, very slowly, get me? They'll all swallow that, providing I vouch for it as coming from Squire via your pater and because it's dramatic, it'll make everybody . . . well . . . decent you know, at least for a term or so!"

"But it isn't true," Horsey said, blinking his owlish eyes, "it isn't a bit true, not a word of it, Palfrey! I've never been to New Zealand and I've never been on a boat, except round the Isle of Wight on a paddle steamer."

Ikey stared at him, half in amazement and half in anger so desperate that he too began to stammer.

"Ttrue?" he said, "well dammit, man, of course it's not true! I made it up, didn't I! I made it up to keep you out of trouble, as Squire asked me. I daresay it sounds mad to you but I know this place and I know how these chaps think! I've been through it all myself and I *know!* You do what I say and spin any yarn you like, so long as we both stick to the same outline."

The boy's face was now almost as white as the pipe-clayed O.T.C. belts hanging on the racks behind him. He said, falteringly, "But I . . . I couldn't, Palfrey! It's jolly decent of you, and I'm grateful, really I am, but it's a lie just the same and I couldn't say that to stop boys like Williams and Vesey Minor kicking me and pouring ink down my neck! It wouldn't be right, don't you see?"

Ikey saw far more than Horsey suspected and more than he would have preferred to see. The boy's rejection of the carefully-thought-out alibi was, in a sense, a revelation to him. He saw, for instance, that one could not always judge by appearances, that heroes sometimes appeared under strange disguises, and that this weed's regard for the truth was likely to prove unassailable. He realised too that it did not spring from self-righteousness but from deeply ingrained lessons learned at home and because, from earliest childhood, Ikey had had the ability to gauge the potentiality of human beings he reassessed Keith Horsey at once, docketing him as a fool and a physical weakling unlikely to collect anything but bruises on his way up the school but also as an individual possessing something quite rare among people—moral courage untarnished by piety. He knew also that he was beaten, that he could never hope to protect Keith Horsey from the Williamses and Vesey Minors of this world and that the best he could do would be to stand by and see fair play within the limits of the code. He said, glumly, "Very well, Horsey, forget what I said! I'll keep an eye on you if I can but it wouldn't help if I interfered too much, you'd only get it worse!", and he opened the door of the bandroom and mooched, hands in pockets, across the quad.

He was faced with the challenge again the following Sunday, the ominous Last Sunday But Four, when new boys, according to prescribed ritual, were required to Scrub-The-Floor with their tooth-brushes and tins of tooth powder. The ritual began with the rising bell and ordinarily Ikey would have paid no attention to it, for he now regarded these practices as the prerogative of The Scruff, that is to say, boys in the Lower Middle School. His disdain, however, was by no means general among other seniors. Some of the more loutish among the Fifth clung to their toys and one of them, a hulking seventeen-year-old, whose idleness accounted for his presence in the Fifth for the fourth term, had elected himself Inquisitor-in-Chief. It was soon clear to Ikey that Piggy Boxall had selected Horsey as his sacrificial lamb, for although Keith, in common with the other new boys, scrubbed his bedspace until it was coated with froth, dust and blanket fluff, Piggy directed him to the bedspace of a boy who had the misfortune to sleep alongside Piggy. This boy protested, not out of sympathy for Horsey but because he did not relish having to stand in the mess of toothpaste but Piggy overruled his objection, standing over the kneeling Horsey and encouraging him with occasional toe-flips.

Ikey watched for a moment in silence. Boxall was a head taller and probably two stone heavier, but he did not intimidate Ikey. His reluctance to intervene stemmed from distaste in becoming involved in such a kindergarten sport

555

and it was only with difficulty that he forced his responsibility to the front of his mind, saying at length, "That's enough, Horsey! Get on and dress now," and when Piggy Boxall demanded of Ikey who was senior Ikey cheerfully admitted that Piggy was but that Horsey had already done his quota and had no business messing up someone else's bedspace. Horsey scuttled off into the wash-room but Boxall seemed disposed to press the point. "You're getting damned bucky for someone who only moved into the Fifth this term!" he said, "I've a good mind to wallop you here and now!"

"You're welcome to try," Ikey said, quietly, as half-dressed boys gathered round, relishing the promise of a fight to relieve the fearful tedium of an autumn Sabbath. "The fact is, Piggy, I'm tired of watching a weed like you take it out on Scruff and as far as Horsey is concerned you'll have to stop picking on him because he happens to be the son of my guardian's new rector and I've been asked to keep an eye on him. Sorry and all that, old man!"

The murmur of conversation in the big room had ceased. Everyone there regarded Ikey Palfrey as an eccentric, given to elaborate jokes of this kind but championship of a first-termer, and a first-termer of Beanpole Horsey's type, was carrying a jest too far, particularly if it entailed challenging the only boy in the dormitory who shaved. They moved closer, interested and expectant but Henley-Jones, senior boy in the House, said, "Well, you can't leave it there, either of you. You'll have to fight and you can't do it today. Sunday fights are taboo."

"I'd be happy to oblige tomorrow," said Ikey, "but only on conditions. If I beat Boxall he doesn't touch Horsey again, not until he's played in."

The nicety of the challenge intrigued them. Henley-Jones said after a moment, "That's reasonable. I'll get the gloves during dinner-break. We haven't had a proper House fight for a year or more but you'll get a hiding, Palfrey."

Boxall said, angrily, "Look here, why do we have to wait until tomorrow? I'll give him his rations now since he's so damned hungry for 'em! It's time someone took

Palfrey down a peg or two!" but Henley-Jones replied, as the five-minute bell rang, "Please yourself about that, Piggy, but if you're caught fighting in the dorm a House perk has to dab whoever he catches and Toothy Gilbert is on duty today. He's about half your size and you'd look damned silly bending over the radiator for him! If I were you I should go about it according to rules."

There was a murmur of agreement. A properly organised fight was infinitely preferable as a spectacle to a dormitory scuffle ending in the contestants getting caned by the duty prefect, which was something they could see any old day. Ikey said, "There's sense in what he says, we'd best make it tomorrow, Piggy!", and he walked back to his own bed.

He had been grateful for Henley-Jones' intervention for it was no part of his plan to leave things to chance and there was something that had to be done if he was to face Boxall in the Fives Court with any chance of beating him. He dressed quickly and went down in the boiler-room to consult Gobber Christow, the school lamp-trimmer. Ikey had a relationship with the school servants that his intimates found difficult to understand. Without hint of patronage he could talk their language and for two years now any favours demanded of them—the purchase of cigarettes, the backing of horses and other infractions of the rules where their services were in demand, Ikey had been chosen to bribe them. It was his familiarity with the world of sculleries, bootholes and furnace basements that had won from Gobber Christow a reluctant admission that he had once been a professional bruiser.

"Gobber," he said, without preamble, "I've got to fight Piggy Boxall tomorrow afternoon. He's a good deal heavier than me and his reach is longer. How would I go about beating him?"

Gobber had been boilerman at High Wood for twenty-five years and thought he knew boys. He screwed up his blood-shot eyes and summoned to mind the image of Piggy Boxall, mentally staking out the distance from solar plexus to chin and equating it with the weight, reach and spunk of Palfrey, a young gentleman who never forgot to tip him at the end of term. Ikey, making a guess at the reason for his deliberation, said, "It's late in term, Gobber, but I could raise a bob or so."

"I don't want no bob," Gobber said, "not till Christmas that is but you can lick that long streak easy enough, if you mind what I say. You'll 'ave to dance about out o' reach of 'im for a round or two and wind him. Then you lets fly a right to the head and his guard goes up. Before it comes down again you land a left on 'is belly-button, hard as you c'n drive and down comes 'is guard again. With any luck he doubles within reach and you c'n weight in left and right, many as you c'n land. Mind all I say and I'll bet on you."

"Would you go over it with me again, Gobber?"

Gobber stirred his tea, swallowed a mouthful and got up from his box.

"I will that," he said, "a dozen times jus' so as you don't forget. Now I'm Boxall, pretty well a head taller . . ." and the lesson continued, the pair dancing a gavotte round the confined space and the ponderous Gobber, blessed with strong stomach muscles, taking punishment without the satisfaction of being able to exploit Ikey's rushes. Afterwards, as they drank more boiler-brewed tea together, Ikey said, "You don't have half a bad time down here, Gobber, with nothing expected of you but to keep the lamps trimmed and the boilers stoked up! I suppose you'd think I was stretching it if I told you I envy you sometimes. The fact is," he went on, forgetting his usual caution, "I'm a bit of a misfit and sometimes I think I don't belong out there at all." But Gobber, with the keen perception of the lowly and middle-aged, replied, "I don't reckon you do neither an' I made dam' certain of it long since but I wouldn't let on if I was you, not even to me! It wouldn't do, you see, for come to think on it you're a bloody sight luckier'n the rest of us! You got the best o' both worlds, so make the most of 'em and don't forget— keep out o' range till he's blown! Meanwhile I'll see if I can get long odds on you, four to one mebbe."

The fight after second school the next day followed the predicted pattern so closely that, looking back on it, Ikey wondered if the boilerman was clairvoyant.

558

Henley-Jones refereed and Ikey endured the storm of jeers from the gallery throughout the first three rounds when the enthusiasm of spectators spent itself in derisive shouts of *"Mix it"* and "Oh, *stand up* to him, Palfrey!" but Ikey was never seriously rattled, bringing to the fight the same patience as he brought to all his complex personal problems. In any case he was in far better training than Boxall and came out of his corner at round four comparatively fresh, whereas the older boy was breathing heavily and resolved to make a speedy finish of it. Driven into a corner Ikey rode out a heavy punch on his shoulder then swung wildly at his opponent's head. Just as Gobber had predicted Boxall's guard shot up, leaving his solar plexus open to attack and the straight left that followed folded him like a penknife, so that several spectators cried "Foul!" but Henley-Jones, revelling in his official role, shouted, "Balls! It was above the belt! Go in and win, Palfrey!" and Ikey stood back to deliver the only telling blows of the match, two lefts and a right to Boxall's head that brought him to his knees.

It was the first technical knock-out ever witnessed at High Wood and they would have made much of him but Ikey slipped away on the excuse of changing and, again making sure he was unobserved, sought out Horsey and led him into the cover of the beech plantation. There was a seat overlooking the cricket pavilion and they sat there in the dusk, Horsey tight-lipped and blinking nervously, Ikey without a mark on his face and triumph in his heart. He said, at length, "Well, you won't have any more trouble from Boxall but you'll still have to take it from the others. I can't fight everybody and I wouldn't if I could. It's accepted that new kids should go through the mill!"

"Why is it?" Horsey asked, unexpectedly, and Ikey, mildly outraged, replied, "If they didn't they'd get bucky and start putting on side."

"It's funny," the boy said, slowly, "we have Chapel twice a day and lessons read from the New Testament, but nobody really listens, do they? I mean, the Head might be reading the call-over list because nobody here actually believes in Jesus Christ!"

Ikey had the same disinclination to discuss Jesus Christ

as any other sixteen-year-old but he could not help wondering at the new boy's detachment, as though he was a kind of a missionary plumped down among a swarm of heathens, appalled by the hopelessness of his situation and the improbability of witnessing justice or mercy. He said, uncomfortably, "It's nothing to do with the Bible. You just got to learn to look after yourself! It's not so hard as it seems at first and it gets easier every term," and then, recklessly, "You'll be spending the hols on the estate and I daresay I'll see something of you. Maybe I can give you a tip or two. You don't have to play everything their way but you have to pretend to, like me."

The boy looked at him curiously. "You mean you don't believe in it either? In all this fighting and bullying? Because if you don't, then why did you fight Piggy Boxall? I didn't ask you to and I wish you hadn't. I think fighting is uncivilised and stupid," and for some reason Ikey was humbled, the mantle of patronage falling from him so that suddenly he felt naked. He said, irritably, "It's no use talking to you, Horsey! Your pater ought not to have sent you to a place like this!" and he got up and stalked through the dusk towards the pool of light shed by the lamps of the quad arch. "Blast the kid," he said to himself, "he'll make a lily of me if I don't bloody well watch out!"

V

At the extreme north-west corner of the mere, beyond the maze of rhododendrons in which Ikey had lost himself in the snow, the ground rose steeply to a great outcrop of sandstone where the older woods fell away, oak, beech, sycamore and thorn giving place to a straggle of dwarf pines and Scots firs that had crept down from the evergreen belt of the Hermitage plateau. It was here that the Shallowford badgers had their sets and from her eyrie at the top of the slope Hazel Potter could watch them lumbering to and fro, like paunched merchants in the streets of a sleepy country town. This was the spot she preferred beyond all others, for nobody ever came here now that Smut had turned horticulturist and it was here, under the

560

overhang of a great, slapsided rock, that she had made her home.

It was unlike any other house in the Valley. Its hearth was a triangle of flat stones and its south side was open to sun and wind but inside it was always dry and warm, with a floor of crushed bracken, a wicker screen that kept out the slanting rain and cavities to store her modest utensils, a pitcher, a few tins, a stock of kindling, a roasting spit and some flour sacks that she used for bedding when the fancy took her to stay here overnight.

In the spring, when the woods below were opening their vast green umbrellas and the birds were busy all day in and about the shrubbery, she spent most of her time up here, composing her prose poems about the creatures she overlooked, cooking a mash of vegetables and rabbit meat in her iron pot and sometimes braiding wild flowers into her hair so that she looked like one of the allegorical goddesses for whom Edwardians blushed at the Royal Academy, the type of floral-crowned beauty painted by popular artists, like Henrietta Rae. When the sun was warm, however, she advanced even further into the world of the painters, throwing off her rags of clothing and sprawling naked on the jutting slab that was her roof. The sun warmed her through and the vantage point gave her a temporary affinity with starlings rushing down from the plateau into the puffs of pot-bellied cloud drifting down the Valley. Cataracts of sounds that were more expressive than words would slip from her tongue to lose themselves in the woods below, heard but unheeded by the stoat, the field mouse and a swarm of tits, wrens and robins in the thickets. She had as much company as she needed, for almost all things living between the red outcrop and the rhododendron forest below had come to accept her long ago. The badgers never gave her a second glance and neither did the lame vixen, nursing cubs in a shallow earth under the wreck of an eighty-year-old pine that had crashed into the Valley. The hedgehog passed her with his belly clear of the ground and the field voles, who frolicked on the stumps of charred firs sometimes scuttled into the cave to look for dry leaves for their nests. During her long watching spells she took careful note of everything that went on around her and because she had the power of remaining utterly still she added a little to her store of secrets every day. She had her favourites, among them the otter, who occasionally left the mere and sunned himself on a rock half-way up the slope; and the old, mad cat, who grinned at her over the remains of a chicken dragged all the way down the escarpment from the most easterly of the Periwinkle runs. She had often heard Will Codsall curse that cat and run for his gun when he caught a glimpse of yellow-white fur in the long grass but she never told Will where it might be trapped at the expense of an old hen. It had to live, she supposed, the same as the white-waistcoated stoat and the brindled water vole and the vixen who also raided Periwinkle runs. Here, where the bracken grew shoulder high, there was always movement and changing colours. Kingcups, willowherb, ragged robin and dwarf red rattle covered the ground near the overspill of the stream at the foot of the slope but nearer the summit grew cowslips, battalions of foxgloves, sea-pinks and wild thyme and in and out of this riot darted a hundred varieties of birds, some as familiar as the golden plover and as impudent as the magpie, others shy summer visitors who came back year after year, like the sand-martin and the monotonous cuckoo, one of the few birds Hazel did not welcome. She was not always absorbed by the panorama or the creatures going about their business between the haze that was the summit of Blackberry Moor and the more definite blur to the south, that was the sandstone cliffs of the Bluff. Sometimes, if the mood came on her, she could forget all else in a long, self-satisfying appraisal of herself, contemplating her golden-brown legs, her flat belly and her high breasts that were a source of special wonder to her for she could not recall anything more regularly formed unless it was the spread of the lower branches of her favourite oak in the meadow a mile south of her eyrie. She would sit cross-legged and study herself minutely, beginning with her flower-decked hair that reached to her waist and ending with a dedicated scrutiny of her supple toes, usually coated with the fine red dust of the rocks. Then she would leap down from the slab and fetch the burnished lid of one of her tins to use as a mirror, holding it up at an angle and glancing side-ways at her shoulders, then moving it in a slow, tilted sweep, until she could catch a distorted glimpse of her rounded buttocks and the deep dimples above them. Usual-ly she was pleased and would shake out her hair, raise her arms and wriggle like a savage beginning a ritual dance, exclaiming with the deepest satisfaction, "Youm bootiful, Hazel! Bootiful, do 'ee yer, now? Youm the most bootiful of all, for youm smooth an' white an' goldy and you baint much fur about 'ee, neither!" If anyone living in the Valley below could have seen and heard her their suspicions that she was mad would have been confirmed and perhaps someone would have set out to capture her and put her away for her own safety, but they would have been making a terrible blunder, for Hazel Potter was not in the least mad but simply primitive and her method of self-appraisal differed little from that of her sisters' or any other woman in the Valley, twisting and cheek-sucking before a bedroom mirror. She was, moreover, probably the happiest woman in the Valley, or any other valley in the West, for her isolated way of life was accepted by her mother Meg and her brother Sam in his cottage below. She never harmed anyone or anything, if one excepted the rabbits she trapped and roasted or the gulls' eggs she gathered and swallowed and even when they did not see her for days at a time no search-parties went to look for her and bring her back to the Dell. They had long since given up sending her to Mary Willoughby's school and she had completely forgotten what little she had learned there, so that at seventeen she could neither read nor write but seemed little the worse for it for she gave Meg far less trouble than had either of her three sisters when they were growing up and quarrelling with one another over men and ribbons. She would appear and disappear like a half-tamed bird and she made no demands upon anyone. Every now and again, usually during spells of bad weather, she would reappear in the Dell and eat sparingly from the family stewpot, or steal one of her sisters' discarded garments, but apart from this she fended for herself and even a conventionally minded soul like Edward Derwent did not remark on her when he caught a glimpse of her flitting across a glade or standing silhouetted against the skyline.

And yet, although exquisitely self-contained, there were moments in the spring of the year when Hazel was vaguely conscious of her isolation, when it made itself known to her by a curious sensation, a faint and remote pricking, located somewhere between her breasts, as though, without leaving a puncture, a sliver of gorse had got under the skin and was trying to work its way out.

At first she paid little attention to it but as the warm April days succeeded one another, and the murmur of the woods swelled so that it reached her rock like the wash of the sea, the pricking became more insistent and sometimes converted itself into a choking feeling in the base of the throat that made her eyes smart, so that she could no longer lay inactive staring down at the green umbrellas and would spring up, pull on her dress and plunge down the pine-studded slope to the rhododendrons and through the green tunnels to the mere and here, if she was lucky, she would see Sam, or Joannie, or old Aaron the osier cutter, and would forget what had brought her here in such a hurry.

It was during one of these brief melancholy spells, on a warm April day, that she saw something break the calm surface of the mere on her side of the islet. She was lying naked on her rock, screened from above and below by gorse and bracken and the landscape, usually so alive, was listless under the noonday sun. At first she thought the wide ripple was caused by the pike that Sam said had lived there since Old Tamer was a boy but soon she saw a swimmer moving slowly across the mere to the western shore. As she watched, surprised and a little alarmed, she saw the figure make a landing near the spot where Smut had hidden from the Heronslea keepers. She recognised him at once, even at this distance, and her heart gave a great leap of pleasure, as a tear, after hovering for half a minute, splashed down her cheek and beaded a hart's tongue fern growing on the edge of the rock. She jumped down into her cave, pulled on her ragged dress and without knowing why held up the shining lid to study her reflection, noting that she had a string of bird's foot trefoil braided into her hair and also that she was smiling and that her eyes were moist. She stood still for a moment, pulling faces at herself and tossing her hair this way and that and said with deliberation, "I ll bring un yer! I'll show un the house, an' mebbe he'd stay on a bit to watch things!"

It was not a light-hearted decision. No one, not even her brother Sam who tramped the rabbit run below three or four times a week, knew of the existence of her house for her instinct had always been to guard the secret against the time when they would come looking for her to put her to work or send her back to that stuffy schoolroom at Deepdene. But The Boy could be trusted, for The Boy was different, half-way to being wild like herself, for if not why should he swim naked across the mere as if the old pike, the underwater bogies and the clutching weeds were not lying in wait to drag him where he would never be seen again? She went swiftly down the slope and through the rhododendron tunnels to a rift in the lakeside foliage, moving cautiously until she could see him towelling himself under a Douglas fir, and as he rubbed he whistled softly through his teeth, flapping his arms as though he was cold. She would have called out to him but at that moment, still flapping, he turned away and reached up to take his shirt and trousers from the lowest branch and she had to smother her giggles for he looked so funny standing there with the filtered sun playing on his long, pale back, lean legs and small chubby behind. She remembered then that men were ashamed of their bodies and with good reason it seemed, so she waited until he had struggled into his trousers, shirt and sweater before crackling twigs underfoot and calling, "Boy! Boy! Dornee know the ole pike'll get 'ee swimmin' in there?"

He looked startled for the moment but when she stepped down to the shore to meet him he smiled and flicked back his dark hair, saying that he had crossed to the islet twice without landing. He seemed to her much broader and taller in his clothes, no longer a boy but a man nearly as broad-shouldered as her brother Sam.

"It's years since I set eyes on you," he said, "where have

you been? They said you were still about but I never saw you, not once!"

"I've seen 'ee many times," she said gravely and he remembered then that she sometimes took it into her head to watch the yard from the meadow behind the house.

"But you're never at the Dell," he said and the truculence in his voice pleased her so that she shook out her hair and twirled her body, saying, "I've got a house o' me orn and I'll tak' 'ee there if you mind to! No one knows it, not even Sam, nor Smut! Tiz mine, fer 'twas I as found un and vurnished un and there I bides as long as I likes!"

It was evident that he did not take her very seriously for he said, carelessly, "Oh, you mean one of those gun hides? Well, there's a dozen of them in the woods. Which is yours?"

She said, pouting, "You follow along, like you did time you was lost, and I'll show 'ee but I'll kill 'ee if 'ee tells, mind!"

He followed her up through the green tunnels and the long, pinestudded slope to the outcrop of rock where she disappeared as completely as if the ground had opened under her feet. A moment later he heard her mocking laughter and looked all round but still could not see her until she climbed half-way out of the cave and showed him where he should enter the wicker screen and scramble over the loose rocks to the overhang. She had her small reward for once inside he looked round in astonishment, noting everything, the fire-blackened stones, the utensils and the flour sacks neatly folded in the corner.

"You actually live here? Sleep here?" he said, unbelievingly.

"On'y when tiz warm," she said carelessly, "other times I go down-along. Do 'ee like my li'l home, Boy?"

He scratched his head looking very puzzled but finally smiled, sat down with his back against her wicker screen and said, "Don't keep calling me 'Boy', Hazel. I've got a name and anyway I'm not a boy any longer, I'm seventeen and I shall be shaving next term!"

"Will 'ee now?" It was information that interested her, so that she tilted her head and searched his chin for evidence. Presumably she found some for she went on, eagerly, "Will 'ee grow a beard then? Like ole Varmer Willoughby's. A bushy one?"

"No," he said laughing, "just a moustache. I'll see how it looks anyway and if I don't fancy it I'll shave it off!"

Suddenly he dismissed the subject of problematic whiskers. "What do you do up here? I mean, aren't you ever lonely? Don't you get sick of you own company?"

"Yiss," she admitted slowly, "but if I'm lonesome I go and have a talk with Sam or the girls; other times, when the wires baint hooked me a coney, I go to the varms and they gives me skimmed milk and home-baked bread!"

"Are they all kind to you?"

"Mrs. Pitts dorn let me go hungry," she said, and then, tiring of so dull a subject, "Do 'ee like it up yer, Boy?"

"Yes," he said, "I think it's a wonderful place to be in summer but my name is Ikey. Call me Ikey, 'Boy' sounds soppy!"

" 'Ikey'!" she repeated slowly, "that's a daft name for gentry, baint it?"

"I'm not gentry," said Ikey firmly but she said, "Oh but you be! Youm Squire's boy and you lives along o' Squire, dornee?"

"I live with him when I'm home from school," Ikey said, patiently, "but I'm not related to him. In fact, I'm no more 'gentry' than you are. Squire Craddock gave me a job years ago and then sent me to school. But surely you knew that, didn't you?"

"Yiss," she said carelessly, "but I forgot. I most always forget. Truth is I forget about you till I zeed 'ee tempting the old pike in the mere!"

He knew then that she must have watched him dry and dress but it did not bother him for in most ways she seemed no older than little Simon or the twins. He was piqued, however, that she had forgotten him so readily for he had never forgotten her or the pleasant days he had spent in her company. Now that he looked more closely at her he saw that she had changed a great deal in the last two years. He had continued to think of her as a child, the rural equivalent of urchins with whom he had run and fought in his scrapyard days but he could now see that she was a woman, moreover the kind of woman his town-bred study partner, Tovey Major, would jest about, might even boast that he had kissed and cuddled and perhaps, in Tovey's own phrase, "run up and down the scales, don't you know?" The thought set his heart pounding, for surely a Blood like Tovey would never miss an opportunity like this, and because of this sudden awareness of her sex he found it difficult to continue to talk to her as though she was a cottager's child and he was duty-visiting. He made the effort, however, saying kindly, "You're quite grown up, Hazel. Is anyone courting you?"

She smiled and by no means innocently. She was familiar with the routine of courting, having watched the antics of her sisters over the years and knew that "courting" implied squeaks, protests, gusts of laughter and stealthy movements in the long grass. She had even had an encounter of her own when the youngest Timberlake boy had cornered her in the barn and run his hands over her before she kicked him in the shins and fled. She said, mildly, "No, I baint courtin'. I keeps to meself mostly", which did not help him very much, for the answer at once relieved and disappointed him. He had gathered from the books and magazines Tovey had introduced into the study that a girl as pretty as Hazel Potter might have a great deal to offer a man of the world, although he did not understand precisely what, or how to begin seeking it. At the same time, he felt under a moral restraint, reflecting that she was, after all, the daughter of Squire's lowliest tenant and perhaps even Tovey would classify a flirtation with Hazel as "infradig-old-man". Then, noticing that she was still watching him intently, he blushed and had a mind to get up at once and leave her absurd "little house" but he found that he lacked the resolution to do anything so final and not solely because he seemed to hear the sound of Tovey's derisive laughter echo in the Valley below. The wonder she had always stirred in him was working its magic again but this time it was not based on an objective admiration of her independence or envy of her way of life. Her mouth, he thought, looked like a rosebud in the early morning and her thick chestnut hair, starred with tiny blue flowers, reminded him of the hair of a goddess in a painting. He said, in a low voice, "You're beautiful, Hazel! You're the prettiest girl in the Valley!"

"Yiss," she said, blandly, "more beautiful that Cis an' Vi an' Pansy." She had watched and absorbed the courting techniques of animals and birds from the rock above. Pride, caprice and ferocity she had seen but never humility on the part of the female. "Woulden 'ee like to kiss me?" she added with shattering directness and at once he was immensely grateful to her for it seemed, by taking the initiative so fearlessly, she had resolved his doubts and also, to some extent, accepted the responsibility. He put his arm round her and turned her warm cheek, kissing her gently but with an air of decision and then, to his dismay, the situation complicated itself again, for the bravado of the act evaporated the moment their lips met and his heart pounded so insistently that he thought he must be ill. For all that, contact with her mouth was the most delightful sensation he had ever experienced, making nonsense of all his triumphs on the playing field. He put up his hand and let it run smoothly down over her hair so that it crackled, as though protesting against the liberty. As he stroked her hair she gave a tiny shudder that somehow increased his delight and there seemed absolutely nothing to say or nothing that would make the least sense. When he had turned her head to begin this extraordinary adventure he had been very conscious of marching forward in step with Tovey Major but now Tovey and all his kind were left behind along the road that led back to his childhood. He was acutely aware of the awful solemnity of the moment and notwithstanding its sweetness and poignancy, he recognised its implications. There would never be another moment quite like this, never another mouth and cheek as soft and sweet as these, and it was this, and not his characteristic caution, that caused his hand to stop half-way in its instinctive move towards her breast and to fall to the bracken floor, for he knew very well what would happen if he touched and caressed that soft roundness; within minutes this beautiful, half-wild creature would be reduced to the status of one of the simpering, broad-hipped blondes in Tovey Major's magazines and that would be to convert a symphony into a discordant jangle.

Instead he sought and took her hand and their fingers interlocked, and as the kiss ended his lips brushed her cheek and found her hair wherein was the scent of everything growing in the Valley.

They sat quite still for a long time, only half aware of the sunplay on the floor of the cave and the restless twitter of birds outside. It crossed his mind that they should make some kind of pledge, a promise that would ensure repetition of this unspoken declaration but he had no idea how to convert his feelings into words and in the end, after kissing her softly once more, he gently removed his arm, saying, "I'll have to be going now, Hazel. I told them at the house I was trying to swim the mere and Chivers will worry if I don't show up."

She said, unemotionally, "You'll come yer agaain? Zoon, mebbe?", and he said he would, at about the same time tomorrow and went out through the tall bracken screen and down the long slope hardly aware of his direction, for every thought that entered his head disappeared at once into a maelstrom of guilt and joy.

She gave him time to pass the rhododendrons before she climbed out of the cave and on to her flat rock, where she could catch occasional glimpses of him as he moved along the northern margin of the lake. In her mind there was no confusion, only the satisfied relish of his lips and the light touch of his hand on her hair. The pricking sensation under her breast had gone and it was some time before it returned to gall her but in its place was a glow that demanded release in words, so that seeing the old, mad cat on a stump partway down the slope, she called, "Did 'ee zee un, Tibb? Did 'ee zee my man, then?" but the cat only turned his head and gave her a long, supercilious glance. He had just disposed of a shrew and the sun was very warm. He had seen Ikey pass but he was not interested in a man without a gun.

CHAPTER SEVENTEEN

I

IT was with a sense of shock that Paul heard the name of Lord Gilroy announced as he sat working in the library one sunny July morning but before the man had been shown in he realised that his visitor must be the successor to the man who had once bearded him in this room and played an unconscious part in Grace's decision to marry.

The old man, the "dry, bloodless old stick," as John Rudd described him, had died a year since and Paul had only a vague recollection of his son, whom he had met once or twice in the hunting field. He found him a great contrast to his dessicated-looking father, a tall, broad-shouldered, chubby-cheeked individual, who looked and dressed more like a prosperous city business man than a landowner. He wore expensively cut country clothes, the kind of clothes city men always don when travelling ten miles outside London and his approach was well-bred, genial and confident, so that Paul got the impression that his visit was friendly and possibly directed at improving relations between the estates. Paul had no quarrel with him and had indeed written him a formal letter when he read of his father's death on the Continent. He offered him whisky which Gilroy promptly accepted.

"I do apologise at interrupting you at work, Craddock," he said glancing at the littered table, "but I'm away up north tomorrow and I gave Owen-Hixon my word I would call, although"—and he smiled, pleasantly—"I must confess it was at his insistence rather than mine! You won't have met Captain Owen-Hixon yet? He'll be opposing your man at the next election, and the local party were lucky to get him! He'll give Jimmy Grenfell a good run for his money, I'm told."

As Paul waited for Gilroy to come to the point it struck

him that father and son were about as unlike one another as was possible in an inbred family like the Gilroys. Whereas the original Lord Gilroy had stood on this same hearthrug, looking and behaving as if he was paying a call on a recalcitrant cottager, his son had the cheerful expansiveness of a company director trying to interest a prospective shareholder in a doubtful bill of goods.

Paul said, hoping to shed light on Gilroy's presence, "The Unionist candidate asked you to call? Didn't he know I was deeply committed to the Liberals?" and Gilroy said laughing, that he did indeed but the candidate had described Squire Craddock as "a lost sheep who might be happy to return to the fold in view of Lloyd George's 'People's Budget', a frontal attack on every landowner in the British Isles."

"Did you agree with him?" Paul asked and Gilroy said that he did not, for he flattered himself that he knew his enemy better. "However," he said cheerfully, "since I'm here I might as well say what I came to say, providing you'll pay me the compliment of listening! Frankly, some of the local committee feel that recent events have caused you to have second thoughts about Liberal policy. They wanted to descend on you with a deputation, the fools, and I give you my word that it was me who stopped them! I remembered the drubbing you gave my father when he called soon after you took over the estate!" and he chuckled, appreciatively. "You were the only person about here who ever sent my father packing with a flea in his ear!"

"It wasn't really me," Paul admitted ruefully, "it was my first wife and I daresay she could do better now. From what I read in the newspapers, however, she seems to expend all her ammunition on the Government!"

Gilroy looked uncomfortable for a moment, as though he had expected Paul to gloss over his oblique reference to Grace but he said, "You are still in touch with her?", and Paul said he was not but that the antics of suffragettes were breakfast-talk all over the country.

"Ah, yes," Gilroy said thoughtfully, "but I can't help feeling that militancy won't get them far, although our people ought not to complain. They have intervened in several important bye-elections already and very much to our advantage. Asquith, I hear, can't speak in public for five minutes without being expertly heckled! However, it wasn't suffragettes that I came to talk about, Craddock."

"Go ahead, by all means," Paul said, deciding that the son was infinitely more likeable than his crusty old father.

"Well," said Gilroy, "there are people on our committee here who find it difficult to believe that a man owning your acreage can stay in step with firebrands like Lloyd George and that pirate Churchill! After all, social progress in an industrial state is one thing but highway robbery is quite another! I imagine you keep in touch with national issues or is your interest in politics purely local?" He paused but when Paul said nothing, he went on, "You don't have to answer my questions, of course, not even out of politeness. You can send me packing as promptly as you sent my father and I'm damned if I'd hold it against you! After all, we may be at war but wars can be fought by gentlemen."

"I don't mind answering your questions in the least," Paul said slowly, "but there's no prospect of me crossing the floor if that's what your committee hopes. I'm not deeply concerned with what happens in Westminster, it's true, for I've always thought of an M.P. as a man who ought to concern himself with his own constituents. After all, that was the original intention, wasn't it?"

"A long time ago," Gilroy replied, "but I'm entirely with you. Have you studied these latest proposals, the way the Chancellor proposes to get the money for this insurance scheme of his? It'll come largely from us, you know. Don't you feel any resentment at all?"

Paul had asked himself this several times during the last few weeks, after the London papers had carried reports of Lloyd George's sensational proposals to raise income tax to 1s. 2d. in the pound, increase death duties by a third on estates of more than £5,000, and slap heavy taxes on land of enhanced value, even if it remained undeveloped but the proposals had not weakened his loyalty to the party as a whole, or to James Grenfell in particular. It would sound, he thought, rather smug to admit this to a far wealthier landowner like Gilroy but the fact was he had never really thought of himself as a wealthy person, and had never been able to interest himself in money as money. He regarded it still as a means of feeding and improving the estate and he could not see how Lloyd George's proposals, that had set most landowners about the ears, could make much difference to the future of the Valley. In any case some kind of insurance scheme was surely due to poor devils cooped up in shops, offices and factories all the year round. He did not say this, however, for it seemed to him a holier-than-thou attitude. Instead, he said, guardedly, "I imagine the Chancellor has to get money from somewhere. You people have been insisting for years that we play snap with the Kaiser as regards naval strength and dreadnaughts can't be built for nothing, Lord Gilroy."

"Indeed they can't," Gilroy replied affably. " 'We want EIGHT And We Won't Wait!' but although I'm not surprised by your attitude—your personal attitude that is—I must admit that I am by its broader implications. After all, it's plain to me looking across the Sorrel that you're as deeply traditionalist as was my father and you're far more attached to the old way of life than I am, who was born to it! How do you marry your cricket-on-the-green notions to the clamour for a New Order, led by men primarily concerned with industrialisation?"

"I've never set my face against change," Paul said, defensively, "and I should have thought that was known in this area. I admit I want to preserve, and even people like Grenfell regard me as a bit old-fashioned but if the old system isn't prepared to bend it will break and I wouldn't like that to happen. I suppose that's why I'm a Liberal."

"Curious," Gilroy said thoughtfully, "for I believe the exact opposite and that's why I vote Unionist. I don't think our system was built to bend but if it's tampered with too much it will break, and then we'll all be in trouble! Still . . . ," and he stood up extending his hand, "I'm bound to say I respect your views, Craddock. I'll fight you when the election comes up and I'll fight damned hard but I hope you'll never regard me as a personal enemy, or associate with me all the party mudslinging that is inevitable!"

"I'm delighted you called," Paul said and meant it, for the feud had always seemed to him very childish. "I take it you will inform the new candidate and the committee that the lost sheep prefers to remain lost!"

"I will indeed," Gilroy said, chuckling, "as a matter of fact I shall rather enjoy doing that, Craddock!" and Paul walked him to the forecourt where his shiny French motor awaited him, a straight-faced chauffeur sitting erect behind the enormous brass steering wheel. The big car moved off smoothly, trailing a cloud of blue exhaust and Paul thought, "Damn it, one can't help liking the chap, but if he's so keen on preservation why the devil does he have to poison the Valley with that stinking contraption?"

Claire came to him, calling "Who was it?" as she crossed the paddock and he said, helping her over the rail and slipping his arm round her waist, "That was only young Gilroy kite-flying. He wanted to know whether I would jettison Grenfell on account of Lloyd George's land piracy!" and her laughter comforted him, for he could not help reflecting how different Grace would have reacted. "It's odd," he said, "the last time a Gilroy called here he succeeded in getting me married! Did you ever hear about that?"

"No," she said, "but before I forget to tell you the twins are talking!"

"That's Simon's idea of talking, to me they only gurgle."

"No," she protested, "Andy can say a word or two—he's already about three months ahead of Steve and he'll be walking in a matter of weeks. Simon has him in the nursery now. He's very good for them, you know, and they worship him," and he forgot all about Gilroy as she talked of the relationship between the three children so that he thought, as soon as she had gone, "She's so different from Grace and I suppose some husbands might be bored with her but I'm jiggered if I am!" and went whistling into the yard calling to Chivers to harness the trap for a seed-buying trip to Paxtonbury.

As though Valley drums had relayed news of Gilroy's

visit to Westminster, Grenfell wired that he was coming down that same week and Paul, meeting him at Sorrel Halt, drove him across Blackberry Moor and listened to lobby gossip that never found its way into the West-country editions of the London newspapers.

He found the Member depressed and glad of a few days' rest in the country, as well as an opportunity to confide in Paul his fears of the outcome of the next election.

"In spite of our majority we're having to fight every inch of the way," he admitted. "We've had to compromise on the new dreadnaughts to get the support we need for social legislation and Irish Home Rule but the P.M. has his hands full with that Cabinet and finds them a difficult team to drive! Some would call the Kaiser's bluff and let him build as many blasted battleships as he likes but at the other end of the scale we have the well-britched, who think L.G. is biting off far more than he can chew! The Lords will throw the budget out, of course, but that only means we shall have to go to the country. I promise you, it's been a devil of a sitting! I can't tell you how glad I am to turn my back on it for a day or so."

He talked, with his customary lucidity, on a wide variety of topics but Paul noticed that he avoided mentioning women's suffrage and the havoc the militants were causing at the public meetings, doing this, he felt, out of motives of delicacy. In the meantime, however, Paul was content to listen, receiving an account of Grenfell's stewardship up to the end of the third year of the Government's span and asking for details of the Chancellor of the Exchequer's proposed new land taxes. Grenfell, he thought, hedged a little on this, as though he shared the local Unionists' suspicions that a man owing fourteen hundred acres might jib at facing a stiff increase of taxes including a levy on increment value and the exploitation of mineral rights, so that when Paul told him of Gilroy's visit he made no attempt to hide his relief. "By George," he said, "I'm delighted to hear that, Paul! I couldn't help wondering if you'd be tempted to ditch us and I suppose one could hardly blame you if you did! Was it loyalty to me that made you spit in his face?"

"No," Paul admitted, "not entirely. If I was that interested in money I wouldn't be down here pouring it into the Valley. I'm all for giving the working chap a larger slice of cake but not, if I'm honest, for philanthropic reasons. Universal suffrage means they'll get the slice one way or another and if it's denied them indefinitely they'll just up and take it! Gilroy and his people don't appear to realise that. They think that they can keep all the advantages of feudalism and still use the short cuts of a highly industrialised society. I notice he's running around in a damned great motor and it wasn't even British made! Maybe you could score a point there in one of your election speeches, James."

Grenfell did not respond to this quip but continued to look preoccupied, so that when they reached the river road Paul reined in, saying, with a smile, "Well, what is it, James? Has it anything to do with the suffragettes?"

The Member looked confused for a moment but then his brow cleared. "You're getting very sharp for your old age, Paul! I always did say you'd make a politician. Yes, it *has* to do with the suffragettes! The fact is, I intend to back them at the recall in the autumn," and when Paul exclaimed in amazement, he went on, hurriedly, "No, wait! I haven't told anyone this because I felt you should be the first to judge my motives. I suppose, knowing your first wife so well, I got in on the ground floor of the controversy but for a long time I wasn't convinced. There was so much else to be done and all of it uphill work. Then it became clear that the Cabinet was very divided on the subject and that many Liberal Members, as convinced as I am that women's suffrage is inevitable, are hoping to hold it at bay as long as possible and maybe pass it to the Tories as a hot potato! Well, some of the colours have faded for me since I graduated from soap-box to the House and discovered how fiendishly difficult the art of government really is but not so much as I can't distinguish black from white! What our people are doing to those women at the moment is a damned outrage! If the Tories did it we should make all the capital we could of their manhandling women in the streets and forcibly feeding in gaol!"

"I've only unpleasant memories and newspaper talk to help me form an opinion," said Paul dryly, "but it does seem to me that some of them enjoy martyrdom! Besides, can we really afford to let a noisy minority blackmail Parliament?"

"One thing at a time, Paul," Grenfell said. "First, are you capable of viewing this issue without prejudice?"

"No," Paul admitted, "I don't suppose I am, for 'The Cause', as they call it, made a bad joke out of my first marriage. For all that I don't still bear a grudge against Grace. Why should I? I'm happier now than ever I was in my life and by every conceivable yardstick Claire is a far better wife and, for that matter, a better mother to Grace's own child. However, no man cares to remember he was once the laughing-stock of everyone about here!"

"That's prejudice for a start," Grenfell said, "for you were never that, Paul! I've always had my finger on the pulse of the Valley and everyone who mattered was deeply sorry for you at the time."

"All right, they were sorry for me but either way I'm not predisposed to suffragettes!"

Grenfell picked up his briefcase, unstrapped it, and took out a buff folder. "Take a look at this," he said, "it's one of several and not the worst by any means! It isn't a fake either, although it was suppressed by the editor whose photographer took it. He thought it might enlist too much public sympathy."

Paul looked at a picture, an eight by six photograph, reproduced on coarse newsprint. It was a close-up of a mêlée outside the Houses of Parliament. In the foreground two bearded policemen were frog-marching a young woman through a mob of bystanders, most of whom appeared to be shouting abuse. The woman had been well dressed but her clothes were in terrible disarray, blouse torn, one shoe gone and hat lying on the ground under the horse of a mounted policeman in the background. The woman was screaming. He said, handing it back, "Well, I must say it doesn't do the London police much credit," and James, dipping into his folder again, handed him another picture, this time printed on glossy paper. It showed a similar scrimmage but in this case a policeman was looking on, whilst three young men in straw hats bundled a middle-aged woman down a flight of stone steps outside a hall. The policeman was grinning and so were several male bystanders standing under a banner reading, *"Liberal Rally, Men Only"*. The most unpleasant aspect of the incident, Paul thought, was not the violence used, although this was shocking but the obvious source of male merriment. The lower part of the woman's body was exposed showing her underclothes as far as her waist and her skirt was ripped almost in half.

"I could show you a lot more," James said grimly, "I've made a collection of them. I think I'll call the dossier *'England, 1909—Under a Liberal Government Pledged to Reform.'*"

Paul said bitterly, "Is there one of Grace?" and James, touching his arm said, "No, but I have an accurate cartoon from the paper she edits. It shows forcible feeding in Holloway. Will you look at it?"

He handed him a small magazine and on the front page was a drawing of a woman held by four wardresses in a tilted chair. A man bending over her was inserting feeding tubes into the prisoner's nostrils. There was a dark smudge where the woman's mouth should have been, arrowed with the words *"Metal Gag."*

"Great God," Paul muttered, "is that what the papers call 'hospital treatment'?"

"I haven't seen forcible feeding," said Grenfell, "but I've seen practically everything else! The police aren't so bad—they're often in a difficult position—it's the public who make me vomit! I've seen young men drag women along the ground holding them round their breasts and some of these poor devils, whose only desire is to want a share in making the country's laws, are half dead when they come out of gaol! I'll tell you something else too! When a man takes his seat in Parliament he soon learns to vote with his head rather than his heart, for it is never much use judging an issue emotionally. However, a line has to be drawn somewhere, unless one is to become a mere voting machine. I've been pushed over that line after witnessing W.S.P.U. lobbying of Members of Parliament. Apart from that I've attended all-male political

579

meetings they managed to penetrate and seen them man-handled by dirty-minded stewards. When I make my next public speech down here I'm pulling no punches! I'm not simply paying lipservice to women's votes, I'm going to attack what's happening inside gaol and out of it!"

"How will that affect your poll?"

"Very adversely, I should say."

"This new man of theirs, Owen-Hixon, is supposed to be a maneater," Paul said. "Do you know anything about him?"

"Yes," said Grenfell, "I know all about him and it'll be touch and go whether I hold the seat! He's fought two strongly held Liberal boroughs and came near to pitching our man out on both occasions. It's odd that Gilroy should have approached you like that but I hope you believe me when I say I would have warned you of my decision in any case. Would you like to think it over for a day or so?"

"Yes, perhaps I would, James," Paul said, "but for a personal reason that isn't affected by my own views. Will you lend me those pictures until tomorrow?"

Grenfell gave him the file and they drove on in silence. Presently Grenfell said, "You were wise, I think, to stay here and accept limitations, Paul. If more of us did that, we wouldn't need a London talking-shop at all!"

Paul noticed at dinner that James paid Claire the same grave courtesy he had shown towards Grace, although Claire's complete ignorance of political issues, which she was not ashamed to admit, meant that she was unable to spark him off, as Grace had done so effortlessly. The conversation was therefore confined to Valley topics and when she had retired to take a final look at the children, James said, puffing at his cigar: "There's not much doubt about your luck having changed, Paul, and you need not have proclaimed your personal happiness back at Codsall Bridge—it shouts at me from all parts of the house!" Afterwards, in the dusk, they walked together through the orchard and across the meadow as far as Hazel Potter's squirrel oak and Grenfell stood for a moment looking down the Valley to the Bluff: "Keep it like this, Paul!" he said suddenly, "don't ever let them change it, so long as you've breath in your body!", and Paul replied, "I made up my mind to that the first day I stood here, James!" and they went slowly back to the house, now lying half invisible in a bowl of violet dusk.

It was after midnight when Paul went up to find Claire still reading in the glow of her bedside lamp. She kept a bedside book called *Rural Anecdotes* and often read a page or two before she slept. Paul knew the book well, a selection of passages from Goldsmith, Cobden, and Borrow, interspersed with lighter passages from Surtees and verses from Wordsworth, Raleigh and Kit Marlowe. He said, throwing Grenfell's bluff file on the bed, "Here's a different sort of reading, Claire! It isn't likely to induce sleep but it's important to me that you see it! I'll tell you why in a moment."

She took the file and looked at the pictures one by one. He saw her mouth tighten once or twice but she made no comment until he had slipped in beside her and, without extinguishing the lamp, settled her head on his shouder. This, for him, was always the most rewarding moment of the day and they would sometimes lie so for half-an-hour before going to sleep, talking of this and that, of the children and domestic problems, of topics like Will Codsall's intention to reclaim more heath land and the comic situation in the Dell, where the Goliath of Bideford was still maintaining his brace of submissive wives, of anything and everything in their tiny world bounded by sea, the Sorrel and railway line. He told her then of Grenfell's decision and of his own dilemma. If women's suffrage was made a platform issue at the coming election how would he stand as Grenfell's chairman at the meetings? Would not people find it curious that he, once cuckolded by The Cause, was publicly advocating it? Then he touched on the real issue. Might not his backing of James in this field imply that he still hankered after his first wife? For this, he admitted, was something of which he must be sure before James returned to London.

She said, after hearing him out, "I think you're being morbid, Paul! It's plain from these pictures that James has made the right decision. I don't know what you think of votes for women but I know how I feel right now! If I was a man, committed to politics, I think I should know precisely what to do."

"And what's that?" he said, shifting slightly so that he could look down at her.

"I should back him for all I was worth!" she said, "and to the devil with what people think or don't think! I'm sure of you now and that's all I care!"

"Turn out the lamp," he said, "and don't reintroduce politics again tonight on pain of getting your bottom smacked!"

She reached out and turned the screw and it was only then that he remembered that the moon was almost full, for the big room was flooded with a light as hard and bright as silver. Yet she disobeyed him after all for just before she slept, she said, as though addressing not so much him but herself, "I suppose I must be as far behind the times as any woman alive! I'll use the vote if we get it but I can't work up much enthusiasm on the subject. Is that why they have to fight so hard do you suppose? Because so many women like me are satisfied to trot between nursery, kitchen and double bed?" He made no reply and his regular breathing told her he was already asleep.

II

The campaign of January 1910 saw the most bitter electioneering in the history of the constituency. Neither candidates nor leading supporters emerged unscathed from the contest.

Captain Owen-Hixon, the new Unionist contender, fought a merciless campaign, appearing, however, in the role of a puff-adder rather than the lion they had been promised. He not only employed conventional ammunition to attack the Government but the brickbats supplied by Grenfell himself after he had openly proclaimed his belief in women's suffrage.

The main issue in the fight was the proposed land taxes and the Unionist, an exceptionally accomplished speaker with a knack of cutting hecklers down to size, hammered out his thesis day after day and night after night, warning the electorate, most of whom looked to agriculture for a living, that the budget would mean all-round contraction on the part of landowners and therefore unemployment among farm labourers in the area. Paul, as the only landowner supporting the Liberals, came in for persistent sniping for Owen-Hixon lampooned him as an amateur farmer, protected from the full effects of the new taxes by a steady flow of capital from a London scrapyard. He implied, and came close to stating openly, that the Shallowford estate was bolstered by profits from the South African War and the jibe was the more lethal because Grenfell had never ceased to denounce the war as a capitalist adventure. Owen-Hixon also made play of an alleged attempt on the part of the Government to sacrifice national safety to a vote-catching policy built on the new insurance scheme, painting lurid pictures of what would happen to Britain when the Kaiser's growing naval strength enabled Germany to challenge the Empire on the high seas. As to Grenfell's sudden infatuation with "the livelier ladies"—the Unionist turned Grenfell's criticism of forcible feeding back upon him by saying that he was puzzled to know why, since his friend felt so strongly on this matter, he was still aligned with Lloyd George, Asquith and Winston Churchill, the principal persecutors of the suffragettes.

In only one exchange did the Liberals come off with the honours and that was at Owen-Hixon's eve-of-poll rally, in the Paxtonbury Corn Exchange, where the heroes were a pair of determined Liberal hecklers. On this occasion Owen-Hixon, carried away by his own eloquence, made a jeering comparison between Lord Gilroy, a landowner with three centuries of tradition behind him and his neighbour Craddock, who, no doubt, would lose interest in farming as soon as the new tax was imposed and seek some other diversion, perhaps milling flour for the suffragettes to throw at Liberal Cabinet Ministers! In the laughter touched off by this sally Henry Pitts, of Hermitage Farm, rose from a gangway seat about a third of the way down the hall and demanded to know of Lord

583

Gilroy, in the Chair, how much he paid his workers on the Heronslea home farm? The question was ruled out of order but Henry remained on his feet, buttressed by the immovable Sam Potter and read out a short list of weekly payments made to Heronslea and Shallowford farm-labourers. The wages showed a difference of around seven shillings a week in favour of Squire Craddock and in the momentary hush that followed this announcement Henry added, genially, "So mebbe tiz as well us didden get an answer from the Chair! Saved ole Gilroy tellin' a string o' bliddy lies, didden it?"

At this the Unionist stewards made a concerted rush for Henry, now standing one seat in from the centre aisle. In their eagerness to eject him, however, they overlooked Sam Potter who threw his chair under the feet of the foremost and floored two others with his fists. Before re-inforcements could be rushed round from the sides of the hall the two Shallowford men had escaped via an exit, Henry felling another steward *en route*. They left the meeting in an uproar and made their way to Liberal headquarters, congratulating one another on the success of their sally. Neither man, out of his cups, was a talkative individual. All Henry said was, "Well, us *told* un, didden us, Sam?" and Sam replied, "Arr, an' us *showed* 'un, didden us, Henry?"

Claire stood beside Paul and Grenfell on the day following the ballot and watched the votes pile up on each table as the boxes were opened by the tellers. By midday the result was announced from the balcony of the Town Hall. James Grenfell had lost his seat by the narrow margin of eighty-seven votes. Captain Owen-Hixon was the new Member for Paxtonbury Vale.

Grenfell, Paul thought, took his defeat stoically. On the way back to Shallowford, as their trap breasted the northern swell of the moor, James said, with a sigh, "Well, Paul, nobody could call it a clean fight but at least it was a lively one! Without you I could never have saved my face, let alone my seat and I'd like you to know I'm grateful for that! Maybe a year or so on the home beat won't do me any harm, for it's my guess we shall be at it again before long. Today's result all over the country is

584

something and nothing, the main issues can never be resolved without a clear-cut majority."

Paul said nothing, feeling far too raw to take pleasure in an inquest but he reflected glumly that Grenfell's championship of suffragettes had cost him far more than eighty-seven votes. It was left to Claire to comment further on the issue and as they turned on to the river road she said, cheerfully, "Well, I wouldn't worry if I were you, James! To my way of thinking you didn't lose out on your policy but on your chivalry and it was about the only spark I saw struck in that mudfight!", and to emphasise her point she squeezed his hand so that Paul, seeing the movement out of the corner of his eye, thought, "By God, if James was lucky enough to find a wife like Claire she'd put him back all right and with a thumping majority!"

As they passed Codsall bridge they saw Eveleigh and his family standing in a forlorn cluster to give the loser a cheer and Grenfell, waving acknowledgement, looked across the winter fields towards the Teazel watershed and said, "The grass roots are right here, Paul. We ought never to forget that, lad!"

III

News of the sudden death of King Edward came to the Valley in the full flush of Maytime; to Paul, who had settled here the summer Edward was crowned, it seemed as if the brief reign completed a personal as well as a national cycle.

The first rumour reached the Valley by one or other of the two telephones in Coombe Bay, and was later confirmed by the heavy black border round the front-page advertisements of the *County Advertiser* but Paul, knowing that some of the tenants living off the main road would be unlikely to see the weekly newspaper for another day, decided to go his rounds, at least, this was the excuse he offered Claire at breakfast. She was not taken in, remembering the long drought of the coronation summer when he had first arrived among them and well knowing his

585

trick of separating the phases of his life into little packages of seasons and years. He would see the death of Edward, she thought, as the end of a Valley era and for an hour or so would want to ride alone, savouring his modest achievements here. She said, kissing him, "Go along then Paul Revere, and proclaim the news among the Potterites and the Codsallites in the Wilderness," and he rode off, taking the river road along the park wall in the direction of Codsall bridge.

He noticed, on passing the Timberlake cottage, that someone had hung a bunch of crepe on the knocker and drawn the parlour blinds, as though the royal corpse lay inside. Old Mrs. Timberlake, allegedly one hundred and four, had died the previous summer, and perhaps it was her late mother-in-law's incredible age linking her with George III, that had prompted Mrs. Timberlake junior to show this special mark of respect to royalty. Yet Paul found himself unable to share in a sense of loss that morning, for the sun was bright, kingfishers flashed along the Sorrel stream, the hedgerows were a riot of flowers and he had never seen King Edward in the flesh. He could think of him with mild affection, however, recalling the headshakes of the wiseacres when the portly, sixty-year-old rake succeeded his mother. Everybody had said he would introduce sweeping changes in the Court and they had been right but some of their other prophecies remained unfulfilled. He had proved an unexpectedly popular monarch and even his weaknesses, the chain-smoking of cigars and his obsession with pretty women, the Turf and rackety characters associated with racing, had endeared him to the mass of English people. He was also said to be the only man alive who could browbeat the German Kaiser, his sabre-rattling nephew across the Channel, and if this was true, it was a pity that he had not ascended his throne earlier and saved everybody a great deal of money by discouraging Wilhelm from building a navy. He thought, as he rode down the Four Winds track, "I suppose we shall have to do something to mark the occasion. Perhaps Parson Horsey will want to hold a special service and if he does I shall have to appear with Claire and the children," and then he saw the oldest Eveleigh boy forking dung and called, "Hullo, there! Is your father about?", and at that moment Marian Eveleigh emerged from the dairy with her daughter, Rachel, a rosy sixteen-year-old, carrying a pail of skimmed milk for the pigs. Marian said, "Good morning, Squire! You've heard the news I suppose?", and Paul said he had and was sorry but all Marian replied was, "Well, to tell 'ee the truth, Squire, I'm surprised 'ee lasted so long! He was very weak in the chest you know!"

She talked, Paul thought, as though the King had lived in one of the tall, red-brick houses in Coombe Bay where the royal bronchitis was a parish topic. It occurred to him that modern communications were already having their effect upon people cut off from the cities, for how would a Tudor peasant have been able to comment on, say, the bronchial tubes of Henry VIII?

Eveleigh himself came out of the byre while they were talking and declared that Edward had proved a better man as King than as Prince of Wales. Paul suspected that Eveleigh, an austere man dedicated to hard work and simple living, was a republican at heart and the farmer seemed to confirm this by adding, "Well, it won't make much difference to me, I reckon! His son'll succeed him and they say he's a quiet sort of chap, don't they, Squire?"

"I believe they do," Paul said, smiling and deciding that Eveleigh was anxious to get on with his work he said good-bye and went on down the gangway between house and barn towards the higher ford. As he passed under the gable of the farmhouse he glanced up at the window of the room where he had looked on the bloody remains of Arabella Codsall but the memory had no power to dull the sparkle of the morning. Eveleigh, and his family of romping, rosy children, had exorcised the ghosts of Four Winds long ago.

He forded the shallow river a mile above the bridge and climbed the edge of the moor to Periwinkle, where Will and Elinor Codsall had heard nothing of the news from London and seemed more deeply impressed by it than the Eveleighs. Elinor's oldest child was now five, and already earning his keep egg-collecting. The farm was nearly double its original acreage, Will having reclaimed a wide strip of moorland and his poultry arks were dotted about the fields like a shanty town. Paul thought, as he gossiped with man and wife, "That was the first real decision I ever made about here—to get Will and Elinor married off and settled on their own and it was a good move, despite what happened afterwards." He remembered his first glimpse of the little woman now standing by Snowdrop's head, a slim, shy, slip of a thing, with hardly a word to say for herself and here she was, the mother of three children, the real master of the farm and the acknowledged poultry expert of the Valley. He wondered if the lumbering Will Codsall resented taking second place to her but decided not, for even now, as they stood in the yard talking, he was looking at her as though he would like to whisk her off into the clover. Codsall said, "Will us be havin' some kind o' funeral service, Squire? Us did for the Ol' Vic, I remember, Parson Bull preached a sermon on her, didden he, midear?" but Elinor said this was a matter between Squire and parson and that he had best get about his work upalong, while she brewed Squire a dish of tea.

He drank her tea and rode down across the great swathe of heather to Hermitage, wondering if any of them were ever put out by his casual visits. After all, they were tenants holding long leases, and were not answerable to him so long as they paid their rent each quarter-day, but as soon as he saw the broad, beaming face of Henry Pitts he knew that he was wrong and that most of them were flattered by his interest in their stock and day-to-day improvements and also that what little remained of their prejudice had disappeared since his re-marriage. Henry called, "Top o' the marnin', Squire! Mr. Grenfell was passin' by yesterday an' I told un, us'll 'ave him back in no time! Us will too, you can depend on it!"

Paul recalled then that Henry's triumphant foray in the Corn Exchange had made him an enthusiastic supporter of Grenfell and that he was now honorary treasurer of the Valley Liberals. Leaving him to his beloved saddlebacks Paul rode into the yard and entered the big kitchen where Martha Pitts and Henry's great tawny wife, Gloria, were apparently enjoying a private joke for they stopped laughing and looked shamefaced when they saw Paul on the threshold. There was always laughter here, he reflected, and enquired after Henry's eldest boy, who had recently broken an arm climbing an elm to get at a rook's nest.

"Oh, er's well enough, Squire," Gloria said casually. " 'Twoulden surprise me if 'er didden come in with t'other one broke tomorrow! Bones mend zoon enough at his age, dorn 'em now?" He told them that rumours of the King's death had been confirmed by the newspapers and at this they both put on straight faces, holding the expressions until Gloria said, nudging her mother-in-law, "Well, if all I yer about 'un be true, he had a wonderful run for 'is money, didden 'er?" and Martha said, "Shhh! Dornee talk like that!" and pretended to be shocked, so that Paul left them hiding his own grin and rode to the top of Hermitage plateau where he could look down over the wide Valley, something he never failed to do when he was this way.

It was a day for remembering. He recalled coming here with Grace on a summer morning, a long time ago it seemed, the day they had punted across to the temple on the islet and made love like lovers meeting by stealth, and he wondered, briefly, where Grace was at this moment, and if she ever thought of him and remembered vistas like the one at his feet. Then a pair of coal-tits distracted him and he watched them flirting on the lower boughs of a chestnut, making a mental note to tell Horace Handcock, the local oracle on all matters ornithological, who had told him only last week, that, whereas the Valley was teeming with great-tits and blue-tits, he had not seen coal-tits hereabouts since he was a boy. The birds seemed almost tame, flitting about Snowdrop's head, darting in and out of the widely-spaced trees. He went down the main ride to the steep-banked lane leading to the mere, finding it alive with all kinds of water birds, moorhens, dabchicks, coots, a mallard and her family, and even a heron, standing like an old post in the shallows near the islet.

Sam's cottage seemed to be half-full of children, although Paul counted but four on the premises. The eldest, his godchild Pauline, was playing with her sister Georgina and the babies, making daisy chains for each of them as Paul called "Catch, Pauline!" and threw a penny which Pauline caught expertly, abndoning her charges to run in and fetch her mother, who Paul noticed was pregnant yet again, the fifth time in eight years. He thought, "Dammit, if they don't call a halt soon I shall have to build on to the cottage!"

"Sam's upalong, hauling timber," Joannie said, pointing towards the northern end of the woods, "did 'ee want un special, Squire?", and Paul said no, he had only looked in to tell them that the King was dead and Joannie said, "Cor! *Be* 'er now? Will Alix have to manage on 'er own then?", and Paul had to explain that Alexandra would not be Queen any more but would live in retirement, while her duties were taken over by the new Queen Mary, King George's wife. Joannie was interested but unconvinced. "Well, I daresay his missus will manage," she said, "but I can't say I call 'er to mind. Sam don't read, you see, so us don't get a paper but he sets a store by Queen Alix because we got her in the parlour," and she led Paul into the tiny front room that seemed never to be used and there on the wall was a gigantic double portrait of the late King and Queen Alexandra, Edward looking half-asphyxiated in a tight, gold-laced gorget and red tunic. "I always thought of 'er as the beautifulest woman I ever set eyes on," Joannie said solemnly, as though she too had died. "I mus' say I'm sorry for *her,* that I am!" and moved by the same instinct as the Timberlakes she pulled down the blind so that the room was almost in darkness despite the brightness of the sun outside.

He left her and went through the wild wood behind the cottage and over the escarpment, to strike the Bluff about half-way up where a briar-tangled path led to the Dell. Only children were there so he put Snowdrop at the path down which the Bideford Goliath had whipped his mistresses, and there, in the level field adjoining the cliff top, he found the Potter girls drawing water from the new well and emptying it into a great wooden pig-trough under the oaks.

They were obviously glad of an excuse to stop work and

came running, their broad, good-natured faces glistening with sweat. "Jem's off across the Teazel to buy wire," they told him in chorus. "He's minded to fence the strip under the trees tomorrow," Violet added, "on account of the pigs fattening quicker if they don't stray. We had to fetch a sow back from Deepdene and it put Jem in a rare old tizzy, didn't it, Cis?" Cis said it had indeed and Paul got the impression that the Potter girls were far more effectively subdued by their hired hand than were the Valley wives by their lawful husbands. He had been discussing the Dell situation only yesterday with Claire, expressing himself in agreement with Parson Horsey that something should be done to regularise the position, particularly as, in the New Year, the Potter sisters had presented Jem with a child apiece to add to the two whose fathers were the subject of much speculation in the Valley. Claire, laughing at his misgivings, told him to let well alone, pointing out that the Dell was paying its way for the first time in living memory. "He seems to have tamed them and that's an achievement," she said, and he had told her she was shameless and that sooner or later Parson Horsey would insist Jem marry one or the other.

"How does your mother get along with that fellow?" he asked and Cis said that Meg looked upon him as a son, Vi adding, resentfully, "An' no wonder, for since Jem come 'er's never done a stroke o' work about the varm, the lazy old slut!"

"Well," said Paul grudgingly, "I must say I've never seen the place looking tidier but Parson Horsey was very shocked indeed when he heard about those babies. It wouldn't surprise me if he doesn't pay you three a visit soon and insist on one of you getting married and living a respectable life, like your sister Pansy."

The girls' faces fell and Violet said, virtuously, "What bizness is it o' the Passon how us arranges things? Jem loves the pair of us equally, dornee, Cis? Besides, Jem won't take no account o' what Passon says, 'er was brought up strict Baptist!"

Paul could think of no reply at all to this so he left them, chuckling as he crossed the cliff fields to call in upon Smut, whose glasshouse was now a blaze of colour and who greeted him cheerily. When Paul told of the death of the King he stood to attention, as though on parade and said, " 'Er's dade is 'er? Then God bless him, Squire, us'll miss him, I reckon!", after which, having paid his respects to the House of Hanover, he drew Paul's attention to a well-stocked wire basket swinging from the cross bar of the greenhouse and said, "Do 'ee think Mrs. Craddock could vind a place fer that on the terrace o' the big house, Squire? I've a few left over and I'd like to maake her a present of un, seein' as she so admired the early ones us had when her was yer last."

"I'm sure she'd be delighted, Smut," Paul said, "but she would want to pay the proper price for it."

"No, 'er worn't, Squire!" said Smut, "for you stood by me like a brother backalong and I'm the last man in the Valley to forget it! Us'll put the basket aside and the boy can drop it off on the way back tonight!"

Smut was sufficiently unprejudiced, Paul decided, to give advice on the situation in the Dell and after thanking him for the gift said: "Can't you persuade your mother to talk Jem into making a choice between Cissie and Violet? She must know that everyone from here to Paxtonbury is sniggering about what is going on down there!"

"Well," said Smut, with a grin that recalled the poacher for a moment, "tiz been goin' on ever since they was young maids, Squire, an' the only diff'rence is that now all us knows where they be whereas us never did in the old days! If you want my advice, Squire, leave things to zettle 'emselves, for not even old Tamer could keep the drawers hoisted on they two, nor their sister Pansy neither till her got 'erself married and was brought to bed once a year reg'lar! The fact is Jem's a match for the two of 'em and they lives in fear an' dread of 'im half the time, which do make for peace an' quiet over there as well as gettin' a yield out o' fields that was left lyin' fallow in Tamer's day!"

"You mean Jem is a brute to them?" said Paul, surprised that such a genial-looking man could terrorise two such experienced harlots as Cissie and Violet Potter, but Smut said he was not, not by any means, and would always defer to Meg, but was not above whopping the girls when they needed it, a privilege the law did not deny any husband in the land!

"But hang it man, Jem isn't married to either one of them," Paul argued. "He's only a hired man as far as I'm concerned."

"Arr, that may be, Squire," Smut conceded, "but they maids have never been partic'lar about churching, 'ave 'em? And since you ask me I woulden wish either one of 'em on any man in the Valley save Jem, who can look after himself! No, Squire, you let the tongues wag, same as they have ever since the girls growed big enough to start 'em waggin'! Us is doin' very well over this side an' tiz all on account o' Jem knowing when to give rein an' when to shorten it!"—and with that Paul had to be content, reflecting that it was precisely the same advice given him by his wife on the subject. He turned the grey on to the cliff path and rode over the shoulder of the Bluff to the head of Coombe Bay's single, broad street, lifting his hand in acknowledgement to almost everyone he met and recalling the first, scorching day he had ridden down to the tiny harbour in the company of John Rudd.

The village was a good deal changed now. Nearly a score of cottages had been gathered into the estate, re-thatched and let on long leases. There had been social changes too, for the low-church Parson Horsey had re-conciled the agricultural church folk and nonconformist fishermen. A sub-post office had opened next door to The Raven, so that it was now possible to send telegrams if despatchers did not mind their contents being broadcast all over the Valley within the hour. One of the ugly Vic-torian villas, where Grace's stepmother Celia had lived, was occupied by a retired army major who collected but-terflies, and the other by an elderly German, called Scholtzer, said to have exiled himself as a protest against the Kaiser's militarism and to save his son from being conscripted into the Prussian army. Paul had spoken to the German once or twice and found him civil enough, a short, fat, moon-faced man, who looked as if he had strayed out of a German band but was, according to John Rudd, a former professor of history at Jena University. He stopped and had a word or two with Abe Tozer,

the smith, and saw Mrs. Walter Pascoe, Pansy Potter that
was, with her tribe of children on the strip of sand where
the nets were drying. Then he turned west, through the
back lanes, intending to cut across the dunes and rejoin
the river road beyond the Four Winds southern boundary,
but on the outskirts of the village he stopped at the
ruined brickworks, recognising a slim, bespectacled youth
engaged in some kind of survey of the derelict area. It
was Sydney Codsall, now nineteen, and articled to Snow
and Pritchard, solicitors of Whinmouth.

It was over a year since he had seen the boy, so he
reined in and hailed him across the ruined wall. Sydney
looked startled and fumbled with the reel of tape he was
holding, so Paul called again, "What's going on, Sydney?
Is somebody thinking of restarting Manson's kilns?"

The boy came towards him reluctantly and Paul realised that, although he had always felt sorry for him, he
was a difficult boy to like. He was a misfit in the Valley
and his year or so in an office since leaving school had
encouraged him to slough off what little influence the
jolly Eveleigh family had had upon him, when he lived at
Four Winds. His face was long and narrow and his carroty hair was sleekly brushed and evidently oiled, for it
gleamed wetly in the afternoon sun. He favoured neither
his father nor mother, Paul thought, and walked alone,
exuding a faint odour of patronage, as though he had been
glad to shed the stigma of sweat and stable straw and
climb into the more genteel atmosphere of streets and
offices. Seeing who it was Sydney touched his cap politely,
composing his sharp features into an expression of cautious humility.

"I'm sorry, I didn't see who was calling," he said in a
reedy voice that recalled Arabella nagging her husband
across the kitchen table. "The fect is, I was busy! I was
sent heah by Mr. Vicary himself!"

"Who is Mr. Vicary?" Paul asked and the boy's expression slipped a little, as though this was a question that
only a fool would ask.

"Why, he's our Chief Clurk, Mr. Craddock, my immediate superior at Snow and Pritchard's. He's not articled, of course, but he had the responsibility of training

me and this is the first assignment I've been given, measuring up so that the deeds can be proved you see." He went on to explain that Manson's heirs had disposed of the property and Paul did not conceal his surprise. He knew Manson had died back in the spring and that his odd bits of property, including the brickyard, had been willed to a relative in London but it piqued him that the solicitors had not approached him to buy the plot, for it was known that he was always in the market for land or cottages adjoining the estate boundaries. He had bought what was now Periwinkle Farm through Snow and Pritchard, and also the cliff land added to the High Coombe holding, and it now struck him that the boy found his presence here embarrassing. He said shortly, "Who bought it, Sydney?" but Sydney's face went blank once more.

"Well I . . . er . . . I'm not at liberty to say, Mr. Craddock! I don't think Mr. Vicary would like me to discuss the firm's business with a third party!"

"Damn it, I'm not a third party, and both you and Vicary should know it! Half the houses hereabouts are on the Shallowford maps and I particularly asked Mr. Snow to tell me when any others came on the market. Do you suppose he forgot about it?"

"I reely couldn't say, Mr. Craddock," replied Sydney, slightly intimidated now, "but I'll certainly tell him you enquired. However"—and Paul was now reminded of Arabella in a malicious mood—"I do assure you it is sold and that the purchaser won't consider re-selling. Shall I make an appointment for you, sir?"

"No," Paul growled, looking across the brick-strewn yard and deciding that it was hardly worth his trouble and then, relenting somewhat, "How do you like working in an office, Sydney?"

"I'm very well suited, thank you," Sydney said primly. "I find the work very much to my taste."

Paul smiled, reflecting that this was the way Arabella might have replied. "Well, that's splendid," he said and rode on, finding his humour slightly soured by the encounter but forgetting Sydney the moment he caught sight of the sun dancing on the shallow river under the Bluff. Sydney, however, did not forget him and pondered the conversation all that day, wondering if Vicary would cover up for him when the Squire raised the matter and deciding that he probably would, for it had been Vicary who had suggested Sydney should lay out some of his savings on the Manson property. Having reassured himself as regards this he began to rejoice in his brush with the Squire, telling himself that he had got the best of it. Sydney Codsall had never heard of the Chinese proverb "Why do you hate me? I have never helped you!" but he would have appreciated its wisdom. It was some years since he had declared secret war on Shallowford and the purchase of the brickyard, and other bits of Manson property, were his opening shots in this war. Vicary, the ageing clerk of Snow and Pritchard, had taken a liking to his junior, seeing in him the makings of a first-class business-man and an astute legal mind. Childless, he had set himself the task of guiding and inspiring the boy for it was no secret that Sydney Codsall would share equally in Martin Codsall's estate when he was twenty-one and at sixty-plus, with small prospect of a pension, an unarticled clerk had to look out for himself. He found the boy quick to learn, very neat and tidy, but, above all, refreshingly lacking in sentiment. When the matter of the Manson property had come up he had counselled Sydney to buy, pointing out that, although the new land taxes made it something of a liability this would be more than compensated by an inevitable rise in the price of building land and that Coombe Bay, a trifling community today, would expand as time went on and seaside holidays came within reach of all. Sydney had thought this sound reasoning and learning that brickyard, cottage and derelict shop were to be had for a little over a hundred pounds, he put his money down straight away. What he would do with his purchases he did not know but whatever it was it must, he felt, yield a profit. In the meantime it added greatly to his status. Perhaps, as time passed, there would be other and better opportunities but in the meantime he could wait. He was only nineteen and there were many examinations ahead; after all, Lloyd George had started life in a solicitor's office and was now Chancellor of the Exchequer.

596

In mid-July that year, Paul, Claire, John Rudd and Maureen travelled to High Wood to attend the annual athletic sports, the last Ikey would take part in, for he was due to leave at the end of term. They took with them six-year-old Simon, who was much attached to Ikey and sick with excitement at the prospect of watching his hero win races and collect cups. "I shouldn't be too sure about it, Simon," Claire warned him, as they climbed out of the carriage and joined the gaily-dressed crowd lining the ropes. "We can't guarantee Ikey will win, he might only come second, or third."

"Really, Mamma, how can you be so stupid?" Simon replied. "Ikey can run further than anyone in the world without even puffing!" and it was Simon rather than Claire who was proved right for Ikey, eighteen now, a double colour and Captain of his House, almost literally walked away with the half-mile, the mile and the steeplechase, as well as winning second place in the long jump and throwing the cricket ball.

Paul listened to the cheers with quiet pride, noting that Ikey was idolised by the smaller boys who screamed their enthusiasm when Ikey's long nicely-judged stride carried him ahead of the field. He thought, as he watched the boy step up to receive five silver cups from the local countess, "By God, it's a miracle! The first time I saw him he was wearing trousers three times too large for him, had a running nose and was driving a cart in a Bermondsey scrapyard! Today nobody could distinguish him from the best dressed of these languid young devils!" Maureen Rudd had other thoughts, recalling her first meeting with Ikey on Codsall bridge when he had been bewildered by the outcome of his plot to help the Squire. She glanced sideways at Claire, cool and elegant in green and white striped silk and showing off a very trim figure indeed for a mother of two expecting a third around Christmas-time. The boy, she thought, must have had an instinct about her; how else could he have known that a mis-spelled letter written on the advice of another woman would restore serenity to the Valley? And again she wondered if anything would be served by bringing it all into the open and telling Claire and Paul exactly how much they owed the boy passing back and forth across the headmaster's lawn to collect his cups but as always she decided to leave well alone and she hoisted Simon level with spectators' shoulders, so he could get a clear view of his hero.

It was during the tea interval, when Ikey was changing, that she asked Paul what Ikey intended to do now that his schooldays were ending and Paul said that as far as he was aware Ikey intended to try for a commission in a cavalry regiment and sit for the Sandhurst exam in the autumn.

"Well, I daresay the life will suit him," she said, without enthusiasm, "he's a sociable type and has plenty of —what do they call it—'Leadership qualities'? Still, the boy's undoubtedly got brains and he'll spend money rather than make it in the Officers' Mess. Couldn't he do something more original?"

"I'll have a word with his headmaster before he leaves," Paul told her and her enquiry set him thinking for, until then, he had never considered Ikey a person with money-making propensities.

Claire was enjoying herself very much in her own way. The mothers and sisters seemed to her a very fashionable set and it wasn't often she got a chance to mix with smartly-dressed women. The setting, she thought, was as remote and rural as the Valley, but today seemed self-consciously so, as if everyone here was taking part in an elaborate pastoral masque. There was an endless flirting of gloves and twirling of parasols, and the women swayed as they walked, wearing bright, fixed smiles and using courtly inclinations of the head. She thought, "If anyone wanted to paint a scene representative of England in the first summer of the new reign they couldn't do better than plant their easel by the long-jump pit and turn out something like Frith's 'Railway Station' or 'At The Seaside'. If they were good enough they might even catch the smugness and the well-fed looks on the faces of that picnicking group over there, or the strained, newly-arrived expression on the face of that little boy's plain sister, sitting alone near the hurdles." Then it occurred to her how very out of touch with the social world she and Paul were becoming down in the Valley and how un-repentant she felt about it, although she wasn't so sure it was altogether right for them to live such an enclosed life. For the first time since she had left London she reminded herself that this voluntary withdrawal on his part had been the rock on which his first marriage foundered and this encouraged her to think that perhaps there was something to be said for Grace after all. Taking advantage of a moment when everyone was talking to somebody else she said, "I'd forgotten people still fol-lowed fashions, Paul! Will you promise me something, while I remember?"

"You look attractive enough to extract any number of rash promises today, Claire," he told her but she said, "No, I'm serious! After the baby's born will you take me to London for the Coronation? I haven't been east of Paxtonbury since we married?"

"Well," he said, "I'll tell you what. Present me with a girl instead of another damned boy and it's a promise! And I don't give a row of beans if it's twins so long as it isn't one of each!"

"I'll see what can be aranged," she said and squeezed his hand as Ikey, looking self-consciously smart in his swallow-tailed coat and three-inch butterfly collar, joined them to say the Head could see Paul now and save him a special journey to school before end of term. So Paul followed him along stone corridors to a heavy, pseudo-Gothic door on which Ikey knocked and said, by way of introduction, "My guardian, sir!" and withdrew, leaving Paul confronted with a thick-set, scrubby-haired man about fifty, who shook his hand absent-mindedly and seated him in an obvious "parents" chair that engulfed him.

Paul had met the headmaster on several previous oc-casions and had found him rather remote, with a tendency to grant an interview with a parent as though it was unavoidable but a crashing bore just the same. Today, however, the man came alive and Paul concluded that his change of manner had some link with Ikey's athletic

599

triumphs for he began by saying, "Delighted you could get over, Mr. Craddock! In view of the fact that Palfrey is leaving this half I should have written in any case, but I appreciate an opportunity to tell you how wrong I was about the lad and how pleased I am to be wrong!" When Paul looked rather nonplussed at this he continued, "The fact is he began rather badly—that time he ran off to London and I admit that I wrote him off as a lad anxious to advertise himself as an individualist!"

"Isn't that encouraged?" asked Paul, deciding that he did not like the man much but the Head disarmed him with a professional smile and said, "Well, to be frank we don't cater to individualists here—not yet, at all events. It was during the last year or so that we began to succeed so spectacularly with your lad."

Paul murmured that his ward (he remembered just in time that "Ikey" was never used at High Wood) had been very happy at the school and that he was relieved to hear him well spoken of by his headmaster.

"Oh, it's rather more than that," the headmaster went on, "the fact is Palfrey has always puzzled me somewhat. He was never any trouble apart from that one time. He pulled his weight and made friends easily enough but frankly, I always had the impression he was . . . well . . . *laughing at us!* Does that sound extravagant?"

Paul thought, privately, "No, I'm damned if it does for he almost certainly was and jolly good luck to him! He got away with it, and I wonder what the old bird would saw if I told him Ikey came here from a London junk yard via my stables?" He said, aloud, "I've been wondering if we're doing the right thing encouraging him to take a commission, Headmaster. Have you any thoughts on the matter?"

The headmaster put on his "careers" look and said, with slight hesitation, "That . . . er . . . rather depends. Has he an army background?"

"I served through the South African War," Paul said, at last beginning to get the measure of the man, but all the Head said was, "Ah, that's not quite the same thing! You were Yeomanry, I expect, and you're his guardian, not his father."

600

"The old bird is fishing now," Paul thought, "but he'll catch nothing from me!" "I'm a relative," he said brazenly, "his sister was my first wife. Perhaps I never told you he was born on the Continent, or that his mother was an Austrian subject?"

The Head seemed vaguely impressed, remarking that the Austrians produced a large number of first-class equestrians, whereupon Paul said promptly that the boy could ride anything and had always had an exceptional flair for horses.

"Then I don't really see how we could improve on the cavalry," the headmaster went on. "After all, it's a pleasant life, particularly in Ireland and India. If he does well enough in Army Entrance he might get a good regiment although there's tremendous competition, I'm told," and when Paul made no reply he added, "Did you have anything else in mind?"

"No," Paul admitted, "I didn't but I think I should prefer him to take up a profession with more future in it."

"But surely there is a future in an Army career, Mr. Craddock?"

"Not in the cavalry," Paul said promptly, "at least, not in my opinion!"

"I'm afraid your opinion isn't generally shared," the Head said kindly, as though applying a gentle damper to a boy who had made a bad gaffe but needed encouragement. "The Chairman of our Governors, Lieutenant-General Manners-Smith, thinks the exact opposite and he was on Buller's staff in the Transvaal."

"I wouldn't wonder," Paul thought, "and got a lot of good chaps killed playing at Waterloo outside Ladysmith!" and suddenly he tired of phrase-juggling and began to wonder if, after all, High Wood was the kind of place he wanted for Simon and the twins when they had passed through Prep School. It had performed a miracle on Ikey but did his own boys stand in need of miracles? He said briefly, "I'll have a talk with the lad during the holidays, Headmaster, and if I need further advice perhaps I could write. If he really wants the Army I won't stand in his way," and he got up, extending his hand. And then another, more important thought struck him and he said, "You spoke well enough of him as a product of the school. How did he show up as a scholar?"

"Oh, average, average," said the Head airily, "but scholarship isn't everything, Mr. Craddock," implying that it counted for rather less than the ability to convert a try into a goal.

The matter was carried a step further early in the holidays as Paul and Ikey rode into Paxtonbury to look at a hunter recommended by Rose Derwent as "being worth a guinea over the odds". They had often travelled this road in company and for each of them it was usually a sentimental journey. Paul recounted the gist of his interview with the Head and Ikey was amused by Paul's confession that he had found the man too pretentious for his taste. "Oh, Sandy Mac is stuffy all right," he said tolerantly, "but he's a trier, a bit like you and I in a way," and when Paul asked what this meant he added, "He's not public school, you see and has to walk pretty carefully. His father was a postman, I believe, and he won a scholarship to a grammar school up north and afterwards went on to win first-class honours at Cambridge. You have to hand it to him for that. It was really why I played along with him."

Paul was intrigued by the boy's eye for the chinks in adult armour and also by his ability to judge people's real worth but the comment reminded him of the Head's remark—"I believe he was laughing at us" and he quoted it, expecting to outface the lad. He evidently failed for Ikey laughed so heartily that he lost a stirrup.

"He said *that?* Old Sandy Mac admitted that to you? Gee-whiz! He must have come close to twigging me after all!"

"The point is," said Paul seriously, "you've been playing charades ever since you went to school and I've been aiding and abetting you! Frankly I think it's been worth it but we don't have to go on playing them indefinitely! You're eighteen now and can make your own decisions!"

"Can I?" The boy was suddenly serious. "I can't you know, not really! Far too much has rubbed off on me. Oh, I'm not complaining, Governor, and I should hate you to think I was, I'm grateful for everything you've done for me but sometimes . . ."

He broke off and kicked his heels against the horse's flanks causing it to break into a trot. Snowdrop automatically increased his pace and when they drew level again Paul saw that the boy s eyes were troubled. "Look here, Ikey," he said, "you don t have to confide everything to me but I'll always listen if you want to and don't ever forget it! I started this conversation with the idea of finding out if you had made up your mind about taking Army Entrance in October and going to Sandhurst. The last time we talked about it you had no doubts. Have you had any since?"

Ikey reined in and both horses stopped near the brow of the hill; another fifty yards and they would top the crest and begin the long descent into the Paxtonbury bowl.

"The Army would cost you money, Governor; it could go on costing you money indefinitely."

"I can afford it and if you really want to take a commission I'll back you. The real issue is—would you prefer to train for something else, for one of the professions? Or would you care to go on to University and make your final decision there?"

The boy said, with a shrug, "It isn't that easy, Governor. At my reckoning I m only about two-thirds a gent; maybe not as much as that, maybe only three-fifths! You couldn't anticipate that when you sent me to High Wood but that's how it happened, a good part of me was still . . ."

"In the scrapyard? That's damned nonsense, Ikey, and I believe you know it!"

"I wasn't going to say 'scrapyard'," Ikey said, gently, "I had that beaten *before* I went to school. But I was happy in the stable-yard and deep down I never wanted or expected anything better."

"I'm hanged if I follow you," Paul grumbled, now more than a little exasperated, "you made a success of High Wood and whether you like it or not you've moved up in the world. What is it you really want?"

"I suppose, more than anything, to justify your investment in me," Ikey said and Paul was instantly sorry for his impatience. "Where would I be now if you hadn't brought me down here?" And suddenly he looked less serious and added, "I can guess—doing a stretch probably, for knocking off the railings of Buckingham Palace or the Monument!"

They rode on in silence for a spell, Paul puzzled and a little disturbed by the boy's view of himself as a partial misfit but the more he thought about it the less credible it seemed for his mind returned to his obvious popularity and the vision of the trim, swallow-tailed youth who had escorted him into the headmaster's study less than a month before. He said finally, "When you were at school were you homesick for the stable-yard, Ikey?"

"Not the stable-yard," Ikey said, "but the freedom that went along with it! A chap outside looking in on a place like High Wood is entitled to imagine it's all beer and skittles but it isn't, you know! Nobody's life is that simple —I mean, there were plenty of times when I was homesick for the days when I didn't have to live up to anything and that's what I mean when I say I'm still only two-thirds a gent. The other third was always back here, deep in the woods."

He was tempted, at that moment, to confess what lay behind this admission, to tell Paul of his long association with Hazel Potter and his identification of her with everything that grew and hunted in the coombes and coverts of Shallowford, but consideration for the man checked him. He had been living with snobs too long not to realise that their kind of snobbery had no place in Paul Craddock's nature but he knew also that there were limits to tolerance and that Hazel Potter, the half-wit of the Valley, was beyond those limits. To say that he had often wished he had stayed a stable-boy with free access to her and her irresponsibilities would be throwing dirt in his benefactor's face yet he was aware that, to some extent, she was the most rewarding person in his life, except for the man riding beside him. As he pondered this he felt a great yearning for her, for the sound of her soft, Devon burr and the broom-thicket scent of her hair, for the security and isolation of her little house over the badger sets and for the touch of her warm lips. He said, suddenly, "Look here, Governor, I don't have to confirm my Army Entrance application until September but I can tell you one thing—I've decided against the cavalry, if only on the grounds of your pocket! A chap I knew at school has an uncle in the Engineers and I met the old boy when he came over one day. The R.E.s are the only up-to-date branch of the Army and if we ever do have a showdown with the Germans or the Russians they'll make rings round the lancers and hussars! And that's not all, either! I don't think I could stick the mumbo-jumbo of what they call a 'good' regiment. If I am to be in the Army then I should certainly want to earn my keep—you know, *really* earn it—and at least I should have an out-door job with a chance to travel at Government expense. I couldn't stick an office life so maybe we have got somewhere with this pow-wow!"

"You mean you want a week or two to think it over?" Paul said, laughing and Ikey said maybe only a day or two, so by common consent they dropped the subject and rode on into the city talking of horses.

V

Every day, wearing his old training sweater and a pair of soiled slacks, Ikey climbed the orchard to the high-banked lane, circled the mere and threaded the rhododendron maze that he now knew as expertly as Hazel. She was always waiting for him, high up on her rock, and would lift her hand when she saw him tackle the steep, pine-studded slope leading to the cave. And when he saw her a sense of urgency would rush down on him and he would set himself at the sandy slope as though he was on the home run of the most important cross-country event of the season for all summer there had been a clock ticking in his heart, setting a term to boyhood.

One day, soon after the conversation on careers, he did not come until evening, after the sun had passed Nun's Head in the west and the bowl below the escarpment was drowsy with summer, as though everything living there had been used up by the heat of the day. She shouted,

605

from her platform, "Where've 'ee been? I've been lookin' out for 'ee zince noon!" and he told her he had been to a tea-party with some of Mrs. Craddock's friends in Coombe Bay and had only now managed to change and steal away. He went through the wicker screen to the little house and because everything there was familiar to him he noticed a stone jar, standing in one of the cavities she had scooped in the soft sandstone.

"What have you got there?" he asked and she told him it was a gallon jar of Meg Potter's hedgerow wine she had stolen from the washroom behind the Potter farmhouse. "Tidden *really* stealing," she added, "for backalong, when 'er was out after blossoms, I went along of her an' helped. Besides, there's nigh on a dozen jars stored there to cool off. 'Er sells it, you zee, over in Whinmouth, so when 'er wasn't lookin' I slipped off with some, thinkin' us'd taake a mug when us was dry!"

He sniffed it, finding that it smelled a little like damp corn. "What does she put in it, Hazel?"

"Oh, all sorts," the girl said carelessly, "zertain nettles 'er knows, cowslips, elderberries, turnips, dandelion, sloes, quinces and I don't know what, fer 'er's proper stingy with 'er book o' charms an' never lets none of us peep, not even me, who couldn't read what's writ there! Would 'ee like to sample it? Tiz rare stuff and good for rheumatics they say."

"I don't have rheumatism yet," he said laughing, "but I'll down a mug if you will," and she produced two earthenware cups, shook the jar and tipped a generous measure into each.

It was like drinking the Valley at harvest time. Clover was there, as a kind of base, but so was every other ingredient Hazel had mentioned and many others besides, including honey. It slipped over the palate like nectar.

"By George!" he exclaimed, "it's marvellous! Better than any drink I ever tasted! Pour me another."

"Tiz heady stuff," she warned him, "us dorn want to zend 'ee 'ome tipsy," but he boasted that he had a good head for liquor and could walk a straight line after half-a-bottle of the Squire's burgundy with brandy to follow so she poured another measure and sat sipping her own, her great brown eyes watching him over the rim of the cup.

When he had finished his second drink and smacked his lips with appreciation she put the stopper on the jar and returned it to the cavity.

"I dorn reckon you'd better have no more, Ikey," she said, "for even our Smut can't taake a pint of it and you've had two gills. 'Ow do it feel? Do it warm your belly and maake your ears sing?"

It would have baffled him to tell her exactly how he felt. There was, it was true, a great glow spreading under his navel and his ears were singing but not unpleasantly so, the murmur of the woods coming to him as a chorus chanted by angels and the evening light, fiiltering into the cave through the gorse, appearing as the radiance of a celestial sunset. He said, giggling, "Let's have another half cup, Hazel—go on, be a sport!", but she refused him and stood with her back to the cavity. He got up then crouching because the roof was low and made a playful grab at her but she pushed him and he staggered, grazing his head on a rock buttress, not heavily, but enough to make him yelp and sink to his knees. She was beside him at once, with her arms round his shoulders, pressing his head to her breast and uttering soothing noises, as she might over a puppy struck by a blundering foot.

" 'Ave I 'urt 'ee? Did 'ee knock yer poor ade on the rock? Tiz gone to your legs, like rough cider! Bide awhile an' I mak 'er some tay!", and she held him like a child, rocking him to and fro while a wave of sweetness passed over him and he forgot the smart of his head in the softness of her breasts and the scent of her hair tumbling about his face. Then the glow in his belly seemed to explode so that its warmth invaded every vein in his body and he broke from her embrace, bearing her backwards and crushing her into the bracken with his weight and covering her face with kisses. She seemed inclined to resist him for a moment for when, breathlessly, he turned his head aside and caught up a handful of her hair, which he pressed against his mouth, she twisted from beneath him and said, "Dornee, Ikey boy, tiz the drink in 'ee!", but he saw to his relief that she was only laughing at him

607

and that her remark was more of a statement than a
protest. He released her, however, rolling on his elbow
and laughing at himself but also at her for she looked
comical squatting back on her arms and looking down at
him like an affectionate wife contemplating a husband far
gone in drink who had returned home and fallen on the
doorstep. She seemed to contemplate him a long time, as
though not sure what to do with him and as she sat
there, head on one side, hands on her knees, he thought
her the most beautiful creature he had ever seen and
blurted out, "I love you so much! I love you, Hazel", and
because, despite the choir and the golden haze, his inner
consciousness was still sharp and clear, his voice sounded
false and stilted so that he slipped back into her vernac-
ular, saying, "Youm mine, Hazel Potter, and I'll kill any
man who touches 'ee, do 'ee hear, now?", and this must
have sobered her for she stood up with a slow, graceful
movement, and without taking her eyes off him, said, "O'
course 'ee would! But I woulden let un, Ikey! *Never,* do
'ee hear? No man but you!"

The effect of the wine on his brain was two-fold, for
while his body presented him as an amorous, half-helpless
clod-hopper his thoughts about her were diamond sharp
and he saw her as he had always thought of her, the
concentration in a woman's body, of all the colours and
scents and fruitfulness of the Valley under the mantle
of summer and desired her not as a woman but as a kind
of key to her world and everything it offered. Yet the
prospect of possessing her seemed to have nothing to do
with his body but was an emphatic gesture of the mind.
He stood up, unsteadily, and because he staggered a little
she took his hands, saying, "You'd best bide a spell,
Ikey, youm drunk as David's sow!" and she giggled as
she propped him against the canting wall and spread her
flour sacks on the bracken at the back of the cave.

"You'll bide tu?" he said and she told him she would
but he was not to worry for he would soon be asleep and
when he awoke he would be none the worse for the drink;
" 'Er dorn carry no ade with 'er," she added. By now,
however, the glow had spread to every part of his body,
so that the atmosphere of the cave became insufferably

hot and he began to struggle with his sweater in an effort to pull it over his head. She said, as though it was the most natural question in the world, "Be 'ee *that* hot then? Do 'ee want to strip to lie down?", and pulled his sweater free after which she removed his trousers by the simple process of unbuckling his belt and hoisting his legs clear. He suffered this indignity without protest, without even thinking of it as an indignity, and watched her make a pillow of his clothes. When the makeshift couch was ready he collapsed on to it and lay flat on his back as she knelt beside him, inspecting his body with a kind of amused tolerance and saying, with the utmost mildness, "Ah, youm a praper-looking man now, Ikey, a praper man to be sure!" He lay staring up at her with slightly glazed eyes and might have succumbed at once to the drowsiness that was already playing tricks with his consciousness, distorting his judgments of sound and distance but then, almost with resignation, she stood upright again and without taking her eyes off him for a moment slipped out of her odds and ends of garments, folded her ragged dress with great care and put it to one side, standing erect between where he lay and the fading light filtering through the gorse screen of the entrance. His drowsiness left him then but he did not move a muscle, remaining on his back looking up at her, marvelling at the tawny smoothness of her long, straight legs and the rim of browned skin where the tide of sunburn had been checked by the dress just above the shallow downsweep of her breasts and above her knees. Then, with a curiously remote expression, half abstracted and half deliberate, she knelt again and began passing her hands over his body, lightly yet with an air of purpose so that the touch of fingers induced in him a state that was a kind of suspension between elation and the richest daydream of his experience. He was aware that they were naked and that she was caressing him with deliberation but he felt no shame or, at that moment, desire. Her manipulation of his senses was without significance and thus made no direct impact on him and he did not move, neither did he reach out to return her caresses. It was only when she placed both hands on his shoulders, leaning over him to kiss his mouth that her

609

presence beyond his reach became intolerable and he pulled her down beside him, kissing her face and breasts and shoulders and slipping his hands down the full length of her back. She said, with a tinge of sadness in her voice but without urgency, "You gonner tak' me now, Ikey? Be 'ee clear-aded enough to know what youm at!" and he said, sharply, "Youm mine, Hazel Potter, I'll tak' 'ee whenever I wants!" and she sighed as he enfolded her and was done with her in a few painful seconds.

He slept then, almost on the instant and she slipped gently from him, aware of the evening chill rising out of the Valley and striking cold on her back. She paused a moment to look down on him, noting the tiny fronds of dead bracken adhering to his chest and hair so that suddenly he looked a boy again, younger by far than her and she hastened to cover him with another of her sacks. She did not regard what had happened as momentous and could contemplate it without fear or regret. She did not invest it with any special significance. He had always been her man and she was aware that men's desires and demands changed as they grew older. It was just that today, unexpectedly, a few draughts of hedgerow wine has hastened his growth and he had moved on, taking her with him as was the order of things. She did not look for a solution to their committal for she had never troubled herself about solutions and explanations of human or animal conduct, taking each new experience as it came and extracting from it what she needed and what life was disposed to give her. It had granted her him and for a long time now she had accepted the inevitability of this bounty and the limitations that accompanied it, for she supposed now that he would demand access to her every time they met and that she would grow accustomed to being seized by him and crushed under him, with dry bracken stalks scratching her back and her body a soft target for his explosive energy. She did not resent this in any way. All she knew of life in the woods and on the moors taught her that violent possession of the female was the unquestionable right of the male and if, beyond this acceptance, there was a single spark of sadness it was struck by his impatience that had involved pain, certainly to her but perhaps also to him. Yet she knew instinctively that this need not always be so, that it would not necessarily be a clumsily contrived act and that perhaps, when the wine was out of him, they could find ways to prolong preliminaries that had brought her infinitely more joy and satisfaction than the climax. She shook out her hair and pulled on the ruin of her dress thinking with yearning of his smooth, white body under her hands and of the way she had gentled every part of him while he lay still staring up at her as though she was an angel appearing out of a cloud. And as she thought this she lifted and studied the hands that had touched him, extending her fingers and bringing them to her lips, smiling secretly as she performed this act of homage. Then, with a final glance at him, she made her way out into the open and through the gorse to the slope. She knew somehow that he would not want to find her there when he awoke.

He got back to his room without disturbing anyone, remembering little of his scramble through the rhododendrons, and round the edge of the mere in almost total darkness. Once or twice he fell and bruised himself and on the climb up the escarpment to the edge of the woods he was clawed by innumerable briars but he struggled on, careless of hurts so long as he could reach the privacy of his room and lock the door against intruders and thought.

She had been right about the comparative harmlessness of the devil's brew that had draw him into this terrifying situation. There was no hangover; his head did not ache and although his mouth felt parched there was no sour taste on his palate as there had been when he, and Manners, and Hicks Minor, had drunk three pints of stout in the fourth form and gone reeling to bed. But the lack of a hangover was a trifling compensation when he was weighed down by so much guilt and shame and by so many desperate fears that rushed at him like gusts of wind from behind every tree. He did not know whether her absence, when he awoke to find himself naked under her sacks, had been a relief or not. He would have found the greatest difficulty, he thought, in meeting her reproachful eyes, but it was pitch dark by then and they could have talked, and she might, somehow, have been able to reassure him, although he doubted very much if she would have forgiven him his handling of her. He thought savagely of his worldly-wise cronies in the Sixth, who boasted so lightly of their conquests of shop-girls and street-walkers. Either they were liars, which he was disposed to believe, or they were made very differently from him, without consciences, and without any sense of moral responsibility toward other people. For a few minutes only after finding himself alone in the cave and the Valley below dark and silent, he had attempted to dismiss the incident as an initiation into the world of men. He had got drunk on Meg Potter's nectar. He had kissed and fondled a girl. And finally he had pushed the encounter to its logical conclusion. After all, she was only a Potter and everyone in the valley knew that the Potter girls were to be had for a shilling. But soon he recognized this as a deliberate distortion of the truth, knowing that what had happened after the wine had started a fire in his loins had not been a casual encounter with an accommodating girl but something approaching a rape, with her a virgin crying out as she was ravished, and, what was worse, ravished by someone whom she trusted. If his memory of all that had taken place had been at all clear he might have found ample self-justification in the fact that it had been she who had undressed him, she who had pushed him down on the floor and then virtually offered herself but the devil of it was he was by no means clear on the details, only upon the fact. That brew of Meg's seemed to have scoured his memory of all that had occurred between his swallowing of the second mugful, and her sharp, single cry as he took possession of her. He could hear that cry now and it tormented him all the way down the sunken lane and across the orchard to the stable-yard. Then, as he reached his room, guilt was driven out by fear and the most urgent of his fears was that she should find herself with a child, his child, whom he would have to acknowledge before Squire, the elegant Mrs. Craddock, Doctor Maureen, Hazel's family and, indeed, the Valley at large! What would follow if this dread possibility materialised he did not know. He would, he supposed, be thrown out of the house, for surely Squire Craddock would be outraged to discover that the protegé upon whom he had lavished so much affection and money had behaved in such a base fashion. Ignorance buttressed his fears for in spite of the long talks over the study fires in his last year at school he still did not know whether a baby was the inevitable sequel to what he had done. He hoped and prayed not, telling himself that if this was the case then the world would be overpopulated in a matter of years, and he clung to this straw of comfort while he pulled off his clothes and stealthily washed himself in cold water. Then, as he climbed into bed, it occurred to him that if the worst happened perhaps he might not be turned out of the house, but reviled and herded to the altar to be married to Hazel Potter out of hand. Possibly her mother and brothers (and almost certainly the Squire and Mrs. Craddock) would insist upon marriage and for a moment the pricks and stabs of guilt and fear ceased to assault him as he tried to picture their life together as man and wife. He supposed he loved her for how else could he have behaved with such criminal recklessness? And he was convinced that she still loved him, in spite of his brutality but he also knew that there was a good deal more to marriage than rolling about on a couple of sacks spread on dried bracken. How and where would they live? How did one earn enough money to maintain a wife and the children resulting from every encounter such as the last?

He found sleep impossible and watched the dawn draw the curtains on his window. Away across the fields, in the yard of the Home Farm, a cock shrilled and birds began to rustle and sing in the creeper above the porch. He got up, sluiced his face and dressed, leaning his elbows on the sill and looking across Big Paddock to the river. It was still only five-thirty and he had an hour or so before people crowded back into his life and addressed him, expecting lucid, everyday replies. He knew that before then he must find some kind of solution to his problems and he thought, for a moment, of flight. Then he remembered that there was no immediate urgency, for a baby, so they said, was nine months in the making and with this though came another, a recollection of something Tovey Major had said about virgins being unable to have children. He was unsure how much reliance could be placed upon this or in what measure it affected him, but he began to cheer up a little, a very little and returned to his bed, lying fully-dressed on the rumpled sheets with his hands clasped behind his head as he searched among his memories for significant details. He found none but some of his fears, and a little of his guilt, began to recede and as the room grew lighter he found to his astonishment that he could look back upon the incident with a certain amount of detachment. The more he succeeded in doing this the less urgent it seemed, and slowly his panic began to subside so that he could think of Hazel with tepid warmth and of his savage use of her with a certain amount of awe. He said, half-aloud, "I shall have to leave here at once for if I don't I know very well what will happen, I'll go to that damned cave again and it will happen as often as I go with or without the jar of hedgerow wine the little fool introduced into the place! After all, it was the liquor that began it all for without that stuff inside me I should have stopped short after kissing her, or maybe fondling her a little. Surely the best thing is to disappear and I can tell Squire first thing I've decided on the R.E.s, and that I need three months' cramming before sitting Army Entrance! I can give him the name of Manners' crammer, near Eastbourne, and go there at once." But then, as he rejoiced in this easy escape route, he remembered Hazel Potter's brown eyes looking across the rim of her mug when he was supping his second gill and he knew that he could not leave without explaining to her why and where he was going. He would have to see her once again, and tell her how sorry he was, and perhaps kiss her but very gently and impersonally on the cheek. He hoped she would understand and agree that things could not be left as they were. If she did not then he would go anyway, leaving her to make the best of it.

He knew where he could find her at this hour. If she had not slept at the cave then she must have gone to the Dell and after what had happened he guessed that she would not remain there long but would make her way back to the woods at first light. He would try the Dell first and if he drew blank he would go to the cave. He slipped out and down the backstairs, cutting round the house and crossing the sloping meadow to enter the scrub on the west side of the Bluff where the field path joined the Dell track. Having made a decision he felt almost lighthearted and it was difficult to remain gloomy in the early morning woods, where it seemed as if every bird in the Valley had congregated to swell the clamour. He waited here, watching a woodpecker at work, and presently he heard her coming along the track and moved behind a bush for his curiosity regarding her had increased rather than diminished and presently she came in view, dawdling along and actually crooning to herself, as though she found the world a particularly pleasant place that morning.

"Damn it," he said to himself, "here's me, worried half out of my wits about her and feeling the biggest cad on earth and here she comes strolling along singing! What the devil am I so bothered about?", and he called, "Hi there! Hazel!"

She stopped, turning her head slowly and her mouth curved in a warm, welcoming smile as he edged out of ambush and stood uncertainly in her path.

"Youm right early, Ikey!" she said, as though she had half-expected him. " 'Ave 'ee come from my little house?" and he said, sulkily that he had not, that he had awakened to find her gone and blundered home in the dark but had not slept a wink because he was worried about what had happened. "It was that awful stuff of your mother's," he excused himself, "and I . . . I'm sorry, Hazel, upon my honour I am! It was a cad's trick and that's a fact!"

She was puzzled by his troubled expression and far more so by his words, for there was nothing, as far as she could remember, to be sorry about. His manner, however, must have enlisted her sympathy for she took his hand as they moved along the path towards the squirrel oak, saying, "Lord, Ikey, what's 'ee long-faced about, boy? You on'y got tipsy, didden 'ee?"

"I . . . I don't mean about getting drunk on that stuff," he protested, indignantly, "I mean . . . well . . . you must *know* what I mean! I wasn't so drunk that I can't re-

615

member what happened and it was the first time ever, you understand?"

"Well," she said, mildly, " 'twas first time for me but what of it? It baint nothing to worry over, be it?"

For several minutes he could make no reply. The gulf between them, between her view of life and the tight, circumscribed code of people who lived in houses, sat at tables and made polite conversation with one another was unbridgeable and the realisation of this renewed his feelings of guilt and apprehension. He said at length, "Look, Hazel love, I . . . I've got to go away, I've got to study to be a soldier and I'll be gone some time! That's why I came to meet you—I thought, well, that maybe you'd think I was staying away from you because of what happened."

She was undismayed by the news. Ever since she had known him he had always been going and coming and the passage of time meant very little to her. He had been with her last evening, he was here now and would be gone tomorrow but he would come back, sooner or later, as he always did and today she felt particularly sure of him. They stopped on the edge of the wood where the heavy timber began its march down the slope to the mere.

"You'll come zoon as 'ee gets 'ome?"

"Yes, of course I will." Suddenly, and inexplicably he felt totally reassured and with reassurance came tenderness and concern. "Hazel," he said, urgently, "why don't you go home and live with Meg and the girls? And why don't you go back to school at Miss Willoughby's? You can't always live in the woods, you know, you're grown up now!"

She said wonderingly, "Go back home? Wi' all that ole racket? Go back to skuel? Now whyfore should I do that?"

"Because I should like you to," he said, "because I want you to . . . I want you to read and write like everyone else. Will you think about it while I'm away?"

"Ooahh," she said, lightly, "mebbe I will, tho' I doan zee much zense in it! Dornee like me as I be?"

"Yes," he said desperately, "of course I like you but . . . well . . . I'm thinking about what's to become of you if you go on living rough and wandering about the way you do."

616

She interpreted this as caution on his part against the possibility of some other young man in the Valley waylaying her and demanding of her what he had been granted and the thought made her smile.

"Giddon," she said scornfully, "I baint afraid o' no one an' a worn't let none of 'em come near me, same as I told 'ee last night! I c'n run faster an' any humping gurt man in the Valley and I keeps meself to meself, mostly! Will 'ee be goin' outalong now? Or shall us go to my li'l house?"

"I'm going now," he said, sighing, and she said, "Ooo, ah," putting up her face to be kissed.

He kissed her gently. Not, as he had promised himself, on the cheek but on the mouth. Her breath was as sweet as the morning air and he held her for a moment until he began to tremble again and stood back, dropping his hands to his sides and looking at the ground, but she did not seem to notice his confusion and said, gaily, "Well, dornee forget then, zoon as 'ee comes back. I'll save what's left in the jar for 'ee. T'won't 'urt fer waitin'!" Then, as in their early days, she was gone, melting into the foliage and he was alone, as bewildered as when he set out but no longer weighed down by shame and fear. He thought, "There's nobody like her, nobody the least like her but I wouldn't have her any different so to hell with everything!" He went slowly down the field to the sunken lane and into the orchard by the stile.

CHAPTER EIGHTEEN

I

CLAIRE must have set her heart on going to London for the Coronation. She had spent the long autumn afternoons of her pregnancy turning the pages of catalogues of children's emporiums, paying particular attention to little girls' frocks and bonnets and when her third child was born, towards the end of the old year, she was delighted, although not much surprised, when she heard Doctor Maureen exclaim, "Glory to God, it's a girl!"

Paul was not in the district when the baby arrived, about 2 o'clock on an unseasonably mild afternoon. He had accepted Maureen's assurances that the event would not occur until the New Year and had embarked, with James Grenfell, on a whirlwind tour of the areas north of Paxtonbury to fight a second election within twelve months. He had been reluctant to go but both doctor and wife persuaded him, the one because, in her own words, "I hate having husbands under my feet at a time when they are less use than a wet clout!", the other because she knew that Grenfell would be fighting the battle of his life and had real need of Paul.

Local passions over the People's Budget had not cooled throughout the summer and Grenfell regained lost ground after the announcement that a Women's Suffrage Bill was to be placed before Parliament; so Paul rode off in the trap, promising to be home before New Year's Day.

The baby gave them very little trouble although she was a plump little thing, tipping the scales an ounce short of seven pounds, more than either of the twins had weighed at birth. She had, Claire noted, an abundance of dark hair, darker even than Paul's and her eyes, now cornflower blue, looked as if they intended to stay blue and not change to grey, as had the eyes of the boys within six months of birth.

"Well, Maureen," she said later that night, "you have to admit she's pretty and Paul will certainly spoil her. He'll be in a real tizzy when he comes home and finds we managed without him."

Maureen said that after breakfast next morning she would post Thirza to watch for Paul at the gates, so about 10 A.M. Thirza was despatched to the ford to give warning of the Squire's approach. An hour or so later he came spanking along the river road at about twice the pony's normal pace and seing Thirza hopping about between the great stone pillars, shouted, "Has anything happened? Is Mrs. Craddock all right?" and Thirza, gasped, "It's a girl, Squire! Prettiest li'l maid you ever did zee!" and without a word he dragged her into the trap and drove furiously up the drive to the forecourt where he left Thirza, now giggling hysterically, to lead pony and trap round to the yard while he went up the stairs three at a time and thumped on the bedroom door, as if alerting occupants of a burning building.

Maureen came out scolding him for his impatience, and telling him that, as the father of four, he ought to know better but then she relented and said, laughing, "As God's my witness she's an angel from heaven, the prettiest baby any of us ever saw, and there's no doubt who's the father! Wait a minute, lad, I'll tell Nurse and you can go in, for they're both doing marvellously."

A moment later he was looking down at the child with an awe that he had not experienced on either of the previous occasions. Thirza and Maureen had not exaggerated. There was nothing of the brick-red, puckered look about this child; she had perfectly formed features, a peach bloom complexion and exquisite little hands and feet. He stood gazing down at her so long that Claire said, "Well, don't I count any more?" and although aware that she was teasing him he blurted his apologies and kissed her a dozen times, saying, triumphantly, "By God, Claire, she's a treasure! She really is! I've always had to pretend to like newborn babies but this one . . . ! Damn it, I'd quite resigned myself to another lump of a boy! Did you have a bad time? Maureen swore she wouldn't arrive for days—I wouldn't have thought of going if I'd dreamed you were so near!"

"She came very quickly and it was about ten times as easy as the twins," Claire reassured him, "so much so that I can't still persuade myself that it's all over. Do you know, Paul, I've got the pleasantest feeling about her. Something tells me she'll never be any trouble to any of us! There's something . . . well . . . something reasonable about her and I'm glad she was born earlier than we reckoned because 1910 was a wonderful year for us and what happens in 1911 is anybody's guess."

He said, stroking her hair, and wondering at both her radiance and resilience, "Every year with you is a good year, Claire, and 1911 will be better than 1910, more sensational anyway, for James is getting us places on the House of Commons stand for the Coronation. Had you forgotten that bargain we made at Ikey's Sports Day?"

"Certainly not," she said, "in fact I've already picked out a dress! It's in the catalogue on the study table, with the corner of the page turned down, so look at it and tell me you approve. But how can James get us seats unless he's re-elected?"

"He'll be re-elected all right," Paul said grimly, "we've got them on the run again! A year on the local doorsteps has worked wonders and I'll wager he goes in with five hundred majority!"

The nurse came back then and shooed him out. Downstairs, before she dashed off to complete her rounds, Maureen told him over a stiff brandy that the birth had indeed proved one of the most casual in her experience and said, raising her glass, "Well, here's long life to the pair of you and that's no conventional toast either! She's a healthy, happy girl and she's made you a wonderful wife, so don't forget to count your blessings, lad!"

"I'm not likely to," he said seriously, "as John could tell you. You never did meet Grace so you can't imagine how different they are but the odd thing is I don't think I should have ever fully appreciated Claire if I hadn't been so much in love with Grace. There's a conundrum to work into one of your fancy theories."

620

"It's not much of a conundrum," Maureen said chuckling but refused to be drawn and hurried away, promising to send John up to "wet the baby's head" immediately after supper.

Paul sat by the log fire stroking the retriever's head and feeling his hand nuzzled for she loved having her ears fondled. The dog was his one permanent reminder of Grace and of the hours they had spent together in this room. Simon, her child, had never interested her much but the dog she had sent him had always remained hers and although she had long since attached herself to Paul she always behaved as if she half-expected Grace to walk through the door again.

It seemed strange to him, sitting here alone with Claire and her new baby overhead and the house quiet after the turmoil of the last two days, that his thoughts should centre not upon Claire but Grace, whose ghost had never been banished from this particular room, although it seemed to have vanished from all other parts of the house. He wondered vaguely what had happened to her, if she had tired of passing in and out of Holloway under the Government's Cat and Mouse act, or whether, by now, she had another husband, perhaps a fellow campaigner who could share her implacable hatred of the old society. He thought, "I wonder if Claire realises how much she owes Grace and how they would behave to one another if they ever came face to face? Claire probably thinks of her, if at all, as a crank, whereas Grace would certainly despise Claire for her domesticity and deference to men. For all that I'm glad Grenfell and his minority have forced the Cabinet to recognise the right of people as intelligent as Grace to vote," and he heaved himself up and fetched his beloved estate record to which he usually turned on these occasions. He wrote, on the last page of the 1910 Section, *"About 2 P.M. on December 29th my wife presented me with a daughter weighing six pounds 15 ounces; she has dark hair and blue eyes"* and then fell to pondering a name embodying the tranquil temperament Claire had prophesied for the child. A string of Biblical names presented themselves—Deborah, Judith, Naomi and Sarah, but none of them appealed and, finally he hit upon the

621

most English of all names, Mary, and savoured it, murmuring, "Mary—Mary, Claire, Craddock", deciding that it had a roundness and simplicity that pleased him. He wrote, feeling sure Claire would confirm his choice, *"I am calling her 'Mary'"* and then, perhaps infected by the inconsequence of Claire's entries, *"Everyone about here describes her as a rare pretty li'l maid and so she be!"*, signing his name under the frivolous entry.

The new year opened in triumph, for Paul's prophecy was fulfilled and Grenfell was returned with over a thousand majority. The sardonic Captain Owen-Hixon disappeared like the Devil in a pantomime but the new Lord Gilroy took his defeat very handsomely, congratulating Paul at the declaration of the poll and promising him "a return match" in the years ahead. "Sour grapes notwithstanding I don't envy your chap," he said, "or any Government taking office to-day! They have so many hot potatoes they can't help but drop some of them! They can't get a clear majority without leaning over backwards to bribe the Irish Home Rulers or the Labourites and what with Ulster, Home Rule, the reform of the Lords, the Navy League outcry, that ass of a Kaiser and the suffragettes, I wouldn't wonder if the more thoughtful among them isn't damned sorry they won!"

The prospects of stormy sessions ahead, however, did not seem to depress James when Paul drove him across the moor to catch the connection for the Cornish express, at Sorrel Halt. A whole year on home ground had revitalised him and his increased majority had boosted his morale, and yet, Paul told himself, he was a very different James from the man who had gone blithely to London after the 1904 bye-election. The struggle to relate conscience and humanity with the cut-and-thrust of life in the House showed in his face, deeply lined at forty-two, and in patches of grey at his temples and he made a jocular reference to the wear and tear on his nerves as they paced the little platform awaiting the train. "I've always said you have the best of it, Paul, guarding the grass roots down here and I don't suppose you'd care to change places, would you?"

"I'd sooner change places with Smut Potter or Norman Eveleigh," Paul said. "I haven't been near London since I went there to try and bring Grace home; that was more than five years ago."

"Well, you'll be combing the straw from your hair in June," James reminded him. "Claire is holding you to your promise to bring her up for the Coronation."

"Oh, I'll do that," Paul told him, "for I can't get out of it now but it'll be a three-day stay and no longer. A drive round to see the decorations, a day watching the toing and froing and another for Claire to show off her new clothes—then home, with the harvest just round the corner!"

"Well," James chuckled, "you were a born townsman but they always say converts are more catholic than the Pope! Here's the train, so good-bye and again, thank you for your loyalty!"

From his seat on the box of the trap Paul watched the train round the long curve and then walked the cob over the moor, congratulating himself on his luck.

II

They had booked a small hotel overlooking St. James' Park and on the day of their arrival, whilst Claire was busy unpacking, Paul sat on the balcony and looked down on the evening idlers moving slowly along the wide paths and across the acres of parched grass. There seemed to be hundreds of thousands of them and the bunting entwining the lamp-posts and the gilded arches catching the last rays of sun in the Mall, reminded him of the day he had crossed a city preparing for Edward's coronation nine years ago. He thought, "I was young and green in those days, with no more than instinct to guide me in leaving this stew and breaking new ground! I hadn't even made up my mind to buy Shallowford then, but now it seems as if I was born there and my father before me! Well, a devil of a lot of water has passed Codsall bridge since those days. People were still flaying poor old Kruger, and Lloyd George, now turning the country upside down with his precious budget, was no more than a comic turn with the Welsh gift of the gab! I wonder if Claire ever hankers after city life? She tried it for a spell but she soon came home and although she says we're developing into a pair of bumpkins I don't believe she really likes cities any more than I do!", and he heard her call from the dressing room and came in to ask if she wanted to go out before dinner.

"Go out? Why, of course I do!" she called, still invisible, "why else do you suppose I've dressed myself up?"

"I didn't know you had," he said. "Come out and let's have a look at you."

"Close your eyes then," she said and he closed them, hearing the pleasant swish of her skirts as she moved into the bedroom and giving a gasp of astonishment that ended in a shout of laughter which he hastily choked back when he saw her frown.

"What's so funny about me?" she demanded, tartly for her, but he moved round her once or twice and was no longer disposed to laugh but rather to wonder how a woman who so seldom got an opportunity of dressing for the town, should succeed so spectacularly when the chance offered itself.

"By George, you're absolutely sensational, Claire!" he told her, sincerely, "I only laughed out of shock! I've never seen you looking like that, not even on your wedding day!"

She was a summer's evening study of white and apple green, with a high-waisted skirt flowing away into a whipped-up torrent of sprigged lace that foamed out behind her like a small, neat wake. Over a tight bodice she wore a green velvet hussar jacket, with frogged lapels and a stiff, turned-up collar. She had on a huge Gainsborough hat, one of the largest hats he had ever seen, worn at a tilt and crowned with green organdie gathered in half-a-dozen loosely tied bows and she was wearing the pearl necklace he had given her after the birth of the twins. In her right hand, clothed in an elbow-length suède glove, she carried a long-handled parasol with a white sword-knot swinging from it. He had noticed, of late, that she had been putting on weight but she was obviously well corseted under her coronation regalia for her figure seemed to him quite perfect, the waist as neat as the day he had first seen her in the yard of High Coombe farm, although even the merciless corset could not conceal the roundness of the hips and the generous contours of the bust. She blushed a little under his scrutiny and said, regretfully, "I didn't realise how much I'd put on since Mary's arrival! I ordered this dress in advance and I suppose it ought to be let out a little."

"Rubbish," he comforted her, "you've only put a little on in the right places and you don't have to apologise to me. I like a woman to look like one, especially when she's my wife! My only complaint is that the hat hides your lovely hair!"

"I could hardly watch the Coronation bareheaded," she said. "After all, it's only once in a lifetime and I don't suppose we shall ever see another king crowned." Then she laughed, adding, "Do stop staring, darling, it can't be that sensational! I bought every stitch of it in Paxtonbury," but he told her that he enjoyed staring and so would everyone else when they went out but that he wished they hadn't got to go out, because she not only looked vice-regal but very provocative indeed.

"I daresay," she told him, "but I'm not available for more than a chaste kiss right now and anyway my breathing is restricted, so do please behave yourself!"

"Well, temporarily," he promised but drew her gently to him, complaining that the corset she was wearing converted her lovely rump into a rampart. She laughed at that and kissed him warmly saying, "Oh, we *are* lucky, Paul! I do love you so much! And this is for bringing me up, because I know you'd far sooner have stayed home!", and she kissed him again, this time on the mouth but skipped away at once sensing that another kiss or two would make him unmanageable.

They went out, walking sedately along the edge of the lake and thence into the Mall, now crammed with sightseers, and from here to the Palace, to stare at the railings and royal standard, and then back again along Constitution Hill to Piccadilly, unrecognisable under a thousand flags and pennants and huge, cardboard portraits of the King and Queen, printed in garish colours and wired

625

against the tug of the breeze. She was so gay, and looked so desirable, that he felt they were well launched on a second honeymoon and Claire, when he told her this, admitted that she was, in fact, far more ready to enjoy herself than she had been on her real honeymoon in Anglesey, four years before.

"Now why should that be for you weren't a particularly nervous bride," he said. "As a matter of fact I was agreeably surprised now I come to think of it."

"Well, I started out terrified I can assure you," she admitted, "because I couldn't hide the fact from myself that I was a country daisy succeeding an orchid! I suppose it didn't show because . . . well . . . you didn't rush me! You probably don't remember, Paul, but you were very patient with me."

"Was I?" he said as they passed into the foyer of their hotel and the commissionaire saluted. "Well, I'm not likely to be so patient on my second honeymoon, my dear," and because it was obvious from the doorman's smirk that he had overheard, Claire whispered urgently, "Shhh, for heaven's sake! I shall blush scarlet when I see that man in the morning."

"It's my belief that you'll have good cause to!" he said, laughing, and in this mood they went in to dinner.

As usual, he was soon heavily asleep. She knew no one who could drop off to sleep so quickly and sleep so soundly, notwithstanding the unfamiliar symphony of rattling carriage wheels and honking motors that was such a contrast to the midnight stillness of Shallowford. She did not feel sleepy, in spite of all the wine they had drunk and the boisterous interlude that had followed. Always, at times like this, she liked to lie still in his arms, and smile at herself and at him and as the increasing flow of traffic rolled under the window she thought, "He really does behave as though he married me this morning! It can't be my new clothes, in spite of the impact they made on him, for he could hardly wait for me to take them off!", and she chuckled, wriggling from under his arms and sitting up, hugging her knees and feeling happier than she ever remembered. It was a very wonderful thing, she thought, to have attained the degree of balance and intimacy that was theirs and had been theirs since the very beginning, and her mind went back to the day soon after his arrival in the Valley, when she had set out to capture him without knowing or even caring what kind of man he really was, or what qualifications she had for marriage to someone with his unusual sense of purpose and singlemindedness. She was glad, looking back, that there had been that near-fatal rift in their association and for the first time in her married life she could contemplate his first wife without jealousy, reflecting that she probably owed her a good deal for seasoning him as man and lover. She must, Claire thought, have been a sensual little minx, for the man now asleep beside her had very little in common with the shy, rather gawky youth she had enticed down by the mere. All his boyishness and uncertainty had been ironed out of him during his first marriage and the unhappy period that followed it yet it had left him with no kind of a grudge against women, as might have been expected. He was masterful but, to her mind, accomplished as a lover and what was more unusual unselfishly so. That, in itself, was a contradiction to all that young women of her generation had been taught to expect of a man once he had got a woman to bed, for how many husbands in the Valley regarded lovemaking as a mutual experience or took pains to ensure that it was so? Precious few, she would say, for the dice were heavily loaded against her sex in this respect, yet it was not so in their marriage and for this she would never cease to be grateful. She leaned over and kissed him lightly and wriggled back into his embrace and as she drifted over the edge of sleep she thought, "If we go on like this I shall have a baby every year and lose my figure altogether but I don't care a row of beans! Not even if they arrive in pairs, like Andy and Steve!"

The next morning they toured the city from Aldgate Pump to Marble Arch and when they had had their fill of sightseeing he asked her if she would care to renew her acquaintance with Uncle Franz and see the scrapyard in all its squalid glory.

"It hardly qualifies as a Coronation attraction," he said, "but the Valley owes it a good deal. If I'd had my way I should have cut myself off from it altogether and it would have taken all of twenty years to put the estate in good heart."

She said she would enjoy meeting Franz and spending an hour among his old iron, so they crossed the river and drove through the sweltering streets to the yard, where Paul noticed that there had been some extensive changes.

The place was as forbidding as ever but there was a certain grandeur about its disorder and multiplicity of its pyramids of junk. Several more acres had been enclosed on the far side and the fires now burned in braziers, mounted on brick hearths. Uncle Franz's shack had given place to a red-brick building with waggon-sheds alongside and among the carts Paul noticed two or three cumbersome motor vehicles, shaped like barges on wheels and called, he was told, "lorries". There was an air of efficiency about the place that had not been there in the earlier, more casual era. Doors in the office building had wooden plaques with *"Foreman"*, *"Weigh In"*, *"Chief Sorter"* and *"Cash"* painted on them; he said to Franz:

"My word, things must be looking up! It used to be just a frowsy dump and now it's a slum empire!"

Franz was his usual chirrupy self, extending to Claire the same Continental courtliness as he had shown Grace and he amused her very much by gravely kissing her hand and telling her that, whilst he was grubbing among scrap in a brick jungle the luckier and more discerning Paul had found "A pearl beyond price in the provinces". Paul said, "Don't take the slightest notice of him, Claire! He talks like that to every woman he meets under sixty! It comes from a lifetime of coaxing housewives to empty their attics!" but to Franz he said, seriously, "You seem to have made a lot of changes round here and I must say the place looks a lot less sleazy than before. Have you taken in more land over there by the viaduct?"

"Another four acres," Franz said casually, "and business was never better, my boy! Thank God for Kaiser Wilhelm and his shining armour! He's the man who put new life into the scrap industry! I don't suppose you ever look at the balance sheets I send you?"

"No," Claire told him, "he doesn't, only the dividend

628

slips and even those have to be brought to his attention by the bank manager."

"Well, you might be interested to know that our turn-over last year was treble that of our best South African War year," said Franz. "If this naval race continues until either us or Germany goes bankrupt you'll die a rich man, Paul, providing, of course, you don't pour the whole of it into those Devon quicksands of yours!"

"At least I do something practical with it," retorted Paul, slightly nettled by the old man's irony, but Claire said, quickly, "Don't tease him about the Valley, Uncle Franz! Ordinarily his sense of humour is good but that's his sensitive spot!" and Paul, suddenly ashamed of his huffiness, was grateful to her for her intervention.

They took Franz back to the hotel for tea and afterwards to a theatre, a musical extravaganza that Paul privately thought ridiculous but which Claire obviously enjoyed. During the interval, as he and Franz smoked a cigar in the foyer, the old man said, affably, "Well, Paul, I must say you should be congratulated on your taste for wives! She's just as pretty as Grace and more tolerant of your eccentricities! You're obviously a happy man."

"Yes I am," Paul admitted readily, "and, in a way, I have to thank you for it, Franz, for I don't suppose I should have bestirred myself to try again if you hadn't jogged my elbow! Claire is a wonderful wife and mother and there's no fear of her disappearing into the blue to join the Militants! Have you seen anything of Grace?"

"Oh, once or twice, for an hour or so," Franz replied, rather too airily Paul thought, "she pops across the river to collect her subscription."

"What subscription? She gets her allowance regularly, doesn't she?"

"Oh, I'm not referring to the hundred a year you allow her," Franz said, laughing, "I mean the subscription I made to the Sacred Cause."

"You subscribe to suffragette funds?"

"Certainly I do, twenty guineas annually!"

"Good God!" exclaimed Paul, genuinely astonished, "I didn't think you cared two straws about votes for women."

"I don't," Franz said, "but I like to see politicians harried and anyway, I admire their spirit."

The thought crossed Paul's mind that the real reason for the wily old Croat's support of a movement that was embarrassing a Liberal Government lay much deeper than this, and had far more to do with his preference for a government inclined to spend even more upon armaments and thus, by inference, upon scrap, but he only said, "How is she, Franz? Still as fanatical?"

"More so I'd say," Franz replied but no longer joking, "their frontline fighters have been getting a very rough handling up here. They don't put everything in the papers."

Paul was going to tell him about Grenfell's championship of the movement and of the photographic evidence he had seen but at that moment the intermission bell sounded and they rejoined Claire in the stalls. The old man refused an invitation to accompany them on the morrow and see the procession from the M.P.s' stand, so they watched him drive off across Leicester Square to his Portman Street home, after he had promised to make another appointment by telephone before they returned home at the end of the week.

That night, when they were alone, Claire said, suddenly, "You can't help liking Uncle Franz, Paul, but . . ." and she hesitated, as though fearing to offend him.

"Under his charm he's rather frightening; is that what you were going to say?"

"Yes, it was, but maybe all people who make money are frightening."

"Well," Paul said, "I don't suppose we should be sanctimonious about it. We put the money he makes to good use in the Valley and have been damned glad of it. I daresay we could struggle along without it now but it seems to me that to reject it would be a rather pompous gesture; all the same, I would do it, if you had strong feelings about it."

She made no immediate reply, sitting on the dressing stool brushing her long hair, so he added, "Well? *Have* you?"

"No," she said, as though she wasn't altogether sure, "but the time could come when I might have. Do you

630

suppose all this battleship building could lead to anything serious; to people actually killing one another, as they did in that war between Russia and Japan?"

"No," he said, "I don't, for in my opinion it's all a game of bluff played by men like Franz and by others, bigger and more ruthless than him! I don't think the Kaiser ever wants to use his dreadnoughts; he simply has then so that he can strut about the decks in fancy dress but our people take him seriously—or they pretend to. No major power could afford that kind of war for more than a week or so!"

"Well, I hope not," Claire said, "but the next time I see Franz I shall ask him that one!"

In the event they did not see Franz again. Within forty-eight hours of parting from him they were on the way home, bolting very much as Paul had bolted six years before. The Coronation procession proved even more spectacular than the newspapers had promised. Watching the cohorts of splendidly uniformed men march past, and hearing the deep-throated roar of the densely-packed spectators as the Royal coach and its escort of Household Cavalry came in view, Paul was gripped by a sense of climax about the spectacle, as though it symbolised the extreme high tide of the Victorian and Edwardian eras and had been deliberately staged to advertise the enormous thrust and weight of British Imperialism. It had seemed enough in the days of the Transvaal War but now, to him at all events, it was even more vociferous and glittering. He said, aloud, "My God! It's like a Roman triumph!" but his voice was lost in the wave of sound that seemed to rock the tall buildings and a moment later the coach and escort were gone, the roar moving forward like a boosted echo.

"Did you say something, dear?" Claire asked when the next military band was still a hundred yards off and Paul said nothing of any consequence but suddenly he felt homesick for the simplicity of a national celebration in the Valley, attended by no more than two hundred people and patronised by the beaming Henry Pitts and the biblical shepherd twins, who asked no more of a national holiday than a tug-of-war between "Outalong" and "Downalong".

631

The next afternoon they were given tea on the terrace at Westminster by a sprucely-dressed James Grenfell, who seemed optimistic about the prospects of getting ahead with the Liberal programme, provided nothing disturbed the existing arrangement with the Irish members and Labourites, whose support gave them their overall majority in the House. They were standing near the West door of the great hall on the point of saying good-bye when Paul saw a party of police dash by, coming from the direction of Westminster Bridge and disappear, whistles shrilling, in the direction of the railings fronting the House.

"Hullo, what's happening there?" he asked and James, looking anxious and uncomfortable, said, "Probably another raid by the Militants, their headquarters are just across the Square and this happens pretty frequently now that the Suffrage Bill looks like being talked out. I'll get a cab, Paul, you should get Claire away."

Although he did not say so it was obvious that he felt there was more than a likelihood of Grace being among the demonstrators and Paul, sharing this misgiving, said, "All right, James, let's get away!" but unexpectedly Claire spoke up, facing them and saying, *"Why?* Why do we have to turn our backs on it? We backed you in two elections on this issue, James, and I think we ought to see for ourselves!" Then, as neither made a reply, "It doesn't matter if Grace *is* there! We ought to judge the issue on more than photographs, James!"

James said, uneasily, "I suppose she's right, Paul, it might be important for you to see what I've seen often enough in the last year or so," so they moved towards the vortex of the disturbance under the statue of Richard I but were soon obliged to link arms to prevent being separated by the crowds now moving in from all directions.

"Sometimes it's no more than a scuffle," James said but they saw at once that it was more than a scuffle today, for the whole area in front of Parliament was boiling like the scene of a revolution, with mounted police laying about them with rolled-up capes and foot police fighting to seal the area in front of the statue where two prison vans were drawn up with doors open and police on the steps. Then a larger section of the crowd swept in from

632

the far side of the Square and they were all three, together with a bearded police sergeant and two younger officers, washed back against the railings, the sergeant losing his temper and shouting to his men, "Get *through* to them, damn you! Use your fists if you have to!" and after a renewed heave Paul was parted from the others and carried closer to the vans as the police drove a passage through the mob enclosing him in the cordon.

Here, the ugliness of the struggle was revealed to him far more vividly than in James' photographs and scenes were being enacted that he would never have associated with an English political demonstration. The cordon reformed behind him and although he looked everywhere he could see no sign of James or Claire and forgot them as he was swept closer to the heart of the riot. He saw about a score of women, most of them well-dressed, grappling with as many police and plain-clothes men and there was no evidence of docility on the part of the suffragettes, or of chivalry on the part of their assailants. It might have been a police descent upon a thieves' kitchen, south of the river. Fists were flailing, hats and umbrellas flying, helmets skidding under the feet of horses and, here and there, police and women were rolling on the ground in a flurry of blue tunics and white petticoats. Paul stood aghast at the brutishness of the spectacle. He saw a middle-aged woman propelled up the steps of the Maria with a punch in the back aimed by a straw-hatted man whose face was distorted with fury and whose nose streamed blood; he saw that one van was already full to overflowing for suddenly a young woman, hair streaming over her shoulders and mouth open in a soundless scream, appeared for an instant at the door before being dragged back by someone inside; he saw an elderly man, whom he identified as a sympathiser by the rosette he wore, wave a banner on which the single word "Votes" was distinguishable and then a mounted policeman tore the banner from him and began using it as a stave to clear the struggling pedestrians from the area about his horse. Then, almost under his feet, he saw a young woman in grey, crouched on hands and knees, hatless and with a mass of dark hair masking her face as she contracted herself to avoid being trampled.

633

He recognised her as Grace even before a young, helmetless policeman seized her by the shoulders and half raised her and he grabbed the man just as someone laid hold of him from behind, so that all four of them, locked in a grotesque chain, lurched and cannoned into the group struggling around the remains of the banner. The din was hellish for by now the cordon had broken and the crowd, predominantly men, were pressing in from all sides so that the van lifted on two wheels and would have overturned but for the plinth of the statue. A certainty that, in a matter of moments, Grace would be crushed to death in the mêlée, gave him the impetus to shoulder the young policeman aside and break free of the restraining hand on his collar. His hat flew off and his collar burst loose but he steadied himself by shooting out his arms and bracing himself against the plinth so that, for a moment or two, he formed an arch over Grace who now lay flat on her face, the man who had been holding the banner crouching almost on top of her. At that moment mounted police moved forward three abreast, clearing a small space under the statue and an inspector, running round the plinth, shouted to Paul, "Get her on her feet, man!" and he shouted back, on impulse, "She's nothing to do with the damned riot! She's my wife, we've been in the House . . . !" and taking advantage of the momentary lull, tore out his wallet and flourished Grenfell's card under the inspector's nose. The man glanced at it and shouted, "Hold hard, there!" as if he had been in the hunting field and to Paul, "Work your way behind the statue! I'll get the van moving! If some of these fools are run over so much the worse for them!"

Paul lifted Grace as the van began to plough through the mob, moving diagonally across the Square so that soon there was space enough to edge round behind the statue where there was a measure of sanctuary after the crowd had streamed away in pursuit of the vehicle. The inspector had forced his way round in their wake and said, breathlessly, "You can vouch for her? She's your wife you say?" and Paul said, savagely, "Yes, and I'm damned if I ever thought I should be ashamed to be English! What the hell has happened to people? Has everyone gone raving mad?"

"It's those women, sir," the inspector said, "it happens

day after day but we weren't prepared seeing it's Coronation week. We thought they would have given over until the celebrations were done. Is she hurt?"

His manner was friendly but by no means anxious until James appeared, also waving a card and announcing that he was an M.P. and intended raising the subject of the riot in the House at the first opportunity. As soon as the link between the unconscious woman and a Member of the House was established the policeman's attitude changed abruptly and he said, a little desperately, "I hope you don't hold me responsible, sir! She was right in the thick of it, and so was this gentleman! You can see for yourself the hopelessness of our job when they start trouble at peak hours! They've been warned often enough, God knows." James said, with a glance at Paul indicating that he was to stay out of the discussion, "Well, this one wasn't, Inspector! I was showing her where English laws are made when this happened!" and the man said, "I'm very sorry, sir, but how can we distinguish? Let's take a look at her; maybe it's only a faint!" And then, as all three of them peered at the limp figure in Paul's arms, Claire rejoined them and the crowd melted away, running towards the Abbey. A helmetless policeman, who seemed to have sized up the situation, bustled up and said, "I've got a cab, sir! Over there by the Members' entrance!" and the inspector, giving him a look of approval, said, "Good work, Crutchley! Get her in first and look for your helmet afterwards!"

James remained for a moment with the inspector while Paul followed the constable across the littered paving stones to the Members' entrance and climbed into a four-wheeler. As they edged through the door he saw Grace open her eyes, then close them again, rather too swiftly. He thought, "Damn it, I don't believe she's hurt at all! She's just using us to make the most of the situation!" and instead of telling the cabby to drive to the nearest casualty ward he gave him the name of their hotel, saying, "All right, Officer, I realise you couldn't help it and I'm a witness to that!" The man saluted and looked very relieved, wiping the sweat and grime from his forehead as James rejoined them.

"Well," he said, as they moved slowly across Whitehall,

"I've given him something to think about but I did it with my tongue in my cheek! The poor devils are in a hopeless position. It's the politicians not the police who should be censured for this kind of thing! Is she hurt, do you think?"

Grace herself answered the question by opening her eyes and subjecting all three of them to an ironic scrutiny. There was, Paul reflected, an element of glee in her expression but as soon as she saw Claire she wriggled out of Paul's grasp, tossed back her hair and said, carelessly, "Well, that's one up for us anyway! I'll wager that inspector has a sleepless night or two! Thank you, James, it was clever of you, and you too, Paul!" and to their amazement she plunged her hands into a sachet fastened to her waistband, extracted a handful of hairpins and began to tidy her hair.

James said, with a note of mild reproof, "I guessed you were spoofing all the time, you little devil! But he didn't, did you, Paul?"

"No, I'm damned if I did!" Paul growled, feeling very foolish and avoiding Claire's glance. "She looked to me as if she was heading straight for martyrdom! The next time I'll do what I intended to do then—keep well clear of a mess like that!" and then he remembered the woman who had been punched in the back and the elderly man with the banner banged over the head with his staff and suddenly he felt neither foolish nor irritated, but almost proud of the way she had used them to save herself from arrest and another spell in gaol and also to hit back at her persecutors. He noticed too that she was much thinner than the last time he had seen her, with her pleasing roundness gone and a strained, white face that reminded him of an undernourished adolescent. Her clothes, well-cut and once smart, were now wildly disordered. The shoulder of the blouse had been ripped across, exposing the strap of her petticoat and her skirt was stained with patches of manure and road dust. He said, with awe in his voice, "Is it worth all that? Isn't there some other way?" and James replied, quietly, "They've tried all the other ways, Paul," and a look of understanding passed between Grace and James so that Paul felt shut out of their confidence.

Claire said, as the cab stopped at the hotel, "You'd

best come in and tidy up, Grace. Then we can all have tea," and when Grace hesitated she added, laughing, "You really do need a wash and brush up! They'll probably arrest you if you go home in that condition," whereupon they all got out and whilst Paul was paying off the cab the two women went through the foyer, causing the commissionaire to open his eyes wide as they passed him on their way to the stairs.

The men remained below, James ordering two stiff whiskies, while Paul went into the cloakroom to make what repairs he could on his burst collar. When he returned James said with a grin, "Leave 'em to it, Paul, they understand one another well enough!" and Paul thought that perhaps he was right for during the cab ride he had been aware of a curious intimacy between the women. He said, "Very well, but afterwards, I'm going straight home, James! Every time I come here something damned unpleasant happens and from now on I'm avoiding this blasted city as if the Great Plague was still raging!" and James told him he was probably well advised to do just that but from now on he hoped Paul would support universal suffrage with more enthusiasm.

"Yes, I'll do that, James," Paul said, slowly, "but out of disgust, rather than conviction! I never thought to see Englishmen behave like that towards demonstrators. On the Continent, perhaps, but not here and not against women, however misguided! As a matter of fact I'm half-persuaded that people like Grace enjoy it in a way. Is that prejudice on my part, would you say?"

"No, not entirely," James said, sipping his drink, "but even if they do I don't see why they should apologise for it. There's self-satisfaction in fighting that hard for something you believe in deeply and sincerely and they'll win, quite soon I believe."

"It can't be soon enough for me," Paul grumbled, "for right now I feel like a bath and not simply to wash the dirt from my body!"

While Grace was in the dressing-room Claire sat in the bedroom sewing up the rent in her blouse and when this was done she set about beating the dust from the heavy folds of the skirt and sponging away the great yellow stain.

She worked methodically, her mind contemplating the unlikely situation, that seemed to her as improbable as a story in a chain-library novel but it did not embarrass her, for instinct told her that Grace had long since renounced any claim on Paul. When she came out drying her hair with a bath robe, she studied her dispassionately, noting her boyish figure, and the prominence of her collar-bone as she slipped on her blouse and stood before the long mirror tidying her hair. There was hardly a trace, Claire thought, of the trim, self-assured young woman who had entertained her to tea at Shallowford in the first year of her marriage. All her curves had disappeared and with them her indifferent, half-vacant air that had seemed at that time close to boredom. Now the lines of the face were taut, the cheek-bones prominent and every movement she made whilst brushing and underpinning her hair was crisp and decisive, as though physical energy was something to be carefully husbanded. Only yesterday, Claire recalled, she had thought of this woman as sensual but she changed her mind now and wondered if dedication to a political cause, to the extent that this woman had dedicated herself, demanded the discipline of a nun entering an order. She thought, "There must be enormous strength of will there for I know myself well enough to realise that I couldn't exchange life with Paul, or the security of the Valley for an abstract idea. I might have done once but not now, not having enjoyed a man's vigour and protection, not having borne him children as she bore him a child. She has resilience, too, she isn't in the least put out by this turn of events and seems almost to take it for granted," and she began to comprehend some of the sources of the failure of the marriage, reasoning that, beside Grace, Paul was an adolescent, with an adolescent's dependence upon flattery. She said, as she handed Grace her skirt, "Would you think it impertinent of me if I asked you if you were happier now, Grace?" and Grace stopped in the act of stepping into her skirt, smiled and said, with the utmost candour, "Certainly not, providing you'll be equally frank with me!"

"I've always been grateful to you," Claire said slowly, "and I don't mind admitting that. There was a time when

638

I was very jealous but that's done with, I'm not jealous now, any more than you are of me! I'm happy and I think Paul is; in fact, I know he is. Yet I know too that he wonders about you sometimes and that he'll be very upset by what happened today."

Grace hitched her skirt and tucked in her blouse so that Claire thought she put on clothes more like a soldier hurrying to parade than a young woman dressing in the presence of another. She had a trick of conducting an intimate conversation like this, on a flat, impersonal level, as though Claire was a recruit to the Cause and she was instructing her in tactics.

"I'm quite sure Paul is happy, Claire, far happier than I could have made him and believe me, I'm grateful to you too! You were the means of soothing my conscience about him. All the same, I still think you should have fought for him in the first place."

"But it wouldn't have worked that way," Claire retorted, although it secretly pleased her to have proof of the fact that she knew Paul so much better than this strange, eclectic creature, "and you haven't answered my question! I've got a reason for asking it."

"I don't want to know reasons," Grace told her, "I made a bad mistake and so did he but I made mine deliberately, so it wasn't fair that he should help pay for it! Am I happier? I don't know, I had never much expectation of happiness so it's difficult to judge. I'm doing what I want to do, I've found a purpose to justify myself so I suppose that's something. The only way I did that when I was a wife was over there," and she inclined her head toward the bed. Claire said nothing, so she went on, as though answering her own questions, "That's half a marriage but Paul isn't a man satisfied with half, is he? I soon found that out and that's what decided me to stop pretending. I imagine it's very different with you for you always belonged in his precious Valley. It's still the whole of his life, I imagine?"

"Yes," Claire told her, it was, that and the children.

"You have children? Yes of course you have, Uncle Franz told me—two girls, wasn't it?"

"Two boys, and now a girl."

"You haven't wasted much time!"

"The first two arrived together—twins—the girl last December."

Grace looked then as if she was trying to make up her mind to say something important but was not sure how it would be received and for a moment Claire suspected that she was going to flaunt her "liberation" by inquiring into the sex relationship of man and wife. Then, suddenly, Claire understood the reason for her hesitation; she was thinking, no doubt, of her own child Simon and said quickly, "You were wondering about your boy?" but Grace shook her head vigorously and replied, "No, that wasn't it! It just occurred to me that a woman like yourself must regard a person like me as a masochist."

Claire had never heard the word "masochist" and frankly admitted as much whereupon Grace laughed and said, "By God, Claire! I was right about you! You were the only person in the world for Paul and I admire your honesty! Not one woman in a hundred would have admitted that in your situation!" and when Claire's expression showed she was unable to follow her reasoning, she went on, "It's just a fashionable word meaning someone who derives pleasure from pain. Some of our people fall over themselves to use all the new words, you know, and I suppose some of them really are masochists. Well, at least my affiliation is not that much of a fad! I'm the person I am simply because I watched my mother driven to suicide by the cruelty of a man and I suppose this is my way of hitting back but perhaps Paul never told you about that?"

"No," Claire said, "he never did."

"Well, if you're interested ask old John Rudd when you get home but I shall have to go now, I'm probably the only one who survived that raid and Headquarters will want a report," and she picked up a yellow straw hat of Claire's from the window seat and said, "Could I borrow this until tomorrow? I lost mine in the scrimmage."

"You can have it, a donation to the Cause," Claire said, "but before you go I would like you to know that both Paul and I campaigned for Women's Suffrage at the last two elections in the West."

"I do know it," Grace said, "for that comes within my terms of reference. However, this isn't the kind of war won on platforms, as you probably noticed outside Parliament this afternoon."

Claire said, "If you'd been arrested and taken to gaol would you have gone on another hunger strike and been forcibly fed?"

"Not necessarily," Claire replied carelessly, "they're so frightened of the prospect of one of us dying in gaol that they've introduced a new method now. They watch us starve for a few days, turn us loose, then arrest us again as soon as we're strong enough to totter along between two fat policemen!"

"It's outrageous," Claire burst out, "how many times have you been in Holloway?"

"I've lost count," Grace said, "but I can tell you how many times I've had the steel gag and been fed through the nostrils. That's something you do remember."

Suddenly Claire felt sick and miserable. The thin, erect figure standing by the window was a rebuke, not only to her but to all of them and contemplation of her, and all that had happened to her over the last few years, made a mockery of the brilliant procession they had watched the previous day. She said, falteringly, "How . . . how long will it go on, Grace?" and Grace, shrugging, said perhaps another two or three years, depending upon all kinds of factors, the staying power of the Militants, the supply of funds, the state of public opinion and the obstinacy of male legislators of both parties. Then, as though bored with the subject, she crammed on the hat and said, "We'll go down now. Paul will be tormenting himself guessing what we're talking about up here!" and she moved for the door but Claire caught her arm and said, "Wait, there is one thing more! We haven't told Simon about you. It isn't easy to explain divorce to a seven-year-old. We shall, of course, but sometimes I wonder . . . well, wouldn't you like to see him? You could, at any time you wished."

Grace gave her another of her long, thoughtful stares before saying, "No, I don't think that would be very wise of me, would it? He's happy and fit, I imagine?"

"Yes, he is," Claire told her, "he gets on well with the

twins but Ikey, the boy Paul more or less adopted, is his great favourite."

"Ah yes, Ikey," Grace said, as it struck her that Claire must be quite unaware of Ikey's role as the link between them. "How is Ikey shaping? I always had great hopes of that boy."

"He's doing very well," Claire told her, "he's in his first year at Woolwich. He was going to be an Engineer but he's changed to the Gunners. Having his own children hasn't made any difference how Paul feels about him."

"No," Grace said, slowly, "it wouldn't, not with people like you and Paul, but . . ." and she stopped, biting her lips so that Claire said, "Well?"

"In a place like the Valley," she said, with less than her former assurance, "Simon won't be in ignorance about me long. If I was in your place I should get Ikey to explain to him and not lose any time about it. It wouldn't help if he heard it from one of the farm hands. Will you do that for me, Claire?"

"Certainly, if Paul agrees," said Claire, although privately she thought the assignment eccentric.

"Paul will agree to anything you suggest," Grace said and suddenly, inexplicably, she bent forward and kissed Claire on the cheek, after which she pulled open the door and marched out into the corridor. "No wonder Paul could make very little of her," Claire thought, as she watched the yellow straw hat bob down the staircase, "for who on earth could? Certainly not me!" and she hurried to catch her up before Grace found the table where Paul and James sat smoking, each looking as sombre and ill-at-ease as an expectant father.

CHAPTER NINETEEN

I

THERE was no persuading him to remain in London another night and catch the 11 A.M. train from Waterloo,
that all Valley travellers used, for it was the only main
line train that stopped at Sorrel Halt. He fled the city like
a fugitive, telling her that this was not the first time but
would be the last. At first she was depressed that their
holiday, which had begun so well, should have ended so
abruptly and on such a dismal note but as the lights of
the tenement houses fell away, and the train ran on into
dark open country she began to share his relief at going
and was soon lulled to sleep by the clack of the wheels.
When she opened her eyes again it was light and she
could smell parched summer woods, a few miles short of
the Devon border.

He had not asked her about her conversation with
Grace and she had not told him, thinking that it would
keep for when he felt less jaded but he remained moody
and silent over breakfast at The Mitre, in Paxtonbury. It
was not until they had hired a horse and trap at the
livery stables, and were breasting the incline on the first
stage of the fifteen-mile journey to the Valley that he began to perk up a little, for she saw him lift his head and
sniff the air like a pointer, as though he was searching the
rendezvous of the west wind and the whiff of Channel
spindrift. He said, as though she had been privy to his
thoughts all the way home, "That glitter and all those
blaring bands! Pomp measured out by the chain mile and
what is the point of it if the vast majority are just lookers-
on? Can you answer me that now?"

She said mildly that she supposed the spectacle itself
was there to be enjoyed by taxpayers, and this, in essence,
was the object the authorities had in mind but he growled,

"Yes, I daresay! Bread and circuses, to keep the mob yammering for more red on the map! But they'll bellow for local blood if given the chance, as you saw outside the House yesterday! Damn it, if we put on a show down here to mark a national occasion every man, woman and child in the Valley would be personally involved in it! But not in London, for London isn't England any more! Monarchs used to make progresses to places like the Valley. Now they use London as a reflecting mirror and a bloody fly-blown one at that!"

He seldom swore in her presence but she said nothing, knowing his mood would blow itself out in a few growls and gusts and that every turn of the trap's wheels would improve his humour and she was right. After a rumble or two he subsided, his features relaxed, and he began to look about him as they tackled the last lap of the interminable hill to the saddle-back where the real moor began. A hundred yards or so below the crest he pulled on to the heather and let the reins drop between his knees. It was then about 8 A.M., and the morning river mist had long since been sucked up by the sun so that the open stretches of the Sorrel winked at the sky and the salt taste of the wind was unmistakable. She saw him grin and stretch himself, and in his sudden enthusiasm he thumped her knee so vigorously that she shouted, "Hi! That'll leave a bruise, you great bully!" but she smiled because she was so relieved the magic had worked again.

"Look at it!" he said. "Six miles wide and twelve deep!"

"And we don't own the half of it," she said, "so stop crowing!"

"It doesn't matter a damn who owns it," he said, "for even old Gilroy's patch is more English than Trafalgar Square! I'll tell you what I have in mind and you're the first to hear of it! We'll put on a coronation show of our own that will be talked about when George and Mary are nudging their jubilee! And I don't mean simply a Valley affair but a *real* show, with brass bands, a sports programme, fatstock competitions, rifle butts, a gymkhana, a cart-horse parade, the lot! We'll get entries from the Paxtonbury territorials, who start their annual camp in a fortnight and from the Yeomanry over in Heronslea Park

644

and we'll get Gilroy to bring his hirelings across the Teazel to get a drubbing from our chaps in everything from pig-skittling to Cornish wrestling! How does that sound for a start?"

"Absurdly ambitious," she said, her lip trembling, "but I'm all in favour if it improves your temper!"

He kissed her then, a great, hearty kiss full on the mouth, like a farmer returning home after a successful day at the market. Back here he was so like a great, hulking boy that she could never think of him as a person born and raised in a city. He said, "By God, we'll show them how to go about things! Get up, Ned!" and he slapped the reins on the cob's back and began the steep descent to the river road.

His enthusiasm infected the entire Valley within a couple of days, as he lunged up and down the estate, dashing off letters to Honorary Secretaries as far afield as Whinmouth and—this astonished everyone who knew him—getting the house connected to the Paxtonbury Telephone Company, so that he could make direct contact with the Gilroy estate and the people and organisations to whom he looked for active co-operation. There had been all manner of free luncheons and sports meetings arranged in the district as part of the national coronation fiesta but most of these had been organised on a local basis. The promise of valuable prizes and free beer worked wonders upon the isolationist spirit of communities half-a-day's journey north, west and east of the Valley so that the event, given good weather, looked like proving the most spectacular since the Heronslea three-day fair at the time of Victoria's first jubilee, a celebration still spoken of by the middle-aged and elderly of the Valley as "the day us all got dead drunk at Gilroy's expense".

The local military organisations proved co-operative, Territorials and Yeomanry entering sports teams in most of the contests, and when it was clear that the number of contestants and spectators was likely to exceed two thousand Paul shifted the venue from Big Paddock to the Codsall stubble fields now lying fallow. Tents and enclosures began to mushroom there within days of his return home and the ringing of the new telephone bell in the hall drove Mrs. Handcock frantic, for she swore that she could never disassociate it in her mind from a fire-alarm. Only the sudden return of Ikey, on a months' furlough, saved her from resignation as Chef Extraordinary, and her husband Horace had to be taken on one side and told to persuade her that the Coronation Jamboree would make Shallowford history, so that her loyalty to the Squire was at stake. Apart from this Horace was a great help to Paul during these feverish days for he was a great authority on the many slumbering feuds that existed between Heronslea and the county border and showed the Squire how to exploit them in the interests of competitive events. Three silver and four brass bands entered in the band contests and there were over a hundred and forty gymkhana entries for a dozen major events. Two hunting packs promised support and rural athletes came in from as far away as Barnstaple, whereas the rifle and clay-pigeon events were so popular that they had to be shot off in heats days in advance. A fifty-yard stretch of the river was dredged for tub-racing and a wrestling ring was built west of the ford. There were all manner of agricultural contests, from fence-splitting to hedging-and-ditching and the inevitable fireworks display advertised a magnificent set-piece of the Spithead Naval Review, with guns firing rocket salvoes over the avenue chestnuts.

John Rudd, although approving of the venture as a whole, shook his head over the probable cost, declaring that it would set the estate back five hundred pounds, but Paul said they could regard it as money spent on advertising and that the Valley as a whole would benefit from new contacts and the opening up of fresh markets in the area. Rudd thought this was eyewash but he did not say so for by then he had had a word with Claire, who described what had happened on their last day in London. Thinking it over he agreed with her that a diversion on this scale was what Paul needed. As for the others, the hard core of the Valley tenantry, they formed a kind of staff about Paul and, notwithstanding the fine weather, work on the farms was shamefully scamped throughout the first week of July. The stolid, conscientious Eveleigh took charge of the sports meeting, Sam Potter the agricultural competitions, and Henry Pitts, glad of such a good excuse to take a holiday, appointed himself Squire's adjutant, with Ikey Palfrey as an aide-de-camp tearing up and down the Valley on his chestnut hunter. And each of these officers had auxiliaries outside the Shallowford area, men like Eph Morgan, the builder, who, as a Welshman, declared himself the only man qualified to supervise the musical programmes, and Tom Williams, the fisherman, who provided tubs for the river-race and cartloads of hazards for the obstacle races. The women of the Valley rallied to Claire's sub-committee so that the smell of baking rose over the Sorrel like a benediction and so much food was prepared that Martha Pitts, carrying her quota into the refreshment marquee, declared that the twelve apostles would be needed to carry away the surplus by the basketful as they had when the five thousand were fed beside Galilee.

The sky began to cloud over on the last day of preparation and it looked as though the spell of fine weather was about to end so that the men worked on frantically after dusk and when it was too dark to swing a mallet assembled to broach the first of the fifteen-gallon casks that had been hauled into the Valley by Whinmouth drays and were now ranged in an imposing row in the refreshment tent. Said Henry Pitts, his cheerful face clouded with anxiety, "All us wants now is a bliddy downpour, an' us looks as if us'll get it!" but to Claire's relief Horace Handcock (whose oracular powers extended to the weather field) licked his thumb, looked wise, and announced majestically that there would be a change of wind during the night and that the sun would shine all the following day. Then Sam Potter, raising his pewter tankard, declared that as the place would be full of foreigners tomorrow he proposed they all take this opportunity to drink the health of the Squire and everybody murmured agreement and downed their pints in one while Claire, glancing across the table at Paul, saw that he was touched by their loyalty and added her silent prayer for a cloudless day.

She was awake and at the window soon after five, watching the grey light creep over the Bluff and cross the river to the little town of tents, booths and enclosures west of the ford. It was childish, she thought, to be so concerned over a country fête of which there were probably a thousand arranged for that day in various parts of the British Isles but it seemed to her an issue of tremendous importance for so much work had gone into the event and not an inconsiderable amount of money. She continued to stand watching the sky while his snores reached her from the bed, and presently the shadows across the river retreated to the Teazel Valley and she saw cotton-wool mist in from the sea, which told her that calm weather could be expected for the surest sign of rain in the Valley was a clear view to the south-west. She went back to the bed and shook him and when he only muttered and rolled over on his back, she slid her hand along the dark stubble of his chin so that the short bristles crackled and he sat up suddenly wide awake and exclaimed, "What's it like?"

"Set fair," she said, "so get up and shave! You forgot to yesterday and your chin is like a quickset hedge!"

He passed his hand across his cheek and grinned, "So I did," he said, swinging his feet to the floor, "I was so damned busy! Have you been lying awake worrying about rain?"

"Yes I have," she said. "I invariably do your worrying for you! Now hurry up, Paul, there's a lot to do before breakfast!"

"Aye, there is that," he admitted, but despite her impatient protest he caught her round the waist as she crossed to the dressing-table and holding her for a moment said, "It wouldn't be any fun without you, Claire! I don't suppose I should lead a different life married or single but it wouldn't be any *fun,* you understand?" and he gave her a bristly kiss on the neck and went whistling along the passage to his tub.

She looked at herself in the mirror, wasting more precious time she told herself but there was time enough to smile at her reflection and say, "Claire Craddock, you're odiously smug and he's smug too! Maybe we're all rather smug down here far away from it all and we'll stay so as long as we can!"

By extending the area of the Jamboree beyond the Valley and inviting entries from districts north of Paxtonbury, east to the county border, and west to Gilroy's estates, Paul had not intended to stress the competitive element but, as Horace Handcock warned him, an occasion like this would unleash local patriotism on a formidable scale and Horace must have known his west-countryman for the Jamboree soon lost its national flavour and entered the arena of local partisanship, with substantial bets being laid on the top score of the various competing units. These units were basically geographical and the intense rivalry between them was not finally resolved until a match had been applied to the set-piece of the new King and Queen. That, however, was very late in the day and in the meantime competition was intense, for superimposed upon geographical backgrounds was the rivalry between the civilians and the Territorials and the Yeomanry, so that sometimes there was a conflict of loyalties. By afternoon the general scheme of the contest had sorted itself out and the amateur bookmakers were at last able to introduce some kind of pattern into their wagers.

The Valley gained a headstart when Rose Derwent, on her steeplechaser Tawnyboy, won the principal event of the Gymkhana. One of Gilroy's stable-lads rode her to a close finish after a pile up at the water-jump and she streaked down the flat with little more than a nose to spare.

Then, to the Valley's surprise and disgust, the famed Goliath of Bideford, a hot favourite for the Cornish wrestling championship, was vanquished in the final by a Horse Artilleryman from Paxtonbury. It seemed that clearing Potter land and digging Potter wells had not provided the right training for this kind of contest, despite the fact that Jem Pollock still looked a magnificent specimen of manhood in his leopard-skin. The men of the Valley, however, seeing him thrown three times in succession in the heats, were not deceived and dispersed wondering if any man, no matter how thick of thigh and broad of chest, could be expected to keep two Potter girls quiescent and still triumph in the wrestling ring. Anyway, he was badly beaten, and several less well-regulated fights threatened to break out between territorials and agriculturalists as a result of the verdict. Jem took his defeat well, declaring his opponent a master of the art but in the dressing tent Cissie and Violet Potter felt ashamed and blamed the issue on Meg's insistence that Jem should enter the contest with a full belly. They had cause to complain. In the interests of the Valley they had denied themselves his comforting presence for almost a week and had looked on glumly that morning when Meg had sent him out fortified by five fried eggs, three pounds of fried potatoes and a dozen rashers of green bacon.

Lord Gilroy's team won the hedging and ditching contest and a West Dorset silver band was judged the winner of the band contest but Sam Potter brought the Valley to the forefront again with his brilliant exhibition of rail-splitting. It was a joy to watch him straddling a great beech log, whirling his woodsman's axe as though it had been a conductor's baton. The sweat poured down his naked back as he worked his way towards the tapering end, occasionally exchanging his axe for wedges and a fourteen-pound sledge until, like a neatly divided apple, the log split down the middle.

A curious thing happened in the final of the clay-pigeon contest where Smut Potter, to everyone's amusement, came face to face with Dave Buller, the Heronslea keeper whose scars had cost Smut three years and eight months behind bars. Paul, when he saw the pair take up their stand, expressed anxiety but John Rudd laughed at him, declaring that Dave bore Smut no malice. And neither did he, it seemed, for when Smut won, he went up to him and wrung his hand saying, cheerfully, "Well, Smut, you baint lost your touch I zee!" and everybody within earshot applauded the keeper's sportsman-like attitude.

Other highlights of the day were the tub race, won by the Yeomanry after all their competitors had capsized and the Ladies' Pancake Tossing sprint, won in fine style by Elinor Codsall, mother of three but still as fleet of foot as when she was a slip of a girl. Ikey increased the Valley's lead before tea by winning the mile, with half a lap in hand but the tug-of-war proved almost as big a disappointment as the wrestling for despite Jem Pollock as anchor, the Territorials dragged the Sorrel men over the mark in a series of expert heaves and pulled into overall second place by going on to win the open relay.

By six o'clock, when points had been totted up after the ankle competition and fancy-dress events (events sporting men discounted and excluded from their wagers) the Valley was only one point ahead and the atmosphere was charged with excitement as competition lined up for the most spectacular event of the day, a two-lap trap-race, with no pettifogging trotting conditions imposed on it and here, it seemed, the Terriers were favourites and a win would give them a clear five-point lead.

The day had been intensely hot, with distant thunder rumbling beyond the Bluff and when the stewards cleared the course word came that Eveleigh's eldest boy, Gilbert, who had been training the Codsall skewball Firefly for the event, had sprained his wrist getting ashore in the tub race and had been obliged to withdraw. In the few minutes left the Valley was canvassed for a substitute but none with any chance of holding off the strong challenge came forward, so that a howl of dismay rose from the ropes as Eveleigh, looking even more unsmiling than usual, began to lead Firefly out of the line-up. Paul, standing alongside the starter, said philosophically, "Well, that's that, John! The Terriers have it in the bag," but John said suddenly, "Look here, they needn't have! You can handle a trap smartly enough, get up there and show 'em," and to Paul's surprise Claire, overhearing the challenge, said, "Do it, Paul! Even if you don't really care who wins everyone else in the Valley does!" So Paul peeled off his coat, donned a steeplechaser's crash hat and climbed into the box to the accompaniment of the biggest cheer of the day but feeling far less confident of his ability to negotiate the bends than were his supporters.

There were five entries but only the Terrier looked dangerous and Paul was relieved to be drawn on the inside, a starting position that seemed likely to exploit Firefly's reputation as a flying starter. He thought, as he picked up the reins, "Good God, this is ridiculous! I feel more nervous than I did out on the Veldt, or fishing those Germans ashore in the cove and all over a footling chariot race in one of my own meadows!"

Then they were off, with Firefly gaining a clear yard in a couple of bounds and he held on to his inside place round the first bend as the ponies went into a stretched gallop on the slight downslope of the flat. The pace was terrifying. Never had he moved so fast behind a horse and he thought, as he dragged Firefly round the second bend and into the straight to complete the first lap, that he must have been an ass to let Henry Pitts and Will Codsall override him on the potential dangers of this event. On the third bend he heard a wild shout, and the splintering of wood behind him but it was not until he had started the final lap that he saw what had happened. Three of the traps had crashed in a wheel-lock on the second bend and were only dragged clear as he pounded straight down on the mêlée with the Terrier drawing level and half-standing in his box as he lashed his pony to overtake at the second bend.

The spectators now seemed to go mad in a body, for as the two traps flashed by neck-and-neck they poured from behind the ropes and capered into the centre of the course, and then, as the two survivors entered the straight again, Paul realised he had the race in hand for the Terrier dropped back and Firefly crossed the finishing line with a length in hand and Paul had to use all his strength to avoid ploughing on into the crowd now scattered all over the track. He said, as an exultant Henry Pitts jumped for the pony's head and brought him to a halt, "The next time you insist on a chariot race you can damned well compete yourself, Henry!" but Henry only banged him on the back and bellowed, "Us 'ave shown 'em, Squire! Us 'ave shown 'em!" and every man, woman and child in the Valley agreed with him, even Claire, who had watched the race with her heart in her mouth feeling sick at the thought that, if Paul had been injured, she would have blamed herself for the rest of a guilty life.

Paul went over to inspect the damage to the others and found, to his great relief, that all three drivers had escaped with bruises, although their vehicles were shattered, two of them beyond repair. The Yeomanry competitor was undismayed for his entry had been official and the trap was on the inventory of the barracks, but Paul felt sorry for the Dorset man, a young farmer now dolefully inspecting the wreck of his gaily-painted rig. "What do you value it at?" he asked, and the man said it was his father's trap and the old man had paid four pounds ten shillings for it at Paxtonbury market only a month ago. "My agent, Mr. Rudd, will give you the money out of funds," he said and feeling magnanimous as winner of such a contest, added, "and here's an extra ten shillings for danger money!"

Over in the east thunder continued to mutter but the rain held off and it was decided to hold the dancing in the open air. Paul went into the refreshment hut for a badly needed drink and was served by a tall, thin, bespectacled young man, whom he did not recognise until Doctor Maureen, sipping a brandy close at hand, told him the volunteer barman was Keith Horsey, son of the rector, still known as New Parson, although he had now occupied Parson Bull's pulpit for more than three years. He went across and talked to the youth, finding him very shy and afflicted by a slight stammer.

"Does Ikey know you are here?" he asked, "you were at school together, weren't you?" and Keith said that this was true but that he had returned home from Oxford only that day and had so far not spoken to Ikey although he had watched him win the mile. Paul said, "There's dancing going on now and a chap your age would be better employed following his fancy. I'll find someone to take on here!" but the boy began to protest and his stammer increased, so that Paul would have left the matter there had not Ikey lounged into the tent at that moment, greeting Keith with genuine pleasure. Paul noticed that the parson's son lost his stammer at once and the way he looked at Ikey, with myopic brown eyes, reminded him of Grace's retriever anticipating an ear-rub in front of the library fire. He thought, smiling to himself, "He's got a way with him has Ikey! There isn't a soul here who doesn't perk up when Ikey walks in and this poor little toad obviously worships

653

him!" and on the pretence of buying Maureen a drink he disposed of Keith for a moment and said, "Take that kid down to the dancing enclosure and make sure he gets a girl! He'll do no good standing here serving drinks for the rest of the night!"

"A girl! Beanpole Horsey with a girl?" said Ikey, laughing, "I know you've just bankrupted the bookies by winning the chariot race, Gov'nor, but don't ask for miracles! Beanpole wouldn't know what to do with a girl if he was locked up with one."

"What sort of chap was he at school?" Paul asked, and Ikey replied a first-class brain but that was about all. "He's a trier all right," he added, "and he's got guts but somehow they don't show. I like him and always have, I'll get working on him tomorrow, Gov," but for some reason Paul persisted, saying, "No, Ikey, not tomorrow, now! All the girls will have gone tomorrow and some girls like the self-effacing type! They don't all fall for the cocky bounders like you!"

"Well," Ikey said, "always willing to oblige, especially after your performance!" and he ambled over to Keith and Paul watched them stand chatting for a few moments after which Keith took off his barman's apron, folded it neatly and left the tent like a poacher's lurcher trotting at its master's heels. It was a trivial incident, perhaps the most trivial of the day, but he was to remember it long after the excitement of the chariot race had faded from his memory.

III

Keith Horsey, now eighteen, would not have survived his first year at High Wood without the patronage of Ikey Palfrey. After fighting for him, and giving him an essential breathing space, Ikey had found it difficult to shed partial responsibility for the ungainly youth and although Horsey was regarded as a useless weed by almost everyone in the school Ikey soon realised that this was by no means the whole truth about the Beanpole. He possessed, for instance, a great deal of moral courage and moral courage was in short supply at High Wood. As it was, buttressed in some measure by Ikey's friendship, Beanpole not only survived but made some kind of impact by his stand against the code of Bloods, notably, that part of it condoning smut and cribbing. In the course of this lonely crusade he collected innumerable beatings, both official and unofficial, but he never yielded ground and no one succeeded in extracting from him so much as a yelp. As Hillman, the Captain of Fortescue, once put it, "It's like walloping a deaf mute and a man can't do it and then sit down to tea and buns with an easy mind." So, in the end, they left him to himself and to Ikey, and the Beanpole shot rapidly up the school to the Sixth where he won the coveted open scholarship to Oxford at the unprecedented age of seventeen and left to read economics and philosophy. Although Ikey had lost touch with him since entering Woolwich the previous year he had by no means forgotten him and was genuinely pleased to see him at the Jamboree. For an hour or more they talked, watching the dancers moving over the clipped turf to the blare of the Yeomanry band and it was not until Ikey saw Rachel Eveleigh partnerless on the far side of the square that he recollected his instructions. Bidding Keith wait for him he lounged across and greeted her.

Rachel was the second daughter of the Four Winds string of children and the most like her placid mother, Marian. She had red-gold hair, a good-natured, slightly freckled face and blue eyes that tonight had something of a snap in them.

"I'm pairing up on Squire's instructions, Rachel," Ikey told her, "do you know Keith Horsey, the parson's son?" and when Rachel admitted that she knew him by sight, "I wonder if you would do Squire a favour and bring him on a bit? He's a nice chap but on the shy side so you'll have to make the running," and to Ikey's surprise Rachel replied in her soft Devon brogue, "I'd love to meet him, he's always seemed a very polite boy and there aren't so many around tonight!" and without waiting to be introduced she walked across the enclosure and stood smiling in front of him while Ikey, temporarily losing the initiative, said, "Er . . . Keith old man, this is Rachel Eveleigh from Four

655

Winds . . . Rachel . . . you've er . . . you've seen him in church, maybe?" Keith said nothing but stood blinking at the girl who took him by the hand with a cheerful, "Come on, this is an easy one, the Military Two-Step. Follow me all the way round!" and Ikey was left standing with his mouth open having always thought of Rachel Eveleigh as hardly less shy than Keith. He did not notice another solitary figure, a boy about his own age wearing spectacles nearly as thick-lensed as Keith's, slightly apart from Rachel when he approached, and who remained to watch the couple merge into the long file of dancers circling the bandstand but Rachel was very much aware of Sydney Codsall, standing by with an expression of baffled irritation on his face for her ready acceptance of Ikey's appeal had been the direct result of a sharp exchange between them earlier that evening.

Sydney Codsall had not wanted to attend the Jamboree, regarding it as a mere chawbacon's carnival with little to offer a man who "worked clean"—that is to say, wore a starched collar and cuffs. He was only there because, of late, he had been cultivating Rachel for reasons that had nothing whatever to do with her amiability, her red-gold hair or her pleasing, freckled face. He had grown up with the Eveleigh family and had no great affection for any of them, having always regarded them as interlopers whom circumstances had contrived to make him a lodger in his own house. He had been glad to break out of the family circle when he became articled to Snow and Pritchard and took lodgings in Whinmouth but his recent foray into the property market had caused him to have second thoughts about abandoning the Eveleighs altogether. A month or two back he had learned by chance that the parcel of land adjoining the brickworks site was registered in the name of a Mrs. Amelia Page and he recalled that Marian Eveleigh had been a Miss Page before her marriage. A little cross-checking during the lunch interval when he was alone in the office had confirmed his guess regarding the ultimate owner of the land, no other than Mrs. Eveleigh, old Mother Page's only surviving child. He also discovered that old Mrs. Page was pushing ninety-three. The land comprised no more than a couple of acres but it had a common boundary with his holding in Coombe Bay and if it could be had cheaply was clearly worth a great deal more to him than to anyone else. Sydney gave matters like these very careful thought and it seemed to him that, whereas a direct approach would probably result in drawing the land-hungry Squire's attention to the parcel, an oblique approach through the most pliable of Marian Eveleigh's daughters might lead to a bill of sale before anyone else was aware that there was another plot of land to be had on the outskirts of the village.

He set to work at once to court Rachel and made what he considered steady progress, for Rachel had never forgotten her father's instructions that they were to be kind to the orphaned Sydney. Soon, or so it seemed to her, kindness cracked the crust of Sydney's aloofness, for he seemed willing to sacrifice precious hours that should have been devoted to study walking her along summer lanes and telling her how much he appreciated the kindness her family had shown him and also—and this interested her rather more—how much more ladylike she was than her sisters. It was some time, however, before Rachel, a modest soul, could persuade herself there were aspects of his attentions that were very puzzling. For one thing he never once tried to kiss her or even to hold her hand; for another all their walks, no matter in which direction, seemed to bring them to the fence surrounding Grannie Page's field, alongside the old brickworks. For some reason Sydney seemed more bemused by the field, which was quite an ordinary-looking field, than by her red-gold hair, her blue eyes, her dimples, or anything about her, including her "ladylike" conversation. It was not until the tea interval at the Jamboree, a month after the sombre courtship had begun, that Sydney confessed to a keen, personal interest in the field and asked her outright if Grannie Page was likely to live much longer and if Rachel thought her mother would be prepared to sell it for, say, ten guineas per acre?

Rachel Eveleigh was a very amiable girl but she was not stupid. Moreover she had the advantage, which Paul Craddock, in his dealing with Sydney, had not, of having lived cheek by jowl with him for years, so that it did not take her more than a moment to price Sydney's courtship at twenty guineas, less solicitor's costs. She had her mother's complaisance but her father's pride. After pondering a moment, in order to be quite certain that she was doing no one an injustice, she lifted her right hand and smacked Sydney's face so hard that he lost his balance on a tussock and fell backwards into the shallow river. By the time he got to his feet she had gone and before he could condemn his stupidity for rushing his fences so recklessly she was dancing with the parson's son, Keith Horsey, and looking very much as if she was making the running. He watched them sourly for half-an-hour but she did not even glance in his direction and before the first rocket soared over the paddock he was bicycling back to Whinmouth, having learned a valuable lesson in tactics but lost a golden opportunity of enlarging his Coombe Bay holdings.

In the meantime Keith Horsey was blithely unaware to whom he owed his adoption by the prettiest of the Eveleigh girls, the titian-haired one, whom he identified as the second unit of a descending row of heads when the family took their places in church. Although shy and ill-at-ease with men he was more relaxed in the presence of women, for he had grown up among church workers who were predominantly female and was thus familiar with feminine topics of conversation. Rachel, who had only taken him in hand as a means of alleviating the smart caused by Sydney's baseness, soon found him agreeable company and was secretly flattered at having one of the gentry all to herself, although she could have wished for one with rather more experience in the art of dancing. By the time the fireworks were due to begin, and the band had disappeared into the refreshment tent, all her toes were bruised and on her right thigh was a tender patch of skin where Keith's knee struck a blow every time they turned. It was very pleasant, however, to find a man ready to admit his shortcomings, especially after a month's courting with Sydney who had never confessed to one. Keith made no excuses for his clumsiness, saying that his cousins had long since given him over as a hopeless hobbledehoy but if he could not dance he at least treated her with an elaborate courtesy that she found very welcome after the fumblings

658

and neighing laughter of partners at village hops she had attended since putting her hair up. Rachel had pride, as her reaction to Sydney's proposal had proved, but like all the sons and daughters of tenant farmers in the Valley she recognised her place in the graded society into which she had been born. On one side of the fence lived Squire, the freeholders, the doctor and the parson, and on the other the tenants, the tradesmen, the cottage craftsmen and the hired hands, in that order of progression. To be asked for a single dance by a young man from the other side of the fence was one thing, and might happen to any girl on an occasion like this, but to dance with a college boy who was also the parson's only son eight times in succession, and then to be escorted by him to the refreshment hut for ices and lemonade, was quite another. By the time the fireworks were started, and Keith still showed no desire to rejoin the gentry, Rachel had decided that the Squire's Coronation Jamboree promised to be a milestone in her life, the more memorable, perhaps, because there had been so few. Then the Valley gods took a hand in the affair. As the third volley of rockets soared forked lightning flickered over the Bluff and seconds later thunder rolled, so that she had every excuse to reduce the space between them; and because he was such a gentleman, and had such nice manners, his hand, cool if bony, took hers and she told the first deliberate lie of her life saying, in reply to his inquiry, "Yes, Mr. Horsey, I *am* frightened of thunder," hoping that he would ask her to address him less formally. He did not but she made progress in another direction for he at once enlarged his hold upon her plump hand and held it tightly for the remainder of the display.

For those in charge of the fireworks it was a race against time. With the fall of dusk the atmosphere over the field became oppressive and the rumbles of thunder beyond the Bluff ever more frequent. Presently, before the set-pieces had been touched off, a few heavy drops of rain splashed down but nobody minded them much for it was not often the Valley could watch a fireworks display and some of the spectators recalled the display here in honour of King Teddy, in October 1902. Among these was Pansy

Pascoe, plain Pansy Potter when watching the last descent of green and crimson balls over the chestnuts. She was here again tonight, with her brood of four, three cooing and ahhing and the fourth, two-year-old Lizzie, asleep in the go-cart, which Pansy now realised she would have to push all the way home to Coombe Bay for Walt, her husband, had been last seen far gone in drink in the refreshment tent with certain other revellers. Pansy was not given to brooding but the link between the firework displays was too obvious to be ignored. In 1902 she recalled, she had been as one with her sisters living a semi-gypsy life in the Dell taking her fun wherever she found it; now she was a woman apart, with a house to keep clean, a husband to cook for and a steadily increasing tribe of children to make impossible demands on her time, so that fun passed her by and she was also losing her figure. She could not help wondering if she had chosen wisely in settling for Walt, simply because he owned a cottage and earned a pound a week, summer and winter. There were times, particularly of late, when she yearned for the cheerful muddle of the Dell as it had been in old Tamer's time, for up there an odd baby or two had never seemed to matter much and children did not get under one's feet as they did in a four-roomed cottage. At the firework display of 1902, she recalled, she had considered herself the sharpest of the Potter girls but tonight she was not so sure, in spite of the rumour that Big Jem, the hired hand, kept Cissie and Violet on a very tight rein. Her thoughts, becoming more nostalgic with every new discharge, were interrupted by an impatient tugging at her arm and in the glare of golden rain she looked down into the face of her eldest boy, Timothy, now rising seven and said, without troubling to ask what he wanted, "Go over there, Timmy, an' dornee be tiresome! No one'll look at 'ee an' iffen they do then who gives a damn, boy?"

Then, as Timothy slipped away, she was aware of the gleam of a waxed moustache at her elbow and sensed the not unwelcome presence of Dandy Timberlake, eldest and by far the sprucest of the Timberlake boys. All the Timberlake boys had a roving eye but Dandy's roved to more purpose than his brothers' and with another pang Pansy

660

recalled larking with him in the hay about a thousand years ago, when everybody in the Valley was free and young and spry. He said, sorrowfully, "I've come to tell 'ee, Panse, Walt's dead drunk and like to stay for the night! How be gonner get the family back home?"

"On shanks' pony," she said grimly, "how else do 'ee think, Dandy?" but she was pleased to see him nevertheless and not much surprised when he said, "If I walked so far with 'ee, would 'ee ask me in for a brew o' tea for old times' sake, Panse?"

She considered; Walt would probably lay up in the barn with all the other over-indulged loyalists and she had always liked Dandy, with his penchant for fancy waistcoats and fierce Kaiser moustaches, the effect of which was softened by a pair of twinkling brown eyes. There could be no harm in him walking her home, cumbered as she was by four children, for it would not be practicable to stop *en route*. If, at journey's end, he claimed a small reward for his services as escort and go-cart pusher was that so unreasonable?

"Mebbe I would at that, Dandy!" she said, "but tiz time us started backalong, for the kids is tired out, baint 'ee, my loves?"

The nature of the reward, she decided, could be left in abeyance and would depend upon how tired she was on arrival, but it might have been otherwise had she known that Dandy had set his sights elsewhere only a few moments before their encounter, having edged along the line of spectators until he stood very close to Violet, her sister, sandwiched between Cissie and Jem, all standing with their faces to the sky. Dandy had always had a slight preference for Vi and seeing that she and Jem were engaged with the fireworks he approached from behind, pinched her bottom, squeezed her hand and let it run lightly upward until it had sufficient purchase to incline her towards him. She turned then and flashed him a smile, for Jem's pitiful performance in the wrestling ring had blown upon embers of resentment in her heart. Like all the Potters she had been born free and tonight she chafed at the bonds of honourable captivity. Jem continued to stare upward and she was so deceived by his air of abstraction that she reached out

661

and touched Dandy, her hand moving tentatively, like the hand of a penniless connoisseur fingering an exhibit in a museum while the curator's back is turned, yet she ought to have remembered that Jem had eyes in the back of his head. He said, quite amiably, and without turning, "I was worsted be that sodger but I could still maake mincemeat o' Dandy Timberlake!" whereupon Dandy moved on to seek Pansy Pascoe and Vi, much piqued, grumbled, "The trouble wi' you, Jem, is youm so bliddy greedy!"

"Ahhh," said Jem, still without taking his eyes off the suspended green balls in the sky, "I daresay I be but that's how it is, Vi midear! I've told 'ee bevore an' I'll tell 'ee again, dornee let me catch either of 'ee we' no man or I'll tan the hide off 'ee, do 'ee mind now?"

"So I should think!" said Cissie virtuously and Violet, reflecting bitterly that her sister had not been tempted, ground her teeth with rage but judged it wise to make no further comment.

Edward Derwent, standing at the foot of the avenue with his wife Liz, his son Hugh and his daughter Rose, watched the rockets soar with more satisfaction than any man in the valley. It was not that he set much store by fireworks, considering them pesky, noisy, unpredictable things but simply that they helped to reveal the fat of the years, particularly the last few years, that had done so much to mellow him. For in that brief span of time Claire had *shown* them. Not only had she married the Squire and presented him with heirs but, almost in passing, she had cured her father's land-hunger, for where was the sense in yearning to own High Coombe when, in a way, he already owned it, together with every other farm in the Valley? His mind returned to the occasion he had last stood here watching fireworks and he recalled his bitter disappointment at the apparent inaccuracy of their assurances that Young Squire was madly in love with his prettiest daughter, and likely to demand her hand at any moment. Well, Young Squire had taken his time but it had come to pass in the end and now he was the Squire's father-in-law, just as they had predicted. As the years passed his pride in his daughter had grown and grown, just like one of his neighbour Willoughby's vegetable marrows earmaked for the harvest festival, and whereas everyone in the Valley had, in some degree, warmed their hands at the glow issuing from the Big House, Derwent had been warmed through and through by events up there. And some of this warmth had passed through him to his wife Liz, she who had tried so hard and so unsuccessfully to fill the shoes of her predecessor, for whereas, in the early days of her marriage, Edward had treated her like a scullery-maid, he now yielded her the respect due to a tolerably efficient housekeeper and with this she was more than content. Silently, as a set-piece of the Battle of Trafalgar began to sputter, Liz Derwent breathed a prayer of thankfulness that things had turned out so well for all of them.

A few yards removed from the families and lovers a thick-set figure sat perched on a shooting stick, also contemplating the fireworks although not as a source of entertainment. Professor Hans Scholtzer, formerly of the University of Jena, liked firework displays because they reminded him that the early Chinese civilisations had shown so much more sense in their use of gunpowder than had their imperial successors in the West. Here, in this remote valley, however, the old German had found something of the peace he had sought all his life and at least once a day he relished it, as he was relishing it at this moment. He hoped with all his heart that the simple folk around him (who reminded him sometimes of peasants he had met in the forest clearings of Lower Saxony) would never be tempted to put gunpowder to other uses and involve themselves in the interminable bickerings of the Hohenzollerns, the Romanoffs and the Hapsburgs, to say nothing of the shifty politicians in Paris. For if they did not only would his peace be shattered but also the peace of the Valley, possibly for generations, and the Kaiser's minions would reach out and pluck the Professor's fine son Gottfried from his studies and enrol him as a private soldier under the Kaiser's double-eagle. The Professor sat on his shooting stick like a carefully balanced toad but in the white glare of the rockets those about him did not see him as a toad but as a caricature of a fat German bandsman, such as they had often seen in the streets of Paxton-bury. His round head shone and his eyeglasses twinkled and every now and again he blew out his cheeks, as though he was flexing his facial muscles for an assault on the trombone.

Then, when everybody had quite forgotten the mutter of thunder over the Bluff, the storm that had been threatening all day burst and rain began to hiss down on upturned faces and lightning shamed the puny flashes over the chestnuts. The Battle of Trafalgar was left to fight its way through to an indecisive finish and everyone ran clear of the trees and made for tents or outbuildings, remaining there while the giant thunderclaps echoed all the way down the Valley and the rain drummed on taut canvas, telling one another what a good thing it was that the storm had held off all day and spared the Squire's Jamboree.

Claire was already in the house when the storm burst, happy to kick off her shoes and shoot her long legs to-wards the empty grate, reflecting that she had been very wise to insist that the helpers' dance was postponed until the debris was cleared from the paddock and stubble field for she did not think she could have kept awake after such a long day in the open. She did not light the lamp but sat sipping hot, sweet tea, watching the lightning play over the chestnuts and hoping Paul would be along soon and they could go to bed. It had been, she reflected, a stupendous success and had done everyone credit, par-ticularly the man who was to foot the bill for all the beer consumed and all the gear hired. There could be little doubt but that everyone had enjoyed themselves immense-ly but then, it did not take very much to amuse the people of the Valley. The men, she reflected, invariably used these occasions to drink, wench, and air their collective rivalries, whereas the women concentrated on displaying their clothes and practised a different kind of rivalry, and Claire, Valley-born, could view these activities without patronage. After all, were the so-called gentry very dif-ferent? Their own life, hers and Paul's, trod an equally narrow circle; they ate, drank, made love, slept and planned the expansion of family and estate, which was only another form of rivalry.

The rain continued to pour down and she wondered how people would get home and how many would stay overnight in the barns and lofts. Well, they were welcome, every one of them, but their presence would mean another early start in the morning, and the thought made her yawn. At last Paul clumped in and greeted her just as she was slipping into a delicious doze.

"It's set in for the night!" he said, "thank God it held off until now! We got most of the fireworks off the ground before the fuses got wet. Is that tea? By thunder I could do with a cup! Is it long made?"

"No," she said, heaving herself out of the chair, "I fell asleep drinking mine—here you are." He stood, feet astride, looking her over with a smile and said, as she handed him his cup, "I couldn't have brought it off without you, Claire. And the food was first-class, everybody says so!" but she was far too sleepy to be flattered and replied "Good! Well drink it up and let's get some sleep, dear." She kissed him on the cheek and drifted off and he looked after her a little ruefully for, in spite of his exertions during the long day, he did not feel tired and would have enjoyed sharing his sense of elation with her. Hearing her footsteps above he pictured her movements, observed so often from a horizontal position for she was a confirmed bedroom potterer and he was always the first to climb between the sheets. Then, in a mood of contemplative sensuality that her presence often brought to him at this hour he lounged across to the bookcase and lifted out a heavy volume in a series called *Famous Paintings of the Western World*. He turned the pages until he came to Rubens' *"Bathsheba Receiving King David's Letter"*, the picture that Grace had shown him the first time she had met Claire in this house. He had never looked at it since but now that he did he saw how accurate Grace's observation had been. Claire *did* look extraordinarily like the fair Bathsheba, with her habit of sitting with knees pressed together at an angle to the chair and a kind of overall ripeness—those had been Grace's words—in every line of her strong, plump, flowing figure. He thought as he closed and replaced the book, "Well, nobody could blame David for trying. . . ." and chuckled, making a mental note to ask

665

Claire how she regarded the old rascal's summary despatch of Uriah to the forefront of the battle.

Perhaps it was reaction from the clamour of the day, or seeing so many familiar faces, of the picture-link with Grace that set his memory bells ringing. He went over to the tall window watching the flicker of lightning playing over the chestnuts and listening to the thunder rolling up to Sorrel source beyond the railway. A feeling of accomplishment warmed him, derived not only from the day's achievements but enclosing the whole cycle of the years he had spent here, every one of them packed with incident. The long procession of the seasons went marching on through the hiss of summer rain and every now and again somebody looked back and lifted a hand in greeting or in farewell—Grace, old Tamer Potter, Parson Bull, Martin and Arabella Codsall, and many, many others, whose names appeared fleetingly in the estate diary and whose destinies, one and all, had been linked with his since he came here, a callow young man with a limp accepting a challenge that seemed, in retrospect, immensely daunting. And then, as he took a final look at the blurred landscape, the roundness and finality of his tenure made an almost physical impact upon him so that he was able to stand outside it and study it as he could observe the detail of the tallest chestnut with every branch and twig illumined by the white glare of lightning. And beyond it, sensed rather than seen, were the decades ahead, years and years possibly of safe, secure living, with the land yielding a richer harvest every summer and his own children and those of the Pitts and Eveleighs and Potters growing up to take their places in the endless and unchanging life cycle of the Valley. Permanence reigned here, permanence, predictability, and within those limits—narrow to some but not to him—was fruitfulness, the rich bounty of the land, claimed and unclaimed, and the bounty of every womb between here and the sea. It was a reassuring thought on which to close an era and he would have lifted out the estate diary and tried to express it in words had not Claire, at that moment, rapped with her shoe on the floor above, reminding him that the day was done and anything new could wait upon tomorrow. Smiling what she would have called "his smug, patriachial smile" he turned out the lamp and added the clump of his boots to the long roll of thunder booming down the sky.

The chronicle of life in the Shallowford Valley will continue in *Post of Honor*, soon to be published by POCKET BOOKS.

...and I don't mind admitting that. There was a time whe...